OF
LOVE
AND
LIFE

Three novels selected and condensed
by Reader's Digest

The Reader's Digest Association Limited, London

The Reader's Digest Association Limited
11 Westferry Circus, Canary Wharf, London E14 4HE

www.readersdigest.co.uk

ISBN 0-276-42815-3

CONTENTS

SOPHIE KINSELLA
CAN YOU KEEP A SECRET?
9

ROSIE THOMAS
IF MY FATHER LOVED ME
163

SARAH-KATE LYNCH
BLESSED ARE THE CHEESEMAKERS
333

Can You Keep a Secret?

Sophie Kinsella

Like all of us, Emma Corrigan is a girl with a few little secrets. Under normal circumstances she would never divulge them to another living soul. But her fear of flying, combined with a brush with danger, finds Emma telling all to the stranger sitting next to her.

But it doesn't really matter; she'll never, ever see him again . . .

one

OF COURSE I HAVE SECRETS. Everyone has a few. It's completely normal. I'm sure I don't have any more than anybody else. I'm not talking about big, earth-shattering secrets. Not the-president-is-planning-to-bomb-Japan-and-only-Will-Smith-can-save-the-world type secrets. Just normal, everyday little secrets.

Here are a few random secrets of mine, off the top of my head:

1. My Kate Spade bag is a fake.
2. I love sweet sherry, the least cool drink in the universe.
3. I have no idea what NATO stands for. Or even what it is.
4. I weigh 9 stone 3. Not 8 stone 3, like my boyfriend Connor thinks. (Although in my defence, I was planning to go on a diet when I told him that.)
5 I've always thought Connor looks a bit like Ken. As in Barbie and Ken.
6. Sometimes, when we're right in the middle of passionate sex, I suddenly want to laugh.
7. I lost my virginity in the spare bedroom with Danny Nussbaum, while Mum and Dad were downstairs watching *Ben Hur*.
8. I've already drunk the wine that Dad told me to lay down for twenty years.
9. Sammy the goldfish at home isn't the same goldfish that Mum and Dad gave me to look after when they went to Egypt.
10. When my colleague Artemis annoys me, I feed her plant

orange juice. (Which is pretty much every day.)
11. I once had this weird lesbian dream about my flatmate Lissy.
12. My G-string is hurting me.
13. I've always had this deep down conviction that I'm not like everybody else, and there's an exciting new life waiting for me just around the corner.
14. I've no idea what this guy in the grey suit is going on about.
15. Plus I've already forgotten his name.

And I only met him ten minutes ago.

'We believe in logistical formative alliances,' he's saying in a nasal, droning voice, 'both above and below the line.'

'Absolutely!' I reply brightly, as though to say: Doesn't everybody? Logistical. What does that mean, again? God. What if they ask me?

Don't be stupid, Emma. They won't suddenly demand, 'What does logistical mean?' I'm a fellow marketing professional, aren't I? Obviously I know these things. And anyway, if they mention it again I'll change the subject. Or I'll say I'm post-logistical or something.

The important thing is to keep confident and businesslike. I can do this. This is my big chance and I'm not going to screw it up.

I'm sitting in the offices of Glen Oil's headquarters in Glasgow, and as I glance at my reflection in the window, I look just like a top business-woman. My hair is straightened, I'm wearing discreet earrings like they tell you to in How-to-win-that-job articles, and I've got on my smart new Jigsaw suit. (At least, it's practically new. I got it from the Cancer Research shop and sewed on a button to replace the missing one.)

I'm here representing the Panther Corporation, which is where I work. The meeting is to finalise a promotional arrangement between the new cranberry-flavoured Panther Prime sports drink and Glen Oil, and I flew up this morning from London specially. (The company paid, and everything!) When I arrived, the Glen Oil marketing guys started on this long, show-offy 'Who's-travelled-the-most?' conversation about air miles and the red-eye to Washington—and I think I bluffed pretty convincingly. (Except when I said I'd flown Concorde to Ottawa, and it turns out Concorde doesn't go to Ottawa.) But the truth is, this is the first time I've ever had to travel for a deal.

OK. The *real* truth is, this is the first deal I've ever done, full stop. I've been at the Panther Corporation for eleven months as a marketing assistant, and until now all I've been allowed to do is type out copy, arrange meetings for other people, get the sandwiches and pick up my boss's dry-cleaning. So this is kind of my big break. And I've got this secret little hope that if I do this well, maybe I'll get promoted. The ad for my job said 'possibility of promotion after a year', and on Monday I'm having my yearly appraisal meeting with my boss, Paul. I looked up 'Appraisals' in the staff induction book, and it said they are 'an ideal opportunity to discuss possibilities for career advancement'.

Career advancement! At the thought, I feel a familiar stab of longing in my chest. It would just show Dad I'm not a complete loser. And Mum. And Kerry. If I could go home and casually say, 'By the way, I've been promoted to Marketing Executive.'

Emma Corrigan, Marketing Executive.

Emma Corrigan, Senior Vice-President (Marketing).

As long as everything goes well today. Paul said the deal was done and dusted and all I had to do was nod and shake their hands, and even I should manage that. And so far, I reckon it's going well. OK, so I don't understand ninety per cent of what they're saying. But then I didn't understand much of my GCSE French Oral either, and I still got a B.

'Rebranding . . . analysis . . . cost-effective . . .'

The man in the grey suit is still droning on about something or other. As casually as possible, I extend my hand and inch his business card towards me so I can read it.

Doug Hamilton. That's right. OK, I can remember this. Doug. Dug. Easy. I'll picture a shovel. Together with a *ham*. Which . . . which looks *ill* . . . and . . . OK, forget this. I'll just write it down.

I write down 'rebranding' and 'Doug Hamilton' on my note pad and give an awkward little wriggle. God, my knickers really are uncomfortable. I mean, G-strings are never that comfortable at the best of times, in my opinion, but these are particularly bad. Which could be because they're two sizes too small.

Which could possibly be because Connor bought them for me, and told the lingerie assistant I weighed eight stone three. Whereupon she told him I must be size eight. Size eight! (Frankly, I think she was just being mean. She *must* have known I was fibbing.)

So it's Christmas Eve, and we're exchanging presents, and I unwrap this pair of gorgeous pale pink silk knickers. Size eight. And I basically have two options.

A: Confess the truth: 'Actually these are too small, I'm more of a twelve, and by the way, I don't really weigh eight stone three.' Or . . .

B: Shoehorn myself into them.

Actually, it was fine. You could hardly see the red lines on my skin afterwards. And all it meant was that I had to quickly cut all the labels out of my clothes so Connor would never realise.

Since then, I've hardly ever worn this particular set of underwear, needless to say. But every so often I see them looking all nice and expensive in the drawer and think, Oh come on, they can't be *that* tight, and somehow squeeze into them. Which is what I did this morning. I even decided I must have lost weight, because they didn't feel too bad.

I am such a deluded moron.

'. . . unfortunately since rebranding . . . major rethink . . . feel we need to be considering alternative synergies . . .'

Up to now I've just been sitting and nodding, thinking this business meeting lark is really easy. But now Doug Hamilton's voice starts to impinge on my consciousness. What's he saying?

'. . . two products diverging . . . becoming incompatible . . .'

What was that about incompatible? What was that about a major rethink? I feel a jolt of alarm. Maybe this isn't just waffle. Maybe he's actually *saying* something. Quick, listen.

'We appreciate the functional and synergetic partnership that Panther and Glen Oil have enjoyed in the past,' Doug Hamilton is saying. 'But you'll agree that clearly we're going in different directions.'

Different directions?

My stomach gives an anxious lurch. He can't be—

Is he trying to pull out of the deal?

'Excuse me, Doug,' I say, in my most relaxed voice. 'Obviously I was closely following what you were saying earlier.' I give a friendly, we're-all-professionals-together smile. 'But if you could just . . . um, recap the situation for all our benefits . . .' In plain English, I beg silently.

Doug Hamilton and the other guy exchange glances. 'We're a little unhappy about your brand values,' says Doug Hamilton.

'My brand values?' I echo in panic.

'The brand values of the *product*,' he says, giving me an odd look. 'As I've been explaining, we here at Glen Oil are going through a rebranding process, and we see our new image very much as a *caring* petrol, as our new daffodil logo demonstrates. And we feel Panther Prime, with its emphasis on sport and competition, is simply too aggressive.'

'Aggressive?' I stare at him, bewildered. 'But . . . it's a fruit drink.'

This makes no sense. Glen Oil is fume-making, world-ruining petrol. Panther Prime is an innocent cranberry-flavoured drink. How can it be too aggressive?

'The values it espouses.' He gestures to the marketing brochures on the table. 'Drive. Elitism. Masculinity. The very slogan, "Don't Pause".' He shrugs. 'We just don't think a joint initiative will be possible.'

No. No. This can't be happening. He can't be pulling out.

Everyone at the office will think it was my fault. They'll think I cocked it up and I'm completely crap.

I can't let this happen. But what do I say? I haven't prepared anything. Paul said it was all set up and all I had to do was shake their hands.

'We'll certainly discuss it again before we make a decision,' Doug's saying. He gives me a brief smile. 'And as I say, we would like to continue links with the Panther Corporation, so this has been a useful meeting in any case.'

He's pushing back his chair. I can't let this slip away! I have to try to win them round. I have to try and shut the deal.

Close the deal. That's what I meant.

'Wait!' I hear myself say. 'I have a few points to make.'

What am I talking about? I have no points to make.

There's a can of Panther Prime sitting on the desk, and I grab it for inspiration. Playing for time, I stand up, walk to the centre of the room and raise the can high into the air where we can all see it.

'Panther Prime is . . . a sports drink.' I stop, and there's a polite silence. My heart is thumping. My face is hot. 'It . . . um . . . it is very . . .' Oh God. What am I doing? Come *on*, Emma. *Think*. Think Panther Prime . . . think Panther Cola . . . think . . . think . . .

Yes! Of course!

'Since the launch of Panther Cola in the late 1980s, Panther drinks have been a byword for energy, excitement and excellence,' I say fluently. This is the standard marketing blurb for Panther Cola. I've typed it out so many zillions of times, I could recite it in my sleep.

'Panther drinks are a marketing phenomenon,' I continue. 'The Panther character is one of the most widely recognised in the world, while the classic slogan "Don't Pause" has made it into dictionaries. We are now offering Glen Oil an exclusive opportunity to join with this premium, world-famous brand.'

My confidence growing, I start to stride around the room, gesturing with the can. 'By buying a Panther health drink, the consumer is signalling that he will settle for nothing but the best.' I hit the can sharply with my other hand. 'He expects the best from his energy drink, he expects the best from his petrol, he expects the best from himself.'

I'm flying! I'm fantastic! If Paul could see me now, he'd give me a promotion on the spot! I come over to the desk and look Doug Hamilton right in the eye. 'When the Panther consumer opens that can, he is making a choice that tells the world who he is. I'm asking Glen Oil to make the same choice.'

As I finish speaking I plant the can firmly in the middle of the desk, reach for the ring pull and, with a cool smile, snap it back.

It's like a volcano erupting.

Fizzy cranberry-flavoured drink explodes in a whoosh out of the can, landing on the desk, drenching the papers in lurid red liquid . . . and oh no, please no . . . spattering all over Doug Hamilton's shirt.

'Fuck!' I gasp. 'I mean, I'm really sorry . . .'

'Jesus Christ,' says Doug Hamilton. 'Does this stuff stain?'

'Er . . .' I grab the can helplessly. 'I don't know.'

'I'll get a cloth,' says the other guy, and leaps to his feet.

The door closes behind him and there's silence, apart from the sound of cranberry drink dripping slowly onto the floor.

I stare at Doug Hamilton, my face hot and blood throbbing through my ears. 'Please . . . Don't tell my boss.'

After all that. I screwed it up.

As I collapse on a bar stool at Glasgow Airport, I feel completely dejected. Doug Hamilton was quite sweet in the end. He said he was sure the stain would come out, and promised he wouldn't tell Paul what happened. But he didn't change his mind about the deal.

My first big meeting. My first big chance—and this is what happens. I feel like giving up on the whole thing. I feel like phoning the office and saying 'That's it, I'm never coming back again, and by the way, it was me who jammed the photocopier that time.' But I can't. This is my third career in four years. It *has* to work. For my own self-worth. For my own self-esteem. And also because I owe my dad four thousand quid.

'So what can I get you?' says an Australian guy, and I look up dazedly.

'Erm . . . a vodka and tonic. Thanks.'

As he moves away, I slump down again in my stool. An air hostess with a French plait comes and sits down two bar stools away.

I don't know how other people manage their careers, I really don't. Like my oldest friend Lissy. She's always known she wanted to be a lawyer—and now, ta-daah! She's a fraud barrister. But I left college with absolutely no clue. My first job was in estate agency, and I only went into it because I've always quite liked looking round houses. But the minute I started, I hated it. So after six months I announced I was changing career and was going to be a photographer instead. My dad lent me the money for a photography course and camera, and I was going to launch this amazing new creative career.

Except it didn't quite happen like that.

I mean, for a start, do you have any idea how much a photographer's assistant gets paid? Nothing. Which, you know, I wouldn't have minded

14

if anyone had actually *offered* me a photographer's assistant's job. I got more and more into debt, and started temping and applying for jobs that actually paid money. And eventually, eleven months ago, I started at the Panther Corporation.

The barman places a vodka and tonic in front of me. I'm just taking a sip when my mobile starts to ring.

My stomach gives a nervous flip. If it's the office, I'll just pretend I didn't hear. But it's not, it's our home number flashing on the screen.

'Hiya!' comes Lissy's voice. 'Only me! So how did it go?'

Lissy is my flatmate and my oldest friend in the world. She has tufty dark hair and an IQ of about 600 and is the sweetest person I know.

'It was a disaster,' I say miserably. 'Not only did I not get the deal, I drenched the marketing director of Glen Oil in cranberry drink.'

Along the bar, I can see the air hostess hiding a smile, and I feel myself flush. Great. Now the whole world knows.

'Oh dear.' I can almost *feel* Lissy trying to think of something positive to say. 'Well, at least they won't forget you in a hurry.'

'I suppose,' I say morosely. 'So, did I have any messages?'

'Oh. Erm . . . your dad did phone, but . . .' She tails off evasively.

'Lissy. What did he want?'

There's a pause. 'Apparently your cousin's won some industry award,' she says apologetically. 'They're going to be celebrating it on Saturday as well as your mum's birthday.'

'Oh. Great.' I slump deeper in my chair. That's all I need. My cousin Kerry triumphantly clutching some silver Best-travel-agent-in-the-world-no-make-that-universe trophy.

'And Connor rang, too, to see how you got on,' adds Lissy quickly. 'He was really sweet—he said he didn't want to ring your mobile during your meeting in case it disturbed you.'

'Really?' At last I feel a lift in spirits. Connor. My lovely, thoughtful boyfriend. My tall, handsome, clever boyfriend, whom *Marketing Week* called 'one of the brightest sparks in marketing research today'.

'He's such a sweetheart!' Lissy is saying. 'He said he's tied up in a big meeting all afternoon but he's cancelled his squash game especially, so do you want to go out to supper tonight?'

'Oh,' I say, with a flicker of pleasure. 'Oh well, that'll be nice.'

I click off and take another sip of vodka, allowing thoughts of Connor to roll round my brain and comfort me. The way his blond hair shines in the sunshine, and the way he's always smiling. And the way he upgraded all the software on my computer the other day without me even asking, and the way he . . . he . . .

My mind's gone blank. This is ridiculous. I mean, there's so much that is wonderful about Connor. From his . . . his long legs. Yes. And his broad shoulders. To the time he looked after me when I had the flu.

I'm so lucky, I really am.

I glance at the clock behind the bar. Forty minutes to go before the flight. Not long now. Nerves are starting to creep over me like little insects, and I take a deep gulp of vodka, draining my glass.

I'm not frightened. I'm just . . . I'm just . . .

OK. I am frightened.

16. I'm scared of flying.

I've never told anyone I'm scared of flying. It just sounds so lame. And I mean, it's not like I'm phobic or anything. But over the last few years, I've gradually got more and more nervous. I know it's completely irrational. I know you have less chance of being in a plane crash than . . . finding a man in London, or something. But still. I just don't like it.

Maybe I'll have another quick vodka.

By the time my flight is called, I've drunk two more vodkas and am feeling a lot more positive. I mean, Lissy's right. At least I made an impression, didn't I? At least they'll remember who I am. As I stride towards the gate, clutching my briefcase, I almost start to feel like a confident businesswoman again. A couple of people smile at me as they pass, and I smile broadly back, feeling a warm glow of friendliness.

I reach the entrance to the plane, and there at the door, taking boarding passes, is the air hostess with the French plait who was sitting at the bar earlier. 'Hi again,' I say smiling. 'This is a coincidence!'

The air hostess stares at me. 'Hi. Erm . . .'

'What?' Why does she look embarrassed?

'Sorry. It's just . . .' She gestures awkwardly to my front.

'What is it?' I say, pleasantly. I look down, and freeze, aghast.

Somehow my silky shirt has been unbuttoning itself. My bra shows. My pink lacy bra. The one that went a bit blobby in the wash. That's why those people were smiling at me.

'Thanks,' I mutter, and do up the buttons with fumbling fingers.

'It hasn't been your day, has it?' says the air hostess sympathetically. 'Sorry, I couldn't help overhearing, earlier.'

'That's all right.' I raise a half-smile. 'No, it hasn't been the best day of my life.' There's a short silence as she studies my boarding pass.

'Tell you what,' she says. 'Would you like an on-board upgrade?'

'A what?' I stare at her blankly.

'Come on. You deserve a break.'

'Really? But . . . can you just upgrade people like that?'

'If there are spare seats, we can. We use our discretion.' She gives me a conspiratorial smile. 'Just don't tell everyone, OK?'

She leads me into the front section of the plane and gestures to a big, wide, comfortable seat.

'Wow,' I whisper, taking in the hushed, luxury atmosphere. This is going to be a completely pleasurable experience from start to finish, I tell myself firmly. I reach for my seat belt and buckle it up nonchalantly, trying to ignore the flutters of apprehension in my stomach.

'Would you like some champagne?' It's the air hostess, beaming.

'That would be great,' I say. 'Thanks!' Champagne!

'And for you, sir? Some champagne?'

The man in the seat next to mine hasn't even looked up yet. He's wearing jeans and an old sweatshirt and is staring out of the window. As he turns to answer I catch a glimpse of dark eyes, stubble, a deep frown etched on his forehead.

'No thanks. Just a brandy. Thanks.'

He has a dry, American voice. I'm about to ask him politely where he's from, but he turns back and stares out of the window again. Which is fine because, to be honest, I'm not much in the mood for talking either.

OK. The truth is, I don't like this.

While we were taking off I counted very slowly with my eyes closed, and that kind of worked. But I ran out of steam at about 350. So now I'm just sitting, sipping champagne, reading an article on '30 Things To Do Before You're 30' in *Cosmo*. I'm trying very hard to look like a relaxed, business-class, top marketing executive. But oh God. Every tiny sound makes me start; every judder makes me catch my breath.

With an outward veneer of calm I reach for the laminated safety instructions and run my eyes over them. Safety exits. Brace position—

Why am I even *looking* at this? How will it help me to gaze at pictures of stick people jumping into the ocean while their plane explodes?

'Excuse me, madam.' An air hostess with red curls has appeared by my side. 'Are you travelling on business?'

'Yes,' I say, smoothing down my hair with a prickle of pride.

She hands me a leaflet entitled 'Executive Facilities'. 'This is some information about our new business-class lounge at Gatwick. Would you be interested?'

'Another time, maybe,' I say. 'And while you're here—I was just wondering. Is that sound normal?'

17

'What sound?' The air hostess cocks her head.

'That sound. That kind of whining, coming from the wing?'

'I can't hear anything.' She looks at me sympathetically. 'Are you a nervous flyer?'

'No!' I say at once, and give a little laugh. 'No, I'm not *nervous*! I just . . . was wondering. Just out of interest.'

'I'll see if I can find out for you,' she says kindly. The hostess moves on, staggering a little as the plane gives a bump.

Why is the plane bumping?

Oh God. A sudden rush of fear hits me with no warning. This is madness. Madness! Sitting in this big heavy box, with no way of escape, thousands and thousands of feet above the ground . . .

Maybe I'll start counting again. Three hundred and forty-nine. Three hundred and fifty. Three hundred and—

Fuck. My head jerks up. What was that bump? Did we just get *hit*?

OK, don't panic. It was just a bump. I'm sure everything's fine. We probably just flew into a pigeon or something. Where was I?

Three hundred and fifty-one. Three hundred and fifty-two—

And that's it. That's the moment. Everything seems to fragment.

I hear the screams like a wave over my head.

Oh God. Oh God Oh God Oh God Oh . . . OH . . . NO. NO. NO.

We're plummeting downwards. The plane's dropping like a stone. A man over there has just shot up through the air and banged his head on the ceiling. He's bleeding. I'm clutching at my seat, trying not to do the same thing, but I can feel myself being wrenched upwards. There's no time to think. My mind can't . . . Bags are flying around, drinks are spilling, one of the cabin crew has fallen over . . .

Oh God. Oh God. OK, it's slowing down now. It's . . . it's kind of . . . back to normal.

'Ladies and gentlemen,' comes a voice over the intercom, and everyone's head jerks up. 'This is your captain speaking.'

My heart's juddering in my chest. I can't listen. I can't think.

'We're currently hitting some clear-air turbulence, and things may be unsteady for a while—'

There's another huge lurch, and his voice is drowned by screams.

It's like a bad dream. A bad roller-coaster dream.

The cabin crew are all strapping themselves into their seats. One of the hostesses is mopping blood on her face. 'Please keep calm,' the captain is saying. 'As soon as we have more information . . .'

Keep *calm*? I can't breathe, let alone keep calm. What are we going to do? I can hear someone behind me reciting 'Hail Mary, full of grace . . .'

and a fresh, choking panic sweeps through me.

We're going to die.

'I'm sorry?' The American man in the next seat looks at me, his face tense and white.

Did I just say that aloud?

'We're going to die.' I stare into his face. This could be the last person I ever see alive. I take in the lines etched around his dark eyes, his strong jaw, shaded with stubble.

'I don't think we're going to die,' he says. But he's gripping his seat-arms, too. 'They said it was just turbulence—'

'Of course they did!' I can hear the hysteria in my voice. 'They wouldn't exactly say, "OK folks, that's it, you're all goners"!' The plane gives another terrifying swoop and I find myself clutching the man's hand in panic. 'We're not going to make it. I know we're not. This is it. I'm twenty-five years old, for God's sake. I'm not ready. I haven't achieved anything. I've never had children, I've never saved a life . . .' My eyes fall randomly on the '30 Things To Do Before You're 30' article. 'I haven't ever climbed a mountain, I don't even *know* if I've got a G spot . . .'

'I'm sorry?' says the man, taken aback, but I barely hear him.

'My career's a complete joke. I'm just a crappy assistant and I just had my first ever big meeting and it was a complete disaster. Half the time I haven't got a clue what people are talking about, I don't know what logistical means, I'm never going to get promoted, and I owe my dad four thousand quid, and I've never really been in love . . .'

I draw myself up short with a jolt. 'I'm sorry,' I say, and exhale sharply. 'You don't want to hear all this.'

'That's quite all right,' says the man.

God. I'm completely losing it.

And anyway, what I just said wasn't true. Because I am in love with Connor. It must be the altitude or something, confusing my mind.

Flustered, I push the hair off my face and try to get a hold of myself. OK, let's try counting again. Three hundred and fifty . . . six. Oh God. Oh God. No. Please. We're plummeting.

'I've never done anything to make my parents proud of me.' The words come spilling out of my mouth before I can stop them. 'Never.'

'I'm sure that's not true,' says the man nicely.

'It's true. Maybe they used to be proud of me. But then my cousin Kerry came to live with us and all at once it was like my parents couldn't see me any more. All they could see was her. She was fourteen when she arrived, and I was ten, and I thought it was going to be great, you know. Like having an older sister. But it didn't work out like that . . .'

I can't stop talking. I just can't stop. Every time the plane bumps or jolts, another torrent of words pours randomly out of my mouth, like water gushing over a waterfall. It's either talk or scream.

'. . . she was a swimming champion, and an everything champion, and I was just . . . nothing in comparison . . .'

'. . . photography course and I honestly thought it was going to change my life . . .'

'. . . eight stone three. But I was planning to go on a diet . . .'

'. . . I applied for every single job in the world. I was so desperate, I even applied to . . .'

'. . . awful girl called Artemis. This new desk arrived the other day, and she just took it, even though I've got this really grotty little desk . . .'

'. . . sweet girl Katie, who works in Personnel. We have this secret code where she comes in and says, "Can I go through some numbers with you, Emma?" and it means "Shall we nip out to Starbucks?". . .'

'. . . the coffee at work is the most disgusting stuff you've ever drunk, absolute poison . . .'

'. . . sometimes, when I'm pissed off with Artemis, I water her stupid spider plant with orange juice, just to serve her right . . .'

'. . . put "Maths GCSE grade A" on my CV, when I really only got C. I know it was dishonest. I know I shouldn't have done it, but I *so* wanted to get the job . . .'

What's happened to me? Normally there's a kind of filter that stops me blurting out everything I'm thinking, that keeps me in check. But the filter's stopped working. Everything's piling out in a big, random stream, and I can't stop it.

'. . . wear G-strings because they don't give you VPL. But they're *so* uncomfortable . . .'

'. . . size eight, and I didn't know what to do, so I just said "Wow those are absolutely fantastic . . ."'

'. . . roasted peppers, my favourite food . . .'

'. . . joined a book group, but I couldn't get through *Great Expectations*. So I just skimmed the back cover and pretended I'd read it . . .'

'. . . I gave him all his goldfish food; I honestly don't know what happened . . .'

'. . . *really* wish I had bigger boobs. I mean, not Page 3 size, not completely enormous and stupid, but you know, bigger . . .'

'. . . perfect date would start off with champagne just *appearing* at the table, as if by magic . . .'

'. . . I just cracked, I secretly bought this huge tub of Häagen-Dazs and scoffed the lot, and I never told Lissy . . .'

I'm unaware of anything around us. The world has narrowed to me and this stranger, and my mouth, spewing out all my innermost thoughts and secrets. I barely know what I'm saying any more. All I know is, it feels good. Is this what therapy is like?

'. . . name was Danny Nussbaum. Mum and Dad were downstairs watching *Ben Hur* . . .'

'. . . works in the market research department. I remember thinking the very first time I saw him, Wow, he's good-looking. He's very tall and blond, because he's half-Swedish, and he has these amazing blue eyes . . .'

'. . . always have a sweet sherry before a date, to calm my nerves . . .'

'. . . Connor's completely wonderful. I'm just so lucky. Everyone's always telling me how great he is. He's sweet, and he's good, and he's successful and everyone calls us the perfect couple . . .'

'. . . I'd never tell anyone this in a million years. But sometimes I think he's almost *too* good-looking. A bit like one of those dolls? Like Ken.'

And now I'm on the subject of Connor, I'm saying things I've never said to anyone. Things I never even realised were in my head.

'. . . gave him this lovely leather watch for Christmas, but he insists on wearing this orange digital thing because it can tell him the temperature in Poland or something stupid. . .'

'. . . took me to all these jazz concerts and I pretended to enjoy them to be polite, so now he thinks I love jazz . . .'

'. . . every single Woody Allen film off by heart and says each line before it comes and it drives me crackers . . .'

'. . . determined to find my G spot, so we spent the whole weekend doing it in different positions, and by the end I was just knackered . . .'

'. . . he kept saying, what was it like, what was it like? So in the end I said it felt as though my whole body was opening up like a flower, and he said, what sort of flower, so I said a begonia . . .'

'. . . can't expect the initial passion to last. But how do you tell if the passion's faded in a good, long-term-commitment way or in a crap, we-don't-fancy-each-other-any-more way . . .'

'. . . knight in shining armour is not a realistic option. But there's a part of me that wants a huge, amazing romance. I want to be swept off my feet. I want something *exciting*. Sometimes I feel as if there's this whole new, thrilling life waiting for me out there, and if I can just—'

'Excuse me, miss?'

'What?' I look up dazedly. 'What is it?'

The air hostess with the French plait is smiling at me. 'We've landed.'

I stare at her. 'We've *landed*?'

This doesn't make sense. How can we have landed? I look around—

and sure enough, the plane's still. We're on the ground.

'We aren't bumping any more,' I say stupidly.

'We stopped bumping quite a while ago,' says the American man.

'We're . . . we're not going to die.'

'We're not going to die,' he agrees.

I look at him as though for the first time—and it hits me. I've been blabbering nonstop for an hour to this complete stranger. God alone knows what I've been saying.

I think I want to get off this plane right now.

'I'm sorry,' I say awkwardly. 'You should have stopped me.'

'That would have been a little difficult.' There's a tiny smile at his lips. 'You were on a bit of a roll.'

'I'm so embarrassed!' I try to smile back but I can't even look him in the eye. I mean, I told him about my knickers. I told him about my *G spot*.

'Don't worry about it. We were all stressed out. That was some flight.' He picks up his knapsack and gets up from his seat—then looks back at me. 'Will you be OK getting back home?'

'Yes. I'll be fine. Thanks. Enjoy your visit!' I call after him.

Slowly I gather my things together and make my way off the plane. I feel sweaty, my hair's all over the place, and my head is starting to throb.

The airport seems so bright and still and calm after the intense atmosphere of the plane. The ground seems so firm. I sit quietly on a plastic chair for a while, trying to get myself together, but as I stand up at last, I still feel dazed. I walk along in a slight blur, hardly able to believe I'm here. I'm alive. I honestly never thought I'd make it back on the ground.

'Emma!' I hear someone calling as I come out of Arrivals. I raise my head in disbelief. Is that . . . No. It can't be, it can't— It's Connor.

He looks heartbreakingly handsome. His skin has that Scandinavian tan and his eyes are bluer than ever, and he's running towards me. This makes no sense. What's he doing here?

As we reach each other he grabs me and pulls me tight to his chest. 'Thank God,' he says huskily. 'Thank God. Are you OK?'

'Connor, what—what are you doing here?'

'I phoned the airline to ask what time you'd be landing, and they told me the plane had hit terrible turbulence. I just had to come to the airport.' He gazes down at me. 'Emma, I watched your plane land. They sent an ambulance straight out to it. Then you didn't appear. I thought . . .' He swallows hard. 'I don't know exactly what I thought.'

'I'm fine. I was just . . . trying to get myself together. Oh God, Connor, it was terrifying.' My voice is suddenly all shaky.

'When you didn't come through the barrier . . . I think I realised for

·the first time quite how deeply I feel about you.'

'Really?' I falter.

'Emma, I think we should . . .'

Get married? My heart jumps in fear. Oh my God. He's going to ask me to marry him, right here in the airport. What am I going to say?

'. . . move in together,' he finishes.

I am such a deluded moron. Obviously he wasn't going to ask me to *marry* him.

'What do you think?' he strokes my hair gently.

'Erm . . .' I rub my dry face, unable to think straight. Move in with Connor. It kind of makes sense. Is there a reason why not? I feel all confused. Something's tugging at my brain, trying to send me a message . . .

And into my head slide some of the things I said on the plane. Something about never having been properly in love.

But then . . . that was just drivel, wasn't it? I mean, I thought I was about to die, for God's sake. I wasn't exactly at my most lucid.

'Connor, what about your big meeting?' I say, suddenly recalling.

'I cancelled it.'

'You cancelled it?' I stare at him. 'For me?'

Oh God, just look at him. He's tall and he's handsome, and he cancelled a big meeting, and he came to rescue me.

It's love. It has to be love.

'I'd love to move in with you, Connor,' I whisper, and to my utter astonishment I burst into tears.

I WAKE UP the next morning with sunlight dazzling my eyelids and a delicious smell of coffee in the air. Something's niggling at me. Have I forgotten something?

As I half listen to Connor clattering around the kitchen, my mind gropes blearily for clues. It's Saturday. I'm in Connor's bed. We went out for supper— Oh God, that awful plane ride . . . He came to the airport, and he said . . . We're moving in together!

I sit up, just as Connor comes in with two mugs and a cafetière. He's dressed in a white waffle robe and looks completely gorgeous.

'Hi,' he says. He hands me my coffee. 'How are you feeling?'

I push my hair back off my face. 'A bit groggy.'

'I'm not surprised. Quite a day yesterday.'

'Absolutely.' I nod. 'So. We're . . . going to live together!'

'If you're still on for it?'

'Of course! Of course I am!' I smile brightly. And it's true. I am. Overnight, I've turned into a grown-up. I'm moving in with my boyfriend.

'I'll have to give Andrew notice . . .' Connor gestures towards the wall, on the other side of which is his flatmate's room.

'And I'll have to tell Lissy and Jemima.'

'And we'll have to find the right place. And you'll have to promise to keep it tidy.' He gives me a teasing grin.

'I like that!' I feign outrage. 'You're the one with fifty million CDs.'

'That's different!'

'How is it different, may I ask?' I plant my hand on my hip, like someone in a sitcom, and Connor laughs.

There's a pause, as though we've both run out of steam, and we take a sip of coffee.

'So anyway,' says Connor after a while, 'I should get going.' Connor is attending a course on computers this weekend. 'I'm sorry I'll miss your parents,' he adds.

And he really is. I mean, as if he wasn't already the perfect boyfriend, he actually *enjoys* visiting my parents.

'That's OK,' I say benevolently. 'It doesn't matter.'

'Oh, and I forgot to tell you.' Connor gives me a mysterious grin. 'Guess what I've got tickets for?'

'Ooh!' I say excitedly. 'Um . . .' I'm about to say 'Paris!'

'The jazz festival!' Connor beams. 'The Dennisson Quartet! It's their last concert of the year. Remember we heard them at Ronnie Scott's?'

For a moment I can't quite speak.

'Wow!' I manage at last. 'The Dennisson Quartet! I do remember.'

They played clarinets. On and on and on, for about two hours.

'I knew you'd be pleased.' Connor touches my arm affectionately.

I give him a feeble smile. The thing is, I probably will get to like jazz one day. In fact, I'm positive I will.

I watch fondly as he gets dressed, flosses his teeth and picks up his briefcase. 'Have a lovely day with your family.' He comes over to the bed to kiss me, and then hesitates. 'Emma?'

'Yes?'

He sits down on the bed and gazes seriously at me. Gosh, his eyes are so blue. 'There's something I wanted to say.' He bites his lip. 'You know we always speak frankly to each other about our relationship.'

'Er . . . yes,' I say, feeling a little apprehensive.

'This is just an idea. You may not like it. I was thinking that perhaps . . .' He stops awkwardly. His face is growing pink.

Oh my God. Is he going to start getting kinky?

'We could start calling each other "darling",' he says in an embarrassed rush.

'What?' I say blankly.

'It's just that . . .' Connor flushes pinker. 'I noticed recently, we never seem to use any . . . terms of endearment.'

I stare at him, feeling caught out. 'Don't we?'

'No.'

'Oh.' Now I think about it, he's right. We don't. Why don't we?

'So what do you think? Only if you want to.'

'Absolutely!' I say quickly. 'I mean, you're right. Of course we should.' I clear my throat. 'Darling!'

'Thanks, darling,' he says, with a loving smile, and I smile back, trying to ignore the tiny protests inside my head.

This doesn't feel right. I don't feel like a darling.

Darling is a married person with pearls and a four-wheel-drive.

'Emma?' Connor's staring at me. 'Is something wrong?'

'I'm not sure!' I give a self-conscious laugh. 'I just don't know if I feel like a "darling". But it may grow on me.'

'Well, we can use something else. What about "dear"?'

Dear? Is he serious?

'No,' I say quickly. 'I think "darling" is better.'

'Or "sweetheart" . . . "honey" . . . "angel" . . .'

'Maybe. Look, can we just leave it?'

Connor's face falls, and I feel bad. Come on. I can call my boyfriend 'darling', for God's sake. This is what growing up's all about.

'Connor, I'm sorry,' I say. 'I don't know what's wrong with me. Maybe I'm still a bit tense after that flight.' I take his hand. 'Darling.'

'That's all right, darling.' He smiles back at me, his sunny expression restored, and gives me a kiss. 'See you later.'

You see. Easy.

Oh God.

It takes me about half an hour to get from Connor's place in Maida Vale to Islington, which is where I live, and when I open the door I find Lissy on the sofa. She's surrounded by papers and has a frown of concentration on her face. She works so hard, Lissy. She really overdoes it.

'What are you working on?' I ask sympathetically. 'That fraud case?'

'No, it's this article,' says Lissy abstractly, and lifts up a glossy magazine. 'It says that since the days of Cleopatra the proportions of beauty have been the same, and there's a way to work out how beautiful you are, scientifically. You do all these measurements . . .'

'Oh right!' I say interestedly. 'So what are you?'

'I'm just working it out.' She frowns at the page again. 'That makes fifty-three . . . subtract twenty . . . makes . . . Oh my God!' She stares at the page in dismay. 'I only got thirty-three out of a hundred!'

'Oh Lissy. That's crap.'

'I know,' says Lissy seriously. 'I'm ugly. I knew it'

'No!' I say, trying not to laugh. 'I meant the magazine's crap! You can't measure beauty with some stupid index. Just *look* at you!' I gesture at Lissy, who has the biggest grey eyes in the world and gorgeous clear pale skin, and is frankly stunning, even if her last haircut was a bit severe. 'I mean, who are you going to believe? The mirror or a stupid mindless magazine article?'

'A stupid mindless magazine article,' says Lissy, as though it's perfectly obvious.

I know she's half joking. But ever since her boyfriend Simon chucked her, Lissy's had really low self-esteem. I'm a bit worried about her.

'Is that the golden proportion of beauty?' says our other flatmate Jemima, tapping into the room in her kitten heels. She's wearing pale pink jeans and a tight white top, and as usual she looks perfectly tanned and groomed. In theory, Jemima has a job in a sculpture gallery. But all she ever seems to do is have bits of her waxed and plucked and massaged, and go on dates with city bankers, whose salaries she always checks out before she says yes.

I do get on with Jemima. Kind of. It's just that she tends to begin all her sentences 'If you want a rock on your finger,' and 'If you want an SW3 address,' and 'If you want to be known as a seriously good dinnerparty hostess.' I mean, I wouldn't *mind* being known as a seriously good dinner-party hostess. It's just not exactly highest on my list of priorities right now. Plus, Jemima's idea of being a seriously good dinner-party hostess is inviting lots of rich friends over, decorating the whole flat with twiggy things, getting caterers to cook loads of yummy food and telling everyone she made it herself, then sending her flatmates (me and Lissy) out to the cinema for the night and looking affronted when they dare creep back in at midnight and make themselves a hot chocolate.

'I did that quiz,' she says now, picking up her pink Louis Vuitton bag.

Her dad bought it for her as a present when she broke up with a guy after three dates. Like she was heartbroken.

Mind you, he had a yacht, so she probably was heartbroken.

'What did you get?' says Lissy.

'Eighty-nine.' She tosses back her long blond hair. 'So Emma, is it true you're moving in with Connor?'

I gape at her. 'How did you know that?'

'Word on the street. Andrew called Rupes this morning about cricket, and he told him.'

'Are you moving in with Connor?' says Lissy incredulously. 'Why didn't you tell me?'

'I was about to, honestly. Isn't it great?'

'Bad move, Emma.' Jemima shakes her head. 'Very bad tactics.'

'Tactics?' says Lissy, rolling her eyes. '*Tactics?* Jemima, they're having a relationship, not playing chess!'

'A relationship *is* a game of chess,' retorts Jemima. 'Mummy says you always have to look ahead. You have to plan strategically. If you make the wrong move, you've had it. Just remember, Emma, *if* you want a rock on your finger, don't move in with Connor.'

Her eyes give a swift, Pavlovian glance to the photograph on the mantelpiece of her meeting Prince William at a charity polo match.

'Still holding out for Royalty?' says Lissy. 'How much younger is he than you again, Jemima?'

'Don't be stupid!' she snaps, colour tingeing her cheeks.

'Anyway, I don't *want* a rock on my finger,' I retort.

Jemima raises her perfectly arched eyebrows as though to say, 'You poor, ignorant fool', and turns to go. 'Oh,' she suddenly adds, her eyes narrowing. 'Has either of you borrowed my Joseph jumper?'

There's a tiny beat of silence.

'No,' I say innocently.

'I don't even know which one it is,' says Lissy, with a shrug.

I can't look at Lissy. I'm sure I saw her wearing it the other night.

'Because I have very slender arms,' Jemima says warningly, 'and I really don't want the sleeves stretched. And don't think I won't notice, because I will. Ciao.'

The minute she's gone, Lissy and I look at each other.

'Shit,' says Lissy. 'I think I left it at work. Oh well, I'll pick it up on Monday.' She goes back to reading the magazine.

OK. So we do both occasionally borrow Jemima's clothes. Without asking. But in our defence, she has so many she hardly ever notices.

'And anyway,' adds Lissy, 'she owes it to me for writing her that letter to the council about all her parking tickets.' She looks up. 'So what are you doing later on? D'you want to see a film?'

'I can't,' I say reluctantly. 'I've got my mum's birthday lunch.'

'Oh yes, of course.' She pulls a sympathetic face. 'Good luck.'

Lissy is the only person in the world who has any idea how I feel about visiting home. And even she doesn't know it all.

But as I sit on the train down, I'm resolved that this time will be better.

I will not: let my family stress me out; feel jealous of Kerry or let Nev wind me up; look at my watch, wondering how soon I can leave.

I will: stay serene and loving and remember that we are all sacred links in the eternal circle of life. (I got that from a Cindy Blaine show.)

Mum and Dad used to live in Twickenham, which is where I grew up. But now they've moved to a village in Hampshire. I arrive at their house, just after twelve, to find Mum in the kitchen with my cousin Kerry. She and her husband, Nev, have moved out too, to a village about five minutes' drive from Mum and Dad, so they see each other all the time.

I feel a familiar pang as I see them, standing side by side by the stove. They look more like mother and daughter than aunt and niece. They've got the same feather-cut hair, they're both wearing brightly coloured tops that show a lot of tanned cleavage, and they're both laughing. On the counter, I notice a bottle of white wine already half gone.

'Happy birthday!' I say, hugging Mum. As I glimpse a wrapped parcel on the kitchen table, I feel a little thrill of anticipation. I have got Mum the *best* birthday present. I can't wait to give it to her!

'Hiya!' says Kerry, turning round in her apron. Her blue eyes are heavily made up, and round her neck she's wearing a diamond cross, which I haven't seen before. Every time I see Kerry she has a new piece of jewellery. 'Great to see you, Emma! We don't see enough of you. Do we, Auntie Rachel?'

'We certainly don't,' says Mum, giving me a hug.

'Shall I take your coat?' says Kerry, as I put the bottle of champagne I've brought into the fridge. 'And what about a drink?'

This is how Kerry talks to me. As though I'm a visitor. But I'm not going to stress about it. Sacred links in the eternal circle of life.

'It's OK,' I say, trying to sound pleasant. 'I'll get it. Can I do anything to help?'

'I don't *think* so . . .' says Kerry, looking critically around the kitchen. 'Everything's pretty much done. So I said to Elaine,' she adds to Mum, '"Where did you get those shoes?" And she said M&S!'

'Who's Elaine?' I say, trying to join in.

'At the golf club,' says Kerry.

Mum never used to play golf. But when she moved to Hampshire she and Kerry took it up together. And now all I hear about is golf matches, golf club dinners, and endless parties with chums from the golf club.

'You could feed Sammy,' mum says, giving me a pot of goldfish food. She frowns anxiously. 'You know, I'm a bit worried about Sammy.'

'Oh,' I say, feeling a spasm of alarm. 'Er . . . why?'

'He just doesn't seem *himself*.' She peers at him in his bowl. 'What do you think? Does he look right to you?'

I follow her gaze and pull a thoughtful face, as though I'm studying Sammy's features. I never thought she would notice.

'He's probably just a bit depressed,' I say at last. 'He'll get over it.'

'OK, well why don't you go and say hello to Dad?' says Mum, sieving some peas. 'Lunch won't be for another ten minutes or so.'

I find Dad and Nev in the sitting room, in front of the cricket. The room has recently been redecorated, but on the wall there's still a display of all Kerry's swimming cups. Mum polishes them every week. Plus my couple of riding rosettes. I think she flicks those with a duster.

'Hi, Dad,' I say, giving him a kiss.

'Emma!' He puts a hand to his head in mock surprise. 'You made it! No detours! No visits to historic cities!'

'Not today!' I give a little laugh. 'Safe and sound.'

Once, just after Mum and Dad moved to this house, I took the wrong train down and ended up in Salisbury. Dad always teases me about it.

'Hi, Nev.' I peck him on the cheek, trying not to choke on the amount of aftershave he's wearing. He's in chinos and a white roll-neck, and has a heavy gold bracelet round his wrist. Nev runs his family's company, which supplies office equipment all round the country, and he met Kerry at some convention for young entrepreneurs. Apparently they struck up conversation by admiring each other's Rolex watches.

'Hi, Emma,' Nev says. 'D'you see the new motor?'

'What?' I peer at him blankly—then recall a glossy new car on the drive when I arrived. 'Oh yes! Very smart.'

'Mercedes 5 Series. Forty-two grand list price.'

'Gosh.'

'Didn't pay that, though.' He taps the side of his nose. 'Thirty-seven two-fifty,' he says triumphantly.

'Right. Wow!' I don't really know what else to say, so I perch on the side of the sofa and eat a peanut.

'That's what you're aiming for, Emma!' says Dad. 'Think you'll ever make it?'

'I . . . don't know. Er . . . Dad, that reminds me. I've got a cheque for you.' Awkwardly I reach in my bag and get out a cheque for £300.

'Well done,' says Dad. 'That can go on the tally.' His green eyes twinkle as he puts it in his pocket. 'It's called learning the value of money. Learning to stand on your own two feet!'

'Valuable lesson,' says Nev, nodding. He takes a slug of beer and grins at Dad. 'Just remind me, Emma—what career is it this week?'

When I first met Nev it was just after I'd left the estate agency to become a photographer. Two and a half years ago. And he makes this same joke every time I see him. Every single bloody—

OK, calm down. Happy thoughts. Cherish your family. Cherish Nev.

'It's still marketing!' I say brightly. 'Has been for a year now.'

There's silence for a few minutes, apart from the cricket commentary. Suddenly, Dad and Nev simultaneously groan as something or other happens on the cricket pitch. A moment later they groan again.

'Right,' I say. 'Well, I'll just . . .'

As I get up from the sofa, they don't even turn their heads.

I go out to the hall and pick up the cardboard box I brought down with me. Then I go out of the front door and through the side gate, knock on the annexe door and push it cautiously. 'Grandpa?'

Grandpa is Mum's dad, and he's lived with us ever since he had his heart operation, ten years ago. At the old house in Twickenham he just had a bedroom, but here he has his own annexe tacked on to the side of the house. He's sitting in his favourite armchair, and on the floor in front of him are about six cardboard packing cases.

'Hi, Grandpa,' I say.

'Emma!' He looks up, and his face lights up. 'Darling girl. Come here!' I bend over to give him a kiss, and he squeezes my hand tight.

'I've got some more Panther Bars for you,' I say, nodding to my box. Grandpa is completely addicted to Panther energy bars, and so are all his friends at the bowling club.

'Thank you, my love.' Grandpa beams. 'You're a good girl, Emma. Now, I read a very worrying newspaper article the other day,' he says as I sit down on one of the packing cases. 'About safety in London. Teenagers with flick knives roam the underground, it said.' He gives me a beady look. 'You don't travel on public transport in the evenings, do you?'

'Hardly ever,' I say, crossing my fingers behind my back. 'Just now and then, when I absolutely have to . . . Anyway. What's all this stuff?' I ask, to change the subject.

Grandpa gives a gusty sigh. 'Your mother cleared out the attic last week. I'm just sorting out what to throw away and what to keep.'

'That seems like a good idea. What about these?' I pull out a bundle of old Christmas cards.

'I never throw away cards.' Grandpa gives me a long look. 'When you get to my age, when the people you've known and loved all your life start to pass away . . . you want to hang on to any memento.'

'I can understand that,' I say, feeling touched. I reach for the nearest card, open it and my expression changes. 'Grandpa! This is from Smith's Electrical Maintenance, 1965.'

'Frank Smith was a very good man—' starts Grandpa.

'You have to throw *some* of them away!' I exclaim. 'And what are these?' I reach into the box again and pull out an envelope of photos. 'Are these actually of anything you really want to—'

Something shoots through my heart and I stop, midstream.

I'm looking at a photograph of me and Dad and Mum, sitting on a bench in a park. Mum's wearing a flowery dress, and Dad's wearing a stupid sunhat, and I'm on his knee, aged about nine, eating an ice cream. We all look so happy together.

Wordlessly, I turn to another photo. I've got Dad's hat on and we're all laughing helplessly at something. Just us three.

Just us. Before Kerry came into our lives.

I still remember the day she arrived. A red suitcase in the hall and an unfamiliar smell of perfume in the air. I walked into the kitchen and there she was, a stranger, drinking a cup of tea. She was wearing school uniform, but she still looked like a grown-up to me. She already had an enormous bust, and gold studs in her ears, and streaks in her hair. Mum kept telling me I had to be very kind to her, because her mother had died. That was why she got my room.

I leaf through the pictures, trying to swallow the lump in my throat. I remember this place now. The park we used to go to, with swings and slides. But it was too boring for Kerry, and I desperately wanted to be like her so I said it was boring too, and we never went again.

'Knock knock!' I look up with a start, and Kerry's standing at the door, holding her glass of wine. 'Lunch is ready!'

I cannot cherish her. I cannot do it. I want to throw my treacle tart at her. We've been sitting round the table now for forty minutes and the only voice we've heard is Kerry's.

'It's all about image,' she's saying now. 'It's all about the right clothes, the right look, the right walk. When I walk along the street, the message I give the world is "I am a successful woman."'

'Show us!' says Mum admiringly.

As we all watch, Kerry starts striding round the room. Her chin is raised, her boobs are sticking out, her eyes are fixed on the middle distance and her bottom is jerking from side to side.

She looks like a cross between an ostrich and one of the androids in *Attack of the Clones*. Oh God. I want to giggle. I mustn't. I mustn't.

'Do you want to have a go, Emma?' says Kerry. 'Copy me?'

'Er . . . I don't think so,' I say. 'I think I probably . . . picked up the basics.' Suddenly I give a tiny snort and turn it into a cough.

'Kerry's trying to help you, Emma!' says Mum. 'You are good to Emma, Kerry.' She beams fondly at Kerry, who simpers back.

I take a swig of wine. Yeah, right. Kerry really wants to help me. That's why when I was completely desperate for a job and asked her for work experience at her company, she said no. I wrote her this long, careful letter, saying I realised it put her in an awkward situation but I'd really appreciate any chance, even a couple of days running errands.

And she sent back a standard rejection letter.

I was so totally mortified, I never told anyone.

'You should listen to some of Kerry's business tips, Emma,' Dad is saying sharply. 'Maybe if you paid attention you'd do a bit better in life.'

'It's only a walk,' quips Nev with a chortle. 'It's not a miracle cure!'

'Nev!' says Mum half reprovingly.

'Emma knows I'm joking, don't you, Emma?' says Nev easily.

'Of course!' I say, forcing myself to smile gaily.

Just wait till I get promoted. Just wait. Just wait.

'Emma! Earth to Emma!' Kerry is waving a comical hand in front of my face. 'Wake up, Dopey! We're doing presents.'

'Oh right,' I say, coming to. 'OK, I'll just go and get mine.'

As Mum opens a camera from Dad and a purse from Grandpa, I start to feel excited. I *so* hope Mum likes my present.

'It doesn't look much,' I say as I hand her the pink envelope. 'But you'll see when you open it . . .'

'What can it be?' Mum says, looking intrigued. She rips open the envelope, opens the flowered card and stares at it. 'Oh, Emma!'

'What is it?' says Dad.

'It's a day at a spa!' says Mum in delight. 'A whole day of pampering. Thank you, love. How thoughtful!' She leans over to kiss me and I feel a warm glow inside. I had the idea a few months ago. It's a really nice day-long package, with free treatments and everything.

'You get champagne lunch,' I say eagerly. 'And keep the slippers!'

'Wonderful!' says Mum. 'I'll look forward to it.'

'Oh dear,' says Kerry, giving a little laugh. She looks at the large creamy envelope in her own hands. 'My present's slightly upstaged, I'm afraid. Never mind. I'll change it.'

I look up, alert. There's something about Kerry's voice. I know something's up. I just know it.

'What do you mean?' says Mum.

'It doesn't matter,' says Kerry. 'I'll just . . . find something else. Not to worry.' She starts to put the envelope away in her bag.

'Kerry, love!' says Mum. 'Stop that! Don't be silly. What is it?'

'Well,' says Kerry. 'It's just that Emma and I seem to have had the same idea.' She hands Mum the envelope with another little laugh.

My whole body stiffens in apprehension. No. She can't have done what I think she's done.

There's complete silence as Mum opens the envelope.

'Oh my goodness!' she says, taking out a gold embossed brochure. 'What's this? Le Spa Meridien?' Something falls out into her hands and she stares at it. 'Tickets to *Paris*? Kerry!'

She has. She's ruined my present.

'For both of you,' adds Kerry, a little smugly. 'Uncle Brian, too.'

'Kerry!' says Dad in delight. 'You marvel!'

'It is supposed to be rather good,' says Kerry with a complacent smile. 'Five-star accommodation . . . the chef has three Michelin stars . . .'

'I don't believe this,' says Mum. She's leafing excitedly through the brochure. 'Look at the swimming pool! Look at the gardens!'

My flowery card is lying, forgotten, amid the wrapping paper.

All at once I feel close to tears. She knew. She *knew*.

'Kerry, you knew,' I suddenly blurt out, unable to stop myself. 'I told you I was giving Mum a spa treat. I *told* you! We had that conversation about it, months ago. In the garden!'

'Did we?' says Kerry casually. 'I don't remember.'

'You do! Of course you remember.'

'Emma!' says Mum sharply. 'It was a simple mistake. Wasn't it, Kerry?'

'Of course it was!' says Kerry, opening her eyes in wide innocence.

'And they're *both* lovely presents. *Both* of them.' Mum smiles at me and I try to smile back. But inside, I feel about ten years old again. Kerry always manages to wrongfoot me. She always has done. Whatever she did, everyone took her side. She was the one whose mother had died. We all had to be nice to her. I could never, ever win.

Trying to pull myself together, I reach for my wine glass and take a huge swig. Then I find myself surreptitiously glancing at my watch. I can leave at four if I make an excuse about trains running late. That's only another hour and a half to get through.

three

ANYWAY. IT DOESN'T MATTER, because I'm going to get a promotion. Then Nev will stop making cracks about my career and I'll be able to pay back Dad. Everyone will be really impressed—and it'll be fantastic!

I wake up on Monday morning feeling totally bouncy and positive, and get dressed in my usual work outfit of jeans and a nice top, this one from French Connection. Well, not exactly French Connection. To be honest, I bought it at Oxfam, but it's practically new! As I skip up the tube steps, the sun's shining and I'm full of optimism.

'Emma!'

I look round to see Katie, my friend from Personnel, climbing the steps behind me, panting slightly. Her curly red hair is all tousled, and she's holding one shoe in her hand.

'What on earth happened?' I say as she reaches the top.

'My stupid shoe,' says Katie disconsolately. 'The heel's just come off.' She flaps it at me. 'God, this day is such a disaster. The milkman forgot to bring me any milk, and I had a *terrible* weekend . . .'

'I thought you were spending it with Charlie,' I say in surprise.

Charlie is Katie's latest man. They've been seeing each other for a few weeks and she was supposed to be visiting his country cottage, which he's doing up at the weekends.

'It was awful! As soon as we arrived, he went off to play golf.'

'Oh right.' I try to find a positive angle. 'Well, at least he's comfortable with you. He can just act normally.'

'Maybe.' She looks at me doubtfully. 'But he said, how did I feel about helping out a bit while he was gone? So I said of course—and then he gave me this paintbrush and three pots of paint and said I should get the sitting room done if I worked fast.'

'*What?*'

'And then he came back at six o'clock—and said my brushwork was careless!' Her voice rises woefully. 'It wasn't!'

'Katie, you're not telling me you actually painted the room.'

'Well . . . yes.' She looks at me with huge blue eyes. 'You know, to help out. But now I'm starting to think . . . is he just using me?'

'Katie, of course he's using you! He wants a free painter-decorator! You have to chuck him. Immediately. Now!'

Katie is silent for a few seconds, and I eye her a bit nervously. Her face is blank but I can tell lots of things are going on beneath the surface. It's a bit like when Jaws disappears underneath the rippling water, and you just know that any minute—

'Oh God, you're right!' she suddenly bursts out. 'You're right. He's been using me! It's my own fault. I should have realised when he asked me if I had any experience in plumbing or roofing.'

'When did he ask you that?' I say incredulously.

'On our first date! I thought he was just making conversation.'

'Katie, it's not your fault.' I squeeze her arm. 'You weren't to know.'

'But what is it about me?' Katie stops still in the street. 'Why do I only attract complete shits? I'm never going to find anyone nice.'

'Don't give up,' I say at once. 'Katie, I just know you're going to find some lovely, kind, wonderful man. I've got a strong feeling about it.'

'Really?' She stares at me. 'You do?'

'Absolutely!' I think quickly for a moment. 'Look, here's an idea. Why don't you try . . . going to have lunch at a different place today. And maybe you'll meet someone there.'

'You think?' She gazes at me. 'OK. I'll try it. The *only* good thing about the weekend,' she adds as we reach the corner, 'is I finished making my new top. What do you think?'

She proudly takes off her jacket and does a twirl, and I stare at her. It's not that I don't *like* crochet . . . OK. It *is* that I don't like crochet. Especially pink, scoop-neck, open-weave crochet tops.

'It's . . . amazing,' I manage at last. 'Absolutely fantastic!'

'Isn't it great?' She gives me a pleased smile. 'So anyway, how about you? Did you have a nice weekend? I bet you did. I bet Connor was completely wonderful and romantic.'

'Actually, he asked me to move in with him,' I say awkwardly.

'Really?' Katie gazes wistfully at me. 'God, Emma, you two make the perfect couple. You give me faith that it can happen.'

I can't help feeling a little flicker of pleasure inside. Me and Connor. The perfect couple. Role models for other people. 'It's not *that* easy,' I say with a modest little laugh. 'I mean, we argue, like anyone else.'

'Do you?' Katie looks surprised. 'I've never seen you argue.'

'Of course we do!' I rack my brain for a moment, trying to remember the last time Connor and I had a fight. I mean, obviously we do *have* arguments. All couples do. It's only healthy.

Come on, this is silly. We must have—

35

Yes. There was that time by the river when I thought those big white birds were geese and Connor thought they were swans. Exactly. We're normal. I knew it.

We're nearing the Panther building now, and as we walk up the pale stone steps I start feeling a bit nervous. Paul will want a full report on how the meeting went with Glen Oil. What shall I say?

Well, obviously I'll be completely frank and honest. Without actually telling him the truth—

'Hey, look.' Katie's voice interrupts me and I follow her gaze. Through the glass front of the building I can see a commotion in the foyer. This isn't normal. What's going on?

As Katie and I push our way through the heavy revolving glass doors, we look at each other in bewilderment. The whole place is in turmoil. People are scurrying about, someone's polishing the brass banister, someone else is polishing the fake plants, and Cyril, the senior office manager, is shooing people into lifts. 'Could you please go to your offices! We don't want you hanging around the reception area. You should all be at your desks by now.' He sounds completely stressed out.

'What's happening?' I say to Dave the security guard, who's lounging against the wall.

He gives us a grin. 'Jack Harper's visiting.'

'What?' We both gawp at him. 'Today? Are you *serious*?'

In the world of the Panther Corporation, this is like saying the Pope's visiting. Or Father Christmas. Jack Harper is the joint founder of the Panther Corporation. He *invented* Panther Cola. I know this because I've typed out blurbs about him approximately a million times. *It was 1987 when young, dynamic business partners Jack Harper and Pete Laidler bought up the ailing Zoot soft-drinks company, repackaged Zootacola as Panther Cola, invented the slogan 'Don't Pause', and thus made marketing history.* No wonder Cyril's in a tizz.

'In about five minutes.' Dave consults his watch. 'Give or take. He wants to have a look round the UK operation.'

'I thought he wasn't active in the business any more,' says Jane from Accounts, who's come up behind us and is listening, agog. 'I thought ever since Pete Laidler died he was all grief-stricken and reclusive.'

'That was three years ago,' points out Katie. 'Maybe he's feeling better.'

'Maybe he wants to sell us off, more like,' says Jane darkly.

'My theory,' says Dave, and we all bend our heads to listen, 'is he wants to see if the plants are shiny enough.' He nods his head towards Cyril, and we all giggle.

Cyril glances up. 'What are you all still doing there?'

'Just going!' says Katie, and we head towards the stairs, which I always use because it means I don't have to bother with the gym. Plus, luckily, Marketing is on the first floor.

We've just reached the landing when Jane squeaks 'Look! It's him!'

A limousine has purred up the street and stopped in front of the doors. As if by clockwork, the lift doors at the other end of the foyer open and out strides Graham Hillingdon, the chief executive, plus the managing director and six others, all looking immaculate in dark suits.

The three of us stand, goggling like children, as the passenger door of the limousine opens. A moment later, out gets a man with blond hair in a navy-blue overcoat. He's wearing dark glasses and is holding a very expensive-looking briefcase. He looks a million dollars.

Graham Hillingdon and the others are all outside by now, lined up on the steps. They shake his hand in turn, then usher him inside, where Cyril is waiting. 'Welcome to the Panther Corporation UK,' Cyril says fulsomely. 'I hope your journey was pleasant?'

'Not too bad, thanks,' says the man, in an American accent.

'As you can see, this is very much a *normal* working day . . .' Cyril glances up and shoos us away in irritation.

Trying not to giggle, the three of us hurry up the stairs.

The atmosphere in the marketing department is a bit like my bedroom used to be before sixth-form parties. People are brushing their hair, spraying perfume, shuffling papers around and gossiping.

I'm just hanging up my coat on the rack when the head of our department, Paul, pulls me aside.

'What the fuck happened at Glen Oil? I had a very strange email from Doug Hamilton this morning. You poured a drink over him?'

I stare at him in shock. Doug Hamilton *told* Paul? But he promised he wouldn't! 'It wasn't like that,' I say quickly. 'I was just trying to demonstrate the many fine qualities of Panther Prime and I . . . I kind of spilled it.'

Paul raises his eyebrows, not in a friendly way. 'All right. It was a lot to ask of you.'

'It wasn't,' I say quickly. 'I mean, it would have been fine, if . . . What I mean is, if you give me another chance, I'll do better. I promise.'

'We'll see.' He looks at his watch. 'You'd better get on.'

'OK. Um, what time will my appraisal be?'

'Emma, in case you hadn't heard, Jack Harper's visiting us today,' says Paul, in his most sarcastic voice. 'But of course, if you think your appraisal's more important than the guy who *founded* the company . . .'

As I scuttle to my desk, Cyril comes into the room, looking hassled.

'Attention!' he says, clapping his hands. 'Attention everyone! This is an informal visit, nothing more. Mr Harper will come in, perhaps talk to one or two of you, observe what you do. So I want you all just to act normally, but obviously, at your highest standards . . . Remember, this department is the hub of the company. The Panther Corporation is renowned for its marketing brilliance!'

He stops and we all stare dumbly at him.

'Get on! Don't just stand there. You!' He points to me. 'Come on. Move!'

Oh, God. My desk is completely covered with stuff. I open a drawer and sweep a whole load of papers inside.

At the next desk, Artemis Harrison is redoing her lipstick. 'It'll be really inspirational to meet him,' she says, admiring herself in her hand mirror. 'Of course, a lot of people think he single-handedly changed the face of marketing practice.' Her eyes fall on me. 'Is that a new top, Emma? Where's it from?'

'Er, French Connection,' I say after a pause.

'I was in French Connection at the weekend.' Her eyes are narrowing. 'I didn't see that design.'

'Well, they'd probably sold out.' I turn away.

'What do we call him?' Caroline is asking. 'Mr Harper or Jack?'

'Five minutes alone with him,' Nick, one of the marketing executives, is saying feverishly into his phone. 'That's all I need. Five minutes to pitch him the web-site idea. I mean, Jesus, if he went for it—'

God, the air of excitement is infectious. With a spurt of adrenaline, I find myself reaching for my comb and checking my lip gloss.

'OK, folks,' says Paul, striding into the department. 'He's on this floor.'

'On with your everyday tasks!' exclaims Cyril. 'Now!'

Fuck. What's my everyday task? I pick up my phone and press my voice-mail code. I can be listening to my messages.

I look around the department—and see that everyone else has done the same thing. We can't *all* be on the phone. This is so stupid! OK, I'll just switch on my computer and wait for it to warm up.

As I watch the screen changing colour, Artemis starts talking in a loud voice. 'I think the whole essence of the concept is *vitality*,' she says, her eye constantly flicking towards the door. 'D'you see what I mean?'

'Er, yes,' says Nick. 'I think we need to be looking at a . . . um . . . fusion of strategy and forward-thinking vision . . .'

God, my computer's slow today. I know what I'll do. I'll be the person getting a coffee. I mean, what could be more natural than that? 'I think I'll get a coffee,' I say self-consciously.

'Could you get me one?' says Artemis, looking up briefly. 'So anyway, on my MBA course . . .'

The coffee machine is near the entrance to the department, in its own little alcove. As I'm waiting for the noxious liquid to fill my cup, I glance up and see Graham Hillingdon walking out of the admin department, followed by a couple of others. Shit! He's coming!

OK. Keep cool. Just wait for the second cup to fill . . .

And there he is! With his blond hair and his expensive-looking suit, and his dark glasses. But no one's even looking at him. Everyone's attention is focused on some other guy. A guy in jeans and a black turtleneck who's walking out now.

As I stare in fascination, he turns. And as I see his face I feel an almighty thud, as though a bowling ball's landed hard in my chest.

It's him. The same dark eyes. The same lines etched round them. The stubble's gone, but it's definitely him. It's the man from the plane.

What's he doing here? And why is everyone's attention on him?

He turns again and I instinctively duck back out of sight, trying to keep calm. What's he doing here? He can't— That can't be—

With wobbly legs, I walk back to my desk. 'Hey,' I say to Artemis, my voice pitched slightly too high. 'D'you know what Jack Harper looks like?'

'No,' she says, and takes her coffee. 'Thanks.'

'Dark hair,' says someone.

I sink into my chair and sip my coffee, not tasting it.

'. . . our head of marketing and promotion, Paul Fletcher,' I can hear Graham saying.

'Good to meet you, Paul,' comes the same dry, American voice.

It's him. It's definitely him.

'Everyone.' Paul is leading him into the centre of the office. 'I'm delighted to introduce our founding father, the man who has influenced and inspired a generation of marketeers—Jack Harper!'

A round of applause breaks out, and Jack Harper shakes his head, smiling. 'Please,' he says. 'No fuss. Just do what you would normally do.'

He starts to walk around the office, pausing now and then to talk to people. Paul is leading the way, making all the introductions, and following them silently everywhere is the blond man.

'Here he comes!' Artemis hisses.

My heart starts to thump, and I shrink into my chair, trying to hide behind my computer. Maybe he won't recognise me.

Fuck. He's looking at me. I see the flash of surprise in his eyes, and he raises his eyebrows. He recognises me.

Please don't come over, I silently pray. Please don't come over.

'And who's this?' he says to Paul.

'This is Emma Corrigan, one of our junior marketing assistants.'

He's walking towards me. Artemis has stopped talking. Everyone's staring. I'm hot with embarrassment.

'Hello,' he says pleasantly.

'Hello,' I manage. 'Mr Harper.'

OK, so he recognises me. But that doesn't necessarily mean he remembers anything I said. A few random comments thrown out by a person in the next-door seat. Who's going to remember that?

'And what do you do?'

'I, um, assist the marketing department and I help with setting up promotional initiatives,' I mumble.

'Emma was in Glasgow only last week on business,' puts in Paul. 'We believe in giving our junior staff responsibility as early as possible.'

'Very wise,' says Jack Harper, nodding. His gaze runs over my desk and alights with sudden interest on my polystyrene cup. He looks up and meets my eye. 'How's the coffee?' he asks pleasantly. 'Tasty?'

Like a tape recording in my head, I suddenly hear my own stupid voice, prattling on. *The coffee at work is the most disgusting stuff you've ever drunk, absolute poison . . .*

'It's great!' I say. 'Really . . . delicious!'

'I'm very glad to hear it.' There's a spark of amusement in his eyes, and I feel myself redden. He remembers. Fuck. He remembers.

'And this is Artemis Harrison,' says Paul. 'One of our brightest young marketing executives.'

'Artemis,' says Jack Harper thoughtfully. 'That's a nice big desk you've got there, Artemis.' He smiles at her. 'Is it new?'

. . . this new desk arrived the other day, and she just took it . . .

He remembers everything, doesn't he? Everything.

Oh God. What the fuck else did I say? I told this man everything about myself. *Everything.* I told him what sort of knickers I wear, and what flavour ice cream I like, and how I lost my virginity, and—

My blood runs cold.

. . . I know I shouldn't have done it, but I so wanted to get the job . . .

I told him about faking the A grade on my CV.

He'll fire me. I'll get a record for being dishonest and no one will ever employ me again, and I'll end up on a 'Britain's Worst Jobs' documentary, clearing up cow poo, saying brightly, 'It's not too bad, really.'

'I'd just like to say that I'm very glad to meet you all,' says Jack Harper, looking around the silent office. 'And also introduce my assistant Sven Petersen.' He gestures to the guy with blond hair. 'I'll be staying here for a few days so I hope I'll get to know a few of you better. As you're aware, Pete Laidler, who founded the Panther Corporation with me, was British.

For that reason, among many others, this country has always been immensely important to me.'

A sympathetic murmur goes round the office. He lifts a hand, nods, and walks away, followed by Sven and all the executives. There's silence until he's gone, then an excited babble breaks out.

I feel my whole body sag in relief. Thank God. Thank *God*.

Honestly, I'm such a moron. Fancy thinking even for a moment that Jack Harper would remember what I said. Let alone care about it! Fancy thinking he would take time out of his busy, important schedule, for something as tiny and insignificant as whether I faked my CV or not! As I reach for my mouse and click on a new document, I'm actually smiling.

'Emma.' I look up to see Paul standing over my desk. 'Jack Harper would like to see you,' he says curtly.

'What?' My smile fades away. 'Me?'

'In the meeting room.'

Paul strides off, and I gaze unseeingly at my computer screen, feeling sick. I'm going to lose my job because of one stupid comment on one stupid plane ride.

Why did I have to get upgraded? *Why* did I have to open my stupid mouth? I'm just a stupid, *stupid* blabbermouth.

Taking a deep breath, I stride across the office and down the corridor to the meeting room, knock on the door and push it open.

Jack Harper is sitting at the conference table. As I come in, he looks up, and his grave expression makes my stomach turn over.

But I have to defend myself. I *have* to keep this job.

'Hi. Can you close the door?' He waits until I've done so, then says, 'Emma, we need to talk about something.'

'I'm aware that we do,' I say, trying to keep my voice steady. 'But I'd like to say my part first, if I may.'

For a moment Jack Harper looks taken aback, then he raises his eyebrows. 'Sure. Go ahead.'

'Mr Harper, I know what you want to see me about. I know it was wrong. It was an error of judgment that I deeply regret. I'm extremely sorry, and it will never happen again. But in my defence . . .' I can hear my voice rising in emotion. 'In my defence, I had no idea who you were on that plane ride. And I don't believe I should be penalised for what was an honest, genuine mistake.'

There's a pause.

'You think I'm penalising you?' says Jack Harper at last, with a frown.

'Yes! You must realise I would never have mentioned my CV if I'd known who you were!'

'Your CV?' Jack Harper's brow clears. 'Ah! The falsified A grade on your résumé.' He gives me a penetrating look. 'You know, a lot of people would call that fraud,' he says.

'I know they would. But it doesn't affect the way I do my job.'

'You think?' He shakes his head thoughtfully. 'Going from a C grade to an A grade . . . What if we need you to do some math?'

'I can do maths,' I say desperately. 'Ask me a maths question. Go on.'

'OK.' His mouth is twitching. 'Eight nines.'

I stare at him, my heart racing, my mind blank. Eight nines. I've got no idea. Fuck. OK, once nine is nine. Two nines are—

'Seventy-two!' I cry, and flinch as he gives a tiny half-smile.

'Very good.' He gestures politely to a chair. 'Now. Have you finished what you wanted to say or is there more?'

I rub my face confusedly. 'You're . . . not going to fire me?'

'No,' says Jack Harper patiently. 'Now can we talk?'

As I sit down, a horrible suspicion starts growing in my mind. I clear my throat. 'Was my CV what you wanted to see me about?'

'No,' he says mildly. 'That wasn't what I wanted to see you about.'

I want to die.

'Right.' I smooth back my hair. 'Well. So, er, what did you . . .'

'I have a small favour to ask you. For various reasons,' says Jack Harper slowly, 'I would prefer it that nobody knows I was in Scotland last week.' He meets my eyes. 'So I would like it very much if we could keep our little meeting between ourselves.'

'Right!' I say after a pause. 'Of course! Absolutely. I can do that.'

'You haven't told anyone?'

'No. No one. Not even my . . . I mean, no one. I haven't told anyone.'

'Good. Thank you very much, I appreciate it.' He smiles, and gets up from his chair. 'Nice to meet you again, Emma.'

Jack Harper opens the door, and holds it politely for me. And I'm halfway out when I stop. 'Wait.'

'What is it?'

'What shall I say you wanted to talk to me about?' I say awkwardly. 'Everyone's going to ask me.'

'Why not say we were discussing logistics?'

For the rest of the day there's a kind of festive atmosphere at work. But I just sit there, unable to believe what just happened. He was a stranger. He was supposed to be a *stranger*. The whole point about strangers is, they disappear into the ether, never to be seen again. Not turn up at the office. Not turn out to be your mega-boss employer.

Well, all I can say is, that's taught me. My parents always said never talk to strangers, and they were right.

I've arranged to go to Connor's flat in the evening, and when I arrive I feel my body expand in relief. Away from the office. Away from all the endless Jack Harper talk. And Connor's already cooking. I mean, how perfect is that?

'Hi!' I say, and give him a kiss.

'Hi, darling!' he says, looking up from the stove.

Shit. I totally forgot to say 'darling'. OK, how am I going to remember this? I know. I'll write it on my hand.

'Have a look at those. I downloaded them from the Internet.' Connor gestures to a folder on the table with a wide smile. I open it.

'Flat details!' I say, taken aback. 'Wow. That's quick.' I sit down on a nearby chair and peer at a blurry photograph of a room, with a sofa and a pot plant, trying to imagine me and Connor living in it together. I wonder what we'll talk about.

Well, we'll talk about . . . whatever we always talk about. Maybe we'll play Monopoly. Just if we get bored or anything.

I turn to another sheet and feel a pang of excitement. This flat has wooden floors and shutters! And look at that cool kitchen . . . Oh, this is going to be so great. I can't wait!

I take a happy slug of wine, and am just sinking comfortably back when Connor says, 'So! Isn't it exciting about Jack Harper coming over?'

Oh God. Please. Not *more* talk about bloody Jack Harper.

'Did you get to meet him?' he adds.

'Um, yes, I met him.' I shrug. 'Anyway—'

'Emma! Aren't you excited?' Connor looks astonished. 'We're talking about the man who took an unknown brand, repackaged it and sold it to the world! He turned a failing company into a huge, successful corporation. And now we're all getting to meet him. This could be the opportunity of a lifetime. To learn from the genius himself! You know, he's never written a book, he's never shared his thoughts with anyone except Pete Laidler . . .' He reaches into the fridge for a can of Panther Cola and cracks it open. Connor has to be the most loyal employee in the world. I once bought a Pepsi when we were out on a picnic, and he nearly had a hernia.

'You know what I would love above anything?' He takes a gulp. 'A one-to-one with him. Wouldn't that be the most fantastic career boost?'

Connor's enthusiastic voice is like salt rubbing into my sore skin. So, let's just see quite how spectacularly I have played this wrong, shall we? I'm sitting on a plane next to the great Jack Harper, creative genius and source of all wisdom on business and marketing. And what do I do? Do I ask him insightful questions? Do I engage him in intelligent conversation? No. I blabber on about what kind of underwear I prefer.

Great career move, Emma. One of the best.

The next day, Connor is off to a meeting first thing, but before he goes he digs out an old magazine article about Jack Harper.

'Read this,' he says. 'It's good background information.'

It's quite a long journey from Connor's place to work, and I haven't got any magazines with me, so I grudgingly start reading the article on the tube. I suppose it is quite an interesting story. How Harper and Pete Laidler were friends and decided to go into business, and Jack was the creative one and Pete was the extrovert playboy one, and they became multimillionaires, and they were so close they were like brothers. And then Pete was killed in a car crash. And Jack was so devastated he shut himself away from the world and said he was giving it all up.

And now I read all this I'm starting to feel a bit stupid. I should have recognised Jack Harper. I mean, I certainly recognise Pete Laidler. For one thing he looks—looked—just like Robert Redford. And for another, he was all over the papers when he died. I can remember it vividly now, even though I had nothing to do with the Panther Corporation then. He crashed his Mercedes, and everyone said it was just like Princess Diana.

I'm so busy reading, I nearly miss my stop and have to make one of those stupid dashes for the doors where everyone looks at you like: You complete moron, did you not know that your stop was coming up?

As I arrive at the office, Paul appears out of his room, snaps his fingers at me and says, 'Appraisal.'

My stomach gives an almighty lurch. Oh God. I'm not ready.

Yes I am. Come on. Exude confidence. Suddenly I remember Kerry and her 'I am a successful woman' walk. I know Kerry's an obnoxious cow, but she does have her own travel agency. Maybe I should give it a go. Cautiously I stick out my bust, lift my head and start striding across the office with a fixed, alert expression on my face.

'Have you got period pain or something?' says Paul crudely as I reach his door.

'No!' I say in shock.

'Well, you look very odd. Now sit down.' He shuts the door, sits down at his desk and opens a form marked Staff Appraisal Review.

'OK. So . . . Emma Corrigan.' He looks at the form and starts ticking boxes. 'Generally, you're doing fine. You're not generally late . . . you understand the tasks given to you . . . you're fairly efficient . . . you work

OK with your colleagues . . . blah blah . . . blah . . . Any problems?'
'Er . . . no.'
'Do you feel racially harassed?'
'Er . . . no.'
'Good. That's it. Well done. Can you send Nick in to see me?'
What? Has he forgotten?
'Um, what about my promotion?' I say.
'Promotion?' He stares at me. 'What the fuck are you talking about?'
'It said in the ad for my job . . .' I pull the crumpled ad out of my jeans pocket. '"Possible promotion to Marketing Executive after a year." It says it right there.' I push it across the desk.
'Emma, that was only for exceptional candidates. You're not ready for a promotion. You'll have to prove yourself first.'
'But if you just give me a chance—'
'You had the chance at Glen Oil.' Paul raises his eyebrows at me and I feel a twinge of humiliation. 'Emma, bottom line is, you're not ready for a higher position. In a year we'll see. Now hop it.'
As I walk dejectedly back to my desk, Artemis looks up with a beady expression. 'Oh, Emma,' she says, 'your cousin Kerry called.'
'Really?' I say in surprise. Kerry never phones me.
'She wanted to know, have you heard about your promotion yet?'
OK. This is now official. I hate Kerry.
'Are you being promoted, Emma? I didn't know that!' Her voice is high and piercing, and I see a couple of people raise their heads.
'No,' I mutter, my face hot with humiliation. 'I'm not.'
'Oh!' Artemis pulls a mock-confused face. 'So why did she—?'
'Shut up, Artemis,' says Caroline. I give her a grateful look.
Another whole year. Another year of being the crappy marketing assistant and everyone thinking I'm useless. Another year of being in debt to Dad, and Kerry and Nev laughing at me. I switch on my computer and dispiritedly type a few words. But suddenly all my energy's gone.
'I think I'll get a coffee,' I say. 'Does anyone want one?'
'You can't,' says Artemis, giving me an odd look. 'Haven't you seen?'
'They've taken the coffee machine away,' says Nick.
'We're getting a new machine!' says Caroline. 'A really nice one, with proper coffee. Ordered by Jack Harper, apparently.'
Jack Harper ordered a new coffee machine?
'Emma!' Artemis is saying impatiently. 'Did you hear that? I want you to find the leaflet we did for the Tesco promotion two years ago. Sorry, Mummy,' she says into the phone. 'Just telling my assistant something.'
Her assistant. God, it pisses me off when she says that.

But to be honest, I'm feeling a bit too dazed to get annoyed.

It's nothing to do with me, I tell myself firmly. He was probably planning to order new coffee anyway—

I stand up with a pile of files in my arms and nearly drop them all on the floor. There he is. Standing right in front of me.

'Hello again.' His eyes crinkle in a smile. 'How are you doing?'

'Er . . . good, thanks.' I swallow hard. 'I just heard about the coffee machine. Um . . . thanks.'

'No problem.'

'Now everyone!' Paul comes striding up behind him. 'Mr Harper is going to be sitting in on the department this morning.'

'Please.' Jack Harper smiles. 'Call me Jack.'

'Right you are. *Jack* is going to be sitting in this morning. He's going to observe what you do, find out how we operate as a team. Just behave normally. And while I've got your attention'—he coughs a little self-consciously—'let me just remind you that our Corporate Family Day is coming up, a week on Saturday. A chance for us all to let our hair down, enjoy meeting each other's families, and have some fun!'

We all stare at him a bit blankly. Until this moment, Paul has always referred to this as the Corporate Fuckwit Day and said he'd rather have his balls torn off than bring any member of his family to it.

'Anyway, back to work, everyone! Jack, let me get you a chair.'

'Just ignore me,' says Jack Harper pleasantly as he sits down in the corner. 'Behave normally.'

Behave normally. Right. Of course. So that would be sit down, take my shoes off, check my emails, put some hand cream on, eat a few Smarties, read my horoscope on iVillage, send an email to Connor, wait a few minutes to see if he replies and then finally get round to finding the Tesco leaflet for Artemis. I don't think so.

As I sit back down at my desk, my mind is working quickly. Jack Harper himself is sitting here, watching me work. Surely I can impress him *somehow*? I leaf through the file of promotional literature, aware that I'm holding my head slightly higher than usual, as though I'm in a posture class. And as I glance around the office, everyone else seems to be in a posture class, too.

'Emma?' says Artemis in a falsely sweet voice. 'Have you found that leaflet I was asking you for? Not that there's *any* hurry—'

'Yes, I have!' I say. I push back my chair, stand up, and walk over to her desk. God, this is like being on telly or something. My legs aren't working properly and my smile is pasted onto my face and I have a horrible conviction I might suddenly shout 'Pants!' or something.

46

'Here you are, Artemis,' I say, and carefully lay the leaflet on her desk.

'Bless you!' she says. Her eyes meet mine brightly and I realise she's acting, too. 'I don't know what we'd do without you, Emma!'

'That's quite all right!' I say, matching her tone. 'Any time!'

Shit, I think as I walk back to my desk. I should have said, 'Teamwork is what keeps this operation together.'

OK, never mind. I can still impress him.

Trying to act as normally as possible, I open a document and start to type as quickly and efficiently as I can, my back ramrod straight. How on earth do people do those fly-on-the-wall documentaries? I feel completely exhausted and it's only been about five minutes.

'Is it normally this quiet?' says Jack Harper, sounding puzzled.

'Er . . .' We all look around uncertainly at each other.

'Please, don't mind me. Talk away like you normally would.' He gives a friendly smile. 'When I worked in an office, we talked about everything under the sun. For instance, what have you all been reading recently?'

'Actually, I've been reading the new biography of Mao Ze-dong,' says Artemis at once. 'Fascinating stuff.'

'I'm just rereading Proust,' says Caroline, with a modest shrug.

'Ah.' Jack Harper nods, his face unreadable. 'And . . . Emma, is it?'

'Um, actually . . .' I swallow, playing for time. I cannot say *Celebrity Doodles—What Do They Mean?* Even though it is actually very good.

'You were reading *Great Expectations*, weren't you, Emma?' says Artemis. 'For your book club.'

'Yes!' I say in relief. 'Yes, that's right—'

And then I stop abruptly as I meet Jack Harper's gaze.

. . . *just skimmed the back cover and pretended I'd read it . . .*

'*Great Expectations*,' says Jack Harper thoughtfully. 'What did you think of it, Emma?'

I don't *believe* he asked me that.

'Well!' I clear my throat. 'I thought it . . . resonated,' I say at last.

'What resonated?' asks Nick.

'The . . . um . . .' I clear my throat. 'The resonances.'

There's a puzzled silence.

'The resonances . . . resonated?' says Artemis.

'Yes,' I say defiantly. 'They did. Anyway, I've got to get on.' I start typing feverishly.

OK. So the book discussion didn't go that well. But I can still do this. I can still impress him—

'I just don't know what's wrong with it!' Artemis is saying in a girly voice. 'I water it every day.' She pokes her spider plant and gazes at Jack

Harper winsomely. 'Do you know anything about plants, Jack?'

'I don't, I'm afraid,' says Jack, and looks over at me, his face deadpan. 'What do you think could be wrong with it, Emma?'

. . . sometimes, when I'm pissed off with Artemis . . .

'I . . . I have no idea,' I say, my face flaming.

OK. So I watered one little plant with orange juice. So what?

'Hey Jack,' says Nick, in a matey, lads-together voice. 'Just in case you don't think we have any fun, look up there!' He nods towards the picture of a photocopied G-stringed bottom, which has been up on the notice board since Christmas. 'We still don't know who it is . . .'

. . . I had a few too many drinks at the last Christmas party . . .

OK, now I want to die. Someone please kill me.

'Hi, Emma!' comes Katie's voice, and I look up to see her hurrying into the office. When she sees Jack Harper, she stops dead. 'Oh!'

'It's all right. I'm simply a fly on the wall.' He waves a friendly hand at her. 'Go ahead. Say whatever you were going to say.'

'Hi Katie!' I manage. 'What is it?'

As soon as I say her name, Jack Harper looks up again, a riveted expression on his face. I do not like the look of that riveted expression. What did I tell him about Katie? What? My mind spools furiously back. What did I say? What did I— I feel an internal lurch. Oh God.

. . . have this secret code where she comes in and says, 'Can I go through some numbers with you, Emma?' and it means 'Shall we nip out to Starbucks?' . . .

I stare desperately at Katie's eager face. Do *not* say it. But she's completely oblivious.

'Could I possibly go over some numbers with you, Emma?'

Fuck.

'I'm not sure that'll be possible today,' I say in a bright, artificial voice.

Katie stares at me in surprise. 'But I have to . . . I really *need* you to go over some numbers with me.'

'I'm quite tied up here with my work, Katie!'

'It won't take long! Just quickly.' Katie is hopping from foot to foot.

'Emma.' At Jack Harper's voice I jump as though I've been stung. He leans towards me. 'Maybe you should go over the numbers.'

I stare back at him for a few moments, unable to speak, blood pounding in my ears. 'Right,' I manage after a long pause. 'OK. I'll do that.'

As I walk along the street with Katie, half of me is numb with horror, and half almost wants to burst into hysterical laughter. Everyone else is in the office, trying as hard as they can to impress Jack Harper. And here I am, strolling off nonchalantly under his nose for a cappuccino.

'Are you OK, Emma?' asks Katie as we push our way through the doors of Starbucks.

'I'm fine!' I say with a kind of shrill hilarity. 'I'm absolutely fine! So . . . why the emergency summit?'

'I *had* to tell you. Two cappuccinos, please.' Katie beams at me excitedly. 'I've got a date. I met a new guy!'

'No!' I say, staring at her. 'Really? That was quick.'

'Yes, it happened yesterday, just like you said! I deliberately walked further than usual in my lunch hour, and I found this really nice place where they were serving lunch. And there was this nice man in the line next to me—and he struck up a conversation with me. Then we shared a table and chatted some more . . . and I was just leaving, when he said did I fancy having a drink some time? So we're going out this evening.'

'That's fantastic!' I say in delight. 'So come on, what's he like?'

'He's lovely. He's called Phillip! He's got these lovely twinkly eyes and he's really charming and polite, and he's got a great sense of humour . . . And I know this sounds really stupid, Emma . . .' She hesitates. 'But I feel you somehow *brought* him to me.'

'Me?' I gape at her.

'You said you knew I'd meet someone. And I did!' Her eyes begin to shine. 'And I wanted to do something for you in return.' She rummages in her bag and pulls out a large piece of orange crochet. 'So I made you this last night.' She looks at me expectantly. 'It's a headscarf.'

For a few moments, I can't move. A crochet headscarf.

'Katie, really, you . . . you shouldn't have!'

'I wanted to. To say thank you.' She looks at me earnestly. 'Especially after you lost that crochet belt I made for you for Christmas.'

'Oh!' I say, feeling a pang of guilt. 'Er, yes. That was . . . such a shame.'

'Oh, what the hell!' Her eyes well up again. 'I'll make you a new belt.'

'No!' I say in alarm. 'No, Katie, don't do that.'

'But I want to!' She leans forward and gives me a hug. 'That's what friends are for!'

It's another twenty minutes before we finish our second cappuccinos and head back to the office. My stomach has started to churn at the thought of facing Jack Harper again. I take a deep breath, close my eyes, take a few steps into the marketing department and open them.

There's a hubbub round Artemis's desk, and no sign of Jack Harper.

'Maybe he's going to rethink the whole company,' someone's saying.

'I've heard this rumour he's got a secret project . . .'

'Where's Jack Harper?' I ask, trying to sound casual.

'He's gone,' says Nick, and I feel a whoosh of relief.

As I sit down at my desk, I feel as light as a helium balloon. Cheerfully I kick off my shoes, reach for my Evian bottle—and stop.

There's a folded piece of paper resting on my keyboard. Slowly I unfold it and stare at the message inside.

Hope your meeting was productive. I always find numbers give me a real buzz.
Jack Harper

It could have been worse. It could have read 'Clear your desk'.

Even so, for the rest of the day, I'm completely on edge. On the dot of 5.30 I stop typing midsentence, close my computer down and grab my coat. I'm not waiting around for him to reappear.

The tubes are miraculously quick for once and I arrive home within twenty minutes. As I push open the front door of the flat I can hear a strange noise coming from Lissy's room. A kind of thumping, bumping sound. Maybe she's moving her furniture around.

'Lissy,' I call as I go into the kitchen. 'You will not believe what happened today.' I open the fridge, take out a bottle of Evian, then wander out into the hall again to see Lissy's door opening.

'Lissy!' I begin. 'What on earth were you—?'

And then I halt, as out of the door comes not Lissy, but a man.

A man! A tall, thin guy in trendy black trousers and steel spectacles.

'Oh,' I say, taken aback. 'Er . . . hi.'

'Emma!' says Lissy, following him out. She's wearing a T-shirt over some grey leggings I've never seen before, is drinking a glass of water and looks startled to see me. 'You're home early.'

'I know. I was in a hurry.'

'This is Jean-Paul,' says Lissy. 'Jean-Paul, my flatmate Emma.'

'Hello, Jean-Paul,' I say with a friendly smile.

'Good to meet you, Emma,' says Jean-Paul in a French accent.

'We were just . . . um . . . going over some case notes,' says Lissy.

'Oh right,' I say brightly. 'Lovely!' Case notes. Yeah, right. Because that would really make a whole load of thumping noises. Lissy is such a dark horse!

'I must be going,' says Jean-Paul, looking at Lissy.

'I'll just see you out,' she says, flustered.

I take a few swigs of Evian, then walk into the sitting room and slump down heavily on the sofa. My whole body's aching from sitting rigid with tension all day. This is seriously bad for my health. How on earth am I going to survive a whole week of Jack Harper?

'So!' I say as Lissy walks back into the room. 'What's going on?'

'What do you mean?' she says shiftily.

'You and Jean-Paul! How long have you two been . . .?'

'We're not,' starts Lissy, turning red. 'It's not . . . We were going over case notes. That's all.'

'OK,' I say, raising my eyebrows. 'If you say so.'

Lissy sometimes gets like this, all shy and abashed. I'll just have to get her pissed one night and she'll admit it.

'So how was your day?' she says, sinking onto the floor.

How was my day? 'A *complete* nightmare.'

'What happened?' Lissy's attention is fully grabbed. 'Tell me!'

'OK.' I take a deep breath. 'OK, remember I had that awful flight back from Scotland last week?'

'Yes!' Lissy's face lights up. 'And Connor came to meet you . . .'

'Yes. Well.' I clear my throat. 'Before that. On the flight. There was this . . . this man sitting next to me. And the plane got really turbulent.' I bite my lip. 'And the thing is, I honestly thought we were all going to die and this was the last person I would ever see, and . . . I . . .'

'Oh my God! You didn't have sex with him.'

'Worse! I told him all my secrets.'

Lissy's looking at me blankly. 'You have *secrets*?'

'Of course I have secrets!' I say. 'Everyone has a few secrets.'

'I don't!' she says at once, looking offended. 'I don't have any secrets.'

'Yes you do!'

'Like what?'

'Like . . . like . . . OK.' I start counting off on my fingers. 'You never told Simon you were hoping he might propose to you . . .'

'I wasn't!' says Lissy, colouring. 'Well, OK, maybe I was . . .'

'You think that sad guy next door fancies you . . .'

'That's not a *secret*!' she says, rolling her eyes.

'Oh right. Shall I tell him, then?' I lean back towards the open window. 'Hey Mike,' I call. 'Guess what? Lissy thinks you—'

'Stop!' says Lissy frantically. 'You've made your point. But I don't understand the problem. So you told some guy on a plane your secrets—'

'And now he's turned up at work.'

'What?' Lissy stares at me. 'Are you serious? Who is he?'

'He's . . .' I'm about to say Jack Harper's name when I remember the promise I made. 'He's just this . . . this guy who's come in to observe.'

'Is he senior?'

'He's . . . yes. You could say he's pretty senior.'

'Blimey.' Lissy frowns, thinking for a few moments. 'Well, does it really matter? If he knows a few things about you.'

'Lissy, it wasn't just a few things.' I feel myself flush slightly. 'It was *everything*. I told him I faked a grade on my CV.'

'You faked a grade on your *CV*?' echoes Lissy in shock.

'I told him about feeding Artemis's spider plant orange juice, I told him I find G-strings uncomfortable . . .'

I tail off to see Lissy staring at me, aghast. 'Emma,' she says at last. 'Have you ever *heard* the phrase "too much information"?'

'I didn't *mean* to say any of it!' I retort defensively. 'It just kind of came out! I'd had three vodkas, and I thought we were about to die. He was just some stranger. I was never supposed to see him again!'

There's silence as Lissy takes this all in. 'What are you going to do?'

'I don't know! I suppose all I can do is try to avoid him.'

'Emma . . .' Lissy clears her throat awkwardly. 'You don't have any secrets from *me*, do you?'

'From *you*?' I say, slightly thrown.

A series of images flashes rapidly through my mind. That weird dream I once had about Lissy and me being lesbians. Those couple of times I've bought supermarket carrots and sworn to her they were organic. The time when we were fifteen and she went to France and I got off with Mike Appleton whom she had a complete crush on.

'No! Of course not!' I say, and quickly take a sip of water. 'Why? Have you got any from me?'

Two dots of pink appear on Lissy's cheeks. 'No, of course I haven't!' she says in an unnatural voice. 'I was just . . . wondering.' She reaches for the TV guide and starts to flip through it, avoiding my gaze.

Wow. Lissy's got a secret. I wonder what it—

Of course. Like she was really going over case notes with that guy. Does she think I'm a complete moron?

I ARRIVE AT WORK the next morning with exactly one aim. Avoid Jack Harper. It should be easy enough. The Panther Corporation is a huge company in a huge building. Even so, as I approach the big glass doors my pace slows down and I find myself peering inside to see if he's about.

I can't see him anywhere. I throw my hair back confidently, walk briskly across the marble floor and start to climb the stairs.

'Jack!' I suddenly hear as I'm nearing the first floor.

I turn round, bewildered, and spot him on the landing above, talking to Graham Hillingdon. My heart gives a huge jump, and I clutch the brass banister. Shit. If he looked down now he'd see me.

Slowly I take a few steps back down the stairs, trying not to click my heels on the marble or move suddenly in case I attract his attention. As soon as I'm out of his view I relax, and I walk more quickly back down to the foyer. I'll go by lift, instead. No problem. I stride across the floor, and I'm right in the middle of the huge expanse of marble when I freeze.

'That's right.' It's his voice. My head swivels round. Where is he now? Which direction is he going in?

'. . . really think that . . .'

Shit. He's coming down the stairs.

Without thinking twice I run to the glass doors and hurry out of the building. I scuttle down the steps, run about a hundred yards down the road and stop, panting.

This is not going well.

I stand on the pavement for a few minutes. There must be a way round this. There must be—

Yes! I have a totally brilliant idea. This will definitely work.

Three minutes later I approach the doors of the Panther building once more, totally engrossed in an article in *The Times*. No one can see my face. This is the perfect disguise!

I push the door open with my shoulder, walk across the foyer and up the stairs, all without looking up. As I stride along the corridor—

'Ow! Sorry!'

I've crashed into someone. Shit. I lower my paper, to see Paul staring at me, rubbing his head.

'Emma, what the fuck are you doing?'

'I was just reading *The Times*,' I say feebly. 'I'm really sorry.'

'All right. Anyway, where the hell have you been? I want you to do teas and coffees at the departmental meeting. Ten o'clock. Oh, and Jack Harper's coming along.'

'What? Do I have to go?' I say before I can stop myself.

'Emma, if you can serve tea and coffee by telepathy,' says Paul sarcastically, 'then you're more than welcome to stay at your desk. If not, would you kindly get your arse in gear and up to the conference room. You know, for someone who wants to advance their career . . .' He shakes his head and stalks off.

I dump my bag and jacket at my desk and hurry back down the corridors to the lifts. One pings in front of me, and the doors open.

No. No. This is a bad dream. Jack Harper is standing in the lift.

Before I can stop myself I take a startled step backwards. Jack Harper puts his mobile phone away, tilts his head to one side and gives me a quizzical look. 'Are you getting into the elevator?' he says mildly.

I'm stuffed. 'Yes,' I say at last and walk into the lift with stiff legs.

The doors close, and we begin to travel upwards in silence. I've got a knot of tension in my stomach. 'Erm, Mr Harper,' I say awkwardly, and he looks up. 'I just wanted to apologise for my . . . for the, um, shirking episode the other day. It won't happen again.'

'You have drinkable coffee now,' says Jack Harper, raising his eyebrows. 'So you shouldn't need to go to Starbucks, at any rate.'

'I know. I'm really sorry,' I say, my face hot. 'And may I assure you, that was the very last time I will ever do such a thing.' I clear my throat. 'I am fully committed to the Panther Corporation, and I look forward to serving this company as best as I can, giving one hundred per cent, every day, now and in the future.' I almost want to add 'Amen'.

'Really.' Jack looks at me, his mouth twitching. 'That's . . . great.' He thinks for a moment. 'Emma, can you keep a secret?'

'Yes,' I say apprehensively. 'What is it?'

Jack leans close and whispers, 'I used to play hookey too.'

'What?' I stare at him.

'In my first job,' he continues in his normal voice. 'I had a friend I used to hang out with. We had a code, too.' His eyes twinkle. 'One of us would ask the other to bring him the Leopold file.'

'What was the Leopold file?'

'It didn't exist.' He grins. 'It was just an excuse to get away from our desks.'

'Oh. Oh right!' Suddenly I feel a bit better.

'So, your colleagues seemed a very pleasant lot,' says Jack. 'A very friendly, industrious team. Are they like that all the time?'

'Absolutely!' I say at once. 'We enjoy cooperating with one another, in an integrated, team-based . . . um . . . operational . . .' I'm trying to think of another long word when I make the mistake of catching his eye. He *knows* this is bullshit. 'OK.' I lean against the lift wall. 'In real life, Paul shouts at me six times a day, and Nick and Artemis hate each other, and we don't sit around discussing literature. We were all faking it.'

'You amaze me.' His mouth twitches again. 'The atmosphere in the admin department also seemed false. My suspicions were aroused when two employees spontaneously started singing the Panther Corporation song. I didn't even know there *was* a Panther Corporation song.'

'Neither did I,' I say in surprise. 'Is it any good?'

'What do you think?' He raises his eyebrows comically.

It's bizarre, but the atmosphere between us isn't remotely awkward any more. In fact, it almost feels like we're old friends or something.

'How about this Corporate Family Day? Looking forward to it?'

'Like having teeth pulled out,' I say bluntly.

'I got that vibe.' He nods, looking amused. 'And what . . .?' He hesitates. 'What do people think about me?' He casually rumples his hair. 'You don't have to answer if you don't want to.'

'No, everyone likes you!' I think for a few moments. 'Although . . . some people think your friend is creepy.'

'Who, Sven?' Jack stares at me for a minute, then throws back his head and laughs. 'I can assure you, Sven is one of my oldest, closest friends, and he's not in the least bit creepy. In fact—'

He breaks off as the lift doors ping. We both snap back into impassive expressions and move slightly away from each other. The doors open, and my stomach gives a lurch. Connor is standing on the other side.

'Hi there!' I say, trying to sound natural.

'Hi,' he says, his eyes shining with excitement, and walks into the lift.

'Hello,' says Jack pleasantly. 'Which floor would you like?'

'Nine, please.' Connor swallows. 'Mr Harper, may I quickly introduce myself?' He eagerly holds out his hand. 'Connor Martin from Research.'

'It's a pleasure to meet you, Connor,' says Jack kindly. 'Research is vital for a company like ours.'

'You're so right!' says Connor, looking thrilled. 'In fact, I'm looking forward to discussing with you the latest research findings on Panther Sportswear. We've come up with some fascinating results involving customer preferences on fabric thickness. You'll be amazed!'

'I'm . . . sure I will,' says Jack. 'I look forward to it.'

Connor gives me an excited grin. 'You've already met Emma Corrigan from our marketing department?' he says.

'Yes, we've met.' Jack's eyes gleam at me.

We travel for a few seconds in an awkward silence. This is weird.

No. It's not weird. It's fine.

'How are we doing for time?' says Connor. He glances at his watch, and in slight horror I see Jack's eyes falling on it. Oh God.

. . . I gave him this lovely leather watch for Christmas, but he insists on wearing this orange digital thing . . .

'Wait a minute!' says Jack, dawn breaking over his face. He stares at Connor. 'Wait a minute. You're Ken.'

Oh no, oh no, oh no, oh no, oh no, oh—

'It's Connor,' says Connor puzzledly. 'Connor Martin.'

'I'm sorry!' Jack hits his head with his fist. 'Connor. Of course. And you two'—he gestures to me—'are an item?'

Connor looks uncomfortable. 'I can assure you, sir, that at work our relationship is strictly professional. However, in a private context, Emma and I are . . . yes, having a personal relationship.'

'That's wonderful!' says Jack encouragingly.

Connor beams and adds proudly, 'In fact, we've just decided to move in together.'

'Is that so?' Jack shoots me a look of genuine surprise. 'That's . . . great news. When did you make that decision?'

'Just a couple of days ago,' says Connor. 'At the airport.'

'At the airport,' echoes Jack Harper after a short silence.

I can't look at him. I'm staring desperately at the floor.

'Well, I'm sure you'll be very happy together,' Jack says to Connor. 'You seem very compatible.'

'Oh we are!' says Connor at once. 'We both love jazz, for a start.'

'Is that so?' says Jack thoughtfully. 'You know, I can't think of anything nicer in the world than a shared love of jazz.'

He's taking the piss. This is unbearable.

'Really?' says Connor eagerly.

'Absolutely.' Jack nods. 'I'd say jazz, and . . . Woody Allen films.'

'We love Woody Allen films!' says Connor in amazed delight.

'Now, Connor, tell me,' says Jack in confidential tones. 'Did you ever find Emma's . . .'

If he says 'G spot' I will die. I will die. I will *die*.

'. . . presence here distracting? Because I can imagine I would!' Jack gives Connor a friendly smile, but Connor doesn't smile back.

'As I said, sir,' he says, a little stiffly, 'Emma and I operate on a strictly professional basis whilst at work. We would never dream of abusing the company's time for our own . . . ends.' He flushes.

God, why does Connor have to be such a *goody-goody*?

The lift pings and relief drains over me. At last I can escape—

'Looks like we're all going to the same place,' says Jack Harper with a grin. 'Connor, why don't you lead the way?'

I can't cope with this. I just can't cope. As I pour out cups of tea and coffee for members of the marketing department, I'm outwardly calm but inside I'm all unsettled and confused. I don't want to admit it to myself, but seeing Connor through Jack Harper's eyes has thrown me.

I love Connor, I tell myself over and over. I didn't mean any of what I said on the plane. I love him. I run my eyes over his face, trying to reassure myself. Connor is good-looking by any standards. His hair is shiny and his eyes are blue and he's got a gorgeous dimple when he smiles.

Jack Harper, on the other hand, looks kind of weary and dishevelled. He's got shadows under his eyes and his hair is all over the place.

But even so. It's as if he's some kind of magnet. Somehow I can't keep my eyes off him.

It's because of the plane, I keep telling myself. It's just because we were in a traumatic situation together, that's why. No other reason.

'We need more lateral thinking, people,' Paul is saying. 'The Panther Bar is simply not performing as it should. Connor, you have the latest research statistics?'

Connor stands up. 'That's right, Paul.' He picks up a clipboard and clears his throat. 'In our latest survey, one thousand teenagers were questioned on aspects of the Panther Bar. Unfortunately, the results were inconclusive.' He presses his remote control. A graph appears on the screen behind him, and we all stare at it obediently. 'Seventy-four per cent of ten- to fourteen-year-olds felt the texture could be more chewy,' says Connor earnestly. 'However, sixty-seven per cent of fifteen- to eighteen-year-olds felt the texture could be more crunchy, while twenty-two per cent felt it could be *less* crunchy . . .'

I glance over Artemis's shoulder and see she's written 'Chewy/crunchy??' on her note pad.

Connor presses the remote control again, and another graph appears. 'Now, forty-six per cent of ten- to fourteen-year-olds felt the flavour was too tangy. However, thirty-three per cent of fifteen- to eighteen-year-olds felt it was not tangy enough.'

Oh God. I know it's Connor. And I love him and everything. But can't he make this sound a bit more *interesting*?

I glance over to see how Jack Harper is taking it and he raises his eyebrows at me. Immediately I flush, feeling disloyal.

'And ninety per cent of female teenagers would prefer the calorie content to be reduced,' Connor concludes. 'But the same proportion would also like to see a thicker chocolate coating.' He gives a helpless shrug.

'They don't know what the hell they want,' says someone.

'We polled a broad cross-section of teenagers,' says Connor, 'including Caucasians, Afro-Caribbeans, Asians, and . . . er . . .' he peers at the paper. 'Jedi knights.'

'Briefly remind us of our target market, Connor,' says Paul.

'Our target market'—Connor consults another clipboard—'is aged ten to eighteen, in full or part-time education. He/she drinks Panther Cola four times a week, eats burgers three times a week, visits the cinema twice a week, reads magazines and comics but not books, is most likely to agree with the lifestyle statement "It's more important to be cool than rich". . .'

'Does he/she eat toast for breakfast?' says somebody. 'Or cereal?'

'I . . . I'm not sure,' says Connor, riffling quickly through his pages.

'I think we get the picture,' says Paul. 'Does anyone have any thoughts on this?'

I've been plucking up courage to speak, and now I take a deep breath. 'You know, my grandpa really likes Panther Bars!' I say.

'What relevance does that have?' says Paul with a frown.

'I just thought I could maybe ask him what he thinks . . .'

'With all due respect, Emma,' says Connor, with a smile that verges on patronising, 'your grandfather is hardly in our target demographic!'

I flush, feeling stupid. Why did Connor have to say that?

'My own view,' Artemis is saying, 'is that if the Panther Bar isn't performing, we should axe it. It's quite obviously a problem child.'

I look up in slight dismay. They can't axe the Panther Bar! What will Grandpa take to his bowling tournaments?

Artemis leans forward. 'If we're going to maximise our concept innovation in a functional and logistical way, then surely we need to focus on our strategic competencies—'

'Excuse me,' says Jack Harper, lifting a hand. It's the first time he's spoken, and everyone turns to look. There's a prickle of anticipation in the air and Artemis glows smugly.

'Yes, Mr Harper?' she says.

'I have no idea what you're talking about,' he says.

The whole room reverberates in shock, and I give a snort of laughter without quite meaning to.

'As you know, I've been out of the business arena for a while.' He smiles. 'Could you please translate what you just said into standard English?'

'Oh,' says Artemis, looking discomfited. 'Well, I was simply saying that, from a strategic point of view, notwithstanding our corporate vision . . .' She falters at his expression.

'Try again,' he says kindly. 'Without using the word strategic.'

'Oh,' says Artemis again, and rubs her nose. 'Well, I was just saying that . . . we should . . . concentrate on . . . on what we do well.'

'Ah!' Jack Harper's eyes gleam. 'Now I understand. Please, carry on.'

He glances at me, rolls his eyes and grins, and I can't help giving a tiny grin back.

After the meeting, people trickle out of the room, still talking, and I go round the table, picking up coffee cups.

'It was very good to meet you, Mr Harper,' I can hear Connor saying eagerly. 'If you'd like a transcript of my presentation . . .'

'You know, I don't think that will be necessary,' Jack says in that dry, quizzical voice. 'I think I more or less got the gist.'

Doesn't Connor *realise* he's trying too hard?

'Now, I'm due in the design studio right about now,' Jack Harper's saying, 'but I don't quite remember where it is . . .'

'Emma!' says Paul sharply. 'Can you please show Jack to the design studio? You can clear up the rest of the coffee later.'

I freeze, clutching an orange cream wrapper. Please, no more.

'Of course,' I manage at last. 'It would be a . . . pleasure. This way.'

Awkwardly, I usher Jack Harper out of the meeting room and we walk down the corridor, side by side. My face is tingling slightly as people try not to stare at us, and I'm aware of everyone else in the corridor turning into self-conscious robots as soon as they see him.

'So,' he says after a while. 'You're moving in with Ken.'

'It's *Connor*,' I say. 'And yes.'

'Looking forward to it?'

'Yes. Yes, I am.' We've reached the lifts and I press the button. I can feel his eyes on me. 'Look. I know I might have made certain . . . comments to you on the plane,' I begin, clenching my fists tightly at my side. 'But what you have to know is that that conversation took place under duress, and I said a lot of things I didn't really mean.'

'I see,' says Jack thoughtfully. 'So . . . you *don't* like double chocolate chip Häagen-Dazs ice cream.'

I clear my throat. 'Some things, obviously, I *did* mean—'

The lift doors ping, and Cyril is standing on the other side of the doors. 'Jack! I wondered where you were.'

'I've been having a nice chat with Emma here,' says Jack. 'She kindly offered to show me the way.'

'Ah.' Cyril's eyes run dismissively over me. 'Well, they're waiting for you in the studio.'

'So, um . . . I'll just go, then,' I say awkwardly.

'See you later,' says Jack with a grin. 'Good talking to you, Emma.'

As I leave the office that evening I feel all agitated, like one of those snow globes. I was perfectly happy being an ordinary, dull little Swiss village. But now Jack Harper's come and shaken me up and there are snowflakes all over the place, not knowing what they think any more.

And bits of glitter, too. Tiny bits of shiny, secret excitement.

Every time I catch his eye or hear his voice, it's like a dart to my chest. Which is ridiculous. Connor is my boyfriend. Connor is my future. He loves me and I love him and I'm moving in with him. So there.

I arrive home to find Lissy on her knees in the sitting room, helping Jemima into the tightest black suede dress I've ever seen.

'Wow!' I say, as I put down my bag. 'That's amazing!'

'There!' pants Lissy, and sits back on her heels. 'That's the zip done.'

Jemima doesn't move a muscle. Lissy and I glance at each other.

'Jemima!' says Lissy in alarm. 'Can you breathe?'

'Kind of,' says Jemima at last. 'I'll be fine.' With a totally rigid body, she totters over to where her Louis Vuitton bag is resting on a chair.

'What happens if you need to go to the loo?' I say, staring at her.

'Or go back to his place?' says Lissy with a giggle.

'It's only our second date! I'm not going to go back to his place!' Jemima says in horror, making a last, desperate effort to bend her body. She manages to scoop up the strap on the end of one of her acrylic fingernails, and triumphantly swings it onto her shoulder.

'What if he suggests dancing?' asks Lissy slyly.

A look of total panic briefly crosses Jemima's face, then vanishes. 'He won't,' she says scornfully. 'Englishmen never suggest dancing.'

'Fair point.' Lissy grins. 'Have a good time.'

As Jemima disappears out of the door, I sink down heavily onto the sofa and reach for a magazine. Then I glance up at Lissy, who's staring at me with a gleeful look on her face.

'Guess what I've got?' She raises her eyebrows tantalisingly, then fishes in her bag. Very slowly she pulls out a large, rusty key ring, to which a brand new Yale is attached.

'What's that?' I begin, puzzledly—then suddenly realise. 'No!'

'Yes! I'm in! Do you want to go this evening?'

'Oh my God! Lissy!'

The key that Lissy is holding opens the door to a private members' club in Clerkenwell that's completely happening and impossible to get into. And Lissy got in!

'Lissy, you're the coolest!'

'No, I'm not,' she says, looking pleased. 'It was Jasper at my chambers. He knows everyone on the committee.'

I take the key from her and look at it in fascination, but there's nothing on it. No name, no address, no logo, no nothing. It looks a bit like the key to my dad's garden shed.

'So who do you think'll be there?' I look up. 'You know, apparently

Madonna's a member. And that gorgeous new actor from *EastEnders*—'

'Emma,' interrupts Lissy. 'You do know celebrities aren't guaranteed.'

'I know!' I say, a little offended. Honestly. Who does Lissy think I am? I'm a cool and sophisticated Londoner. I don't get excited by stupid celebrities. I was just *mentioning* it, that's all. 'In fact,' I add, 'it probably spoils the atmosphere if the place is stuffed full of famous people. I mean, can you think of anything worse than sitting at a table, trying to have a nice, normal conversation, while all around you are movie stars and supermodels and pop stars. . .'

There's a pause while we both think about this.

'So,' says Lissy casually. 'We might as well go and get ready.'

'Why not?' I say, equally casually.

Not that it will take long. I mean, I'm only going to throw on a pair of jeans. And quickly wash my hair, which I was going to do anyway.

And maybe do a quick face mask.

An hour later Lissy appears at the door of my room, dressed in jeans, a tight black corset top and her Bertie heels, which I happen to know always give her a blister. 'What do you think?' she says, in the same casual voice. 'I mean, I haven't really made much effort—'

'Neither have I,' I say, blowing on my second coat of nail polish. 'I mean, it's just a relaxed evening out. I'm hardly even bothering with make-up.' I look up and stare at Lissy. 'Are those false eyelashes?'

'No! I mean . . . yes. But you weren't supposed to notice. They're called natural look.' She goes over to the mirror and bats her eyelids at herself worriedly. 'Are they really obvious?'

'No!' I say reassuringly. 'Come on, let's go.'

'We can't!' Lissy looks at her watch. 'It's too early.'

'Yes we can. We can be just having a quick drink on our way to *another* celebrity party.'

'Oh yes.' Lissy brightens. 'Cool. Let's go!'

It takes us about fifteen minutes by bus to get from Islington to Clerkenwell. Lissy leads me down an empty road near to Smithfield Market, full of warehouses and empty office buildings. Then we turn a corner, and then another corner, until we're standing in a small alley.

'Right,' says Lissy, standing under a street lamp and consulting a tiny scrap of paper. 'It's all hidden away somewhere.'

'Isn't there a sign?'

'No. No one except members knows where it is. You have to knock on the right door and ask for Alexander. It's their secret code.'

Secret code! This gets cooler and cooler. As Lissy squints at an intercom set in the wall, I look idly around. This street is completely nondescript.

In fact, it's pretty shabby. Just rows of identical doors. But hidden behind this grim façade is the whole of London celebrity society!

'Hi, is Alexander there?' says Lissy nervously. There's a moment's silence, then as if by magic, the door clicks open.

Looking apprehensively at each other, we make our way down a lit corridor pulsing with music. We come to a stainless-steel door and Lissy reaches for her key. As the door opens, I casually rearrange my hair.

'OK,' Lissy mutters. 'Don't look. Don't gawp. Just be cool.'

'All right,' I mutter back, and follow Lissy into a large, dim room.

Somehow we manage to sit down, stow our bags and pick up the list of cocktails, all the time rigidly staring at each other. God this is a strain. I want to look around. I want to *see* the place.

'Lissy,' I hiss. 'I'm going to have a look round.'

'Really?' Lissy stares at me anxiously, as though I'm Steve McQueen announcing he's going over the wire. 'Well . . . OK. But be *discreet*.'

OK. Here we go. A quick, non-gawping sweep. I allow my eyes to skim swiftly round the room. Low lighting . . . lots of purple sofas and chairs . . . a couple of guys in T-shirts . . . three girls in jeans and jumpers . . . a guy with a beard reading *Private Eye* . . . and that's it.

This can't be right. Where's Robbie Williams?

'Who did you see?' hisses Lissy, still staring at the cocktail menu.

'I'm not sure,' I whisper uncertainly. 'Maybe that guy with the beard is some famous actor?'

Casually, Lissy gives him a look. 'I don't think so,' she says.

'Well, how about the guy in the grey T-shirt?'

'Mmm . . . no. I don't think so.'

There's silence as we look at each other.

'Is *anyone* famous here?' I say at last.

'Celebrities aren't guaranteed!' says Lissy defensively.

'I know! But you'd think—'

'Hi!' A voice interrupts us and we both look round, to see two of the girls in jeans approaching our table. One of them is smiling at me nervously. 'I hope you don't mind, but my friends and I were just wondering—aren't you that new one in *Hollyoaks*?'

Oh, for God's sake.

Anyway. I don't care. We didn't come here to see tacky celebrities showing off. We just came to have a nice quiet drink together.

We order strawberry daiquiris and some luxury mixed nuts (£4.50, for a small bowl. Don't even *ask* how much the drinks cost).

'How's your work going?' I ask, as I sip my drink.

'Oh, fine,' says Lissy with a shrug. 'What about your man?'

I know at once she means Jack, but I don't want to admit that's where my mind has leapt to, so I attempt a blank look and say, 'Who, Connor?'

'No, you dope! Your stranger on the plane. The one who knows everything about you. Have you managed to avoid him?'

'No,' I admit. 'He won't bloody leave me alone.'

Lissy gives me a close look. 'Emma, do you fancy this guy?'

'No, of course I don't,' I say hotly. 'He just . . . disconcerts me. But I only have to get through until Friday. Then he'll be gone.'

'And then you'll be moving in with Connor.' Lissy takes a sip of her daiquiri. 'You know, I reckon he's going to ask you to marry him!'

I feel a tiny lurch in my stomach, which is probably just my drink going down or something.

'You're so lucky,' says Lissy wistfully. 'You know, he put up those shelves in my room the other day without even asking!'

'I know. He's just . . . great.' There's a pause, and I start to shred my paper coaster into little bits. 'I suppose the only *tiny* little thing would be that it's not that romantic any more.'

'You can't expect it to be romantic for ever,' says Lissy. 'Things change.'

'Oh, I know that!' I say. 'We're two mature, sensible people, and we're having a loving, steady relationship. Which, you know, is just what I want out of life. Except . . .' I clear my throat awkwardly. 'We don't have sex *that* often any more . . .'

'That's a common problem in long-term relationships,' says Lissy knowledgeably. 'You need to spice it up. Have you tried handcuffs?'

'No! Have you?' I stare at Lissy, riveted.

'A long time ago,' she says with a shrug. 'They weren't all that . . . Um . . . why not try doing it somewhere different. Try doing it at work!'

Now, that's a good idea. 'OK!' I say. 'I'll try that!'

Suddenly I'm filled with fresh enthusiasm. This is a brilliant plan. I'll shag Connor at work tomorrow, and it will be the best sex we've ever had, and the sparkle will come back, and we'll be madly in love again. Easy. And that will show Jack Harper.

No. This is nothing to do with Jack Harper. I don't know why that slipped out.

There's only one tiny hitch to my scheme. Which is that it's not quite as easy to shag your boyfriend at work as you'd think. I hadn't quite appreciated before how *open* everything is in our office. By eleven o'clock the next morning I still haven't managed to put a game plan together.

We can't do it in the loos. The girls' loos always have people in there, gossiping and putting on their make-up, and the men's loos . . . yuck.

We can't do it in Connor's office because the walls are completely made of glass and there aren't any blinds or anything. Plus people are always coming in to get stuff out of his filing cabinet.

I can't email him for suggestions, because it's crucial that I surprise him. The shock element will be a huge turn-on and make it really sizzling hot. Plus there's a tiny risk that if I warn him he'll go all corporate on me and insist we take an hour's unpaid leave for it, or something.

I'm just wondering whether we could creep out onto the fire escape when Nick comes out of Paul's office saying something about margins.

My head jerks up. There's something I've been trying to pluck up courage to say to him since that big meeting yesterday. 'Hey Nick,' I say as he walks by. 'Panther Bars are your product, aren't they?'

'If you can call them a product,' he says, rolling his eyes.

'Are they going to axe them?'

'More than likely.'

'Well, listen,' I say quickly. 'Can I have a tiny bit of the marketing budget to put a coupon ad in a magazine? It won't be very expensive, I promise. No one will even notice.'

'Where?'

'*Bowling Monthly*,' I say, flushing slightly. 'My grandpa gets it.'

'Bowling *what*?'

'Please! Look, you don't have to do anything. I'll sort it all out.' I stare at him entreatingly. 'Please . . . please . . .'

'Oh all right!' he says impatiently. 'It's a dead duck, anyway.'

'Thanks!' I beam at him, then, as he walks off, reach for the phone and dial Grandpa's number.

'Hi Grandpa!' I say as his answering machine beeps. 'I'm putting a money-off coupon ad for Panther Bars in *Bowling Monthly*. So tell all your friends! You can stock up cheaply.'

'Emma?' Grandpa's voice suddenly booms. 'I'm here! Just screening.'

'Screening?' I echo, trying not to sound too surprised.

'It's my new hobby. Have you not heard of it? You listen to your friends leaving messages and laugh at them. Most amusing. Now Emma, I was meaning to ring you. I saw a very alarming piece on the news yesterday, about muggings in central London.'

Not this again. 'Grandpa—'

'Promise me you don't take London transport, Emma.'

'I, er . . . promise,' I say, crossing my fingers. 'Grandpa, I have to go, really. But I'll call again soon. Love you.'

As I put the phone down I feel a tiny glow of satisfaction. That's one thing done. But what about Connor?

'I'll just have to go and fish it out of the archives,' Caroline is saying across the office, and my head pops up.

The archive room. Of course. Of course! No one goes to the archive room unless they absolutely have to. It's way down in the basement, and it's all dark with no windows. It's perfect.

'I'll go,' I say, trying to sound nonchalant. 'If you like. What do you have to find?'

'Would you?' says Caroline gratefully. 'Thanks, Emma. It's an old ad in some defunct magazine. This is the reference . . .' She hands me a piece of paper and I take it, feeling a thrill of excitement. As she walks away, I demurely pick up my phone and dial Connor's number.

'Hey Connor,' I say in a low, husky voice. 'Meet me in the archive room. I've got something I want to show you.'

'What?'

'Just . . . be there,' I say, feeling like Sharon Stone.

Ha! Office shag here I come!

I hurry down the corridor, but as I pass Admin I'm accosted by Wendy Smith, who wants to know if I'd like to play in the netball team. So I don't actually get to the basement for a few minutes, and when I open the door, Connor is standing there, looking at his watch.

That's rather annoying. I'd planned to be sitting there waiting for him, one leg crossed over the other and my skirt hitched up seductively.

Oh well. 'Hi,' I say, in the same husky voice.

'Hi,' says Connor, with a frown. 'Emma, what is this? I'm really busy.'

'I just wanted to see you. A lot of you.' I push the door shut with an abandoned gesture and trail my finger down his chest, like an aftershave commercial. 'We never make love spontaneously any more.'

'What?' Connor stares at me.

'Come on.' I start unbuttoning his shirt with a sultry expression. 'Let's do it. Right here, right now.'

'Are you *crazy*?' says Connor, pushing my fingers out of the way and hastily rebuttoning his shirt. 'Emma, we're in the office!'

'So what? Come on, Connor!' I shimmy close to him and pull one of his hands inside my bra. 'Don't you find this exciting? Just the thought that someone could be walking down the corridor right now . . .'

I come to a halt as I hear a sound. I think someone *is* walking down the corridor right now. Oh shit.

'I can hear footsteps!' Connor hisses, and pulls sharply away from me, but his hand stays exactly where it is, inside my bra. He stares at it in horror. 'I'm stuck! My bloody watch. It's snagged on your jumper!' He looks frantically around. 'Where are some scissors?'

'You're not cutting my jumper,' I say in horror.

'Do you have any other suggestions?' He yanks sharply again.

I give a muffled shriek. 'Ow! Stop it! You'll ruin it. If you'd—'

I break off. There are definitely footsteps approaching.

'Fuck!' Connor's looking around distractedly. 'Fucking . . .'

'Calm down! We'll just shuffle into the corner,' I hiss. 'Anyway, they might not even come in—' I freeze as the door opens.

No. God, no. I feel light-headed with shock.

Jack Harper is standing in the doorway, holding a big bundle of old magazines. Slowly, his eyes run over us, taking in Connor's angry expression, his hand inside my bra, my agonised face.

'Mr Harper,' Connor begins to stutter. 'I'm so very sorry. We're . . .' He clears his throat. 'Can I just say how mortified I am . . .'

'I'm sure you are,' says Jack. His face is blank and unreadable. 'Perhaps the pair of you could adjust your dress before returning to your desks?'

five

JACK HARPER LEAVES TODAY. Thank God. Thank God. Because I really couldn't cope with any more of . . . of *him*. If I can just keep my head down and avoid him until five o'clock and then run out of the door, then everything will be fine. Life will be back to normal and I will stop feeling as if my radar's been skewed by some invisible magnetic force.

I don't know why I'm in such a jumpy, irritable mood. Although I nearly died of embarrassment yesterday, things are pretty good. First of all, it doesn't look like Connor and I are going to get the sack for having sex at work, which was my immediate fear. And secondly, my brilliant plan worked. As soon as we got back to our desks, Connor started sending me apologetic emails. And then last night we had sex. Twice. With scented candles.

I think Connor must have read somewhere that girls like scented candles during sex. Maybe in *Cosmo*. Because every time he brings them out, he gives me this 'Aren't I considerate?' look and I have to say, 'Oh! Scented candles! How lovely!'

I mean, don't get me wrong. I don't *mind* scented candles. But it's not as if they actually do anything, is it? They just stand there and burn. And then at crucial moments I find myself thinking, 'I hope the scented candle doesn't fall over,' which is a bit distracting.

Anyway. So we had sex. And tonight we're going to look at a flat together. So my life is coming together nicely. I don't know why I'm feeling so pissed off. I don't know what's—

I don't want to move in with Connor, says a tiny voice in my brain.

No. That can't be right. Connor is perfect. Everyone knows that.

But I don't want to—

Shut up. We're the Perfect Couple. We have sex with scented candles.

The phone rings on my desk, interrupting my thoughts.

'Hello, Emma?' comes a familiar dry voice. 'This is Jack Harper.'

My heart gives an almighty leap of fright. I haven't seen him since the hand-in-bra incident. 'Oh,' I say. 'Er . . . hi!'

'Would you mind coming up to my office for a moment?'

I clear my throat. 'Should I . . . bring anything?'

'No, just yourself.' He rings off.

I feel a coldness in my spine. He's going to fire me after all.

Oh, well. There's nothing I can do. I take a deep breath, stand up and make my way up to the eleventh floor. There's a desk outside his door, but no one is sitting at it, so I go straight up to the door and knock.

'Come in.'

Cautiously I push the door open. The room is huge and bright and panelled, and Jack is sitting at a circular table with six people I've never seen before gathered round on chairs. The atmosphere is a bit tense. Have they gathered to watch me being fired?

'Hi.' Jack's face crinkles in a smile. 'Emma . . . relax. There's nothing to worry about. I just wanted to ask you something.'

'Oh, right,' I say, taken aback. Now I'm totally confused.

Jack reaches for a piece of paper and holds it up so I can see it clearly. 'What do you think this is a picture of?' he says.

Oh fuckety fuck. This is like when I went for that interview at Laines Bank and they showed me a squiggle and I said I thought it looked like a squiggle. Everyone is staring at me. I so want to get it right. If only I knew what right was. I stare at the picture. It's a graphic of two round objects. Kind of irregular in shape. I have absolutely no idea what they're supposed to be. None at all. They look like . . . they look like . . .

Suddenly I see it. 'It's nuts! Two walnuts!'

Jack explodes with laughter. 'Well, I think that proves my point.'

'Aren't they walnuts?' I look helplessly around the table.

'They're supposed to be ovaries,' says a man with rimless spectacles.

'*Ovaries?*' I stare at the page. 'Well, yes. Now you say it . . .'

'The ovaries are simply *part* of a range of symbolic representations of womanhood,' says a thin guy defensively. 'Ovaries to represent fertility, an eye for wisdom, this tree to signify the earth mother . . .'

'The point is, the images can be used across the entire range of products,' says a woman. 'The health drink, clothing, a fragrance . . .'

'The target market responds well to abstract images,' adds Rimless Spectacle Guy. 'The research has shown.'

Jack looks at me again. 'Would *you* buy a drink with ovaries on it?'

'Er . . .' I clear my throat, aware of a couple of hostile faces pointing my way. 'Well . . . probably not.'

'Jack, three creative teams have been at work on this,' the woman says earnestly. 'We can't start from scratch. We simply cannot.'

Jack looks at her. 'We are not selling a drink with ovaries on it.' He exhales sharply. 'OK, let's take a break. Emma, would you be kind enough to assist me in carrying these folders down to Sven's office?'

He marches me down the corridor, into a lift, and presses the ninth-floor button. After we've descended for about two seconds he presses the emergency button and we grind to a halt. Finally, he looks at me.

'Are you and I the only sane people in this building? What happened to instincts?' His face is incredulous. 'No one knows a good idea from a terrible one any more. Ovaries!' He shakes his head.

I can't help it. He looks so outraged and the way he says 'Ovaries!' suddenly seems the funniest thing in the world, and before I know it I'm laughing. For an instant Jack looks astounded, and then his face crumples and suddenly he's laughing too. His nose screws up when he laughs, like a baby's, and somehow this makes it seem a million times funnier.

'Emma?'

'What?' I look up, still laughing, until I realise that Jack's stopped. He's looking at me, with an unreadable expression on his face.

'Why are you with that guy?' he asks.

My gurgles peter out. 'What do you mean?' I say, playing for time.

'Connor. He's not going to make you happy. Or fulfil you.'

I stare at him, feeling wrongfooted. 'Who says?'

'I've sat in meetings with Connor. I've seen how his mind works. He's a nice guy—but you need more than a nice guy. My guess is, you don't really want to move in with him. But you're afraid of ducking out.'

I feel a swell of indignation. 'Actually, you're quite mistaken,' I say cuttingly. 'I'm looking forward to moving in with him.'

Jack's shaking his head. 'You need someone who excites you.'

'Connor *does* excite me!' I give him a defiant look. 'I mean . . . when you saw us last, we were pretty passionate, weren't we?'

'Oh, that.' Jack shrugs. 'I assumed that was a desperate attempt to spice up your love life.'

I stare at him in fury. 'That was . . . a spontaneous act of passion!'

'Sorry,' says Jack mildly. 'My mistake.'

'Anyway, why do you care?' I fold my arms. 'What does it matter to you whether I'm happy or not?'

There's a sharp silence, and I find I'm breathing rather quickly.

'I've asked myself that same question,' says Jack. He shrugs. 'Maybe it's because we experienced that extraordinary plane ride together. Maybe it's because you're the only person in this whole company who hasn't put on some kind of phoney act for me.'

I would have put on an act, I feel like retorting. If I'd had a choice!

'I guess what I'm saying is . . . I feel as if you're a friend,' he says. 'And I care what happens to my friends.'

'Oh,' I say, and rub my nose. I'm about to say politely that he feels like a friend, too, when he adds, 'Plus anyone who recites Woody Allen films line for line *has* to be a loser.'

I feel a surge of outrage on Connor's behalf. 'You don't know anything about it!' I exclaim. 'You know, I wish I'd never sat next to you on that stupid plane! You go around behaving as though you know me better than anyone else—'

'Maybe I do,' he says, his dark eyes glinting.

I stare back at him, feeling a breathless mixture of anger and exhilaration. I suddenly feel like we're playing tennis. Or dancing.

'You do not know me better than anyone else!' I retort.

'I know you won't end up with Connor Martin.'

'You don't know that.'

'Yes I do.' He's starting to laugh.

'No you don't! If you want to know, I'll probably end up marrying Connor. And anyway, this is my personal life. You're my boss, and you only met me last week, and frankly this is none of your business!'

Jack's laughter vanishes and he looks as though I've slapped him. Then he takes a step back and releases the lift button. 'You're right,' he says in a completely different voice. 'I overstepped the mark and I apologise.'

I feel a spasm of dismay. 'I . . . I didn't mean—'

'No. You're right.' He stares at the floor for a few moments. 'So, I leave for the States tomorrow. It's been a very pleasant stay, and I'd like to thank you for all your help. Will I see you at the drinks party tonight?'

'I . . . I don't know,' I say. This is awful. I want to put it back to the way it was before, all easy and joking. But I can't find the words.

We reach the ninth floor, and the doors open.

'I think I can manage these from here,' Jack says.

Awkwardly, I transfer the folders to his arms.

'Well, Emma,' he says in the same formal voice. 'In case I don't see you later on . . . it was nice knowing you.' He meets my eyes and a glimmer of his old, warm expression returns. 'I really mean that.'

'You too,' I say, my throat tight.

I don't want him to go. I don't want this to be the end. I feel like suggesting a quick drink. God, what's *wrong* with me?

'Have a good journey,' I manage as he shakes my hand. Then he turns on his heel and walks off down the corridor.

I feel leaden for the rest of the day. Everyone else is talking about Jack Harper's leaving party, but I go straight home, and I'm sitting on the sofa, staring into space when Connor lets himself into the flat.

I look up as he walks into the room, and immediately I know something's different. Not with him. He hasn't changed a bit. But I have.

'Hi,' he says, and kisses me lightly on the head. 'Shall we go?'

'Go?'

'To look at the flat on Edith Road. We'll have to hurry if we're going to make it to the party. Oh, and my mother's given us a house-warming present. It was delivered to work.'

He hands me a cardboard box. I pull out a glass teapot and look at it blankly. 'Connor,' I hear myself saying. 'I can't move in with you.'

'What?' Connor stares at me. 'Has something happened?'

'Yes. No.' I swallow. 'I've been having doubts for a while. About us.'

'*What?*' Connor rubs his face. 'Emma, are you saying you want to . . .?'

'I want to break up,' I say, staring at the carpet.

'But . . . this is ridiculous! It's ridiculous!' Connor's pacing around the room like a rattled lion. Suddenly he looks at me. 'It's that plane journey. You've been different ever since that plane ride down from Scotland. You've been edgy, you've been tense . . .' Connor squats down in front of me and takes my hands. 'Emma, I think maybe you're still suffering some kind of trauma. You could have counselling.'

'Connor, I don't need counselling!' I jerk my hands away. 'But maybe you're right. Maybe that plane ride did'—I swallow—'affect me. Maybe it brought my life into perspective and made me realise a few things. And one of the things I've realised is, we aren't right for each other.'

Slowly Connor sinks down onto the carpet, his face bewildered. 'Is there someone else?'

'Of course not!' I look straight into his eyes. 'I want to break up.'

'I don't believe you!' he says, shaking his head. 'I *know* you, Emma! You wouldn't just throw away something like that. You wouldn't—'

He stops in shock as, with no warning, I hurl the glass teapot to the floor. We both stare at it, stunned.

'It was supposed to break,' I explain after a pause. 'And that was going to signify that yes, I would throw something away. If I knew it wasn't right for me.'

'I think it *is* broken,' says Connor, picking it up and examining it. 'At least, there's a hairline crack. But we could still use it—'

'No. We couldn't.' I clench my fists. 'It would never work properly.'

'I see,' says Connor after a pause.

And I think, finally, he does.

'Well . . . I'll be off then,' he says at last. 'I'll phone the flat people and tell them that we're . . .' He stops, and roughly wipes his nose.

'OK,' I say, in a voice that doesn't sound like mine. 'Can we keep it quiet from everyone at work?' I add. 'Just for the moment.'

'Of course,' he says gruffly. 'I won't say anything.'

He's halfway out of the door when abruptly he turns back. 'Emma, here are the tickets for the jazz festival. I know how much you've been looking forward to hearing the Dennisson Quartet.' He pushes the brightly coloured tickets roughly into my hand.

'I . . . I . . .' I swallow. 'Connor . . . I just . . . I don't know what to say.'

'We'll always have jazz,' says Connor in a choked-up voice, and closes the door behind him.

So now I have no promotion *and* no boyfriend. And puffy eyes from crying. And everyone thinks I'm mad.

'You're mad,' Jemima says, approximately every ten minutes. It's Saturday morning, and we're in our usual routine of dressing gowns, coffee, and nursing hangovers. Or in my case, break-ups. 'You do realise you had him?' She frowns at her toenail, which she's painting baby-pink. 'I would have predicted a rock on your finger within six months.'

'I thought you said I'd ruined all my chances by agreeing to move in with him,' I retort sulkily.

'Well, in Connor's case I think you would have been safe and dry.'

'Do you think I'm crazy?' I say, turning to Lissy. 'Be honest.'

'Er, no,' says Lissy unconvincingly. 'Of course not!'

'You do!'

'It's just . . . you seemed like such a great couple.'

'I know we looked great on the outside. But the truth is, I never felt I was being myself. It was always a bit like we were acting.'

'That's *it*?' interrupts Jemima, staring at me as though I'm talking gibberish. 'That's the reason you broke up?'

'It's a pretty good reason, don't you think?' says Lissy loyally.

Jemima stares at us both blankly. 'Of course not! Emma, if you'd just stuck it out and acted being the perfect couple for long enough, you would have *become* the perfect couple.'

'But . . . but we wouldn't have been happy!'

'You would have been the perfect couple,' says Jemima, as though explaining something to a very stupid child. '*Obviously* you would have been happy. And anyway, everyone pretends in a relationship.'

'No they don't! Or at least, they shouldn't.'

'Of course they should! All this being honest with each other is overrated. My mother's been married to my father for thirty years, and he still has no idea she isn't a natural blonde.' She disappears out of the room.

I exchange glances with Lissy. 'Do you think she's right?' I say.

'No,' says Lissy uncertainly. 'Of course not! Relationships should be built on . . . on trust and truth.' She pauses, and looks at me anxiously. 'Emma, you never told me you felt that way about Connor.'

'I . . . didn't tell anyone.'

This isn't quite true, I immediately realise. But I'm hardly going to tell my best friend that I told more to a complete stranger than to her, am I?

'Well, I really wish you'd confided in me more,' says Lissy earnestly. 'Emma, let's tell each other *everything* from now on. We shouldn't have secrets from one another, anyway. We're best friends!'

'It's a deal!' I say, with a sudden warm burst of emotion.

'So . . .' Lissy gives me a sidelong look. 'Did your chucking Connor have anything to do with that man from the plane?'

I take a sip of coffee. 'No,' I say without looking up. 'Nothing.'

We both watch the television screen for a few moments.

'Oh, OK!' I say, suddenly remembering. 'So if we're asking each other questions . . . what were you *really* doing with that guy Jean-Paul? And don't tell me you were looking at case notes, because that wouldn't make all that thumping, bumping noise.'

'Oh!' says Lissy, looking cornered. 'OK. Well . . . we were . . .' She avoids my gaze. 'We were . . . um . . . having sex.'

'What?' I stare at her, disconcerted.

'Yes!' She clears her throat. 'We were having passionate . . . raunchy . . . animalistic sex.'

There's something wrong here. Why is she lying? What on earth was she doing in there? What's more embarrassing than sex, for God's sake? I'm so intrigued I almost feel cheered up.

To be honest, it's not the greatest weekend of my life, but by Monday morning, I'm feeling better. I *haven't* made a mistake. My new life starts today. I'm going to forget all about love and romance and concentrate on my career. Maybe I'll even look for a new job.

At least no one at work knows about me and Connor yet, I think as I walk up the office stairs. That would make things a million times harder. To have people coming up to me and saying—

'Emma, I'm so sorry to hear about you and Connor!'

'What?' My head jerks up in shock and I see a girl called Nancy.

'It was such a bolt from the blue! Of all the couples to split up . . .'

I stare at her dazedly. 'How . . . how do you know?'

'Oh, everyone knows!' says Nancy. 'You know there was a little drinks do on Friday night? Well, Connor came to it, and he got quite drunk. And he told everyone. In fact, he made a little speech! It was quite touching, really. About how the Panther Corporation felt like his family, and how he knew we would all support him through this difficult time. And you, of course,' she adds as an afterthought. 'Although since you were the one who broke it off, Connor's really the wounded party.'

I cannot believe this. Connor gave a speech about our break-up. After promising to keep it quiet. And now everyone's on *his* side.

I head for the new coffee machine and am staring into space, trying to get my head round this, when a tremulous voice interrupts me.

'Emma?' I look up and my heart sinks. It's Katie. 'Is it true?'

'Yes,' I say reluctantly. 'It's true. Connor and I have broken up.'

'Oh God.' Katie's breathing becomes quicker and quicker.

Shit. She's hyperventilating. I grab an empty sugar bag and shove it over her mouth.

'I've been having panic attacks all weekend,' she manages, between breaths. 'You and Connor were *the* couple. I mean, if you can't make it, why should the rest of us bother even trying?'

'Katie, we weren't *the* couple!' I say. 'We were *a* couple. It went wrong, and . . . and these things happen. Come on, you haven't told me how your date with Phillip went yet. Cheer me up with some good news.'

Katie's breathing has gradually calmed, and she removes the bag from her face. 'Actually, it went really well,' she says. 'He's so charming. And gentle. And we like the same things.' A bashful smile spreads across her face. 'In fact, he's lovely. And we're going to see each other again!'

'You see?' I squeeze her arm. 'You and Phillip will probably be a far better couple than Connor and I ever were. Do you want a coffee?'

'No thanks, I've got to go. We've got a meeting with Jack Harper about personnel. See you.'

'OK, see you,' I say absently. About five seconds later, my brain clicks into gear. 'Wait a second.' I hurry down the corridor and grab her shoulder. 'Did you just say Jack Harper? He left on Friday.'

'No he didn't. He changed his mind. He's upstairs.'

Suddenly my legs won't work properly.

'Why . . .' I clear my throat. 'Why did he change his mind?'

'Who knows?' Katie shrugs. 'He's the boss. He can do what he likes, can't he? Mind you, he seems very down to earth. He was really nice to Connor after he gave his little speech . . .'

I feel a fresh jolt.

'Jack Harper heard Connor's speech? About us breaking up?'

'Yes! And afterwards he said something really nice like he could imagine just how Connor was feeling. Wasn't that sweet?'

I need to sit down. I need to think. I need to . . .

'Emma, are you OK?' asks Katie in dismay. 'God, I'm so insensitive—'

'No. It's fine,' I say dazedly. 'I'm fine. I'll see you later.'

My mind is whirling as I walk into the marketing department. He'll think I chucked Connor because of what he said to me in the lift, won't he? He'll think it was all because of him. Which it wasn't. It so *wasn't*.

At least, not completely . . .

Maybe that's why . . . *No*. It's ridiculous to think that his staying has anything to do with me. Ridiculous.

As I near my desk, Artemis looks up from a copy of *Marketing Week*. 'Oh, Emma. There's a message for you from Jack Harper. Could you please take the'—she squints at a Post-It on her desk—'the Leopold file to his office. He said you'd know what it was. But if you can't find it, it doesn't matter.'

I stare at her, my heart hammering in my chest. The Leopold file. *It was just an excuse to get away from our desks . . .* It's a secret code. He wants to see me. Oh my God. Oh my God. I have never been more excited and thrilled and petrified. All at once.

I sit down and with trembling fingers take out a blank file. I wait until Artemis has turned away, then write '*Leopold*' on the side of it.

Now what do I do? Well, it's obvious. I take it to his office.

I'm about to push my chair back when I suddenly have a paranoid thought. What if someone stops me and asks what the Leopold file is?

Quickly, I open a new document, invent a fancy letterhead and type a letter from a Mr Ernest P. Leopold to the Panther Corporation. I send it over to print, stroll over to the printer and whisk it out before anyone else can see what it is. Not that anyone else is remotely interested.

As I walk along the corridors my stomach is churning. Why does Jack

Harper want to see me? Because if it's to tell me he was right all along about Connor, then he can just . . . Suddenly I have a flashback to that awful atmosphere in the lift, and my stomach turns over. What if it's really awkward? What if he's angry with me?

I don't have to go, I remind myself. He did give me an out. I could easily phone his secretary and say, 'Sorry, I couldn't find the Leopold file,' and that would be the end.

For an instant I hesitate on the marble stairs, my fingers tightly clutching the cardboard. And then I carry on walking.

As I near the door of Jack's office I see Sven sitting at the desk outside. 'Hi,' I say. 'Er . . . Mr Harper asked me to bring up the Leopold file.'

Sven looks at me, and for an instant it's as if a little silent communication is passing between us. He knows, doesn't he? He probably uses the Leopold file code himself. He picks up the phone and after a moment says, 'Jack, Emma Corrigan here with the Leopold file.' Then he puts down the phone, and without smiling, says, 'Go straight in.'

I walk in. Jack's sitting behind a big wooden desk. When he looks up, his eyes are warm and friendly. I feel myself relax just the teeniest bit.

'Hello,' he says.

'Hello,' I reply, and there's a short silence.

'Here's the Leopold file.' I hand him the cardboard folder.

'The Leopold file.' He laughs. 'Very good.' Then he opens it and looks at the sheet of paper in surprise. 'What's this?'

'It's a . . . it's a letter from Mr Leopold of Leopold and Company.'

'You composed a letter from Mr Leopold?' He sounds astonished. '"From the office of Ernest P. Leopold",' he reads aloud, and his face crinkles in delight. 'I see he wishes to order six thousand cases of Panther Cola. Quite a customer, this Leopold.'

'It's for a corporate event,' I explain. 'They normally use Pepsi, but recently one of their employees tasted Panther Cola, and it was . . .'

'So good they simply had to switch,' finishes Jack. '"May I add that I am delighted with all aspects of your company, and have taken to wearing a Panther jogging suit, which is quite the most comfortable sportswear I have ever known."' To my surprise, his eyes are shining slightly. 'You know, Pete would have adored this.'

'Pete Laidler?' I say hesitantly.

'Yup. It was Pete who came up with the whole Leopold file manoeuvre.' He taps the letter. 'Can I keep it?'

'Of course,' I say, a little taken aback.

He folds it up and puts it in his pocket, and for a few moments there's silence. 'So,' says Jack at last. He raises his head and looks at me with an unreadable expression. 'You broke up with Connor.'

My stomach gives a flip. I don't know what to say.

'So.' I lift my chin defiantly. 'You decided to stay.'

'Yes, well . . .' He stretches out his fingers and studies them briefly. 'I thought I might take a closer look at some of the European subsidiaries.' He looks up. 'How about you?'

He wants me to say I chucked Connor because of him, doesn't he? Well, I'm not going to. 'Same reason.' I nod. 'European subsidiaries.'

Jack's mouth twitches reluctantly into a smile. 'I see. Are you OK?'

'I'm fine. Actually, I'm enjoying the freedom of being single again.' I gesture widely with my arms. 'You know, the flexibility . . .'

'That's great. Well then, maybe this isn't a good time to . . . I know you must be hurting right now, but I was wondering . . .' He pauses for what seems like for ever, and I can feel my heart thumping hard against my ribs. 'Would you like to have dinner some time?'

He's asked me out. He's asked me out. I can't move my mouth.

'Yes,' I say at last. 'Yes, that would be lovely.'

'Great!' He pauses. 'The only thing is, my life is kind of complicated right now. And what with our office situation . . .' He spreads his hands. 'It might be an idea to keep this to ourselves.'

'Oh, I completely agree,' I say quickly. 'We should be discreet.'

'So shall we say . . . tomorrow night? Would that suit you?'

'Tomorrow night would be perfect.'

'I'll come and pick you up. If you email me your address. Eight o'clock?'

'Eight it is!'

I head back to the marketing department, trying as hard as I can to keep my face dispassionate and calm. But excitement is bubbling away in my stomach and a huge smile keeps licking over my face.

Oh my God. I just . . . I can't believe—

Oh, who am I kidding? I knew this was going to happen. As soon as I heard he hadn't gone to America. I knew.

I have never seen Jemima look quite so appalled.

'He knows all your secrets? What on earth do you mean?'

'I sat next to him on a plane, and I told him everything about myself.'

I frown at my reflection in the mirror and tweak out another eyebrow hair. It's seven o'clock, I've had my bath and I've blow-dried my hair.

'And now he's asked her out,' says Lissy. 'Isn't it romantic?'

'You're going out with a man who knows everything about you,' says Jemima, looking aghast. 'Are you *crazy*?'

'I *knew* you fancied him,' says Lissy for about the millionth time. 'I knew it. Right from the moment you started talking about him.' She looks at my reflection. 'I'd leave that right eyebrow alone now.'

'Really?' I peer at my face.

'Emma, you don't tell men all about yourself! You have to keep something back! Mummy always told me, you should never let a man see your feelings or the contents of your handbag.'

'You're not being very helpful, Jemima,' puts in Lissy. 'Come on. You've been on loads of dates with rich businessmen. You must have some good advice!'

'All right.' Jemima sighs. 'The first thing is to look well groomed.'

'Why do you think I'm plucking my eyebrows?' I say with a grimace.

'Fine. OK, the next thing is, you show an interest in his hobbies. What does he like?'

'Dunno. Cars, I think. He has all these vintage cars, apparently.'

'Well then!' Jemima brightens. 'That's good. Pretend you like cars.'

'I can't,' I say, taking a glug from my pre-date relaxer glass of Harvey's Bristol Cream. 'I told him on the plane that I hate vintage cars.'

'You did *what*?' Jemima looks as if she wants to hit me. 'Emma, I'm sorry, I can't help you. This is a disaster. You're completely vulnerable. It's like going into battle in a nightie.'

'You're so cynical, Jemima,' says Lissy. 'I think it's really romantic! They're going to have the perfect date, because there won't be any awkwardness. He knows what Emma likes, what she's interested in.'

'Well, I wash my hands of it,' says Jemima. 'What are you going to wear?' Her eyes narrow. 'You're not going to borrow anything of mine.'

'No!' I say indignantly. 'Honestly Jemima, I do have my own clothes.'

'Fine. Well. Have a good time.'

Lissy and I wait until her footsteps have tapped down the corridor and the front door has slammed.

'Right!' I say excitedly, but Lissy lifts a hand.

'Wait.'

We both sit completely still for a couple of minutes. Then we hear the sound of the front door being opened very quietly.

'She's trying to catch us out,' hisses Lissy. 'Hi!' she says.

'Oh hi,' says Jemima, appearing at the door of the room. 'I forgot my lip gloss.' Her eyes do a quick sweep of the room.

'I don't think you'll find it in here,' says Lissy innocently.

'No. Well. OK. Have a nice evening.' Again her footsteps tap down the corridor, and again the front door slams.

'Right!' says Lissy. 'Let's go.'

We unpeel the Sellotape from Jemima's door, and Lissy makes a little mark where it was.

'You should have been a spy,' I say, watching her.

'OK,' she says, her brow furrowed in concentration. 'There have to be some more booby traps.'

'Oh my God!' I point up. A glass of water is balanced on top of the wardrobe, ready to drench us if we open the door.

'That cow!' says Lissy. She waits until I've put the water down safely, then reaches for the door. 'Ready?' She takes a deep breath, then opens the wardrobe door. Immediately, a loud, piercing siren begins to wail. '*Wee-oo wee-oo wee-oo . . .*'

'Shit!' she says, banging the door shut. 'Shit! How did she do that?'

'It's still going!' I say agitatedly. 'Make it stop!'

We both jab frantically at the wardrobe, searching for an off switch.

'I can't see a button or anything . . .'

Abruptly the noise stops, and we stare at each other, panting slightly.

'Actually,' says Lissy after a long pause. 'Actually, I think that might have been a car alarm outside.' Looking a bit sheepish, she reaches for the door again, and this time it's silent. 'OK,' she says. 'Here goes.'

'Wow!' we breathe as one as she swings the door open.

Jemima's wardrobe is like a treasure chest. It's new, shiny, gorgeous clothes, one after another, all neatly folded or hung on scented hangers.

'So!' says Lissy with a grin, and reaches for a white sparkly dress. 'What look would Madam like this evening?'

In the end, I go for this amazing red top of Jemima's with slashed shoulders, over my own black DKNY chiffon trousers (from the Notting Hill Housing Trust shop) and Jemima's silver high heels from Prada.

'You look amazing!' says Lissy as I do a twirl. 'Completely fab!'

'Do I look too smart?'

'Of course not! You're going out to dinner with a multimillionaire.'

'Don't *say* that!' I exclaim, feeling nerves clutch my stomach. I look at my watch. It's almost eight o'clock.

'Fuck!' Lissy's looking out of the window in the sitting room.

As I follow her gaze, I almost can't breathe. An enormous posh car is waiting outside our house. I mean, *enormous*. It's silver and shiny, and looks incredibly conspicuous in our tiny little street.

And all at once I'm really scared. What am I doing? Look at the world he lives in—and look at the world I live in.

The buzzer goes, and we jump. I feel like I might throw up.

'Hi,' I say into the intercom. 'I'll . . . I'll be right down.' I put the phone down and look at Lissy. 'Well,' I say in a trembling voice. 'This is it!'

Lissy hugs me tightly. 'Just have a lovely time.'

'I will.' I make my way down the stairs, open the door, and Jack's standing there, wearing a jacket and tie. He smiles, and all my fears fly away. Jemima's wrong. This isn't me against him. This is me *with* him.

'Hi,' he says, smiling warmly. 'You look very nice.'

'Thanks.' I reach for the car door handle, but a man in a peaked cap rushes forward to open it for me. 'Silly me!' I say nervously.

I can't quite believe I'm getting into this car, sitting on this plushy seat. Me. Emma Corrigan. I feel like a princess. I feel like a movie star.

'Are you OK?' says Jack.

'Yes! I'm fine!' My voice is a nervous squeak.

'Emma,' says Jack. 'We're going to have fun. I promise. Did you have your pre-date sweet sherry?'

How did he know—? Oh yes. I told him on the plane.

'Yes, I did actually,' I admit.

'Would you like some more?' He opens the bar and I see a bottle of Harvey's Bristol Cream sitting on a silver platter.

'Did you get that especially for me?' I say in disbelief.

'No, it's my favourite tipple.' His expression is so deadpan, I can't help laughing. 'I'll join you,' he says, as he hands me a glass. 'I've never tasted this before.' He pours himself a deep measure, takes a sip, and splutters. 'Are you serious?'

'It's yummy! It tastes like Christmas!'

He shakes his head. 'I'll stick to whisky if you don't mind.'

'OK,' I say with a shrug. 'But you're missing out.' I take another sip and grin happily at him. I'm completely relaxed already.

This is going to be the perfect date.

We ARRIVE AT A RESTAURANT in Mayfair that I've never been to before. In fact I'm not even sure I've been to Mayfair before. It's so completely posh, why ever would I?

'Mr Harper. Miss Corrigan,' says a man in a Nehru suit, appearing out of nowhere. 'Please come this way.'

Wow! They know my name!

We're shown to a table in the corner of an ornate room. A waiter helps me into my chair and fluffs a napkin over my knee, while another pours out some water, and yet another offers me a bread roll. Exactly the same is happening on Jack's side of the table. We have six people dancing attendance on us! I want to catch Jack's eye and laugh, but he looks unconcerned, as if this is perfectly normal.

Perhaps it *is* normal for him, it strikes me. Oh God. Perhaps he has a butler who makes him tea and irons his newspaper every day.

'So,' I say, as all the waiting staff melt away. 'What shall we have to drink?' I've already eyed up the drink that a woman at a neighbouring table has got. It's pink, with slices of watermelon, and looks delicious.

'Already taken care of,' says Jack with a smile, as one of the waiters brings over a bottle of champagne, pops it open and starts pouring. 'I remember you telling me on the plane, your perfect date would start off with a bottle of champagne appearing at your table as if by magic.'

'Oh,' I say, quelling a tiny feeling of disappointment. 'So I did.'

'Cheers,' says Jack, and lightly clinks my glass.

'Cheers.' I take a sip, and it's delicious champagne. It really is. All dry and delicious. I wonder what the watermelon drink tastes like.

Stop it. Jack's right. Champagne is the perfect start to a date.

'The first time I ever had champagne was when I was six years old—'

'At your Aunt Sue's,' says Jack with a smile. 'You took all your clothes off and threw them in the pond.'

'Oh right,' I say, halted midtrack. 'Yes, I've told you, haven't I?'

So I won't bore him with that anecdote again. I sip my champagne and quickly try to think of something else to say. Something that he doesn't already know. *Is* there anything?

'I've chosen a very special meal, which I think you'll like,' says Jack, with a smile. 'All preordered, just for you.'

'Gosh!' I say, taken aback. 'How . . . wonderful.'

A meal specially preordered for me! Wow. That's incredible.

Except . . . choosing your food is half the fun of eating out, isn't it?

Anyway. It doesn't matter. It'll be perfect. It *is* perfect.

OK. Let's start a conversation. 'So what do you like doing in your spare time?' I ask, and Jack gives a shrug.

'I hang out. I watch baseball. I fix my cars . . .'

'You have a collection of vintage cars! That's right. Wow. I really . . .'

'You hate vintage cars.' He smiles. 'I remember.'

Damn. I was hoping he might have forgotten.

'I don't hate the cars themselves,' I say quickly. 'I just hate the people who . . .' Shit. That didn't quite come out right. I hate to admit that Jemima could be right about anything. But it would have been a lot easier if I could just have said brightly, 'Oh, I adore vintage cars!'

As I'm gulping some water, a plate of roasted peppers somehow materialises in front of me. 'Wow!' I say in delight. 'I love roasted peppers.'

'I remembered.' Jack looks rather proud of himself. 'You said on the plane that your favourite food was roasted peppers.'

'Did I?' I stare at him, a bit surprised. Gosh. I don't remember that. I mean, I *like* roasted peppers, but I wouldn't have said—

'So I called the restaurant and had them make it specially for you. I can't eat peppers,' Jack adds, as a plate of scallops appears in front of him, 'otherwise I would join you.'

I gape at his plate. Oh my God. Those scallops look amazing.

I take a bite of roasted pepper. It's delicious. And it was very thoughtful of him to remember. But I can't help eyeing up his scallops. They're making my mouth water. And look at that green sauce! God, I bet they're succulent and perfectly cooked . . .

Suddenly Jack claps a hand on his pocket. 'My mobile,' he says. 'Emma, would you mind if I took this?'

'Of course not,' I say. 'Go ahead.'

When he's gone, I just can't help it. I reach over, and spear one of his scallops. I close my eyes as I chew it, letting the flavour flood through my taste buds. That is just divine. That is the best food I've ever tasted in my life. I'm just wondering whether I could get away with eating a second one, if I shifted the others around his plate a bit, when Jack sits back down in his place, a strained expression on his face.

There's silence and I cast around for something to say. 'I have a confession to make,' I say, gesturing to his plate. 'I pinched one of your scallops.'

'That's OK,' he says abstractedly, and begins to fork the rest of them into his mouth.

What's happened? Where's the banter gone? He's completely changed.

By the time we've finished our tarragon chicken with rocket salad and chips, my entire body is tensed up with misery. This date is a complete disaster. I've made every effort possible to chat and joke and be funny. But Jack's taken two more calls and the rest of the time he's been broody and distracted. I might as well not be there.

'I'll just go and freshen up,' I say, as our main-course plates are removed, and Jack simply nods.

The Ladies is more like a palace than a loo, with gold mirrors, plushy chairs and a woman in uniform to give you a towel. For a moment I feel a bit shy about phoning Lissy in front of her, but she must have seen it all before, mustn't she?

'Hi,' I say, as Lissy picks up. 'It's me.'

'Emma! How's it going?'

'It's awful,' I say dolefully. 'It all started off brilliantly. We were laughing and joking, and the restaurant's amazing, and he'd ordered this special menu just for me . . .' I swallow hard.

'It sounds wonderful,' says Lissy in astonishment. 'So how come—?'

'So then he had this call on his mobile.' I blow my nose. 'And ever since, he's barely said a word to me.'

'Maybe he's worried about something, but he doesn't want to burden you with it,' says Lissy after a pause.

'That's true,' I say slowly. 'He does look pretty hassled.'

'Maybe something awful has happened but he doesn't want to ruin the mood. Just try talking to him. Share his worries!'

'OK,' I say, feeling more cheerful. 'OK, I'll try that. Thanks, Lissy.'

I walk back to the table feeling slightly more positive. As I sit down, I give Jack the warmest look I can muster. 'Jack, is everything OK?'

'It's fine,' he says curtly. 'Thanks.' His tone is very much 'subject closed' but I'm not going to give up that easily.

'Have you had some bad news?'

'No.'

'Is it . . . a business thing?' I persist. 'Or some kind of personal . . . ?'

Jack looks up, a flash of anger in his face. 'I said, it's nothing. Quit it.'

Great. That puts me in my place, doesn't it?

'Would you both care for dessert?' A waiter's voice interrupts my thoughts, and I give him a strained smile.

'Actually, I don't think so.' I've had enough of this evening. I just want to get it over and go home.

'She does want dessert,' says Jack, over my head.

What? *What* did he just say? The waiter looks at me hesitantly.

'No I don't!' I say firmly.

'Come on, Emma,' says Jack, and now his warm, teasing tone is back. 'You don't have to pretend with me. You told me on the plane, you say you don't want a dessert, when really, you do.'

'Well, this time, I really don't.'

'It's specially created for you.' Jack leans forward. 'Häagen-Dazs, meringue, Bailey's sauce on the side . . .'

Suddenly I feel completely patronised. How does he know what I want? He has no idea about me. None at all.

'I'm not hungry,' I push my chair back.

'Emma, I know you. You want it, really—'

'You *don't* know me!' I cry angrily. 'Jack, you may know a few random facts about me. But that doesn't mean you know me!'

'What?' Jack stares at me.

'If you knew me, you would have realised that when I go out to dinner with someone I like them to listen to what I'm saying and not tell me to "quit it" when all I'm doing is trying to make conversation . . .'

'Look.' Jack rubs his face. 'A few things are going on in my life at the moment, they're very important—'

'Fine. Well, let them go on without me.' Tears are stinging my eyes as I stand up and reach for my bag. 'Thank you for dinner,' I say, as one of the waiters magically appears at my side with my coat.

'Emma,' says Jack in disbelief. 'You're not seriously going.'

'I am.'

'Give it another chance. Please. Stay and have some coffee.'

'I'm going.' I gulp. 'Thank you very much,' I add to the waiter. 'How did you know I wanted my coat?'

'We make it our business to know,' says the waiter discreetly.

'You see?' I say to Jack. '*They* know me.'

There's an instant in which we stare at each other.

'Fine,' says Jack at last, and gives a resigned shrug. 'Fine. Daniel will take you home. He should be waiting outside in the car.'

'I'm not going home in your car! Goodbye. And thanks very much,' I add to the waiter. 'You were all very attentive and nice to me.'

I hurry out of the restaurant to discover it's started to rain. I stride along the streets, feeling raindrops mingling with tears on my face. I don't have an umbrella. I have no idea where I am, or where . . .

Hang on. There's a bus stop. I look down the numbers and see one that goes to Islington. Well, fine. I'll take the bus home.

It's one of those bus shelters with a roof and little seats, and I sit down, thanking God my hair won't get any wetter. I'm just staring blankly at a car advertisement, wondering what that Häagen-Dazs pudding tasted like, when a big silver car purrs up at the pavement.

I don't believe it.

'Please,' says Jack, getting out. 'Let me take you home.'

'No,' I say, without turning my head.

'You can't stay here in the rain.'

'Yes I can. Some of us live in the real world, you know.'

The next moment Jack has arrived in the bus shelter. 'I know I was terrible company this evening,' he says. 'And I'm sorry. I'm also sorry I can't tell you anything about it. But my life is . . . complicated. And some bits of it are very delicate. Do you understand?'

No, I want to say. No, I don't understand, when I've told you every single little thing about me. 'I suppose,' I say, with a tiny shrug.

'I'm sorry the evening was a disappointment to you,' says Jack.

'It wasn't,' I say, suddenly feeling bad. 'I just . . . I had such high hopes! I wanted to get to know you a bit, and I wanted to have fun . . . and I wanted one of those pink cocktails, not champagne . . .'

Shit. *Shit.* That slipped out before I could stop it.

'But . . . you like champagne!' says Jack, looking stunned. 'You told me. Your perfect date would start off with champagne.'

I can't quite meet his eye. 'Yes, well. I didn't know about the pink cocktails then, did I?'

Jack laughs. 'Fair point. Very fair point. And I didn't even give you a choice, did I? Oh Emma. I'm sorry.' He shakes his head. 'I wanted to get to know you too. Will you give me another chance?'

A big red double-decker bus rumbles up to the bus stop, and we both look up. 'I've got to go,' I say, standing up. 'This is my bus.'

'Emma, don't be silly. Come in the car.'

'No. I'm going on the bus!' The automatic doors open, and I step onto the bus. I show my Travelcard to the driver and he nods.

'You're seriously considering riding on this thing?' says Jack, stepping on behind me. He peers dubiously at the usual motley collection of night bus riders. 'Is this *safe*?'

'You sound like my grandpa! Of course it's safe.'

'Hurry up!' says the driver to Jack. 'If you haven't got the money, get off.'

'I have American Express,' says Jack, feeling in his pocket.

'You can't pay a bus fare with American Express!' I say, rolling my eyes. 'And anyway, I think I'd rather be on my own, if you don't mind.'

'I see,' says Jack in a different voice. 'I guess I'd better get off,' he says to the driver. Then he looks at me. 'You haven't answered me. Can we try again? Tomorrow night. And this time we'll do whatever you want.'

'OK.' I try to give a noncommittal shrug but as I meet his eye I find myself smiling too. 'Eight o'clock. And leave the car behind,' I add firmly. 'We'll do things my way.'

'Great! I look forward to it. Good night, Emma.'

As he turns to get off, I climb the stairs to the top deck of the bus. I head for the front seat and stare out at the rainy London night. If I stare for long enough, the streetlights become blurred like a kaleidoscope. Like fairyland. I can feel the bus lurch as we turn corners, but I'm barely aware of where we're going. Until after a while, familiar sights impinge on my consciousness, and I realise we're nearly at my street. I gather myself, reach for my bag, and totter along to the top of the stairs.

Suddenly the bus makes a sharp swing left, and I grab for a seat handle, trying to steady myself. Why are we turning left? I look out of the window, and blink in astonishment. Surely we're not—

But we are. I peer down through the window, dumbfounded. We're in my tiny little road. And now we've stopped outside my house. I hurry down the stairs, nearly breaking my ankle, and stare at the driver.

'Number 41 Ellerwood Road,' he says with a flourish.

'What's going on?' I look at the driver. 'Did he *pay* you?'

'Five hundred quid,' says the driver, and winks at me. 'Whoever he is, love, I'd hold on to him.'

'Thanks,' I say dazedly. 'I mean, thanks for the ride.'

Feeling as though I'm in a dream, I get off the bus and head for the front door. But Lissy has already got there and is opening it.

'Is that a *bus*?' she says, staring. 'What's it doing here?'

'It's my bus,' I say. 'It took me home.'

'I don't believe it!' says Lissy slowly, gazing as it disappears round the corner. She turns to look at me. 'So . . . it was OK in the end?'

'Yes,' I say. 'Yes. It was . . . OK.'

OK. Don't tell anyone. Do *not* tell anyone you were on a date with Jack Harper last night. As I arrive at work the next day I feel almost convinced I'm going to blurt it out by mistake.

'Hi,' says Artemis as I sit down at my desk.

'Hi,' I say, forcing myself not to add anything else.

I'm supposed to be doing some filing this morning, but instead I find myself taking out a piece of paper and starting a list of possible date venues where I can take Jack tonight.

1. Pub. No. Far too boring.
2. Movie. No. Too much sitting, not talking.
3. Ice skating. I have no idea why I put that, since I can't even skate. Except it was in *Splash*.

God, I've run out of ideas already. How crap is this? I stare at the sheet blankly, half tuning into the idle conversation going on around me.

'. . . really working on some secret project, or is that just a rumour?'

'. . . company in a new direction, apparently . . .'

'. . . *is* this Sven guy anyway? I mean, what function does he have?'

'He's with Jack, isn't he?' says Amy, who works in Finance but fancies Nick so is always coming into our office. 'He's Jack's lover.'

'*What?*' I say, snapping the end of my pencil. Jack gay? Jack gay?

That's why he didn't kiss me good night. He only wants me to be a friend. He'll introduce me to Sven and I'll have to pretend to be all cool with it, like I knew all along—

'Is Jack Harper gay?' Caroline is saying in astonishment.

'I just assumed he was,' says Amy with a shrug.

'I don't think he *looks* gay!' I say, trying to sound light-hearted.

'He's not gay,' chimes in Artemis authoritatively. 'I read an old profile of him in *Newsweek*, and he was dating the female president of Origin Software. And it said before that he went out with some supermodel.'

Relief floods through me. I knew he wasn't gay. Honestly, do these people have nothing better to do than engage in mindless speculation about people they don't know?

'He's pretty sexy, don't you think?' says Caroline with a wicked grin.

'Apparently, he hasn't had a relationship since Pete Laidler died,' says Artemis crisply. 'So I doubt you've got much of a chance.'

'Bad luck, Caroline,' says Nick, with a laugh.

Just for an instant, I find myself imagining what would happen if I stood up and said, 'Actually I had dinner with Jack Harper last night.' They wouldn't even believe me, would they?

'Hi, Connor,' comes Caroline's voice, interrupting my thoughts.

Connor? My head jerks up in dismay.

He's approaching my desk, a wounded look on his face. 'Hi,' he says.

'Hi,' I reply awkwardly, and there's silence. All the gossip about Jack has petered out. I know everyone in the office is listening to us.

'I only came up', says Connor at last, 'because I'd put us down to do a stint on the Pimm's stall together at the Corporate Family Day. Obviously I thought we'd be—' He breaks off, looking more wounded than ever. 'Anyway. But I don't mind going through with it. If you don't.'

I'm not going to be the one to say I can't bear to stand next to him for half an hour. 'I don't mind,' I say.

'Fine.'

'Hey,' says Nick, coming over towards us with a wicked, eyes-gleaming, let's-shit-stir expression. 'I saw you with someone last night.'

My heart gives a huge, terrified bound. Fuck! Fuck, fuck, OK . . . OK . . . It's OK. He's not looking at me. He's looking at Connor.

Who the hell was Connor with?

'That was just a friend,' says Connor stiffly. 'It's far too early to be thinking of . . . moving on. Isn't it, Emma?'

'Er, yes.' I swallow several times. 'Absolutely. Definitely.'

Oh God.

Anyway. Never mind. I'm not going to worry about Connor. I have an important date to think about. And thank goodness, by the end of the day I have at last come up with the perfect venue. There is one tiny little hitch—but I'll overcome it.

It only takes me about half an hour to persuade Lissy that when they said 'The key shall in no circumstances be transferred to any non-member' in the rules, they didn't really mean it. At last she hands it to me, an anxious expression on her face. 'Don't lose it!'

'I won't! Thanks, Liss.' I give her a hug.

'You remember the password, don't you?'

'Yes. Alexander.'

'Where are you going?' says Jemima, coming into my room all dressed up to go out. She gives me a critical look. 'Nice top. Where's it from?'

'Oxfam. I mean, Whistles.'

'I was meaning to ask,' Jemima says, narrowing her eyes. 'You two didn't go into my room last night, did you?'

'No,' says Lissy innocently. 'Why, did it look like we had?'

Jemima was out until three, and by the time she got back everything was back in place. Sellotape and everything.

'No,' admits Jemima reluctantly. 'Nothing was out of place. But I just got a *feeling*. As though someone had been in there.'

I pull a face at her behind her back as she leaves and start putting on my mascara. 'What's the time?' I ask.

'Ten to eight,' says Lissy.

Suddenly the buzzer goes, and we both look up.

'He's early,' says Lissy. 'That's a bit weird.'

We hurry into the sitting room and Lissy gets to the window first. 'Oh my God,' she says, looking down to the street below. 'It's Connor.'

'*Connor?*' I stare at her in horror. 'Pretend we're not in!'

'Too late,' says Lissy, and pulls a face. 'Sorry. He's seen me.'

Shit. I pelt downstairs and open the door.

There, standing on the doorstep, is Connor, wearing the same martyred expression. 'Hi,' he says. 'Here are some of your things. I thought you might need them.'

'Er, thanks,' I say, grabbing the box, which seems to contain one bottle of L'Oréal shampoo and some jumper I've never seen in my life.

'No problem,' says Connor. He gives a heavy sigh. 'Emma . . . I was thinking perhaps we could use this as an opportunity to talk. Maybe we could have a drink, or supper even.'

'Gosh,' I say brightly. 'I'd love that. I really would. But to be honest, now isn't a completely brilliant time.'

'Are you going out?' His face falls.

'Um, yes. With Lissy.' I glance surreptitiously at my watch. It's six minutes to eight. 'So anyway, I'll see you soon.'

'Why are you so flustered? Is something going on?'

At that moment, Lissy appears behind me at the door. 'Um, Emma, there's a very urgent phone call for you,' she says. Unfortunately Lissy is the worst liar in the world.

'You're trying to get rid of me!' says Connor, in bewilderment. Then, staring at my outfit. 'Hang on a minute . . . are you going on a date?'

My mind works quickly. If I deny it, we'll probably get into some huge argument. But if I admit the truth, maybe he'll stalk off in a huff.

'You're right,' I say. 'I've got a date.'

There's a shocked silence. Connor, to my dismay, sinks heavily down onto the garden wall. 'You told me there wasn't anyone else!'

'There wasn't! But . . . there is now. And he'll be here soon . . . Connor, you really don't want to get into this.' I grab his arm and try to lift him up, but he weighs about twelve stone. 'Connor, please.'

'I suppose you're right.' At last Connor gets to his feet. 'I'll go.'

He walks to the gate, his back hunched in defeat. Then, to my horror, he turns back. 'So, who is it?'

'It's . . . it's someone you don't know,' I say, crossing my fingers behind my back. 'Look, we'll have lunch soon and have a good talk.'

'OK,' says Connor, looking more wounded than ever. 'I get the message.'

I watch, unable to breathe, as he shuts the gate behind him and walks slowly along the street. Keep walking, keep walking . . . don't stop . . .

As he finally rounds the corner, Jack's silver car appears at the other end of the street. I sink onto the stone wall. I think I need a drink. And I've only got mascara on one set of eyelashes, I abruptly realise.

The silver car pulls up in front of the house, and out gets the same uniformed driver as before. He opens the passenger door, and Jack steps out. 'Hi!' he says, looking taken aback to see me. 'Am I late?'

'No! I was just . . . um . . . sitting here. Anyway!' I say, hastily standing up, 'Actually, I'm not quite ready. Do you want to come up for a minute?'

'Sure,' says Jack with a smile. 'That would be nice.'

'And send your car away,' I add. 'You weren't supposed to have it!'

'You weren't supposed to sit outside your house and catch me out,' retorts Jack with a grin. 'OK, Daniel, that's it for the night.'

'This is Lissy, my flatmate,' I say as the driver gets back into the car. 'Lissy, Jack.'

'Hi,' says Lissy with a self-conscious grin, as they shake hands.

As we make our way up the stairs to our flat, I'm suddenly aware of how narrow they are, and how the cream paint on the walls is all scuffed and the carpet smells of cabbage. Jack probably lives in some enormous grand mansion. He probably has a marble staircase.

But so what? We can't all have marble. Anyway, you probably trip on it all the time, and it probably chips really easily—

'Emma, if you want to get ready, I'll fix Jack a drink,' says Lissy, with a smile that says, He's nice!

'Thanks,' I say, shooting back an 'isn't he?' look. I hurry into my room and hurriedly start applying mascara to my other eye.

A few moments later there's a little knock at my door. In comes Jack, holding out a glass of sweet sherry. 'Oh, thanks!' I say gratefully.

'I won't come in,' he says politely.

'No, it's fine.'

Jack takes a sip of what looks like whisky, and looks around my room in fascination. 'So this is your room. Your world.'

'Yes.' I flush slightly, unscrewing my lip gloss. 'It's a bit messy—'

'It's very homey.' I can see him taking in the bed covered with clothes, the fish mobile, and a new skirt hanging on the wardrobe.

'Cancer Research?' he says puzzledly, looking at the label.

'It's a shop,' I say, a little defiantly. 'A secondhand shop.'

'Ah.' He nods in tactful comprehension. 'Nice bed cover,' he adds.

'It's ironic,' I say hastily. 'It's an ironic statement.'

God, how embarrassing. I should have changed it. Maybe it wasn't such a great idea to let Jack come in here. He's picking up my Perfectil vitamins, and examining them. I mean, what's so interesting about *vitamins*? Now he's looking at Katie's crochet belt.

'What's this? A snake?'

'It's a belt,' I say, screwing up my face as I put in an earring. 'I know. It's hideous. I can't stand crochet.'

I turn to see him looking in fascination at my exercise chart, which I put up in January after I'd spent the entire Christmas eating Quality Street. '"Monday morning",' he reads aloud. '"Brisk jog round block. Forty sit-ups. Lunch time: yoga class. Evening: Pilates tape. Sixty sit-ups."' He takes a sip of whisky. 'Very impressive. You do all this?'

'Well, I don't exactly manage every *single* . . . I mean, it was quite an ambitious, you know . . . er . . . Anyway!' I spritz myself with perfume. 'Let's go!' Honestly! Why on earth is he so *interested* in everything?

As we head out into the balmy evening and walk up to the main road, I feel light and happy with anticipation.

'So,' says Jack. 'An evening out, Emma-style.'

'Absolutely!' I stick out my hand and hail a taxi, and give the name of the road in Clerkenwell off which the little alley runs.

'We're allowed to go by taxi, are we?' says Jack mildly as we get in.

'As a very special treat,' I say with mock severity.

As we whiz along Upper Street, I feel quite proud of myself. It just shows I'm a true Londoner. I can take my guests to little places off the beaten track. And who knows, Madonna might be there this evening!

After about twenty minutes we get to Clerkenwell. I insist on paying the taxi fare, and lead Jack down the alley.

'Very interesting,' says Jack. 'So where are we heading?'

'Just wait,' I say enigmatically. I head for the door, press the buzzer.

'Hello?' comes a voice.

'Hello,' I say casually. 'I'd like to speak to Alexander, please.'

'Who?' says the voice.

'Alexander,' I repeat. Obviously they have to double-check.

'Ees no Alexander here.'

'You don't understand. Al-ex-and-er,' I enunciate clearly.

'Ees no Alexander.'

Maybe I got the wrong door. I mean, I remember it as being this one—but maybe it was this other one with the frosted glass. Yes. That one looks quite familiar, actually.

'Tiny hitch.' I smile at Jack, and press the new bell.

There's silence. I wait a few minutes, then try again, and again. There's no reply. Fuck. I am a moron. Why didn't I check the address?

'Is there a problem?' says Jack.

'No!' I say at once, and smile brightly.

I look up and down the street, trying not to panic. Which one was it? Then, through an arch, I spy another alley, almost identical to this one.

I feel a huge thud of horror. Am I in the right *alley*, even? I dart forward and peer into the other alley. It looks exactly the same.

OK, I'll call Lissy! She'll tell me. I pull out my mobile and dial home, but immediately it clicks onto the answering machine.

'Hi, Lissy, it's me,' I say, trying to sound light and casual. 'A tiny little hitch: I can't remember exactly which door the club is behind. So if you get this, could you give me a call? Thanks!'

I look up to see Jack watching me. 'Everything OK?'

'Just a slight glitch,' I say, and give a relaxed little laugh. 'There's this secret club along here somewhere, but I can't quite remember where.'

'Never mind,' says Jack nicely. 'These things happen.'

I jab the number for home again, but it's engaged. Quickly I dial Lissy's mobile number, but it's switched off.

'Emma,' says Jack cautiously. 'Would you like me to make a reservation at—?'

'No!' I jump as though stung. Jack's not going to reserve anything. I've said I'll organise this evening, and I will. 'No thanks. It's OK.' I make a snap decision. 'Change of plan. We'll go to Antonio's instead. It's a bit out of the way, in south London. But it's really nice.' I stride purposefully towards the main road and, thank God, a taxi's coming along with its light on. I flag it down, open the door for Jack and say to the driver, 'Hi, Antonio's on Sanderstead Road in Clapham, please.'

OK, it should *not* take this long to get from Clerkenwell to Clapham. We should have got there ages ago. I mean, it's only down the road!

After about half an hour, I lean forward and say to the driver yet again, 'Is there a problem?'

'Traffic, love.' He gives an easy shrug. 'What can you do?'

I sink back on my seat, feeling my stomach churning with frustration. I can't make small talk. I'm using every ounce of concentration in willing the taxi to go faster. I stare out of the window, giving an inward cheer every time the postcodes on the street signs get closer to where we want to be. SW3 . . . SW11 . . . SW4!

OK. Calm down, Emma. Here's the street. We're finally here.

'So this is it!' I say. 'Sorry it took a while.'

'No problem,' says Jack. 'This place looks great!'

As I hand the fare to the taxi driver, I have to admit I'm pretty pleased we came. Antonio's looks absolutely amazing! There are fairy lights decorating the familiar green façade, and music and laughter spilling out of the open door. I can even hear people singing inside.

'Hi!' I say as I push the door open. 'Antonio!'

'Emma!' says Antonio, who's standing by the door holding a glass of wine. '*Bellissima!*' He kisses me on each cheek, and I feel a flood of warm relief. He'll make sure we have a wonderful time.

'This is Jack,' I say, grinning at him.

'Wonderful to meet you!' Antonio kisses Jack too, and I giggle.

'So, could we have a table for two?'

'Ah . . .' He pulls a face of regret. 'Sweetheart, we're closed!'

'What?' I stare back at him, baffled. 'But . . . people are here!'

'It's a private party! My nephew's wedding. Another night, I'll give you the best table we have. You call in advance . . .'

I can't even look at Jack. I dragged him all the way down to bloody Clapham for this. I have to redeem this situation. Quickly.

'We'll go to the pub,' I say as soon as we're outside on the pavement. 'I mean, what's wrong with just sitting down with a nice drink?'

'Sounds good,' says Jack mildly, and follows me as I hurry down the street to a sign reading The Nag's Head, and push the door open. I've never been in this pub before, but surely it's bound to be fairly—

OK. Maybe not.

This has to be the grimmest pub I've ever seen in my life. I cannot have a date with Jack in here. I just can't.

'Right!' I say, swinging the door shut again, 'Let's just grab a taxi and head back to town!'

I stride to the edge of the pavement and stick out my hand.

During the next three minutes not a single car passes by. Not just no taxis. No vehicles at all.

'Kind of quiet,' observes Jack at last.

Suddenly I want to burst into tears. I want to sink down on the pavement and bury my head in my hands and sob.

'How about pizza?' says Jack, and my head jerks up in sudden hope.

'Why? Do you know a pizza place round—?'

'I see pizza for sale.' He nods at one of the grotty takeaway places. 'And I see a bench.' He gestures to the other side of the road, where there's a tiny railed garden with paving and trees and a wooden bench. 'You get the pizza.' He smiles at me. 'I'll save the bench.'

I have never felt so mortified in my entire life. Ever.

Jack Harper takes me to the grandest, poshest restaurant in the world. And I take him to a park bench in Clapham.

'Here's your pizza,' I say, carrying the hot boxes over to where he's sitting. 'I got margarita, ham and mushroom and pepperoni.'

'Perfect,' says Jack with a smile. He takes a large bite, then reaches into his inside pocket. 'Now, this was supposed to be your going-home present, but since we're here . . .'

I gape as he produces a small, stainless steel cocktail shaker and two matching cups. He unscrews the top of the shaker and to my astonishment, pours a pink, transparent liquid into each cup.

'I don't believe it!' I gaze at him wide-eyed.

'I couldn't let you wonder all your life what it tasted like, could I?' He hands me a cup and raises his towards me. 'Your good health.'

'Cheers.' I take a sip of the cocktail . . . and oh my God it's yummy. Sharp and sweet, with a kick of vodka.

He's being so nice to me. He's pretending he's having a good time. But what does he think inside? He must despise me.

'Emma, are you OK?'

'Not really,' I say in a thick voice. 'Jack, I'm so sorry. I really am. I honestly had it all planned. We were going to go to this really cool club where celebrities go, and it was going to be really good fun . . .'

'Emma.' Jack puts his drink down and looks at me. 'I wanted to spend this evening with you. And that's what we're doing.' Slowly he leans towards me and my heart starts to pound. Oh my God. Oh my God. He's going to kiss me. He's going to—

'Arrgh!' I leap up in total panic. A spider is running up my leg.

With one brisk swipe, Jack brushes the spider off onto the grass, and I subside back on the bench, my heart racing.

And of course, the mood's completely ruined. Great. Just marvellous.

'I don't suppose you're afraid of spiders,' I say to Jack, giving an awkward laugh. 'I don't suppose you're afraid of anything.'

Jack gives a noncommittal little smile in return.

'*Are* you afraid of anything?' I persist.

'Real men don't get afraid,' he says jokily.

In spite of myself, I feel a tiny prickle of discontent. Jack's not the best person in the world at talking about himself.

'So, where did you get this scar?' I ask, gesturing to his wrist.

'It's a long, boring story.' He smiles. 'You don't want to hear it.'

I do! my mind immediately says. I do want to hear it. But now he's just staring ahead into the distance, as if I'm not even there.

Did he forget about kissing me? Should I kiss him? No. No.

'Pete loved spiders,' he says suddenly. 'Kept them as pets.'

'Really?' I pull a face.

'Crazy. He was a crazy fucking guy.' He exhales sharply.

'You . . . still miss him,' I say hesitantly.

'Yes. I still miss him.'

There's another silence. 'Did he leave any family?' I say cautiously, and immediately Jack's face closes up.

'Some,' he says.

'Do you see them still?'

'Occasionally.' He exhales sharply, then turns and smiles. 'You have tomato sauce on your chin.' As he reaches up to wipe it away, he meets my eyes. Slowly, he's bending towards me. Oh my God. This is it, this is really it. This is—'

'Jack.'

We both leap in shock. I turn round, and stare in utter disbelief. Sven is standing at the gate of the tiny garden. What the fuck is he doing here?

'Great timing,' murmurs Jack. 'Hi, Sven,' he calls.

I stare at Jack. 'But . . . how did he know where we were?'

'He called while you were getting the pizza.' Jack sighs and rubs his face. 'I didn't know he'd get here this quickly. Emma . . . something's come up. I need to have a quick word with him. It won't take long.'

'OK,' I say with a little shrug. After all, what else can I say? But inside, my whole body is pulsing in frustration, bordering on anger.

Jack and Sven stand by the gate having an animated conversation in low voices. I take a sip of cocktail and casually shift along the bench so I can hear better.

'. . . plan B . . . back up to Glasgow . . .'

'. . . urgent . . .'

Their voices descend even lower, and I can't hear a word. Then Jack breaks off and comes towards me. 'Emma . . . I'm really sorry about this.' He sits down beside me. 'But I'm going to have to go.'

'*Go?*' I stare at him in dismay. 'What, now?'

'I'm going to have to go away for a few days. I'm sorry. But . . . it's pretty important. Sven's ordered a car for you to take you home.'

Great, I think savagely. Thanks a lot, Sven. 'That was really . . . thoughtful of him,' I say, and trace a pattern in the dirt with my shoe.

'Emma, I really have to go,' says Jack, seeing my face. 'But I'll see you when I get back, OK? At the Corporate Family Day. And we'll . . . take it from there.'

'OK.' I try to smile. 'That would be great.'

'I had a good time tonight.'

'So did I,' I say, staring down at the bench. 'I had a really good time.'

'We'll have a good time again.' Gently he lifts my chin. 'I promise.'

He leans forward and this time there's no hesitation. His mouth lands on mine, sweet and firm. His stubble is rough against my face. His arm creeps around me and pulls me towards him, and my breath catches in my throat. I find myself reaching under his jacket, feeling the ridges of muscle beneath his shirt. Oh God, I want this. I want more.

He pulls away, and I feel as if I've been wrenched out of a dream.

'Emma, I have to go.'

My mouth is prickly wet. I can still feel his skin on mine. My entire body is throbbing. This can't be the end. It can't.

'Don't go,' I hear myself saying thickly. 'Half an hour.'

What am I suggesting? That we do it under a *bush*?

'I don't want to go.' His dark eyes are almost opaque. 'But I have to.' He takes my hand, and I cling onto his.

'So . . . I'll . . . I'll see you.' I can barely talk properly.

'I can't wait.'

'Neither can I.'

'Jack.' We both look up to see Sven at the gate.

'OK,' calls Jack. We stand up and I discreetly look away from Jack's slightly strange posture.

I could ride along in the car and—

No. *No.* Rewind. I did not think that.

When we reach the road, I see two silver cars waiting by the pavement. Sven is standing by one, and the other is obviously for me. As the driver opens the door for me, Jack touches my hand briefly. I want to grab him for a final snog, but I manage to control myself.

'Bye,' he murmurs.

seven

WE'LL TAKE IT FROM THERE. Every time I think about it, my stomach gives an excited little fizz. I can't think about anything else. The Corporate Family Day is a company event, I keep reminding myself. Not a date. But . . . you never know what might happen next.

On Saturday morning I get up extra early, exfoliate all over, Immac under my arms, rub in my most expensive body cream and paint my toenails. Just because it's good to be well groomed. No other reason.

I choose my Gossard lacy bra and matching knickers, and my most flattering bias cut summer dress. Then, with a slight blush, I pop some condoms into my bag. Simply because it's always good to be prepared.

I look in the mirror, give my lips a final coat of gloss and spray Allure all over me. OK. Ready for sex. I mean, for Jack.

I mean . . . Oh God. Whatever.

The family day is happening at Panther House, which is the Panther Corporation's country house in Hertfordshire. They use it for training and conferences and brainstorming days, none of which I ever get invited to. So I've never been here before, and as I get out of the taxi I have to admit I'm pretty impressed. It's a nice big old mansion, with lots of windows and pillars at the front.

I follow the sounds of music and walk round the house to find the event in full swing on the vast lawn. Brightly coloured bunting festoons the back of the house, tents are dotted across the grass, a band is playing on a little bandstand and children are shrieking on a bouncy castle.

'Emma!' I look up to see Cyril advancing towards me, dressed as a joker with a red and yellow pointy hat. 'Where's your costume?'

'Costume! Gosh, um . . . I didn't realise we had to have one.'

This is not entirely true. Yesterday evening at about five o'clock, Cyril sent round an urgent email to everyone in the company: A REMINDER: AT THE CFD, COSTUMES ARE COMPULSORY FOR ALL PANTHER EMPLOYEES.

But let's face it, what can they do about it now?

'Sorry,' I say vaguely, looking around for Jack. 'Still, never mind . . .'

'You people! It was on the memo, it was in the newsletter . . .' He takes hold of my shoulder as I try to walk away. 'Well, you'll have to take one of the spare ones.'

'What?' I look at him blankly. 'What spare ones?'

'I had a feeling this might happen,' says Cyril with a note of triumph, 'so I made advance provisions.'

A cold feeling starts to creep over me. He can't mean—

I give a desperate wriggle, but his hand is like a clamp on my shoulder. He chivvies me into a tent, where two middle-aged ladies are standing beside a rack of . . . oh my God. The most revolting, lurid man-made-fibre costumes I've ever seen.

'No,' I say in panic. 'Really. I'd rather stay as I am.'

'Emma, this is a fun day,' snaps Cyril. 'And part of that fun derives from seeing our fellow employees and family in amusing outfits. Which reminds me, where is your family?'

'Oh.' I pull the regretful face I've been practising all week. 'They . . . actually, they couldn't make it.'

Which could be because I didn't tell them anything about it.

'Well. You'll have to mingle with other families. Here we are. Snow White.' He shoves a horrendous nylon dress towards me.

'I don't want to be Snow White—' I begin, then break off as I see Moira from Accounts miserably being pushed into a big, shaggy gorilla costume. 'OK.' I grab the dress. 'I'll be Snow White.'

I almost want to cry. My beautiful flattering dress is lying in a calico bag, ready for collection at the end of the day. And I am wearing an outfit that makes me look like a six-year-old with zero taste.

As I emerge disconsolately from the tent, the band is briskly playing the 'Oom-pa-pa' song from *Oliver*. I spot Paul, walking along on the grass dressed as a pirate, with three small children hanging off his legs.

'Uncle Paul! Uncle Paul!' one is shrieking. 'Do your scary face again!'

'Hi, Paul,' I say miserably. 'Are you having a good time?'

'Whoever invented Corporate Family Days should be shot,' he says without a flicker of humour. 'Get the hell off my foot!' he snaps at one of the children, and they all shriek with delighted laughter.

'Mummy, I don't *need* to spend a penny,' mutters Artemis as she walks by dressed as a mermaid, in the company of a commanding woman in a huge hat.

This is so weird. People with their families are completely different.

'Emma!'

I look up, and see Katie. She's dressed in a bizarre carrot costume, holding the arm of an elderly man with grey hair. Her father, I suppose. Which is a bit weird, because I thought she said she was coming with—

'Emma, this is Phillip!' she says radiantly. 'Phillip, meet my friend Emma. She's the one who brought us together!'

Wh— what? *This* is Phillip? But he has to be at least seventy!

In a total blur, I shake his hand, which is dry and papery just like Grandpa's, and manage to make a bit of small talk about the weather. But all the time I'm in total shock.

Don't get me wrong. I am not ageist. But he's an old man! He's *old*!

'Isn't he lovely?' says Katie fondly, as he goes off to get some drinks. 'He's so thoughtful. Nothing's too much trouble. I've never been out with a man like him before!'

'I can believe that,' I say, my voice a little strangled. 'What exactly is the age gap between you two?'

'I'm not sure,' says Katie in surprise. 'I've never asked. Why?'

Her face is shiny and happy and totally oblivious. Has she not *noticed* how old he is?

'No reason!' I clear my throat. 'So, er . . . remind me. Where exactly did you meet Phillip again?'

'You know, silly!' says Katie mock-chidingly. 'You suggested I should try somewhere different for lunch, remember? Well, I found this really unusual place, tucked away in a little street.'

'Is it . . . a restaurant? A café?'

'Not exactly,' she says thoughtfully. 'You go in and someone gives you a tray, and you collect your lunch and then eat it sitting at all these tables. And it only costs two pounds! And afterwards they have free entertainment! Sometimes it's bingo or whist, sometimes it's a singsong round the piano. I've made loads of new friends.'

I stare at her for a few silent seconds. 'Katie,' I say at last. 'This place. It couldn't possibly be . . . a day-care centre for the elderly?'

'Gosh,' she says slowly, and screws up her brow. 'Now you mention it, I suppose everyone is kind of quite . . . mature. But honestly, Emma, you should come along.' Her face brightens. 'We have a real laugh!'

'You're still *going* there?' I stare at her.

'I go every day,' she says in surprise. 'I'm on the social committee.'

'Hello again!' says Phillip cheerily, reappearing with three glasses. He beams at Katie and gives her a kiss on the cheek, and she beams back. And suddenly I feel quite heart-warmed. OK, it's weird. But they do seem to make a really sweet couple.

'The man behind the stall seemed rather stressed out, poor chap,' says Phillip, as I take my first delicious sip of Pimm's.

Mmm. There is absolutely nothing nicer on a summer's day than a nice cold glass of—

Hang on a minute. Pimm's. Shit. I promised to do the Pimm's stall with Connor, didn't I? I glance at my watch and realise I'm already ten minutes late. Oh, bloody hell. No wonder he's stressed out.

I apologise to Phillip and Katie, then hurry to the stall. There I find Connor dressed as Henry VIII, with a huge red beard stuck to his face. He must be boiling. 'Sorry I'm late,' I mutter, sliding in beside him.

'That's all right,' he says stiffly.

For the next few minutes we're too busy serving Pimm's to talk. Then the queue melts away and we're left on our own.

Connor isn't even looking at me. He's chopping a bundle of mint as though he wants to kill it. Why is he in such a bad mood?

'So, did you have a nice time the other evening?'

That's what this is all about. 'Yes, I did, thanks,' I say after a pause.

'It's someone at work, isn't it?' Connor suddenly says, and my stomach gives a small plunge. 'That's why you won't tell me who it is.'

'It's not that! Look, Connor, can't you just respect my privacy?'

'I'll work it out.' His jaw sets grimly. 'It won't take me long.'

I feel a flicker of uncertainty. What if he guesses? I start to slice up a lemon, constantly scanning the crowd. Where is Jack, anyway?

'I've got it,' says Connor suddenly, and I look up to see him staring at me triumphantly. 'It's Paul, isn't it?'

'What?' I gape back at him, wanting to laugh. 'No, it's not Paul! Why on earth should you think it was Paul?'

'You keep looking at him.' He gestures to where Paul is standing nearby, moodily swigging a bottle of beer. 'Every two minutes!'

'I'm not looking at him,' I say hurriedly. 'I'm just looking at . . . I'm just taking in the atmosphere. Look, you're never going to—'

'Is it Nick?' His eyes narrow. 'You and he have always had a bit of a spark going.'

'No!' I say impatiently. Honestly. Clandestine affairs are hard enough, without your ex-boyfriend subjecting you to the third degree.

'Oh my God,' Connor says in a lowered voice. 'Look.'

I look up, and my stomach gives an enormous lurch. Jack is walking over the grass towards us. He's dressed as a cowboy, with leather chaps and a checked shirt and a proper cowboy hat.

He looks so completely and utterly sexy, I feel quite faint.

'He's coming this way!' hisses Connor. 'Quick! Tidy up that lemon.'

'Hello, Emma. Enjoying the day?' says Jack with a smile.

'Hello,' I say, my voice about six notches higher than usual. 'Yes, it's . . . lovely!' With trembling hands I pour out a glass of Pimm's.

'Emma! You forgot the mint!' says Connor.

'It doesn't matter about the mint,' says Jack, his eyes fixed on mine.

'You can have some mint if you want it,' I say, gazing back.

'It looks fine just the way it is.' His eyes give a tiny flash.

This is so unreal. We can't keep our eyes off each other. Surely it's completely obvious to everyone else what's going on?

'So, Emma,' says Jack casually. 'Just to talk work briefly. That extra typing assignment I asked you about. The Leopold file.'

'Er, yes?' I say, flusteredly dropping an ice cube onto the counter.

'Perhaps we could have a quick word about it before I go?' He meets my eyes. 'I have a suite of rooms up at the house. Say . . . one o'clock?'

'Right,' I say, my heart pounding. 'OK.'

He saunters off, holding his glass of Pimm's, and I stand staring after him, dripping an ice cube onto the grass. A suite of rooms.

That can only mean one thing. Jack and I are going to have sex.

And suddenly, with no warning, I feel really, really nervous.

'I've been so stupid!' exclaims Connor, abruptly putting down his knife. 'Emma, I know who your new man is.'

I feel a huge spasm of fear.

'It's Tristan from Design, isn't it?'

As soon as our stint on the stall is up, I escape from Connor and go and sit under a tree with a glass of Pimm's, glancing at my watch every two minutes. I can't quite believe how nervous I am about this. Maybe Jack knows loads of tricks. Maybe he'll expect all kinds of amazing manoeuvres that I've never even heard of.

I mean . . . I don't think I'm *bad* at sex. You know. Generally speaking. All things considered. But what sort of standard are we talking about here? Jack Harper is an international multimillionaire. He must have dated models and gymnasts . . . women with enormous perky breasts . . . kinky stuff involving muscles I don't even think I *possess*.

OK, just stop. I'll be fine. It'll be like doing a ballet exam. My old ballet teacher always used to say to us, 'As long as you keep your legs nicely turned out and a smile on your face, you'll do splendidly.' Which I guess kind of applies here, too.

I glance at my watch and feel a fresh spasm of fright. It's one o'clock. Time to go and have sex. I stand up, and do a few surreptitious limbering-up exercises. Then I begin to walk towards the house. I've just reached the edge of the lawn when a shrill voice hits my ears.

'There she is! Emma! Cooee!'

That sounded just like my mum. Weird. I stop briefly, and turn round, but I can't see anyone. It must be a hallucination.

'Emma, turn round! Over here!'

Hang on. That sounded like Kerry.

I peer bewilderedly at the crowded scene, my eyes squinting in the sunshine. I can't see anything. And then suddenly, like a Magic Eye, they spring into view. Kerry, Nev, and my mum and dad. Walking towards me. All in costume. Mum is wearing a Japanese kimono and holding a picnic basket. Dad is dressed as Robin Hood and holding two fold-up chairs. Nev is in a Superman costume and holding a bottle of wine. And Kerry is wearing an entire Marilyn Monroe outfit, including platinum-blonde wig, and complacently soaking up the stares.

What are they *doing* here? I didn't tell them about the Corporate Family Day. I know I didn't. I'm *positive* I didn't.

'Hi, Emma!' says Kerry as she gets near. 'Like the outfit?'

'Who are you supposed to be, darling?' says Mum. 'Is it Heidi?'

'I . . .' I rub my face. 'Mum . . . What are you doing here? I never—I mean, I forgot to tell you.'

'I know you did,' says Kerry. 'But your friend Artemis told me all about it the other day, when I phoned.'

I stare at her, unable to speak. I will kill Artemis. I will murder her.

'So what time's the fancy-dress contest?' says Kerry, winking at two teenage boys who are gawping at her. 'We haven't missed it, have we?'

'There . . . there isn't a contest,' I say, finding my voice.

'Really?' Kerry looks put out.

So this is why she's come here, is it? To win a stupid competition. 'You came all this way just for a fancy-dress contest?' I can't resist saying.

'Of course not!' Kerry quickly regains her usual scornful expression. 'Nev and I are taking your mum and dad to Hanwood Manor. It's near here. So we thought we'd drop in.'

'We've brought a picnic,' says Mum. 'Now, let's find a nice spot.'

I watch dumbly as Mum shakes out a plaid picnic rug and Dad sets up the two chairs. 'So, is Connor here?' asks Mum.

'Ssh! Don't Mention Connor!' says Dad in his Basil Fawlty voice.

I try to smile, but my face won't quite do it. It's ten past one. Jack will be waiting. What can I do?

As Dad passes me a plate and a glass of wine, I see Sven.

'Sven,' I say quickly. 'Um, Mr Harper was kindly asking earlier on about my family. And whether they were here or not. Could you possibly tell him that they've . . . they've unexpectedly turned up?' I look up at him desperately and his face flickers in comprehension.

'I'll pass on the message,' he says. And that's the end of that.

I once read an article called 'Make Things Go Your Way', which said if a day doesn't turn out as you intended, you should go back, charting the differences between your Goals and your Results, and this will help you learn from your mistakes. OK. Let's see.

Goal: Look like sexy, sophisticated woman in flattering dress.

Result: Look like Heidi/Munchkin extra in lurid puffy nylon sleeves.

Goal: Make secret assignation with Jack.

Result: Make secret assignation with Jack then fail to turn up.

Goal: Have fantastic sex with Jack in romantic location.

Result: Have peanut-barbecued chicken drumstick on picnic rug.

Overall Goal: Euphoria.

Overall Result: Complete misery.

All I can do is stare dumbly down at my plate, telling myself this can't last for ever. Dad and Nev have made about a million jokes about Don't Mention Connor. Kerry has shown me her new Swiss watch, which cost £4,000, and has boasted about how her company is expanding yet again. And now she's telling us how she played golf with the chief executive of British Airways last week and he tried to head-hunt her. 'But I said to him, if I *needed* a job . . .' She tails off. 'Did you want something?'

'Hi there,' comes a dry, familiar voice from above my head.

Very slowly I raise my head, blinking in the light.

It's Jack. Standing there against the blue sky in his cowboy outfit. He gives me a tiny, almost imperceptible smile, and I feel my heart lift. He's come to get me. I should have known he would.

'Hi!' I say, half-dazedly. 'Everyone, this is—'

'My name's Jack,' he cuts across me pleasantly. 'I'm a friend of Emma's. Emma . . .' He looks at me. 'I'm afraid you're needed.'

'Oh dear!' I say with a whoosh of relief. 'Oh well, never mind.'

'That's a shame!' says Mum. 'Can't you at least stay for a quick drink? Jack, you're welcome to join us, have a chicken drumstick.'

'We have to go,' I say hurriedly. 'Don't we, Jack?'

'I'm afraid we do,' he says, and holds out a hand to pull me up.

'Sorry, everyone,' I say.

'We don't mind!' says Kerry. 'I'm sure you've some vital job to do, Emma. In fact, I expect the whole event would collapse without you!'

Jack stops. Very slowly, he turns round. 'Let me guess,' he says pleasantly. 'You must be Kerry.'

'Yes!' she says in surprise. 'That's right.'

'And Mum . . . Dad . . .' He surveys the faces. 'And . . . Nev?'

'Spot on!' says Nev with a chortle.

'Emma must have told you a bit about us,' says Mum with a laugh.

'Oh . . . she has,' agrees Jack, looking around the picnic rug again with a kind of odd fascination on his face. 'You know, there might be time for that drink after all.'

What? *What* did he say?

'Good,' says Mum. 'It's always nice to meet friends of Emma's!'

I watch in disbelief as Jack settles comfortably down on the rug. He was supposed to be *rescuing* me from all this. Not joining in.

'So, you work for this company, Jack?' says Dad, pouring him a glass of wine.

'In a way,' says Jack after a pause. 'You could say . . . I used to.'

'Are you between jobs?' says Mum tactfully.

'You could put it like that, I guess.' His face crinkles in a little smile.

'Oh dear!' says Mum sympathetically. 'What a shame. Still, I'm sure something will come up.'

Oh God. I'm really not at all sure I like this.

'I saw Danny Nussbaum the other day in the post office, Emma,' adds Mum, briskly slicing some tomatoes. 'He asked after you.'

Out of the corner of my eye I can see Jack's eyes brightening.

'Danny and Emma used to step out together,' Mum explains to Jack with a fond smile. 'Such a nice boy. Very *bookish*. He and Emma used to study together in her bedroom all afternoon.'

I cannot look at Jack. I cannot.

'You know . . . *Ben Hur's* a fine film,' Jack suddenly says in thoughtful tones. 'A very fine film.' He smiles at Mum. 'Don't you think?'

I am going to kill him.

'Er . . . yes!' says Mum, a bit confused. 'Yes, I've always liked *Ben Hur*. So, Jack,' she adds sympathetically as she hands him a paper plate. 'Are you getting by financially?'

'I'm doing OK,' Jack replies gravely.

Mum looks at him for a moment. Then she rummages in the picnic basket and produces a Sainsbury's quiche, still in its box.

'Take this,' she says. 'And some tomatoes. They'll tide you over.'

'Oh no,' says Jack at once. 'Really, I couldn't—'

'I won't take no for an answer. I insist!'

'Well, that's truly kind.' Jack gives her a warm smile.

'You want some free career advice, Jack?' says Kerry.

'Now, you want to listen to Kerry,' puts in Dad proudly. 'She's our star! She has her own company.'

'My own travel agency,' says Kerry with a complacent smile. 'Started from scratch. Now we have forty staff and a turnover of just over two million. And you know what my secret is?'

'I . . . have no idea,' says Jack.

Kerry leans forward and fixes him with her blue eyes. 'Golf. Business is all about networking. I'm telling you, Jack, I've met most of the top business people in the country on the golf course. Take any company. Take *this* company.' She spreads her arm around the scene. 'I know the top guy here. I could call him up tomorrow if I wanted to.'

I stare at her, frozen in horror.

'Really?' says Jack, sounding riveted. 'Is that so? I'm impressed.'

'Perhaps Kerry could put in a good word for you, Jack!' exclaims Mum in sudden inspiration. 'You'd do that, wouldn't you, Kerry love?'

'Mr Harper?' A voice interrupts and I breathe in relief. We all look up to see Cyril bending awkwardly down to Jack.

'I'm extremely sorry to interrupt, sir,' he says. 'But Malcolm St John is here and would like a very brief word.'

'Of course,' says Jack, and smiles politely at Mum. 'If you could just excuse me a moment.'

As he carefully balances his glass on his plate and gets to his feet, the whole family exchanges confused glances.

'Giving him a second chance, then!' calls out Dad jocularly to Cyril.

'I'm sorry?' says Cyril, taking a couple of steps towards us.

'That chap Jack,' says Dad, gesturing to Jack, who's talking to a guy in a navy blazer. 'You're thinking of taking him on again, are you?'

Cyril looks stiffly from Dad to me and back again.

'It's OK, Cyril!' I call lightly. 'Dad, shut up, OK?' I mutter. 'He owns the company.'

'What?' Everyone stares at me.

'He owns the company,' I say, my face hot. 'So just . . . don't make any jokes about him.'

'The man in the jester's suit owns the company?' says Mum, looking in surprise at Cyril.

'No! *Jack* does! Or at least, some great big chunk of it.' They're all still looking completely blank. 'Jack's one of the founders of the Panther Corporation!' I hiss in frustration. 'He was just trying to be modest.'

'Are you saying that guy is Jack Harper?' says Nev in disbelief.

'Yes!'

There's a flabbergasted silence. As I look around, I see that a piece of chicken drumstick has fallen out of Kerry's mouth.

'Jack Harper—the multimillionaire,' says Dad, just to make sure.

'*Multimillionaire?*' Mum looks totally confused. 'So . . . does he still want the quiche?'

'Of course he doesn't want the quiche!' says Dad testily.

Mum's eye starts flicking around the picnic rug in slight agitation. 'Quick!' she says suddenly. 'Put the crisps into a bowl.' She hastily starts straightening the rug. 'Brian! Crumbs on your beard!'

'So how the hell do *you* know Jack Harper?' says Nev.

I colour slightly. 'We've worked together and he's kind of become a . . . a friend. But listen, don't act any differently,' I say quickly, as Jack starts coming back towards the rug.

Oh God. Why am I even bothering? As Jack approaches, my entire family is sitting bolt upright, staring at him in awe-stricken silence.

'Hi!' I say, as naturally as possible, then quickly glare around at them.

'So . . . Jack!' says Dad self-consciously. 'Have another drink! Is this wine all right for you? Because we can easily nip to the wine shop, get something with a proper vintage.'

'It's great, thanks,' says Jack, looking a little baffled.

'Jack, what else can I get you to eat?' says Mum, flustered. 'Emma, give Jack your plate!' she snaps. 'He can't eat off paper.'

Jack meets my eye with a quizzical expression. 'I take it my cover's been blown,' he says with a grin.

'Jack!' exclaims Kerry, who has regained her composure. She thrusts out her hand. 'Good to meet you properly.'

'Absolutely!' says Jack. 'Although . . . didn't we just meet?'

'As *professionals*,' says Kerry smoothly. 'One business-owner to another. Here's my card, and if you ever need any help with travel arrangements, please give me a call. Or if you wanted to meet up socially . . . perhaps the four of us could go out some time! Play a round? Couldn't we, Emma?'

I stare at her blankly. Since when have Kerry and I ever socialised together?

'Emma and I are practically sisters, of course,' she adds sweetly, putting her arm round me. 'I'm sure she's told you.'

'Oh, she told me a few things,' says Jack, his expression unreadable.

He takes a bite of roast chicken and starts to chew it.

'We grew up together, we shared everything.' Kerry gives me a squeeze and I try to smile, but her perfume is nearly choking me.

'Isn't that nice!' says Mum in pleasure. 'I wish I had a camera.'

Jack doesn't reply. He's just giving Kerry this long, appraising look.

'We couldn't be closer!' Kerry's smile grows even more ingratiating. She's squeezing me so hard, her talons are digging into my flesh.

Jack swallows his chicken, then looks up. 'So, I guess it must have been a pretty tough decision for you when you had to turn Emma down,' he says conversationally to her. 'You two being so close, and all.'

'Turn her down?' Kerry gives a tinkling laugh. 'I don't know what—'

'That time she applied for work experience in your firm and you turned her down,' says Jack pleasantly.

That was a secret. That was supposed to be a secret.

'What?' says Dad, half laughing. 'Emma applied to Kerry?'

'I . . . I don't know what you're talking about!' says Kerry, a little pink.

'I *think* I have this right,' says Jack. 'She offered to work for no money . . . but you still said no.' He looks perplexed. 'Interesting decision.'

Very slowly, Mum and Dad's expressions are changing.

'But of course, fortunate for us here at the Panther Corporation,' Jack adds cheerfully. 'We're *very* glad Emma didn't make a career in the travel industry. So I guess I have to thank you, Kerry! You did us a big favour.'

Kerry is completely puce.

'Kerry, is this true?' says Mum sharply.

'You never told us about this, Emma.' Dad looks taken aback.

'I was embarrassed, OK?' I say, my voice jumping a bit.

'Bit cheeky of Emma to ask,' says Nev, taking a huge bite of pork pie. 'Using family connections. That's what you said, wasn't it, Kerry?'

'Cheeky?' echoes Mum in disbelief. 'Kerry, if you remember, we lent you the money to start that company. You wouldn't *have* a company without this family.'

'It wasn't like *that*,' says Kerry, darting an annoyed look at Nev. 'There's been a . . . . a crossed wire. Some confusion!' She gives me another smile. 'Obviously I'd be *delighted* to help you with your career, Ems. You should have said before! Just call me at the office.'

I gaze back at her, full of loathing. I cannot *believe* she is trying to wriggle out of this. She is the most two-faced cow in the entire world.

'There's no crossed wire, Kerry,' I say, as calmly as I can. 'We both know exactly what happened. I asked you for help and you wouldn't give it to me. And fine, it's your company and it was your decision and you had every right to make it. But don't try and say it didn't happen.'

'Emma!' says Kerry, with a little laugh, and tries to reach for my hand. 'Silly girl! I had no idea! If I'd known it was important . . .'

I jerk my hand away and stare back at Kerry. I can feel all the old hurt and humiliation building up inside me. 'Yes you did!' I hear myself crying. 'You *knew* how desperate I was! Ever since you've arrived in this family you've tried to squash me down. You tease me about my crap career. You boast about yourself. I spend my entire life feeling small and stupid. Well, fine. You win, Kerry! You're the star and I'm not. You're the success and I'm the failure. But just don't pretend to be my best friend, OK? Because you're not, and you never will be!'

I finish, and look around the rug, breathing hard. I have a horrible feeling I might burst into tears at any moment.

I meet Jack's eye and he gives me a tiny way-to-go smile. Then I risk a brief glance at Mum and Dad. They're both looking paralysed. The thing is, our family just doesn't *do* loud, emotional outbursts.

In fact, I'm not entirely sure what to do next myself.

'So, um . . . I'll be going, then,' I say, my voice shaking. 'I'll be off. Come on, Jack. We've got work to do.' With wobbly legs, I turn on my heel and head off, stumbling slightly on the grass.

'That was fantastic, Emma,' comes Jack's voice in my ear. 'You were absolutely . . . logistical assessment,' he adds more loudly as we pass Cyril.

'I've never spoken like that in my life,' I say. 'I've . . . operational management,' I add, as we pass a couple of people from Accounts.

'I guessed as much,' he says. 'Jesus, that cousin of yours . . .'

'She's a total—spreadsheet,' I say quickly as we pass Connor. 'So . . . I'll get that typed up for you, Mr Harper.'

Somehow we make it into the house and up the stairs. Jack leads me along a corridor, produces a key and opens a door. And we're in a large, light, cream-coloured room. With a big double bed in it.

For a still moment there's silence. Jack's gazing at my flushed face. I'm staring back, my rib cage rising and falling, blood beating in my ears. Then suddenly he bends forward and kisses me.

His mouth is opening mine, and he's already tugging the elastic sleeves of my Snow White costume down off my shoulders, unhooking my bra. I'm fumbling for his shirt buttons. Oh my God, this is quick. His hands are . . . his fingers are . . . I'm panting helplessly . . . We're going so fast I can barely register what's happening. This is nothing like Connor. This is nothing like I've ever—

'Wait,' I manage to say. 'Wait, Jack. I just need to tell you something.'

'What?' Jack looks at me with urgent, aroused eyes. 'What is it?'

'I don't know any tricks,' I whisper, a little gruffly. 'You know, you've probably had sex with zillions of supermodels and they know all sorts of amazing . . .' I tail off at his expression. 'Never mind.'

'I'm intrigued,' says Jack. 'Which tricks did you have in mind?'

'I didn't!' I say, growing hot. 'That's the whole point, I don't *know* any.'

'Neither do I,' says Jack, totally deadpan. 'I don't know one trick.'

I feel a sudden giggle rise inside me. 'Yeah, right.'

He pauses thoughtfully. 'Oh, OK. Maybe one.'

'What?' I say at once. 'Tell me!' And I can't help giggling out loud.

'Show, not tell,' he murmurs against my ear.

I'm in love. For the first time in my entire life, I'm totally, one hundred per cent in love! I spent all night with Jack at the Panther mansion. I woke up in his arms. We had sex about ninety-five times and it was . . . perfect. (And tricks didn't even seem to come into it. Which was a relief.)

But it's not just the sex. It's everything. It's the way he had a cup of tea waiting for me when I woke up. It's the way he turned on his laptop especially for me to look up all my Internet horoscopes and helped me choose the best one. He knows all the crappy, embarrassing bits about me which I normally try and hide from any man for as long as possible . . . and he loves me anyway.

So he didn't exactly *say* he loved me. But he said something even better. We were lying there this morning, just staring up at the ceiling, when all at once I said, without quite intending to, 'Jack, how come you remembered about Kerry turning me down for work experience?'

'What?'

'How come you remembered about Kerry turning me down?' I swivelled my head slowly to look at him. 'And not just that. Every single thing I told you on that plane. About work, about my family, about Connor . . . everything. You remember it all. And I just don't get it.'

'What don't you get?' said Jack with a frown.

'I don't get why someone like you would be interested in my stupid, boring little life,' I said, my cheeks flushing with embarrassment.

Jack looked at me silently for a moment. 'Emma, your life is not stupid and boring.'

'Of course it is! I never do anything exciting, I never do anything clever, I haven't got my own company, or invented anything—'

'You want to know why I remember all your secrets?' interrupted Jack. 'Emma, the minute you started talking on that plane—I was gripped.' And he leant over and kissed me.

Gripped! Jack Harper was gripped by my life! By me!

As I arrive home, I'm glowing all over. A light bulb has switched on inside me. Jemima is wrong. Men and women aren't enemies. Men and women are *soul mates*. And if they were just honest, right from the word go, they'd all realise it. Everyone should share their secrets straight away!

I float up the stairs and unlock the door of our flat.

'Lissy!' I call. 'Lissy, I'm in love!'

There isn't any reply, and I feel a twinge of disappointment.

I hear a thumping sound from her room, and stand completely still in the hallway, transfixed. And then I see it, through the door of the sitting room. On the floor, next to the sofa. A black leather briefcase. It's Jean-Paul. He's in there. Right this minute! What are they *doing*?

I just don't believe her story that they're having sex. But what else could it be? What else could it possibly—?

OK . . . Just stop. It's none of my business. If Lissy doesn't want to tell me what she's up to, she doesn't want to tell me. Feeling very mature, I walk into the kitchen and pick up the kettle.

Then I put it down again. *Why* doesn't she want to tell me? We're best friends! It was *she* who said we shouldn't have any secrets.

All of a sudden, a little thought occurs to me. Suppose I *hadn't* seen the briefcase? Suppose I'd just walked into the flat perfectly innocently, like I normally do, and happened to go straight to Lissy's door and happened to open it? Nobody could blame me then, could they?

I come out of the kitchen, listen intently for a moment, then quickly tiptoe back towards the front door.

Start again. I'm walking into the flat for the first time.

'Hi, Lissy!' I call self-consciously. I walk down the corridor, arrive at her door and give the tiniest of knocks.

There's no response from inside. The thumping noises have died down. I stare at the blank wood, feeling a sudden apprehension.

Am I really going to do this? Yes, I am. I just *have* to know.

I grasp the handle, open the door—and give a scream of terror.

The image is so startling, I can't make sense of it. Lissy's naked. They're both naked. She and the guy are tangled together in the strangest position I've ever, ever . . . Her legs are up in the air, and his are twisted round her, and they're both scarlet in the face and panting.

'I'm sorry!' I stutter. 'God, I'm sorry!'

'Emma, wait!' I hear Lissy shout as I scuttle away to my room, slam the door and sink onto my bed. I almost feel sick. I should *never* have opened that door. They were having sex! But I mean, what kind of weird, contorted sex was that? Bloody hell. I never realised. I never—

I feel a hand on my shoulder, and give a fresh scream.

'Emma, calm down!' says Lissy. 'It's me! Jean-Paul's gone.'

'Lissy, I'm sorry,' I gabble, staring at the floor. 'I'm sorry! I didn't mean to do that. I should never have . . . your sex life is your own affair.'

'Emma, we weren't having sex, you dope!'

'You were! I saw you! You didn't have any clothes on.'

'We did have clothes on. Emma, look at me!'

Apprehensively, I raise my head, and gradually my eyes focus on Lissy, standing in front of me. Oh. Oh . . . right. She's wearing a flesh-coloured leotard. 'Well what were you doing if you weren't having sex?' I say, almost accusingly. 'And why are you wearing that?'

'We were dancing,' says Lissy, looking embarrassed.

'*Dancing?* But . . . why were you dancing?' This makes no sense at all. Lissy and a French guy called Jean-Paul dancing in her bedroom? I feel like I've landed in the middle of some weird dream.

'I've joined this group,' says Lissy after a pause. She bites her lip. 'It's some lawyers who've got together and formed a . . . a dance group.'

For a few moments I can't quite speak. Now that my shock's died down, I have this horrible feeling that I might possibly be about to laugh. 'You've joined a group of . . . dancing lawyers.'

'Yes.' Lissy nods.

An image pops into my head of a bunch of portly barristers dancing around in their wigs and I can't help it, I give a snort of laughter.

'You see!' cries Lissy. 'That's why I didn't tell you. I *knew* you'd laugh!'

'I'm sorry!' I say. 'I'm sorry! I think it's really great!' Another hysterical giggle bursts from me. 'It's just somehow the idea of dancing lawyers . . .'

'We're not all lawyers,' she says defensively. 'There are a couple of merchant bankers, too, and a judge . . . Emma, stop laughing!'

'I'm sorry,' I say helplessly. 'Lissy, I'm not laughing at you, honestly.' I try desperately to clamp my lips together. But all I can see is merchant bankers dressed in tutus, clutching briefcases, dancing to *Swan Lake*.

'It's not funny!' Lissy's saying. 'It's just a few like-minded professionals who want to express themselves through dance.'

'I'm sorry,' I say again, wiping my eyes. 'I think it's brilliant. So are you having a show, or anything?'

'It's in three weeks. That's why we've been doing extra practices.'

'Three weeks?' I stare at her. 'Weren't you going to *tell* me?'

'I . . . I hadn't decided,' she says, scuffing her dancing shoe on the floor. 'I was embarrassed.'

'Don't be embarrassed!' I say in dismay. 'Lissy, I'm so sorry I laughed. I think it's brilliant. And I'm going to come and watch.' I give her a curious look. 'Lissy, I never knew you could dance.'

'Oh, I can't,' she says at once. 'I'm crap. It's just a bit of fun. D'you want a coffee?' As I follow her into the kitchen, she gives me a raised-eyebrow look. 'So, you've got a bit of a nerve, accusing *me* of having sex. Where were you last night?' She flicks on the kettle.

'With Jack,' I admit with a dreamy smile. 'Having sex. All night. Oh God, Lissy. I'm completely in love with him.'

'In *love*? You've only known him five minutes.'

'That doesn't matter! We're already complete soul mates. There's no need to pretend with him . . . and the sex is amazing . . . and he's *interested* in me. You know, he asks me questions all the time, and he seems really genuinely fascinated by the answers.'

'So where is he now?' says Lissy, shaking coffee into the cafetière.

'He's going away for a bit. He's going to brainstorm some new concept with a creative team.'

'What?'

'I dunno. He didn't say. It'll be really intense and he probably won't be able to phone me. But he's going to email every day,' I add happily. 'You know, I've got this whole new theory about relationships. It's so simple. Everyone in the world should be more honest with each other. Everyone should share! Men and women should share, families should share, world leaders should share!'

'Hmm.' Lissy looks at me for a few moments. 'Emma, did Jack ever tell you why he had to rush off in the middle of the night that time?'

'No,' I say in surprise. 'But it's his business.'

'Did he tell you what those phone calls were about on your first date?'

'Well . . . no.'

'Has he told you anything about himself other than the bare minimum?'

'He's told me plenty!' I say defensively. 'Lissy, what's your problem?'

'I don't have a problem,' she says mildly. 'I'm just wondering . . . is it you who's doing all the sharing?'

'What?'

'Is he sharing himself with you?' She pours hot water onto the coffee. 'Or are you just sharing yourself with him?'

'We're sharing with each other,' I say, looking away. Which is true, I tell myself firmly. Jack's shared loads with me! He's told me . . . He's told me all about . . .

Well, anyway. He probably just hasn't been in the mood for talking very much. Is that a crime?

'Have some coffee,' says Lissy, handing me a mug.

'Thanks,' I say, a touch grudgingly, and Lissy sighs.

'Emma, I'm not trying to spoil things. He does seem really lovely—'

'He is!' I cannot help beaming at her. 'Lissy, he's perfect!'

eight

FOR THE NEXT COUPLE OF WEEKS, nothing can pierce my happy glow. Nothing. Paul's sarcastic comments bounce off me like bubbles. I don't even notice when Artemis introduces me to a visiting advertising team as her personal secretary. They can all say what they like. Because what they don't know is that when I'm smiling at my computer it's because Jack has just sent me another funny little email. What they don't know is that the guy who employs them all is in love with me. *Me*. Emma Corrigan. The junior.

'Hey!' says Nick, looking up from his phone. 'Jack Harper's going to be on television!'

'What?' I feel a jolt of surprise. How come he didn't tell me?

'OK, folks,' says Paul, coming out of his office. 'Jack Harper has done an interview on *Business Watch*, and it's being broadcast at twelve. A television is being set up in the large meeting room. Anyone who would like to can go along and watch there. But we need one person to stay behind and man the phones.' His gaze falls on me. 'Emma. You can stay, OK?'

'No! I mean . . . I want to watch!' I say in dismay. 'Can't someone else stay behind? Artemis, can't you stay?'

'*I'm* not staying!' says Artemis at once. 'Honestly, Emma, don't be so selfish. It won't be at all interesting for you.'

'Yes it will!'

'No it won't.' She rolls her eyes. 'You've barely even spoken to him.'

'I have!' I say before I can stop myself. 'I have! I . . .' I break off, my cheeks turning pink. 'I . . . once went to a meeting he was at . . .'

'And served him a cup of tea?' Artemis gives a little smirk.

I stare at her furiously, blood pounding through my ears, wishing I could think of something really scathing that would put Artemis down.

'Enough, Artemis,' says Paul. 'Emma, you're staying here, and that's settled.'

By five to twelve the office is completely empty. Apart from me, a fly and a whirring fax machine. Disconsolately I reach into my desk drawer and take out an Aero. And a Flake for good measure. I'm just unwrapping the Aero and taking a big bite when the phone rings.

'OK,' comes Lissy's voice down the line. 'I've set the video.'

'Thanks, Liss,' I say through a mouthful of chocolate. 'You're a star.'

'We'll watch it again tonight. Jemima's going to put the video on in her room too, so we should definitely catch it.'

'What's Jemima doing at home?' I say in surprise.

'She's taken a sickie so she can do a home spa day. Oh, and your dad rang,' she adds cautiously.

'Oh right.' I feel a flicker of apprehension. 'What did he say?'

I haven't talked to Mum or Dad since the debacle at the Corporate Family Day. I just can't bring myself to. It was all too painful and embarrassing. When Dad rang here on the following Monday, I said I was really busy and I'd call him back, and never did.

'He'd seen the trailer for the interview,' says Lissy. 'He recognised Jack and just wondered if you knew about it. And he said . . .' She pauses. 'He really wanted to talk to you about a few things.'

'Oh.' I stare at my note pad, where I've doodled a huge spiral over a telephone number I was supposed to be keeping.

'Anyway, he and your mum are going to be watching it,' says Lissy. 'And your grandpa.'

Great. Just great. The entire world is watching Jack except me.

When I've put the phone down, I go and pour orange juice into Artemis's spider plant. And some photocopier toner for good measure. Then I feel a bit mean. It's not the plant's fault, after all.

'Sorry,' I say out loud, and touch one of its leaves. 'It's just—'

'Talking to your mystery man?' comes a sarcastic voice from behind me, and I turn round in shock to see Connor standing in the doorway.

'Connor!' I say. 'What are you doing here?'

'I'm on my way to watch the TV interview. But I just wanted a quick word.' He fixes me with an accusing stare. 'You lied to me.'

Oh shit. Has Connor guessed?

'I've just had a little chat with Tristan from Design.' Connor's voice swells with indignation. 'He's gay! You're not going out with him!'

Connor didn't *seriously* think I was going out with Tristan from Design, did he? I mean, Tristan could not look more gay if he wore leopardskin hot pants and carried a handbag.

'No,' I say, managing to keep a straight face.

'Well!' says Connor. 'I don't see why you feel it necessary to lie to me.' He gives me his most wounded-martyr look and starts walking away.

'Wait!' I say suddenly. 'Hang on a minute! Connor, could you do me a real favour?' I wait until he turns, then pull a wheedling face. 'Could you possibly man the phones here while I quickly go and watch Jack

Harper's interview?' I know Connor isn't my number one fan at the moment. But I don't exactly have a lot of choice.

'I can't believe you're even *asking* me that!' says Connor incredulously. 'You *know* how important Jack Harper is to me! Emma, I really don't know what you've turned into.'

After he's stalked off, I sit there for twenty minutes. I take several messages. I file a couple of letters. And then, suddenly, I've had it. I love Jack. He loves me. I should be there, supporting him. I pick up my coffee and hurry along the corridor to the meeting room.

'What are *you* doing here?' says Artemis, as I arrive at her side.

'No taxation without representation,' I hear myself responding, which perhaps isn't exactly appropriate but it shuts her up.

I crane my neck so I can see over everyone's heads, and my eyes focus on the screen—and there he is. Sitting on a chair in a studio, in jeans and a white T-shirt. The man I love. God, I want to kiss him.

'What have they asked him so far?' I murmur to Artemis.

'They're talking to him about how he works. His inspirations, his partnership with Pete Laidler, stuff like that.'

'Of course it was tough after Pete died,' Jack's saying. 'It was tough for all of us. But recently . . .' He pauses. 'Recently my life has turned around and I'm finding inspiration again. I'm enjoying it again.'

He has to be referring to me. He has to be. I've turned his life around! Oh my God. That's even more romantic than 'I was gripped'.

'You've already expanded into the sports drinks market,' the male interviewer is saying. 'Now I believe you're looking to expand into the women's market.'

There's a *frisson* around the room.

'We're going into the women's market? Since when?'

I stare at the screen, instantly recalling those people up in Jack's office. That's what the ovaries were for. Gosh, this is quite exciting.

'Can you give us any further details about that?' the male interviewer is saying. 'Will this be a soft drink marketed at women?'

'It's very early stages,' says Jack. 'But we're planning an entire line. A drink, clothing, a fragrance. We have a strong creative vision.'

'What's your target market this time?' asks the man. 'Sportswomen?'

'Not at all,' says Jack. 'We're aiming at . . . the girl on the street.'

'The "girl on the street"?' The female interviewer sits up, looking slightly affronted. 'What's that supposed to mean?'

'She's twenty-something,' says Jack after a pause. 'She works in an office, takes the tube to work, goes out in the evenings and comes home on the night bus . . . just an ordinary, nothing-special girl.'

'But the Panther brand has always been associated with men,' chips in the woman, looking sceptical. 'With masculine values. Do you really think you can make the switch to the female market?'

'We've done research,' says Jack pleasantly. 'We know our market.'

'Research!' she scoffs. 'You round up a load of women in some focus group and ask them a few questions! How does that tell you anything?'

God, why is she being so aggressive? I think indignantly.

'That's only a small part of the picture,' says Jack evenly.

'Oh, come on,' the woman says, leaning back and folding her arms. 'Can a company like Panther—can a man like you—*really* tap into the psyche of, as you put it, an ordinary, nothing-special girl?'

'Yes. I can!' Jack meets her gaze square-on. 'I know this girl.'

'You *know* her?' The woman raises her eyebrows.

'I know what her tastes are, what colours she likes, what she eats and drinks. I know what she wants out of life. She's size twelve but she'd like to be size ten . . .' He spreads his arms as though searching for inspiration. 'She eats Cheerios for breakfast and dips Flakes in her cappuccinos.'

I look in surprise at my hand, holding a Flake. I was about to dip it into my coffee. And . . . I had Cheerios this morning.

'We're surrounded these days by images of perfect, glossy people,' Jack is saying with animation. 'But this girl is real. She has bad hair days, and good hair days. She wears G-strings even though she finds them uncomfortable. She writes out exercise routines, then ignores them. She pretends to read business journals but hides celebrity magazines inside.'

Just . . . hang on a minute. This all sounds a bit familiar.

'That's *exactly* what you do, Emma,' says Artemis. 'I've seen your copy of *OK!* inside *Marketing Week.*' She turns to me with a mocking laugh and her gaze lands on my Flake.

'She loves clothes but she's not a fashion victim,' Jack is saying on screen. 'She'll wear, maybe, a pair of jeans . . .'

Artemis stares in disbelief at my Levis.

'. . . and a flower in her hair . . .'

Dazedly I lift a hand and touch the fabric rose in my hair.

He can't be talking about—

'Oh . . . my . . . God,' says Artemis slowly.

'What?' says Caroline, next to her. She follows Artemis's gaze, and her expression changes. 'Oh my God! Emma! It's you!'

'It's not,' I say, but my voice won't quite work properly.

A few people start nudging each other and turning to look at me.

'She reads fifteen horoscopes every day and chooses the one she likes best . . .' Jack's voice is saying.

'It is you! It's exactly you!'

'. . . she scans the backs of highbrow books and pretends she's read them . . .'

'I *knew* you hadn't read *Great Expectations!*' says Artemis triumphantly.

'. . . she adores sweet sherry . . .'

'Sweet *sherry*?' says Nick, turning in horror. 'You cannot be serious.'

'It's Emma!' I can hear people saying on the other side of the room.

'It's not Emma!' says Connor all of a sudden, with a laugh. 'Don't be ridiculous! Emma's size eight, for a start. Not size twelve!'

'Size *eight*!' Caroline giggles. 'That's a good one!'

'Aren't you size eight?' Connor looks bewildered. 'But you said . . .'

'I . . . I know I did.' I swallow, my face like a furnace. 'But I was . . .'

'Do you really buy all your clothes from thrift shops and pretend they're new?' says Caroline, looking up with interest from the screen.

'No!' I say defensively. 'I mean, yes, maybe . . . sometimes . . .'

'She weighs one hundred thirty-five pounds, but pretends she weighs one hundred twenty-five,' Jack's voice is saying.

What? *What?* My entire body contracts in shock. 'I do not!' I yell in outrage at the screen. 'I do not weigh anything like a hundred and thirty-five pounds . . .' I tail off as the entire room turns to stare at me.

'. . . hates crochet . . .'

There's an almighty gasp from across the room. 'You hate crochet?' comes Katie's disbelieving voice.

'No!' I say, swivelling in horror. 'That's wrong! I love crochet!'

But Katie is stalking furiously out of the room.

'She loves Abba,' Jack's voice is saying, 'but she can't stand jazz . . .'

Oh no. Oh no oh no . . .

Connor is staring at me as though I have personally driven a stake through his heart. 'You can't stand . . . *jazz*?'

It's like one of those dreams where everyone can see your underwear and you want to run but you can't. I can't tear myself away. All my secrets. All my personal, private secrets. Revealed on television. I'm in such a state of shock, I'm not even taking them all in.

'She wears lucky underwear on first dates . . . she borrows designer shoes from her flatmate and passes them off as her own . . . when she goes out, she can play sophisticated, but on her bed . . .'

I'm suddenly faint with fear. No. No. *Please* not this . . .

'. . . she has a Barbie bed cover.'

A huge roar of laughter goes round the room, and I bury my face in my hands. I am beyond mortification.

'Is she sexy?' the interviewer is asking, and my heart gives a huge jump. I stare at the screen, unable to breathe for apprehension.

'She's very sexual,' says Jack at once, and all eyes swivel towards me, agog. 'This is a modern girl who carries condoms in her purse.'

OK. Every time I think this can't get any worse, it does.

My *mother* is watching this. My *mother*.

'But maybe she hasn't reached her full potential. Maybe there's a side of her that has been frustrated . . .'

I can't look at Connor. I can't look anywhere.

'Maybe she's willing to experiment. Maybe she's had—I don't know— a lesbian fantasy about her best friend.'

No! No! My entire body clenches in horror. I have a sudden image of Lissy watching the screen at home, wide-eyed, clasping a hand over her mouth. I will never be able to look her in the eye again.

'It was a *dream*, OK?' I manage desperately, as everyone gawps at me. 'Not a fantasy. They're different!'

'She believes in love and romance. She believes her life will one day be transformed into something wonderful and exciting. Sometimes she feels frightened.' He pauses, and adds in a softer voice, 'Sometimes she feels unloved. But she's brave and good-hearted and faces her life head on . . .' He shakes his head dazedly and smiles at the interviewer. 'I'm . . . I'm so sorry. I guess I got a little carried away. Could we—?'

His voice is abruptly cut off by the interviewer.

Carried away. This is like saying Hitler was a tad aggressive.

'Jack Harper, many thanks for talking to us,' the interviewer starts saying. 'Next week, we'll be chatting to the charismatic—'

Someone leans forward and switches the television off. For a few seconds the entire room is silent. Everyone is gaping at me. Some faces are sympathetic, some are curious, some are gleeful and some are just Jeez-am-I-glad-I'm-not-you.

Now I know how zoo animals feel. I am never visiting a zoo again.

'But I don't understand,' comes a voice from across the room, and all the heads swivel avidly towards Connor, like at a tennis match. He's staring at me, his face red with confusion. 'How does Jack Harper know so much about you?'

Oh God. I know Connor got a really good degree from Manchester University and everything. But sometimes he is so slow on the uptake.

The heads have swivelled back towards me again.

'I . . . Because we . . .' I just can't say it out loud. But I don't have to.

'No,' Connor gulps. 'No. I don't believe it.'

'So how long has this been going on?' exclaims some guy.

It's as if he opened the floodgates. Suddenly everyone in the entire room starts pitching questions at me.

'Is that why he came to Britain? To see you?'

'Are you going to marry him?'

'You don't *look* like you weigh a hundred and thirty-five pounds . . .'

I can't cope with this. I have to get out of here. Now.

Without looking at anyone, I get to my feet and stumble out of the room. I enter the empty marketing department, where phones are ringing shrilly. The habit's too ingrained, I can't ignore them.

'Hello?' I say, picking one up.

'So!' comes Jemima's furious voice. '"She borrows designer shoes from her flatmate and passes them off as her own."'

'Look, Jemima, I'm sorry,' I say feebly, and put the phone down.

No more phones. Get bag. Go. As I zip up my bag with trembling hands, a couple of people who have followed me into the office are picking up some of the ringing phones.

'Emma, your granddad's on the line,' says Artemis. 'Something about the night bus and he'll never trust you again?'

'You have a call from Harvey's Bristol Cream publicity department,' chimes in Caroline. 'They want to know where they can send you a free case of sweet sherry?'

'How did they get my name? How? Has the word spread already?'

'Emma, I have your dad here,' says Nick. 'He says he needs to talk to you urgently.'

'I can't,' I say numbly. 'I have to . . .' I grab my jacket and almost run out of the office and down the corridor to the stairs. Everywhere, people are making their way back to their offices after watching the interview, and they all stare at me as I hurry by.

Someone grabs my arm. 'Hey, can you tell me which charity shops you go to?' It's a girl I don't even recognise.

'I adore Barbie dolls too!' Carol Finch from Accounts is suddenly in my path. 'Shall we start a club together, Emma?'

I back away, then start running down the stairs. But people keep accosting me from all directions.

'I didn't realise I was a lesbian till I was thirty-three . . .'

'Leave me alone!' I yell in anguish. 'Everyone just leave me alone!'

I sprint for the entrance, run outside and down the road, not looking right or left. At last I come to a halt, sink down on a bench and bury my head in my hands.

I have never been so embarrassed in all my life. And I'm so shocked and bewildered I feel as though I can barely keep my balance on this bench. In the space of a few minutes, my world has turned upside-down. I thought Jack loved me. I thought he. . . I thought he and I . . .

A searing pain suddenly hits me, and I bury my head in my hands.

Jack used me. He just wanted to find out what a girl-on-the-street was like. For his target market. For his stupid new women's line.

That's why he asked me out to dinner. That's why he found every-thing I said so interesting. That's why he was gripped.

It wasn't love. It was business.

As I sit on the tube going home, tears pour down my face, landing in big wet drips on my skirt. People are staring at me but I don't care. Why should I care? I've already suffered the worst embarrassment possible.

I feel so stupid. So *stupid*.

'Don't worry, darling!' says a large lady sitting to my left, wearing a voluminous print dress covered with pineapples. 'He's not worth it! Now you just go home, wash your face, have a nice cup of tea . . .'

'How do you know she's crying over a man?' chimes in a woman in a dark suit aggressively. 'That is such a clichéd, counterfeminist perspec-tive. She could be crying over a piece of music, world famine, the polit-ical situation in the Middle East.' She looks at me expectantly.

'Actually, I *was* crying over a man,' I admit.

The tube stops, and the woman in the dark suit rolls her eyes at us and gets out. The pineapple lady rolls her eyes back.

'World famine!' she says scornfully, and I can't help giving a half-giggle. 'Now, don't you worry, love.' She gives me a comforting pat on the shoulder. 'Have a nice cup of tea and a few chocolate digestives and a nice chat with your mum. You've still got your mum, haven't you?'

'Actually, we're not really speaking at the moment,' I confess.

'Well then, your dad?'

Tacitly, I shake my head.

'Well, how about your best friend? You must have a best friend!' The pineapple lady gives me a comforting smile.

'Yes,' I gulp. 'But she's just been informed on national television that I've been having secret lesbian fantasies about her.'

The pineapple lady stares at me silently for a few moments.

'Have a nice cup of tea,' she says at last, with less conviction. 'And . . . good luck, dear.'

I make my way slowly back from the tube station to our street. How am I going to face Lissy after what Jack said on television? How?

I've known Lissy a long time. And I've had plenty of embarrassing moments in front of her. But none of them comes anywhere near this.

This is worse than the time when I threw up in her parents' bathroom. This is even worse than the time she saw me kissing my reflection in the mirror and saying 'Ooh, baby' in a sexy voice.

As I open the front door of the flat, there she is, coming out of the kitchen. I can already see it in her face. She's completely freaked out.

So that's it. Not only has Jack betrayed me. He's ruined my best friendship, too. Things will never be the same again between me and Lissy. It's just like When Harry Met Sally. Sex has got in the way of our relationship, and now we can't be friends because we want to sleep together.

No. Scratch that. We don't want to sleep together. We want to— No, the point is we don't want to— Anyway. Whatever. It's not good.

'Oh!' she says, staring at the floor. 'Gosh! Um . . . hi, Emma!'

'Hi!' I reply in a strangled voice. 'I thought I'd come home. The office was just too . . . too awful . . .' I stop, and there's the most excruciating silence for a few moments. 'So . . . I guess you saw it,' I say at last.

'Yes, I saw it,' says Lissy, still staring at the floor, 'And I . . .' She clears her throat. 'If you want me to move out, then I will.'

A lump comes to my throat. I knew it. After twenty-one years, our friendship is over. One tiny secret comes out—and that's the end. 'It's OK,' I say, trying not to burst into tears. 'I'll move out.'

'No!' says Lissy awkwardly. 'I'll move out. This isn't your fault, Emma. It's been me who's been . . . leading you on.'

'What?' I stare at her. 'Lissy, you haven't been leading me on!'

'Yes I have.' She looks stricken. 'I feel terrible. I've been walking around half-dressed. No wonder you were frustrated!'

'I wasn't frustrated,' I say quickly. 'Lissy, I'm not a lesbian.'

'Emma, please!' Lissy grabs my hand. 'Don't be ashamed of your sexuality. And I promise I'll support you, whatever choice you make—'

'Lissy, I don't need support! I just had one dream, OK? It wasn't a fantasy, it was just a weird dream, and it doesn't mean I'm a lesbian, and it doesn't mean I fancy you, and it doesn't mean anything.'

'Oh.' There's silence. Lissy looks taken aback. 'Oh, right.'

There's a long pause, during which Lissy looks intently at her fingernails and I study the buckle of my watch.

'So, did we actually . . . ?' says Lissy at last.

Oh God. 'Kind of,' I admit.

'And . . . was I any good?'

'What?' I gape at her.

'In the dream.' She looks straight at me, her cheeks bright pink. 'Was I any good?'

'Lissy . . .' I say, pulling an agonised face.

'I was crap, wasn't I? I was crap! I knew it.'

'No, of course you weren't crap!' I exclaim. 'You were . . . you were really . . .' I cannot believe I'm seriously having a conversation about my best friend's sexual prowess as a dream lesbian. 'Look, can we just leave the subject? My day has been embarrassing enough already.'

'Oh. Oh God, yes,' says Lissy, suddenly full of remorse. 'Sorry. Emma. You must be feeling really . . .'

'Totally and utterly humiliated and betrayed?' I try to give a smile. 'Yup, that's pretty much how I feel.'

'Did anyone at the office see it, then?' says Lissy sympathetically.

'Did anyone at the office *see* it?' I wheel round. 'Lissy, they *all* saw it. It was *awful*.' I close my eyes as fresh mortification washes over me. 'I have never been more embarrassed in my entire life. I have never felt more . . . exposed.' My voice is wobbling more and more, and then, with no warning, I give a huge sob. 'Oh God, Lissy. You were right. I feel such a complete *fool*. He was just using me, right from the beginning. I was just a . . . a market research project.'

'You don't know that!' she says in dismay.

'I do! Of course I do. That's why he was gripped. It was because he realised he had his target customer, right next to him. The kind of normal, ordinary girl-on-the-street he would never normally give the time of day to!' I give another huge sob. 'I mean, he said it on the television, didn't he? I'm just a nothing-special girl.'

'You are not,' says Lissy fiercely. 'You are *not* nothing-special!'

'I am! That's exactly what I am. I'm just an ordinary nothing. And I was so stupid, I believed it all. I honestly thought Jack loved me. I mean, maybe not exactly loved me.' I feel myself colour. 'But . . . you know.'

'I know.' Lissy looks like she wants to cry herself. 'I know you did.' She gives me a huge hug. 'Come on,' she says. 'You need a drink.'

We go onto the tiny, overgrown balcony and sit in a patch of sun, drinking the schnapps that Lissy got duty-free last year.

'I should have known a millionaire like that would never be interested in me,' I say, staring into my glass.

'I can't believe it was all made up,' says Lissy, sighing for the thousandth time. 'It was all so *romantic*. Changing his mind about going to America, and the bus, and bringing you that pink cocktail . . .'

'But that's what makes it so humiliating. He knew I wanted excitement and intrigue and a big romance. He just fed me everything he knew I'd like. And I believed it—because I wanted to believe it.'

'You honestly think the whole thing was one big plan?'

'Of course it was a plan,' I say tearfully. 'He deliberately followed me around; he watched everything I did; he wanted to get into my life! Look at the way he came and poked around my bedroom. The truth is, a man like that doesn't get to the top without being ruthless and trampling over people. It just doesn't happen.'

'Is that Emma?' comes a piercing voice, and Jemima appears on the balcony in a white robe and face mask. 'So! Miss I-never-borrow-your-clothes. What have you got to say about my Prada slingbacks?'

Oh God. There's no point lying about it, is there?

'They're really pointy and uncomfortable?' I say with a little shrug.

'I knew it! I knew it all along. You *do* borrow my clothes.'

'Oh shut up about your stupid clothes,' says Lissy. 'Emma's really upset. She's been betrayed by the man she thought loved her.'

'Well, surprise, surprise, let me just faint with shock,' says Jemima tartly. 'I could have told you that was going to happen. I *did* tell you! Never tell a man all about yourself. It's bound to lead to trouble.'

'You said she wouldn't get a rock on her finger!' exclaims Lissy. 'You didn't say, he will pitch up on television, telling the nation all her private secrets. You know, Jemima, you could be a bit more sympathetic.'

'No, Lissy, she's right,' I say miserably. 'If I'd just kept my stupid mouth shut, then none of this would have happened.' I reach for the schnapps bottle. 'Relationships *are* a battle. They *are* a chess game. And what did I do? I just threw all my chess pieces down on the board at once, and said, "Here! Have them all!"' I take a gulp of my drink. 'The truth is, men and women should tell each other nothing. *Nothing.*'

'I couldn't agree more,' says Jemima. 'I'm planning to tell my future husband as little as possible—' She breaks off as the cordless phone in her hand gives a shrill ring.

'Hi!' she says, switching it on. 'Camilla? Oh. Er . . . OK. Hang on.' She puts her hand over the receiver. 'It's Jack!' she mouths.

I stare back in utter shock.

'Tell him Emma doesn't want to speak to him!' hisses Lissy.

'No! She *should* speak to him,' hisses back Jemima. 'Otherwise he'll think he's won.'

'Give it to me!' I say, and grab the phone out of Jemima's hand, my heart thumping. 'Hi,' I say, in as curt a tone as I can muster.

'Emma, it's me,' comes Jack's familiar voice, and with no warning, I feel a rush of emotion that almost overwhelms me. I want to cry. I want to hit him, hurt him . . . But somehow, I keep control of myself.

'I never want to speak to you again,' I say. I switch off the phone.

'Well done!' says Lissy.

An instant later the phone rings again.

'Please, Emma,' says Jack, 'just listen for a moment. I know you must be very upset. But if you just give me a second to explain—'

'Didn't you hear me?' I exclaim, my face flushing. 'You used me and you humiliated me and I never want to speak to you again, or see you, or hear you or . . . or . . .'

'Taste you,' hisses Jemima, nodding urgently.

'. . . or touch you again. Never ever. Ever.' I switch off the phone, march inside and yank the line out of the wall. Then, with trembling hands, I get my mobile out of my bag and, just as it begins to ring, switch it off.

As I emerge on the balcony again, I'm still half shaking with shock. I can't quite believe it's all ended like this. In one day, my entire perfect romance has crumbled into nothing.

'Are you OK?' asks Lissy anxiously.

'I'm fine. I think.' I sink onto a chair. 'A bit shaky.'

'Now, Emma,' says Jemima, examining one of her cuticles. 'I don't want to rush you. But you know what you have to do, don't you?'

'What?'

'You have to get your revenge!' She looks up and fixes me with a determined gaze. 'You have to make him pay.'

'Oh no.' Lissy pulls a face. 'Isn't it better just to walk away?'

'What good is walking away?' retorts Jemima. 'Will walking away make him wish he'd never crossed you?'

'"Living well is the best revenge." George Herbert,' says Lissy.

Jemima stares at her blankly for a few seconds. 'So anyway,' she says at last, turning back to me. 'I'd be delighted to help. Revenge is actually quite a speciality of mine, though I say it myself . . .'

I avoid Lissy's eyes. 'What did you have in mind?'

'Scrape his car, shred his suits, sew fish inside his curtains and wait for them to rot . . .' Jemima reels off instantly, as though reciting poetry.

'Did you learn that at finishing school?' says Lissy, rolling her eyes.

'I'm being a feminist, *actually*,' retorts Jemima. 'We women have to stand up for our rights. You know, before she married my father, Mummy went out with this scientist chap who changed his mind three weeks before the wedding, can you believe it? So one night she crept into his lab and pulled out all the plugs of his stupid machines. His whole research was ruined! She always says, that taught Emerson!'

'Emerson?' says Lissy, staring at her in disbelief. 'As in Emerson Davies?'

'That's right! Davies.'

'Emerson Davies who nearly discovered a cure for smallpox?'

'Well, he shouldn't have messed Mummy about, should he?' says Jemima, lifting her chin mutinously. She turns to me. 'Another of Mummy's tips is chilli oil. You somehow arrange to have sex with the chap again, and then you say. "How about a little massage oil?" And you rub it into his . . . you know.' Her eyes sparkle.

'Your *mother* told you this?' says Lissy.

'What is your *problem*, Lissy? Do you think you should just let men walk all over you and get away with it? Great blow for feminism.'

'I'm not saying that,' says Lissy. 'I just wouldn't get my revenge with . . . chilli oil! *If* I was going to stoop so low as get my revenge, which I never would because personally I think it's a huge mistake . . . I'd do exactly what he did. I'd expose one of *his* secrets.'

'Actually . . . that's rather good,' says Jemima grudgingly.

'Humiliate *him*,' says Lissy. 'Embarrass *him*. See how he likes it.'

They both turn and look at me expectantly.

'But I don't know any of his secrets,' I say.

'You must do!' says Jemima.

'I don't,' I say, feeling a fresh humiliation. 'Lissy, you had it right all along. Our relationship was completely one-sided. I shared all my secrets with him—but he didn't share any of his with me.'

'You must know *something*!' says Jemima. 'You slept with him, for goodness sake! He must have some secret. Some weak point.'

'An Achilles' heel,' puts in Lissy, and Jemima gives her an odd look.

'It doesn't have to be to do with his feet,' she says, and turns to me, pulling a 'Lissy's lost it' face. 'It could be anything. Think back!'

I close my eyes obediently and cast my mind back. But my mind's swirling a bit, from all that schnapps. Think back . . . Jack's secrets . . .

Scotland. Suddenly a coherent thought passes through my mind. I feel a tingle of exhilaration. I do know one of his secrets. I do!

'What?' says Jemima avidly. 'Have you remembered something?'

'He . . .' I stop, feeling torn. I did make a promise to Jack. But then, so bloody what? Why on earth am I keeping any stupid promise to him? It's not like he kept my secrets to *himself*, is it? 'He was in Scotland!' I say triumphantly. 'The first time we met after the plane, he asked me to keep it a secret that he was in Scotland.'

'Why did he do that?' says Lissy.

'I dunno.'

'What was he doing in Scotland?' puts in Jemima.

'I dunno.'

There's a pause.

'Hmm,' says Jemima kindly. 'It's not the *most* embarrassing secret in the world, is it? I mean, plenty of smart people live in Scotland. Haven't you got anything better? Like . . . does he wear a chest wig?'

'Of course he doesn't wear a chest wig,' I retort.

'Well then, you'll have to make something up,' says Jemima. 'You know, before the affair with the scientist, Mummy was treated very badly by some politician chap. So she made up a rumour that he was taking bribes from the Communist party, and passed it round the House of Commons. She always says, that taught Dennis a lesson!'

'Not . . . Dennis Llewellyn?' Lissy says, she looks aghast.

'Er, yes, I think that was him.'

'The disgraced Home Secretary? The one who spent his whole life fighting to clear his name and ended up in a mental institution?'

'Well, he shouldn't have messed Mummy around, should he?' says Jemima. A bleeper goes off in her pocket. 'Time for my footbath!'

As she disappears back into the house, Lissy rolls her eyes.

'She's nuts,' she says. 'Totally nuts. Emma, you are *not* making anything up about Jack Harper.'

'I won't!' I say indignantly. 'Who do you think I am? Anyway, who am I kidding? I could never get my revenge on Jack. He's a huge, powerful millionaire.' I take a miserable slug of my drink. 'And I'm a nothing-special . . . crappy . . . ordinary . . . nothing.'

nine

THE NEXT MORNING I wake up full of sick dread. I feel exactly like a five-year-old who doesn't want to go to school. A five-year-old with a severe hangover, that is.

'I can't go,' I say, as 8.30 arrives. 'I can't face them.'

'Yes you can,' says Lissy reassuringly, doing up my jacket buttons.

'What if they're horrid to me? Can't I just stay at home with you?' I grab her hand beseechingly. 'I'll be really good, I promise.'

'Emma, I've explained to you,' says Lissy patiently. 'I've got to go to court today.' She prises my hand out of hers. 'But I'll be here when you get home. And we'll have something really nice for supper. OK?'

'OK,' I say in a small voice. 'Can we have chocolate ice cream?'

'Of course we can,' says Lissy. 'Now, go on. You'll be fine!'

Feeling like a dog being shooed out, I go down the stairs and open the front door. I'm just stepping out of the house when a van pulls up. A man gets out, holding the biggest bunch of flowers I've ever seen, and squints at the number on our house.

'Hello,' he says. 'I'm looking for an Emma Corrigan.'

'That's me!' I say in surprise.

'Aha!' He smiles, and holds out a pen and clipboard. 'Well, this is your lucky day. If you could just sign here . . .'

I stare at the bouquet in disbelief. Roses, freesias, amazing big purple flowers, fantastic dark red pompom things, dark green frondy bits, pale green ones that look just like asparagus . . .

OK, I may not know what they're all called. But I do know one thing. These flowers are expensive.

There's only one person who could have sent them.

I grab the card, rip it open, and scan down the long message, not reading any of it until I come to the name at the bottom. *Jack.*

I feel a huge dart of emotion. After all he did, Jack thinks he can fob me off with some manky bunch of flowers? All right, huge, deluxe bunch of flowers. But that's not the point.

'I don't want them, thank you,' I say, lifting my chin.

'You don't *want* them?' The delivery man stares at me.

'No. Tell the person who sent them, thanks, but no thanks.'

'What's going on?' comes a breathless voice beside me, and I look up to see Lissy gawping at the bouquet. 'Oh my God. Are they from Jack?'

'Yes. But I don't want them,' I say. 'Please take them away.'

'Wait!' exclaims Lissy. 'I've never *seen* flowers as amazing as this.' She looks at the man. 'So what will happen to them?'

'Dunno.' He shrugs. 'They'll get chucked away, I suppose.'

'Gosh.' She glances at me. 'That seems like an awful waste . . .'

'Lissy, I can't *accept* them!' I exclaim. 'I can't! He'll think I'm saying everything's OK between us.'

'No, you're quite right,' says Lissy reluctantly. 'You have to send them back.' She touches a pink velvety rose petal. 'It is a shame, though . . .'

'Send what back?' comes a sharp voice behind me. Oh, for God's sake. Now Jemima has arrived in the street. 'You're not sending those back!' she cries. 'I'm giving a dinner party tomorrow night. They'll be perfect.' She grabs the label. 'Smythe and Foxe! Do you know how much these must have cost?'

'I don't care how much they cost!' I exclaim. 'They're from Jack! If I keep them, I'm basically saying, "I forgive you."'

'Not necessarily,' retorts Jemima. 'You could be saying "I can't be bothered to return your stupid flowers, that's how little you mean to me."'

There's silence as we all consider this.

The thing is, they *are* pretty amazing flowers.

'So do you want them or not?' says the delivery guy.

'Emma, if you send them back you look weak,' says Jemima firmly.
'You look like you can't bear to have any reminder of him in the house.
But if you keep them, then you're saying, "I don't care about you!"'

'Oh, God, OK!' I say, and grab the pen from the delivery guy. 'I'll sign
for them. But could you please tell him that this does *not* mean I forgive
him, nor that he isn't a cynical, heartless, despicable user.'

The delivery guy looks at me blankly. 'Love, I just work at the depot.'

'I know!' says Lissy suddenly. She grabs the clipboard back and prints
WITHOUT PREJUDICE clearly under my name.

'What does that mean?' I say.

'It means "I'll never forgive you, you complete bastard . . . but I'll
keep the flowers anyway."'

It's one of those amazingly bright, crisp mornings that make you feel
that London really is the best city in the world. As I'm walking from the
tube station to work, my spirits can't help rising a little.

Maybe everyone at work will already have forgotten about the whole
thing. I mean, let's get a bit of proportion here. It wasn't *that* big a deal.
It wasn't *that* interesting. I push open the glass door to the foyer with a
small spurt of optimism, and walk in, my head held high.

'. . . a Barbie bedspread!' I immediately hear from across the marble.

'. . . shagging Jack Harper all along?' comes a voice from above me.

'It's Connor I feel sorry for,' someone replies. 'That poor guy . . .'

'. . . pretended she loved jazz,' someone else is saying.

OK. So they haven't forgotten. Clenching my fists at my sides, I make
my way up the stairs and along the corridor. Everyone I pass either blatantly stares at me or pretends they're not looking when they are, and at
least five conversations are broken off as I approach.

As I reach the door to the marketing department I take a deep breath,
then walk in, trying to look as unconcerned as possible.

'Hi everyone,' I say, taking off my jacket and hanging it on my chair.

'Emma!' exclaims Artemis in tones of sarcastic delight. 'Well I never!'

'Good morning, Emma,' says Paul, coming out of his office and giving
me an appraising look. 'You OK? Anything you'd like to . . . talk about?'
To my surprise he looks as if he genuinely means it.

'No,' I say, my face prickling. 'Thanks, but I'm OK.'

'Good.' He pauses, then adopts a more businesslike tone. 'All right, then, carry on. And the rest of you.' Paul looks around the office warningly. 'Remember what I said.'

'Of course,' says Artemis at once. 'We all remember!'

Paul disappears into his office again, and I stare rigidly at my computer as it warms up. As calmly as possible I click onto my emails, and give a small gasp of shock. I normally get about ten emails every morning, if that. Today I have ninety-five.

Dad: I'd really like to talk . . .
Carol: I've already got two more people for our Barbie Club!
Moira: I know where you can get really comfy G-strings . . .

I scroll down the endless list and suddenly feel a stabbing in my heart. There are three from Jack. My hand hovers uncertainly over my mouse. Does he deserve at least a chance to explain?

'Oh Emma,' says Artemis innocently, coming over to my desk with a carrier bag. 'I've got this jumper I wondered if you'd like. It's a bit too small for me but it's very nice. And it should fit you, because'— she pauses, and catches Caroline's eye—'it's a size eight.'

Immediately both of them erupt into hysterical giggles.

'Thanks, Artemis,' I say shortly. 'That's really sweet of you.'

'Oh Emma, I meant to say,' Nick adds, sauntering over to my desk. 'That new secretary in Admin. Have you seen her? She's quite something, isn't she?' He winks at me and I stare at him blankly for a moment, not understanding. 'Nice spiky haircut,' he adds. 'Nice dungarees.'

'Shut up!' I cry furiously, my face flaming red. 'I'm not a . . . I'm not . . . Just fuck off, all of you!'

My hand trembling with anger, I swiftly delete each and every one of Jack's emails. He doesn't deserve anything. No chance. Nothing.

I rise to my feet and stride out of the room, breathing hard. I head for the ladies' room, slam the door behind me and rest my hot forehead on the mirror. Hatred for Jack Harper is bubbling through me like lava.

'Emma!' A voice interrupts my thoughts and I give a start. Katie has come into the Ladies without me hearing. Her face is reflected in the mirror next to mine, and she isn't smiling. 'So,' she says in a strange voice. 'You don't like crochet.'

Oh God. Oh God. What have I done? I've unleashed a side of Katie that no one's ever seen before.

'Katie,' I say, my heart thumping hard. 'I never meant—'

'Emma, don't even start.' She lifts her hand. 'There's no point.' She gives an eerie smile. 'You know, I was pretty upset yesterday. But after work I went straight home and called my mum. And do you know what she said to me?'

'What?' I say apprehensively.

'She said . . . she doesn't like crochet either.'

'*What?*' I wheel round and gape at her.

'And neither does my granny.' Her face flushes, and now she looks like the old Katie again. 'Or any of my relatives. They've all been pretending for years, just like you. It all makes sense now!' Her voice rises in agitation. 'You know, I made my granny a whole sofa cover last Christmas, and she told me that burglars had stolen it. But I mean, what kind of burglars steal a crochet sofa cover?'

'Katie, I don't know what to say . . .'

'Emma, why couldn't you have told me before? All that time. Making stupid presents that people didn't want.'

'Oh God, Katie, I'm sorry!' I say, filled with remorse. 'I'm so sorry. I just . . . didn't want to hurt you.'

'I know you were trying to be kind. But I feel really stupid now.'

'Yes, well, that makes two of us,' I say a little morosely.

I still can't quite believe how everything has turned upside-down, just like that. Everything I believed in has turned out to be false. Oh God. My eyes are pricking again.

'I think you're really brave,' says Katie, watching me. 'I'm amazed you even came in today. I would have been *far* too embarrassed.'

'Katie,' I say, turning to face her. 'Yesterday I had all my most personal, private secrets broadcast on TV.' I spread my arms widely. 'How could anything possibly be more embarrassing than that?'

'Here she is!' comes a ringing voice behind us, and Caroline bursts into the Ladies. 'Emma, your parents are here to see you!'

No. I do not believe this. I do not believe this.

My parents are standing by my desk. And the entire office is staring at them, as though they're some kind of rare creature.

Scratch that. The entire office has now turned their heads in order to stare at *me*.

'Hi,' I say in a voice that has suddenly gone rather husky.

'Emma!' says Dad, making an attempt at his normal jovial voice. 'We just thought we'd . . . pop in to see you.'

'We brought you a little present,' says Mum brightly. 'Some flowers for your desk.' She puts the bouquet down awkwardly. 'Look at Emma's desk, Brian. Isn't it smart! Look at the . . . the computer!'

'Splendid!' says Dad, giving it a little pat.

'We were just saying, the other day,' continues Mum, 'how *proud* you should be of yourself, Emma. Working for a big company like this.'

'Absolutely!' says Dad. 'You've done very well for yourself, Emma.'

I'm so taken aback, I can't even open my mouth. I meet Dad's eye, and he gives a strange, awkward little smile. And Mum's hands are trembling slightly as she puts the flowers down.

They're nervous, I realise with a jolt of shock. They're both *nervous*.

I'm just trying to get my head round this as Paul appears at the door of his office. 'So Emma,' he says. 'You have visitors, I gather?'

'Er . . . yes,' I say. 'Paul, these are . . . um . . . my parents.'

'Enchanted,' says Paul politely. 'Perhaps, Emma, you'd like to take your parents out for—shall we call it an early lunch?'

I look up at the clock. It's a quarter to ten.

'Thanks, Paul,' I say gratefully.

This is surreal. I should be at work. And instead I'm walking down the street with my parents. I can't even *remember* the last time it was just the three of us, no Grandpa, no Kerry, no Nev.

'We could go in here,' I say, as we reach an Italian coffee shop.

'Good idea!' says Dad heartily, and pushes the door open. 'We saw your friend Jack Harper on television yesterday,' he adds casually.

'He's not my friend,' I reply shortly.

We sit down at a wooden table and a waiter brings us each a menu, and there's silence. Oh God. Now *I'm* feeling nervous.

'So . . .' I begin. 'What . . . brings you to London?'

'We just thought we'd like to visit you,' says Mum, looking through her reading glasses at the menu. 'Now, shall I have a cup of tea, or— what's this? A frappelatte?'

'I want a normal cup of coffee,' says Dad, peering at the menu with a frown. 'Do they do such a thing?'

'If they don't, you'll have to have a cappuccino and spoon off the froth,' says Mum. 'Or an espresso and just ask them to add hot water.'

I don't believe this. They have driven two hundred miles. Are we just going to sit here and talk about hot beverages all day?

'Oh, and that reminds me,' adds Mum casually. 'We've bought you a little something, Emma. It's a car.' She looks up at the waiter who's appeared at our table. 'Hello! I would like a cappuccino, my husband would like a filter coffee if that's possible, and Emma would like—'

'A *car*?' I echo in disbelief.

'Car,' echoes the Italian waiter, and gives me a suspicious look.

'I'd . . . I'd like a cappuccino, please,' I say distractedly. 'Mum . . .' I put a hand to my head as the waiter disappears. 'What do you mean, you've bought me a car?'

'Just a little run-around. You ought to have a car. It's not safe, you travelling on all these buses. Grandpa's quite right.'

'But . . . but I can't afford a car,' I say stupidly. 'I can't even . . . What about the money I owe you? What about—?'

'Forget the money,' says Dad. 'We're going to wipe the slate clean.'

'What?' I stare at him, more bewildered than ever. 'But we can't—'

'Forget the money,' says Dad, a sudden edge to his voice. 'I want you to forget all about it, Emma. You don't owe us anything. Nothing at all.'

I honestly cannot take all this in. I look confusedly from Dad to Mum. Then back to Dad. Then, very slowly, back to Mum again.

And it's really strange. But it almost feels as though we're seeing each other properly for the first time in years. As though we're seeing each other and saying hello and kind of . . . starting again.

'We were wondering what you thought about taking a little holiday next year,' says Mum. 'Just the three of us, we thought.' She gives me a tentative smile. 'It might be fun! You don't have to, of course, if you've got other plans.'

'No, I'd like to!' I say quickly. 'I really would. But . . . but what about . . . ?' I can't even bring myself to say Kerry's name.

There's a tiny silence, during which Mum and Dad look at each other.

'Kerry sends her love, of course!' says Mum brightly, as though she's changing the subject completely. She clears her throat. 'You know, she thought she might visit Hong Kong next year. Visit her father.'

'Right,' I say dazedly. 'Good idea.'

'We feel, Emma,' says Dad, and stops. 'We feel . . . that perhaps we haven't been . . . that perhaps we haven't always noticed—'

'Cappu-ccino,' says the waiter. 'Filter co-ffee, cappu-ccino—'

'Thank you!' interrupts Mum. The waiter disappears again, and she looks at me. 'Emma, what we want to say is . . . we're very proud of you.'

Oh God. Oh God, I think I'm going to cry.

'Right,' I manage.

'And we . . .' Dad begins. 'That is to say, we both, your mother and I' —he clears his throat—'we've always . . . and always will . . . both of us . . .' He pauses, breathing rather hard, and wipes his perspiring face with a napkin. 'The fact of the matter is that . . . is that . . .'

'Oh, just tell your daughter you love her, Brian!' cries Mum.

'I . . . I . . . love you, Emma!' says Dad in a choked-up voice. 'Oh Jesus.' He brushes roughly at his eye.

'I love you too, Dad,' I say, my throat tight. 'And you, Mum.'

'You see!' says Mum, dabbing at her eye. 'I knew it wasn't a mistake to come!' She clutches hold of my hand, and I clutch hold of Dad's hand, and for a moment we're in a kind of awkward group hug.

'You know . . . we're all sacred links in the eternal circle of life,' I say with a sudden swell of emotion.

'What?' Both my parents look at me blankly.

'Er, never mind. Doesn't matter.' I release my hand, take a sip of cappuccino, and look up. And my heart nearly stops.

Jack is standing at the door of the coffee shop.

My heart is hammering in my chest as I stare at him. He puts out a hand, the door pings, and suddenly he's inside.

As he walks towards our table, all the old feelings of pain and humiliation threaten to take over and turn me to jelly again. But I'm not going to let them. I'm going to be strong and dignified.

'Ignore him,' I say to Mum and Dad.

'Who?' says Dad, turning round in his chair. 'Oh!'

'Emma, I want to talk to you,' says Jack, his face earnest. 'Please.' He sits down at an adjoining table. 'I want to explain. I want to apologise.'

'There's no explanation you could possibly give me.' I look fiercely at Mum and Dad. 'Pretend he isn't there. So, Mum. How's the golf?'

'It's . . . er . . . fine, thanks.' Mum shoots a glance at Jack.

'Don't look at him!' I mutter. 'And Dad?' I persevere.

'It's . . . also fine,' says Dad stiltedly.

'Where do you play?' asks Jack politely.

'You're not in the conversation!' I cry, turning furiously on my chair. There's silence.

'Dear me!' says Mum suddenly in a stagy voice. 'Just look at the time! We're due at the . . . the sculpture exhibition. Lovely to see you, Emma.'

'You can't go!' I say in panic. But Dad's already placing a £20 note on the table while Mum stands up and puts on her white jacket.

'Just listen to him,' she whispers.

'Bye, Emma,' says Dad. And they're gone.

I cannot believe they have done this to me.

'So,' says Jack, as the door pings shut. 'Emma, please.'

Determinedly I shift my chair round, so I can't see him. I'm staring straight at the wall. That'll show him.

The only thing is, now I can't reach my cappuccino.

'Here.' I look round to see Jack is holding out my cup to me.

'Leave me alone!' I say angrily, leaping to my feet. I grab my bag and stalk out of the coffee shop, into the busy street. A moment later, I feel a hand on my shoulder.

'We could at least discuss what happened . . .'

'Discuss what?' I wheel round. 'How you betrayed me?'

'I appreciate I embarrassed you. But . . . is it really such a big deal?'

'Such a big *deal*?' I cry, nearly knocking over a lady with a shopping trolley. 'You came into my life. You fed me this amazing romance. You made me fall in lo—' I halt myself abruptly. 'You said you were gripped by me. You made me . . . care for you . . . and I believed every word!' My voice is starting to wobble treacherously. 'I believed it all, Jack. But all the way along, you were just using me for your stupid research.'

Jack stares at me. 'No,' he says. 'No, wait. You have this wrong.' He grabs my arm. 'That's not the way it was. I didn't set out to use you.'

'Of course you did!' I say, wrenching my arm out of his grasp, jabbing the button at a pedestrian crossing. 'Don't deny it was me you were talking about in that interview. Every detail was me.'

'OK. I don't deny I had you in mind. I don't deny you filtered into . . . But that doesn't mean . . .' He looks up. 'I have you on my mind most of the time. That's the truth, I have you on my mind.'

The pedestrian crossing starts bleeping, telling us to cross. This is the cue for me to storm off and him to come running after me—but neither of us moves. I *want* to storm off, but somehow my body isn't doing it.

'Emma, when Pete and I started the Panther Corporation, you know how we worked?' Jack's dark eyes are burning into mine. 'You know how we made our decisions? Gut instinct. Would *we* buy this? Would *we* like this? Would *we* go for this? During the past few weeks, I've been immersed in this new women's line. And all I've found myself asking myself is . . . would Emma like it? Would Emma drink it? Would Emma buy it? Yes, you got into my thoughts. Yes, you fed into my work. Emma, my life and my business have always gotten confused. But that doesn't mean my life isn't real.' He hesitates. 'It doesn't mean that what we had . . . we have . . . is any less real.'

He takes a deep breath and shoves his hands in his pockets. 'Emma, I didn't lie to you. I didn't *feed* you anything. I was gripped by you the minute I met you on that plane. The minute you looked up at me and said, "I don't even *know* if I've got a G spot!" I was hooked. Not because of business . . . because of *you*. Because of who you are. Every single tiny detail.' The flicker of a smile passes over his face. 'From the way you pick out your favourite horoscope every morning to the way you wrote the letter from Ernest P. Leopold. All of it.'

His gaze is fixed on mine, and my head is all confused. For an instant I feel myself wavering. Just for an instant.

'That's all very well,' I say, my voice shaking. 'But you embarrassed me. You *humiliated* me!' I start striding across the road again.

'I didn't mean to say so much,' says Jack, following me. 'I was . . .' He shakes his head. 'I don't know, goaded, I got carried away . . .'

'You got carried *away*?' I feel a renewed surge of outrage. 'Jack, you told the world about my underwear . . . and my sex life . . . and my Barbie bed cover and you *didn't* tell them it was ironic . . .'

'Emma, I'm sorry—'

'You told them how much I weigh!' My voice rises to a shriek. 'And you got it *wrong*!'

'Emma, really, I'm sorry—'

'Sorry isn't good enough!' I wheel round furiously to face him. 'You don't know what it was like for me. Everyone was laughing at me. Everyone was teasing me. Artemis was teasing me—'

'I'll fire her,' Jack cuts me off firmly.

I'm so shocked, I give a half-giggle, then turn it into a cough.

'And Nick was teasing me—'

'I'll fire him too. How about this: anyone who teased you, I'll fire.'

This time I can't help giggling. 'You won't have a company left.'

'So be it. That'll teach me. That'll teach me to be so thoughtless.'

For a moment we stare at each other in the sunshine. My heart's beating quickly. I'm not quite sure what to think.

'Emma, I want to make this up to you,' he says. 'Could we have lunch? A drink?'

'I don't know,' I say, rubbing my nose.

'Things were going so well, before I had to go and fuck it up.'

'Were they?' I say.

'Weren't they?' Jack hesitates. 'I kind of thought they were.'

My mind is buzzing. There are things I need to say. There are things I need to get into the open. A thought crystallises in my head.

'Jack . . . what were you doing in Scotland? When we first met.'

At once, Jack's expression changes. His face closes up and he looks away. 'Emma, I'm afraid I can't tell you that.'

'Why not?' I say, trying to sound light.

'It's . . . complicated.'

'OK, then.' I think for a moment. 'Where did you go rushing off to that night with Sven? When you had to cut our date short.'

Jack sighs. 'Emma—'

'Or the night you had all those calls? What were those about?'

This time, Jack doesn't even bother answering.

'I see.' I'm trying to stay calm. 'Jack, did it ever occur to you that in all our time together, you hardly told me anything about yourself?'

'I . . . guess I'm a private person,' says Jack. 'Is it such a big deal?'

'It's quite a big deal to me. I shared everything with you. All my thoughts, all my worries, everything. And you shared nothing with me. You didn't even tell me you were going to be on television.'

'It was just a dumb interview, for Chrissakes!'

'I told you my secrets,' I say stubbornly. 'You didn't tell me any of yours.'

Jack sighs. 'With all due respect, Emma, I think it's a little different—'

'What?' I stare at him in shock. 'Why should it be any different?'

'You have to understand. I have things in my life that are very sensitive . . . complicated . . . very important . . .'

'And I *don't*?' My voice bursts from me like a rocket. 'You think my secrets are less important than yours? You think I'm less hurt by you blurting them out on television? Because you're so huge and important and I'm—what am I, again, Jack?' I can feel my eyes glittering with tears. 'A nothing-special girl? An "ordinary, nothing-special girl"?'

Jack winces, and I can see I've hit home. 'I didn't mean to use those words,' he says, rubbing his forehead. 'The minute I said them, I wished I could take them back. Emma, you *have* to know I didn't mean—'

'I'm going to ask you again!' I say, my heart pounding. 'What were you doing in Scotland?'

There's silence. As I meet Jack's eyes, I know he's not going to tell me. He knows this is important to me and he's still not going to tell me.

'Fine,' I say, my voice lurching slightly. 'That's fine. I'm obviously not as important as you. I'm just some amusing girl who provides you with entertainment on flights and gives you ideas for your business.'

'Emma—'

'The thing is, Jack, that's not a real relationship. A real relationship is two-way. A real relationship is based on equality. And trust.' I swallow the lump in my throat. 'So why don't you just go and be with someone on your level, who you can share your precious secrets with? Because you obviously can't share them with me.'

I turn sharply before he can say anything else, and stalk away.

I don't get home until much later that evening. But I'm still smarting from our argument. I open the door of the flat to find Lissy and Jemima in a full-scale argument about animal rights.

'The mink like being made into coats—' Jemima is saying as I push open the door to the living room. She breaks off and looks up. 'Emma! Are you all right?'

'No. I had a huge row with Jack.'

'With *Jack*? You saw him?'

'He came to . . . well, to apologise, I guess.'

'What happened?' says Lissy, hugging her knees. 'What did he say?'

'He said . . . he didn't ever mean to use me,' I say. 'He said I got in his thoughts. He said he'd fire everyone in the company who teased me.' I can't help giving a half-giggle.

'Really?' says Lissy. 'Gosh. That's quite romant—' She coughs, and pulls an apologetic face. 'Sorry.'

'He said he was really sorry for what happened, and he didn't mean to say all that stuff on the TV, and that our romance was . . . Anyway. He said a lot of things. But *then* he said . . .' My heart beats with fresh indignation. 'He said his secrets were more important than mine.'

There's a huge gasp of outrage.

'No!' says Lissy.

'Bastard!' says Jemima. 'What secrets?'

'I asked him about Scotland. And rushing off from the date.' I meet Lissy's eyes. 'And all those things he would never talk to me about. He said it was too "sensitive and complicated".'

'Sensitive and *complicated*?' Jemima is staring at me, galvanised. 'Emma, this is perfect. You find out what it is—and then you expose it!'

I stare at her, my heart beating hard. God, she's right. I could do it. I could get back at Jack. I could make him hurt like I've been hurt.

'But I have no idea what it is,' I say at last.

'You can find out!' says Jemima.

'There's definitely some kind of mystery,' says Lissy thoughtfully. 'He has all these phone calls he won't talk about, he rushes off mysteriously from your date—'

'He rushed off mysteriously?' says Jemima avidly. 'Where? Did he say anything? Did you overhear anything?'

My mind flashes back to that evening. Sitting on the bench, sipping the pink cocktail. Jack and Sven talking behind me in low voices . . .

'It was nothing much,' I say reluctantly. 'I just heard him say something about Plan B . . . and something being urgent . . . And they said something about flying back up to Glasgow.'

Jemima looks beside herself. 'Emma, I do not believe this. You've had this information all this time? This has to be something juicy. It *has* to be. If only we knew more.' She exhales in frustration. 'You didn't have a Dictaphone or anything with you?'

'Of course I didn't! It was a date! Do *you* normally take a Dictaphone on a . . .' I tail off incredulously at her expression. 'Jemima. You don't.'

'Not *always*,' she says, with a defensive shrug. 'Just if I think it might come in . . . Anyway. That's irrelevant. The point is, you have information,

Emma. You have power. You find out what this is all about—and then you expose him. That'll show Jack Harper who's boss.'

I stare back at her determined face, and for a moment I feel exhilaration bubbling through me. That would show him. Then he'd see I'm not just some nothing, nobody girl. *Then* he'd see.

'So . . .' I lick my lips. 'So how would I do it?'

'First we try to work out as much as we can ourselves,' says Jemima. 'Then, I've got access to various . . . people who can help get more information.' She gives me a tiny wink. 'Discreetly.'

'Private detectives?' says Lissy in disbelief. 'Are you for real?'

'And then we expose him! Mummy's got contacts at *all* the papers. A very good place to start is rubbish bins,' adds Jemima knowledgeably. 'You can find *all* sorts of things looking through somebody's trash.'

And all of a sudden sanity comes flying in through the window.

'Rubbish bins?' I say in horror. 'I'm not looking in any rubbish bins! In fact, I'm not doing this, full stop. It's a crazy idea. I want to forget about it.' My face closes up. 'I want to move on.'

'No you don't!' retorts Jemima. 'Don't be stupid, Emma. This is your big chance for revenge. We are *so* going to get him.' I have never seen Jemima look so animated in my life. She reaches for her bag and gets out a tiny lilac Smythson notebook, together with a Tiffany pen. 'Right, so what do we know? Glasgow . . . Plan B . . .'

'The Panther Corporation doesn't have offices in Scotland, does it?' says Lissy thoughtfully. 'I might go and look some stuff up on the Internet, just out of interest.'

'Look, just stop it, both of you!' I say. 'If Jack doesn't want to tell me what his secret is . . . then I don't want to know.'

As I pad into the kitchen the next morning to make a cup of tea, I'm fully resolved. I'm not even going to *think* about Jack from now on. He can keep his stupid secrets. Finito. Fin. The End.

'OK. Jack's big secret. I have three theories.' Lissy arrives breathlessly at the door of the kitchen in her pyjamas, holding her legal pad.

'Only three?' says Jemima, appearing behind her in her white robe, clutching her Smythson notebook. 'I've got eight!'

'I don't want to hear any theories,' I say. 'Look, this has been really painful for me. Can't you just respect my feelings and drop it?'

They both look at me blankly for a second, then turn back to each other. '*Eight?*' says Lissy again. 'How did you get eight?'

'Easy-peasy. But I'm sure yours are very good too,' says Jemima kindly. 'Why don't you go first?'

'OK,' says Lissy with a look of annoyance, and clears her throat. 'Number one: he's relocating the Panther Corporation to Scotland. He was up there reconnoitring, and didn't want you spreading rumours. Number two: he's involved in some kind of white-collar fraud . . .'

'What?' I stare at her. 'Why do you say that?'

'I looked up the accountants who audited the last Panther Corporation accounts, and they've been involved in a few big scandals recently. Which doesn't *prove* anything, but if he's acting shadily. . .' She pulls a face.

Jack a fraudster? No. He couldn't be. He couldn't.

Not that I care one way or the other.

'Can I say that both of those sound highly unlikely to me?' says Jemima with raised eyebrows.

'Well, what's your theory, then?' says Lissy crossly.

'Plastic surgery, of course!' she says triumphantly. 'He has a face-lift and he doesn't want anyone to know, so he recuperates in Scotland. *And* I know what the B is in Plan B.'

'What?' I say suspiciously.

'Botox!' says Jemima with a flourish. 'That's why he rushed off from your date. To have his fine lines smoothed. The doctor suddenly had a spare appointment, his friend came to tell him—'

What planet does Jemima come from?

'OK, Miss Marple,' says Lissy, rolling her eyes. 'So what are your other seven theories?'

'Let me see . . .' Jemima turns the page of her notebook. 'OK, this one's rather good. He's in the Mafia.' She pauses for effect. 'His father was shot, and he's planning to murder the heads of all the other families.'

'Jemima, that's *The Godfather*,' says Lissy.

'Oh.' She looks put out. 'I thought it seemed a bit familiar.' She crosses it out. 'Well, here's another one. He has an autistic brother . . .'

'*Rain Man*.'

'Oh. Damn.' She pulls a face and looks at her list again. 'So maybe not that after all . . . or that . . .' She starts crossing entries out. 'OK. But I do have one more.' She raises her head. 'He's got another woman.'

I stare at her, feeling a jolt. I never even thought of that.

'That was my last theory, too,' says Lissy apologetically.

'You *both* think it's another woman?' I look from face to face. 'But . . . but why?' Suddenly I feel really small. And stupid. Has Jack been playing me along? Have I been even *more* naive than I originally thought?

'It just seems quite a likely explanation,' says Jemima with a shrug. 'He's having some clandestine affair with a woman in Scotland. He was paying her a secret visit when he met you. She keeps phoning him, maybe they were having a row, then she comes to London unexpectedly, so he has to dash off from your date.'

I get a pint of milk from the fridge and slam it shut, my hands trembling slightly. Sensitive and complicated. Is that code for 'I'm seeing someone else?' Well, fine. Let him have another woman. I don't care.

'If you're going to get revenge—' says Jemima.

'I don't *want* to get revenge, OK?' I say, turning round to face her. 'It's not healthy. I want to . . . heal my wounds and move on.'

She gives me an impressive look. 'Emma, I'm not going to let you sit back and allow yourself to be mistreated by some bastard man.'

I stare at Jemima, feeling a few tiny qualms. 'Jemima, you're not actually going to do anything about this.'

'Of course I am,' she says. 'I'm not going to stand by and see you suffer. It's called the sisterhood, Emma!'

Oh God. I have visions of Jemima scraping Jack's car with a nail file.

'Jemima . . . don't do anything,' I say in alarm. 'Please.'

'You'll thank me later—'

'No I won't! Jemima, you have to promise me you're not going to do anything stupid.'

She tightens her jaw mutinously.

'Promise!'

'OK,' says Jemima at last, rolling her eyes. 'I promise.'

'She's crossing her fingers behind her back,' observes Lissy.

'*What?*' I stare at Jemima in disbelief. 'Promise properly! Swear on something you really love.'

'All right, you win,' says Jemima sulkily. 'I swear on my Miu Miu ponyskin bag, I won't do anything. But you're making a big mistake.'

She saunters out of the room, and I watch her, a bit uneasily.

'That girl is a total psychopath,' says Lissy, sinking down onto a chair. 'Why did we ever let her move in here?' She takes a sip of tea. 'Actually, I remember why. It was because her dad gave us a whole year's rent in advance—' She catches my expression. 'Are you OK?'

'You don't think she'll actually do anything to Jack, do you?'

'Of course not,' says Lissy reassuringly. 'She's all talk. She'll probably bump into one of her ditzy friends and forget all about it.'

'You're right.' I give myself a little shake. 'You're right.' I pick up my cup and look at it silently for a few moments. 'Lissy, do you really think Jack's secret is another woman?'

Lissy opens her mouth.

'Anyway, I don't care,' I add defiantly, before she can answer.

'Sure,' says Lissy, and gives me a sympathetic smile.

As I arrive at the office, Artemis looks up from her desk with a bright-eyed glance. 'Morning Emma!' She smirks at Caroline. 'Read any intellectual books lately?'

Oh, ha ha-di-ha. So, so funny. Everyone else at work has got bored with teasing me. Only Artemis still thinks it's completely hilarious.

'Actually, Artemis, I have,' I say brightly. 'It was called "What to do if your colleague is an obnoxious cow who picks her nose when she thinks no one's looking."'

There's a guffaw around the office, and Artemis flushes a dark red.

'I don't!' she snaps.

'I never said you did,' I reply innocently, and switch on my computer.

'Ready to go to the meeting, Artemis?' says Paul, coming out of his office with a magazine in his hand. 'And by the way, Nick,' he adds ominously, 'before I go, would you mind telling me what possessed you to put a coupon ad for Panther Bars in'—he consults the front cover—'*Bowling Monthly* magazine? I'm assuming it was you, as this is your product?'

My heart gives a little swoop, and I lift my head. Shit. Double shit. I didn't think Paul would ever find out about that.

Nick shoots me a dirty look and I pull an agonised face back. 'Well,' he begins truculently. 'Yes, Paul. Panther Bars are my product. But—'

Oh God. I can't let him take the blame. 'Paul,' I say in a trembling voice, half raising my hand. 'Actually, it was—'

'Because I want to tell you.' Paul grins at Nick. 'It was bloody inspired! I've just had the feedback figures, and bearing in mind the pitiful circulation . . . they're extraordinary!'

I stare at him in astonishment. The ad worked?

'What the *fuck* compelled you to advertise a teenage bar to a load of old codgers?'

'Well!' Nick adjusts his cuff links, not looking anywhere near me. 'Obviously it was a *bit* of a gamble. But I simply felt that maybe it was time to . . . experiment with a new demographic . . .'

Hang on a minute. *What's* he saying?

'Well, your experiment paid off.' Paul gives Nick an approving look. 'And very interestingly, it coincides with some Scandinavian market research we've just had in. If you'd like to see me later, to discuss it—'

'Sure!' says Nick with a pleased smile. 'What sort of time?'

'Wait!' To my own astonishment, I leap to my feet in outrage. 'The *Bowling Monthly* ad was my idea. *Wasn't* it, Nick?' I look directly at him.

'Maybe we discussed it,' he says, not meeting my eye. 'I don't really remember. But you know, something you'll have to learn, Emma, is that marketing's all about teamwork . . .'

'Don't patronise me! This wasn't teamwork. It was totally my idea. I put it in for my grandpa!' Damn. I didn't mean to let that slip out.

'First your parents. Now your grandpa,' says Paul, turning to look at me. 'Emma, remind me, is this Bring Your Entire Family To Work week?'

'No! It's just . . .' I begin, a little hot under his gaze. 'You said you were going to axe Panther Bars, so I . . . I thought I'd give him and his friends some money off so they could stock up. I tried to tell you at that meeting, my grandfather loves Panther Bars! And so do all his friends. If you ask me, you should be marketing Panther Bars at *them*, not teenagers.'

There's silence. Paul looks astonished. 'You know, in Scandinavia, they're coming to the same conclusion,' he says. 'So why does this older generation like Panther Bars so much, Emma? Do you know?'

'Yes, of course I know.'

'It's the grey pound,' puts in Nick wisely. 'Demographic shifts in the pensionable population are accounting for—'

'No it's not!' I say impatiently. 'It's because . . .' Oh God, Grandpa will kill me for saying this. 'It's because they don't pull out their false teeth.'

There's a staggered pause. Then Paul throws back his head and roars with laughter. 'False teeth,' he says, wiping his eyes. 'That is sheer bloody genius, Emma. False teeth!'

I feel the blood beating in my head. I've got the strangest feeling. Like something's building up inside me, as though I'm about to—

'So can I have a promotion?'

'What?' Paul looks up.

Did I really just say that? Out loud?

'Can I have a promotion?' My voice is trembling slightly, but I hold firm. 'You said if I created my own opportunities I could have a promotion. That's what you said. Isn't this creating my own opportunities?'

Paul looks at me for a few moments, blinking, saying nothing.

'You know, Emma Corrigan,' he says at last. 'You are one of the most . . . one of the most *surprising* people I've ever known.'

'Is that a yes?' I persist.

There's silence. The entire office waiting to see what he'll say.

'Oh, for God's sake,' he says, rolling his eyes. 'All right! You can have a promotion. Is that it?'

'No,' I hear myself saying, my heart beating even more furiously. 'It was me who jammed the copier that time. In fact . . . all the times. And that bottom . . .' Amid agog faces, I walk to the pin-board and rip down the photocopied, G-stringed bottom. 'That's mine, and I don't want it up there any more.' I swivel round. 'And Artemis, about your spider plant.'

'What?' she says suspiciously.

I stare at her, in her Burberry raincoat and her designer spectacles, and her smug, I'm-better-than-you face.

OK, let's not get carried away. 'I . . . I can't think what's wrong with it.' I smile at her. 'Have a good meeting.'

For the rest of the day, I am totally exhilarated. I'm actually going to be a Marketing Executive! But it's not just that. I feel like a new person. Goodbye old, crap Emma, who hides her Oxfam bags under her desk. Hello new, confident Emma, who proudly hangs them on her chair.

I rang Mum and Dad to tell them I was getting promoted, and they were so impressed! And then I had a nice long chat with Mum about Jack. She said some relationships were supposed to last for ever and some were only supposed to last a few days, and that was just the way life was. Then she told me all about some chap in Paris who she'd had some amazing forty-eight hour fling with. She said she knew it could never last, but that made it all the more poignant.

Then she added I needn't mention any of this to Dad.

Gosh. I'm actually quite shocked. I always thought Mum and Dad . . . At least, I never . . . Well. It just goes to show.

But she is right. Some relationships are meant to be short-lived. Jack and I were obviously never going to get anywhere. And actually, I'm very sorted out about it. In fact, I'm pretty much over him.

My whole new life begins today. I expect I'll meet someone new tonight at Lissy's dancing show. Some tall, dashing lawyer. Yes. And he'll come and pick me up from work in his fab sports car. And I'll trip happily down the steps, not even *looking* at Jack, who will be standing at his office window, glowering . . .

No. Jack won't be anywhere. I am over Jack. I have to remember this. Maybe I'll write it on my hand.

LISSY'S DANCING SHOW is being held in a theatre in Bloomsbury set in a small gravelled courtyard, and when I arrive I find the entire place crammed with lawyers in expensive suits using their mobile phones. No one is making the slightest attempt to go into the auditorium yet, so I head backstage, to give Lissy the bouquet I've bought for her. (I was originally planning to throw it onto the stage at the end, but it's roses, and I'm a bit worried it might ladder her tights.)

I catch sight of Lissy sitting on a stool in one of the dressing rooms. Her face is heavily made up and her eyes are all huge and glittery, and she's got blue feathers in her hair.

'Oh my God, Lissy!' I say, halting in the doorway. 'You look amazing!'

'I can't do it.'

'What?'

'I can't do it!' she repeats desperately, and pulls her cotton robe round her. 'I can't remember anything. My mind is blank!'

Suddenly her face changes expression, and she breaks off and rushes through an adjoining door. The next moment I can hear her retching. She appears again, pale and trembling.

I peer at her anxiously. 'Liss, are you all right?'

'I can't do it,' she says. 'I can't.' She seems to come to a sudden decision. 'OK, I'm going home.' She starts reaching for her clothes.

'You can't!' I say in horror. 'Lissy, you'll be fine! Think about it. How many times have you had to stand up in a big court and make some really long speech in front of loads of people, and if you get it wrong an innocent man might go to jail?'

Lissy stares at me as though I'm crazy. 'Yes, but that's *easy!*'

'Well, if you pull out now, you'll always regret it. You'll always look back and wish you'd gone through with it.'

There's silence. I can practically see Lissy's brain working underneath all the feathers and stuff. 'You're right,' she says at last. 'OK. I'll do it. Just . . . Emma, if I ever say I want to do anything like this again, you have to stop me. Whatever I say. Promise you'll stop me.'

'I promise,' I say hastily. 'I promise.'

Bloody hell. I have never seen Lissy like that before in my life. As I walk back out into the courtyard, I'm thudding with nerves myself. A horrible image comes to me of Lissy standing like a startled rabbit, unable to remember her steps. And the audience just staring at her. The thought of it makes my stomach curdle.

OK. If anything goes wrong I'll pretend to have a heart attack. Everyone will look at me for a few seconds but the performance won't stop because we're British, and by the time everyone turns back to the stage, Lissy will have remembered her steps.

And if they rush me to hospital or anything, I'll just say, 'I had these terrible chest pains!' No one will be able to prove that I didn't.

And even if they *can* prove it, I'll just say—

'Emma.'

'What?' I say absently. And then my heart stops.

Jack is standing ten feet away. As his eyes meet mine, I feel the hurt rushing back into my chest. Don't react, I tell myself. Closure. New life.

'What are you doing here?' I ask.

'I found the flyer for this on your desk.' He lifts a piece of paper, not taking his eyes off mine. 'Emma . . .' He walks forward until he's only a couple of feet away, his face frank. 'What you said. It stayed with me. I should have shared more with you. I shouldn't have shut you out. I owe you an explanation, at least.'

'You owe me nothing!' I lift my chin proudly. 'It's over, Jack. And we might as well both just . . . Aargh! Let go!'

Jack has grabbed my arm. 'I came here tonight for a reason, Emma,' he says gravely. 'I came to tell you what I was doing in Scotland.'

I feel the most almighty bound of shock, which I hide as best I can. 'I'm not interested in what you were doing in Scotland!' I manage, wrenching my arm away.

'Emma, I want to tell you.'

'Well, maybe I don't want to know!' I reply defiantly.

We're facing each other like a pair of duellers. My rib cage is rising and falling quickly.

Of course I want to know. He knows I want to know.

'Go on then,' I say at last, and give a grudging shrug.

In silence, Jack leads me over to a quiet spot, away from all the crowds. As we walk, my bravado ebbs away. In fact, I'm a bit apprehensive. Do I really want to know his secret? What if it's fraud, like Lissy said? What if he's doing something dodgy and wants me to join in?

'OK.' Jack turns to face me. 'Here it is.' He takes a deep breath. 'I was in Scotland to visit someone.'

My heart plummets.

'A woman,' I say before I can stop myself.

'No, not a woman!' His expression changes, and he stares at me. 'Is that what you thought? That I was two-timing you?'

'I . . . didn't know what to think.'

'Emma, I do not have another woman. I was visiting . . .' He hesitates. 'You could call it . . . family.'

My brain gives a huge swivel. *Family?* Oh my God, Jemima was right, I've got involved with a mobster. OK. Don't panic. I can escape. I can go in the witness protection scheme. My new name can be Megan. No, Chloe. Chloe de Souza.

'To be more precise . . . a child.'

A child? My brain lurches again. He has a child?

'Her name is Alice.' He gives a tiny smile. 'She's four years old.'

He has a wife and a family I don't know about, and that's his secret. I knew it, I knew it. 'You . . .' I lick my dry lips. 'You have a child?'

'No, I don't have a child.' Jack stares at the ground for a few seconds. 'Pete had a child. He had a daughter. Alice is Pete Laidler's child.'

'But . . .' I stare at him in confusion. 'But I never knew Pete Laidler had a child.'

'Nobody knows.' He gives me a long look. 'That's the whole idea.'

This is so completely and utterly not what I was expecting.

'But . . . but how can nobody know about her?' I say stupidly. We move even further away from the crowds to sit on a bench.

'Pete was a great guy.' Jack sighs. 'But commitment was never his strong suit. By the time Marie—that's Alice's mom—found out she was pregnant, they weren't even together any more. Pete supported her financially—but he wasn't interested in the child. He didn't even tell anybody he'd become a father.'

'Even you?' I stare at him. 'You didn't know he had a child?'

'Not until after he died.' His face closes up slightly. 'I loved Pete. But that I find very hard to forgive. So a few months after he died, Marie turns up with this baby.' Jack exhales sharply. 'Well. You can imagine how we all felt. But Marie was positive she didn't want anyone to know. She wanted to bring Alice up just like a normal kid, not as Pete Laidler's love child. Not as the heiress to some huge fortune.'

My mind is boggling. A four-year-old getting Pete Laidler's share of the Panther Corporation. 'So she gets everything?' I ask hesitantly.

'Not everything, no. But a lot. Pete's family have been generous. And that's why Marie's keeping her away from the public eye.' He spreads his hands. 'I know it'll come out sooner or later. But when they find out about her, the press will go nuts. She won't be normal any more. Some kids could cope. But not Alice. She has asthma, she's kind of frail.'

As he's speaking, my mind fills with memories of the papers after Pete Laidler died. Every single one had a picture of him on the front page.

'I'm overprotective of this child.' Jack gives a rueful smile. 'I know it. Even Marie tells me I am. But . . . she's all we've got left of Pete.'

I gaze at him, suddenly moved. 'So, is that what the phone calls were about?' I ask tentatively. 'Is that why you had to leave the other night?'

Jack sighs. 'They were both in a road accident a few days ago. It wasn't serious. But . . . we're extrasensitive, after Pete. We just wanted to make sure they got the right treatment.'

'Right.' I give a little wince. 'I can understand that.'

There's silence for a while. My brain is trying to slot all the pieces together. Trying to work it all out. 'But why did you make me keep it a secret that you'd been in Scotland? Nobody would know, surely.'

Jack rolls his eyes ruefully. 'That was my own dumb stupid fault. I'd told some people I was going across to Paris that day. Then I walk into the office . . . and there you are.'

'Your heart sank.'

'Not exactly.' He meets my eyes. 'It didn't know which way to go.'

I feel a sudden colour coming to my cheeks and awkwardly clear my throat. 'So, er . . .' I say, looking away. 'So that's why . . .'

'All I wanted was to avoid you piping up, "Hey, he wasn't in Paris, he was in Scotland!" and start some huge intrigue going.' Jack shakes his head. 'You'd be amazed at the ludicrous theories people will put together when they don't have anything better to do. I'm planning to sell the company . . . I'm gay . . . I'm in the Mafia . . .'

'Er . . . really?' I say. 'Gosh. How stupid of people!'

'Emma, I'm sorry I couldn't tell you this before,' Jack says in a low voice. 'I know you were hurt. I know it felt like I was shutting you out. But . . . it's just not something you share lightly.'

'No!' I say immediately. 'Of course you couldn't have done. I was stupid.' I scuff my toe awkwardly on the gravel, feeling a bit shamefaced. I should have known it would be something important.

'Only a handful of people know about this.' Jack meets my eyes gravely. 'A handful of special, trusted people.'

There's something in his gaze that makes my throat feel a bit tight. I stare back at him, feeling blood rising in my cheeks.

'Are you going in?' We jump, and look up to see a woman in black jeans approaching. 'The performance is about to start!' she says.

'I . . . I have to go and watch Lissy dancing,' I say.

'Right. Well, I'll leave you then. That was really all I had to say.' Slowly Jack gets to his feet, then turns back. 'There's one more thing.' He looks at me for a few silent moments. 'Emma, I realise these last few days can't have been easy for you. You have been the model of discretion throughout, whereas I . . . have not. And I just wanted to apologise. Again.'

'That's . . . that's OK,' I manage.

Jack turns again, and I watch him walking slowly away over the gravel. He came all the way here to tell me his secret. His big, precious secret. He didn't have to do that. Oh God. Oh God . . .

'Wait!' I hear myself calling out, and Jack immediately turns. 'Would you . . . like to come too?'

And his face creases into a smile.

As we crunch over the gravel together, I feel a little shaft, half of hope, half of apprehension. For a long while neither of us says anything. I'm breathing rather fast.

Suddenly Jack's gaze falls with interest on my hand. 'I am over Jack,' he reads aloud.

Fuck. My entire face flames with colour.

I am never writing anything on my hand again. Ever.

'That's just . . .' I clear my throat again. 'That was just a doodle. It—'

A shrill ring from my mobile interrupts me. Thank God.

'Emma, you're going to love me for ever!' comes Jemima's piercing tones. 'I've sorted everything out for you!' she says triumphantly.

'*What?*' I feel a twinge of alarm. 'Jemima, what are you talking about?'

'Getting your revenge on Jack Harper, silly! Since you were just sitting there like a total wimp, I've taken matters into my own hands.'

For a moment I can't quite move. 'Er, Jack, excuse me a minute.' I shoot him a bright smile. 'I just need to . . . take this call.' With trembling legs I hurry to the corner of the courtyard, well away from earshot.

'Jemima, you promised you wouldn't do anything!' I hiss. 'You swore on your Miu Miu ponyskin bag, remember?'

'I haven't *got* a Miu Miu ponyskin bag!' she crows triumphantly. 'I've got a *Fendi* ponyskin bag!'

She's mad. She's completely mad.

'Jemima, what have you done?' I demand. 'Tell me what you've done.'

'An eye for an eye, Emma! Now, I'm sitting here with a very nice chap called Mick. He's a journalist, he writes for the *Daily World* . . .'

My blood runs cold.

'A *tabloid journalist?*' I manage at last. 'Jemima, are you *insane?*'

'Don't be so narrow-minded and suburban,' she scolds. 'Tabloid journalists are our *friends*. They're like private detectives, but for free! Mick's done loads of work for Mummy before. He's marvellous at tracking things down. And he's *very* interested in finding out Jack Harper's little secret. I've told him all we know, but he'd like a word with you.'

I feel quite faint. This cannot be happening.

'Jemima, listen to me. I don't want to find out Jack's secret, OK? I just want to forget it. You have to stop this guy.'

'I won't!' she says like a petulant six-year-old. 'Emma, don't be so pathetic! Mummy always says—' There's the sudden screeching of tyres. 'Oops! Tiny prang. I'll call you back.'

The phone goes dead.

I am numb with horror. Frantically I jab her number into my phone, but it clicks straight onto messages.

'Jemima,' I say as soon as it beeps. 'Jemima, you have to stop this! You have to—' I stop abruptly as Jack appears in front of me.

'It's about to start,' he says. 'Everything all right?'

'Fine,' I say in a strangled voice. 'Everything's . . . fine.'

As I walk into the auditorium I'm almost light-headed with panic. What have I done? I have given away Jack's most precious secret in the world to a morally warped, revenge-wreaking, Prada-wearing nutcase.

OK. Just calm down, I tell myself. She doesn't actually know anything. This journalist probably won't find out anything.

But what if he does? What if he somehow stumbles on the truth? And Jack discovers it was me who pointed them in the right direction? I feel ill at the thought. *Why* did I ever mention Scotland to Jemima? *Why?*

New resolution: I am never giving away a secret again. Never, ever.

In fact . . . I am never talking again, full stop. All talking ever seems to do is get me into trouble. If I hadn't opened my mouth on that stupid plane in the first place, I wouldn't be in this mess. I'll become a mute.

'Is this Lissy?' says Jack, pointing to a name in the programme, and I jump in fright. I follow his gaze, then give a silent nod.

'Do you know anyone else in the show?' he asks.

I give a 'who knows?' shrug.

'So . . . how long has Lissy been practising?'

I hesitate, then hold up three fingers.

'Three?' Jack peers at me uncertainly. 'Three what?'

I make a little gesture with my hands that is supposed to indicate 'months'. Then I make it again. Jack looks totally baffled.

I feel in my pocket for a pen—but I haven't got one. OK, forget not talking. 'About three months,' I say out loud.

'Right.' Jack nods, and turns back to the programme. His face is calm and unsuspecting, and I can feel guilty nerves rising through me again.

OK. Think rationally. I'll just keep trying Jemima's mobile and as soon as I get through I'll explain in words of one syllable that she has to call this guy off and if she doesn't I will break her legs.

A low, insistent drumbeat starts playing over the loudspeakers and I give a start of fright. I'm so distracted, I'd actually forgotten what we were here for. The auditorium is becoming completely dark, and around us the audience falls silent with anticipation. The beating increases in volume but nothing happens on stage; it's still pitch-black.

Pow! Suddenly there's a gasp as a dazzling light fills the auditorium. Music fills the air, and a figure appears on stage in a black, glittering costume, twirling and leaping. Gosh, whoever it is, they're amazing.

Oh my God. It's Lissy.

I am pinioned to my seat by shock. Everything else has been swept away from my mind. I cannot keep my eyes off Lissy.

I had no idea she could do this. No idea! I mean, we did a bit of ballet together. And a bit of tap. But we never . . . How can I have known someone for over twenty years and have no idea they could dance?

She just did this amazing slow, sinewy dance with a guy in a mask who I guess is Jean-Paul, and now she's leaping and spinning around with this ribbon thing, and the whole audience is staring at her, agog, and she looks completely radiant. I'm *so* proud of her.

To my horror, tears start to prick my eyes. And now my nose is starting to run. I don't even have a tissue. This is so embarrassing.

I feel something nudging my hand. I look up, and Jack's offering me a hanky. As I take it from him, his fingers curl briefly round mine.

When the performance comes to an end, I'm on a total high. Lissy takes a star bow and both Jack and I applaud madly, grinning at each other.

'Don't tell anyone I cried,' I say, above the sound of applause.

'I won't,' says Jack, and gives me a rueful smile. 'I promise.'

At the exit, people are streaming across the courtyard to a lit-up room on the other side.

'Lissy said I should meet her at the party,' I say to Jack. 'So, er . . . why don't you go on? I just need to make a quick call.'

'Are you OK?' asks Jack, giving me a curious look. 'You seem jumpy.'

'I'm fine!' I say. 'Just excited.'

I wait until he's safely out of earshot, then dial Jemima's number. Straight onto messages. I dial it again, trying to ignore my thrusting panic. Messages again.

OK. I'll just have to go to the party and act normally, keep trying her on the phone and, if all else fails, wait until I see her later. There's nothing else I can do. It'll be fine. It'll be fine.

The party is huge and bright and noisy. I take a glass of wine and start edging into the crowd. Suddenly I spot Lissy, looking flushed and shiny and surrounded by a load of good-looking lawyer-type guys, one of whom is blatantly staring at her legs.

'Lissy!' I cry. She turns round and I give her a huge hug. 'I had no idea you could dance like that! You were amazing!'

'Oh no. I wasn't,' she says at once, and pulls a typical Lissy-face. 'I completely messed up—'

'Stop!' I interrupt. 'Lissy, it was utterly fantastic. *You* were fantastic.'

'But I was completely crap in the—'

'*Don't* say you were crap!' I practically yell. 'You were fantastic. Say it. *Say* it, Lissy.'

'Well . . . OK.' Her face reluctantly creases into a smile. 'OK. I was . . . fantastic!' She gives an elated laugh. 'Emma, I've never felt so good in my life! And guess what, we're already planning to go on tour next year.'

'But . . .' I stare at her. 'You said you never wanted to do this again, ever, and if you mentioned it again, I had to stop you.'

'Oh, that was just stage fright,' she says with an airy wave of her hand. Then she lowers her voice. 'I saw Jack, by the way.' She gives me an avid look. 'What's going on?'

My heart gives a huge thump. Should I tell her about Jemima? No. She'll only get all hassled. 'Jack came here to talk to me.' I hesitate. 'To . . . tell me his secret.'

'You're joking!' breathes Lissy, hand to her mouth. 'So—what is it?'

'I can't tell you.'

'You can't *tell* me?' Lissy stares at me in incredulity. 'After all that, you're not even going to *tell* me?'

'Lissy, I really can't.' I pull an agonised face. 'It's . . . complicated.'

'Well, all right,' says Lissy a bit grumpily. 'I suppose I can live without knowing. So . . . are you two together again?'

'I dunno,' I say, flushing. 'Maybe.'

'Lissy! That was fabulous!' A couple of girls in suits appear at her side. I give her a smile and move away slightly as she greets them.

Jack is nowhere to be seen. Should I try Jemima again?

Surreptitiously I start getting out my phone, then hastily put it away again as I hear a voice behind me calling 'Emma!'

I look round, and give a huge start of surprise. 'Connor! What are you doing here?' I say in astonishment.

'Lissy sent me a flyer,' he replies. 'I'm glad I've run into you,' he adds awkwardly. 'I'd like to talk to you, if I may.'

He draws me towards the door, away from the main crowd.

'Emma.' He clears his throat as though he's about to start a formal speech. 'I get the feeling that you weren't always . . . totally honest with me in our relationship.'

This could be the understatement of the year.

'You're right,' I admit, shamefacedly. 'Oh God, Connor—'

'It doesn't matter. That's water under the bridge. But I'd be grateful if you were totally honest with me now.'

'Absolutely,' I say, nodding earnestly. 'Of course.'

'I've recently . . . started a new relationship. Her name's Francesca.'

'Good for you!' I say. 'Connor, I'm really pleased. Where did you—?'

'I wanted to ask you about sex,' Connor says, cutting me off in a rush of embarrassment.

'Oh! Right.' I feel a twinge of dismay.

'Were you honest with me in bed?' His face is growing pillar-box red. 'Or were you faking it?'

Oh no. Is that what he thinks? 'Connor, I never ever faked an orgasm with you,' I say, lowering my voice. 'Hand on heart. I never did.'

'OK.' He rubs his nose. 'But did you fake anything else?'

I look at him uncertainly. 'I'm not sure I know what you—'

'Were there any'—he clears his throat—'any particular techniques I used that you only pretended to enjoy?'

Oh God. *Please* don't ask me that question.

'You know, I really . . . can't remember!' I hedge.

'Emma, tell me!' he says, with sudden passion. 'I'm starting a new relationship. I should be able to . . . to learn from past mistakes.'

I gaze back at his shiny face and suddenly feel a huge pang of guilt. He's right. I should be honest. I should finally be honest with him.

'OK,' I say, and move closer to him. 'You remember that *slidey* thing you used to do with your tongue? Well, sometimes that kind of made me want to . . . laugh. So if I had one tip, it would be don't do—'

His expression changes. Fuck. He's already done it.

'Francesca said . . .' Connor says in a voice as stiff as a board. 'Francesca told me that really turned her on.'

'Well, I'm sure it did!' I backtrack madly. 'Women are all different.'

'She said she loved jazz, too. Was she *lying*?' He stares at me bewilderedly. 'Do *all* women have secrets?'

Oh no. Have I ruined Connor's trust in all of womankind for ever?

'Of course they don't!' I exclaim. 'Honestly—' My words wither on my lips as I glimpse a familiar flash of blonde hair at the hall's entrance.

My heart stops. That can't be—

'Connor, I have to go,' I say, and start hurrying towards the door.

'She told me she's size ten!' Connor calls helplessly after me. 'What does that mean? What size should I really buy?'

'Twelve!' I shoot back over my shoulder.

It is. It's Jemima. Standing in the foyer. What's she doing here?

The door opens again and I experience such a shock, I feel faint. She's got a guy with her. He's got a camera and is looking around interestedly.

No. She can't have done.

'Emma,' comes a voice in my ear.

'Jack!' I wheel round, to see him smiling down at me, his dark eyes full of affection.

'You OK?' he says, and gently touches my nose.

'Fine!' I say a little shrilly. 'I'm great!'

I have to manage this situation. I have to.

'Jack—could you get me some water?' I hear myself saying. 'I'll just stay here. I'm feeling a bit dizzy.'

Jack looks alarmed. 'You know, I thought there was something wrong. Let me take you home. I'll call the car.'

'No. It's . . . it's fine. I want to stay. Just get me some water. Please,' I add as an afterthought.

As soon as he's gone I tear into the foyer, almost tripping in my haste.

'Emma!' Jemima looks up brightly. 'Excellent! I was just about to look for you. Now, this is Mick, and he wants to ask you some questions.' She heads into a small, empty office that leads off from the foyer.

'No!' I say, grabbing her arm. 'Jemima, you have to go. Now. Go!'

'I'm not going anywhere!' Jemima jerks her arm out of my grasp and rolls her eyes at Mick, who's closing the door of the office behind me. 'I told you she was being all hissy about it.'

'Mick Collins,' Mick thrusts a business card into my hand. 'Delighted to meet you, Emma. Now, there's no need to get worried, is there?'

'Look, there's been a misunderstanding,' I say, forcing myself to sound polite. 'I'm afraid there's no story.'

'Well, let's see about that, shall we?' says Mick with a friendly smile.

'No!' I turn to Jemima. 'I told you I didn't want you to do anything. You promised me!'

'Emma, you are such a wimp.' She gives Mick an exasperated look. 'Do you see why I've been forced to take action? I told you what a bastard Jack Harper was to her. He needs to learn his lesson.'

'Absolutely right,' agrees Mick and puts his head on one side as though measuring me up. 'Very attractive,' he says to Jemima. 'We could think about an accompanying interview feature. My romp with top boss. You could make some serious money,' he adds to me.

'No!' I say in horror.

'Emma, stop being so coy!' snaps Jemima. 'You want to do it really. This could be a whole new career for you, you realise.'

'I don't want a new career!'

'Well then you should! Do you *know* how much Monica Lewinsky makes a year?'

'You're sick,' I say in disbelief. 'You're a totally sick, warped—'

'Emma, I'm just acting in your best interests.'

'You're not!' I cry, feeling my face flame red. 'I . . . I might be getting back together with Jack!'

There's a thirty-second silence. I stare at her, holding my breath. Then it's as if the killer robot jerks into action again, shooting yet more rays.

'Even *more* reason to do it!' says Jemima. 'This'll keep him on his toes. This'll show him who's boss. Go on, Mick.'

'Interview with Emma Corrigan. Tuesday, fifteenth of July, nine forty pm.' Mick has produced a small tape recorder and is holding it towards me. 'You first met Jack Harper on a plane. Can you confirm where this was flying from and to?' He gives me a soothing smile.

'Stop it!' I yell. 'Just leave! Leave!'

'Emma, grow up,' says Jemima impatiently. 'Mick's going to find out what this secret is whether you help him or not, so you might as well be—' She stops abruptly as the door handle rattles, then turns.

The room seems to swim around me.

As the door slowly opens, I can't breathe. I can't move.

'Emma?' says Jack, coming in, holding two glasses of water in one hand. 'Are you feeling OK? I got you both still and sparkling because I wasn't quite . . .' His voice dies away. With a flicker of bewilderment he takes in Mick's card, still in my hand. Then his gaze falls on the turning tape recorder and something slides out of his face.

'I think I'll just make myself scarce,' murmurs Mick. He sidles out of the room. Nobody speaks for a few moments.

'Who was that?' says Jack at last. 'A journalist?' He looks as though someone just stamped on his garden.

'I . . . Jack . . .' I say huskily. 'It's not . . . it's not . . .'

'Why . . . ?' He rubs his brow, as though trying to make sense of the situation. 'Why were you talking to a journalist?'

'Why do you *think* she was talking to a journalist?' chimes in Jemima.

'What?' Jack's gaze swivels to her with dislike.

'You think you're such a big-shot millionaire! You think you can use little people. You think you can give away someone's private secrets and completely humiliate them and get away with it. Well, you can't!'

She takes a few steps towards him, lifting her chin with satisfaction. 'Emma's been waiting for a chance to get her revenge on you, and now she's found it! That *was* a journalist, if you want to know. And he's on your case. And when you find your little Scottish secret plastered all over the papers, then maybe *you'll* know what it feels like to be betrayed! And maybe you'll be sorry. Tell him, Emma! Tell him!'

But I'm paralysed.

The minute she said the word Scottish I saw Jack's face change. It kind of snapped. He almost seemed winded with shock. He looked straight at me and I could see the growing disbelief in his eyes.

'You might think you know Emma, but you don't,' Jemima is continuing. 'You underestimated her, Jack Harper.'

Shut up! I'm screaming internally. *It's not true! I would never . . .*

But nothing in my body will move. I can't even swallow. I'm pinioned, staring helplessly at him with a face I know is covered with guilt.

Jack turns on his heel, pushes the door open and walks out.

For a moment there's silence in the tiny room.

'That showed him!' says Jemima, smacking her hands triumphantly.

It's as though she breaks the spell. Suddenly I can move again. I can draw breath. 'You . . .' I'm almost shaking too much to speak. 'You stupid . . . stupid . . . thoughtless . . . bitch!'

The door bursts open and Lissy appears, wide-eyed.

'What the hell happened here?' she demands. 'I just saw Jack storming out. He looked absolutely like thunder!'

'She brought a journalist here!' I say in anguish, gesturing at Jemima. 'A bloody tabloid journalist. And Jack found us all closeted here, and he thinks . . . God know what he thinks.'

'You stupid cow!' Lissy slaps Jemima across the face.

'Ow! I was helping Emma get vengeance on her enemy.'

'He's not my *enemy*, you stupid . . .' I'm on the verge of tears. 'Lissy . . . what am I going to do? What?'

'Go,' she says. 'You can still catch him. Go.'

I pelt out of the door and through the courtyard, my chest rising and falling rapidly, my lungs burning. When I reach the road I look frantically left and right. Then I spot him, down the road.

'Jack, wait.'

He's striding along with his mobile phone to his ear, and at my voice he turns round with a taut face.

'So that's why you were so interested in Scotland.'

'No!' I say, aghast. 'No! Listen, Jack, they don't know. All Jemima knows is that you were there. She was bluffing. I haven't said anything.'

Jack gives me a long look, then starts striding again.

'It was Jemima who called that guy, not me!' I cry desperately, running after him. 'I was trying to stop her . . . Jack, you know me! You *know* I would never do this to you. Yes, I told Jemima about you being in Scotland. I was hurt, and I was angry, and it . . . came out. And that was a mistake. But . . . but you made a mistake too, and I forgave you.'

He's not even looking at me. He's not even giving me a chance. His silver car pulls up at the pavement and he opens the passenger door.

'Jack, that's not why I asked about Scotland! I didn't want to *sell* your secret!' Tears are streaming down my face. 'I didn't even want to *know* such a big secret. I just wanted to know your little secrets! I just wanted to know you . . . like you know me.'

But he doesn't look round. The car door closes with a heavy clunk, and the car moves away. And I'm left on the pavement, all alone.

A spasm of pain runs through my body and I close my eyes, almost unable to bear it. If I could just turn back time . . . if I'd been more forceful . . . if I'd marched Jemima and her friend off the premises . . . if I'd spoken up more quickly when Jack appeared . . .

But I didn't. And it's too late. I force myself to turn around and make my way slowly back up to the party.

I find Lissy and Jemima still in the little office, Jemima cowering in terror as Lissy lays into her.

'. . . selfish immature little bitch! You make me sick, you know that?'

I once heard someone say Lissy was a Rottweiler in court, and I could never understand it. But now, as I watch her striding up and down, her eyes blazing in fury, I'm actually pretty scared myself.

'Emma, make her stop shouting at me!' pleads Jemima.

'So . . . what happened?' Lissy looks at me, her face alight with hope.

'He's gone,' I say in a wobbly voice, and take a deep breath. 'Where's her friend?' I jerk my thumb at Jemima.

'He got thrown out,' says Lissy with satisfaction. 'He was trying to take a picture of Justice Hugh Morris in his tights.'

'Jemima, listen to me.' I force myself to meet her unrepentant blue gaze. 'You cannot let him find out any more. You *cannot*.'

'It's OK,' she says sulkily. 'I've already spoken to him. Lissy made me. He won't pursue it.'

'How do you know?'

'He won't do anything that would piss Mummy off. He has a pretty lucrative arrangement with her.'

'Jemima, this is a warning. If anything of this gets out—*anything* at all—I will tell everyone you got your Donna Karan coat from a discount warehouse shop.'

Jemima gasps in horror. 'I didn't!' she says.

'You did. I saw the carrier bag,' Lissy chimes in. '*And* we'll make it public that you never really cook the food at your dinner parties.'

Jemima claps a hand over her mouth.

'. . . and your pearls are cultured, not real . . .'

'. . . and that photo of you meeting Prince William is faked . . .'

'OK!' says Jemima, practically in tears. 'OK! I promise I'll forget all about it. I promise. Can I go now?' She looks imploringly at Lissy.

'Yes, you can go,' says Lissy contemptuously, and Jemima scuttles out.

As the door closes, I stare at Lissy. 'Is that photo of Jemima and Prince William really faked?'

'Yes! Didn't I tell you? I once did some stuff for her on her computer, and I opened the file by mistake—and there it was. She just pasted her head onto some other girl's body!'

I can't help giving a giggle. Then I sink into a chair, feeling suddenly weak, and for a while there's silence.

'Wouldn't he even listen?' says Lissy at last.

'No. He just left.'

'But he gave away *all* your secrets. You only gave away one of his.'

'You don't understand. What Jack told me, it's not just anything. It's something really precious to him. He came all the way here to tell me. To show me that he trusted me with it.' I swallow hard. 'And the next moment he finds me spilling it to a journalist.'

'But you weren't!' says Lissy loyally. 'Emma, this wasn't your fault!'

'It was!' Tears are welling up in my eyes. 'If I'd just kept my mouth closed, if I'd never told Jemima anything in the first place . . .'

'She would have got him anyway,' says Lissy. 'He'd be suing you for a scraped car instead. Or damaged genitals.'

The door bursts open and a guy looks in. 'Lissy! There you are. They're serving food.'

'Thanks, Colin.' She turns to me. 'Do you want something to eat?'

'I'm not really hungry,' I say. 'But you go. I'll . . . just go home.' I try to smile as cheerfully as I can. 'Don't worry, Lissy, I'll be fine.'

And I am planning to go home. But when I get outside I find I can't bring myself to. Instead, I head towards the auditorium. The door is unlocked and I walk straight in and make my way to a seat. And as I stare at the silent blackness of the empty stage, two fat tears make their way out of my eyes. I cannot believe I've fucked up so monumentally. I can't believe Jack really thinks I would—

Suddenly there's a creaking sound. The door is slowly opening.

I peer uncertainly through the gloom as a figure comes into the auditorium and stops. In spite of myself, my heart starts to thud with unbearable hope. It's Jack. It has to be Jack. He's come to find me.

There's a long, agonising silence. I'm taut with apprehension. Why won't he say anything? Why won't he speak?

'Oh Francesca . . .'

'Connor . . .'

What? I peer again, more sharply, and feel a crash of disappointment. I am such a moron. It's not Jack. It's not one figure, it's two. It's Connor and what must be his new girlfriend—and they're snogging.

'Do you like this?' I hear Connor murmuring.

'Mmm . . .'

'Do you really like it?'

'Of course I do! Stop quizzing me!'

'Francesca, be honest, OK?' Connor's voice rises in agitation. 'Because if that means no, then—'

'It doesn't mean no! Connor, what's your problem?'

'My problem is, I don't believe you.'

'Why the hell don't you believe me?' She sounds furious.

Suddenly I'm filled with remorse. This is all my fault. Not only have I wrecked my own relationship, now I've wrecked theirs too.

I clear my throat. 'Er . . . excuse me?'

'Who the fuck's that?' says Francesca sharply. 'Is someone there?'

'It's me. Emma. Connor's ex-girlfriend.'

A row of lights goes on, and I see a girl with red hair staring at me belligerently, with her hand on the light switch.

'What the hell are you doing? *Spying* on us?'

'No!' I say. 'Look, I'm sorry. I didn't mean to . . . I couldn't help overhearing . . .' I swallow. 'The thing is, Connor isn't being difficult. He just wants you to be honest.' I summon up my most understanding, womanly expression. 'Francesca . . . tell him what you want.'

Francesca stares at me incredulously, then looks at Connor.

'I want her to piss off.' She points at me.

'Oh,' I say, taken aback. 'Er, OK. Sorry.'

Hastily I pick up my bag and hurry towards the exit, flicking the light switch as I pass, then step out into the courtyard.

I freeze. I don't believe it. It's Jack.

It's Jack, coming towards me, striding fast across the courtyard, determination on his face. I haven't got time to think, or prepare.

He reaches me with a crunch of gravel, takes me by the shoulders, and gives me a long, intense look. 'I'm afraid of the dark.'

'What?' I falter.

'I'm afraid of the dark. Always have been. I keep a baseball bat under the bed, just in case.'

I stare at him in utter bewilderment. 'Jack—'

'I've never liked caviar. I got the scar on my wrist by cracking open a bottle of beer when I was fourteen. When I was a kid I used to stick gum under my Aunt Francine's dining table. I lost my virginity to a girl named Lisa Greenwood in her uncle's barn, and afterwards I asked if I could keep her bra to show my friends.'

I can't help giving a snuffle of laughter, but Jack carries on regardless, his gaze fixed on mine.

'I've never worn any of the ties my mother has given me for Christmas. I've always wanted to be an inch or two taller than I am. I . . . I don't know what codependent means.' He draws breath and gazes at me. His eyes are darker than I've ever seen them. 'I met a girl on a plane. And . . . my whole life changed as a result.'

Something hot is welling up inside me. My throat is tight, my whole head aching. I'm trying so hard not to cry, but my face is contorting all by itself. 'Jack,' I swallow desperately. 'I didn't . . . I really didn't . . .'

'I know,' he cuts me off with a nod. 'I know you didn't.'

'I would never—'

'I know you wouldn't,' he says gently. 'I know you wouldn't.'

And now I can't help it, tears start flooding out of my eyes in sheer relief. 'So . . .' I wipe my face, trying to gain control of myself. 'So does this mean . . . that we . . . ?' I can't bring myself to say the words.

There's a long, unbearable silence.

'Well, you might want to hold back on your decision,' says Jack at last, and gives me a deadpan look. 'Because I have a lot more to tell you. And it isn't all pretty.'

I give a shaky laugh. 'You don't have to tell me anything.'

'Oh, I do,' says Jack firmly. 'I think I do. Shall we walk?' He holds out an arm, and after a pause, I take it.

'So . . . where was I?' he says, as we step down into the courtyard. 'Oh, OK. Now this you really *can't* tell anybody.' He leans close and lowers his voice. 'I don't actually like Panther Cola. I prefer Pepsi.'

'No!' I say, shocked.

'In fact, sometimes I decant Pepsi *into* a Panther can—'

'No!' I give a snort of laughter.

'It's true. I told you it wasn't pretty . . .'

Slowly we start to walk around the edge of the dark, empty courtyard together. The only sound is the crunching of our feet on the gravel, and Jack's dry voice, talking. Telling me everything.

It's amazing what a different person I am these days. I'm a new Emma. Far more open than I used to be. Far more honest. Because what I've really learned is, if you can't be honest with your friends and colleagues and loved ones, then what is life all about?

The *only* secrets I have nowadays are tiny little essential ones. And I hardly have any of those. I could probably count them on the fingers of one hand. I mean, just off the top of my head:

1. That Greek-style cake Lissy made for my birthday was the most disgusting thing I've ever tasted.
2. I borrowed Jemima's Ralph Lauren swimsuit to go on holiday with Mum and Dad and bust one of the straps.
3. I had this really weird dream last week, about Lissy and Sven.
4. I've secretly started feeding Artemis's spider plant 'Rebuild' plant food.
5. I'm *sure* Sammy the goldfish has changed again. Where did that extra fin come from?
6. I know I have to stop giving out my 'Emma Corrigan, Marketing Executive' card to strangers, but I just can't help it.
7. Last night, when Jack said 'What are you thinking about?' and I said 'Oh nothing . . .' that wasn't quite true. I was actually planning the names of all our children.

But the thing is, it's completely normal to have the odd little secret from your boyfriend. Everyone knows that.

SOPHIE KINSELLA

Sophie Kinsella, like her heroine Emma Corrigan, knows all about keeping secrets and has only just revealed the most astonishing one about herself. 'I'm actually someone else!' she recently disclosed. Having written several family dramas under her real name, Madeleine Wickham, she had decided that she wanted to write something more light-hearted. 'But I thought that my publishers might discourage me, so I decided to submit the book under a pseudonym.' Her first Sophie Kinsella novel, *The Secret Dreamworld of a Shopoholic*, was a runaway success, and she has since written two more *Shopoholic* novels.

The inspiration for *Can You Keep a Secret?* had been in the back of the author's mind for some time. 'Maybe it was due to keeping my own secret for so long but I just loved the idea of someone becoming so frightened in a situation—and a plane is such a falsely intimate setting—that they would bare their every secret to a complete stranger. It doesn't really matter because you know that you are never going to see them again. But then, "Oh my God. It's him!"'

Life for Sophie Kinsella/Madeleine Wickham is extremely busy. She is a wife and mother to two young sons, Freddy and Hugo, and when I met her she was preparing for a book promotion tour in New York and then Canada. 'It's hard leaving my family,' she told me. 'But it's all part of

being an author these days. For months you sit at home, all alone, writing your novel, and then, once it is finished, you have to become a very public person. It's quite a contrast. Once, after my first *Shopoholic* novel was published, I was asked to be the "entertainment" at a company Christmas party. I guess, because I write comedy, they thought I was also a stand-up comedienne! Which I most definitely am not. I was tempted to accept just to see the look on their faces when I simply read out passages from my book!'

The film option for *Can You Keep a Secret?* has recently been bought by Paramount Pictures and the author is keeping her fingers crossed that the film actually gets made. 'I've had a number of my books optioned for either telly or film but I really hope that this one makes it, as the story would work so well dramatised.'

And she should know. She is currently writing a screenplay in conjunction with Rocket Pictures, Elton John's film company. 'It's early days yet, but it is called *Seven Ways to Keep Your Wife* and it is, of course, a romantic comedy, but written from the man's point of view.'

Now that Sophie Kinsella is such a success story, I wonder whether the author will ever write as Madeleine Wickham again? 'Who knows?' she answered, with a smile. 'Maybe. Or I might possibly reinvent myself all over again!'

Jane Eastgate

ROSIE THOMAS

If My Father Loved Me

When Sadie learns that her father is dying she rushes to his bedside. As she sits holding his hand, she knows there is much that is left unsaid between them, much that she still does not understand about their shared past. And she knows, too, that the cold, aloof relationship she had with her father has affected all her male relationships—especially with her son Jack. Can Sadie change the pattern of the past?

ONE

'MY FATHER WAS A PERFUMER and a con artist,' I said. 'You would like him. All women do.'

I was telling Mel this, my dear friend Mel, on what was then still an ordinary night.

We had arranged to meet in a new restaurant and I had got off the tube one stop early and walked for ten minutes to reach it. It was that tender time between winter and very early summer that is too fragile and understated, in the city, to count as a proper spring. The sky was pale grey, almost opalescent, and shafts of light like cathedral pillars struck down between the concrete buildings.

When I arrived Mel was already at the table, waiting for me. She was wearing her leather jacket and her hair frizzed out in black spirals all round her face. Her trademark red lipstick was still fresh, not yet blotted with eating and drinking. She stood up when she saw me and we hugged, laughing with the pleasure of seeing one another and to acknowledge the small festivity of a new restaurant, the stealthy approach of summer and also the fact that life was kind to us both.

As we sat down Mel said, 'Let's get a bottle of wine and order some food, then we can talk.'

Mel and I have been saying this, or a near version of it, all through the five years that have gone by since we met. The talk is always the most important ingredient, although food and wine are right up there too. It was our interest in cooking that brought us together, on a week's master class hosted by a celebrity chef at some chichi hotel in the

Midlands. The first time I saw Mel she was wearing her black curls bundled up under a white cook's cap in a way that was all about business and nothing about looking fetching, and I liked her immediately. She was quietly laying out her knives while our fellow students were crowded up at the front trying to catch the chef's attention. (And that was just the *men*, Mel said.)

She looked confident and successful. It turned out that she knew how to cook and wasn't afraid of the bad-tempered prima donna who was supposedly there to inspire us. I wasn't the only one who warmed to her, as it turned out, but it was to my room that she brought a bottle of wine on the second evening and it was to me she chose to open her heart. I learned that Mel Archer was trying to come to terms with the knowledge that she was never going to have a child of her own, let alone replicate her fecund mother's perfect family. It was causing her pain, like a bereavement.

In my turn I told her that I was newly divorced. I was hard up and quite depressed and I had a daughter who was trying single-handedly to re-create the cliché of the teen rebel queen, as well as a six-year-old son who was going through an awkward phase. The one that had lasted since he was four days old.

We were both going through a difficult time in our lives.

'We should swap problems,' Mel said.

She made me laugh, and we opened another bottle and the talk went on. At the week's end we came back to London with some overblown new recipes, a shared sense of relief that we would never have to work in a commercial kitchen under our master chef's direction, and a friendship that would endure.

'What are you going to eat?' Mel asked now, as we studied the menu.

'The pasta, I think.'

I always choose what I want to eat very quickly. While I waited for Mel I looked down the line of tables. On one side was a noisy quartet of old friends; on the other were three young women, one of whom was leaning forward through a veil of cigarette smoke to say to the others, 'Just wait and see, he'll be regretting it within, like, six weeks.' The red nail polish she was wearing looked the same shade as Mel's lipstick.

'What do you think of this menu?' Mel was saying. 'Scallops and mushrooms is always a good combination, I'm going to have that.'

A young waiter took our order and Mel chose a bottle of Fleurie from the list. A different waiter came and poured the wine. We clinked our glasses before we drank.

'How's Jack?' Mel asked. She shook a Marlboro out of the packet and lit it, then leaned back in her chair to look at me. Jack is my son.

'Not bad,' I said cautiously. 'And Adrian?'

'So-so.'

Adrian was Mel's current boyfriend, if that's a word you can still use when you aren't young any more. Mel and I have both turned fifty and we are therefore invisible except in the technical sense to, say, the nice-looking young waiter who took our order.

I don't remember anyone mentioning the fact to me when I was as young as my daughter Lola, but you don't feel yourself growing older. You reach an age—which probably varies according to your personal circumstances, but in my case was twenty-seven—and there you are, fully formed. And inside my skin I remain twenty-seven years old. It's a shock, when riding the escalator in Selfridges or somewhere, to confront an unexpected mirror and be obliged to check the discrepancy.

We've talked about this, of course, Mel and I. Being invisible to waiters doesn't bother us. What is alarming is the possibility that when we do start to feel our age, it might all happen at once. What if we go from being twenty-seven to being sixty-seven in a day, suddenly crumbling into old ladies as the light falls on us like Rider Haggard's *She*?

Joking about our worries is something we have always been able to do together. What else should we do?

I lifted my glass of wine again. 'Here's to now,' I said.

Being old hasn't happened yet, that's what the toast means, in spite of our awareness that it will, that it must.

'To now,' Mel echoed happily.

The waiter came with our food. We sampled our own portions and then traded forkfuls. Mel chewed attentively and pronounced my ravioli stuffed with aubergine to be drab, and I agreed with her.

'Go on,' I said.

We had started talking about Adrian and I was watching her face as she relayed her concerns. I also wanted to enjoy the restaurant's brightness and the animated faces of the other diners.

And there is another presence, too. A shadow at the back of the room, a black silhouette beyond the restaurant plate glass, waiting.

I can smell him, even, although I haven't put the awareness anywhere close to words. It's still only premonition, a cloudy scent stirring in the chambers of my head, but he is *there*.

I don't know it yet but it's not an ordinary night.

Mel sighed. 'You know, Adrian always makes me feel that he would like me to pat his cheek and say *well done*, or on the other hand *don't worry*. He needs approval all the time. It's tiring.'

'Maybe the reassurance he really needs is that you're not going to leave him.'

'I can't give him that assurance, unfortunately.'

We have been here before. We exchanged smiles.

'Fucked up by my happy family history,' Mel said, only half joking.

Mel has never married. She is the middle child of five siblings, petted by two older brothers and idolised by two younger ones. Her father was a fashionable Harley Street gynaecologist, and her parents had a house in the country as well as a Georgian gem in London. Her widowed mother now lives in some style in South Kensington and her brothers do the kinds of thing that the sons of such families usually do. Mel insists that her childhood was so idyllic and her father such a wonderful influence that she has never found a man to match him.

'What was your childhood like?' she asked me, when we first met and we were finding out about each other.

'It was ordinary,' I lied. 'There isn't much to tell,' I said, 'except that my mum died very suddenly when I was ten. I lived quietly with my dad and then eventually I grew up.'

'That's very sad,' Mel said warmly.

'Yes,' I agreed. I didn't volunteer any more, because I don't like to talk about my childhood. The past is gone and I am glad of it.

'What are you going to do?' I ask now, eating my ravioli.

'About Adrian? End it, or wait for it to end, I suppose.'

'You don't love him.'

'No. But I like him and I enjoy his company, quite a lot of the time.'

'Isn't that enough?'

She looked at me, tilting her head a little. 'You tell me. *Is* it enough?'

I gave the question proper consideration. When Lola was eleven and Jack was three, and I was married to Tony, I fell deeply in love with a man called Stanley. It wasn't that I didn't care for my husband, because I did. Almost from the day I met him he made me feel that I was at anchor in some sheltered harbour while the storms raged out at sea, and for years I believed that was what I wanted. But sometimes I longed for the danger of towering waves and the wild wind filling my sails.

Stanley was gale force, all right. He was eight years younger than me. He was a not very successful actor who made ends meet by doing carpentry and he came to do some work in our kitchen. He was handsome and funny, utterly unreliable and unpredictable, and he stirred a longing in me that I have never known before or since. He would turn up and tell me that I was beautiful and intoxicating, and that I was all he had ever wanted. Happiness and wonder at seeming to mean so much to someone like Stanley made me suspend my natural disbelief. It was as if nothing else mattered. Not my children, my husband, or our well-rubbed and fingermarked everyday world. What I wanted, *all* I wanted, was this passion and delight.

After two months of agonising I left Tony for Stanley and took the children with me. I truly believed that there was nothing else I could do. Lola accepted this as a *fait accompli* and although she never warmed to Stanley, she and I still managed to stay friends. But Jack was already an insecure child and the upheaval tipped him severely off-balance. At twelve, he still hasn't recovered his equilibrium.

Tony and I sold our house, and I bought a much smaller one with my half of the money and Stanley came to live in it with us. For a few months I was shockingly happy. But then, slowly and inevitably, things began to go wrong. Stanley did less carpentry and spent more time in the pub. Then he went off with a travelling production of *The Rocky Horror Show* and met Dinah, who was playing Janet.

I was afraid that I would die without him, but I also thought that to be abandoned was no more than I deserved.

It's not a very original story and I'm not proud of it. I'm sorry for what I did and regret that I can't put it right, not for Jack and Lola, or Tony either. But even so, what I really think—now that Mel has asked me—is that you can compromise in love as in all other things. If you have to, that is. But it's much better not to. If all you are doing is rubbing along with someone, then you would be better off alone.

'No, it's not enough,' I said.

'Of course it isn't,' she agreed.

Mel and I knew that we were fortunate, because we'd often discussed it. We had evenings like this one. We could do our work, eat out, book holidays, choose films, argue about politics, cook meals, laugh and talk a lot. True love in addition would have been magnificent, but I didn't want to sacrifice any of the above for an ersatz version of love.

I also thought that maybe Mel herself thought a little differently from me. She would say that she was still looking for a man to replace her daddy. Whereas I had run so far and so fast from mine that by now I had shaken off all male bonds altogether. Except for Jack, of course.

Mel's thoughts must have been travelling along a path parallel to mine. 'Tell me about *your* father. I don't think you ever have, not properly. What was he like? Do you look like him?'

Her questions made me shiver.

I had been thinking about him as I walked through the opalescent evening. I could feel his shadow here in the restaurant. Yet there was no reason for this tonight of all nights, other than premonition.

I told her, reluctantly, that my father was a perfumer, and a con artist.

Mel fixed all her formidable attention on me, ready to be fascinated.

'You would like him. All women do. He was a perfumer's "nose",' I added.

With only the one obvious exception, myself, women did find Ted Thompson utterly magnetic. He was a good-looking man, for one thing, with the looks of a Forties movie star. But the real basis for his success with women was his interest in them. He had a stagy trick of cupping his target's upturned face in his hands and then breathing in the warmth of it as if the skin's scent were the most direct route to knowing its owner. He would close his eyes, frowning in concentration, then murmur, 'I could create such a perfume for you. The top notes sweet and floral to reflect your beauty but with the firmest base, cedarwood with earth tones, for your great strength.'

Or some such nonsense, anyway.

'His job was to mix essences, the building blocks of scent, to create perfume. He told me it was like painting a picture, making the broad brushstrokes that give the first impression and then filling in the details, the light and shade, to create the fragrance that lingers in the memory.'

As I talked I was thinking about the words from my childhood, ambergris and musk and vetiver. I recalled them the way other children might remember television programmes or ice-cream flavours.

'Why did I never know that? It sounds highly exotic.'

'Yes.'

It was exotic, in its way, Ted's world. But you couldn't describe my growing up on the edge of it as anything of the kind.

'What about the other thing? The con artist bit?'

'That's a manner of speaking. Perfume is nothing more than a promise in a bottle, Ted used to say. It exists to create an illusion.'

'I have just realised something. You never wear it, do you?'

'No,' I said. My discomfort was growing. I didn't want to talk to Mel about my father.

'I prefer the smell of skin,' I smiled. I remembered the way Lola and Jack used to smell when they were babies.

'What's the real reason?'

'There's no other reason,' I said.

I put down my knife and fork, placing them very precisely together between uneaten half-moons of ravioli.

Mel stared at me for a moment, then she lightly held up her hand. If I didn't want to talk about my father she wasn't going to force me to. But in the little silence that followed I understood that Mel was hurt by my reticence, that she was wondering whether our friendship was really as close as she had let herself believe.

I wanted to reach out and take her hand, to assure her that I hid nothing except my history, and this no longer mattered to me. But I didn't do it and the moment passed. The waiter came and took our plates away, and we exchanged some news of Caz and Graham, my oldest friends whom Mel had met many times, and discussed the government's ridiculous plans for the tube. The atmosphere between us warmed again.

Then we studied the pudding menu together. Mel spotted it first and her face puckered with delight. She pointed the item out to me.

Pecan, almond and walnut pie (contains nuts).

Mel and I collected menu misspellings and absurdities. The addition of this latest one helped us to forget the doubts I had raised by putting a wall round my past. Maybe some time I could talk to Mel about Ted and the way I grew up, and maybe even should do so. But not now, I thought. Not yet.

'I'm going to put my nut allergy behind me and have that,' I said.

'Split it with me?'

'Done.'

The familiar rhythms of the evening were restored, and it was eleven o'clock before we found ourselves out in the street again. Mel turned the collar of her leather jacket up. 'Call me later in the week?'

'I will,' I promised, quickly hugging her. 'You're a good friend.'

I saw the white flash of her smile. She touched my shoulder, then turned and walked fast up the street. Mel always walked quickly. She filled up her life, all the corners of it.

I retraced my steps more slowly to the tube station. I liked travelling on the underground late at night and watching the miniature dramas of drunks and giggling girls and hollow-eyed Goths and couples on the way to bed together. I never felt threatened. I even liked the smell of Special Brew and Kentucky Fried Chicken, and the homely detritus of trampled pages of the *Evening Standard* and spilled chips.

The walk at the other end was much quieter. The houses in my street had steps leading up to the front doors, and as I walked under the clenched-fist branches of pollarded lime trees, I had glimpses of basement kitchens barred by area railings, although most of the downstairs windows were already dark. I reached my steps and walked up, my house keys in my hand. The lights in our house were all on. Lola must still be up.

I turned the Yale key and the door swung open. Jack was sitting on the bottom stair, his arms were wrapped round his knees and his chin rested between them. His eyes fixed on mine.

'Jack? What are you doing? Where's Lola?'

My voice sounded sharp. The main feeling I had at the sight of him, out of bed at almost midnight, was irritation. He should be asleep now.

'Lola's in her room.'

'So should you be.'

'Why?'

It should be obvious even to a twelve-year-old boy that midnight is not a suitable time to be sitting around on the draughty stairs in a house in which the central heating has gone off for the night. I sighed. 'Please, Jack. It's late. Just go to bed.'

He stood up then, pulling his pyjama sleeves down to cover his fists. He said, 'There's some bad news. Granddad has had a heart attack.'

I turned, slowly, feeling the air's resistance. 'What?' I managed to say.

Upstairs a door clicked and Lola materialised at the head of the stairs. 'Mum, is that you?' She ran down to me.

'What?' I repeated to her, but my mind was already flying ahead.

That was it. Of course, it was why he had been in my thoughts tonight. I had smelt his cologne, glimpsed his shadow out of the corner of my eye even in the slick light of a trendy new restaurant.

I looked from one to the other. 'Tell me, quickly.'

'The Bedford Queen's Hospital rang at about nine o'clock. He was brought in by ambulance and a neighbour of his came with him. He had had a heart attack about an hour earlier. The Sister I spoke to says he is stable now.' There were tears in Lola's eyes. 'Poor Granddad.'

'We tried to call you,' Jack said accusingly.

But I'd forgotten to take my mobile phone out with me. I put to one side my regrets for this negligence. 'Is there a number for me to call?'

'On the pad in the kitchen.'

I led the way down the stairs to the basement.

'My father. Mr Ted Thompson,' I said down the phone to a nurse on Nelson Ward in the Bedford Queen's Hospital. She relayed the information that Lola had already given me. 'Should I come in now?' I asked. I didn't look at them, but I knew that Jack and Lola were watching my face. We hadn't seen their grandfather since Christmas. We observed the conventions, meeting up for birthdays and Christmases, prize-givings, and anniversaries, and we exchanged regular phone calls, but not much more. That was how it was. Ted had always preferred to live on his own terms.

The nurse said that he was comfortable now, sleeping. It would be better to come in the morning.

'I'll be there first thing,' I said, and hung up. Lola put a mug of tea on the counter beside me.

'Thank you,' I said.

Jack lifted his head. 'Is he going to die?'

He was over eighty. Of course he was going to die. If not immediately, then soon. This was reality, but I hadn't reckoned with it because I wasn't ready. There was too much unsaid and undone.

'I don't know.'

I held out my arms and Lola slid against me, resting her head on my shoulder. Jack stood a yard away, his arm out of one pyjama sleeve. He was twisting the fabric into a rope.

'Come and have a cuddle,' I said to him. He moved an inch closer but his head, his shoulders, his hips all arched away from me.

After a minute I pushed a pile of ironing off the sofa. Lola and I sat down to finish our tea and Jack perched on a high stool.

Lola sniffed. 'I don't want him to die, I love him.'

'So do I,' Jack added, not to be outdone.

It was true. My children had an uncomplicated, affectionate relationship with Ted. They teased him, gently, for being set in his ways. In a corner of myself I envied the simplicity of their regard for each other.

I stroked Lola's hair. 'Let's all go to bed,' I suggested. 'Granddad's asleep. If anything changes they'll ring us. We'll see him tomorrow.'

I followed Jack up the stairs into his bedroom. I sat on the end of the bed and he lay on his back with his arms folded behind his head.

'Are you all right?' I asked.

'Can we tell Dad what's happened?'

'Of course. In the morning.'

I leaned down and kissed him, but he gave no response.

The air in Lola's room was thick with smoke and joss.

'Lo. Have you been smoking in here?' Obviously.

'We've been sitting worrying, waiting for you to get back.'

'I know. I'm sorry.' Did all mothers have to apologise so often?

'Good night, Mum.'

'Good night, darling. I love you.'

In my own bedroom I turned on the bedside light and drew the curtains. Then I lay down on my bed, still fully dressed. I stared at the ceiling, trying to picture my father's face. All I could see was his shadow.

'Don't die,' I ordered the dark shape. 'Not until I've had a chance to talk to you.'

TWO

THEY HAD PUT HIM in a small room off the main ward. There he was, lying on his back, his head propped on pillows. I saw that his profile had become a sharper, bonier version of the one I knew.

I hesitated at the door but he opened his eyes and turned his head to look straight at me. 'Hello, Sade. Sorry about this. Damned nuisance.'

I smiled at him. 'Hello, Dad.'

All night and as I drove out of London I had been dreading this moment. I had been afraid of how he would look and of what we would say to each other with the spectre of death in the room. Now that I was actually here I saw that he was hooked up to wires and tubes ran into his arms, and my fear was not in speaking of painful matters, but that he might go away before we had a chance to talk at all.

There was a red plastic chair beside his bed. I sat down and took one of his hands, lacing my fingers with his. We had so rarely touched each other. Somewhere deep inside my head I could feel the pressure of tears, but I knew I wasn't going to cry. 'How do you feel?'

He ran his tongue over his lips. 'Rough as a bear's back.'

'What happened?'

'Chest pain. I rang Jean Andrews and she came right over.'

I knew Mrs Andrews. She was Ted's neighbour. It would have been Mrs Andrews who came here with him in the ambulance.

'Why didn't you call me?'

He moistened his lips again. 'I thought I'd see the quack first, let him take a shufti. Might all have been a false alarm.'

The vocabulary made my neck stiffen, just a little, as it always did.

Ted had served in the RAF during the war, working on the maintenance of Spitfires. He was never too specific about his exact rank and responsibility, but when on the back foot he still reached for words like prang and crate and willco, as if this threadbare old slang could lend him some extra strength or status.

He lived increasingly in the past, like many old people, although the difference with Ted was that the geography of that other country was largely imaginary. My fingers tightened on his. 'I'm here now,' I said.

'How's my cutie? And Jack?'

When she was a little girl Ted always called Lola his cutie. He was delighted to have a granddaughter, although he protested that it made him feel old. 'She's going to be a heartbreaker,' he used to say.

'Lola's just fine. She's going to come in and see you later, or maybe tomorrow. And Jack's OK, although he doesn't like school that much.'

'Neither did I when I was his age. I used to sit next to a boy called Peter Dobson. He and his chums used to lie in wait for me after school and pull my books out and run off with my comics.'

'I don't think things have changed for the better.'

A nurse came in. He was young, dressed in a white jacket and trousers. He glanced at the whiteboard over the bed and I followed his eyes. A note in bright blue magic marker declared that this was Edwin Thompson, 'Ted'. 'Hello, Teddy-boy,' the nurse said, examining the bags that leaked fluids into my father's arm. 'My name's Mike. How are you feeling?'

'I feel as you would expect, having had a heart attack last night,' Ted answered. I smiled. Ted didn't like being patronised, even in hospital.

'And who is this young lady?'

'I'm his daughter.'

'Well, now then, I need to do your dad's obs and then the doctors are coming round. Could I ask you to wait in the visitors' room?'

'I'd like to talk to his doctor.'

'Of course. Not a problem.'

I walked up the ward, past bedridden old men, to sit and wait in a small side room. A long hour later, the nurse put his head round the door. 'Doctor will see you now, in Sister's office.'

As I passed I saw Ted lying on his back, his eyes closed.

The consultant cardiologist was a woman, younger than me. She held out her hand, with a professionally sympathetic smile. 'Susan Bennett,' she said, and we shook hands.

I sat down in the chair she indicated.

I remembered the shadow that had slid into the restaurant last night and found myself repeating over and over in my head, *don't, please don't say it, just let him get better . . .*

Susan Bennett explained that it had been a serious attack, bigger than they had at first suspected. There was no likelihood of long-term recovery, she said, given the damage that had already occurred to the heart muscle. The question was when rather than if the end would come, and how to manage the intervening time.

'I see,' I murmured. The voice in my head had stopped. All I could hear was a roaring silence.

'I'm sorry to have to give you bad news,' she said gently.

'Does he know?'

'We haven't told him what I've just told you, if that's what you mean.'

'He's over eighty,' I said, as if his age somehow made the news slightly less bad. What I actually meant was to deplore the total of years that he and I had allowed to pass, until we had unwittingly reached this last minute where his doctor was telling me that Ted was going to die soon.

She nodded anyway. 'If there is anyone else, any other members of the family, it might be a good idea if they came in to see him soon.'

'How long is it likely to be?'

'I don't know,' Susan Bennett said. I liked her for not pretending omniscience. 'We'll do what we can to keep him comfortable.'

I walked slowly back to his bedside. His eyes flickered open as soon as I sat down. He wasn't asleep—he had been waiting for me.

'Did you hear what that nurse called me? *Teddy-boy*,' he muttered in disgust.

'I know.' We both smiled. I leaned over his hand as I took hold of it again. Please don't die, I wanted to beg him. As if it were his choice.

'What did the doctor say?'

'That you have had a heart attack. They're monitoring you and waiting to see what will happen over the next few days.'

'Yes?'

'She sounded optimistic.'

Coward, coward, coward.

Ted nodded, lying wearily against his pillows. He was looking away from me, out of the window at the grey angle of building and the narrow slice of cloudy sky that was the only view from his bed.

If he asks anything else, I resolved, I will tell him the truth. Then we can hold each other. I will put my arms round him and help him and look after him, whatever is coming.

The silence stretched between us. I rubbed the skin on the back of Ted's hand with the ball of my thumb, noticing how loose and papery it felt. He didn't say anything, but the muscles of his chin and throat worked a little, as if he wished that he could.

The last few times we had seen each other, Ted reminisced about the war and about the make-do years that followed it when he was first married to my mother. I thought that maybe I could reach out to him now by talking about the past, even though it was such a quagmire. 'Do you remember that day when you took me in to the Phebus labs?' I said. 'I must have been six or seven, I should think.'

'Old Man Phebus,' Ted said quietly.

I can't remember why Ted took me to work with him on that particular morning. Maybe my mother was ill, or had to go somewhere where she couldn't take me. We travelled there by bus, and I sat close up against my father in the blue, smoky fug on the top deck. It must have been the school holidays because there were children out playing on the bomb-site next to the small warehouse building in Dalston, on the fringe of the East End, which was home to Phebus Fragrances.

Anthony Phebus was Ted's earliest mentor in the perfume business. Ted always called him the Old Man. Ted had started working for him not long after I was born, as a bookkeeper, although of course he didn't actually have any bookkeeping skills or relevant office experience.

'I learned on the job,' he liked to say with a wink. 'Always the best way. You don't know what you're going to be able to do until you have to do it, and when you have to it's surprising what you *can* do.'

In any case, Ted Thompson didn't stay long with the ledgers and filing cabinets in the outer office. Anthony Phebus's business was as a commercial fragrance supplier. In his laboratory, with a tiny staff, the old man would mix and sniff and frown and adjust and finally come up with formulae that he would sell to perfume houses or cosmetics manu-facturers. Quite soon after joining the company Ted was helping him to do it. Phebus Fragrances was a long way down the scale from Chanel or Guerlain, but the Old Man did enough business to survive.

When we arrived Mr Phebus was at his desk in an untidy cubbyhole of an office, but he stood up straight away and came round to shake my hand. I was frightened of his eyebrows. They were white and jutted straight out from his forehead like a pair of bristly hearth brushes.

'So, Miss Sadie, you work hard and make my fortune for me today?'

I looked up at Ted for confirmation and he gave me a wink.

The 'lab', as Ted always referred to it, was a windowless room lined with ex-Works Department metal shelves. On the shelves were hun-dreds of brown glass screw-top bottles. Each bottle was labelled or numbered in the Old Man's neat, foreign-looking script. In the centre of the room was a plain wood table, a line of notepads and pens, a pair of scales and some jars of what looked to me like flat white pencils.

'This is where we make our magic, eh?' Mr Phebus laughed. 'Where your good father learns to make dreams for beautiful women.'

I didn't like the reference to beautiful women or their dreams, not in relation to my father. The only women he should have anything to do with were Mum and me. I kept my mouth shut and waited.

'Sit down here, miss,' Mr Phebus said and I slid into a seat. As well as having alarming eyebrows, I thought he talked in a funny way, as though 's's and 'th's were 'z's. When I was older I learned that the Old Man had been a chemist in Warsaw, but he had come to London before the war. He started work with a cosmetics house and he turned himself from a chemist into a perfumer by sheer hard work.

'Your father, Mr Ted here, he has what we call a nose,' Mr Phebus grandly announced.

I remember looking at my father's face and realising it was a hand-some one compared with Mr Phebus's, and feeling proud of my father's youth and good looks. But his nose seemed relatively unremarkable. 'So have I,' I retorted, pressing the end of mine and squashing it.

'We shall see,' the Old Man said.

The three of us sat down at the plain wood table and Ted gave me my own jar of the flat white pencils. Now I could see that they were in fact strips of thick blotting paper. Mr Phebus was setting a line of the little glass bottles between us. He unscrewed the top of one with a flourish and slid the tip of his blotter gently into the liquid in the bottle.

'Now you,' he said. I copied him exactly as he lifted the blotter to his nose and breathed in. His eyebrows twitched and I looked again at Ted, wanting to laugh. My father pressed his forefinger against one nostril and winked again. I sniffed hard at my dipper, as Mr Phebus had done. A dense, sweet cloud instantly filled my nose and rushed up through the secret insides of my face until it seemed to squeeze its fingers round my brain. 'What is that?' I whispered.

Mr Phebus said, 'That is lavender. It will be one of the top notes of the scent we are working on today.'

'Lavender's blue, dilly dilly.' I had heard the song on *Listen with Mother* and I was pleased to make this unexpected connection. But Mr Phebus held up his hand and frowned. We were working. He unscrewed another bottle and we went through the same process. This one was nasty as well as strong. The stink was sharp, like cats or the lavatories at my school, and I screwed up my face in disgust.

'Cassia,' Mr Phebus said. 'Very important. You must remember that not all perfume essences smell sweet and pretty. We often use these sensual animal stinks like musk and civet for our base notes, to anchor the structure. Men and women are animals too, you know.'

I frowned at him, battling my incomprehension.

The door opened and a woman with her hair swept up on the top of her head looked in at us. 'Phone call for Mr Thompson,' she said.

I shivered with pleasure at the importance of this. We didn't have a telephone at home. Ted sprang up and went out, but Mr Phebus went on unscrewing bottles and motioning to me to dip and sniff. Some of the smells were like flowers pressed and squeezed to make them power-ful instead of sweet and gentle, others were surprising, reminding me of orange peel, or Christmas, or the sea at Whitstable where we had spent a summer holiday. By the time my father came back there were ten used white dippers on the table in front of me and I was beginning to feel slightly queasy.

'Now, miss,' Mr Phebus said, pulling at the thistly tuft of one eyebrow. 'Can you remember which one was lavender?'

Ten dippers with their tips turned translucent by the oils now lay on the table in front of me. Reluctantly I picked up several in turn and sniffed at them again. My head felt muzzy and too full of potent fumes. I was hopelessly confused. I took a wild guess. 'That one?'

'No, that one is jasmine.'

Ted laughed and sat down again on the wooden chair beside mine. I felt that I had let him down.

'Don't worry, you can learn the difference if you try hard enough,' Mr Phebus said. 'I managed it. I spent many years of hard work, memoris-ing thousands of notes, which is what we call the different basic scents. But your father here'—he paused for effect, with his eyebrows pointing at me—'he is a natural. He smells a note only once and he remembers it. And he knows, because the artistry is in his heart and in his mind, he knows how to coax from these bottles the dreams of women.'

Women and their dreams, again. I was torn between pride in my father and a new discomfort that rubbed at the margins of my under-standing. I didn't like the feeling of insecurity that came with it.

'Of course, he still has very much to learn. *Many* years of practice.'

Ted laughed out loud delightedly. 'Better get on with it, then.' He was always enthusiastic in those days. He rubbed his hands and smacked his lips, full of raw appetite for life. I didn't recognise his hunger then for what it was, but I already knew that my mother entirely lacked what Ted possessed. I loved her, of course, and I took for granted her devotion to me, but she wasn't thrilling in the way my father was. She was always there and I never noticed her constancy until she wasn't any longer. One morning she was at home and that same afternoon she was never coming back. That's how sudden her death was from the brain haemor-rhage. Afterwards, when I thought about her, I would remember her quietness and restraint. It was as if even before she left us altogether she occupied only the corners of her own life.

Mr Phebus said, 'Let's have Black Opal three and four, then.'

Ted brought some bottles from the shelves and the two of them began nosing and muttering together. They talked about heart and base notes, and sparkle and synthesis, and the names of natural essences and the chemical polysyllables of synthetics rolled off their tongues. I didn't remember the tongue-twisting chemicals, but the mysterious-sounding beauty of naturals—vetiver and musk and mimosa—stayed with me.

They were still with me now as I sat by my father's bed and held his dry hand. Only the names, not the scents. I was not an artist like Ted.

I was talking too much, I realised. It would be tiring for him.

'How old were you?' he asked, restlessly moving his legs and frowning with the effort of recollection.

'Six, or seven.'

'Back in '56, then.'

I was pleased that he knew the year of my birth. 'Yes.'

'We were working on contract for Coty.' His hand moved a little in my grasp, as if he were trying to reach for something, and then fell back again. 'I don't remember the day. It must have been boring for you.'

We're so polite to each other, I thought. We are like a rough sea swirling under a thin skin of ice.

'It wasn't boring,' I told him. 'I loved it.'

And it was true. The impression of that day stayed with me for years.

'He was a good perfumer, the Old Man. I learned everything I needed to know from him. No business sense, though. None at all.'

I had to lean closer to catch his words. His voice seemed to be fading and his eyes were gradually falling shut. I had to stop myself from grasping his hand and shaking it hard to keep him with me. I watched the shallow rise and fall of his chest. He had fallen asleep.

I went down to the visitors' car park, where I could use my mobile phone, and called Lola to relay the news.

'Oh God, Mum, I'm sorry. Poor Granddad. I'd better ring in and cancel my shift,' she said at once. Lola worked in a bar during university holidays. We agreed that she would collect Jack from school in her car and they would come straight up to the hospital.

Next I telephoned Penny at the Works, as we call the book bindery and small print shop we jointly own. Penny and I have been business partners for twelve years. I have always loved the physical weight and dimensions of fine books, the texture of paper, and the variety and intricate grace of typefaces, and Penny possesses the rare combination of design flair and business acuity. We work well together and although there are no great riches in what we do, we make an adequate living.

'Don't worry,' Penny told me. 'Don't even think about anything here, I'll handle it. And I'm here if you need me, OK?'

178

Next I spoke to Caz. Caz has been my friend since we lived in adjacent rooms in a decrepit student house thirty years ago. We were married in the same year, and she and Graham had their two boys in quick succession, not long after Tony and I had Lola.

'What can I do?' Caz said, as soon as I told her the news. If there is ever a favour to be done, Caz is always the first to volunteer.

'Will you have Jack, if I have to stay over at the hospital? If Lola can't hold the fort, that is?'

Jack didn't currently get on all that well with Dan and Matthew, Caz's boys, but in this emergency he would have to make the best of it.

'Of course,' she assured me. 'Call me as soon as there's any news.'

Finally I dialled Mel's office direct line. After I had told her what had happened she said, 'That's quite strange, isn't it? The way we were talking about him last night?'

'Yes.'

'Do you want me to come up and keep you company?' It was a generous offer. Mel worked for a big head-hunting company and I could guess at the rapid mental diary reshuffling she must be doing, although there wasn't the faintest hint of it in her tone.

'No. But thank you.'

I hurried back to my father's bedside.

Ted was still asleep. I took my seat once more beside him but didn't try to hold his hand in case I disturbed him.

The hours passed slowly until, at the distant end of the afternoon, Lola appeared. In this airless room my daughter looked supernaturally beautiful and healthy, with her bright eyes and polished skin, as if all the threats of mortality had been airbrushed out of her face. I clung to her, breathing in her sweet and perfectly familiar smell. Jack sidled in in her wake, and after a quick glance at Ted, he leaned against the window and stared out. I hugged him too and he submitted briefly, although I could still feel the tense curve of his body arching away from me.

Lola took a framed photograph out of her nylon rucksack. It was of herself and Jack and me, taken last year in Devon. For once we were all smiling, looking straight into the camera. She placed the picture on Ted's locker, angled so that he could see it when he woke up. 'I thought he might like it,' she said, 'if he wakes up when we aren't here.'

The love implicit in the simple gesture touched me and I felt sorry that I hadn't thought of it myself. 'A very good idea.'

'How is he?'

Out of the corner of my eye I saw Jack's head half turn at Lola's question. He wanted to hear but didn't want me to see him listening.

'Holding his own,' I said. I would tell them Dr Bennett's verdict later, out of Ted's earshot.

Lola nodded. 'Go and get a cup of tea, Mum. We'll be here.'

When I returned to the room, carrying a polystyrene cup of tea, Lola said, 'He woke up.'

'Yes?'

'We chatted for a bit, Jack, didn't we?'

'Yeah. He asked Lo about uni and me about school. He was OK. Then he just sort of shut his eyes and went to sleep again. He didn't see the photo, though.'

This was a long speech for Jack. Hope began sliding through my veins. Outside on the main ward there were relatives gathered round the beds of the old men, and a woman in a green overall was offering tea and biscuits. It wasn't over. In a week or two, maybe, I could be driving Ted home. I would bring him back to my house and slowly, slowly, we would stitch up the weave of forgiveness.

Anything was possible. Everything was possible.

The three of us settled round his bed. On one side Lola stroked his hand and talked to him about her house-share friends at university. She talked easily and I knew that Ted would like the sound of her voice with its regular gurgles of laughter. Jack leaned on the windowsill watching the birds coming to roost among the huge metal cylinders on the hospital roof. I sat still and watched the rise and fall of Ted's chest. It already felt like routine to be sitting here. Was it only yesterday at this time that I had been walking through the shimmering evening to meet Mel?

Time passed slowly. The ward quietened as the visitors drifted away. A new nurse, just arrived on night duty, introduced herself and changed one of the packs of fluid that drained into Ted's arm. 'How is he?' I asked, thinking of the monitors at the nursing station.

'There's no change.'

That meant there was no deterioration. I smiled my gratitude at her.

At nine o'clock I told Lola and Jack that they should go home. It was over an hour's drive and Jack had school in the morning.

Lola bent over and kissed her grandfather's forehead, then touched her fingertips to his lips. 'See you later, Granddad,' she whispered.

Jack touched the small steeple of bedclothes over his feet and snatched his hand back. 'Bye,' he mumbled. He followed his sister to the door and then hovered, torn between the impulse to rush back to Ted's side and the need to keep his own distance from me and his sister. 'Bye,' he said again, and turned to follow Lola.

'Drive carefully,' I warned automatically. 'I love you both.'

'Yes, Mum.'

I sat down yet again. An hour dragged by and Ted rolled his head on the pillows and feebly shifted his legs. The Night Sister suddenly appeared with the first nurse. They moved rapidly around him, checking his fluids and the tubes that led into him, and calling him by name.

'What's happened? What's wrong?' My voice was sharp and loud.

'There are some new signs. The doctor's coming.'

I was squeezed out of my place at his side. Ted's eyes were wide open now and I could see how much it hurt him to breathe.

'Dad? Dad, I'm here . . . I . . .'

I couldn't finish what I was saying because the doctor arrived and I was edged further away to make room for him. I stood obediently outside the room until the doctor came out again. He was wearing a dark blue shirt under his white coat and a name tag that read Dr Raj Srinivasar. He indicated that we should step a little distance away.

'Doctor?'

'I'm sorry. The undamaged portion of your father's heart muscle has been working very hard since the attack and we have been helping him with drugs to stimulate the heart's natural rhythm. But I am afraid even this is gradually failing him now. I think Dr Bennett explained?'

I bent my head. 'Yes.'

It had been human but utterly vain to hope, of course. I closed the door of the little room and took my place in the chair once more.

He was awake and he didn't look as if he was in pain. He licked his lips and his neck muscles worked as if to squeeze words out of his ruined heart. 'You've been a good girl,' he whispered.

Automatically, defensively, I muttered, 'Not really.'

I wasn't ready for Ted's praise and in my unpreparedness I couldn't have assured him in return that he had been a good father.

I would have snatched my answer back if only I could, but Ted surprised me. He let his head fall further back against the pillows and laughed. It was a small coughing echo of his old laugh, but still there was no mistaking it. He said one more thing after that, on a long breath. I thought it was 'my girl'.

As the minutes ebbed and I waited I knew that now it was too late for us to make our spoken allowances to each other. He lay with his eyes closed and the rise and fall of his chest grew shallower until I could no longer see it. I pressed my face against his cheek. Tears began to run out of my eyes and into the sheet. I put my arm under his shoulder as if I were going to lift him up and held him close against me. As I wept I told him, the angry words and the bitter words threading with the words of love, that I loved him and I hated the childhood he had given me, and I would always love him, an interior dialogue I had rehearsed many times before. He didn't answer and I didn't expect him to. I knew that he was dead.

THREE

THE CHAPEL WAS LIGHT AND BARE, with tall, plain windows. Rows of wooden seats faced a pair of non-committal flower arrangements. The atmosphere was subdued, naturally enough, but also utilitarian. The light-wood coffin under a purple drape was utilitarian too, which was inappropriate for Ted, whose life had been many things but never that.

'I haven't got to sit through it, have I?' I could hear him snort in the half-irritable, half-jovial way that he adopted in his later years. 'Just do the necessary and make sure all and sundry get a drink at the end of it.'

Mel was sitting a few seats behind me. She had never met Ted, but she insisted that she wanted to come, out of respect and to keep me company. Caz and Graham were with her. They had met him a handful of times, at my wedding and the children's birthday parties.

'I liked your dad. Of course I'm coming to his funeral,' Caz declared.

Ted had liked her, too. I remember him flirting with her at my wedding reception. He had probably cornered her in some alcove, before cupping her round face between his two hands and breathing in the scent of her skin as if she were some exotic flower. 'I could create such a perfume for you,' he would have murmured in her ear. This routine would not have worked with Caz, of course. But it worked like a dream with plenty of others. More than I would want to remember.

Lola and I sat on either side of Jack in the front row of seats. Lola blotted her tears with a folded Kleenex and glanced down at the two black feathered wings of mascara printed on the tissue. Jack sat upright and stared straight ahead of him, dressed in school uniform.

When I broke the news to him, on the morning after Ted's death, he said, 'I see.' And after a moment's thought, 'It's very final, isn't it?'

'Yes. Although he's still here in a way, because we remember him and because we'll go on talking about him as long as we are alive.'

Jack gave me one of his withering looks, as if he saw right through this threadbare platitude, but he didn't pass any comment.

Apart from the six of us, the other mourners were Ted's two first cousins on his mother's side, who had come down from Manchester. There was no other family left. Then there was a handful of Ted's neighbours, led by the large and forthright Jean Andrews, and the landlord and a couple of regulars from the pub Ted used to go to. I had never met any of these people before, but they filed up to me at the chapel door, and shook my hand and told me how sorry they were. A great character, your dad, they said. Thank you, I murmured. And yes, he was.

There was also an old woman wearing a ratty fox fur over a shapeless bag of a coat and a crumpled black felt hat with a bunch of silk-and-wire lilies of the valley pinned to one side. *Muguet*, Ted called the flower. It was one of his favourites. The woman had nodded to me as she walked in, but she didn't introduce herself or offer condolences.

There were perhaps twenty-five people in all. Muted piped organ music whispered around us.

On being given the nod by the crematorium officiator, one of the cousins hobbled to the lectern to read that passage from Canon Henry Scott Holland about not having gone away, but being in the next room, still with you. I thought it was a fine and comforting piece of writing, but unfortunately untrue. Ted *was* completely gone, his movie star looks, his laugh and his perfumes, all off and away out of our reach.

Lola's shoulders shook and she pressed the Kleenex to her face. I reached round Jack to rest my hand in the smooth dip between her shoulder blades.

After the reading there was a hymn, 'All Things Bright and Beautiful', which I had chosen for no more significant reason than that Ted sometimes hummed it while he was shaving. He would turn his face from side to side, catching the best of his reflection in the mirror above the bathroom basin as he whisked on the soap lather with an old bristle brush. Then, with his lips twisted aside, he would razor long, crisp channels through the white foam.

After the hymn the officiator gave a short address. I had provided as much background as I could about Ted and his life, and it was a good attempt at a tribute, given that he had never met him. He spoke of Ted's popularity, his love of life and its opportunities, and his gifts as a perfumer. We were just shuffling to our feet again, to the first notes of the organ voluntary that the cousins had suggested to accompany the coffin's slow slide between the curtains, when Jack scrambled past me. I thought for a second that he might be going to be sick, but he pushed me back when I went to follow him. He marched up to the lectern and took his place behind it, and the recorded music was abruptly switched off. Lola and I glanced nervously at each other.

Jack cleared his throat. 'My granddad,' he began. We waited in silence. 'My granddad told me when I was a little kid that pigeons are vermin.'

After another beat of silence I heard from the back of the room a snuffle that might have been suppressed laughter. Jack didn't blink.

'At our other house before . . . before Mum and me and Lola moved, they used to sit on all the upstairs windowsills, and Granddad didn't like all the . . . all the . . . mess they left. He pointed at it when I was going to bed one night and said they were dirty. And I looked at their feet, and they were all, like, scabby. Their plumage was dirty as well.'

This all came out in a breathless rush, his gaze fixed on the back of the room.

'I said, are all birds dirty, then? And he said, I remember it really well, he said no, birds are beautiful, they've got the gift of the air, all the freedom of the sky and it's just the poor pigeons who live in London and eat rubbish and everything and sit on top of *our* dirt that makes them dirty. So they're vermin in the same way as rats, because rats are really clean creatures, in fact. He told me that as well. Anyway . . .'

Jack paused and now he did look at his audience, letting his eyes slide over us. He had got into his stride. We all sat without moving.

'Anyway, after that I got interested in birds. I liked the idea of the freedom of the sky. I wanted to think about them not being all vermin with diseased feet from living on our mess. So I started watching them and learning about them, and he was right, they are beautiful. Sea birds especially because the sea belongs to them as well as the sky, if you think about it. So it's because of him. That I like birds. I owe it to him.' He nodded sideways to the coffin under the purple drape. 'That's what I wanted to say, actually. Granddad knew about things. He didn't always let you know that he knew, but he still knew. He was interesting, like that.'

The rush of confidence subsided as quickly as it had come. Jack's gaze returned to the floor. After a few long seconds of silence, the officiator cleared his throat and stepped forward, and at the same moment Jack's head jerked up and he swung round to face the coffin. 'I love you, Granddad,' he blurted out. There were tears on his eyelashes. Then he turned round and marched back to his place between Lola and me. I tried to put my arm round his shoulders but he shook it off.

The piped music started up again. The curtains at the back of the chapel parted slowly and the coffin slid forward. I kept my eyes fixed on it, feeling the faint tremors of Lola's weeping.

Then I began to think about my mother.

I could remember her calling me in from the garden—*Sadie? Sa-aa-die!*—where I was playing some complicated only-child's game.

I was ten when she died. I have so few memories of her and yet this tiny moment was suddenly crisp and rounded out with the sound of a radio playing in a neighbour's garden, and the suburban scents of dusty shrub borders and cooking. It was as if I were standing there beside the rosebushes again, torn between playing and responding to her call.

Yes? I answered now, silently, but there was no more. It was strange that Ted himself, who had been so vividly alive all my life, should seem absent from these proceedings, while my shadowy mother, dead for more than forty years, was close at hand.

I wish I had been able to go to my mother's funeral. I think Ted sent me to a neighbour's, although I can't remember the precise circumstances. He excluded me, anyway, and later he swept my mother out of our lives and made it as if she had never existed.

Ted's coffin had travelled the full distance. The curtains swished shut behind it and the organ voluntary wheezed to an end.

Afterwards we walked out into the bright daylight. The family and neighbours already knew that there was to be a gathering back at Ted's house, and there was a slow movement towards the parked cars.

The old woman in the black hat was waiting with the sun showing up the dust on her defiant fox fur. She came towards me with her head tilted expectantly. She had purply-red lipstick and powdered cheeks. 'You'll be his daughter,' she said. 'I am Audrey.'

This meant nothing to me. 'Thank you for coming,' I murmured. 'Would you like to join us for a drink, back at . . .'

But Audrey had already turned her attention to Jack. 'And you're his grandson. I liked what you said about him. You were quite right, Ted knew about things and it was one of the games he liked to play, not letting you know what he knew and then surprising you when you least expected it. Birds, or whatever it might be.'

Jack nodded, looking at her and sizing up the unwinking fox eyes and sharp fox faces that hung down over her bosom. I turned away because I had to speak to the undertakers, and when I had finished doing that, Audrey was nowhere to be seen.

'She went,' Jack said and shrugged, when I asked him.

After the crematorium, the neighbours and pub friends and Ted's small family reassembled at his small red-brick terraced house. Everyone came back, except the mysterious Audrey. Caz and I had made an early-morning lightning swoop on Marks & Spencer's and bought in enough finger-food to fill several trays. She worked her way

185

round the guests with these while Graham and I followed with gin, Scotch or wine. The atmosphere lightened as people ate and drank, and then grew positively jolly.

The noise level rose. The pub landlord told a couple of jokes, on the grounds that they had been favourites of Ted's, and everyone laughed.

Jack sat on the stairs and read a book while people trod past him on the way to the bathroom. He glowered when anyone tried to speak to him or congratulate him on his impromptu speech, particularly me. Lola's tears had dried up. She moved between the groups, with the attention of one or two of the younger pub men fixed on her. She caught my eye once and winked. Caz and Graham still circulated with drink and food, and Mel just circulated.

After a while I glanced at my watch. It was well past the lunch hour and I wanted to look in at work before the end of the day because there was some urgent finishing to do. I raised my eyebrows at Graham, who is used to standing in for a husband at times like this.

When I called Tony to tell him that Ted was gone, he had said how sorry he was, then asked immediately when the funeral was to be.

'Sadie, that's the one day I can't come. I've got to go to Germany for a big client meeting.'

I knew he would have come, if he possibly could. Tony is like that. 'Don't worry. Graham and Caz will be there. We'll organise it together.'

'I know they'll support you. But I'm truly sorry I can't be there too.'

'It can't be helped,' I said. I would have liked Tony to be here as well, for my own sake as well as Lola's and Jack's. But there was no point in regretting his absence now, or at any other time.

When we were first divorced, Jack and Lola both spent plenty of time with their father and it worked well. But in the last five years, since Tony met his new partner and particularly since the birth of their twin girls, the visits have become less regular, simply because Tony has less time to spare for children who can already feed and dress themselves. Lola is fairly sanguine about it, but Jack minds.

Graham glanced around the room, judging the atmosphere. 'A few words, maybe?' he suggested to me in a whisper.

I cleared my throat and stepped into the middle of the room while he rattled a spoon against a plate.

I had no idea what I was going to say, so I thanked everyone again for coming, and lifted my glass that had one and a half mouthfuls of red wine in it. Luckily everyone else's glasses were well charged.

'To Ted.'

The echo began as a muted, respectful chorus. But the next thing I saw was the faces all around me breaking into smiles and there was a sudden little wave of clapping, and some stamping and cheering. *Ted, Ted, Ted.* Jack's white face poked round the hallway door.

'My father,' I added to the chorus. It wasn't my unmemorable words that had provoked this, of course. It was Ted himself and I was being made aware of his popularity for perhaps the last time.

I looked around me, searching for a synthesis between my knowledge of him and what all these other cheerful, rational friends felt. There was his dented old armchair but even as I stared at it I couldn't shift the cold wedge that separated my memories of Ted from everyone else's.

I shook my head and looked for the faces of my children and my old friends. They jumped out of the gloom at me, full of warmth and life. This is what matters now, not *then*, I rationalised. History's gone.

I found myself with my fingers wrapped round my now empty glass, fondly beaming back at all of them. And my smile must have been particularly noticeable because there was another surge of clapping and cheering. How Ted would have *loved* all this.

It was another moment before everyone noticed that they were involved in an outbreak of spontaneous celebration, but when they did the applause gently faded into shuffling and coughing. This was a funeral, after all. Still smiling, Jean Andrews began dabbing her eyes.

My short speech and the clapping were taken as the signal for everyone to make a move. 'If only he could have been here,' Jean Andrews sighed as she squeezed into her coat.

Half an hour later Caz's and Graham's Volvo followed Mel's Audi down the road. Lola and Jack and I were left standing on Ted's doorstep. The children looked at me, waiting for a lead.

'Let's go home,' I said, double-locking the door.

In the traffic on the M1 Lola told me, 'I think that went really well.'

'Yes, it did.'

I glanced in the rearview mirror. Jack's head was tilted against the passenger window. There was no telling what he thought.

It was after five o'clock when I finally reached work, but that didn't matter. Penny and I are self-employed and we put in the hours to suit ourselves. Her house is the end one of a pretty Georgian terrace, but it's East- rather than West-End Georgian. The houses themselves were once fine but have become dilapidated and even recent gentrification hasn't improved the immediate surroundings, which are grimy, traffic-clogged and unsafe after dark. Not that that worries Penny.

I walked down a small cobbled alleyway past the side of her house, under a sign that reads 'Gill & Thompson Fine & Trade Bookbinders'. The old brick outbuilding, backing onto a murky stretch of the Regent's Canal, opposite some gasometers, was one of the main reasons why Penny bought the house. It had originally been a coal depot, where the long barges down from the Midlands unloaded their cargo, but together we cleaned it up and converted it into a book bindery.

That was what I did, and do. I am a bookbinder, in the way that Ted was a perfumer. But without the mystery, of course.

I opened the door into the shop part of the bindery. Across the counter that divides it from the workshop I saw Penny. She was standing over a stitched book, rounding out the spine ready for backing. When she heard the door closing she looked up over her half-moon glasses and said, 'Hi.'

I walked round the counter end and took my apron off its hook. 'I'm glad that's over,' I said, tying the strings round my middle.

My job was lying at the end of my bench. The dark blue cloth-covered book boards for Ronaldshay's three-volume *Life of Lord Curzon* that we were restoring for a regular customer of ours. The finishing still remained to be done, ready for collection tomorrow.

'Are you OK?' Penny asked.

I picked up the first board and stroked the cloth with my thumb. It was a good job, clean but nothing flashy. 'Yes.'

'You needn't have come in, you know. I could have done *Curzon*.'

'I know.' I smiled at her. Penny's a good finisher. 'But I wanted to.'

It was the truth. The bindery, with its ordered clutter and smells of glue and skins, is a soothing place.

Penny nodded and went back to her tap-tapping with the little Victorian hammer I had found at a bindery sale and bought for her. I switched on the heating element in the Pragnant machine. The gold lettering on the spine was all that remained to be done. I decided that I would do the title in two pulls, and then put the author's name and the volume number together in the third panel. Using tweezers, I dropped the letters and spacers for *The Life of* one by one into the slot of the type holder and checked them. The characters have to be placed upside-down and it's easy to make mistakes.

The work absorbed me. Penny and I settled into the easy silence that we often enjoy when we are on our own in the bindery. It's different when Andy and Leo, our part-timers, are there. They like to play music and talk about the jobs in hand. It's still comfortable, but different.

I measured the available space on the book's spine with my dividers, then checked it by eye. However carefully and accurately the lettering is placed, if the result looks wrong to the eye then it is wrong. I put the board back on the stand and slipped the foil out of the way and made a blind pull, just an impression of the letters lightly tapped into the cloth that I could rub away if they were misplaced. When I examined the result I saw they were indeed in the wrong position. About a millimetre too high. I rolled the bar down by what I calculated to be the right amount and did another blind pull. This time it was exactly right.

Even though this was a routine job, I still had to summon up some courage to make the gold pull. If I got it wrong there was no chance of a repair. The boards would have to be made and covered all over again, and with the margins Penny and I operate on, and the backlog of work waiting to be done, we can't afford the time. I took a steadying breath and pressed the operating lever forward. The type kissed the blue cloth and I pressed harder, and the gold tape frazzled as the letters burned out of it. I eased the handle back and bent forward to see the result.

There it was, *The Life of* in strong, gold, block capitals on the dark blue cloth. I'd gone in a little too heavy, perhaps, and laid on a touch too much foil, but I could fix that. I stood back in a glow of satisfaction.

'Good,' I said. However many times I do it, finishing always gives me the most pleasure of all the stages of binding a book.

Penny completed her rounding and backing job with a final burst of tapping. She took off her glasses and ran her hand through her short hair. 'How did it go?'

What do you say about a funeral? 'It was . . . well, processed. Jack made a speech, though.'

'*Did* he?' Penny was surprised, not surprisingly.

'About pigeons. It was Ted who set off his interest in birds by telling him about the way pigeons live in London. He made a whole address out of it at the ceremony.'

'I think that's very appropriate.'

She was right. I was proud of Jack.

'And then, at the drinks afterwards, everyone clapped and sort of cheered and tapped their feet when I made a toast to Ted.' I took up the second cover and squinted at the panel where I would place the blocking, not wanting to expose my feelings to Penny.

'Ah.' She put her book in the press. It was a good edition of Keats's *Letters* that we were restoring. Tomorrow she would paste a backing on the spine and cut the endpapers. I planned to hand-finish the leather binding with gold and blind tooling, the full works.

'I'm going to head inside,' she said. 'Evelyn's going out and she wants me to give Cassie her tea and put her to bed.'

'See you tomorrow,' I said.

I made the pulls for the second and third volumes, then set up the type for *Lord Curzon*. I loved the quiet in the bindery on evenings like this. Behind me, the tall window that looked out over the canal darkened and the pale struts of the supports of the gasometer opposite briefly glowed like the skeleton of a spaceship.

If I was thinking about anything as I worked it was Penny. We had met as art students at Camberwell and had learned the principles of bookbinding together. After the course I found a job as a very junior assistant to Arthur Bromyard, one of the great artist-bookbinders, while Penny went into a busy and aggressive trade bindery where most of the other workers were men. She was bullied there and responded by becoming even more superficially prickly and defensive than she had been at Camberwell. We stayed friends, but she was scathing about what she regarded as my sheltered and arty-farty existence under Mr Bromyard's gentle tutelage, and I thought she was wasting her talents banging out dozens of legal buckram-bound law reports day after day.

I blocked in the rest of the title and the author's name and the volume number on each of the three books, then laid out the results on the bench to examine them. Perfect, even though I had to pass the verdict myself. Within the constraints of time and resources, of course.

Once the books were glued into their covers I could go home. Half an hour later, as I began turning the screw of the old wooden press on the glued boards, I heard the door open. A second later Cassie burst round the corner of the bench. 'Sadie! Sadie!' she shouted.

Cassie was nearly three, the daughter of Penny's partner Evelyn and a musician from Grenada. A year ago the lovely but distracted Evelyn had left Jerry and brought herself and Cassie to live at Penny's.

'*What* are you doing here?' I demanded.

'Seeing you,' Cassie yelled triumphantly.

I swung her off the floor and she sat astride my hip. She was wearing a zip-up fleece over Tellytubby pyjamas. 'Why?'

'Because you are silly.'

I reached for my duster and dropped it over my head and face. 'How about now?'

This was greeted with hoots of laughter. She twitched the duster off my face and rubbed her boneless button nose against mine.

I cleared a space on my bench and gently sat her down. I didn't really like seeing Cassie in the bindery. There were too many instruments of harm in here, too many knives and mallets and jars of glue. I blew a raspberry against her plump, brown neck and told her to sit still.

Penny came in with a tea towel over her shoulder.

'Pen . . .' I began.

She held up her hands. 'I know, I know. But she wanted to come and see you on her own. I was watching her all the way.'

Penny was incapable of refusing Cassie anything. She loved the child with an absorbed, half-unbelieving passion. I loved her too; the familiar weight of a baby in my arms, the softness and tenacity and scent of her. I missed my own children's infant selves and Cassie filled some of the space they had left empty.

'I'm just finishing,' I capitulated. 'Do you want to stay here with me, Cass, and then I'll carry you up to bed?'

'No bed.'

'Yes, bed.'

'We'll see,' she bargained and I could hear her mother's sweet cajoling voice. Evelyn always got what she wanted. After checking that *Curzon* was properly positioned, I hoisted Cassie into my arms again, locked up, and walked to the back door of the house to find Penny.

The ground-floor rooms interconnected and together they functioned as kitchen, living area and bindery office. Penny was sitting at the computer making up invoices. This was usually my job.

'I'll do those tomorrow,' I said.

I put Cassie down and she immediately ran away to find Evelyn.

'Sade, tell me why you're rejecting all offers of help and sympathy?'

I played for time. 'Am I?'

I felt fraudulent, that was why. I had hardly cried yet for Ted and I couldn't map even the outlines of what his loss meant to me. What could I look for from my friends, when I couldn't locate my own grief? All I felt was numb, and exhausted to realise that my relationship with my father, that old disabling argument between love and bitterness, wasn't going to end with the mere fact of his death.

Penny sighed. 'Never mind,' she said gently. 'Why don't you stay and have a glass of wine?'

My own children would be waiting for me at home. 'Thanks. Not tonight.'

'See you tomorrow, then.'

After I had tucked Cassie up in bed, as promised, I walked home along the canal towpath. The gates that gave access to it were locked at dusk, but the railings were easy to climb. Muggers and junkies hung out down there, but tonight I wanted the silence and solitude of the path instead of threading the longer way through the busy streets.

Lola was on the phone. She mouthed 'hello' at me as I came in. When she hung up she said, 'Mum, that was Ollie. I said I'd go and meet him and Sam for a drink, is that OK with you?'

She had stayed in with Jack, waiting for me to come back. Having her at home in university holidays had great benefits for me, although I tried not to take advantage of this too often. And I was glad that she felt like going out with her friends tonight. She had cried enough for Ted. I smiled at her. 'Of course it is. Where's Jack?'

'He said he was going to bed.'

'Did he talk to you?'

'What do you think?'

'I think he didn't talk to you.'

Lola and I have always discussed everything. I feared sometimes that because I didn't have a husband I admitted too many of my anxieties to her, but her response was always that she would rather know what affected me because whatever it was actually affected all three of us.

She picked up her denim jacket now, with its badges and graffiti, and stitched-on bits of ribbon. 'Are *you* all right?' she asked.

'Yes. Yes, I am.' So I didn't share everything with her.

Lola whirled out of the house. I went upstairs, knocked softly on Jack's door and, when there was no answer, turned the knob. The light was out but something told me he wasn't asleep. 'Jack?'

There was no answer, but I picked up the darkness of rejection in the room. 'Good night,' I whispered.

FOUR

HE WALKED OFF UP THE ROAD, very slowly, his bag slouched across his back and the soles of his trainers barely lifting off the pavement.

It was the third day of the summer term and every morning so far Jack had refused to get out of bed. Then, when I finally hauled him out from under the covers, he refused to get dressed. He didn't speak, let alone argue; he just did everything very, very slowly.

'Jack, you have to go to school. Everybody does. It's a fact of life.'

He shrugged and turned away. While I stood over him, he had got as far as putting on his school shirt and it hung loose over his pyjama bottoms. I could see faint blue veins under the white skin of his chest and his vulnerability made me want to hold him, but I knew if I tried to touch him he would pull away.

'Downstairs in five minutes, please.'

Five minutes turned into fifteen as he ate his toast, very slowly.

'You're going to be late.' I couldn't hide the irritation.

'Oh *no*.'

'For God's sake,' I snapped, 'what's the matter with you? If you won't talk to me how can I help you? What's wrong?'

Jack looked around the kitchen as if surveying his life, and then said out of a pinched mouth, 'Everything.'

The bleakness of this was unbearable.

I tried to touch his hand but he pulled away as if my fingertips might burn him.

I took a breath. 'Jack, listen. It just *seems* like everything, you know. It isn't so bad. There are lots of things you enjoy and look forward to.' Although if he had pressed me to name them, I couldn't have got much beyond seagulls. 'And you've got us, Lola and me, and your dad as well. If we try and work out what's most wrong, I can help you.'

There was a small silence. Then he said flatly, 'You?'

I understood that *everything* mostly meant his life in this house, with me and without his father.

It wasn't that he didn't see Tony: the three and a half weeks since Ted's death had spanned the school Easter holidays and the two of them had been away together for three days' fishing in Devon. Once or twice a month Jack went over to Twickenham to spend a night with Tony and his second family, but that wasn't the same as having a father who lived in the same house.

Everything wasn't school and friends or the lack of them. The trouble was home, and home was mostly me.

The silence extended itself. The need to cry burned behind my eyes. I couldn't make the world right for Jack, my unlucky child, I couldn't even make the dealings between us right.

'I'm sorry,' I managed to say.

He pushed back his chair and stood up. 'Going to school,' was his only response.

I went with him to the door and watched him until he was out of sight. I longed to go with him and shield him through the day, to turn his *everything* into nothing that mattered and let us both start again, but I couldn't heal the breach between Jack and me. Ted was dead and gone but somehow his damned legacy was right here in our house.

I was angry as well as impotent. I snatched up my bag and went to work, and when I arrived I made a mess of cutting some endpapers out of some special old hand-marbled paper. Penny kept her head down over her work, and, although I could sense Andy and Leo glancing at each other, I didn't look their way.

When I got home again Lola had already gone out to her bar job. In two days' time she would be going back to university and she was trying to earn as much money as she could. Jack was sitting in front of the television, looking grubby and utterly exhausted.

'How was your day?' I asked. I was going to make shepherd's pie for supper, his favourite.

'All right.'

'What lessons did you have?'

'The usual ones.'

He didn't take his eyes off the screen but I didn't think he was really watching it. I threw three potatoes in the sink and began peeling. 'So, it was a pretty uneventful day, then?'

He twisted his shoulders in a shrug, and I started browning the meat and vegetables. The next time I looked he had fallen asleep.

We ate dinner together—at least he sat at the table with me, but he had a bird book open beside his plate. He ate ravenously, as if he hadn't seen food since breakfast time.

But the next morning, to my surprise, he put up less resistance to getting up and getting dressed. Maybe he was beginning to accept the inevitable, I thought. Maybe the tide had changed.

That day Colin came into the bindery. He lived with his mother, somewhere on an estate that lay to the east of Penny's house, and he was a regular visitor. He pushed the door open, marched in and laid a heavy carrier bag on the counter. We took it roughly in turns, without actually having drawn up a rota, to deal with Colin, and today it was my turn.

'Morning!' he shouted. He had an oversized head that looked too heavy for his shoulders and his voice always seemed too loud for the space he was in.

'Hello, Colin. How are you today?'

'All the better for getting this finished.' He began hauling magazine clippings, jottings on lined paper and sketches out of his bag. Penny and the others were suddenly completely absorbed in their jobs.

My heart sank. Colin had been writing a book ever since he first came in to see us, and would regularly turn up with fragments of it that he wanted us to discuss. It was going to be a cookery book, and he had chosen us to be his publishers. Penny and I had often tried to explain to him the difference between binding an interesting collection of personal recipes and publishing a cookery book, but he took no notice.

I spotted a flaccid curl of bacon rind sticking to one of the papers, and had to stop myself from taking a brisk step backwards. 'Colin, we're not book publishers. I told you that, didn't I?'

He gazed around him with an ever fresh air of surprise and bewilderment. 'Yes, you are. I know you are. Look at all your books.'

'We just put covers on them. We restore old books.'

'Exactly.' Colin nodded triumphantly. 'So you can put covers on mine. I'll pay you, you know.'

'I know, Colin. But we aren't publishers. Putting a cover on . . . on your *manuscript* won't get it into the bookshops. You have to . . . well, you have to have the text edited, then marketing people would have to look at designs for it, and thousands of copies would have to be printed, and then salesmen would have to sell it to booksellers . . .' I felt weary at the mere thought of all this effort.

'Exactly.'

'But we don't do any of these things, Colin.' I reached out for his plastic bag and very gently began putting the rancid, greasy pages into it.

He watched me for a second or two, then he grabbed the bag from me and began hauling the contents out again. 'My book's important, I'm telling you.' His voice was rising. We tussled briefly with the bag, and the bacon rind dropped in a limp ringlet on the counter.

'I'll tell you what, Colin,' I said reluctantly, to stop him shouting. 'There's something we could do for you, if you'd like it.'

'What?'

I took him by the arm and showed him a photographer's portfolio in dark navy-blue cloth with a lining of pale-green linen paper. 'We could make you a beautiful case like this, and you can put your recipes in it.'

'Can I choose the colour?'

'Of course. Any colour you like, Colin.' Including sky-blue pink.

He expressed a preference for red. Promising that he would call in again tomorrow to see how the job was progressing, he left.

'Christ on a bike,' Penny muttered as the four of us raised our eyebrows at each other. 'Anyone want a coffee?'

Jack was sitting in his armchair again when I got home from work, apparently absorbed in *Neighbours*. He looked dirtier and even more exhausted than he had done yesterday. It was Lola's last night at home before going back to university. She was ironing, also with her eyes fixed on the television. I let my bag drop to the floor.

'Good day, Mum?' Lola asked.

'Er, not bad, thanks. What about you?'

She nodded. 'Yeah.'

'Jack?'

Just the way that he shrugged his shoulders made me want to yell at him. I took a deep breath and began rummaging in the freezer. It was going to have to be defrost du jour tonight, because I didn't have the energy to start a meal from scratch.

As soon as *Neighbours* was over Jack went upstairs. I sat on the sofa and watched the six o'clock news, and when Lola finished ironing she brought over two glasses of red wine and joined me.

'I'll miss you,' I said, as I always did when she was about to go off. I did rely on her, more than I should have done, for companionship but also for the lovely warmth of her life that I enjoyed at second hand—the parties and nights out clubbing that she'd describe in tactfully edited detail the next day, the friends who dropped in and lounged around the kitchen, and the certainty that anything was possible.

'I know, Mum. I'll miss you too. But I'll be back for the weekend in a couple of weeks.'

'So you will. Is there any more of that red? How does he seem to you, the last couple of days?'

'He' was always Jack in Lola's and my conversations.

'Very quiet.'

'But he's been making less fuss about school the last two days. Maybe the worst's over.'

Lola said, 'I hope so.'

Jack ate most of the dinner, finishing Lola's portion even after he had devoured his own second helping.

'Hey, bruv. Is school food getting even worse?' Lola teased.

'I was hungry, OK? What's wrong with that?'

'I never said there was anything wrong. Sorry I asked.'

After dinner Lola went out to meet some friends and Jack retreated again. He didn't answer when I knocked on his door. I called out good night and told him to sleep well.

Lola saw Jack and me off in the morning and said goodbye. She would drive herself north later in the day.

Colin came in twice to the bindery, and on the second visit he was aggrieved to discover that we hadn't even started work on his box.

'There are twelve other jobs ahead of yours,' Penny told him.

'Well, I've had some more thoughts about how I want it.'

'Don't you want to hear our estimate first of what it's going to cost?'

I was trying to signal to her to go easy, but Colin was grandly insisting that cost didn't matter to him. His money was as good as anyone else's. The phone rang and I picked it up. A voice asked for Mrs Bailey.

'Speaking.' At the same time I was frowning because although Jack and Lola went under Tony's name, after the divorce I had deliberately gone back to being just Sadie Thompson again.

'This is Paul Rainbird, at the school.'

'Is something wrong?' Paul Rainbird was Jack's head of year. I felt a rush of blood in my ears.

'No, nothing at all. I wanted to ask how Jack is.'

'Why?'

'We haven't seen him for three days. Is he ill?'

The lack of protest in the mornings, the dirtiness and exhaustion and his appetite in the evenings fell belatedly into place. Anxiety for Jack overtook the usual nagging concern. 'I'd better come in and see you.'

Mr Rainbird said he would be at school until six that evening. I looked at my watch. Ten to four. Colin was reluctantly shuffling out.

'Jack's been bunking off,' I told Penny. 'I've got to go and see his teacher.'

The school wasn't far from our house, so it didn't take me long to drive there. As I parked the car there were streams of children coming out of the gates. I pushed my way against the current. There were so many different statements being made within the elastic confines of school uniform, so much yelling and kicking and threatening and ganging up. Survival was the prize of the fittest—and you could see which kids were the natural survivors. They were the cool ones and the disciples of the cool ones, with others who hung around on the fringes and took their cues from them. The rest straggled on in ones and twos, keeping out of the way.

Lola had been the coolest of cool. She had achieved this by breaking every school rule and defying me daily about her clothes and her hair, and her attitudes and the company she kept. But even then, on some deeper level we had still been allies. We were both women and for all our differences we had the comfort of being the same.

In my mind's eye now I saw Jack, and he was smaller and paler than all these children, and *different*. Different even from the wary singles. I clenched my fists into tight balls, wanting to defend him.

I found my way to the Year Seven office at the end of a green corridor.

'Sit down, Mrs Bailey,' the teacher said, as he shook my hand.

'Thompson,' I murmured. 'I'm divorced from Jack's father.'

Briefly my eyes met the teacher's. Mr Rainbird nodded, registering my statement. He was wearing a blue shirt and his colourless hair almost touched his collar. He looked tired. If, without knowing him, I had been forced to guess his occupation I would have said English teacher in a large comprehensive school.

'Is Jack being bullied?' I asked.

'Has he said so?'

'He hasn't said anything. I know he's not happy at school, not the way my daughter Lola was, but I didn't know it was as bad as this.'

'I remember Lola.' Mr Rainbird nodded appreciatively. 'Although I never taught her. How's she getting on?'

'Fine. She's studying at Manchester now.'

There was some shouting and crashing outside the door, but the teacher seemed not to hear it. 'I don't think he's being bullied,' he said. 'Jack doesn't stand out enough, either in a bad way or a good way. He's a loner, but that seems to be out of choice. He's very quiet, very serious. His work is adequate, as you know, although he doesn't try very hard. He gives the impression of absence. But mostly only mental absence, at least until this week. Has anything changed for him lately, at home?'

'His grandfather died, at the very end of last term.'

The teacher looked at me. He had a sympathetic, creased, battle-worn face. I thought he must be somewhere in his late forties.

'Yes, I remember now. Does Jack miss him badly?'

I tried to answer as accurately as I could. 'Not in the everyday sense, because . . . well, he didn't live nearby. But now that he's gone, yes, I think so. It's another absence in Jack's life.'

I realised that I had dashed here in the hope that Mr Rainbird would be able to offer me explanations for the way Jack behaved. But this was what he was looking for from me, his mother.

'What about his dad?' he asked.

'Tony remarried and had two more children. They live the other side of London. He sees Jack and Lola as often as he can, but he does have a lot of calls on his time. Jack lacks a male role model.'

Mr Rainbird half smiled. 'Some people would say that's no bad thing.'

I knew he said it not as a teacher, but as himself. I wondered if he was married and whether his wife thought all men were monsters.

I smiled back. 'In Jack's case, a father figure would be helpful.'

The root of Jack's problem was with me, but the root of *that* problem went back much further. Back beyond Stanley, even Tony. I could do relationships with women, I reckoned, but I got it wrong with men. From Ted onwards. I blinked back a surge of irrational tears.

'So, what should we do?' Mr Rainbird asked. He was looking down at his hands and I knew it was to give me a chance to recompose myself.

I stared hard at a pile of exercise books until I had my face under control. 'I'll go home and talk to him. I'll try to get to the root of this.'

'I'll talk to him too. Maybe between us we can work out what the problem is. What do you think he's doing instead of being at school?'

I shook my head. 'I don't think he's doing anything. I think he's . . . just killing time.' He was waiting for this to be over, dreaming of when he could change something for himself. I remembered how that was.

We both stood up and Mr Rainbird went to open the door for me. 'Are you all right?' he asked.

'Yes, thanks.' I wondered how distraught I actually looked.

'We'll speak again, then.' He didn't attempt any empty reassurances and he didn't make authoritarian demands. I liked him. We shook hands a second time and I retraced my path out to the gates.

Jack was sitting in his accustomed place. There was plenty of evidence of toast, cheese, jam and yoghurt having been eaten. It was no wonder that he came home hungry. He would probably have had almost nothing to eat since breakfast.

I turned off the television and sat down. I could feel Jack waiting tensely for me to say something.

'I've just been to see Mr Rainbird,' I said.

He flinched, just a little. I waited, but he didn't volunteer anything.

'I want you to tell me why you haven't been to school for three days.'

His face was a crescent of misery. I had been keeping my imagination in check but now it broke loose and galloped away from me. I pictured drug deals, shifty kids who hung around by the canal, a leering fat man beckoning from a doorway. The images catapulted me out of my chair and I grabbed Jack by the arms and shook him hard. 'Where've you been?' I yelled. 'Who have you been with?'

He stared at me. His eyes had rings under them. 'Nowhere.'

'You must have been somewhere.'

'I walked around. Sat on a bench. Then I came home.'

'For three whole days?'

He nodded, mute and despairing.

I sank back on my heels and tried to take stock. If he had let some pervert befriend him, I thought, if he had been sniffing glue out of a brown-paper bag, or buying crack, would he give me a clue? 'That must have been horrible,' I said. 'You must have felt lonely.'

He said, 'I watched the pigeons. They're filthy. Did you know that there are hardly any sparrows left in London?'

I closed my eyes for a second. I didn't know whether to be relieved or infuriated. 'Let's not talk about birds right now, Jack. Let's try to work out exactly what it is about going to school that makes you so miserable. Is someone picking on you? A teacher? Other kids?'

'Not really. They think I'm sad. But I think they're even sadder.'

The rock of his unhappiness held glinting seams of mineral disdain. Jack was sharp-witted and he wouldn't have much time for losers, even though he might currently consider himself to be one.

'All of them? Everyone? Isn't there anyone you like or admire?'

'Mr Rainbird's OK. Some of the boys are all right. People like Wes Gordon and Jason Smith. But they wouldn't be interested in me. And the rest are dumb.'

This was the most information he had volunteered in about six months. I supposed Wes and Jason would be the cool ones, big, blunt-faced boys surrounded by hangers-on like those I had seen swaggering out of school this afternoon. I couldn't see Jack in their company any more than he could see himself. I pushed my luck. 'Go on.'

His face contracted with irritation. It was just like watching a hermit crab pull back into its shell. 'That's all,' he snapped. 'You always want stuff. I'll go back to school on Monday if that's what you want.'

'I want you to want to go. What I want isn't important.'

His head lifted then and he stared at me. 'Is that so?' he sneered.

I was still catching my breath when the doorbell rang. Jack turned the television on again and increased the volume.

It was Mel on the doorstep, with two carrier bags and an armful of red parrot tulips. I had forgotten that she had promised to cook us supper. She took one look at my face. 'You'd forgotten I was coming.'

'No. Well, yeah. I'm sorry. I've just been having a set-to with Jack.'

'Do you want me to go away again?'

'Depends on what's in the bags.'

'Sashimi-grade bluefin tuna. Limes, coriander, crème fraîche, a tarte aux poires from Sally Clarke's, a nice piece of Roquefort . . .'

I opened the door wider. 'Come right inside.'

Mel breezed into the kitchen. Her polished brightness lifted my spirits by several degrees.

'Hi, Jackson.'

Jack quite liked Mel. 'Hi,' he muttered.

'I've come to cook you and your mum some dinner. However, that's going to be tricky if I can't hear myself think.'

'Oh. Right.' He prodded at the remote and Buffy went from screeching to mouthing like a goldfish.

Mel busily unpacked fish and cheese. 'Great. How's school?'

I tried to signal at her but she missed the gesturing.

'It's shit,' Jack said.

'So no change there, then.'

I thought I caught the faintest twitch of a smile on his face before it went stiff again. 'No. None.' He eased himself out of the room.

While Mel started making a lime and coriander butter I poured us both a drink and told her what had happened.

'I'm worried. Really worried,' I concluded. 'I never get to the root of anything with Jack. He clams up or shuts himself in his room. I never know what he's thinking. What must it have been like for him, wandering around with nowhere to go for three days?'

'Worrying won't help,' Mel said. She came round the worktop and wound her arms round me. The touch was comforting.

'I think he'll be all right, Sadie. I've got no grounds for saying so, but I still think it. Remember what Lola was like when we first met?'

'How could I forget?'

'Right, then.' She let go of me. 'Now, do the veg for me, please.'

I did as I was told, dropping little peas and fingernail-sized beans into the steamer. 'Let's talk about something else,' I suggested.

'How about me?'

'Perfect.'

Mel shimmied the length of the worktop, rapping the knife point on jars and pans. 'I met someone.'

'No.' This wasn't exactly an infrequent occurrence.

She stopped dancing and held up her hand. I had been so preoccupied that it was only now I noticed that her face was as bright as a star. 'Yes,' she said. 'I really have met someone.'

While she told me about this latest one we finished off the cooking, tasting and discussing and amending, as we had done many times before. These were the evenings I liked best, the companionable times of making unhurried food in a warm kitchen while the light turned to dark outside. I lit a pair of yellow candles and the glow wiped out all the dust and shabby corners, and shone on Mel's star face and the orange-red tulips she had brought.

Mel flipped the tuna off the griddle. 'It's ready.'

I went to the foot of the stairs and called Jack. He appeared almost at once, changed out of his school clothes and with wet hair combed flat from the shower. He sidled to his chair and sat down. Immediately he started wolfing down the fish.

'Are you hungry?' Mel asked.

'Yes.' He glanced at me. 'Didn't get anything to eat at lunchtime.'

'And why's that?'

'I should think Mum told you.'

'Yeah. So, what amazing things did you do that were worth missing school for?' Mel leaned forward, her attention focused on him. There was no censure, only friendly interest.

'Nothing,' Jack muttered.

'Really? It sounds deadly boring.'

He nodded and went on eating. By the time the pudding came, he even joined briefly in our conversation, speaking slowly, as if he weren't quite used to the sound of his own voice. After we finished and he said good night, Mel and I opened another bottle of wine.

'Thanks, Mel. For being so nice to Jack.'

'I wasn't nice, I was ordinary.' This was true. Mel had a gift for being ordinarily warm and inclusive.

'You look very happy,' I said. 'This Jasper must be good news.'

'I am happy. I wish you were.'

I felt some of the protective walls around me shifting, as if Mel's darts might pierce them. I didn't like it.

'What did you mean, when you said your father was a con artist?'

What did I mean? There was the pressure inside me, building up inside my skull, threatening to break through the bones. 'Ted was a great nose, a fine perfumer, but that wasn't enough for him.' I chose the words carefully, biting them off with my tongue and teeth. 'He always wanted something more. He wanted to be rich and he never was. He wanted glamour but except for the illusion of perfume his life was humdrum. He thrived on secrecy, the nose-tapping and winking kind that is all to do with deals, scams, setting up little businesses. I think he must have lived through his fantasies and the reality was always disappointing. Women ultimately disappointed him. His daughter did, too.'

Mel leaned back in her chair. '*You* are his daughter. You talk about the relationship as if it involves someone else.'

That was truer than she realised. Somewhere within the numbness around Ted's death there was raw grief, yet I could only touch the outlines of it. As if it didn't belong to me, but to someone I knew.

'Mel, I'm not you. I didn't grow up in your family.'

'What about his house? Are you going to go and sort it out?'

'Yes.' It came to me now that my reluctance to do this formed part of the numbness. Of course I feared going back to his house and unlocking the memories, but sooner or later I would have to.

Mel insisted, 'I'll come and help you.'

'Yes. Thank you.'

I knew I didn't want anyone else to be there, not even Lola or Jack. It wasn't just furniture and clothes and memories I had to deal with. It was the way the very scent of the place shook my soul.

FIVE

I UNLOCKED THE FRONT DOOR of Ted's house and gently pushed it open.

The silence pressed on my ears and in an effort to dispel it I walked to the kitchen and rattled around opening cupboards. There was the tin tea caddy from our old house, with pictures of the Houses of Parliament rubbed away where his thumb and palm had grasped it so many times. Inside, I knew, was the teaspoon with an RAF crest on the handle.

I rummaged around for some rubbish sacks and went upstairs. I was here to go through Ted's belongings. I didn't want to keep many of his possessions—there were more than enough memories already.

The blue-tiled bathroom was a comfortless narrow space that reminded me again of Ted humming 'All Things Bright and Beautiful' as he shaved. Me perched on the edge of the bath at our old house, gazing at him, trying by the sheer power of concentration to draw some attention to myself. It must have been infuriating for him.

There was a bottle on the wooden shelf over the basin. I reached for it, unscrewed the cap and automatically sniffed. The scent of his cologne rushed into my nose and mouth and eyes, and my obedient brain performed its trick of instant recall. The here and now dropped away, and there was my father wearing a dark blazer and a lightly checked shirt with a cravat, paisley-patterned. He was freshly shaven, with his skin taut and shiny where he had rubbed and patted it with the cologne. His thick hair was slicked back with some kind of brilliantine.

I still didn't like his cologne. Maybe it represented the way he wanted to be, or perhaps with his love of secrecy he just relished putting up another smoke screen. But to me it still smelt like a lie. I screwed the lid back on the bottle and reached to replace it on the shelf. Then I remembered that I was here to sort out his belongings and dropped it into a rubbish sack instead.

203

I cleared the bathroom cupboard. I worked methodically, telling myself that these were only inanimate things, the inevitable remnants we would all leave behind, some day.

Next I went to the bedroom. I took his jackets and suits off their hangers and piled them up, thinking that maybe they would do for Oxfam. The cuffs were frayed and the trousers bagged, but they were all dry-cleaned and brushed. Ted was always a dapper dresser. I folded up his thick white silk evening scarf and put it aside, thinking that Lola might like to have it.

In the drawers of the tallboy there were socks and pants, and a coil of ties and paisley cravats. I put aside his RAF tie, frayed at the edges where he had tied the knot so many times, and consigned the rest to the disposal pile, along with all his well-polished but worn shoes.

I was up to my wrists in his old clothes now and the scent of him was everywhere, but I told myself it was just a job to be done. I kept at it and the pile of black rubbish sacks mounted up on the landing.

The bottom drawer of the tallboy was half full of papers. Reluctantly I knelt down and began to sift through them. They were mostly old bills, but in a manila envelope I found a handful of photographs. There was one of my mother and me, in the back garden of the old house. I was perhaps four years old, scowling under the brim of a sunhat. Faye was characteristically looking into the distance away from the camera, as if she wished herself elsewhere. I had seen this picture before and almost all the others in the envelope, including one of Ted looking rakish and handsome in front of an MG. Somebody else's MG, although he managed a proprietorial air. There were also four or five photographs of women.

One of them caught my attention. She had a plump face with a round dimpled chin and her hair was drawn up at the sides with combs. The lipsticked margins of her smile spread fractionally beyond the true contours of her lips, giving her a slapdash, come-and-get-me look.

Auntie Viv.

Viv wasn't the first of Ted's girlfriends or 'aunties' as I was taught to call them when I was little. But she was memorable because she was friendlier to me than any of the others.

I sat down on the green candlewick cover of Ted's bed. I was Jack's age again.

'Sadie, this is Auntie Viv.'

My father was smiling at the woman who had followed him into the hallway of our house in Dorset Avenue, Hendon.

'Hello, love.' Auntie Viv grinned at me. She had silvery blonde hair and was wearing a tight skirt with a fan of creases over the thighs, and high heels that tilted her forward and made her bum stick out.

'Hello,' I muttered. I didn't want any more aunts. I wanted my father sitting with just me in the evenings to watch *Hancock's Half Hour* or maybe even helping me with my French homework. I wanted my mother back as well, of course, but even I knew that there was no point in dwelling on this one.

Auntie Viv made me sit beside her on the sofa. Ted brought out the gin bottle and the best glasses with diamonds and stars incised on them.

'Give her a little one,' Viv suggested and, to my amazement, Ted poured me a small glass of sweet Martini.

'Cheers, love,' Viv said, and took a gulp of her gin and tonic. She scissored her fingers—red varnished nails, lots of rings—in my short, wavy hair. 'Hasn't she got lovely hair? Is it natural?'

I thought this was a stupid question. I was twelve. As if I would be able to choose to have my hair permed or dyed. 'Yes,' I said stiffly, but I couldn't help yielding a little to Viv's admiration. They made an unfamiliar pair of sensations for me, the being admired and the yielding.

'Auntie Viv's a ladies' hairdresser,' Ted explained. 'We're planning a little business venture together. A range of exclusive hair-care products.'

'Shampoos, setting lotion, conditioner,' Viv said dreamily. 'Your dad's going to create them for me. My own range.'

'Really?' I asked. 'Will they be in Boots?'

Ted gave me one of his cold, quelling looks but Viv nodded. 'Of course they will. And in all the salons. With my expertise in the field of hairstyling and your dad's genius as a fragrance artist—he *is*, you know—we will be creating something every woman will want.'

I was impressed. Ted splashed some more gin into Viv's glass. They settled down for a business talk, but Viv told me that I should listen in. The ideas of the younger market were always important, she said.

I listened eagerly for a while. Viv had a lot of ideas for names and the shapes of the bottles and packages. She drew sketches in a notebook, tore out the leaves and handed them to Ted and me for our approval. She wanted to call the shampoo Vivienne.

They both drank a couple more large gins and I drained the sticky dregs of my Martini. The drink made me sleepy, and my arms and legs felt like plasticine when I shifted on the sofa. After a while Viv went into the kitchen, wobbling a little on her high heels, and made a plate of cream crackers with slices of cheese and a blob of pickle on top. Viv turned on the television. She sat close up against Ted and let one of her shoes swing loose from her nyloned toes.

'Hop off to bed, now, Sadie,' Ted said, when we finished eating.

I began to protest, but he fixed me with his icy grey stare.

'Good night, pet,' Viv murmured. 'See you soon.'

That was the beginning of quite a good time. Ted went out in the evenings even more, and I assumed that when he wasn't at home with me he was with Viv. She was safe territory, I felt. She brought me her *Woman* and *Woman's Own* when she had finished reading them. She chatted about lipsticks and clothes. One evening she brought a glass bottle with a bulb spray out of her handbag. She sprayed the insides of my wrists and showed me how to rub them together to warm the skin.

'What do you think?' Her face was pink with excitement.

I thought the perfume was wonderful. It smelt of cloves and carnations, and it made me think of velvet dresses and candlelight reflected in tall mirrors. Ted stood watching us, one eyebrow raised.

'It's called Vivienne,' she whispered. 'He created it for me. Better than an old shampoo, don't you think?'

'Yes,' I managed to say. I glanced at my father but he was looking fondly at Viv. After that I always knew when Auntie Viv had been in the house. The perfume lingered in the cushions and curtains of the front room, and in the bathroom, and round the threshold of Ted's bedroom.

There were evenings at home when Ted and she worked on their hair products. Tubs of chemicals appeared on the dining table and there were snippets of card and colour charts too, and spiral-bound books of different kinds of lettering. I particularly liked the letters. I found some greaseproof paper and laid it over the biggest, curliest set of letters. I traced off my name, Sadie Faye Thompson, playing about with the spacing until the balance pleased me. At my elbow Ted and Viv were arguing because Viv thought it was taking him too long to produce her prototype shampoos, but I barely heard them.

I began to talk about my Auntie Viv to the other girls at school, boasting a little about how young and pretty she was, and showing them what she did to my hair. It was growing and she had cut a soft fringe instead of the way I used to wear it, pulled to one side with a hair clip.

The beginning of the end came on Viv's birthday.

I made her a card, using my special lettering. It said 'Auntie Viv' on the front with a red heart. Inside I wrote, 'Wishing you many happy returns of the day. With all my love, Sadie.' I picked some roses from the garden and tied them with a ribbon.

Ted told me he was taking Viv for a night out.

'Where's the birthday girl?' he fretted while we waited. At last a taxi drew up outside.

Viv was wearing a short, tight dress in a patterned cream material. I started singing 'Happy Birthday' as soon as Ted opened the door, but then they were kissing each other and the sound sort of petered out in my mouth. She hugged me anyway, once they were finished.

Ted had a present for her. It was a big box done up with ribbons and shiny paper, and Viv fell on it with a little gasp. She shook it and held it up to listen to it as if it might be ticking, and then undid the wrapping, very slowly, to tease us.

There was a white box inside and out of a nest of filmy tissue paper came a shoe. It had a silver heel like a real stiletto blade and the rest of it was exactly the same cream colour as her dress. 'How lovely,' she murmured, but I saw a little pout crease her lipstick. 'But, darling, I thought it was going to be my shampoo and conditioner. You promised me they were going to be ready.'

'Try them on,' Ted ordered. She did as she was told, and I saw the shoes were a perfect fit.

Then I fetched the card and roses I had hidden in my bedroom. 'Here you are,' I said.

'Look what she's done,' she cried to Ted. 'Isn't that the loveliest thing you ever saw?'

I saw his face as he examined the card. His mouth pursed and his eyes went flat. At first I didn't understand why he was angry, but then it came to me. Ted was jealous because she seemed to like my gift more than his shoes. There was something else too, something more complicated. Ted didn't want me making any offering to Viv that didn't include him. She belonged to him and I belonged to him, but he wanted to keep us separate because that gave him greater power over both of us.

I blinked. I felt as if in a matter of seconds I had slid from being a child in the dark all the way into adulthood. I felt strangely elated. It seemed that I had power too—the power to arouse jealousy. I smiled serenely at Ted, from within the shelter of Viv's scented hug.

'Very nice,' he said, shooting his wrist out of his white shirt-cuff and examining his watch. 'It's time we were going, darling.'

'Oh, Ted.' Viv suddenly sparkled. 'I've got an idea. Let's take Sadie out with us tonight.'

'We can't do that.'

'Why not? It's my birthday, after all, so you should let me choose.'

Her pout was still pretty and seductive but with my new illuminated vision I could see that there was a steely core in Viv. I nestled against her, enjoying the sight of my omnipotent father's discomfort. I would still have sided with him in the end, in anything that really mattered, but I couldn't help being pleased and intrigued by the new perspectives.

Viv patted my bottom and giggled. 'Go upstairs and put something nice on, Sadie, and we'll hit the town.'

I didn't have anything that would have fitted Viv's notion of nice, or my own for that matter, but I did my best. When I came down again Viv took a zip purse out of her handbag, tilted my head to the light and applied a quick coat of mascara to my almost invisible eyelashes.

'Now,' she told Ted. 'You can take your girls out and show them a good time.'

In the back of Ted's Ford Consul, flashing past the houses in Dorset Avenue in the midsummer dusk, I felt as if I'd gone to heaven.

The evening, as it turned out, was closer to hell.

To begin with Ted was morose and Viv was determinedly, skittishly cheery. She kept winking at me as if we were conspirators. The three of us sat at a round table in the corner of a beery, smoky place that was somewhere between a pub and a nightclub. In another corner there was a dais with a piano and a microphone stand. While Ted was at the bar a pianist came on in a dinner jacket. Ted and Viv had big glasses of gin, with ice and little slivers of lemon in them. I had a smaller measure of sticky-sweet Martini. We all clinked our glasses and said cheers before we drank. I felt happy—a kind of shiny, explosive new happiness. I loved Viv and I wanted the three of us to live together in a world that had mysterious and exotic places like this in it.

I sipped my drink and watched everything. Ted and Viv knew lots of people, Ted especially. Men came over to the table and kissed Viv, and then leaned over to murmur in Ted's ear. The women who accompanied them mostly had tight, low-cut dresses like Viv's, and backcombed hair. Ted and Viv were drinking hard. Rounds of drinks were sent over by friends sitting at other tables and Viv blew kisses at the men to say thank you.

After the pianist bowed off the platform there was dancing. Some couples jived and other, younger ones swayed and wriggled on their own. Mostly, though, people sort of waltzed in unsteady clinches. Ted and Viv got up and danced together but then a man cut in on them and swept Viv into a showy routine. When I looked for Ted I saw he was dancing with another blonde woman, holding her hips close against his with his hand on her bottom. Viv came back to our table first. She flounced down and made a 'so what' face in my direction.

When Ted came back she demanded, 'What's all that about?'

'All what?' he said coldly.

'That cow.' Viv sniffed.

'Don't be so common.'

The temperature of everything changed. From being the pouting belle of the evening Viv turned tremulous and uncertain. She pulled her chair tight up against Ted's but he was watching the dancers instead of paying any attention to her.

All of a sudden Viv stood up and almost ran away towards the Ladies. Ted's eyes didn't follow her. Instead he leaned heavily towards me, the elbow of his blazer smearing drops of drink spilt on our table. 'All right there, Princess? What d'you make of this, then?' His voice was slurred.

I tried to smile but I was distracted by the red faces looming everywhere, all gaping mouths and bristly hair.

A minute later, it seemed, Viv was back again. She had been crying. Her eyes were teary and smudged. She grabbed Ted by his sleeve and began pulling him to his feet. He jerked her wrist and she tried to slap his face. When she couldn't get her hand to connect she wrenched off her shoe and tried to stab him with the silver dagger heel. The red faces all turned in our direction. My head was swimming but I was mortified to see my father and Auntie Viv fighting in public.

'I want to go home,' I blurted out. My words seemed to drop into a sudden pool of silence and the speeded-up film slowed to a dead stop.

Then a woman at the next table leaned across. 'You take her home, Ted. She ought to be safe in her bed. What would Faye think?'

The mere mention of my mother's name in this place made tears run burning out of my eyes. Now Viv and I were both weeping.

'You mind your own business,' Ted snapped at the woman. But he and Viv let go of each other. Ted walked away and we followed him as best we could past the crowded tables to the door.

All the way home in the car my father and Auntie Viv shouted ugly things at each other. But every time I closed my eyes the car and the passing lights spun round so sickeningly that I didn't care what else was happening. When we got inside the house I managed to get myself upstairs and into the bathroom before I threw up.

Much later, when I lay shivering under the blankets, I could still hear the two of them storming at each other downstairs.

I didn't see Auntie Viv after that. I missed her, and the *Woman's Own*. 'Isn't she going to come and see us any more?' I asked Ted at last.

'No,' he admitted. He looked depressed, but he tried to cover it up. 'Plenty more fish in the sea, eh? And she had no business acumen whatsoever. Anyway, you're my girl. That's quite enough for me.'

This was blatantly untrue, of course, although I still wanted to believe him and was disappointed when the next auntie arrived. She was thin, and wore matador pants and called herself Maxine. She had a strong aversion to jealous, beady-eyed, twelve-year-old daughters and she didn't mind showing it. But, I thought, I wasn't a kid any more. I wouldn't let Maxine know that I cared about anything.

I put Viv's photograph back into the manila envelope. One of the other photographs, of a woman with wind-blown hair sitting on a stone wall, stirred a faint memory but I couldn't recall a name. I put the envelope aside to be kept along with Ted's evening scarf, his silver-backed hair-brush, a brass cigarette lighter and a leather address book. It didn't take me long to clear the rest of the room. Everything that didn't go in the rubbish bags or onto the Oxfam pile could be left to the house-clearance people. And once the house was empty, it could go on the market.

Ted's solicitor and I had already talked about his will. Half of his estate was to come to me and the other half was to be divided between Lola and Jack. Apart from the house, which was mortgaged, and a couple of thousand pounds in the bank, he didn't have anything else.

In the living room I checked the bookcase. There were paperbacks of Ludlum, Higgins and Le Carré, a few military biographies and, lying flat on the bottom shelf, three volumes bound in dark brown calf. They each had Ted's initials, ELT for Edwin Lawrence Thompson, blind tooled on the front. Inside were pages of notes, all in Ted's handwriting. These were Ted's fragrance notes and formulae. Some of them had the names of customers against them—occasionally Yardley or Coty, more often ET&P, which had been the name of his company. The P stood for Partners, although I wasn't aware that he had actually had any. One for-mula was labelled 'for Janice, August 1963', another just 'Linda'.

They weren't young any longer, these women of Ted's who had danced and kissed and promised all through his best years. Maybe they weren't even alive now. But the perfumes that he had devised for them were still here after forty years, perfectly preserved in the dense pages of notes. I snapped the book shut, but still the ghosts of his women and his work and Ted himself swam up at me. And even when I had dragged the sacks of rubbish out to the dustbin and parcelled up his clothes for the charity shop and locked the door, I didn't feel any sense of relief. The pressure inside my skull was there again, and it was as if a dam might burst and release some black flood tide that would wash me away.

I got home just before Jack arrived back from school. He came in and sat down in front of the television. I made us a pot of tea and a plate of toast, and he devoured it with his eyes fixed on the screen.

'What did you do at school today, Jack?' I asked. I assumed that I would have heard from Mr Rainbird if he had bunked off again.

A shrug.

'Did you have Biology?' Biology was the only subject for which he had any enthusiasm.

He gave me a dry look. 'It's Thursday.'

'Ah. Would you like some more toast?'

'No, but I'll have more tea, if there is any.'

Encouraged by the normality of this exchange I refilled our mugs and went to sit by him. The slope of his shoulders and his bony wrists made my longing to gather him up in my arms so strong that I had to clench my fists to stop myself. It was one of the paradoxes of parenthood, I thought, that the demonstrative love I had yearned for as a child was utterly rejected by my own son.

'I was up at Granddad's today. Sorting out his things. I brought some bits and pieces back with me, I don't know whether you and Lola want to keep anything?'

He slid out of the armchair and leaned on the table while I unpacked the box. My hands shook a little. He clicked the lighter once or twice but couldn't make it ignite, and glanced without much interest at the books of notes. I shook the photographs out of the envelope and spread them out to show him the picture of his grandmother and me in my sunhat. The aunties' forgotten smiles beamed out of the sheaf at us.

'Some of Ted's girlfriends,' I said unnecessarily.

Jack picked up the picture of the woman sitting on a stone wall and studied it for a minute. 'She was at the funeral,' he said.

Now I remembered the woman in the dusty fur. 'I thought I recognised something in the picture. What was her name?'

'Audrey,' Jack said.

That's right. 'You'll be his daughter,' she had said. 'I'm Audrey.'

Now Jack was flipping through the address book. 'Here,' he said.

Sure enough, there was the name, no surname, almost the first entry. There was no address either. Ted must have known her well.

Jack said, 'Do you know what? She must live really near to us. Look.' The first digits of the telephone number were the same as ours. 'You should call her and ask if she wants any of this.'

'Yes,' I agreed in surprise. 'Yes, I could do that.'

After Jack had gone up to his bedroom I rang Tony.

'Hello, Sade. Everything OK?' His voice sounding exhausted and at the same time utterly familiar.

I see Tony only rarely but I still feel that I know him better than anyone else. Even when I was leaving him for Stanley I still loved him in that well-rubbed, faintly exasperated way of long-standing couples.

'I'm worried about Jack,' I said.

'Sadie, you're always worried about Jack. What's happened?'

I told him.

'Yeah, OK. That's legitimate worry.'

I felt a rush of relief at being able to talk to him. 'What shall we do?'

'I'll talk to him. Is he coming to us this weekend?'

'If he wants to. Does that suit you and Suzy?'

'I'll check with her.' We always made our arrangements in this polite, considerate way. It was Tony's nature to be thoughtful and I did my best to be so because I was the one who had caused all this dislocation. He asked, 'Do you think it's anything to do with your dad dying?'

'Yes, partly.' It also had to do with other, longer-standing problems in Jack's life, mostly connected to me. In the pause while we both listened to the noise of young children in the background, I endured the familiar twist of guilt and regret at having left my husband.

'Sadie?'

'What?'

'It may be the wrong time to say this. You won't want to hear it, anyway. But do you think you might be trying to love Jack too much? Do you think he might respond if you gave him some extra space?'

'Extra space?' I repeated angrily. 'What kind of a tired old cliché is that? And what do you know, Tony, about how much space I do or don't allow Jack? You see him every other weekend at the most.'

'The events that resulted in this situation weren't dictated by me.'

I bit my tongue, but in spite of my good intentions I still retorted, 'I *know* that, Tony, for God's sake. You can't resist a reminder, can you?'

My relief at being able to discuss our son turned to anger with myself for the waste of all our joint history and achievements. If Tony and I were still a solid couple, how much more comfortable would Jack therefore be, with himself and the rest of the world?

Even as I speculated, I knew that if I were to feel guilty for the rest of my life, I still couldn't undo what was done.

I wondered if Ted had been thinking along the same lines while he lay in his hospital bed and held on to my hand.

I would never know, now.

Tony's voice at the other end of the line almost made me jump. 'I've got to go and help Suzy with the girls,' he said. 'I'll give Jack a call and sort out about the weekend. I'm not supposing for a minute that my

involvement will solve any problems for him, but I'll do what I can.'
'Thanks,' I said.
'I love Jack too, you know. And you as well, if that counts for anything.'
'Thanks,' I repeated, blinking at sudden tears. 'Bye, then.'

SIX

EVELYN AND PENNY WERE BOTH in the kitchen when I called in on the evening of the day after my trip to Ted's house. Cassie was sitting on her booster seat at the table, doing her favourite puzzle.

It had been another long day and Colin had only just gone home after a lengthy visit to check up on the progress of his book. I had given the job to Andy, who had made a start on cutting the boards, but this wasn't nearly fast enough for Colin. 'I don't like being without my recipes, you know,' he complained. 'What if I wanted to cook one of them?'

'You could take it away with you right now,' Andy offered.

He wasn't enjoying the job and he took the view that as we'd never be paid for the work the standard didn't matter too much.

Colin certainly refused even to consider an estimate.

'Don't be stupid,' he crowed. 'If I took it away you couldn't get on with publishing it, could you?'

I wasn't sorry when the end of the day finally arrived and I could make a ten-minute visit across the yard.

Evelyn was standing at the cooker dreamily stirring pasta sauce for Cassie's supper, holding her flowing velvet sleeve out of the way with her free hand. ''Lo, Sadie,' she murmured.

Penny was peering at her computer monitor by the front window. It was VAT time but I could sense that her attention wasn't on the company books. The atmosphere in the kitchen didn't feel comfortable.

Evelyn spooned the pasta into Cassie's bowl. We put the puzzle to one side. 'Looks *good*,' I told her. 'Can't I have some?'

She wagged her head from side to side and laughed. 'No.'

There was burnished yellow late-afternoon sunlight sliding through the side windows. Evelyn curved her slender body against the door frame and gazed out across the yard to where a seat stood against a whitewashed brick wall. After a minute she drifted outside and sat on the bench with her face turned up to the evening sun.

I said, 'Pen, why don't you go and sit in the sun with Evelyn for ten minutes? Cassie and I are eating pasta.'

'Not you.' Cassie chortled. 'Mine.'

Penny took off her reading glasses and pinched her nose. 'Yes, I think I will,' she said. She shouldered her way out into the yard and I saw her sit down next to Evelyn, who didn't move up to make room.

I concentrated on persuading Cassie to use her spoon. The child's soft chin and cheeks were coated with tomato sauce and there was a globule stuck in her black eyelashes. 'Mucky baby,' I told her.

'Sadie-la-aaaady,' she retorted and I took the opportunity to post a loaded forkful into her open mouth. Between her spoon and my fork, we had emptied the dish by the time Evelyn came into the kitchen again. Two patches of red showed high up on her cheekbones. 'Come on, Cass. Bathtime now,' she said. Without a glance at me she swept the child into her arms and carried her away up the stairs, her long skirt swirling behind her in a blur of colour and flowery scent.

Penny came in when she had gone and took a two-thirds-full bottle of wine out of the fridge. 'Drink?'

'Yes, a quick one.' I was thinking of Jack who would already have been home for an hour. Penny's hand was shaking as she sloshed wine into two glasses.

'What's wrong?' I asked about a minute later, when Penny had already drunk half of hers.

'Nothing's wrong.'

'Ah.'

It had always been hard to get Penny to talk about her feelings, but since meeting Evelyn, she had been more open. Happiness had lowered her guard. For this reason I pushed a bit harder now. 'Is it Evelyn?'

'What do you mean? Is what Evelyn?'

Her wineglass was empty so I filled it again. I hadn't touched mine yet. 'You don't have to keep everything to yourself, you know.'

Penny's laugh sounded more like a cough or a groan. 'You can talk.'

It was true. I hadn't spoken to Penny or anyone else about what was happening to me. I hardly cried for my father; it seemed that I couldn't. It was more that a cloud of grief loomed over me, like a storm that threatened but refused to break.

I said gently, 'We're not talking about me right now.'

Penny sighed. 'Evelyn wants another baby.'

I couldn't see a problem in having a second Cassie for us all to lavish affection on. 'Well?' I said. 'There are ways of doing it, aren't there?'

'She wants it to be Jerry's. So Cassie can have a real brother or sister.'

I had met Jerry when he called to see Cassie. He had a high, rounded forehead, a nose that ran in a straight line from that brow to its tip, and thick black hair that he wore in a helmet of tiny braids. He was six foot four and extremely beautiful. With such parents it was no wonder that Cassie was exquisite. 'That's not impossible either, is it?'

Penny gave the scornful laugh again. 'Can you see Jerry obediently doing the business and then popping round here with the result in a jam jar? No. She wants to start fucking Jerry again.' Penny didn't use words like that, or only very seldom. Her face was stiff with the effort of containing her misery.

'Is that what she really wants? To start sleeping with Jerry again?'

'She says it would only be until she gets pregnant.'

'And you don't believe her?'

'I don't know.' She shook her head and I could see that she was losing the battle for control. 'I don't know what I'd do without her. Without the two of them.'

I moved to put my arms round her. I cupped the back of her head with one hand as if she were Cassie, and drew her forehead to rest against my shoulder. She sobbed just once, a terrible sound that seemed torn out of her chest as I rubbed her back and muttered useless soothing words. I was thinking, as I stroked her hair, that it was a long time since I had known or even dreamed of passion like Penny's. Maybe Tony was right, maybe I did channel too much of my leftover yearning towards Jack because I had nowhere else to direct it.

'Sorry,' Penny snuffled. 'I love her so much. It's stupid, isn't it?'

'I know. And no, it isn't. It's wonderful.'

'I think I'd like to talk to her on my own when she comes down again. Do you mind?'

I straightened her shoulders and rubbed away the tears from under her eyes with my thumbs. 'I'll see you tomorrow,' I said.

'Thanks, Sadie.'

Jack was in his usual position in front of the television when I got home. We went through the regular question-and-evasion routine while I put together some supper. As I was putting knives and forks on the table I pushed to one side the small pile of Ted's belongings. The address book had been lying on top of the silk evening scarf and now it slid off onto the floor. I bent down to retrieve it.

Jack was watching me. 'Are you going to ring Granddad's friend? From the funeral?'

I looked down at the little brown leather book. I had been intending to fill the fifteen minutes before supper with calls to Caz and Mel, but now I picked up the phone and flipped open the address book at A.

The ringing tone at the other end went on until I was on the point of hanging up again, but then a voice answered, 'Yes?'

Just that. I was sure it was her, but I asked anyway. 'Is that Audrey?'

'Who's this?' the voice demanded.

'It's Sadie Thompson. Ted's daughter.'

There was a pause, and then a cool chuckle. 'Is it, now?'

I plunged on. I noticed at the same time that Jack was listening hard. I explained to Audrey that I had been clearing out the house, had kept some of Ted's belongings, wondered if she would like a memento of him. 'I could drop round to see you, maybe?'

'All right,' she said, after another yawning interval. She gave me an address which was only about ten minutes' walk away and we arranged that I would call in early on Tuesday evening the following week.

'I'll come with you, if you like,' Jack offered after I had rung off.

I gazed at him in delight. 'Great,' I said.

The weekend came and went. Lola came home, mainly for a twenty-first party on the Saturday night. She arrived late on Friday evening and we sat together for an hour and shared a bottle of wine, and I listened and laughed while she talked about her escapades. There was a geography student who was really, really fit but he liked to go hiking in the Pennines at the weekends and she wasn't sure if she could handle this.

The next day I went to the supermarket, tried to do an hour's tidying up in the garden, paid some bills and cleaned the kitchen floor. I was functioning normally, but the comforts of normality evaded me. The tasks I set myself seemed pointless and I felt stiff with loneliness.

That evening I asked a neighbour's daughter to baby-sit Jack while I had supper with Caz and Graham. I didn't get back until 1.00am. Jack was in bed but Lola was still not home.

Later, the noise of my daughter coming in after the party woke me up. I knew it was very, very late but I willed myself not to look at the clock and see the worst.

Neither child emerged from bed until lunchtime again the next day, and then they sat round in their nightclothes eating cereal and yawning, and annoying each other.

'You must have been so wasted last night,' Jack needled. 'You knocked half the furniture over when you came in.'

'I wasn't.'

'It was *five* o'clock.'

'We were just chilling round at someone's place, OK? If you weren't such a sad specimen you'd know what it's like.'

'No, he wouldn't, Lola. He's twelve, not twenty,' I said, but they both ignored me. In the end I left them to it and went over to Mel's house. There were vases of fat blood-red peonies on her tables and her polished oak floorboards with their overlay of pale rugs were completely free of dust. Mel herself was unmade-up and looked even better than with her painted-on public face. If I hadn't liked her so much I would have felt jealous. When she passed close to me I could smell her perfume, a strong, sweet waft of tuberose today. In fact, scents seemed to rise up all around me lately, as if by taking the lid off Ted's cologne bottle I had unstoppered not just his but a thousand genies.

She gave me a cup of tea and we sat in her sunny kitchen to drink it. I noticed that there was an empty champagne bottle standing on the floor by the bin and Mel's glance followed mine.

'Jasper was here last night. Do you know what? He *cooked* for me. It was pan-fried brill, herbed crust, pak choi . . .' We caught each other's eye and laughed. 'And, as you know, it's the sexiest thing a man can do. Expertly cook for you and feed you and then expertly take you to bed.'

So that was why she looked so luminous. 'First time?' I asked.

She nodded. 'Definitely not the last if I have any choice in the matter.'

We talked about it a little, but in much less detail than Mel usually went in for. 'It's really good,' she said disbelievingly. 'But I'm just going to wait and see what happens. I don't want any games or stuff.'

I smiled. Mel was queen of dating game-play and to hear her talking like this was something new. 'Tell me more about him.'

He was forty-six, a bit younger than Mel, but not significantly so. He was a graphic designer, not loaded but not broke either. He was divorced, with an eighteen-year-old daughter who lived with her mother and he got on fine with both of them. He'd been involved with someone until recently, but it had fizzled out. Mel and he had met at a PR party, and he had asked for her number.

'He's interesting, and funny, and interested. He's . . .' she hesitated and I waited for the punch line that would diminish him just enough to set up Mel's self-protection in advance. 'He's lovely,' she concluded.

'That's good,' I said quietly. 'When can I meet him?'

'Soon,' she said and I knew she didn't want to share him just yet.

Back at home, Lola had packed her belongings into her car, ready for the return trip to Manchester. I waved goodbye until the car was out of sight, then made Jack some supper. After I'd checked and signed his homework sheet, he retired to bed with his birdwatchers' diary.

That was the weekend. Nothing had changed since the evening a few weeks before when I walked through the spring dusk to meet Mel; the only real difference was that the real Ted had slipped absolutely beyond my reach. Until now I had always been able to tell myself that some day I would set matters to rest between us. But now the opportunity was completely lost and I was left only with unwelcome recollections of my childhood and an angry urge to go back and break through the silence that lay like a blanket inside Ted's old house, to pull it apart and make a clamour with my demands and my questions. It was this, I knew, that drew me to the inimical Audrey. I wanted to know her.

I wanted to know what she knew.

On Tuesday evening Jack and I walked to her house. It was June, and the daylight streets were noisy with children wheeling in tight circles on bicycles and rattling over the kerbstones on skateboards. The air was rank with the fumes of diesel, but there was still sweetness in it.

Turnmill Street turned out to be leafy and gentrified. Most of the early-Victorian houses were fully smartened up with crisp white paint and window boxes and brass or blue enamel numbers, and so I knew which house was Audrey's long before we reached it.

It stood almost in the middle of the terrace. The stucco of the gatepost was a scabby mess of rotting plaster reminiscent of peeling skin, and in the front garden there was an old bath and some ancient sodden cardboard boxes. The house itself looked like a decaying tooth in the white smile of the terrace. Buddleia sprouted out of the walls and the windows were so nearly opaque with dirt that the loops of torn curtain inside were hardly visible.

There was no bell push so I tapped on the door and then, when there was no response to that, I hammered with my closed fist.

The door swung open suddenly and Audrey stood there. 'Oh, it's you,' she said, as if she wasn't expecting us. 'Do you want to come in?' She addressed the invitation to Jack rather than me.

'Yes, please,' he said smartly, peering into the shadows inside.

We followed her down a dusty hallway to the back of the house. In a long narrow room that looked out onto the back garden were a sink and an oven, a folding-leaf table and some upright chairs, two ancient armchairs, a radio and an old portable television set. This was obviously where Audrey spent her time. Piles of yellowing newspapers were built up on every surface. And everywhere I looked there were cats.

'Do you like animals as well as birds?' Audrey asked Jack.

He nodded.

'He's Jack, too.' She pointed to an enormous black and white cat who occupied one of the armchairs.

My Jack squatted down to the animal's level and stroked him. 'Is he the leader?' he asked.

'He certainly is. All the others have to get his say-so before they so much as yawn.'

'How many cats have you got?' Jack wondered.

'Eleven, last time I counted.'

I might as well have faded into the yellowish wallpaper. I looked round at the sediment of Audrey's life, trying to imagine her as she must have been thirty or forty or however many years ago it was, when Ted knew her. She had a strong-boned face with a slightly hooked nose, and, although her mouth was stitched with vertical seams now, the lower lip was still full. I thought she would once have been beautiful.

'That's cool,' Jack said.

Audrey filled a kettle and lit the gas. 'What about you?'

'Cats? None,' he said.

Audrey and he were exchanging looks. 'I do what I want. I live how I like,' she told him. I had the sense that huge chunks of their conversation were taking place in some dimension to which I was not admitted.

Jack nodded and smiled, one of his rare flashes of admiring approval. Then he darted a glance at me. *Not like you*, the look said.

Audrey made a pot of tea. While she was busy with this I took Ted's silver cigarette case and the flashy 1950s cigarette lighter out of my bag and laid them on the table.

'Have a Hobnob,' Audrey told Jack.

He settled back with his cup of tea and a biscuit, and one of the cats leapt onto his lap. He looked as thoroughly at ease as if he lived there.

'So,' Audrey said to me, having ignored me since I walked in through the front door. 'I suppose by now you've seen his will?'

I nodded.

'Did he leave anything for me?'

'No.' Surprise pinched my throat but I managed to add, 'I'm sorry, were you expecting him to?'

Audrey shrugged. 'I thought he might have done the decent thing at the end. But I wasn't exactly expecting it, no.'

'How did you and Ted know each other?'

'We met.'

There was a silence as Audrey's mouth folded into a smile. I thought she was like some rusty and cut-rate Mrs Danvers, holding the keys to rooms that had been locked up for too long. I was afraid of the lumber piled up within those rooms, but even so I was driven to open them up. How else was I going to learn about Ted? 'And how did you meet?'

The folds of her smile deepened. 'In the usual way. And I lent him money to start up in business.'

Not another one, I thought. Ted's history was one long story of borrowing money to set up businesses. Even I knew that much. If only his expertise as a businessman had matched his phenomenal memory for essences. 'You weren't the only one,' I said.

'He never paid me back.'

'You weren't alone in that either, I'm afraid.' She was going to ask me for money from Ted's estate to settle some ancient debt.

Audrey suddenly struck an attitude on the mat in front of her gas fire. 'We were planning to conquer the world together. Paris, Rome, Rio, New York. Shops in the best quarters. Jewelled flasks containing drops of our golden liquid that women would commit murder to possess and lead men to their own deaths from desire. A life of rose petals and peacocks and diamonds, that was what Ted and I intended.'

Auntie Viv and her suburban dreams of setting lotions and conditioners had nothing on this. Audrey was slightly mad, I realised, but my son was looking at her with fascinated admiration.

'And what did my money buy? *I've* no idea,' she said.

'There isn't any money now. At least until his house is sold,' I said.

Audrey gave a cackle of laughter. 'You don't say.' She wiped her eyes, and sat down. 'Oh, but they were good days. The best. No one knew how to have a good time the way Ted did. I remember once he took me to Paris. It was a big thing in those days, overnight on the Golden Arrow from Victoria. We stayed in a hotel that seemed all gilt and ormolu, and we went to a meeting with a fragrance house in the rue de Rivoli. Ted bought me a little suit, hound's-tooth check, specially for it.'

'When was this?'

Jack was less interested in these reminiscences. He stood up and sloped across to the back door. 'Can I go out in the garden?'

'The key's in the lock,' Audrey told him. He went outside and his shadow flicked across the dirty glass of the window.

'It must have been, let's see, 1958 or so.'

Before my mother died. Audrey saw me making calculations and coolly amended, 'Or thereabouts. I can't really remember.'

I said coolly, 'I didn't know you were a girlfriend of Ted's.'

Audrey sat up straight, offended. 'I wasn't his *girlfriend*.'

'I see.' Although I didn't. 'Sorry.' She wanted me to think she had been a business associate, was that it? Travelling to Paris together to visit a fragrance house. Now here she was, holed up with her cats in this decaying house, and Ted himself was dead. It was a pathetic picture and I regretted my lack of warmth for her.

Then Audrey gave another cackle of laughter. 'You don't know much about your dad.' It wasn't a question. I could only shake my head in agreement. 'He went to great lengths to shield you, he did.'

I looked her in the eye. Her gaze didn't flicker. There was nothing in the least pathetic about Audrey, I now decided.

'It felt more like neglect than shielding,' I murmured.

Audrey shrugged her indifference. 'I suppose it may have done. Does it matter, now he's dead and gone?'

I thought back to Dorset Avenue and the empty hours of waiting for Ted or of wishing, when he was there, that he wouldn't go out again so soon. I had never been interesting enough to capture his attention, never believed that I would be glamorous enough to do so. Ambergris, musk and vetiver. I thought of Ted's volumes of fragrance notes stacked where I had left them in my kitchen. The formulae for his spells. He had never tried to cast one for me. 'Yes, it does,' I said abruptly.

The back door creaked open and Jack reappeared, his face shining. 'It's amazing,' he said. 'It's like a zoo. Come and see.'

The garden was maybe thirty feet long. All down one side there were rough hutches and cages made of wood struts and chicken wire, and inside the cages were rabbits and guinea pigs. Jack tugged me along to the end of the line and showed me a hedgehog, and a small ball of russet-brown fur that turned out to be a sleeping fox cub.

'His mother must have been trapped or poisoned.' Audrey sniffed. 'I found him half dead near the bins beside the supermarket. Can't have him indoors because of the cats. But I'm going to save him.'

The rest of the garden was a mess of bowls filled with stinking scraps, bones, corn, vegetable peelings. I wondered what the neighbours thought of Audrey's reeking menagerie.

'I put out food for the foxes and hedgehogs,' she was telling Jack. 'Birds like it as well, of course. You see the odd magpie and jay, as well as pigeons. They soon learn to beware of the cats.' As the two of them wandered along the line of cages together, I watched and felt left out of a club that I didn't want to belong to.

At last I had to tell Jack that it was time to go. He followed me reluctantly back inside the house and I showed Audrey the cigarette case and the other small possessions of Ted's that I had brought with me. She looked each one over and put it back on the table. 'I don't want any of these. I've got plenty of memories.'

Stung, in spite of my determination not to be, I packed the things back into my bag. 'That's fine, then.'

'Were there any photographs?' she asked.

'There was one of you, sitting on a wall. I should have brought it.'

'Yes. Well, you'll be on your way, then?'

She accompanied us back through the dusty tunnel of the house and opened the front door. Bright, clean light streamed in.

'Come and see me again,' she said, but the command was issued to Jack, not me.

'Yeah,' he said. 'I'll bring your photo if you like.' We had got to the gatepost when he suddenly wheeled and ran back. 'Wait. Wait a minute. You know at the funeral? You were wearing a fox fur, weren't you? You like foxes, don't you, so didn't you think that was cruel?'

'It was already dead when I got it, poor thing. I like to give it an outing now and again, particularly to funerals, so it can take a look at the world. Nothing wrong with that, is there?'

'No,' he agreed, apparently satisfied.

Later, when we were back home, I took the three volumes of Ted's notes down from the shelf and browsed through the pages once again, looking for Audrey's name. I couldn't see it, but there were plenty of other names, and the formulae that had promised desirability and passion and dreams to so many women. The clouds of fragrance seemed to rise out of the pages, nudging and beckoning me.

SEVEN

THE DAYS OF EARLY SUMMER gently trickled away, like dry sand through my fingers. I went to work every day, did whatever needed to be done there, saw Cassie if I was lucky and came home again. Colin's cookery book took handsome shape; Leo and Andy did the paste-up between them and the folded sheets were made ready for stitching.

Jack went to school, following daily protests that had by now become routine. Some evenings he came home late, telling me that the biology teacher had invited him to join the school's new ornithology club. No further information about the Bird Club was forthcoming and I didn't press him. If things were even approximately working, I didn't want to start asking why or how.

I didn't see Mel. She was busy at work and her limited free time, I guessed, was spent with Jasper. Caz and Graham had announced they had decided to move to a smaller house and were house-hunting. The boys would be leaving home soon, and they would no longer need such a big house. In the evenings, when Jack had retreated from the supper table, I began reading my way through Ted's calf-bound notes.

There were pages and pages of lists. The old familiar perfume words leapt out at me—lilac, chypre, amber—as I frowned over the jottings and tried to imagine what he was imagining as he smelt and scrawled and worked his way towards a new fragrance. As I turned the pages my admiration for Ted's gift steadily grew.

He could take a brief and devise a perfume to order. On the one hand it was a dry and commercial business, but on the other it was pure romance. He could sell the formula to one of the cosmetics houses, or he could make up the perfume himself and retail it in his Mayfair shop. Or, if he was in the throes of a seduction, he could mix just enough to fill a single phial and present it to the latest of his women as if it were a bouquet of flowers. No wonder he had been so successful with that face-cupping routine. What woman could resist it?

In those quiet evenings that I spent reading my father's notebooks I realised how much I would have liked there to have been a perfume marked 'for Sadie'. I searched all the way through, but there was no word-picture and list of ingredients marked 'for Faye', either. I wondered if my mother had once been breathless and flirtatious, and as mesmerised by Ted's charm as one of the aunties. She must have been, I thought, and I wished I could remember her like that.

Near the beginning of the first volume of notes I did come across the description of a fragrance with no name. The first word Ted reached for in the word-picture he painted for that particular fragrance was 'mystery'. Then, to enlarge on the notion he wrote 'multi-layered, teasingly complex. A veiled woman with the curves of her body showing through rich folds of velvet. Heady with smoke and incense.' I knew for sure that this wasn't a description of my mother. Then I noticed what I hadn't seen before. At the bottom of the last page, the formula was labelled simply with a tiny pencilled 'A'. Maybe the initial stood for Audrey.

The reading and musing and the effort of comprehension that went with it brought pictures of Ted flashing into my mind. I saw him at his work, in the cubbyhole of a lab behind his showroom in South Audley Street. He was holding a paper dipper to his nose and smelling, not just with his nose but with his entire mind and being. This was at the height of Ted's grand period. He was busy playing the role of master perfumer who kissed the hands of Mayfair ladies and promised them the scent of desire itself, caught in a crystal bottle.

The shop was called Scentsation. I visited it only two or three times in the few months that Ted owned it, but my memories of the place are vivid. The shop itself was no more than a narrow corridor, but it was lined with mirrors set between dark mahogany panels. The counter was mirrored too, and the floor was black marble tiles that were polished to a savage glitter. From the ceiling hung a gilt chandelier blazing with candle-shaped lamps. The little gold points of light were reflected and reflected again in the mirrors, so that the confined space became a magic box of illusion.

In this perfumed and hushed atmosphere Ted worked with a sales assistant called Valerie, and when she spoke her name she gave it the French pronunciation, *Valérie*. She wore a little charcoal-grey suit and her hair was done up in a chignon finished with a black velvet bow. When she moved along behind her counter her fragrance, which was also the shop's, drifted a little more strongly in her wake.

On mirrored shelves under the counter and on glass strips against the mirrored walls, sat boxes and bottles of Ted's ready-made fragrances, the name of the shop printed on them in elaborately curled lettering.

On these signature perfumes Ted had bestowed oddly simple and rustic names, like River and Sky and Leaf and Rain. I didn't think the names sounded right for the hall of mirrors. They ought to have been more of the Ecstatic or Masquerade or Cause Célèbre variety. It turned out that Ted was just a long way ahead of his time, of course. But it also meant that his Mayfair days of 1964 were short-lived.

He loved them, though, while they lasted.

I remember him in a grey suit with a chalk stripe and a pale, shimmery tie. I had called in at Scentsation for a reason, which was that I was going shopping. Daphne from school was having a record party for her birthday—singles piled up on her bedroom Dansette and maybe even some boys because, after all, we were fourteen at last—and I wanted to buy the blue-green smock-cut dress I had seen on the way to the shop.

I sidled into the shop, a lumpy schoolgirl wearing her skimpy school uniform. Valerie gave me a cool nod as she looked me up and down.

'Is my dad here?'

'Hello, Sadie. Just come from school? I'll see.' She knocked at the door that led into the smelling room and inclined her chignoned head to catch the response from within.

After a moment Ted materialised in his grey suit. He looked surprised and faintly irritated to see me. 'Oh, Sadie. Yes, what is it?'

I looked from my father to Valerie and then back again. 'I want to go shopping. You know, Daphne's party. I told you, remember? And you promised that you would give me the money . . .' My voice trailed away. Money was never an easy topic to bring up with him; it was something to be avoided if at all possible. He had probably only made the promise in the first place to keep me quiet at some other inconvenient moment. 'I've seen the dress I want,' I ventured.

But he was already looking past me and out through the shop's tall, plate-glass window. I turned and saw a woman looking in at us. By the time she had strolled to the door, Ted was holding it open for her.

The customer looked groomed and poised and rich. She had silver-gilt hair cut in a smooth bell that curved in to her jawline from beneath a neat pillbox hat worn perched on the back of her head. The hat was made from the same lavender-blue tweed as her suit, and her court shoes and handbag were fine grey suede. Valerie stood back against the shelves but I was trapped in the main part of the shop.

'Mrs Ingoldby,' Ted murmured. 'Can I help you with anything today?'

'I was thinking,' the woman answered, 'about the scent we discussed. My own scent. I would like . . . something *exotic*. But not . . . *obvious*. A fragrance that will murmur my name, never shriek it.' She was picking up little glass bottles, and putting them down again, haphazardly.

'Very well put,' Ted twinkled. 'If you would like to . . .' He gestured to the innermost corner of the shop where two fragile gilt chairs were drawn up to a small table. As Mrs Ingoldby swayed towards the nearest chair, Ted shot a glance over her head at me.

You, make yourself scarce, the look said.

Ted drew out the little chair for her and while she settled herself he took out a leatherbound notebook and uncapped his fountain pen. His eyes were fixed on Mrs Ingoldby again, now with a much friendlier gleam in them. 'Let's talk about exactly what you would like. Because I could create such a fragrance for you. Such grace and suppleness . . .'

'I'll come back later,' I managed to say, into the space between my father and Valerie. I marched out of the shop and into the street.

I stayed away an hour, walking up and down Oxford Street. When I got back to Scentsation, Mrs Ingoldby had gone. Ted looked as surprised to see me as he had done the first time round—he must have forgotten my earlier visit.

'I want to buy a dress for Daphne's party,' I said loudly. 'I've seen the one I want and it costs five pounds.'

Ted must have had some big success with Mrs Ingoldby because he walked to the till, rang something up and took a five-pound note out of the cash drawer. 'There you are,' he said.

I stared, surprised by his rapid capitulation.

'Go on.' Ted nodded towards the shop door. 'Get want you want.'

One of the formulae in the notebooks, I supposed, would be for Mrs Ingoldby's perfume. I wondered if Ted's alchemy had restored her husband's flagging interest, brought her a new lover or simply made her feel more beautiful and desirable than all her friends—whatever it was she was hoping for when she came to Scentsation. In other words: if her perfume was a promise in a bottle, whether that promise had been kept.

'Are you going?' Caz asked.

She was standing on a stepladder and opening the high cupboards in her kitchen. She would take a milk jug or a gravy boat from the piled shelves, look closely at it, and then replace it on the shelf.

'How many milk jugs can one woman use, Caroline?' I teased her.

'Well.' She laughed and hesitated. 'You never know, do you? Three? Six? Vicars coming to tea and all that.'

Caz and Graham had sold their house, for the asking price, to the second family who came to look at it. After three weeks' frantic hunting they had found exactly the smaller new place they wanted, and Caz was realising that if there was going to be any room for the four of them to live in it she would have to weed out some of their belongings.

'So, are you going?' She was talking about the party that Penny's Evelyn's ex had invited us to, next weekend.

'Yeah,' I said. 'I'll be there if I can get a sitter.'

'Matt or Dan could come over, I should think.'

I glanced out of the window. After a show of reluctance Jack had come to Caz's with me, but when Graham and the two boys suggested a game of tennis in the park his face twitched into an involuntary smile. 'Yeah? Doubles?'

Graham said, 'Men's four. We'll leave these two to their cupboards.'

They would be back soon and Caz was planning a barbecue supper in the garden. We had done a similar thing dozens of times before, although nowadays Jack didn't always want to join in. He had become shy around Caz's boys. And then when Graham and the two boys were together I sometimes saw Jack watching them with a blank expression that didn't quite conceal his jealousy. He would have liked to be playing football or fiddling with the barbecue with his own father, of course. And I wished it for him, too.

When Jack and the others came back Matt and Dan lounged into the kitchen and went straight to the fridge. Jack sidled round the table in their wake and Matt flipped the cap off a chilled bottle of Beck's and handed it to him. Jack glanced quickly from me to Caz.

'Matt, he's only twelve,' Caz remonstrated.

'It's a beer, not crack. And we had a hard game, Jackson, didn't we?'

Jack had flushed with pleasure. 'Cheers, mate,' he muttered and gulped at the beer. His Adam's apple bobbed in his skinny throat.

'Who won?' I asked him.

He twitched one shoulder at me. He looked small standing between Caz's big, fair-haired, sunny-faced boys.

'Jack and me did,' Dan said. 'He's a demon at the net. Just needs to grow another six inches or so.'

Jack aimed a weak punch at him, but he couldn't hide his pleasure. I tried to catch his eye and give him a smile but he was looking away.

When we had finished eating, Matt and then Daniel stood up and said they would have to go. It was Saturday night and they had people to meet in bars, and then clubs to head for. They both touched Jack on the shoulder as they passed.

'See you later. Thanks for the game,' Dan said.

'Later,' Matt echoed.

'Yeah. See you.' Jack didn't smile but his eyes followed them as they left, and his quiet good mood seemed to evaporate.

I would have liked to sit out in the warm darkness, talking to Caz and Graham, but by ten o'clock I was driving home again with my silent Jack. I turned over in my mind the various ways I might initiate a conversation about our family and his dislocation from it. Or from me, if I was going to be honest. 'Jack? Will you try to tell me what I can do to make things better for us all? Because if you don't tell me, I can't help you have the kind of life you want. Can I?'

'What do I *want*?' he echoed and the sarcastic emphasis fully acknowledged the gulf between whatever it was he did want and the likelihood of him getting it. I remembered that perspective, of course.

'Yes,' I said firmly, expecting more silence. But his head snapped round so sharply that I thought I could hear his vertebrae cracking, and he was glaring full at me. 'I want to live in a family with my dad,' he shouted. 'I don't want to live with you always sighing and asking niggling questions like I don't know what you're trying to get at, right, just because I'm not the way you want me to be. You're not what I want either, do you ever think of that? I want to live in a family and do the stuff that I like. I like birds and animals, even Dad knows that, and

Granddad did as well. Just because you don't care about the difference between a pigeon and a grebe it doesn't mean it's nothing, you know, it doesn't *mean* that. It's important.' He twisted round in the passenger seat and the rage came off him in waves that felt hot enough to scald.

I tightened my hands on the wheel. 'Do you want to go and live with your dad?' I asked.

I hated the idea, but if that was what Jack really wanted, I resolved, I'd go along with it.

'No,' Jack said scornfully. 'I want a family, not to have to live with one half or the other.'

'We have talked about this, haven't we? Tony and I don't live together, but it doesn't mean we don't love *you*, Jack. And I know I don't understand about birds. But you know other people who do, don't you? You go to Bird Club now.'

A black BMW convertible with the top down swept past and the blast of music that pulsed out of it vibrated right through our silent vehicle.

'Yeah,' Jack flatly agreed, when the booming bass line had faded away. 'I go to Bird Club.'

EIGHT

'THE PARTY? YEAH, in the back there.'

The barman pointed towards the stairs at the rear of the pub and I eased my way through the crowd of Saturday-night drinkers.

The upstairs room was packed with people. There were white girls in skimpy T-shirts that showed their bellybutton rings, black men with dreadlocks, tattooed people, smoke, earrings and studs and pins, and a blast of solid, sweaty heat larded with noise. At the far end on a low platform a DJ was working the decks. The band hadn't come on yet.

The first face I recognised was Cassie's because she was towering over everyone else. She was perched high up on Jerry's shoulders, swaying to the rhythm of her father's dancing and giving the crowd her Queen wave. The next person I saw was Graham. He was leaning against the wall with a pint in his hand, looking conspicuous in his weekend uniform of corduroys and a pressed shirt. I edged my way over to him.

'Christ,' he said. From this vantage point I could see Caz dancing with a fat man I didn't recognise and just beyond her was Evelyn. Evelyn's hair was parted in the middle and fell round her face in Pre-Raphaelite waves. She was wearing a skirt that swirled round her ankles and a tiny vest and she moved dreamily, with a smile curving her lips.

'Christ,' Graham muttered again. I took this as a general statement that he would prefer to be at home stoking the barbecue.

'Where's Penny?' I asked.

'She's here somewhere. Let me get you a drink.'

'Thanks, Graham. I'll just go and see if I can find Pen.'

She was in the middle of the room, with Kathy and Dee who were two of her gay friends.

'Thanks for coming, Sade,' she shouted in my ear. Kathy and Dee draped an arm apiece over my shoulders and hugged me.

'I didn't know you were going to bring Cassie.' She was the only child in the room. Jack was at home with Matt as baby sitter.

Penny frowned. 'I didn't either. It's a ridiculous idea to bring a baby to a gig like this. Evelyn just announced that she was coming with us because Jerry wanted her here.' Penny shrugged. Her face was contused with unhappiness. 'But it's only for one night,' she said, taking a gulp from a glass of vodka and looking at me for reassurance.

'Of course it is,' I said. I patted her shoulder and left her with Dee and Kathy.

Graham gave me a glass of wine. I waved to Leo who was nuzzling his girlfriend in a niche beside the bar. Penny's friends and supporters were out in force tonight. I drank my wine, danced with Graham and then with Caz's partner, who turned out to be a music critic with a mordant sense of humour. My ears got attuned to the noise and I began to enjoy myself. After a while I saw Mel easing her way between the dancers to join us, followed by a big bear of a man with a smile as broad as a soccer pitch. Jasper. Instantly I realised that Mel had deliberately engineered the meeting with Jasper to happen in this low-key way because she didn't want there to be any build-up to the encounter.

'I was right about that dress, wasn't I?' Mel crowed, after the introduction had been made. Mel had made me buy a sliver of a fire-red dress with a deep V front last time we met for lunch.

I looked down at myself and smiled. 'Yes, you were.'

Mel and Jasper were standing close together, but not quite touching. I could sense how much they *wanted* to touch each other, and the resultant crackle of static across the inch of space between them was almost audible. Jasper was gorgeous. I was envious, but benignly so. He was a good dancer too, I discovered, when the time came for him to ask me.

Finally the DJ bawled that he was taking a break and the band began tuning up. I watched Jerry, minus Cassie now, as he adjusted his mike. Under the lights his dark skin shone as if it had been polished. Then, in the line-up behind him, I caught sight of someone else I knew, the man holding a trumpet. It took me a second to place him, because he was wearing a black T-shirt with a white Marilyn Monroe image instead of his schoolteacher's blue shirt, but then I had him worked out. It was Mr Rainbird from Jack's school.

'All right, friends,' Jerry crooned into the mike. 'Here we go now. One, two, three.'

They launched raggedly into 'Mustang Sally'. I leaned back against the bar and laughed at the happy absurdity of it. It was Penny's Evelyn's ex's and Mr Rainbird's soul band. They had plenty of brass and enthusiasm, and Jerry's voice wasn't bad at all. Soon everyone was dancing.

Mel inclined her head to mine. 'What do you think?' I shouted.

She rolled her eyes. 'The big time beckons Jerry.'

I danced with Jasper again, and with Andy. It was a really good party. I was enjoying myself so much that it made me realise I didn't get out enough these days.

I caught a glimpse of Evelyn and Cassie. They were twirling in dizzy circles and Cassie's head was thrown right back in the last transports of exhausted delight. I turned away again to talk and dance some more. A few minutes later I heard Cassie's screaming over the thump of music.

Frantically I pushed my way to the spot where I had last seen her. She was lying on the floor, her face mottled and her heels drumming. Relief brought my breath back. It was nothing more than a temper tantrum brought on by tiredness. Evelyn was stooped over her, pulling her upright. Penny was trying to get past Evelyn to Cassie.

'No,' Cassie screamed and drummed her heels even harder.

Penny had her arms round Evelyn and was trying to stop her hauling on Cassie. Evelyn let go of Cassie to try to fend Penny off.

Seeing my chance, I stepped in and scooped the child up. Her body was rigid. 'Cassie! Cassie, it's all right. Come to Sadie-lady.'

She took a deep breath to go on yelling but then thought better of it. She went limp and heavy in my arms.

'What are you doing?' Evelyn demanded, but not very aggressively. We were all pleased the tantrum had blown itself out.

'I'll take her for a few minutes,' I said. 'You two go and, you know, have a dance. Enjoy the party. Cassie will be fine with me.'

Penny's arms were still round Evelyn. She murmured in her ear and stroked the waves of hair back from her cheek. Evelyn nodded, pouting a little, and let her head fall on Penny's shoulder.

I carried Cassie away towards a door at the side of the room. As I made my way I saw that Mr Rainbird was watching me go.

The door opened onto a fire escape. There was a metal platform from which a single flight of metal stairs led down to the alley alongside the pub. I let the heavy door swing shut behind us and sank down on a step. 'Here we are,' I murmured against her sweaty head. 'Here we are now.' She sighed and curled herself closer against me. I sat quietly, watching the cats around the overflowing wheelie bins in the alley below and then looking up at the stars. Cassie fell asleep.

The door behind me creaked open. A man's legs appeared at the corner of my vision and then folded as whoever he was sat down on the step beside me.

'Hello,' Mr Rainbird said.

'I didn't know you were a musician,' I remarked.

'I'm not. I'm a part-time trumpeter in a pub soul band.' His voice was full of amusement. 'Is she yours?'

I laughed. 'Thank you, that's flattering. No, she's the daughter of my business partner's girlfriend. And Jerry,' I added as an afterthought.

'Ah. Right. I saw her on Jerry's shoulders earlier on. When I saw you carrying her out I thought maybe you and he . . .'

I really laughed this time and, turning my head, was surprised by how close Mr Rainbird was sitting. 'No,' I said.

'Right. Jerry's probably not an ideal boyfriend. Or father, actually.'

There was a long but perfectly comfortable silence.

'Anyway. It suits you, sitting there holding her like that. How's Jack?'

'He seems OK. Thanks. He goes to school, very unwillingly. But on the other hand he stays late quite often, at Bird Club.'

'Bird Club?'

'Yes.'

After another silent interval I asked him, 'How long have you been playing the trumpet in Jerry's band?'

'Only about a year. We play four, maybe five gigs a month.'

Cassie sighed and threw her legs out, and I gently shifted her weight so she lay on the side away from Mr Rainbird. This had the unintended effect of making us seem even closer together.

'How's Lola at Manchester?'

'You've got a very good memory.'

'Actually, I've got a pretty lousy memory. I remember everything you said to me that day, though.'

It occurred to me that Mr Rainbird might be making a play for me. 'Lola's fine,' I said quietly.

'And Jack is coming on the school journey, isn't he?'

I had had to persuade him quite hard, but in the end Jack had agreed to go with the rest of the Year Sevens on the school holiday to Cherbourg. 'Yes,' I said. And then, 'I'm going to take a few days off at the same time. I'm going up to Suffolk, actually.'

This plan took me completely by surprise. Jack would be safely elsewhere, so I could easily slip away to Suffolk on my own. As soon as I had said it, the idea hammered in my head. Auntie Angela, one of the very few aunties with whom I had kept in touch, lived up on the east coast. She hadn't been well enough to come to the funeral. If I went up to see her, I knew she would talk to me about the old days.

In all the years that had gone by, I had wanted to know less rather than more about our history: Ted's and mine, and Faye's. I felt damaged by it and wanted to rub it out, smoothing away the ingrained lines of bitterness. But I was increasingly aware that Ted's death had changed all that. The scent of the past fumed around me as thick as mist, it teased my subconscious and made me give public voice to plans that I hadn't conceived even in my dreams. The trail was drawing me to Suffolk and it seemed I had no choice but to follow where it led.

I'd forgotten, momentarily, about Mr Rainbird.

'To Suffolk? If I weren't escorting kids to Cherbourg I'd come too.'

I turned to look straight at him. He had neat, unremarkable features with fine laughter lines at the corners of his eyes. It was a good face and I wondered why I hadn't noticed this before.

He said quickly, 'It's where I come from. Near Ipswich. I could . . . I could have shown you some nice country pubs.'

I breathed in hard, making myself concentrate, and the distracting waft of perfume faded a little. 'That would have been nice. But Cherbourg beckons, doesn't it?'

'Oh God, yes. Trying to stop them doing all the things school trips are really about for just long enough to pick up some French vocabulary or a few cultural impressions. I shouldn't be saying this, should I?'

'It's nothing I don't know already. I'm Lola Bailey's mother, remember.'

'And Lola turned out fine. Much more thanks to you than to the school, I suspect.'

We both hesitated, but neither of us chose this moment to mention Jack. The bass vibration that shook the step and the closed door at my back had now stopped. I heard a guitar tuning up.

Mr Rainbird rose to his feet. 'I've got to go and play the trumpet.'

232

'Thanks for keeping me company.'

'Sadie? May I call you Sadie?'

'Of course.'

'Shall I give you a ring?'

I remembered the evening in the new restaurant with Mel. I looked around my life then and thought this is good, this is what I want—family and friends, work and the calm satisfaction generated by these things. But the weeks since then seemed to have stripped away several layers of comfortable, thick, nerveless skin. I felt exposed now, and shivery with a kind of feverish, naked anticipation. Wait a minute, I wanted to say. I like the idea, or at least the *idea* of the idea, but I've got something else to work out first. There's a scent to follow.

Mr Rainbird was looking down at me, waiting. Jerry would be back at the mike for the closing set. I temporised, 'How about if I call you?'

'OK,' he said at once. He took a notebook out of his pocket, scribbled down a number, tore out the leaf and handed it to me. 'Don't lose it.' These were the authentic tones of a teacher, but I didn't mind that. He opened the fire-escape door and went inside.

I sat watching the cats again, but Cassie stirred restlessly and after a minute or two she began to cry. It was almost eleven and I knew that the music licence only extended to midnight. If I took Cassie home and put her in her own bed, Penny and Evelyn could come back later to relieve me.

The atmosphere inside was even thicker and Jerry had cranked up the volume by another twenty decibels or so. Cassie flinched.

'Where were you?' Mel asked as I edged around the room.

'Out on the fire escape with this one.'

She smiled. '*And* the rather nice-looking trumpet player.'

Mel never missed a thing. My guarded instincts made me shrug noncommittally. 'He's Jack's head of year. I'm going to take Cassie home and put her to bed. I'll call you tomorrow.' I kissed her good night.

Caz and Graham had gone. Penny and Evelyn were together, at least, dancing in the thick of the crowd. Evelyn's eyes now had exactly the same overexcited glitter that Cassie's had held earlier.

'You're an angel,' Penny murmured. Her face was a solid dark red. 'I can't leave Eve here, can I?'

I hurried through the knots of glassy-eyed people and out into the night. My car was parked at the corner and I lowered the sleepy child into the back, trussed her into the baby seat I kept there for her, and drove to Penny's house. I let myself in and carried Cassie upstairs. When she saw her bed she stretched her arms out, as if to embrace its security. Her head flopped on the pillow and she gave a sigh. I settled the quilt round her and went down to the kitchen to make myself a cup of tea. It was 1.00am when I heard a black cab ticking outside.

Penny and Evelyn came in with a waft of smoky air and the exaggerated movements of people who have had plenty to drink. Evelyn came straight to me. She smelt of the party.

'She's fast asleep,' I said.

'There,' Evelyn said to Penny. 'I told you everything would be fine.' There was a smile of vindication in her voice, but at least it was a smile.

'Thanks to Sadie,' Penny answered.

'Yes, thanks to Sadie.' Evelyn's fingers musingly stroked my hair. 'She is a heroine. Always a heroine, Sadie is.' She drifted away again, back to Penny, and curved the willowy arc of her body against Penny's hips.

'I'm going home,' I said redundantly. Everything was all right here, for another night at least.

NINE

THERE WERE THREE BUSES lined up at the school gates. Children swarmed on and off, yelling and shoving, while teachers counted heads against lists. Jack was already in his seat in the front bus, reading. My heart ached for his solitariness in the excited mass of kids. A week could be a very long time to a lonely twelve-year-old, as I well knew.

Finally the bus driver climbed into his seat. When the engine started up Jack's head lifted. I stood upright and waved, with a wide grin pasted to my face. Jack smiled back and at the very last second, as the bus turned away at an angle, he blew me a kiss.

I watched until the bus was out of sight. Then I swung round and almost collided with Mr Rainbird. 'Don't worry. I'll keep an eye on him,' he promised.

'You don't need to do that. No, wait a minute. I didn't mean to sound ungrateful, I just hope he won't need any special attention.'

Mr Rainbird was holding a clipboard. The second bus noisily pulled away. 'Did you lose my number?' he said.

It was ten days since the party. The scrap of paper was still folded inside my wallet. 'No.'

'Well?'

'I . . .' There was too much memory and also too much present tense in my head. Jack and Lola marched in my thoughts alongside Audrey and Penny, and Auntie Angela who was waiting to see me up in Suffolk. My mind was already focused on the drive there. 'I'm sorry,' I said.

'Sir? Sir?' Two huge boys wearing barge-sized trainers were scuffling beside the third bus. I recognised Wes and Jason from Jack's form.

'Yes, what is it?'

'Sir, Miss Clarkson said we was on the wrong bus, yeah? But it's the only one left now.'

'Just get on it, then, and we'll sort it out later.' Mr Rainbird sighed.

'Have a good week,' I said.

'Thank *you*, Sadie. And the same to you. Don't forget our agreement.'

I assured him I wouldn't forget and didn't add that merely recollecting didn't mean that I would actually ring. The doors had closed behind him before I realised I was grinning. I was playing a withholding game, that was it. Whether or not I called this man in the end, I was still—after so long—back in the dance.

All these things—Ted's death, the crowding in of memories, my unlooked-for rebirth as a desirable woman—these were all connected. The stopper was out of the bottle and the perfume was spilled. There would be no closing it up until evaporation was complete.

It was another hot day. Later I drove up the crowded motorway past Colchester and on towards Ipswich. At the end of the afternoon I reached the hotel I had booked. It was a red-brick battlemented place that faced the crinkled sullen blue of the North Sea.

After I had unpacked I went out for a walk along the harbour wall, enjoying being alone. I could feel myself slowly uncoiling and expanding with the luxury of choice, the lure of my empty room. I ate a solitary dinner and with the sound of waves washing on the shingle I slept better than I had done for weeks.

The next day I drove half a dozen miles inland to the village where Auntie Angela now lived. Her modern bungalow was in a little close. I put my finger to the bell push and waited for her to open the door.

'Good gracious,' Angela said, when she at last appeared.

It was twenty years since we had last met, a little while after Lola was born. Angela's exclamation meant that I didn't look like a young mother any longer. And on my part, if I had passed her in the street I don't think I would have recognised her. In the Dorset Avenue days she had been plump, with soft dimply arms, but now she was hugely fat. Her face was a broad moon of flesh, with concentric circles wobbling round a tiny central boss of features. 'Come on inside, then,' she said.

I followed her through the narrow hallway to the living room.

I knew that after Ted Angela had married a chef and they had had two daughters before the chef left her and emigrated to Australia. Angela had had a hard life. 'You've been quite a stranger,' she said.

The abrasive touch in this reminded me of Audrey. Ted must have liked his women to be cheeky, and it was just time's wear and tear that turned a pretty girl's taunting into sharpness.

'Well. I'm sorry about your dad,' she added more gently.

I rummaged in my bag. 'I thought you might like to have this, to remember him by,' I said and handed her a photograph that I had had copied and framed. It was of Ted smiling in his RAF tie and a blazer, taken some time in the late Fifties. He looked very handsome and wholly untrustworthy.

Angela studied it for a minute, then put it aside. 'Always a lovely boy, Ted was. A lovely boy.'

She went to the kitchen to make coffee, which I carried through to the living room on a tray. Then we sat and talked about the years that had intervened since I had last seen her.

'Are you on holiday up here, then?' she asked, sipping her coffee.

'In a way,' I answered.

She pursed her mouth so it turned into a little purple-red bud in the mottled plain of her face. 'You're looking for something.'

It wasn't a question so I didn't try to deflect it. 'It's more that I wanted to talk about Ted. I know it's too late to change anything now that he's dead, but I want to hear someone else's version of him.'

Audrey. You should be asking *Audrey* this, a voice intoned in my head. And how was it that I could remember Angela perfectly well, and Viv and Maxine and all the others, and Audrey not at all? Why *was* that?

I told Angela, 'My memories are all distorted, you see. I'm angry with him because I think he neglected me. But if I could see past that, if I could understand why, I might mind less.'

Angela nodded. She had finished her coffee and now sat with her bulk spreading across a sofa, her hands laced across her front. 'Well. I don't know what I can tell you, dear. Your father was just a boyfriend to me, you know. Older than anyone else I'd been with, a bit suave with his car and the scent and so on. I always thought he was dead gorgeous. I'd have waited for him longer than the six months or whatever it was. But he didn't want me when he came out. A clean break was what he was after. And then I met Michael and that was that.'

236

I was listening not just with my head now but with the whole surface of my skin, my new thinner skin.

'I remember you so well, back then. Fifteen, you were and your eyes big enough to see everything that went on but as innocent as a kid of eight. That was Ted's way. He didn't want you touched by all that.'

Apprehensiveness was crawling like nausea in my chest. 'All what?'

'What are you asking me?' Angela blinked.

I spoke carefully. 'What do you mean about waiting for him to come out, and my father not wanting me to be touched by it?'

She was trying to work out the extent of my ignorance. 'You really don't know, do you?' she said eventually.

'No. What is it, exactly, that I don't know?'

She looked straight back at me, making a decision. 'Your dad went to prison. For fraud. He served three months of a six-month sentence that summer you spent in France.'

My first sensation was relief. I had been afraid of something much darker. Ted had always been a fraud; this was only a confirmation. 'I see. How much more do you know?'

'Not much. He embezzled some money, not a lot, something to do with the shop he had in Mayfair.'

'Scentsation.'

'Daft name, I always thought. Well, he was caught and tried and found guilty, and that was the time I knew him. And when he was in prison he wrote to me to say it was finished.'

'I see,' I said again. The scale of his concealment was beginning to dawn on me.

The months leading up to that summer had no particular resonance. I remembered vaguely that Ted was often absent and when he did come home late at night he was irritable, sitting with his piles of paperwork and answering in monosyllables if I tried to talk to him. But none of that was unusual. I fended for myself, doing my homework at the living-room table and making a sandwich for supper.

It was just before the end of the summer term that Ted announced he had some business to do and he'd be away from home.

I left my seat, wanting to hold on to his arm and stop him going anywhere. 'Don't,' is all I managed to say.

Ted gave me a quelling stare. 'Don't make a fuss, Sadie. It's all sorted out. You're going on holiday, to the South of France.'

I'd never been abroad. I stared at him, mistrust forming like ice at the margins of a winter pond. 'Aren't you coming too?'

He frowned. 'I can't. I told you, I've got business to do. But you'll be staying with a friend of mine. You'll have a good time, believe me.'

I wanted to believe what he told me but I didn't trust him. 'How long am I going for?' I whispered.

'I don't know yet. A couple of weeks, maybe longer.'

He would have been hoping for a not guilty verdict, I now realised. Ever the optimist, my father.

So I went to the South of France, to Grasse, the summer I was fifteen, and stayed there for three months.

Now Angela leaned forward across the coffee tray and tapped me on the knee. 'Not upset, I hope?'

I shook my head experimentally. 'But why didn't he tell me?'

'I don't know, dear. Maybe you were the one thing he did have that he wanted to keep nice. He wasn't a bad man, your dad, you know. He just used to get carried away with all his ideas.'

'Thank you for telling me,' I said.

I looked at my watch. I wanted to get away from here so I could weigh up what this new information meant. A con artist. My father *was* a perfumer and a con artist. That was how I had described him to Mel and it turned out to be closer to the truth than I knew.

Angela shuffled to the door with me. She put her arms round me and kissed my cheek and I could feel the powdery softness of her skin.

'I was always fond of you, Sadie.'

Angela had remembered my birthday until I was well into my twenties and Christmas cards still arrived faithfully every year. To me she had been just one of the procession of aunties, but I had meant more to her, perhaps simply because of my vulnerability that summer.

I rested my hands on her arms. 'I know, Angela. Thank you. I'll try to be a better friend from now on.'

I made her promise that she would come and stay with us in London soon. She stood on the doorstep watching as I drove away.

I reversed my route back to the coast and parked the car facing a wide shingle beach. I walked to the water's edge and turned towards the sun, stepping aside from the waves and following the spits of hard wet sand that lay between the shining stones.

I didn't know why Ted had concealed so much from me, or why he was so harsh in his handling of a child. *He wasn't a bad man, you know,* Angela had said. *He didn't want anything to touch you.*

I was harsh in my response to him too, because that was the adult way I had learned to contain the past and its deficits. All I had seen was his selfishness and his charm, that poisoned and perfumed chalice, directed everywhere and at everyone except for me. But it was possible that what Angela said was true and, given this new chink of insight, I began to think that maybe he had loved me in his own way and had done his best to protect me. Perhaps if I found out what had really happened between us I would be able to forgive him.

As I walked on, I began thinking again about Grasse.

Auntie Angela had put me on the boat train at Victoria and I reached the Gare du Nord in Paris at midday the next day. I climbed awkwardly down from the high carriage with my suitcase bumping my shins. For two frozen minutes I stood listening to station announcements that I couldn't understand. Then a woman who looked a little like Valerie from Scentsation appeared. She said in strongly accented English that I must be Sadie Thompson and I was so relieved to be rescued that my eyes filled with tears.

The Frenchwoman told me that she was a friend of a friend of my father's. She took me to a café and bought me steak frites and a salade verte, then there was another train and a night in a stuffy couchette. Next morning I looked out of the window and saw the Mediterranean for the first time. Philippe Lesert was waiting to meet me at Nice station. He took my suitcase as if it weighed nothing and opened the passenger door of a dusty 2CV for me. We drove away from the startling blue-whiteness of the coast, past farms and flower meadows and little houses with ochre tiled roofs.

At last Philippe pointed out medieval Grasse on its hill ahead of us, but we turned aside before we reached it and came to a halt outside a house set in fields full of flowers. The house was ugly, too tall for its width, but it had pistachio-green shutters and tubs of marigolds, and kitchen herbs at the back steps. Philippe opened the car door for me again, just as if I were someone who mattered. I stepped out and the cool, elegant scent of jasmine folded itself around me. The waves of perfume filled my head with wonder and I said in amazement, '*Oh*.'

'Is strong, yes?' Philippe laughed.

Philippe spoke a little English. He was eighteen, three years older than me, and because of the suitcase-carrying and door-opening, and also because of the way he talked to me as if I were one of his friends and not just some inconvenience, I already thought he was wonderful.

'You smell at dawn, when we pick flowers. Then, ah.' Philippe blew on his fingernails and shook his hand as if it were burning. His eyebrows made black circumflexes. '*Voilà, maman, la petite est arrivée.*'

Madame Lesert came down the steps. She was wearing a coarse apron and wiping her big hands on a cloth. She was short, not much taller than me, wide-hipped with thick, strong legs and feet sheathed in dusty clogs. I learned later that she was a widow who ran her husband's fields of flowers grown for the perfume industry with autocratic efficiency. Philippe was her only child and she was protecting his birthright. She patted my shoulder in greeting. '*Alors, Sadie, bienvenue. Tu as faim?*'

She didn't speak a word of English. All through the weeks that I lived under her roof her remedy for my shyness and melancholy and home-sickness was food. *Tu as faim?* I can hear her voice now, and smell her thick vegetable soups and good roast chicken.

I had been travelling for over thirty-six hours. I nodded and managed a watery smile.

She took me upstairs to my bedroom at the top of the house. There was an iron bedstead, and a china ewer and basin on a wooden stand, and as I looked around I was so interested in it all that I forgot my misery for a minute or two. When I had unpacked Philippe called to say that *le déjeuner* was ready. I sat opposite him and next to Madame, and we ate tomato salad that tasted of pure sunshine. They must have seen how exhausted I was, because they didn't ask questions or bewilder me with information. They ate slowly, exchanging a few calm words, and I knew at once that this was how they always behaved together and that I was accepted. I listened and watched the sunlight on the bare stone floor and felt some of the stiffness leak out of my body.

That night I slept on a feather mattress, with my head on a strange, long, hard French bolster, and I woke up the next morning just as it was getting light. I pattered barefoot over the bare floorboards to the window and then I unhooked the shutters and leaned out. There were twenty or thirty women fanning out between the jasmine bushes. They wore headscarves and aprons and some of them had babies tied in shawls on their backs. Round their waists were open sacks and they moved up and down the rows of bushes, picking off the white starry flowers and dropping them into their sacks.

And the scent.

I understood Philippe's quaint gesture now. The jasmine perfume was strongest at dawn and it rose up to me at my window in great billows of voluptuous sweetness. I knew then what perfume meant.

Breakfast was bread and honey that tasted of lavender. Philippe dipped chunks of bread into his flat bowl of coffee. I thought this was a very strange thing to do, and it would have been frowned on at home, but I copied him and he grinned encouragement at me.

I soon discovered that the days followed a very simple routine and I loved that after the loneliness and uncertainty of life at home with Ted. Madame Lesert and Philippe were always up before it was light, because that was when the pickers came chattering down the track to the fields. Once the sun had heated up and the jasmine's unearthly perfume began to fade, they gathered at rough tables under a sun awning. Philippe and Madame weighed each picker's sack and wrote the figures down in a notebook. Afterwards Philippe carried out jugs of coffee and unmarked bottles of red wine, and Madame and I brought baskets of bread and tomatoes and cheese. I listened to the incomprehensible chatter and the laughter that went with it as the women ate and drank.

After the pickers had streamed away again down the track, Philippe drove the sacks away to the perfume house up in Grasse. While Madame frowned over the accounts, I attended to the household chores, sweeping the stone floors, washing dishes and feeding the hens. None of this felt remotely like work.

Later in the day there was cooking. Madame taught me how to make bread and chop vegetables for soup, and which herbs to pick to flavour which dishes. After a little while I acquired a few French words and stock phrases, and whenever I used them she would puff out her red cheeks in admiration and reinforce my efforts with a voluble response.

In the afternoon heat, she used to sit in her armchair in the coolest corner of the kitchen and listen to music on her radio. I preferred to sit outside with my back against the house wall and my legs stretched out in front of me, idly watching the lizards run over the stones and the butterflies settling briefly on the rosemary bushes. With the exception of Sundays every day at the Leserts' was exactly the same.

On Sundays we put on neatly pressed clothes and went to Mass in the little church in the village. Madame and Philippe knew every single person in the congregation, and the ritual of handshaking and kissing afterwards seemed to go on even longer than the service itself.

The only other break to routine came when we drove in the 2CV up the steep road to Grasse. Madame liked to go to the market for the few items of food that she didn't produce herself, and she would walk around the stalls with a wide wicker basket, frowning and testing the lemons in her capable fingers or sniffing the saucisson that the stallholder held out for her approval.

In the evenings after dinner, which was eaten early because we were such early risers, she would sew or frown over the newspaper for an hour and then, by nine o'clock, she would be getting ready to go up to bed. Sometimes Philippe used to comb his black hair back from his handsome face and disappear with a wink at me. I knew he would be going to meet a girl but even so I couldn't be jealous. For the first time in my life I felt an utterly benign and selfless love: a special smile from him, a teasing joke, a good-night kiss on one cheek and then the other, that was all I looked for.

I didn't hear from Ted, but Madame assured me, with Philippe's help, that he was occupied with his business and all would be well. And because I was happy with the Leserts I accepted what I was told and didn't speculate any further.

Then, after the jasmine harvest ended, a letter came with an English stamp. Philippe and Madame conferred over it and called me and said that in one week's time my father would be waiting for me at home.

I felt a leap of joy, and at the same time sadness at the thought of leaving the Leserts. 'Can I come back and visit you again?' I begged.

'Bien sûr, chérie,' Madame said.

Exactly a week later Philippe took me and my suitcase to the station. It was an affectionate but unemotional parting from both my friends. I don't think they ever guessed how momentous that summer had been for me. I didn't expect letters from them and there were none. I knew they weren't the letter-writing kind.

When I finally reached Dorset Avenue again, Ted was at home. I put my suitcase down, feeling almost shy at seeing him.

'Good Lord, Sadie,' he said. I wanted to hurl myself against him, and hug and be hugged in return, but he held me at arm's length and said, 'How tall and brown you are. I'm not sure I'd have recognised you.'

I bit my lip. This was a compliment, but it emphasised the distance that the summer had put between us. 'I'm still the same,' I mumbled. Ted looked thinner. 'How are you? Where have you been?' I said.

'Around and about,' he said, in the voice that told me not to ask any more questions. I followed him to the kitchen and put the kettle on. I opened the fridge to look for milk and found that it was empty.

So there was an entirely new perspective to the picture, like one of those images that can be either a candlestick or two facing profiles, depending on how you look at it. Ted had banished me or he had tried to save me from the humiliation of knowing my father was in prison.

I had walked a long way down the glittering beach. Ted felt very close at hand now. I couldn't *see* him because his shape, the genie that had escaped from the bottle, was changing all the time.

But my face was wet with tears at last and I could hardly see the way as I walked on, leaving my solo footprints in the sand.

TEN

I BANGED ON THE DOOR of Audrey's house and waited. After a long while the door swung open and Audrey confronted me.

'Yes?'

'I was just passing, so I thought I'd call, on the off chance that you might be in,' I said with approximate truth.

Her full lips crimped as if to acknowledge a glimmer of humour in this but the amusement was private, not to be shared with me.

'May I come in?' I persisted.

'All right.'

I followed her down the hallway again and into the narrow room at the back of the house. The air was thick with the smell of cat food.

'Push him off there,' Audrey said, gesturing to Jack the cat, but I chose an upright chair at the corner of the table.

'I've been up in Suffolk for a few days,' I said conversationally, when Audrey had taken the armchair instead and hoisted Jack's bulk onto her lap. 'I went to look up Angela, one of Ted's girlfriends, and she told me some things I didn't know about Ted. Some quite startling things, in fact. For instance, I didn't know that he had been in prison,' I said.

'And were you surprised to hear it?' Audrey said flatly.

Audrey betrayed no surprise whatsoever. I had been right to deduce that it was Audrey I should be talking to about the past. Whoever she was and whatever she had been to Ted, she knew much, much more than she was so far prepared to give away. 'No,' I said. 'Not really.'

'I see.'

The cat, sensing that some moment of drama had passed, started kneading the bobbled fabric of her trousers.

'I brought you this. You asked if there were any photographs.'

I handed over the same picture of Ted that I had given to Angela. I had searched my house for the photograph of Audrey herself, the young woman sitting on a low stone wall with the wind blowing hair round her face, but I'd been unable to find it. I thought it must have been swept up in a pile of papers, and I was ashamed of my carelessness. Audrey looked at the picture for a long moment, then put it down.

'Why have you come? Not just to drop in a photograph, I imagine?'

I sat forward on my chair. 'Since Ted died,' I explained, 'I feel him in my head all the time. He's gone and I never asked enough questions about him while he was still alive, and I never talked to him about what put us apart from each other. You know that about us, don't you?'

Audrey inclined her head very slightly. Her thin grey hair was pulled back from her face, showing her bones. Her ringless hand stroked the cat's fur, head to haunch, head to haunch, in long deliberate sweeps. I looked at her, trying to catch a smile in her eyes in order to return it. But Audrey's face was closed tight and the only emotion I could discern was anger. Ted had borrowed money from her and had never returned it, and therefore it was hardly surprising that she felt no warmth towards him or me. Yet somehow I didn't think this was the whole story.

I plunged on, talking almost at random in the hope that the flood of words would carry me towards what I wanted to say. 'I've come here because I don't know much about Ted's life. He hid everything from me, even a prison sentence. But if I can find out some more about the time between when my mother died until I grew up and left home, I might understand more about who he really was and why we lost each other. It might help to exorcise the past.'

Audrey shifted the cat's weight and it flexed its claws in warning across her knees. 'I thought you were going to say exorcise *him*.'

'No, I didn't mean that.' I gathered my resources for a further admission. 'I thought he didn't love me.'

I had barely time to register what a wail of bitterness this sounded before Audrey snapped back, 'Did it occur to you that he thought just the same about you?'

I stared at her in astonishment. I was going to say, no, he couldn't possibly have imagined that I didn't love him. But then I thought, it's like Jack and me. However much I tried to hug him close to me, however hard I tried to compensate for having left his father, he pulled away from me and withdrew into himself. I had broken up his family and, whether he did it consciously or otherwise, he made me pay dues for that. Had I made Ted pay, too, for Faye's death and what came afterwards?

I said, 'I hadn't seen it in exactly that light. But maybe you are right. I'd like to know more and try to understand these things better.'

I thought for a moment Audrey might relent and talk to me. Her hand lifted in mid-stroke while she considered the options. Then she smoothed the cat's fur even more deliberately and the creature closed its eyes in supine contentment. 'Your father borrowed money from me, put it into a shop, lost it, never paid me back. He made promises, which he broke. What else are you expecting to hear?'

'Was it because of your money that he went to prison?'

'No.'

'Whose was it, then?'

'Why are you so anxious to know all this? I can't help you, anyway.'

There was nothing to be gained from this. Audrey wasn't going to tell me about Ted. But I couldn't stop myself from asking one more question. 'Did you know my mother and father before she died?'

'No,' Audrey said. Her wide mouth puckered, the vertical creases round it deepening as she bit off the monosyllable.

'But you said . . .'

'I don't remember dates. And I don't remember a whole lot of other things, nowadays. Do you know how old I am?'

The question was delivered with all the go-on, be-amazed bravura of a pub granny. But I didn't believe for a minute that Audrey was forgetful, let alone senile. She was too cunning, and too careful.

'No,' I said.

'And I'm not going to tell you,' she wound up triumphantly. The cat bounded off her lap and headed for one of the bowls by the back door.

I picked up my bag and stood up. 'All right,' I conceded. 'Thank you for the chat, anyway. I'd better go. I've got things to do at home. Jack's been in France and he's coming back the day after tomorrow.'

'That's right,' Audrey agreed.

I had let myself out and closed the peeling green door behind me before the implication of this properly struck me. By the time I reached home my suspicion was hardening into a certainty.

The next day was Saturday. I moved the furniture around in Jack's bedroom and hoovered in the corners before pushing everything back into place again, and I pinned up the corners of his curling bird posters and dusted the books. In the evening I went to the cinema with Caz and Graham, and we came back and ate a late last scratch supper in their old kitchen. They were moving out in three days' time and they were both tetchy with the strain of it. Everything was changing.

On Sunday afternoon I drove over to school to collect Jack. As soon as I saw him emerge from the bus I skipped through the crowd and put my arms round him. He wriggled away after the briefest submission to my hug and a just-discernible returned pressure.

'Did you have a good time?' I asked, as I carried his holdall to the car.

'It was OK.'

Back at home, Jack glared at his sparkling bedroom. 'It's all moved around in here.'

245

'I had a cleanup. I didn't throw anything out, I just dusted.'

He whirled round to face me. 'Don't touch my stuff. This is my room and you should leave it alone.'

I closed the door, although of course there was no one else in the house to overhear anything. 'Let's talk about this.'

'No.' He had already taken his binoculars out of his backpack and was resuming his study of the pigeons.

I said quietly, 'If we don't talk to each other about anything at all, except to ask if supper's ready or to argue about house cleaning, the silence will just grow deeper, and in the end we won't know how to break it, ever. I'm your mum, Jack, and I care about you more than anything in the world. When I was your age I was very unhappy, too. Your gran died—you know that—and there was Granddad and me left in the house on our own. Just like this.' I made a gesture that took in the two of us and the four walls. 'Only Granddad was never there for me to talk to.'

'Why?'

The monosyllable took me by surprise. He *was* listening, then.

'It didn't suit him to have a child to look after and he was selfish about his own pleasures. He had girlfriends and he liked to go out with them. And I was jealous and therefore probably quite demanding. We drifted further and further apart as I grew up, and even right at the end I wanted to tell him that I loved him and I couldn't manage it. So I'm telling you now that I love you and I'll always be here. If you'll let me.'

Jack said nothing. I could feel his confusion and also his stubbornness. I knew I *was* the enemy to Jack. Maybe the best thing I could do for him was accept it and not mind too much.

'You're always here, Mum,' he said. He made a little enclosing movement with his hands to indicate that I fenced him in with my anxiety and possessiveness. Perhaps Tony was right and I did try too much.

I smiled and stood up. 'And always will be.'

He took up his binoculars again in evident relief. 'Am I going to Dad's next weekend?' It was the weekend he was due to go.

'Yes. If you want to, of course.'

He nodded. 'Yeah. I do.'

'Good.' I kissed the top of his head quickly, before he could avoid it. 'Let's unpack your things and put them in the machine. I'm making penne with tuna for supper.' One of his favourites.

'OK.' He sighed.

The damp clothes in his bag smelt of sea water. After some prodding Jack admitted that they had had sailing lessons in the harbour, and long hikes with map-reading tests, and that Wes and some of the others had got drunk on red wine bought at the hypermarché. 'Dean Gower puked up in the bunk room,' he said. 'It was all red.'

'Lovely.'

'Mr Rainbird cleared it up. He was OK about it.'

'Was he? What was the best bit of the trip?'

'There was a huge colony of guillemots on some cliffs near the centre.'

The next morning Jack went to school without a word of protest. He said he would be late back, because he was going to Bird Club.

I put the finishing touches to Colin's book, while Penny was working on a stack of law reports. Cassie was perched on a stool playing with her Duplo at the end of her bench because her childminder was ill and Evelyn couldn't miss her morning's class. She was training to be a reflexologist. 'My work,' Cassie said seriously. 'I'm busy, thank you.'

At midday Colin arrived. 'Is my book ready?' he asked even though I had telephoned only an hour earlier to say that it was waiting for him.

'Here you are,' I said and put the heavy volume into his hands. He took the book out of its slipcase, pursing his lips as he checked his name and flipped the thick creamy pages. 'It looks very nice,' he said and a smile briefly transformed his thick features.

'I hoped you would be pleased,' I said.

'Yes. Yes, I'm quite pleased, as a matter of fact. My mum will like it.'

'What's this man?' Cassie asked loudly.

'This is Colin,' I told her. 'He's a customer of ours.'

'Colin,' she repeated.

Rather surprisingly, because he rarely betrayed any interest in anyone or anything except his own concerns, Colin strode round to Cassie's side of the bench. Penny and I took two steps closer to her.

'What's your name?' he asked her.

She told him in a clear voice.

'Do you want to see my book?'

'Yes, please. It's red,' Cassie said. She reached out to touch it as soon as he placed it on the bench but he hoisted it out of her reach.

'No dirty fingermarks, thank *you*.'

She rested her chin on her clenched fists and looked at the pages with obedient interest as he turned them over for her.

'Writing,' Cassie said, pointing at the titles with her chubby finger.

'Yes, it's writing,' Colin agreed. 'Now I can get on with my cookery. It's been quite a nuisance that it's all taken so long, I can tell you.'

He tucked the book into its case and slid the whole thing into a plastic supermarket bag that he drew from inside his mac. 'I'll be off, then.'

I handed him a sealed envelope. 'Our invoice,' I said discreetly.

He frowned and drew himself up. 'What's this?'

'It's our bill. For binding your recipes.' I had given some thought to this tricky question. In the end I had decided on £110 although it didn't reflect anything like the amount of time spent on the job.

His frown intensified as he unfolded the single sheet of paper. 'A hundred and ten *pounds*?'

'That's right.'

'Books don't cost that much. Do you think I was born yesterday?' He took out his wallet and counted out two tenners and five pound coins. 'There you are. That's for you.'

'Thank you,' Cassie prompted me.

I bit the insides of my cheeks. 'Right, Colin,' I managed to say. 'Thank you.' I took the money to the till and rang up the sale.

Colin sailed to the door with his book. 'Bye, Cassie,' he said, ignoring Penny and me. 'I'll be seeing you again.'

'Bye-bye.' Cassie beamed and gave him her wave.

Penny and I kept our faces straight until the door closed behind him. Cassie gazed at the two of us and then happily joined in the laughter.

'I think you should be glad of the twenty-five quid,' Penny gasped. 'Andy bet me a fiver you wouldn't get anything out of him at all.'

That day I finished work early and drove straight to Turnmill Street.

Ever since Audrey had said *That's right* I had been guessing that Bird Club was a fiction and Jack was spending his after-school hours with her. So I parked the car and waited. Ten minutes later I saw Jack in the distance. He walked straight up to Audrey's house and turned in at the gate.

I locked the car and took five steps towards the house before I stopped. I tried to reconcile uncomfortable feelings: I didn't want Jack to have secrets from me, any more than I wanted to keep what I knew from him. I was jealous of Audrey because my son chose to spend his after-school hours with her and unhappy, but not very surprised, to discover that he needed to lie about his whereabouts. But I knew that if I tried to confront Audrey with this now, I might reveal too much of myself to her. I wheeled round and made my way back towards the car. I would go home and wait until Jack appeared for supper.

At six o'clock I heard Jack's key in the lock. He came downstairs and took out a carton of orange juice from the fridge while I sat at the table and waited.

'Hi, Mum,' he said in the end, registering my failure to ask how his day had been. 'What's up?'

While I told him he stood with his head hanging. 'You shouldn't have been watching me,' he said.

'I'm sorry it looks like that. But if you hadn't been going to Audrey's without telling me it couldn't have happened, could it?'

'No.'

'Why didn't you tell me?'

He glared at me. 'Because I didn't want you to know, all right? I like it at Audrey's. I feed the animals and play with the cats. Anyway, I knew you wouldn't want me going there. I'm not sure why and it doesn't bother me much. You would have to go and find out, wouldn't you?'

He was right, in part, and I felt a distinct surge of admiration for my son's reasoning. It was Audrey who was the problem.

I cooked supper and we sat at opposite ends of the table to eat it. Jack read a bird book and I frowned at the *Evening Standard*. When he had cleared the table and put our plates and cutlery in the dishwasher, Jack said he was going to bed.

I waited until I was sure he was safely in his room, then dialled Audrey's number.

The abrupt way she said 'Yes?' was becoming familiar.

'I want to talk to you about Jack.'

'Is that so?' she said, spiky with hostility.

'I know that he was at your house today, Audrey. I think he's been visiting you quite a lot lately, hasn't he?' I took a breath to keep my voice steady. 'Perhaps you could tell me why you let Jack spend his afternoons with you when he's been telling me that he's at an ornithology club at school. I don't think it's correct for you to establish a relationship with him that's based on a falsehood. I don't . . .'

'Why does what's *correct* matter so much to you?'

'Because I'm his mother. It's my responsibility to teach him to tell the truth. I try to give him the right guidelines.'

Audrey sniffed. 'You like control, Sadie. You like your child to be where you want him to be and act the way you want him to act. But he doesn't care to be controlled by you or anyone else. I didn't know he was lying to you, as it happens. But I can't say I'm surprised to hear it. How did you find out where he was today?'

'I saw him arrive. I was parking my car at the end of the street, on my way to see you.'

'And now you know. Does that make you feel better?'

'No,' I said. I had been imagining that Jack and I were just at adolescent cross-purposes. I thought I could put matters right between us by an effort of will. But now an abyss had opened up and as I peered down from the edge of it I was afraid that I might lose him altogether.

'I'm sorry for assuming you were party to the lie,' I managed to say. Actually, I thought that Audrey was likely to have understood the situation perfectly clearly, but I still shouldn't have made the accusation.

She ignored the apology anyway. 'What are you going to do, then? Forbid him to come round to my place?'

'I don't think I can do that, can I? I could ask you to make sure that your influence on him is a positive one.'

Audrey gave a derisive hoot. 'Jack's old enough and more than intelligent enough to make his own judgments about influence. You're a priggish woman, Sadie, do you know that?'

'Maybe I am,' I breathed, stunned by her aggression.

'Good night,' Audrey said calmly. And she hung up.

I walked round the kitchen, steadying myself. My anger slowly subsided as I made myself a cup of tea and sat down at the table, trying to disentangle the threads of truth from the mess of resentment.

I did need to control my life, because I had grown up in confusion. Lola had rebelled against that control in all the usual ways, and Jack was choosing to make his protest in a different manner. And although I was a bit of a prig, with my ideas about duty and truth, I loved my children.

I would hold on to that.

ELEVEN

ON THE FOLLOWING FRIDAY evening I drove Jack over to his father's house in Twickenham. As soon as Tony opened the door to us he held out his arms to Jack and they stood swaying together in a long hug.

'Go on in, son,' Tony said when they finally broke apart. He kissed me lightly on the cheek too.

'Bye, Mum,' Jack called and vanished into the house.

'Are you coming in for a drink?' Tony asked. 'Suzy's just putting the girls to bed.'

I smiled at him. 'I won't, thanks. I've got to get back.'

'OK.' My ex-husband looked relieved and also embarrassed by his relief. Suzy and I didn't have much in common except Tony himself, and our encounters were always slightly uncomfortable. 'I'll bring him back on Sunday evening, then.'

'Thanks.' This was our usual arrangement. 'Have a good time.'

Even after all these years, it felt strange to be walking away from Tony. I still loved him and I knew his face and the shape of his hands and the weight of his body as well as I know my own.

We met when I was still at art college. I went to a party, wandered into the kitchen in search of a drink and there was Tony. He was standing at the sink washing glasses, smoking a cigarette between clenched teeth and talking volubly out of the other side of his mouth to a girl with spiky eyelashes painted on her lower lids.

'Here's a glass,' he told me, squinting through the smoke and handing one over, 'and there's the Vino Collapso. Pour me one as well, will you?'

It wasn't love at first sight. We moved in the same circle and kept bumping into each other. In the end he asked me out. Very quickly, amazingly, he fell in love with me. I was wary to begin with and then I eagerly gave way. Tony was working in advertising. He was never late, he never cancelled. He offered me delicious safety and the reassurance of unconditional love after Ted's shiftiness, and I grabbed hold of him. It was only much later that I discovered safety wasn't what I wanted after all.

Stanley, on the other hand, was a showcase of theatrical attitudes and unpredictability. On Valentine's Day he carved our entwined initials into every stripped pine floorboard and door panel in our living room, and a month later he completely forgot my birthday.

Ted adored him. Of course he did, because they were so alike. 'He's a bit of a shyster, your boyfriend,' he'd say. 'But he's bloody good fun.'

Tony and Stanley were the male polar opposites that drew my wavering compass needle, after I left Ted behind. Once Stanley had gone I was trying to make up to Lola and Jack for the dismantling of their family and there hadn't been much time or space left over for lovers.

But I still felt twenty-seven under the skin, whatever the external evidence might suggest to the contrary. It wasn't too late.

When I reached home I opened my purse and extracted the folded piece of paper with Mr Rainbird's telephone number written on it. Without giving myself time to think further, I dialled the number.

'Hello. It's Sadie Thompson here,' I said when he answered.

'Yes, I recognise your voice.'

I rested my forehead on my free hand, wondering what I thought I was doing. 'How are you?'

'Very well, thank you. I'm just doing some marking.' We listened to the distance between us and tried to work out what to say next. I was relieved when he took the initiative. 'I was wondering if you would like to see a film or have dinner with me?'

'Yes, I would, thank you. Maybe both? We could go to the cinema and have dinner afterwards, perhaps?' This is right, this is how it goes.

'Are you by any chance free tomorrow evening?'

'Well, yes,' I said. 'As it happens, I am free.'

'I'll come and pick you up. Would about six suit you?'

I gave him my address.

Jack's head of year, eh?' Caz said. She and Graham were in the new house and were taking her milk jugs out of their packing case nests.

'Mm.' I unwrapped a china cat and put him on the mantelpiece.

'What's he like?'

'Rather crumpled, quizzical, sympathetic. Like an English teacher, in fact. One of the kids got drunk on the school trip and threw up everywhere. Jack said Mr Rainbird cleared it up and was quite nice about it.'

Caz straightened up from her packing case and blew upwards so her fringe lifted off her forehead. 'God. Grab him.'

'Caz, we're going to a film. He hasn't asked me to marry him.'

'Would you like him to?'

I started a laugh but it got caught in my throat. 'No. Not at all. I'm an independent woman. I'm happy to stay the way I am.'

Caz raised an eyebrow. 'That sounds like Mel's mantra. "Men, who needs them? Use 'em and lose 'em."'

'And look what's happened to *her*.' Mel and Jasper had gone to Paris for a long weekend.

Caz nodded. 'Yeah . . . Yeah. Well, It's nice for some, I must say. Here are you and Mel, both going out to dinners and having an exotic time and the possibility of interesting sex. I'm jealous.'

We both looked out through the patio doors into the small garden where Graham was irritably stowing garden tools in a lopsided shed. My eyes met Caz's and we laughed, duly acknowledging but not needing to calibrate the prolonged and intricate compromises of marriage against the daily tiny exposures of being single.

'You wouldn't really want to swap places, would you?'

'No. I couldn't deal with all that business of having to wear matching underclothes,' Caz said.

Mr Rainbird rang the doorbell at four and a half minutes past six. I invited him in and he followed me down the stairs to the kitchen.

'You look . . . very nice,' he said.

I felt flattered, because he clearly meant it. 'Thank you. So do you.'

He was wearing a linen jacket over a plain T-shirt and the crisp line at the nape of his neck suggested that he had just had a haircut. He patted his elbows. 'The other jacket's the corduroy one with leather patches.'

'Really? I think of you in the Marilyn T-shirt.'

'That's just my gig outfit.' He looked pleased that I remembered, though. I gave him a glass of wine.

'Where's Jack?' he asked.

'Gone to his dad's for the weekend.'

'Ah.' I couldn't tell whether he was relieved at this news. 'What will he think about me taking you out like this? Does he know?'

I liked the way he chose to bring this up immediately. I had been asking myself the same question and the answer was almost certainly horrified. 'No, not yet. But I'll tell him all about it tomorrow.'

Mr Rainbird nodded. 'I'll hope for a good report, then.'

We drove to the local multiplex in his car, a green Morris Minor estate complete with timbered sides. I admired it and he grinned.

'It belonged to my dad. He was going to sell it, but I wouldn't let him. I swapped him my Honda in the end, just to keep his in the family. I'm not very interested in cars, I just like this one.'

'So do I. Is your dad still alive? What did he do?'

'Yeah, he is. He was a teacher, too. Physics. And my mum taught home economics. It was DS, domestic science, in those days.'

'I remember.'

'She died last year. I miss her, but not as much as he does. They were married for fifty years and they were always each other's best friend. I remember you telling me that Jack's grandfather died last term. Was that your father?'

'Yes.'

He waited, but when I didn't volunteer anything he didn't press me any further. There was a choice of three films and we settled unanimously on the starry adaptation of a Booker prize-winning novel. Mr Rainbird bought the tickets and I judged that it would be inappropriate to offer to pay for my own.

I liked the film, but I couldn't have answered many questions about it afterwards. I was smiling as we walked out at the end with all the other couples, blinking slightly in the glare of lights.

Mr Rainbird lightly touched my elbow. 'I thought we might eat at Casa Flore?'

This was an excellent choice, our neighbourhood non-pretentious old-fashioned Italian restaurant. Even Mel approved of it.

It was full, but he had booked a table. We sat opposite each other in a corner between the Technicolor painting of the Amalfi sunset and the shell sculpture that doubled as a wall lantern.

'Jack seemed to enjoy the Cherbourg holiday,' Mr Rainbird said, looking at me over the leatherbound menu.

'Did he?' I was pleased to hear this. 'He didn't have a lot to say about it when he got home, except for the guillemot colony on the cliffs and someone throwing up in the bunk room.'

'Yes, that last was definitely the highlight of the trip for most of them. He didn't say much while we were there either, but he was part of it all. Jack's an observer but he's not an isolate.'

'Thank you for looking out for him,' I said.

'It was a pleasure,' Mr Rainbird answered and again I knew that this was the truth. There was an openness about him, a transparency that didn't in any way suggest simplicity.

We ordered our pasta and scallopa Milanese, and when they arrived I was surprised to get the full peppermill and bella-signora treatment from the waiter, a first in all the times I had eaten here with Lola and Jack or Caz and Graham. Either I was more attention worthy because I appeared to be half of a couple, or I just looked different tonight.

We discussed the film. Mr Rainbird had read the book, and he talked about it in a way that made me want to read it too. I thought he was probably a very good teacher. We went on to talk about what we had both been reading lately, and then I told him about the business of bookbinding. I mentioned Colin's volume of recipes and how a carrier bagful of magazine clippings had become something quite imposing.

He laughed at the story, then said, 'It was generous of you to do that.'

'I couldn't afford to do it too often.'

Mr Rainbird smiled. 'Just the same, it sounds to me as though you have the balance of your life about right.'

'In most things,' I agreed. 'And you?'

A small silence shivered between us, made more noticeable by the clamour of the restaurant. 'More or less,' he agreed.

I wanted to know more. 'Are you in a relationship?'

'I split up with my girlfriend about six months ago. We'd been together ten years. God, that's a long time, isn't it?'

'About two-thirds as long as I was married to Tony. Did she leave?'

'No, I left her. We both knew it wasn't working any longer. But when it finally came to separating she wasn't very happy.'

I liked the strength of mind that his decision implied. 'Did you have someone else?' I asked.

'No. I still don't.'

I found myself looking as if for the first time at the shape of his face. There was a new noise in my ears that I identified as the circulation of my blood. The sudden awareness that I was attracted to someone—to *him*—was so startling that it left me without anything to say.

We had shared a bottle of Montepulciano and had become absorbed in our conversation. I saw his hand lift slightly from where it rested on the tablecloth, as if he were going to cover mine with it, but then decided that this wouldn't be the right move after all. He lifted the wine bottle instead and poured the last drops into my glass, then called for the bill. I offered to pay half but he shook his head.

'It'll be my turn next time, then.'

'I'd like that,' he said. We seemed to have passed the point where it was necessary to negotiate whether or not there'd be another time.

We walked back to the car and Mr Rainbird drove me home. It was another warm city night. The pavements surged with people all the way and the roads pulsed with steady gouts of traffic.

'I'll call you,' he said, when we drew up outside the house. He kissed me lightly on the cheek.

'I'd like that,' I said.

I noticed that he waited while I fumbled with my keys and let myself in, and only drove off when the front door shut safely behind me.

Tony brought Jack home again at five o'clock the next evening. As soon as Jack came into the house I could feel his resentment gathered inside him like a black ball. Tony followed behind, accepting my invitation to come in for a cup of tea. Downstairs in the kitchen, Jack was already glaring into the depths of the fridge.

'Did you have a nice weekend?'

'There's no cheese spread.'

'No,' I agreed.

'I'm going upstairs.'

'Don't you want a cup of tea with Dad and me?'

'No.'

'Jack . . .' Tony remonstrated but I shook my head at him.

When Jack had gone I made myself busy with cups and Marmite toast, which was what Tony and I always used to eat for Sunday tea. He laughed when he saw the jar. 'You're such a creature of habit.'

'No, I'm not. Not any more.' I meant it. Habit seemed to have been forcibly taken away from me in the last few weeks.

I carried the tray over to the stool next to the sofa where Tony was sitting. It felt normal to be sitting knee to knee with him, passing cups and plates. Comfortable, even.

'How was he?' I asked.

'Moody, I suppose that's the word.'

'No, really?'

'Come on, Sade, don't be sarky. He'll be all right in the end,' he said. Tony was always the same: good-humoured, optimistic and admirably loyal, even to me.

'That's what Lola says too. She'll be home next week.' I was happy to think that there was a whole long summer of her company ahead.

'She told me. We had a long talk on the phone yesterday.'

I nodded. Lola and her father had always managed to sustain a relationship separate from me. In the beginning, when everything about our divorce hurt more than it did now, I had felt jealous of their continuing closeness and affection, but now it reassured me.

Tony put his empty cup back on the tray. 'Well. I'd better head for home. I've got to finish a presentation for tomorrow, and Suzy's had a long weekend with the girls.'

'Of course. Thanks for having Jack. He misses you. Not that it's your fault,' I said hastily. 'I didn't mean that, it's just the way it is.'

Tony hugged me. 'Don't worry so much.' We liked each other, Tony and I, and there were times when I did wish we were still together, living in a comfortably battered house like Caz and Graham, mildly bickering, and yet vegetably entwined like ancient tree roots.

He called goodbye upstairs to Jack on his way out.

Jack appeared at the head of the stairs, his small figure outlined against the light in the stairwell. I could see the conflict between his wish to run downstairs to his father, and his anger with him for leaving and me for always being there. 'Bye,' he said. He turned away again before the door closed behind Tony.

He claimed that he had homework, so I let him eat his supper in his bedroom.

Mel called much later, to tell me about the pictures she and Jasper had looked at together and the dinner up in Montmartre with all the lights of Paris laid out just for them.

'How wonderful,' I said.

'It was.' Mel chuckled. 'Weird, isn't it? I looked at him across the table and I thought, it's you. After all this time, it's *you*.' Mel had always been so certain that none of her men would ever measure up to her father, let alone assume a bigger role. 'And I'm scared, Sadie.'

'What are you afraid of?'

'I'm afraid of wanting him too much. I'm afraid I'll love him so much that I'll die if some night I wake up and he isn't here.'

And it was true, I could hear the shiver of fear in her voice. 'But then if it's so valuable, how could I *not* be frightened of losing it all? I didn't know that this is how it feels to be in love.'

Mel sounded humble, even awed—my dismissive, comical Mel who had always been so certain that she would never love anyone as much as she had loved her daddy.

'That's how it happens,' I said.

We made a date to have dinner together later in the week.

'Suzy makes bacon in the mornings,' Jack said at the breakfast table. His eyes looked small, as if he had slept too much.

'Really?' I wasn't going to rise to that one. I was writing overdue cheques for the telephone and electricity, to stave off the threatened disconnections. 'What have you got on at school today?'

He didn't answer.

'What time will you be home?'

A cunning look crossed his face. He poured milk into a bowl, slopping some of it on the table as he put the carton down. 'Why? Will you be here?'

'You know what time I usually get in. I have to work, Jack.'

'I'm going to Audrey's after school.'

I put my Biro down in the clutter covering the table. Jack took a slow spoonful of cereal and deliberately, sloppily chewed on it while he stared defiance at me.

'What about your homework?'

'I'll do it there. Audrey helps me. She's at home, isn't she?'

'OK.' I found the envelope for the electricity bill and stuffed the counterfoil and my cheque into it. There was no point in arguing this issue. Let him go to Audrey's, if that was what he wanted. 'Make sure you're back for supper.' I got up from the table to search for a stamp. Perhaps I was getting tired of loving Jack too much.

'I don't want to go to school.'

'Don't, then,' I said. I put the letters into my bag.

By the time I was ready to leave the house, Jack was there before me. 'Say hi to Audrey for me.' I smiled.

He shrugged and hoisted his bag onto his shoulder. I watched him as he trailed away up the road and turned the corner.

As I drove to the Works I was thinking that I could turn the Audrey situation round, if I was clever enough.

TWELVE

WE SAT IN ANOTHER NEW RESTAURANT, Mel and I. This one had been Mel's choice. It was very smart and much more expensive than the places we usually went to. 'This is my treat,' she said, as we settled at our table. 'I wanted to come here first with you.'

It was one of Mel's gifts to make you feel that you were the very person in all the world she longed to be with at that moment.

She fitted in well with these surroundings. There were pale cream walls, leather seats and as a centrepiece a six-foot flower arrangement featuring tropical leaves and blooms like exotic birds. The tall glass windows were partly frosted but they gave enough of a view of the street to make the diners feel a privileged, soft distance from the real world. Black-suited waiters with proper French accents brought us menus and good bread, and blue glass bottles of mineral water.

'How lovely,' I sighed. I felt that I had worked hard today and achieved nothing. On top of that there was a tube strike, and we had both had to fight our way here through hot seething streets. But in the restaurant's plush calm it was easy enough to forget all this.

'And how modish,' Mel said, studying the menu. 'Everything's retro.'

The food was old-fashioned French. I ordered frog's legs and Mel chose an endive salad with Roquefort. We both ordered the côte de boeuf with sauce béarnaise to follow.

'And it's got to be a serious burgundy to go with all that, don't you think?' Mel was looking at the wine list.

'You *are* pushing the boat out.'

She debated her choice at some length with the sommelier and then made the decision. This was my friend at her eager, inquisitive best, enjoying her surroundings and opportunities, and I loved watching her.

'It's because I'm so happy. I want to wrap my arms round everything.' Her eyes travelled over my face. 'Is it all right to say that to you?'

'Yes.' Of course it was, even though I felt a little pang of jealousy.

'I'm still scared too. Sadie, he wants me to meet his daughter.'

'That's good, isn't it?'

'Yes, it's good.'

Her agreement still left a curlicue of doubt hanging in the air.

'Mel, she's his. You'll love her for that reason alone. And there's no chance that she won't love you back as soon as she sets eyes on you.'

Our first courses were reverently placed in front of us. I carved the muscles of my frog's legs off the little bones and took a slippery mouthful. The taste of garlic and butter reminded me of the long-ago summer in Grasse when I had first realised how good food could be.

'Can I try some of that?'

We traded forkfuls.

'This is serious cooking.' But even though she was eating Mel was also listening intently to what I said. 'I'm sure you're right. I hope his daughter and I will like each other. But, you know—'

I did know. The prospect of meeting Jasper's daughter, the loved child of a woman he had once loved, would be disturbing, however welcome the idea might also be.

She hesitated, then said, 'There's a part of me that mourns, how sad, how wasteful for the two of us not to have found each other until now, when it's too late for us to have our own child together.'

'Does he want one?'

Mel shook her head. 'No. He says he's already got everything he wants in the offspring department, in Clare.'

'Then he's lucky.' I wondered briefly if Mr Rainbird hoped for children of his own, after spending his working life surrounded by other people's. 'Go and meet Clare. She'll be someone new to love even though she isn't your own child, and maybe there's some way she can even become a kind of substitute, in time, in a small way.'

It was easy enough for me to say, because I had known the absorbed intensity of pregnancy and the intimacy of feeding my babies, and because Lola and Jack were within every fibre of me, and always would be. Mel had never known this connection and it was wrong of me to envy her, even a little bit, for what she was enjoying today.

'Thanks, Sadie.' She was smiling, her red lipstick a generous slash of colour against the tasteful monochromes of the restaurant's decor.

I did love her. Her friendship mattered to me more than almost anything else in the world. 'You're welcome.'

'I don't want to talk about myself through the whole of the next course as well. It's your turn now. Tell me something.'

On that night when Ted was taken ill, I had deflected her questions about him, and Mel had noticed that I did so and minded that I withheld something of myself from her. I wanted to offer her something now to make up for that, but there was also more—the thought of confiding in her about my father had become inviting rather than impossible.

'Do you remember I told you that my father was a con artist?'

'A perfumer and a con artist,' Mel said, leaning back in her chair.

'It was more true than I realised. I found out some more about him,' I said. 'He went to prison.' I told her about going to Suffolk to see Angela.

'Does knowing that make you feel any different?' she said.

'No.' I wasn't shocked or dismayed, which is what Mel was meaning.

'And so what is it that you do feel?'

This made me think more carefully. 'In the dark,' I said at length.

That was just what it was. Ted had put up so many smoke screens. It can't have been just my mother and me he hid from, but his other women too, and his creditors. I was beginning to think that behind the puffs of coloured smoke that drifted at the far end of the hall of mirrors where my father dwelt, there had been only a void. There was nothing solid there and perhaps nothing so very significant to hide either, except my father's fear of being exposed for what he really was.

It was fitting that his great gift was as a perfumer, the creator of illusion, and it was sad that even his gift had come to almost nothing except some mostly forgotten fragrances, and three volumes of notes.

I looked into Mel's face across the plates and glasses, with the muted noise of the restaurant like a shell held to my ear.

For the first time I felt pure sympathy for him, and it was like having a hand pushed deep inside my chest cavity. Poor Ted, I thought, with the fingers tightening round my heart. He had juggled so hard, for so long, and the fear of dropping those spinning balls must have been ever present. He had been dexterous enough to go to *prison* and still manage to keep the whole episode from me. The Ted of my childhood, the RAF slang and the blazers and the cars and the shop in South Audley Street, had only been balls in the air.

'You can turn the lights on, you know, if that's what you want,' Mel said, cautiously. 'I'll tell you what I'd do, if I were in your place.'

'What's that?'

'You know the date, for a start. I'd go to the archives and look up the local newspaper. It would all have been reported there.'

The *Hendon & Finchley Times*. 'You're right,' I said. 'Of course it would.'

'Shall I come with you?'

She was offering to stand by me, if I needed to look at anything that might be difficult to confront alone.

'I don't know. I'll ask you if I think I need you, but I'm not used to going public about my life. I felt ashamed of being different from other kids so I always kept quiet. It's not like your family, is it?'

'Not superficially, no. But my father was so powerful, his influence hobbled us all. Look at me, I'm only just finding out how to fall in love with a man who isn't him. We're our fathers' hostages, both of us.'

She put the last morsel of beef into her mouth and leaned smilingly back in her chair. 'And listen to me, I'm talking about myself again. That's enough about me. What do *you* think about me?'

This was one of Mel's favourite self-knowing jokes and it did have bite because she was interested in herself. She had all the self-confidence that came from being her daddy's princess. With the added charge of being in love, Mel shone as brilliantly as the midday sun reflected off a sheet of mirror glass.

'I'll tell you after I've eaten the tarte tatin.'

Mel ordered us a glass of Barsac apiece to go with our puddings and we toasted each other.

'To many more dinners,' she said. 'Even when we're old and grey.'

'Especially when we're old and grey. I'll tell you what I think. That you're the best friend any woman could have. Let's drink to friendship.'

Mel squeezed my hand. 'Thank you, Sadie,' she said. 'You too.'

She paid the bill with a reckless flourish. 'Thank *you*,' I responded.

I made my way home through the chaotic streets. The tube entrances were still barred and the two buses that swayed past were crammed to the doors. In any case, I was happy enough to walk. I felt buoyed up by the evening and by having opened a small chink for Mel to look into. It hadn't been so difficult after all.

'To friendship,' I repeated aloud, to the cats and the parked cars, as I finally waltzed round the corner into my street.

As the next few days turned out, it was just as well that I had the dinner with Mel to buoy me up.

Lola was working as a temp receptionist because it paid better money than bar work, but it also meant that she had to be up, washed, dressed, and out of the house by eight thirty every morning. She wasn't prepared to curtail her nightlife, however, and so she was always tired and hung-over and irritable.

Jack was sleepwalking through the last days of the school year. He spent most of the after-school hours at Audrey's and in the limited time he did spend at home he either lay on his bed or glowered at the local bird population through his binoculars. He hardly ever spoke to Lola and me except to snap at us.

I telephoned Audrey and held out an olive branch. I thought I might be able to demystify her in Jack's eyes somehow, by making her part of the family. 'Why don't you come and have Sunday lunch with us? You've been so hospitable to Jack and I would love to see you here.'

'Why?'

'Well . . .' Her lack of social emollience disconcerted me, but perhaps I usually erred on the side of being too conciliatory. 'Because we would.'

'All right. I'll come on Sunday, then.'

I told Jack about the arrangement and he whipped round at me with fury glittering in his face. 'Can't you just leave me alone?'

'It's only lunch, Jack. You're spending such a lot of time round at Turnmill Street I thought it was fair to invite Audrey back here.'

'You can't let me have anything to myself, can you?'

I tried too hard; Tony and Mr Rainbird had both seen that. 'OK. I'll call her and cancel,' I said. I didn't want Jack to feel I was caught in a playground squabble with Audrey.

'Don't be stupid. She already thinks you're weird enough.'

'*Audrey* thinks *I'm* weird?'

'Oh, Mum.' Jack sighed. 'Just forget it. Like you said, it's only lunch.'

Sunday with Audrey kept its place in the diary.

I did some research into summer holidays. In the past we had been to a cottage in Cornwall, to Wales and the Lake District and, when we had a couple of fatter years at the Works, to an apartment on Skopelos. This year, with the genie out of its bottle and all the smoke and scent swirling around me, I really did want to go back to Grasse.

There wasn't a lot of money in the budget, but after hunting for a day or two I found a campsite between the town and Cannes that offered camping, caravans and some farm buildings converted into holiday lets.

'Is there a pool?' Lola asked. 'Any bars, or clubs?'

'There's a pool at the site, look,' I said, showing her the picture. 'There are plenty of bars in Grasse and clubs in Cannes. Although it must all be completely different from the way I remember it.'

'OK,' she said.

Jack just shrugged. I booked the first two weeks of the school holidays and considered us lucky to have found somewhere in the South of France that I could more or less afford.

I also spoke to Mr Rainbird.

'It seems a very long time since we saw each other,' he remarked, after we had exchanged the initial courtesies.

'I know. I'm sorry.'

'Shall we remedy this?'

I hesitated. 'How do I tell Jack that I'm dating his head of year?'

'Just that would do, wouldn't it?' There was some amusement in his voice but also the faintest edge of impatience.

'Jack and I aren't having a particularly easy time at the moment. He's angry with me, for all kinds of reasons, most of them justified.'

'Sadie, kids are often angry. Do you want us to go out again?'

I listened to his breathing. 'Yes.'

'OK. Good. So do I.'

But. I waited to hear what the *but* was going to be.

'So, if what you're saying is that before you and I go any further you want to find the right way to tell Jack that we're going to the cinema, I'll just wait for you to do that and then call me, shall I?'

No but at all.

Mr Rainbird, I thought, you're quite a class act. It was a second before I caught myself giggling. I said with the vibration of laughter in my throat, 'Yes, please. I promise I will.'

'Good night then,' he said and I could hear that he thought all this was quite funny too. I liked the fact that he didn't take it too seriously, but that he didn't entirely make light of it either.

Lola was in, for once. I had thought she was absorbed in the television, but she looked up immediately. 'Was that Mr Rainbird?'

I had told Lola about my evening with him and she was fascinated. 'Yes.'

She grinned. 'Good for you, Mum.'

On the Friday morning before Audrey was due to come for lunch, I drove to the newspaper library, which was housed in a north suburban street, not so very far from Dorset Avenue itself.

I was already waiting in the lobby when the staff opened the reading room. A red, leatherbound volume of the *Hendon & Finchley Times* was put on the desk in front of me.

I opened the cover and looked at the yellowed front page of the first paper: HENDON SCOUTMASTER'S HIGH AWARD. CHIEF RABBI VISITS KINGSBURY.

It was like peering into another century rather than a mere forty years back. There were interviews with local girls who had 'passed with flying colours' the selection tests to become air hostesses. Every wedding in the borough seemed to be covered in minute detail, and I read incredulously that 'gay bachelors have had their day. Now it's gay spinsters and gay wives.'

Those were the days when gay had nothing to do with damned homos, as Ted used to grumble in his old age. I was still smiling at this when I turned another page and I knew immediately that this was the story that I had come to find: HENDON MAN GUILTY OF FRAUD.

The case was reported in some detail. The Middlesex Quarter Sessions chairman, W. H. Gascoigne, QC, had found Ted guilty of a 'particularly low type of offence'. He was accused of obtaining the sum of £344 8s 8d by virtue of a forged receipt of purchase.

I read more quickly, with a prickling of discomfort at the nape of my neck that spread up and over my scalp like a too-tight cap.

Ted had undertaken to supply Messrs Bourne & Hollingsworth Ltd with an exclusive sample range of fine fragrances under the Scentsation trade name and he had presented his financial backer, a Mrs Caroline Ingoldby, with a receipt for the purchase of perfumery materials in con-nection with the manufacture of the said fragrances. She had advanced him the money in good faith, and believed that they might have a joint business future. The delivery date for the consignment of perfume had not been met, however, and when the store had insisted on receipt of the goods or cancellation of the contract, Thompson had applied to Mrs Ingoldby for further funds to solve 'unforeseen production problems'. Mrs Ingoldby had become suspicious and had caused the original invoice to be examined. It had proved to be a forgery.

Thompson had claimed that he had some business debts and had every intention, he said, of fulfilling the order to the department store and settling his financial shortfall from his share of the resulting profits. He pleaded guilty to the charge and expressed his sincere regret for the matter and was sentenced to six months' imprisonment. An earlier offence of embezzlement had been taken into account.

I read the article carefully, twice over.

Everyone I knew back in those days must have known. Miss Avery, my headmistress, and the other teachers, the girls in my class, they would all have read or heard about my father going to prison. I sat in my library seat and what struck me at that moment was the strength of my determination not to confront the truth.

I must have seen but somehow managed to ignore the other girls' whispers and the sympathetic glances of the teachers.

I didn't want to know what Ted had done or where he was, and there-fore I had remained completely ignorant. Such tenacity betrayed the understood fragility of my world. If Ted had let me down, I had no one else to turn to. And so what he did had to be right and what he said had to be true. From my adult perspective, the mental contortions that this must have involved felt utterly exhausting.

A perfumer and a con artist, I had told Mel, and the admission rose up from a deep well in my consciousness. I *had* known, really, all along.

THIRTEEN

IT WAS THE THIRD WEEK IN JULY and the leaves on the trees in our road were already browning and crisping at the edges with the heat. In spite of this, Audrey was wearing her fox fur. I opened the front door on Sunday morning and there she was, standing on the front step with the dusty pelt fluffed up around her chin, like a suit of armour.

'Hello, Audrey. Come on in.'

She peered past me into the hallway. 'Quite a big house, this,' she remarked. She had a good look into the room that led off the hall, then craned back her head to see up the stairs.

'Is it? I suppose it is. Shall I take your fur?'

'No, thank you.'

'Come on downstairs, then. I thought we might have a drink in the garden before lunch.'

Jack was hovering in the kitchen. I had been feeling nervous on his behalf, anticipating how it might be for him to encounter Audrey on his own tricky ground, but I saw now that there was no need for anxiety. He gave Audrey a quick, relieved smile and she tapped him reassuringly on the shoulder and I realised then that I was the one they were mutually wary of. I went to the fridge and took out a bottle of white wine.

Lola came in and Audrey's glance travelled over her fringed miniskirt and suntanned bare legs.

'We met at the funeral.' Lola smiled.

'That's right. Aren't you cold?'

I steered everyone out into the garden and we sat down at the table in the shade of the cherry tree. Audrey sipped at her wine, pursing her full lips as if she disapproved of the taste of it. 'You're pretty well set up here,' she said, looking around at the overgrown garden and the rear wall of the back extension, which urgently needed repointing.

Her comment irritated me. But the dilapidation on my patch was, admittedly, nothing compared with the state of Audrey's own house. I felt a spasm of sympathy. 'We don't have a menagerie in our garden, though,' I said brightly.

'Do you remember the cub?' Jack asked me.

'The cub?'

'The first time we went to Audrey's there was a fox cub.' He was amazed that I actually didn't remember.

'Really?' Lola was interested. 'A baby fox? How cute is that?'

'Oh, yes,' I recalled too late.

'Well, Audrey fed him on milk and scraps and stuff, and he got bigger and bigger and really strong. We used to shut the cats in the house and let him out in the garden, and he ran around and sniffed everything but he still went back in the cage for his food. Then we let the other cats out, except for Jack because he's like the most threatening, and the cub was well big enough to stand up to all of them. There was some snarling and spitting and stuff, but basically they left him alone. Then we decided it was time for Jack and him to go head to head.'

Lola was looking from her brother to Audrey and back again, and I could see her interest. 'What happened?'

'We opened the cage, right? And the cub came out and went straight up to Jack and sniffed him. Audrey thinks it was because he never had his mother to teach him what to be afraid of and so he'll go for anything. Jack hissed and fluffed his fur up, right, like cats do, and the cub ran and Jack sprang after him and then they did this sort of fight and the cub nipped the back of Jack's neck, behind his ear. You never heard such a noise of yowling and yapping. Audrey got them apart and the cub ran back in his cage and Jack sort of slunk into the house.'

'One-all draw.' Lola laughed.

I was enjoying Jack's story, or rather I was enjoying hearing him tell the story. Audrey just sat there listening and watching Jack.

'Yeah. And since then, they totally ignore each other. The cub's taller than Jack now, anyway. We leave his cage open all the time and he spends less and less time there. He'll be making his own way soon.'

One more fox to go foraging through the dustbins at night, I thought.

'That's really sweet.' Lola sighed.

'So, are we ready for lunch?' I asked, sounding like some 1950s hostess.

We moved inside and arranged ourselves at the table. It had occurred to me that with her enthusiasm for animals Audrey might be vegetarian, so I had made a tomato and feta tart and a dish of roasted vegetables.

She sniffed at the runny innards of her slice of tart. 'What's this?'

I explained and she sniffed again. 'I see.'

'Is there something you don't like, Audrey?'

She chuckled. 'I was expecting roast beef and Yorkshire. Or a nice bit of lamb, maybe. That's what Sunday lunch means to me.'

'Oh dear. I thought you might not like eating animals.'

'Why not? Animals eat each other.'

Jack corrected her earnestly. 'Not herbivores. Sheep and cows are herbivores, actually.'

Audrey favoured him with a benign glance. 'Proper animals, then.'

'There is a natural food chain, you know,' Jack told me. 'Carnivores have their place.'

'Next time, I promise Beef Wellington.' I smiled.

Conversation over lunch didn't exactly go with a swing. I tried everything I could think of without much response from Audrey. Jack and she made asides to each other, to do with conversations they had had on other occasions, but in spite of her reservations about my food I noticed that she cleared her plate quite quickly.

I removed the first course and served the pudding, a lemon polenta cake that was one of Lola's favourites. She gobbled up her helping and eased away from the table. 'Mum, is it OK if I go out? Leave the clearing up, I'll do it later.'

I nodded. As she said goodbye, Lola asked Audrey if she could come round some time to see the fox cub.

'If you make sure you ring up first,' Audrey told her. 'I don't like unexpected callers.'

Jack scowled at his sister's retreating back. He didn't want to be left at the table on his own, caught between me and Audrey, but I thought it would do him no harm to stay where he was and see it through. I was telling Audrey that we were going off next week on holiday, to Grasse.

'Grasse?'

'Yes. Ted sent me off there to stay with a friend of his, that summer when he was, er, away.'

I looked at her and waited, but she said nothing.

'Would you like another little helping of my polenta cake?'

'No, thank you. Too much foreign food doesn't agree with me.'

'I'll make us some coffee, then, shall I?'

Jack began to collect plates and even slotted a few haphazardly into the dishwasher. The angle of his shoulders and the way his head hung told me how uncomfortable he was. I should have risen above my feelings and let his friendship with this prickly old woman run its natural course without intrusion from me.

I carried the coffee tray to the table.

Audrey accepted a cup and dipped her head to smell it before taking a swallow. 'That's very good,' she said and I found that I was disproportionately pleased with the note of approval. I settled more comfortably into my chair.

Audrey reached down for her cracked old brown leather handbag and began fishing round in the contents. 'Since you're taking such an interest in your father, this late in the day, I thought you might like to look at this,' she said. She passed an empty bottle across the table.

It was a beautiful little *flacon*, made of smoked glass and shaped like a teardrop, with overlapping petals of silver and mother-of-pearl cupping the base. The stopper was a smaller fluted teardrop of glass set in a silver collar. I touched the glass stopper, testing the fit.

'Go ahead,' Audrey commanded.

I withdrew the stopper and sniffed. The perfume, whatever it had once been, was dead and gone. 'What is it?' I asked.

'One of your father's fragrances. He called it Innominata. Nameless, if you like.'

'Did he create it for you?'

Yes, of course he did. The face-cupping routine.

Audrey nodded. Then her mouth crimped with a mixture of pain and triumph that made me uncomfortable. I really should have left well alone, I thought.

'Why Nameless?' I asked, for the sake of something neutral to say.

'Because it suited me,' Audrey snapped. Jack, who had wandered across to the fridge, turned in surprise.

I handed the bottle back. So Ted had created a perfume for her, but not for my mother or me. I knew and Audrey knew, and there was more triumph than pain showing in the pucker round her mouth. She was formidable, I thought. There was a steely strength in her that I hadn't fully appreciated. She would have been a match for Ted. More than a match, probably.

'When did he make it for you?' I asked.

'Nineteen fifty-six.'

It was a very precise answer, given that she had claimed to be so vague about dates. The timing was right for the position of the formula in Ted's volumes of notes. Another thought came to me. 'I found a photograph, among his things.'

'You gave it to me.'

I frowned, and then remembered that she must mean Ted's film star picture. 'No, not that one. This is one of you, sitting on a wall somewhere. Only I'm afraid I've gone and lost it. I'd love you to have had it.'

Jack dropped something on the worktop behind me and I heard the scuffle he made to mop up a spill.

'I have got it,' Audrey said.

I frowned again, as Jack sidled round into my field of vision.

'Er, Mum? I gave it to her. I thought it wouldn't matter.'

Audrey smiled, pleased with this evidence of Jack's concealment. It linked the two of them against me.

I kept my voice light. 'Well, that's fine. It's Audrey's picture. You should have mentioned it to me, though, Jack. I was worrying about how I could have been so careless with it.'

'Sorry,' he muttered.

Audrey drained the last of her coffee. 'It's been very interesting,' she said. 'But I must get home now. The animals can't be left too long.'

'We must do this again.' I smiled. Jack fidgeted near my elbow, indicating his displeasure at this suggestion. 'And I'll give you a lift home.'

Audrey stood up and adjusted the hook that fastened her fur. 'I'll walk, thanks. I'm used to walking.' I went with her to the front door. Audrey's stiff bearing indicated that I shouldn't try on anything as bogus as kissing her goodbye. We nodded at each other instead. She said goodbye to Jack and we watched her part of the way down the road.

My plan to defuse her appeal to Jack by drawing her more closely into the circle didn't seem to have worked at all, and when I considered it now it seemed in any case like a cheap manoeuvre.

I didn't see Mr Rainbird in the press of children when I collected Jack and his belongings at the end of term. I called him that evening instead. 'We're going to France for two weeks' holiday,' I explained.

'I hope you'll be impressed by Jack's command of the language, after Cherbourg.'

'I'm sure I shall be. I wondered if you are still interested in us going out together?'

'Sadie, I thought I'd made that clear.'

'So how about the Tuesday evening a week after we get back?' I gave him the date.

'I'll just consult my diary.' Our passports and air tickets were laid out on the table in front of me and I slipped them into a folder while I waited. 'That looks good to me,' he said.

'I'll look forward to it,' I told him. And it was true.

We flew to Nice. The airport was being rebuilt and the white light reflecting off raw concrete made us all blink, and when I tried to catch the ozone sparkle of the turquoise sea all I could smell was dust.

We collected our rental car and Lola did her best to navigate the route towards Grasse. At last we turned inland, and drove up the broad valley I remembered so well. I could see Grasse on the hill, and the outline of the hills beyond was familiar against the sun-drained sky, but everything else had changed. Where there had once been meadows there were now rashes of white and ochre villas, and building sites that heralded new supermarkets and a drive-thru' McDonald's. Jack and Lola had gone quiet in the heat.

'Soon be there,' I said brightly.

The campsite was up a winding road on a steeper section of the hillside. There were mimosa trees overhanging the gate, some of the branches still plumed with powdery dead flowers, and banks of nettles beyond the driveway. I understood, when the concierge showed us to our apartment in the converted barn, why the place was cheap. But to my relief there was a wide view of the valley that reduced the sprawl of building to toppled white sugar cubes, and there was even a grey-blue smudge of sea on the horizon. Lola flung her suitcase on her bed, took out her bikini and went straight to the pool. Four boys who had been playing water volleyball stopped to watch her as she settled down to read on one of the bleached sunbeds lined up round the pool.

Jack took possession of his cupboard of a room, meticulously laying out his binoculars and notebook, and a guide to the birds of the region. I kicked off my shoes and sat on our tiny terrace, letting the sun soak into my bones. When I closed my eyes the scent, a mixture of baked dust and thyme and the faintest suggestion of flowers, was more familiar than any landscape could be.

We spent the next three days sunbathing and eating and reading—at least Lola and I did, while Jack flitted under the trees or sat on a rock with his binoculars—and on the fourth we drove up to Grasse and visited the old stone-flagged flower market that I had loved so much when I was fifteen. We wandered around for a while, then ordered crêpes and salad at a restaurant in the shade of the stone arches. There were citrus trees in pots against the medieval walls, and a view down steep steps to an alley snaggled with iron balconies and washing lines. Even in the middle of the day it was cool here out of the sun.

'It's beautiful.' Lola sighed. 'You're right. I'm glad we came.'

I smiled at her.

Later, while they were eating ice cream, I slipped inside the restaurant and looked for a public telephone. I found one, next to the *toilettes*. I riffled through the dogeared pages of the local directory, certain that I would find nothing. Yet here was the name, clearly listed.

Philippe Lesert.

I dialled the number.

'*Oui?*' It was a heavy, rather tired-sounding voice. I began my explanation of who I was but he interrupted me in disbelief. '*Sadie? C'est toi?*'

'*Oui, Philippe.*'

We laughed at one another's surprise. I tried to explain and apologise for my long silence and sudden reappearance, but Philippe wouldn't hear of it. 'And you are right here in Grasse?' he repeated.

'Yes. Yes, on holiday with my children.'

'We must make a rendezvous, please. I should like very much to meet your husband and family.'

'Only my son and daughter.'

I learned that his wife Stéphanie was a writer of children's books and was unfortunately so busy this week that he could not ask me to their home. But, perhaps, I would meet him for lunch?

We made a date for three days' time.

'Who were you talking to, Mum?' Jack wanted to know.

'An old friend. Someone I knew the first time I came here.'

Jack and Lola made the face they always made at each other following any suggestion that I might have had a life that predated them.

Two more days passed. It was hot and windless, and I sat on the terrace with my book and stared out over the valley towards the sea. Lola had made friends with the volleyball boys and went down with them to the beach in Cannes. Jack didn't want to go to the beach. He wandered up the steep incline to the rocky ridge overlooking the valley and watched birds. The other families at the site played noisy ball games together and lit barbecues or drove to the sea, but it was as if we three were on separate holidays within the envelope of a family trip. Yet it was a solution of a kind, I decided, since even Jack seemed reasonably content.

On the third day I drove to meet Philippe for lunch in a restaurant up in the old town. When I walked into the dim interior a man stood up at a corner table. 'Sadie, I would have known you anywhere.'

He kissed me on both cheeks and held my hands between his. I wasn't so sure that I would have recognised him. He was still slim but his black hair had turned grey and he was smaller and much sadder-looking than I remembered. For all Philippe's gallantry, I guessed that if he were being truthful he would have said the same about me.

There was a bottle of champagne in an ice bucket beside the table and Philippe poured me a glass. 'To 1965,' he said, and I echoed the toast.

The lunch was like any other reunion between two people who haven't met for almost forty years. There were points of recognition so intense that it seemed as if no time at all had intervened and there were huge chunks of separate histories to sketch in. Philippe told me he had sold most of the family land for real-estate development. There was no money to be made from growing flowers for perfume; synthetic perfume essences were produced in labs, and a tiny soupçon of *jasmine de Grasse* might be added, he said, if the accountants' figures allowed for it.

Philippe now worked as a marketing director for one of the big perfume houses. 'Maman was the last of us to live the old way,' he told me.

Marie-Ange Lesert had died nine years ago. After that, Philippe sold the remaining few hectares to one of the last three jasmine farmers left in Grasse. 'It's all gone, everything that you and I remember,' he said. His dark eyes were so shiny that I thought he was about to cry.

'And I do remember it so well,' I said. Madame with her red, brawny arms and her feet in clogs, the smell of cooking and jasmine and roses, and the calm welcome she gave to a withdrawn English teenager.

The champagne was going to my head. 'You were the first love of my life,' I told Philippe. 'Did you know that?'

He inclined his head, smiling. 'One should notice these things. But not act on them. You were far too young and a guest besides.'

I found that I was blushing.

I told Philippe about how I loved paper and print and old books, and he listened and watched my face.

'I think you must very much resemble your father. You have the same vitality of intention, the same devotion to your materials and methods.'

The warmth that suffused me wasn't just because of the champagne. Was I like Ted? I was startled to realise it, but I was flattered by the comparison. 'Do you know anything about him? Do you know how your mother and he were connected?'

He spread his hands. 'I'm so sorry, no. I never thought to ask Maman. But this is why you are here in Grasse, isn't it? Now he is dead and you are mapping his history, because it is a way that you can make him live.'

'Yes.'

'I remember the same, when Maman died. I keep all her boxes of papers and her trinkets at my house, for no reason except—ha—they were hers. Stéphanie thinks I am a little crazy.'

We had finished the champagne and after Philippe had paid the bill, we were the last diners to leave the restaurant. Then I walked with him through the dusty streets. We said goodbye on the steps of his office, where he kissed me and rested his hand for a minute on my arm. 'Don't leave it for another forty years, please, Sadie.'

'I won't,' I promised him.

I walked back to my car and started the engine. On the way home I made a detour along the dusty track to the Leserts' home. The house was exactly the same—tall, blinkered with green shutters and set in a patch of trodden dust edged with nettles and clumps of goose grass—but the flower field had shrunk to a tenth of its old size and now it lay within a corral of holiday homes and garden swings and swimming pools. Some of the jasmine and centifolia roses still flowered, and the scent of them was the same as it always had been.

I sat quietly for a minute or two, thinking about that summer. I had been happy here, and the warmth of the place and its people had offered me reassurance when I needed it. The Leserts had given me the resolve to go back to London and my life with Ted.

I started the engine and drove back to the campsite. Jack and Lola were both waiting for me.

'So, Mum, how did it go with the French love interest?'

They were exchanging the look again.

'It wasn't like that at all,' I protested. I kept the truth, which was that it could have been, entirely to myself. It was a fresh, revitalising piece to add to my happy memories.

On the last day Jack and I went for a walk together, up the hillside to his lookout place on the ridge of rock. It was early in the morning, still cool with a hint of mist and the resinous scent of pine in the air.

'OK,' Jack sighed when I asked if I could accompany him.

I scrambled up the steep ravine in Jack's wake, breathing heavily and sweating in spite of the cool air. Finally, we reached the rock band and Jack sprang straight up the sloping ledges to the ridge summit. I followed more carefully, testing the outcrops of stone before trusting them with my weight. I am not good at heights and I didn't look down until I was sitting at the top next to Jack.

The view was worth the climb. Beneath us, the carpet of real estate spilled down to the sea, and to the left were the medieval towers of Grasse. But beyond the ridge another landscape was revealed. There were peaks of jagged rock here, ink-blue in the shadows, and ochre or warm peach in the strengthening sun. Birds wheeled round the exposed faces and traced punctuation marks against the sky. I turned my back on the valley and watched. Jack had the binoculars to his eyes and I could feel the thread of his concentration like a wire under tension.

After about fifteen minutes, I was shifting my position, realising how hard the rock was under my haunches, when Jack drew in a sharp breath. He jerked to his feet with his binoculars raised. I followed the direction of his gaze. Two huge birds soared across the rock face, quite close at hand. I saw the flash of white tails banded with black, domed heads briefly etched against the stone as they wheeled and rose majestically above the cliff and into the blue space beyond. I watched until they were no more than black dots in infinity. Jack stood for seconds more, straining forward as if he could catch them.

As he lowered his binoculars, Jack gave a deep sigh. And when he turned his face to me his eyes were shining with rapture.

'What were they?'

'They were golden eagles,' he whispered. He looked incredulous and enchanted, as if he had been given the best present of his life.

After a moment he slipped his binoculars into the case. I understood that any other sightings could only be an anticlimax now. We reversed our route down the rock band and he held out his hand to help me down the slope. 'Have you seen a golden eagle before?' I asked.

His eyes were still brilliant as they held mine. He was breathing hard, as if he had been running. 'You only get them in the north of Scotland.'

'Did you know they were here?'

'No. I didn't expect it. But you get . . . what is it? A feeling that something's going to happen? Not with your brain, but down your spine?'

'A premonition.'

'Yes,' Jack said happily. 'A premonition, that's it.'

We made our way back to the campsite down the dry earth channels left by the winter rain. 'Thanks, Mum,' he said.

Lola was sitting outside, drinking coffee. 'Where have you two been?'

She looked fondly at Jack while he spilled out the story, and I sat and listened and watched the two of them. It had been a good holiday, surprisingly good. Even if we hadn't followed the nuclear families' pattern of picnics and barbecues and ball games.

FOURTEEN

PENNY'S AND EVELYN'S RELATIONSHIP had evidently taken a serious downward turn while I was away. On my first day back at the Works there was no sign of Cassie, or Evelyn.

'Where's Cassie?' I asked. Andy and Leo were both at their benches.

Penny didn't look up from gluing a binding. 'With her mother.'

There was a scissoring snap as Leo brought down the guillotine blade on a stack of card. I got on with my work and waited until eleven o'clock when the men took their mugs of coffee outside for ten minutes.

'What's happened?'

Penny did lift her head now. There were deep lines round her eyes and at the corners of her mouth. 'She's living with Jerry again.'

'Why?' I asked.

'Partly because she wants to get pregnant. Partly because she's not sure about being gay. Or she's not sure about being gay and with me.'

There was so much pain in her face that I could hardly look at her. I went round the end of my bench and put my arm round her shoulders.

Penny sagged and let her forehead rest against me.

'It may still work out,' I said, forcing conviction into my voice. 'Evelyn loves you in her way, and Cassie adores you.'

'We'll see,' my friend said.

Andy and Leo came in, shuffling awkwardly, knowing that everything was wrong, and afraid, as young men are, of what might be required of them if they had to help out.

Life was no more comfortable at home either. Lola had decided that she was going on holiday again, with her boyfriend Sam this time, and she needed to earn the money to pay for it. She was doing full-time reception work and a part-time bar job as well, so we hardly ever saw her.

I was seeing plenty of Jack, though, and he was impossible. It was as if the holiday in Grasse, and especially the glimpse of the golden eagles, had opened a window that he couldn't bear to have closed again. 'London's a shithole,' he snapped, when I tried to talk to him. 'It stinks. Why do we have to live here? I hate it.'

The long holidays were always a problem for Jack. It was difficult to come up with ways to entertain a solitary child who lived in the middle of the city and whose only real interest was birdwatching.

'You'll grow up and then you'll be able to choose where you live,' I said as patiently as I could.

Everyone grows up in the end, even though at Jack's age I had found that just as hard to believe as he did now.

And London did stink that August.

It was very hot, a windless and humid heat that left the exhausted streets hazed with dust and clogged with litter. And the traffic was worse than I had ever known it. The transport strikes had become so frequent that they ran into one another, and no one ever knew whether it was worth plunging into the suffocating underground to try for a tube, or if it was better to stand outside in the heat, gazing down the lines of grid-locked cars in the hope that a bus might materialise.

The heat didn't engender any sense of lassitude, though. Instead, the whole city seemed to simmer with rage and aggression. As I sat in the car, trying to get to or from the Works, I listened to the radio news reports of street violence breaking out in Brixton and Homerton and Goldhawk Road. Whenever I set out on foot, even if I was only going as far as the high street, people pushed and jostled each other on the pavements. Anger seemed to seep from the very cracks in the brickwork until a miasma of threat hung everywhere, and for the first time in my life I felt afraid of London, of my own place.

Jack started spending more and more of his days at Audrey's.

In spite of my misgivings, I was glad that he was somewhere, doing something, with somebody.

On the evening that I had arranged to meet Mr Rainbird for dinner, Jack was sprawled in the stifling kitchen watching television. I had insisted that he come back home from Audrey's by six o'clock and Lola was due back from work any minute but hadn't actually arrived yet.

'I've got to go,' I told him, 'or I'll be late. Lola'll be back soon. Will you be OK?'

He didn't look at me. 'Yeah. Where're you going?'

I could have told him, but I chickened out. I didn't have time to go into it now; I would have to tell him later that I had been on a hot date with his head of year. 'To have dinner,' I said.

'Who with?'

'Just a friend. Listen, Jack, will you ask Lo to ring my mobile as soon as she gets in?'

'Yuh.'

I felt the accustomed twist of guilt as I left. I shouldn't be going out to have a good time, should I, and leaving my child on his own?

Lola called as I was almost at the door of the Italian restaurant.

'You'll stay in the house with him?'

'Yeah. OK.' Lola didn't sound delighted at the prospect, on a rare night off. 'Have fun, Mum. Don't do anything I wouldn't do.'

'Plenty of scope, then.'

After this ritual exchange I dropped my phone back into my bag and pushed open the door of the restaurant. Mr Rainbird was sitting at the corner table, waiting for me.

When we had finished dinner and spun out two cups of espresso apiece, what seemed like a long time but also a matter of mere minutes later, he drove me home. Darkness had brought no relief from the heat;

if anything, the night seemed even more oppressive than the day.

'What a hell's kitchen,' Mr Rainbird murmured, as he tried to nose the bonnet of the Morris into an unrelenting stream of traffic coming at us from the left. I was well fed and relaxed with red wine, and I watched the shops and cars sliding by with calm detachment.

I had told him that Jack didn't yet know who I was out with and he sighed, signalling disapproval, but when we reached home he parked the car a tactful distance from my front door. He switched off the engine and the lights and we were left cocooned in the smell of creased old leather as the ticking and whirring of the motor gradually subsided. Mr Rainbird took me in his arms and kissed me.

It was a nice kiss. I hesitated and then I kissed him back. Our tongues touched and seemed to match. I relaxed, but what I began to feel was the opposite of relaxation. I put my hand on his arm, then moved it along his shoulder until my fingers touched the nape of his neck.

It was Mr Rainbird who pulled back. When I opened my eyes I caught the glimmer of his smile. 'I think we should call it a night, Ms Thompson.'

Anxiety and pre-embarrassment crawled along my spine, and I sat upright. Had I misread the signals after all?

Then I saw that he was teasing me, but with affection and also a definite shading of regret. He had a better sense of time and place than I did, that was all. 'Too old for snogging in the car?' I smiled.

'Nope. But, you know.' He nodded in the direction of my house.

'Yes. You're right. Thanks. And thank you for a wonderful evening.' I meant it.

'I'll call you tomorrow,' he said.

The hall lights were all off when I walked in, but I knew at once that there was someone watching me in the darkness. 'Jack?'

I groped along the wall and found the light switch. I jumped at the sight of Jack standing motionless on the stairs, staring down at me.

'What are you doing?' Alarm made my voice sharp.

'Did you have a good time?' he countered just as sharply.

The tone of his voice warned me, and I saw now that his face was taut and waxy with accusation. I sighed. 'Yes.'

'I asked Lola who you were with.'

Lola had known. I hadn't asked her to keep my arrangements to herself, not specifically, because I had just assumed that Jack wouldn't be that interested. Even as I was making these rapid calculations I recognised the scale of my mistake. At Jack's age I had been more interested in my father's doings and whereabouts than anything else in the world, as a matter of self-preservation. Ted was all I had. It shouldn't come as a surprise that Jack felt the same about me.

'You should have told me you're going out with a *teacher* from my *school*. I hate being treated like a kid. I hate secrets,' he blurted out.

Of course he did. So did I. I knew the insecurity that untruths bred, so how could I inflict the same on my son?

I put my bag down and climbed the stairs towards him. 'Jack, I'll tell you everything. *Please* let me tell you.'

He started backing away from me, retreating towards his room. I followed with my hand stretched out to him as if I were trying to soothe a frightened animal. Jack reached his bedroom door. He half sat and half fell against his bed, lifting an arm to ward me off. 'Go away.'

'Jack, it's OK. Listen. It's not a secret. I like your teacher and I think he likes me. I'm sorry you felt excluded. I was afraid you'd be embarrassed and I was trying to find the right time to talk to you about it.'

'Embarrassed.' Jack repeated the word flatly. Then he swung round to stare out of his window. 'Suzy's pregnant again. She's had tests. It's a boy.'

I caught my breath in sympathy. This was very hard. Jack had taken the birth of the twins hard enough, those dear little scarlet-faced babies with their tiny clenched fists and black eyelashes, but at least he had been able to tell himself that they were only girls. *He* was Tony's son.

Now there was fresh unwelcome proof that Tony and Suzy had sex with each other and as a result he wouldn't be the best-loved boy any longer. There would be another, probably more satisfactory claimant.

On top of this, tonight, there was the possibility that his mother and his teacher were also thinking about having sex. Even his sister never stopped talking about her miraculous new boyfriend.

Embarrassing barely described it.

'Dad rang. He wanted me and Lola to know first.' Jack made an angry face. Tony always tried to do the right thing in these matters.

'So where's Lo now?'

Jack did the shrug. 'In her room.'

I listened to the sounds of the house. There was no muffled bass thud of music vibrating through the floorboards. Lola had retired to bed. She would be upset at Tony's news, too. Lola's sadness and jealousy wouldn't last long because there were too many other things going on in her life, but they would be real enough tonight.

I sat down on the bed beside Jack. 'I'm sorry about Dad and the new baby. But I suppose we should have been expecting it.'

'Hm. They're going to call it Hugo. *Hugo*,' he repeated in disbelief.

'Are they really? Well. At least being called Hugo is one thing you don't have to cope with,' I said.

I might have been mistaken but I thought I saw the beginnings of a smile, before Jack remembered that he didn't do smiles.

I looked at his bedside clock. 'It's midnight. Time we went to bed. We can talk more tomorrow.'

He turned his head. 'Are you going to see him again?'

'Yes, I think so. Would you mind that?'

The shrug again.

'I love you best in all the world,' I told him truthfully. He made no response to that.

Outside Lola's door I stood and listened for a long minute. I tapped gently and whispered, 'Lo?' When there was no answer I knew she was asleep. Lola wouldn't hear me without answering.

I went quietly along the landing to my own room and lay down. The day had been too long and too complicated for me to try to set it straight before I slept.

Next morning I left for work before Jack or Lola had emerged from their rooms. Penny and Andy were already at their benches when I arrived. It was Leo's day at college.

In the middle of the morning Colin appeared at the front counter. We all tried to ignore him but he rapped on the countertop with a coin. 'Shop!' he called briskly. 'Nobody working here today?'

I gave in. 'Hello, Colin. Three of us are working, if you look closely. And we're pretty busy.'

He hoisted a bulging carrier bag and dumped it on the counter. 'Got another book. I want to discuss it with you.'

I put down my job and walked to the front of the shop. Even in the heatwave Colin was still wearing a grey jumper. He smelt sharply unpleasant and I resisted the impulse to take a step backwards.

'I'm afraid we're not scheduling any new work at the moment, Colin.'

'That's rubbish.'

'It's not, actually. And we lost money on the last book, you know.'

'I paid you. I'm on benefit, you know. I'm on the sick. I have to watch what I spend.'

'I understand.'

'Good. So.' He began shovelling dogeared magazines out of his carrier bag and as they spilled over the counter I scooped them up and tried to force them back at him.

'Colin. Listen to me. We can't do any more for you.'

I thought he hadn't heard because for several more seconds we continued our tussle. Then suddenly his arms dropped to his sides and his thick lips parted as he stared at me in silence.

'I'm sorry,' I said. Suddenly my skin prickled and I wanted very much to get Colin out of here. I smiled and put my hand to his elbow. 'We've just got a lot of work on right now and we can't handle any more even from our best customers. Phew. Isn't it hot in here? Let's collect up your things, look, and go outside. We can chat out there, can't we?'

He took the carrier bag and meekly allowed me to steer him out into the yard. When I glanced back I saw that Penny and Andy had moved as one to the bindery door, to keep me in sight.

'You've already got your beautiful book,' I reminded him. 'Your mum must have been impressed with that.'

At the gate, Colin hesitated, then looked at the back door of the house. 'Where's that kiddie of yours?'

'She's not mine. She and her mum moved away.'

Colin peered down at me. He looked genuinely concerned and upset. 'Oh dear. That's a pity. You must miss her.'

'Yes. Quick, here comes your bus. Bye now, Colin.'

I waited until he had lumbered on board and the doors had hissed shut behind him.

Penny and Andy watched me come back down the yard.

'Was it just me, or did our Colin seem rather sinister today?' I asked.

'It's the heat. Makes everyone weird,' Andy judged.

We went back to work. The atmosphere in the bindery was depressed, so I was relieved when it was time to go home. I was looking forward to spending the evening with Jack. We were going to talk about his father and the new baby, and I'd tell him about Mr Rainbird and me so that he wouldn't need to feel that I was keeping secrets from him.

I got in at ten past six to find the house empty and close-smelling. At seven o'clock Jack still hadn't returned.

I dialled Audrey's number, assuming he was there. I hung on and on. I would let it ring all night, I decided, if that was what it took.

'Yes?'

'It's Sadie here. Is Jack with you?'

'Yes.'

'Can I speak to him, please?'

Silence. I heard Audrey putting the receiver down and walking away.

'Mum,' Jack said at last in a heavy voice.

'Do you know what the time is? You're supposed to be home now.'

'What?'

Jack sounded as if he didn't have any idea of the time, barely even knew who I was. 'Jack,' I said clearly. 'I'm coming to pick you up.'

'Mum . . .'

Two minutes later I was driving towards Turnmill Street.

I banged on Audrey's peeling front door and when nobody came I crouched down and peered through the letterbox. It gave me a view of the murky hallway and its piles of junk.

'Jack!' I shouted, but nothing stirred.

I banged and shouted again through the letterbox. Then I saw Audrey emerge and walk slowly up the hallway. The door jerked open.

'Didn't you hear me knocking?' I asked. 'I've come to pick Jack up.'

Audrey looked pale. Her hair hung in grey wisps beside her jaw. She hesitated, then half turned away from me. 'Jack?' she called, into the dim house. 'Jack?'

I saw him backlit against the yellow glow from the end room, but he didn't come any closer. I had no choice but to slip past Audrey into the hallway. When I reached him I saw that his eyes were puffy with crying.

'What's wrong? What's happened?'

Jack's mouth twisted as he bit his lip, trying to hold back more tears. 'The cub's dead,' he whispered.

'The cub?' I repeated stupidly.

He couldn't stop himself crying and it was to Audrey, standing close behind me, that he looked for comfort, not me.

'Come on.' She took Jack's arm. 'Come on now.'

'He was run over. We found him lying in the street,' he sobbed.

The fox cub, of course. Nothing more serious than that. Relief flooded warmly through my veins. 'Oh dear. That's very sad.'

Jack flung himself as far from me as possible in the confined space. 'Sad? Is that all you can say?' He hid his face against Audrey and wept, while she stared coldly into my eyes and stroked his hair.

I said as gently as I could, 'It's time we went home now.'

He didn't even look round. 'I'm not coming. I want to stay here.'

Audrey's glance glittered like chips of ice. I kept my dismay at the idea submerged as far as possible. 'You haven't got any pjs here, no toothbrush, nothing. You can stay another time.' I was getting this all wrong, I knew, but I had no idea how to make it right.

He shook his head violently. 'No,' he snarled.

This wasn't just about the fox cub, of course. It was because of Tony's new baby son, and Lola and Sam, and me and Mr Rainbird. Audrey's house had become a retreat from all of this and the drama of the cub's death made him feel even more part of it.

'Come with me,' I said. 'Now.' I took hold of his hand and tried to draw him away from Audrey but he snatched himself out of my grasp.

'I. Am. Staying. Here,' he said.

My hands fell to my sides. I could not stand here and do battle with Audrey for possession of my child. I'd have to back down temporarily.

I took a deep breath and smiled. 'All right. You can stay with Audrey until tomorrow morning. I'll pick you up at nine o'clock.'

Jack rubbed his eyes with his knuckles. Audrey's full mouth loosened and curved with triumph.

There was much more to this for her than a night's sleepover. The depth of rivalry between Audrey and me went way back into history, the thick roots twisted in the earth of the past and Ted's devious doings. I felt in my pocket for my car keys. 'Good night, Jack,' I said softly.

'Say good night,' Audrey told him while I waited.

'Night, Mum.'

'I'm sorry about the fox cub.'

'OK.'

I drove home and sat with my hands loose in front of me at the kitchen table, just waiting and thinking. I wanted to seize Jack and bodily carry him out of Audrey's ambit, but the fact that I couldn't do that didn't mean that I wouldn't bring him home.

FIFTEEN

IN THE MORNING I STOOD on Audrey's step with a carrier bag containing Jack's clothes for the day. I knocked and called but the only response I got was from Audrey, who finally spoke up from the other side of the closed door. 'Jack's staying here with me and the animals.'

'He can't.'

'Why is that, if it's what he wants?'

'I don't know that it is what he wants.'

I wrestled in my mind with lurid images of drugging or hypnotic suggestion, while behind me the morning business of Turnmill Street went on regardless. The postman worked his way along the street, but didn't turn in at Audrey's gate.

I called again through the letterbox. 'Audrey? Can I talk to him for a second, please. I won't make him come out if he doesn't want to.'

Minutes passed, then Jack came into view. He didn't look as though he had been drugged or hypnotised, nor even particularly forlorn. He seemed calm, with Jack the cat rubbing and twisting round his ankles.

'Mum, what do you want?'

'To talk to you. Don't make me do it through this slot.'

'I want to stay here because Audrey and me are both unhappy about the cub dying. What else would I be doing today anyway?'

'You'd be at home. Where you belong. And I'm sorry the cub got run over too. I'm just less sad than I would have been . . . oh, if something bad had happened to you, or Lola, or Dad.'

Jack said, 'You've got to go to work, haven't you?'

'Yes,' I admitted. There was always that pressure.

'I'm staying here,' he repeated.

I considered the situation. There wasn't anything I could do, for the time being, short of breaking the door down. Jack was apparently well and comfortable, and probably enjoying the sense of power that defiance gave him. 'All right. See you later,' I said.

I marched down the path and back to where I had parked the car. It took me nearly an hour to reach the Works. A truck had shed its load at the Highbury roundabout and the resultant chaos had added to the usual congestion. When I finally turned into the yard I saw Evelyn sitting sunning herself. Her hair tumbled prettily round her face.

'Hi, Sadie.' She sighed in her soft voice. 'How're you doing? Everything sweet?'

A familiar one-legged teddy bear was lying on the bench beside her.

'You're back,' I said unnecessarily. I was already tending towards the house door, hungry for the sight of Cassie.

'Sadie-lady!' Cassie was in her booster chair at the kitchen table, squeezing raisins between her fat fingers as if she had never been away.

I scooped her up and swung her round. She threw her head back and laughed with delight, and I realised then how much I had missed her. Evelyn was watching us from the doorway.

'Play. Let's play,' Cassie imperiously demanded.

'I've got to work, Cass, or Penny'll want to know why. Tell you what. I'll come across at teatime and read you a story. I promise.' And how simple that was, I thought, compared with my negotiations with Jack.

As I passed the child back to her mother, Evelyn's long hair caught between us and briefly lifted off her face to reveal a shiny purple swelling over her cheekbone and under her eye. I glanced away at once but she knew I had seen it. 'Clumsy, aren't I?' she said brightly. 'I walked smack into a lamppost when I'd had a couple of drinks.'

I nodded sympathetically, accepting the lie while I wondered with a beat of horror if there had been any threat to Cassie.

Penny was busy at her bench but she looked up when I came in. The lines of misery round her eyes and mouth were all rubbed out.

'So,' I murmured.

Andy and Leo waved vaguely to me, absorbed in their separate tasks.

'I won't bloody well let anyone lay a finger on either of them ever again,' Penny swore in a fierce voice. 'He'll have to kill *me* first.'

'I hope not,' I said.

At lunchtime I told her about Jack and Audrey as we sat in the shade of the bindery wall. 'What shall I do?' I said.

'I'd say don't force the issue. Have you talked to Graham and Caz? Or Mel? Whatever happens you're not on your own. You've got all of us to help you out, remember.'

I was glad of Penny's assurance. She knew the core of isolation and the chill that went with it, because it was hers too. Caz and Graham didn't because their roots were so closely entwined, and Mel had never experienced it because the warmth of her family always insulated her.

'I do remember,' I said gratefully to Penny.

After work, I found myself yet again on the step at Turnmill Street. There was no response to my knocking. All I could think of was how much I wanted to get Jack home again, yet I had packed a bag with some more of his clothes and some other belongings so that he would have the comforts he might need from home if he did stay.

I knocked as hard as I could, then leaned forward so that my forehead rested against the door. 'Audrey! I want to speak to my son. Open this door immediately or I'll call the police.'

The door opened and I peered into the gloom. Audrey was there.

'He doesn't want to speak to you.'

'I've had enough of this.' I pushed hard at the door, getting my shoulder up against it. Audrey resisted with surprising strength and the door almost slammed in my face before I could shove back again. I heard a rattle as she swiftly slotted the chain into place. I was locked out.

'This house is my property,' Audrey said calmly through the gap. 'And Jack's my guest. Why can't you let him be? You don't own him. We're watching *Animal Hospital*. I'll tell him to phone you later.'

I took a breath. This exchange was so irrational that it was surreal.

'Listen to me, Audrey. Nobody owns anybody else and I wouldn't claim that they do. I am Jack's mother, though, and I'm responsible for his safety and his well-being. And a lot of other things besides, but let's keep it simple for now. I'm not convinced that he's safe with you, especially since you seem to need to lock him in.'

'The chain's to keep you out, not him in. And if he wants to take a break from life with you maybe you should ask yourself why. Don't worry, I'll take good care of him.'

'Let me talk to him.'

'We're watching *Animal Hospital*.'

Bugger *Animal Hospital*. 'Jack?' I called into the crack. 'Can you hear me? I've brought some clothes and your GameBoy. Is there anything else you need before you come home tomorrow?'

There was no answer.

'Open the door, please, Audrey, so I can hand you the bag.'

'Leave it on the step. I'll pick it up when you've gone.'

I drove home through the dark blue August twilight, shaking from my confrontation with Audrey. I had been made to feel powerless in relation to my own child and I vowed that wouldn't continue. If I was going to have to fight to bring Jack back, then so be it.

When I pulled up I saw that most of the lights in our house were on although Lola had warned me it was one of her bar-job nights. I let myself in and the smell of soy and ginger wafted to meet me. In the kitchen I found Caz sitting at the table with a glass of wine. Graham and Jasper were leaning against the counter also holding glasses of wine, and Mel was stirring the contents of a frying pan.

I blinked. 'Is it my birthday? I wasn't expecting a surprise party.'

'It wouldn't really be a surprise party, would it, if you were expecting it?' Graham remarked reasonably. Caz shushed him and came round to me with a drink. I swallowed a gulp and Mel blew me a kiss.

'Penny called me. She said you're worried about Jack and from the sound of it I don't blame you. I rang Caz, and we thought we'd all come round and cook some food for you and have a case conference. Lola let us in before she went to work.'

I sat down shaking. 'Thank you,' I said. Caz patted my shoulder.

I looked round the circle of faces in the candlelight, and I was touched by this demonstration of friendship.

Jasper was sitting opposite me. He looked across at Mel then said, 'Clare didn't speak to me for two months after her mother and I split. Not a word. I thought I'd lost her for good.'

'What happened?' Caz asked.

'We made it up eventually, but it took time. Then she became very possessive of me for a while and hostile to my girlfriend. She went in for a couple of heavy relationships herself and they both ended badly.'

'And now?'

'We like each other again.' Jasper looked less confident than I had seen him before. 'At least, I like her. Love her very much.'

The eerily positive picture of his family history had been painted for Mel in the early days of their relationship. Nothing was really that simple, I was thinking, and we couldn't solve one another's problems. But we could draw comfort from comparisons, and we could get together and drink wine by candlelight.

At that moment the phone rang and I got up to answer it.

'Hello, Mum.' Jack's voice sounded small and clear. Audrey was true to her word, then.

'Hello. Hold on for a minute, I'll take this upstairs.'

I went up to the living room and picked up the phone. 'Are you there, Jack? What are you doing?'

'Not much. We've been watching TV. It's so hot.'

'Do you want to come home? Shall I come round and pick you up?'

'No, Mum.'

There was a silence. I wasn't sure what to say next. In the end I went for the obvious. 'I miss you. Is there anything you need?'

'I'd like my binoculars. And my bird book. It's on my table.'

'Jack. You're not *staying* there.'

'Yes, I am.'

I bit back the sharp contradiction. If I was going to fight, I would have to use more subtle weaponry than a telephone slanging match. 'I'll bring them tomorrow.'

'Thanks,' he said, still in the same clear voice. He sounded older, as if he were discovering unexpected resources. 'Who's with you?'

'Just Caz and Graham and Mel and Jasper.'

'Oh. That's nice.' After another silence he said, 'Well. Good night, then.'

'Good night. I love you, you know. You can call me as soon as you want to come home, any time, even if it's in the middle of the night.'

Reluctantly I hung up and made my way downstairs. I met Mel coming up. 'Jack?' she asked me.

'Yes. What are they doing downstairs?'

'They're fine.' Mel steered me back into the living room. Her face was shadowed with concern. 'I met Clare, you know.'

I exhaled. 'I'm sorry. I should have asked you about it. It's just . . .'

'I didn't mean that,' she said, sitting down. 'Meeting her gave me a new perspective, that's what I want to say. Because I wanted so much for her to like me, and because it was so important, to me and to him, I felt disabled, I got it all wrong. I was trying too hard *not to try too hard.*'

I was laughing now, in spite of wanting to take all this seriously.

'No, listen. I'm telling you this because of Jack and you. Trying to make a go of it with Clare made me aware of how difficult all this must be for you. With kids it seems the more you want something to work, the more seized-up the relationship gets. Right?'

'Yes. Like handling pastry too much. You can go on working on it and hoping to make it better until you bring it to the point of ruination.'

Mel ran her fingers through her hair until it crackled. 'My God, that's frightening. I was scared to death of Jasper's Clare and she's a nineteen-year-old girl. It must be even more complicated with Jack, when you love him so much. And for Jasper, with Clare.'

I groped for Mel's hand and held on to it. 'Clare is scared too,' I said. 'She's afraid you'll turn out not to be good enough for her father. She's afraid that he'll love you too much and therefore love her less.'

Mel drew up her knees and rested one cheek on them, looking hard at me. 'You've been through all this.'

'In a way.'

We squeezed each other's hands.

'It doesn't stop, does it?' Mel murmured. 'Learning and loving.'

'No. Even though we're as old as we are. It doesn't stop.'

'Good,' she said.

We found that the party in the kitchen had changed gear. The table had been cleared and Graham was shuffling a pack of cards. We played pontoon for fifty-pence stakes and I forgot about Jack for an hour. I lost a fiver, drank too much wine and laughed a lot.

When Lola got back from her bar job, she joined the game. Luck was on her side, as always. As she raked a pile of coins into her pocket she beamed around the table. 'A lot easier than bar work,' she said.

As the others left we all agreed that we should do this more often. It had been a good evening, against the odds: I felt the warmth of it around me as I locked the front door and turned off the lights.

Lola slipped into my room as I got ready for bed. 'Are you really worried?' she asked. She wanted to pitch her own anxiety by estimating mine, so I smiled and shook my head.

In the morning, I had a hangover. I left the mess from last night littering the kitchen table, and hunted for Jack's bird book and binoculars. Lola had already gone to work.

Outside, the sun's glare made my eyes throb. I banged and shouted at

Audrey's front door. I was bending down to peer through the letterbox when I heard a car draw up.

When I turned, a young policewoman was coming in through Audrey's gate. Fear stiffened my back. Why were the police here?

'Good morning,' the WPC said pleasantly. 'Is this your house?'

'No. No, it isn't. My son's . . . staying here.'

'I see.' She was looking at the debris scattered in the garden. 'We have had a call from one of the neighbours. Somebody has been seen several times, shouting and hammering at the door. And there is a child on the premises who doesn't usually live here. Is that right?'

The relief I felt briefly shifted into anger. Self-satisfied, bourgeois, bloody Turnmill Street, I thought. Some busybody had it in for Audrey because her paintwork and garden maintenance didn't conform to local standards. 'That would be my son, yes,' I said pleasantly.

'Shall we just have a word with him, then?'

This put me in a difficult position. I could knock on the door, but we might well stand here hoping for a response until the sun fried us both to a crisp. I decided that candour was the best resort. 'I don't honestly know about that. He's being a bit rebellious. He's a teenager, you see. Well, almost. He's decided to stay here with, with . . .' My voice trailed away. I realised I didn't even know Audrey's surname. 'A family friend. He's upset because his fox cub died. And he won't come out, which is why I have been banging on the door, actually.'

The driver of the panda car was now coming to join his companion.

'His fox cub,' repeated the policewoman. 'Your son is twelve?'

'That's right.'

'Let's see, shall we?'

She rapped smartly on the door, which opened at once to reveal Audrey. Her eyes travelled straight from the police to me and I knew she would assume this was my doing.

'Good morning,' the policewoman said again. 'Are you all right?'

I realised that they were just as prepared for her to be a thuggish twelve-year-old's hostage as they were for Jack to be a kidnap victim.

'Yes, thank you. Is there some problem?'

'We understand you have this lady's son staying with you?'

Audrey's cold glance rested on me. 'That's correct,' she said.

'Where is he now?'

She lifted her chin. 'Well, he's here, isn't he? Jack!' she called into the dim recess of the house.

Jack came down the stairs slowly, reluctantly, one step at a time. His face was a troubled mask.

'I didn't call the police, Jack. One of the neighbours did,' I told him.
'What's going on here?' the WPC asked.
He shrugged. 'Nothing.' He wouldn't look at me.
The officers were losing interest. No one was hurt or being held captive here. I could tell they were preparing to withdraw when Audrey made the tactical error of protesting too much. 'What harm can it do, if he wants to stay here with me?'
The policeman spoke for the first time. 'By rights, he should be at home with his mum.'
'I'm fine here,' Jack mumbled. My heart twisted in sympathy: he couldn't be seen to lose face by coming with me, nor did he want to reject me under the gaze of the police and the growing knot of spectators.
The two officers glanced at each other but they were moving off, past the geological strata of decaying cardboard. They had had enough.
'I think your lad'll be back home as soon as he gets tired of all the attention,' the WPC said, kindly enough. Then they peeled away to the panda car, settled themselves inside and cruised off down the street.

Mr Rainbird said when I called him, 'Damn. I've got a gig with the band tonight. But listen, why don't you come along and we can have a drink or something to eat afterwards? It's not exactly an irresistible proposition, but maybe if you're not doing anything else . . .?'
His honesty disarmed me, as it always did. It was Friday and Lola had gone up north to stay the weekend with Sam. 'I'll come.'
He gave me directions and I promised to be there for the second set.
When I arrived, the pub was hotter than a Turkish bath. Jerry was on stage, singing 'Destination Anywhere', and the pub's red and blue lighting was throwing purple slashes across his handsome face. The colours reminded me of Evelyn's bruises and I had to look away. I felt that I was betraying Penny and Evelyn and Cassie just by being there.
Mr Rainbird saw me and smiled when he lowered his trumpet.
I searched for a space at the bar and bought myself a drink. The ice cooled the back of my throat and I rested the frosted glass against my forehead. This was the first empty moment of the day and even in this inferno I was glad of an interlude of peace.
The music was good, and I let it wash over me in big, lavish waves.
By the time the set ends I have downed another icy drink. The band plays 'Wait 'til the Midnight Hour' for the encore and I am sorry when we have clapped and stamped our way to the final bars. The bar staff are calling time and the pub doors stand wide open.
Then Mr Rainbird is standing right in front of me. 'Shall we go?'

We are walking down the street together. It feels so cool out here. He puts one arm round my shoulders. His trumpet case is in the other hand. It's nice, walking like this, in step and with the music still in our heads. We are humming the same tune and just moving together, in no particular direction and in no hurry. Under a wide horse-chestnut tree Mr Rainbird stops and puts down his trumpet case. He stands in front of me and a street lamp throws his shadow across my face.

He puts his hands on my shoulders and looks down at me. Then he kisses me, and after a minute I lock my arms round his neck, holding him close, tipping my head back and opening my mouth to his.

When we move apart we do so very reluctantly.

He says, 'Sadie, would you like to come home with me?'

I think about this and the thought makes my veins feel as though they are running with honey, not vodka and ice.

I begin composing a sentence. 'Mr Rainbird . . .' I say by mistake. Of course I know his name. It's just that up until now, in my head, he has stayed partly connected to school and Jack and a public role.

He puts one finger over my lips, silencing me. 'I have just asked you to come to bed with me. It's all right to use my first name.'

Laughter begins in the pit of my stomach and bubbles upwards. Somewhere a thread is severed and his teacher persona drifts away.

'It's Paul, by the way,' he adds considerately.

'I know,' I insist, but I can hardly get the words out. Suddenly we are both laughing so hard that we have to hold each other up.

SIXTEEN

YOU DON'T FORGET how to make love, I discover, any more than you forget how to laugh. It's just that lately I haven't been doing enough of either.

Tonight, though, goes some way towards making up the shortfall.

I lie in Paul Rainbird's arms, salved by slippery skin against skin, after an interlude of eager touch and taste that has made me cry and laugh, with my eyes shut and my mouth open against his. I can tell from his breathing that he is still awake and listening, like me, to the night noises from beyond the open windows. In here, in Paul's white-painted room, the sirens, speeding cars and shouting voices are as distant and unthreatening as the cries of sea birds. Gulls, terns and guillemots, Jack would say.

Even the thought of Jack slides through my head without making me draw up my knees to ease the stab of anxiety. Sleep is coming at me in big waves now. He strokes my hair and I fall asleep.

In the morning, I woke up with his arms still round me. It took me a few seconds to work out where I was. Paul's face was creased with sleep and his hair stuck out in rakish wings.

'Hello,' I said.

He sat upright and rubbed his face, and I could see full consciousness coming back. I watched to see if realisation was going to be followed by a flicker of dismay, but all I could see was happiness. I put my fingers to his cheekbones and the angle of his jaw, mapping his face.

We stared into each other's eyes. I kept telling myself, Jack is at Audrey's and Lola's with Sam. The absence of responsibility made me feel lightweight, as if I might drift upwards away from the sheets and pillows, if I didn't have Paul Rainbird's arms and legs to hold me down.

Later, we got up and padded around in his kitchen. Paul had given me a clean T-shirt to wear and I sat on a stool watching him make coffee and toast. 'How's Jack? Is he at his dad's this weekend?' he asked.

'Um, no.' I told him what was happening.

'I wanted to tell you about it,' I concluded. 'My good friends came round the other evening and we had a conference. They were very supportive and I was grateful, but I was thinking that you were the person I really wanted to talk to.'

'Because I was his head of year?'

'No. Because you're you.'

'Really?'

There was a hesitancy about him, a reluctance to take anything for granted, that touched me.

I touched his hand across the table top. It was an ordinary morning, a baking August Saturday in the inner city, but something out of the ordinary was happening. 'Yes. Tell me something, Paul.' It seemed to be the first time I had used his name. 'Didn't you want children of your own? Don't you still want them now?'

'I did, with Jane. She did, with me. But the time was never right for both of us at once, so it never happened. I don't regret it now because I think we'd have split anyway.' Tactfully he considered what he was about to say, then said it regardless. 'And so as far as the present goes, I teach enough kids from fractured families. I see what it's like.'

'Like Jack.'

He laughed. 'Not much, no. On another scale, actually. Some kids—not all, of course, but some—are like a different species. I try to teach them *Macbeth* and creative writing, and the difference between an adjective and an adverb, yes. Mostly it's utterly pointless. They're angry, some of them, and violent, but it's bred out of deprivation and neglect and brutality that Jack could hardly conceive of. So no, I don't yearn too much for fatherhood. I fear the responsibility of it.'

He spoke simply, almost flatly. 'Very occasionally you do get through to one or two of them. One of them says, Yes, I see. Or, I liked that, sir. And you know they'll remember whatever it was you were trying to convey long after they've left school. Maybe even until their dying day. That compensates for all the rest of the mindless argy-bargy that teaching's about nowadays. There was a moment with Jack, in fact.'

'Was there?' I was startled.

'I gave him a poem to read. "The Windhover". It's about a bird.'

I'd never heard of it. In front of Paul I was slightly ashamed of the fact that, to me, books had always represented calf bindings and tooled designs, rather more than windows into an infinity of knowledge.

'Jack told me he didn't understand most of it and that didn't bother him. But it described what the bird in flight looked like and, because Jack knew all about that, he felt that he could trust the poet for having got that much right. And he said the words and the rhythm also made him feel what it was like to *be* a bird in flight. He decided that the point of a poem was to tell you something you knew, and then to use that to introduce you to something you didn't know and were pleased to find out about. I thought that was quite impressive.'

So did I. Warmth spread along my spine and filled my throat, and I recognised the feeling as pride. 'Thank you,' I said to Paul.

He fidgeted uncomfortably. 'Just doing my job,' he said.

'And doing it well,' I persisted. I found myself wanting to chip away at his self-deprecation. I suspected that he was a brilliant teacher, I knew that he was a pretty good trumpeter and I had just found out that he was surprisingly good in bed. The last thought, coming unexpectedly into my mind, made me blush.

Paul took my hand and held on to it. 'What do you want to do now, Sadie? Would you like to spend the rest of this lost weekend with me?'

I totted up my responsibilities. I had to keep in touch with Jack and I had to let Lola know where I was. That was all. 'Yes, please,' I said.

We walked in the park and ate a picnic of takeaway sandwiches in the shade of a huge horse-chestnut tree. All around us were couples lying openly entwined on the grass, and babies in buggies shaded by little frilled parasols, and groups of noisy softball players. This afternoon's benign version of the city was much more familiar to me than the threatening version that had recently hatched out of the weird, prolonged hot spell.

In the early evening, when the metal disc of the sun slid to a lower angle but the air still seemed to heat your lungs as you sucked it in, Paul and I drove through the sullen crowds to Audrey's house.

Paul stood quietly by the peeling gateposts while I performed the now familiar ritual of banging on the door and shouting through the letterbox. No one answered, although I knew they were both in there.

I put down on the doorstep a box of fresh fruit and vegetables, and some clean clothes. I called good night to Jack through the slot, told him to telephone me if he needed anything and retraced my steps. Paul and I walked in silence back to the car.

'Let's go home to my house,' I said, as we drove away.

We sat in the garden under the tree and watched the light fade. I didn't want to talk and Paul understood that without my having to explain it. When it was fully dark we went upstairs together.

I woke in the night, confused to find a man's body in my bed. I fell asleep again and was gripped by a nightmare.

I am in a closed space, with no space beyond it. The walls squeeze me and I know with complete certainty that there is no calling for help because there is no one to hear. I am alone, and the desolation of it wrings tears out of my eyes and a terrible wail from my throat.

I woke up, still hearing the wail. I was tangled in the bedcovers and I fought to free myself.

Paul sat bolt upright. 'You are safe,' he said. 'You are safe now.'

He held me gently until the nightmare released its grip.

'I'm sorry,' I mumbled.

'It was a bad dream. Everyone has bad dreams.'

We lay down again. It was still dark but I could hear the tentative notes of the day's first bird singing.

'Tell me why you have bad dreams,' Paul said. 'Tell me what's the worst thing that ever happened to you.'

'That sounds like some party game gone badly wrong.'

I knew that I was pulling up the drawbridge while Paul lay still and waited. But the nightmare's desolation clung around me and I found myself wanting to push it away. I made myself say, 'My mother died.'

293

That was just how it was. One day she was there and the next she was gone. There had been no interlude of illness.

'What happened?'

'A cerebral haemorrhage, I believe.'

I came home from school one afternoon and instead of my mother waiting for me with a glass of orangeade, I found our neighbour, Mrs Maloney. She told me that my dad would be home soon and in the meantime why didn't I watch the television?

I asked her where Mum was and she said I was to be good and my dad would tell me all about it.

I didn't ask any more because I already feared what I must hear.

After a long hour he came in and told me she was dead.

I tried to be brave and not to ask too many questions, because that was plainly what was expected of me.

After her death, instead of being comfortingly present, Ted became less and less accessible. From a mature viewpoint I could excuse his absence as to do with his own grieving, but as a child I took it personally. I began to fear that he would disappear as abruptly as Faye had done, so I clung about him, watching him for signs of fatal illness, checking that he wasn't preparing to go out and leave me.

All this was in the days before the first auntie made her appearance, of course. Mrs Maloney was supposed to look after me, but I hated her smell and her lugubrious manner, and the way she snooped around our house when Ted was out. I was supposed to go to her house for my tea after school and wait there until he came back, but then he often left me stranded there until nine or ten o'clock or even the whole night.

I had my own door key to our house, so after a while instead of going to Mrs Maloney's I began to let myself in and do my homework. It was lonely, but better than being in the other house.

Mrs Maloney came to look for me one afternoon and tried to tell me off, but I stood up to her. I said I wanted to be in my own home and she could tell my dad if she wanted, or we could keep it just between the two of us. I knew that he paid her for minding me and she didn't want to lose the money. Ted had enough to worry about, I told her righteously, and I was perfectly all right where I was.

That was how we left it for a while. Then one evening Ted said he had to go away on business for a few days the following week.

'How long for?' I asked, trying to pretend I didn't care.

'I told you. Just a few days. You'll be fine with Mrs Maloney.'

I lay awake at night praying that he wouldn't go, but he did.

I let myself into our house on the first day he was away and scented the cold, unused air. There wasn't much food, but I made myself a kind of meal from bread and tinned meat. Then I sat down to watch television. Mrs Maloney came and knocked at the door.

'Go away,' I told her. She had a key, but I slid the bolts.

'Just you listen to me, you little madam. Your dad's gone off with his fancy woman and he'll be back when it suits him. You're to do as you're told and come with me to my place, do you hear?'

I didn't know what a fancy woman was, but I could guess. The thought made me feel sick. 'Go away,' I repeated.

When she went, at last, I crept upstairs and lay under my bedcovers. I was shivering so hard I thought my jaw would crack.

That was the first of nine days.

I went to school and came home again. In between times I bolted myself in and waited. I watched television, read books and slept as much as I could, which wasn't much. The silent house was full of noises. I heard my mother's voice calling me. I would hear Ted's key in the lock and I'd jump up and run trembling to the front door, only to find that there was no one there. In the darkness there were footsteps coming closer and I cringed under my covers for fear of burglars. My whole body ached with the effort of listening and trying not to hear.

Mrs Maloney covered herself by knocking at the door whenever she passed and, I supposed, by noting when the lights went on and off.

As the days crept by I felt odder and odder. I ran out of bread and milk, and then everything fresh. For a whole weekend I didn't speak to anyone. Then something had happened to the Ascot heater in the bathroom, because the water stayed cold.

When I went back to school on Monday morning I knew that I looked strange. I was hungry and cold all the time, but the sight of school dinners made me feel sick. None of the teachers noticed, though.

I began to wish I had stayed with Mrs Maloney, but I wasn't going to go knocking at her door and ask her to take me in. By this time I was afraid that Ted would never come back, that he was dead too.

Then, on the evening of the second Friday, without any warning, I heard his key in the lock. I knew with a heart's leap that this time it really was him, not just my imagination or Mrs Maloney trying to get in. I ran to the front door and dragged back the bolts.

Ted was there, with his leather suitcase in his hand and the waft of his cologne coming at me. He was frowning. 'Hello, there. What's this, Sadie? I thought you'd be up the street.'

'I . . . I just wanted to be home for a bit.'

295

'Come on then, let me get inside.'

I was blocking the doorway. I jumped aside, and he went upstairs, and even from the back he looked tired and older than the nine days' difference. I heard him turning on the taps in the bathroom. 'Damn pilot light's gone out,' he said. A few minutes later there was hot water again.

When he came downstairs I went and stood in front of him.

'I thought you weren't coming back,' I said, accusingly.

'What's this? I told you I'd be back. Mrs Maloney was here to look after you.' He was blustering. We both knew he had done wrong to leave me, although he would never admit it. He patted my shoulder. 'Are you hungry? Shall we get fish and chips?'

I was ravenous and suspicious. 'Can I come with you?'

'I insist that you do.'

We drove to the chippy in the car, and ate our supper straight from the newspaper at the kitchen table.

For a while after that my father was at home more in the evenings. I began to relax, although I was never quite off my guard. In fact, I never trusted Ted again, not really, although I tried to, and although I loved him, in my way. I was quick to place my trust elsewhere, as soon as I thought I was grown up. I gave it to Tony, then I made the mistake of falling violently in love with someone else. My family, Jack and Lola, suffered from the mistakes I had vowed never to make.

'That's it, really. That's all that happened,' I concluded. But I turned my face against Paul's shoulder and he held me to him.

'I understand now why you're so upset about Jack.'

'It's quite different,' I protested.

'Yes, of course,' Paul gently agreed.

The nightmare's miasma had receded and my limbs were beginning to feel heavy. I found it difficult to keep my eyes open.

'But it touches quite a lot of chords, doesn't it? Jack running away from home and locking himself in a place where you can't reach him?'

'I don't know how to deal with it. I love him so much, he must know that, but I don't know how to get to him.'

'We'll find a way,' Paul said.

I adored that we. I hadn't heard it like this, spoken in the vulnerable small hours by a man I trusted, since Stanley left.

On the Sunday morning, it was my turn to make the coffee and toast. Paul's eyes rested on me as I trod the overfamiliar route between toaster and kettle and fridge, and just once he put out his hand to stroke my hip as I brushed past him. The single touch made me shiver with recollection and anticipation. I almost spilled the milk.

He carried the breakfast tray out into the garden for me. I peeled an orange and divided it into segments. I offered one to him. He took the crescent and ate it.

'I had an idea, after you fell asleep last night,' he said.

He had been lying awake, thinking about me.

I smiled at him. 'Go on.'

'If Jack won't come out and you can't get in, maybe you should move the goalposts. Doing something always feels better than doing nothing. Maybe you should let him know that you're close and that you won't ever give up or let him go, however hard he tries to make you?'

I knew he had put his finger on something. Jack was testing me, to see how long and how hard I would hang on. It was as if he were saying to me, unconsciously, *Don't let me down. However hard I push you, don't show me what I fear, which is your rejection or your indifference.*

'I think you're right,' I said.

'So let's go and show Jack we're with him. Let's have a picnic in the garden. Deck chairs, Sunday papers, sandwiches, that sort of thing.'

'What if Audrey calls the police?' But she wouldn't do that. She knew she was on tricky ground after our last encounter with the law. 'And if you're there, won't that make Jack more hostile?'

'If we're there together, Sadie, you're letting Jack know that you've got a life of your own that has a huge space in it for him. And that's the truth, isn't it?'

I nodded. It was the truth. I wanted Paul to be there and there was also a touch of anarchy to his proposal that appealed to me.

'Let's do it.'

There was a strip of shade beneath the wall that separated Audrey's rubbish-tip garden from the next-door neighbours rectangle. We sat in the folding chairs that I had hauled out of my cellar. Paul read the *Observer* while I flicked through the supplements. I knew we were attracting attention, from inside and outside the house, but if I happened to catch anyone's eye, as they parked cars, or walked past with shopping bags, I just nodded and smiled. Nothing moved behind Audrey's shrouded windows, but I knew she and Jack were watching.

When lunchtime came Paul strolled round the corner to a bakery and came back with a brown bag. We were eating our picnic when the people from the other side emerged from their house.

'Hello?' the woman said pointedly. She was wearing pearl earrings and a blue sundress, and her husband was in salmon-pink Lacoste.

Paul and I introduced ourselves and I explained about Jack and Audrey, as lightly as I could.

'We heard that the police were here,' the woman said. I wondered if she was the one who had called them.

'Yes. No need for that, of course. Jack's just going through one of those adolescent phases. Audrey's a sort of family friend.'

The man looked at the garden, as if to say that I must be a fine friend. The woman clearly felt this was too confrontational. She said quickly, 'Well, we know all about adolescent phases. I'm Gilly, by the way, and this is Andrew.'

I told them our names and Paul added pleasantly that he was one of Jack's teachers, so they wouldn't assume he was his father. Gilly asked which school and when he told her she said oh yes, she'd heard it was very good. 'We're fee-payers, for our sins,' she added.

It was rather like being at a dinner party. I was thinking that just because we ate sandwiches from the deli and talked about schools, Gilly assumed we were on the same side, whereas Audrey with her cats and a garden full of cardboard never would be. My sympathy was with her.

'Well,' Gilly concluded, 'we'd better get a move on, we're going out to lunch. Let us know if we can do anything to help, won't you?'

As they were getting into their car they stopped to talk briefly to a man who was trimming his hedge and I saw Andrew nodding in our direction. The news of our sit-in would travel fast.

The afternoon trickled by in a daze of heat.

It was surprisingly pleasant, idling in the semi-shade, doing nothing in Paul's company. Midafternoon I walked round the corner to find a pub that was open and as I strolled back I saw a small movement behind the tattered curtains at an upstairs window. Jack was checking up on my whereabouts.

Paul was talking to two young men. They were both in Spandex cycle shorts and tight vests, and their bikes were resting against the party wall. He introduced them as Tim and Gavin from next door.

'I was just saying to your friend, we do worry about the old lady,' the slightly less muscular one confided to me. 'We offered to do some tidying up out here in the garden for her, but she wouldn't let us. I'm surprised she's letting you sit around on her property, as a matter of fact.'

'We'll have to see what happens,' I said neutrally.

'Well, you want your boy to come home, don't you? Is there anything we can bring you, by the way, while you're out here?' Gavin asked.

'A cup of tea would be very welcome, thank you,' Paul said.

They brought out a tray, and while we were all sitting drinking our tea Gilly and Andrew came back.

'It's a street party!' Gilly cried. 'I've always said we should do one for the Jubilee.' She had clearly enjoyed a few Pimmses, and her husband's face was a dark reddish colour that was at odds with his polo shirt.

'I'm going to come and join you,' she said suddenly and tripped across the geological strata of cardboard in her sandals. 'Bring out a bottle of nice white vino, Andrew, and a few glasses.'

Five minutes later our numbers were increased by the man who had been trimming his hedge. He didn't know Tim and Gavin, so Gilly introduced them as well as Paul and me. His name was Mike and he had a loud voice and a highly confident manner.

'Have you heard the news?' he boomed, accepting a glass of Andrew's Sauvignon.

'No, what?' Andrew asked.

'There's been a street fight over on the Ullswater Estate. A pack of skinheads set on some Muslim kids, or vice versa. Stone-throwing, knives, casualties, police in riot gear. It's still simmering over there.'

In this crowded inner-city borough, the toughest areas and the most expensive often lay next to each other. The Ullswater was barely half a mile from the far end of Turnmill Street. Paul and I exchanged looks. Now that it was actually erupting, it had seemed inevitable all along that violence would boil out of the city's overheated cauldron. We all listened, but the street was eerily quiet with purple shadows lying under the dust-coated trees.

Two blond children emerged from Mike's gate, one of them riding an expensive bike. They came across the road to us.

'Are those your bikes?' the boy on the bike asked Tim and Gavin.

The four of them clustered round to exchange technical information. The garden was getting quite crowded. In my bag, my mobile rang.

'Mum,' Jack hissed. 'Who are those prats with the bike? What are all those people doing in Audrey's garden?'

This was the first contact of the day and Jack had voluntarily initiated it. Even if it was only to make a protest. Clever Paul Rainbird, I thought.

I said airily, 'Just hanging out. Why don't you join us?'

'Don't be stupid. And what's Mr Rainbird doing here?'

'Keeping me company. Is that OK?'

'Shit,' Jack said despairingly. But he didn't say it wasn't.

After another bottle of Andrew's good wine, Tim and Gavin said they had to get ready to go out. Fifteen minutes later Paul and I were alone in the garden again. 'I think we should call it a day,' he said.

I went to the front door and called through the letterbox into the listening space of the house, 'Audrey, I hope you don't mind too much that we were here today. You've got some good neighbours. 'Night, Jack. I love you. Call me any time you want. I'll see you tomorrow.'

The next evening Paul and I resumed our vigil. Mike's wife Andrea came across to say hello because, she said, Mike had told her all about what was going on and she didn't want to miss anything.

'There's Jack now,' Paul said. I swung round and saw my son's face at the downstairs window. He was watching us with surprise and, I thought, a degree of satisfaction. All this was happening because of him.

'Hello, Jack,' I called.

Jack responded with a quick, embarrassed smile.

When he disappeared from the window, I was convinced that he was about to come back to me.

But when the front door did open, it was Audrey who stood there. 'What are you doing in my garden?'

We fell silent. I took one step forward. 'Audrey, let me try to explain. We're not trying to invade you. I just want Jack to know that he's also got a life to live with us. It doesn't mean he can't spend time with you, of course. I want him to come home, that's all.'

Audrey half turned and behind her we saw Jack, standing in the gloom at the foot of the stairs, looking serious and determined.

'Jack?' Audrey said.

Before he could answer quick footsteps came along the pavement and bounced in at the gate. 'Mum? Jack?' Lola asked. 'What's happening?'

Paul and Andrea stood aside. 'Hello, bruv,' she said. 'I brought you some sweets and magazines and stuff.' She held the package out to him.

Then Jack came out onto the step and took it. 'Thanks, Lo.'

He hovered, poised between us, his family and the regular world, and Audrey's fastness. I felt his indecision and also the tug of his loyalties. It would be easy for him now to step outside, and much more difficult to cleave to Audrey and the lonely house.

There was a whisper in my head, *go on Jack*. But I wasn't willing him to step my way.

Jack would be all right, I knew that much now. He wasn't helpless or full of fear, as I had been. He was loyal to Audrey and he wouldn't be seen to climb down. For the time being he had made the right choice.

He stood up straight. 'Thanks, Lo,' he repeated. 'And you, Mum. But I'm staying here, you know?'

I saw the flash in Audrey's eyes. 'You are on private property,' she warned. The door closed with a firm click, shutting us out.

Andrea murmured good night and tactfully dispersed leaving just Paul and Lola and me in the garden.

I took Lola's hand. 'Jack will be fine.'

'I know that.'

We were subdued by the taste of Audrey's loneliness and her need to hold on to Jack. Lola turned to Paul. 'Hi, Mr Rainbird.'

He smiled at her. 'Hi, Lola. You can call me Paul, now you're out in the real world.'

'I'm not sure I'm that crazy about the real world,' she said sadly.

'If anyone's up to dealing with it, Lola, that person is you.'

She brightened up. 'Really? Well. Thanks. Look, Mum, I've got to go. I promised I'd meet Kate.' As ever, Lola had her own priorities.

'Go on, then. It was good that you came over tonight.'

Lola hoisted her bag, ready to depart. She looked straight at Paul. 'I'm glad you're taking care of my mum.'

'I will do my best,' he said gravely.

When we were on our own again Paul said, 'Do you want to go now?'

I nodded and started folding the chairs. I knew better than to ask Jack to come with me. Instead, I went to the door and crouched on the step. I could just see Jack's eyes through the slot.

'I'm proud of you,' I said. Then I pushed my fingertips past the flap. Jack's touched them at once. We told each other good night.

'I'll be back tomorrow after work,' I said.

Another hot day crept by at the Works. We didn't have much paid work on, but that wasn't unusual for August.

I catalogued our supplies of paper and calf while Penny worked on a set of leather display boxes for a local jeweller. Leo and Andy were both on holiday.

Throughout the heatwave Evelyn had been putting Cassie to bed for the hottest part of the afternoon and letting her stay up later in the evenings. Today she slept until past four o'clock, and Penny and I heard her irritably wailing when Evelyn finally brought her downstairs again. When the end of the day came I went across the yard to look in at the house and found her in her wet red starfish-patterned swimsuit, standing up on a chair sailing toy boats in the sink full of water. 'See, ships,' she shouted to me. Waves slopped into the puddles on the floor.

Evelyn was sitting at the table, looking tired and peevish. 'Sadie, d'you mind keeping your eye on Cassie for a minute? I want to make a phone call and have a fag in peace. She's been a nightmare all afternoon.'

I had promised to meet Paul at Turnmill Street straight after work, but it wouldn't matter if I was a few minutes late. 'Sure,' I said.

'This your ship,' Cassie told me, handing me a wooden yacht with a sodden triangle of sail. My sandals squelched in the puddles.

'Thank you. It's a beauty.'

We sent the boats gliding across the tiny lake. She was leaning so far forward that I hooked my fingers under the slippery straps of her swimsuit in case she toppled headfirst into the water.

After about fifteen minutes Evelyn wandered back again. She was still holding the telephone handset and a packet of cigarettes.

'Eve, I've really got to go,' I said.

'What? Oh, right. Is Penny still not here?'

'She was just finishing some gluing. She shouldn't be long,' I said. I kissed the top of Cassie's head. 'See you tomorrow, Cass.'

I dried my hands on a tea towel. Evelyn was sitting at the table again. She didn't look round when I said good night, just sighed a response.

I could see Paul as I parked my car and walked up Turnmill Street. 'I thought you weren't coming,' he said.

He wouldn't kiss me under the eyes of Audrey's house and probably the rest of Turnmill Street, but I knew he wanted to.

'Here I am.' I smiled.

We went into the garden and I called a greeting through the letterbox to Jack, then we settled in the folding chairs. After we had exchanged the news of our separate uneventful days, we divided the *Evening Standard* between us and read the reports of the clashes on the Ullswater Estate. There had been an attempted robbery at a Bangladeshi-run curry house. A fight between rival gangs had broken out in the street outside the restaurant and the violence had then spread across the estate. A couple of cars had been torched, and some shops had been looted.

There was an acrid mass of frustration and an indefinable anxiety balled within my own chest. It was so stifling and airless tonight. I was listlessly folding the newspaper when my mobile rang.

Penny's voice was so jagged with panic that I sat up sharply and sent the contents of my bag spilling over the ground. 'Cassie's disappeared.'

'What? When?' My heart lurched and started hammering in my chest.

'After you left. Evelyn thought she'd come across to be with me in the bindery, but I hadn't seen her since before her sleep. She's gone.'

She had been there, in the kitchen. Wet in her red swimsuit. Evelyn listless and sulky with the phone and her packet of cigarettes.

'How long?'

'An hour. We're searching. The police are coming. Did you see anyone? Anything at all, before you left?'

I made the pictures, a little innocent loop of film, play over in my head. The boats in the sink, the empty yard, Evelyn sitting at the table. Nothing unusual. 'No. I'm on my way,' I gabbled. Paul had been gathering up the contents of my bag, and I grabbed it from him, almost falling over the chair in my haste.

'I'll drive you,' he said at once, not yet knowing where or why.

I called a rapid goodbye to Jack and then we were in the car. Paul trod on the accelerator and we shot forward. 'Cassie,' I said. I saw his knuckles go white as his hands gripped the wheel.

There was a police car outside Penny's house. When I ran into the kitchen I found an officer trying to talk to Evelyn who was weeping hysterically. 'A red swimsuit.' She choked. 'With a pattern of starfish.'

A little knot of neighbours was gathered in the yard, and a white-faced Penny was directing them to take a street each.

'Jerry? Could Jerry have taken her?' I shouted.

'No. Jerry's coming. He hasn't got her.'

Two more policemen came round the side of the house, moving with massive calm. I ran out of the yard towards the canal towpath.

There was no one there. The water was an unrippled sheet of khaki. I stared wildly up and down the path, then knelt down at the water's edge, trying to see into the depths. All I could see were Cassie's limbs flailing and her mouth filling with water as she sank out of sight.

'Oh, please, God,' I whispered.

Paul's hand touched my shoulder. 'You go that way, I'll go the other.'

I scrambled up and made off towards the lock. The band of shade beneath the bridge dropped across my face and I touched the crumbling brickwork. There was nothing on the no-man's-land under the opposite pier except broken glass. I ran on round the corner. A fisherman was sitting there, his beefy bare arms livid from the sun. 'Have you seen—?'

'That kiddie not found yet?' he cut in. I shook my head.

The man said, 'I'll walk on up this way for you.'

'Thank you,' I panted. The sight of him stirred something in my mind. Whatever it was glimmered like a fish in deep water and I pressed my fists against my temples in a vain attempt to hook it.

I ran back in the other direction. Paul was shouting the question to a narrowboat full of startled people. They shook their heads in answer, smiles fading on their faces.

'Nothing,' Paul said to me, as the boat chugged off.

The shoulders and arms and legs of the people on board were all bare and sunburnt, like the fisherman's. Then the submerged memory flickered again and I jerked my head in pursuit. This time I had it.

Only two hours ago. I was driving away from Penny's. My attention was focused on getting to Turnmill Street but out of the corner of my eye I caught a glimpse of a man wearing a beige knitted cardigan. It had been Colin, at his usual bus stop, opposite. I was sure of that.

I snatched at Paul's wrist. I was already running and he pounded in my wake. 'I've thought of something.'

In the house, Evelyn was still crying hysterically. Penny was sitting on her chair beside the computer, answering police questions.

I dashed across the yard and took my address book. There was an address for Colin, but no telephone number. It was a long shot. 'Quick. We can check this ourselves,' I called to Paul.

He thumbed the pages of the *A-Z* as I drove. 'Here it is. Left at the end, straight on, under the railway bridge. Left here.'

I stopped the car outside a cheerless block of flats, concrete-faced with ugly blue-painted slabs beneath the windows.

We dashed up a flight of stone steps to a first-floor landing. Colin's door was one of a pair. I pressed the bell. From the other side of the flimsy door his loud, blurry voice demanded, 'Who's this?'

'Colin, it's Sadie. From the bookbinders.'

There was the sound of bolts being slid back, then the door opened on a chain. Colin's thick nose appeared in the gap.

'It's me, Colin. Let me in.'

'I can see it's you. You can't be too careful, you know.'

He took the chain off and I edged into the hallway, with Paul right behind me. The air was thick with Colin's body odour.

'Who are you?' Colin demanded.

'My name's Paul. I'm Sadie's friend.'

I sidestepped very slowly and carefully towards an open doorway. I could hear the *plink-plink* of a child's musical box. The cramped room was almost entirely filled with a sofa and a huge television.

On the sofa Cassie was sitting, wide-eyed, gripping the musical box. Beside her was a little old woman, her dentures bared in a smile.

'Sadie-lady,' Cassie said. She let the musical box drop and slid off the sofa. The old woman caught the discarded toy and set it carefully on the sofa arm. I saw that there were framed photographs on the windowsill and on top of the television, all of them of a little girl.

I held out my hand to Cassie, smiling at her as calmly as I could. With the other hand I extracted my mobile phone from my pocket and gave it to Paul. He stepped smoothly back into the hallway. I held

Cassie's warm, sticky hand in mine for a second, then I stooped down to her level. 'Hello,' I whispered. I couldn't see any fear or pain reflected in her wide brown eyes. She looked surprised and mildly curious.

There was no sign of the red swimsuit. She was dressed up like a living doll in a lemon-yellow smocked-front dress with a matching hand-knit cardigan, tiny white ankle socks and white leather bar shoes.

Colin's mother smiled. 'She wasn't properly dressed, you know. But she looks a picture now, doesn't she? These are some of my Susan's things. Lucky that I'd kept them all this time, isn't it?'

I lifted Cassie into my arms and held her tight. I could just hear Paul, outside the flat, talking rapidly. He had found Penny's number, stored in my phone. *Yes, yes. She's fine. Safe, yes. No. Nothing at all.*

I started trembling with relief. From all around the room the huge eyes of the other child gazed down at us. She looked nothing like Cassie—she had a thin little face and pale straight hair. The only point of similarity was the clothes.

I turned slowly to face Colin. 'Why did you take her away? Didn't you know how worried everyone would be?'

His cheeks turned a dull red and his lower lip protruded. His mother wound up the musical box and set it tinkling again.

'I was coming to see you and Penny about my new book and the kiddie was there in the yard. She said she wanted to play. It was hot so I walked her down to the canal. You can easily walk from there to here. Although generally I prefer to take the bus because it's safer.'

He told his story without hesitation and I replayed the route in my mind's eye. The canal route was direct. By road it was twice the distance.

'I used to have a sister, you see,' Colin confided. 'But she died.'

His mother pulled herself to her feet. She was tiny and as frail as a bird. She said, 'Don't talk about that now, love, or it'll get us all upset. Let me put the kettle on. We'll have a nice cup of tea.'

'All right,' Colin mumbled and she patted his hand. 'I brought her home to say hello to my mum, you know.'

The words fell unemphatically in the thick, sour-smelling air, but the sadness in them weighed down on me. I tried to imagine what life must be like for the two of them, walled up in this tiny flat. I also thought about Jack and me. I understood that whatever might and whatever would happen from now on, I must stand back and give him room to flourish. Children who don't have enough light and space around them grow up spindly and lopsided, just like plants deprived of sunlight.

Paul came back and stood beside me. 'We should take her back home now,' he murmured in my ear.

I held on tight to Cassie, who was beginning to squirm with impatience. 'We'll have to be off,' I said brightly.

'Wouldn't you like a cup of tea?' Colin's mother asked, politely. Her grip on reality seemed fragile. She didn't understand who we were.

'We can't, this time.'

'Wait a minute, then.'

She reached for a Boots plastic bag, which she handed to me. When I opened it I saw the red swimsuit and Cassie's canvas shoes. 'You can keep the things she's wearing. As a present from Colin and me.'

Penny and Evelyn were waiting on the pavement outside the house. Evelyn was still crying as she opened the rear door of the car to reach her daughter. Together she and Penny held Cassie and the three of them made a tangle of arms and wrists and hair. Jerry loomed directly behind, frowning, his hands hanging loose at his sides.

'Let's go inside,' Penny murmured. A police panda car waited in front of the house and now an officer was coming towards us.

Evelyn said to Cassie, 'Let's take that pretty yellow frock off, shall we? You don't want it to get all dirty, do you?'

The policeman wanted me to make a statement. He took off his cap and I sat down facing him at the kitchen table. In the background Penny mechanically switched on the kettle.

I told him what had happened at Colin's and he wrote it down.

'I see. You glimpsed the man at the bus stop and he is a customer of yours. He knows the child.'

'A little. Hardly at all.'

'Anything else?'

I shook my head and the policeman closed his notebook. There were plenty more urgent matters to attend to, tonight and every night. The policeman picked up his cap and straightened it on his head. 'Keep a closer eye on her in future, please.'

'My feelin's pre-cisely,' Jerry growled.

After the policeman had gone and before Evelyn and Cassie came back, Penny squared up to Jerry. In a small, even voice she said to him, 'Listen to me, Jerry. What happened today was terrifying for us all, but it's over and thank God Cassie came to no harm. Evelyn doesn't always know what she wants, but she's learning to trust her instincts. She loves Cassie and so do I. I love Evelyn too, but I care for Cassie more than I have ever cared for anything, or anyone, in my whole life. I will not let anyone harm a hair on her head, or Evelyn's. Not now, or in the future.' Her voice dropped even lower, but the intensity in it made me shiver. 'And that includes you.'

Jerry shifted on his feet. I saw his eyes slide in my direction, then settle on Paul. He struggled with himself for a moment and then evidently decided that he didn't want any further discussion of this in front of his trumpeter. He lifted his hands and laughed, making an exaggerated backing-off movement. 'Hey. Whatever you say, my lady.'

'I do say.'

'You just take proper care of my women from now on, right?'

To Jerry they *were* his women. Penny didn't even deign to blink. Jerry turned and clapped Paul on the shoulder. 'Thank you, my man, for what you did tonight. I'll be seein' you at the gig on Friday, is that right?'

Paul said yes, he would be there, then I said we ought to go. Penny followed me outside. 'Thank you, Sadie, thank you for finding her,' she whispered, and she took both my hands in hers and pressed her lips to each set of knuckles in turn.

The gesture touched me deeply. 'What did I do? Nothing. Say good night to Cassie for me.'

'I will,' Penny said. 'Thank you, both of you.'

Paul drove me home, but at the door he said, 'I think I'll leave you to yourself this evening.'

He was perceptive. I did want to be on my own for a while. I nodded, then I kissed him on the mouth. 'Good night. I'll see you tomorrow.'

I wandered through the quiet house. Rain was forecast, and occasional flickers of lightning whitened the sky followed by the bass mumble of thunder. There was a small sheaf of post waiting for me on the kitchen table—Lola must have put it there. I opened the first envelope and saw that the estate agents who were handling the sale of Ted's house were confirming an offer at the asking price. The purchasers were in a hurry and wanted an early completion.

Ted's volumes of notes stood on the bookshelf, and I took one down and turned the pages. Lavender, verbena, bergamot, sandalwood. The perfume formulae kept their secrets from me, as remote now as the seductions they had been designed to promote. I didn't care. I had my own memories of him and of past times. Good times and bad times, sometimes so closely intertwined that I couldn't separate them.

I closed the book and replaced it beside its companions. 'Good night,' I said, aloud. It was Ted I was speaking to, and for once I felt the closeness of our connection, without wishing for anything to be different.

The phone's sudden ringing makes me jump. 'Hello?'

'Sadie? Is that you? Your voice is a bit strange,' Mel says.

'I'm fine.'

And I truly am, I realise.

'I want you to be the first to hear my news.' Mel's voice is so tight with happiness it's like the skin of a ripe peach, ready to split and spill its juice.

'What is it?' I ask, although I already know.

'Jasper has asked me to marry him.'

'Mel, that's wonderful.' I'm smiling; there are creases at the corners of my eyes and bracketing my mouth. 'Did you say yes?' I wonder.

'Not yet.'

'What?'

'Oh, Sade. I wanted to think about it, taste it before I swallowed it. I was too happy to answer properly. Does that sound crazy?'

'No.' It sounds like Mel.

'I am going to tell him tomorrow night. Wish me luck?'

'I wish you much more than luck. I wish the two of you happiness and more happiness, and contentment for ever. It's what you deserve.'

'Thank you, my dear friend,' she murmurs and then blurts out, 'I want you to be happy too.'

As you do, when your own world is so full of joy that you long for it to be reflected down the hall of mirrors and into eternity.

'I am,' I tell her gently.

SEVENTEEN

AT FIRST, FROM UNDER THE SKIN of sleep, I thought it was the thunder that had woken me.

Then I was properly awake, coming to with the cold certainty that something terrible was about to happen. Cassie was safe but there was more to come, there was an even bigger threat trapped in the brooding air. I could smell it and taste it. The phone began to ring.

I hardly recognised Jasper's voice. He was hoarse and his words were disjointed. *It's Mel. Oh, Sadie. What if she dies . . . She looks so . . .*

'Tell me.' My own voice had taken on the edge of panic.

'She was coming to see me. Oh God, I should have gone to her . . .'

'Jasper. What's happened?'

'She was knifed. In her chest. The blade punctured her lung. She lost so much blood. She . . . she might not live. Sadie, I . . .' He was crying.

'When?'

'Ten. This evening. Yesterday, now. I'm sorry, I'm not . . .'

'Jasper, I'm coming.'

'It was a robbery, you know? Nothing to do with Mel at all. She'd just gone to get some champagne for . . . They ran in, tried to grab money. It went wrong. They, the police, told me. One of them had a knife, a very sharp knife with a long thin blade.'

I had a vision of Mel lying on the off-licence floor with her hair fanned about her head and bright blood spilling. Feet milling around her body and her lipstick another slash of red in her death-white face.

'I'm coming.'

I drove through the dead-of-night streets to the hospital.

Jasper was sitting in a grey-walled side room that smelt of anguish. He stood up as soon as he saw me and we held tight to each other.

'Come on,' I whispered at last. 'Tell me as much as you know.'

They were operating on Mel, he said. The long thin blade had missed her heart, but her left lung had been punctured and then collapsed. She had lost a huge amount of blood. Mel's mother was on her way.

'Did the police get them?' I asked.

'Not yet.'

I tried to swallow but my throat was dry. 'It will be on the security cameras. They'll catch them.'

'I suppose so,' Jasper said. It didn't matter much to either of us at that moment, only Mel mattered, but it was something to say.

Silence seeped between us as we waited.

Outside there were flashes of lightning followed almost instantly by long rolls of thunder. As I sat staring at the dull red floor, I thought of the knife thrust as another lightning bolt, discharging the static threat that had built up all this hot summer under the canal bridges and between crawling cars and at the dark end of fetid alleyways.

And this had happened to Mel, the most vital person any of us knew.

'I don't know what I'll do if she dies,' Jasper said suddenly. It was a simple statement of the truth. He didn't know and nor did I.

I took his hand again and massaged it between mine. 'She isn't going to die.' I spoke firmly, refusing to admit anything else even though the opposite possibility hammered in all the chambers of my mind.

Jasper stood up and walked down the corridor. I could hear him asking a question of someone out of sight. When he came back he shook his head and my heart almost stopped. 'No news yet.'

I breathed again.

A young Indian couple came in. They nodded patiently at us and took the two seats furthest away. The young woman was beautiful, with delicate features, but there were silent tears running down her face. Like us, they were waiting for news.

After a few more minutes I looked up to see Lois Archer. She was wearing a silky two-piece with a cashmere wrap and a little beaded handbag over her arm. Her huge frightened eyes with mascaraed lashes took in the four of us and the bleak room. 'Sadie? What's going to happen now? I was playing bridge with the girls. I couldn't get a taxi . . .'

We both stood up and Jasper guided her to a chair. 'You're here now, that's all that matters. All we can do is wait,' I told her.

In a low voice Jasper repeated what he knew. Lois was trembling but she held her head up. 'How can it have happened?' she whispered. I knew she had been asking herself this all the way here.

Jasper said, 'We don't know. The police will find out. I'm going to fetch you a cup of coffee, Lois. It will make you feel better.'

With Lois to take care of, with someone who needed his support, Jasper was more himself again. He seemed to have grown back to his normal size. I thought then how we are all made who we are by our needs as much as by our strengths.

'He seems a good man,' Lois murmured when he'd gone.

'He is.'

'If only Steven were here.'

Steven was Mel's legendarily charismatic father. The only man Mel had ever loved, she told me. Up until now.

I bit the inside of my cheek to stop the tremors. 'Yes.'

And then suddenly Ted was there. My own father. I felt his presence as strongly as Lois's beside me, smelt his cologne and heard his entirely familiar voice that I would now never hear again except in my memories. 'Well, my girl,' he said. 'This is a shaky old do, isn't it?'

I tilt my head, listening and gazing at the images in my mind's eye.

We are in the kitchen of our old house, the one that Tony and I shared, and into which Stanley erupted with the mission to build kitchen cupboards. Neither of them is here now, though. Tony has already moved out and Stanley has absented himself in the pub. It's Ted I'm looking at and at Jack standing on my father's lap, rocking up and down, pretending to ride a horse. He is about three, with fat babyish legs emerging from a pair of green shorts.

Ted has never been physically demonstrative with my children, any more than he was with me. But today Jack has demanded a connection and Ted has yielded. He looks uncomfortable; but at least he's here. My marriage is ending and he has come to talk to me about it. He has rallied round in a crisis, as he would put it.

Lola is in the room too, a smouldering, angry adolescent presence. Clothes, hairstyle, language all designed to provoke.

I put a drink at my father's elbow. 'Yes,' I agree, choosing my words with care. 'It's a big decision and I didn't make it lightly . . .'

In fact, I am shell-shocked by my wilful destruction of our family when it had been my strongest intention to preserve its security for Lola and Jack. And yet—I am convinced that I am doing the right thing, because I am so helplessly and passionately in love.

I am turning to my father, looking to him as a fellow traveller. Ted will comprehend what I feel, surely, with his history? I need his understanding, his wisdom, and most of all to know that he doesn't condemn me for what I have done. He takes a sip from the gin and tonic that I have prepared for him, replaces the glass on the table. 'Think of your children, Sadie,' he says. 'Is this what they want?'

There is a clatter behind me. Lola slamming down a knife or the kitchen scissors. I dread her scathing response. I take a breath, count five long seconds, then tell the truth: 'It's what *I* want.'

It's like uttering a blasphemy. I have never deliberately made such a choice before, let alone articulated it. In this instant I feel free and powerful and—in spite of all the pain I cause and feel—I am happy.

My father shakes his head. 'That's not the point. You're a mother. Your responsibility is to these two and then to your husband.'

The hypocrisy makes me gasp. But *you* do what you want and always have, I want to shout at him. Isn't anyone else allowed to do the same? Yet I don't shout, or even speak.

In the silence that follows, the last drops of my longing for his approval turn to chips of ice.

In the end it is Ted who breaks it. He says sorrowfully to Jack, 'Come on, then, old son. That's enough of that. Let's you and me go out in the garden and look at the birds.'

I'm sure neither of the children remembers that day and it's quite likely that Ted didn't either. But after that I was always angry with him. We were cordial to each other, there was almost nothing that was different, not on the surface, but I cut him off. I became implacable.

I finally knew that I was on my own, instead of wishing and longing to be otherwise and all the time coming up against the brick wall of disappointment. That understanding helped me to survive the loss of

Stanley; I was strong because I reckoned I was invulnerable—as long as I had Lola and Jack, and the company of friends.

I wanted to tell Ted all about this when I drove up to his bedside, but I never found the words. I should have explained that I was wrong to be angry, because we are all flawed. Even my glamorous father, the perfumer and con artist, whom I wished to be perfect. I wanted to tell him that I regretted my selfishness. But it was too late.

It has taken me until now to understand this sequence properly.

I'm sorry, I tell him. I am truly sorry. And I did—do—love you.

Jasper came back with three polystyrene beakers clutched like a sloppy bouquet in front of him. Carefully he handed one each to Lois and me, then sat down. I sipped the weak liquid and the minutes creaked by.

At last a nurse looked in. She asked if we were waiting for news of Melissa Archer and when Jasper said yes she asked us to follow her into an office where the doctor was looking through a sheaf of notes.

He spoke drily, unemphatically, but the words flared in my head.

Repaired. Transfusion. Optimistic. Recovery, he said.

Mel was going to live, I understood. Lois groped for my hand and I put my arm out to support her. I realised how tiny and light she was, and that she was quivering like a bird.

Jasper rubbed his hand over his face. I could feel the wash of relief in him, a big, heavy tide, with no undertow of happiness yet. That would come later. 'Can we see her?' he asked.

'Only two of you,' he apologised. 'And then only a couple of minutes. She's very tired.'

Of course she was tired. But only people who are alive feel weary. Everything was going to be all right.

'You two go on,' I said to Lois and Jasper. 'Give her a kiss from me.'

I drove back through the thin drizzle. The security that my home offered had never felt so welcome. I went slowly up the stairs and lay down on my bed, intending to get up in a minute and undress properly. I pulled the covers round my shoulders and let my eyes close.

When I woke up again I was aware first that it was broad daylight, then that there was someone snugly fitting like a spoon against my back. I thought in sleepy confusion that it must be Paul, but when I stirred he stirred too and I knew it was Jack.

'Mum.'

I turned over and looked into my son's wide eyes. 'You're home.'

'We heard the early news on the radio. I came straight away because I thought you'd want me to be here.'

'I do.'

'Do you know how Mel is?'

'She's going to be all right.' I stroked his hair.

'It would be against the laws of nature for someone like Mel to die, wouldn't it?'

This thought had passed through my mind many times last night. 'I'm not sure that there are any laws, Jack. It's frightening.' I was speaking to him like an adult. We had passed a milestone.

'There are in nature,' he said calmly.

We lay still for a few minutes, lapped in quiet. It was only hours since I had watched Cassie playing with her boats in the sink. An afternoon, an evening, a night and half a lifetime seemed to have intervened.

'It's quite cool outside. It smells of autumn,' Jack remarked. After another pause he went on, 'It's cool to be home as well. I've had enough of Audrey's. I want to go up the park. I might see Wes and the others.'

'OK,' I ventured. 'Good. Do you want some breakfast now?'

'Haven't you got to go to work?'

'I think Penny'll understand if I don't make it this morning.'

'Yeah. All right, then. I'd like a bacon sandwich with red sauce.'

One of his favourites. I sat up. 'We'll both have one.'

Jack lay back against my pillows and watched me rummage around for clean clothes. The threads of life were tight. They might sometimes become unravelled, but this morning they were still intact and they knitted us all together in love and friendship.

I went on into the bathroom, and in my happiness I didn't even blink at the mess of smeared make-up that Lola left in her wake.

There were so many chairs crammed in round my table that they had to stand at slight angles to each other, like crooked teeth in an over-crowded jaw. People pressed their knees together between the table legs, shouting to make themselves heard above the rising noise.

Mel sat at the head of the table with Jasper opposite her at the foot. We were celebrating their engagement. It was five weeks since the night in the off-licence and she had been home from hospital for almost three. 'I would have died if I'd had to stay in there any longer,' she said.

She was much thinner and there were grey streaks among the tight coils of black hair, but most noticeably of all she had stopped wearing lipstick. Now you noticed the curve of the top lip and the fullness of the lower one, rather than just the bright crimson. I thought she looked more beautiful than ever as she sat watching the faces around her.

Then when her eyes reached Jasper it was like shutters opening to the inside of her skull. The look was so naked that I had to glance away, as if I had been caught spying.

Jasper sat with Lois on his right and on Lois's other side was Mr Rainbird. She rested her leaf-dry hand first on Paul's arm, then turned the other way to murmur to Jasper. She seemed even more fragile than on the night at the hospital, but she could still turn on the considerable wattage of her charm, especially near personable men.

Caz was beckoning me into the kitchen, so I went to join her.

We were ready to serve our pudding.

When we planned the celebration dinner we knew that Mel's favourite, Chocolate Nemesis, had to be on the menu. And on top of the rich, dark square I had piped two big interlinked sugar-pink hearts and a cupid's arrow.

Caz and I lifted the cake board and I balanced it flat-palmed at shoulder height. Caz clapped her hands for attention. Everyone's eyes turned.

I rotated my wrist and lowered the cake in front of Mel. She sprang half out of her chair to admire it, forgetting the great sickle-shaped wound that ran from her spine to her breastbone. The pain showed before she managed a smile.

'Be careful, darling,' Lois called.

'I am just greedy,' she murmured. Then she looked up at me. 'Sadie, thank you. It's beautiful.'

I stood next to her, facing the table, my fingers just resting on her shoulder. Lola and Sam sat at one corner, their two chairs wedged in a space only strictly big enough for one. They had left the festivities of the first week of university term specially for the party. Paul Rainbird sat with his elbow hooked over his chair back, smiling when his eyes met mine. I had begun, I realised, to look for him to be there.

Jack had asked if he could sit next to Jasper. 'He seems all right,' he said, which coming from him was the highest praise.

Graham made sure that everyone had a full glass of champagne. There was a waiting pause while I suddenly wondered if I was going to be able to speak at all because my throat was tight.

'We might so easily not have been here tonight,' I began. 'But we *are* here and that's mostly because Mel has been so brave. Jack said to me on the day after it happened, people like Mel don't just go and die. It's against the laws of nature.'

Jasper was looking at her as if there were no one else in the room, or anywhere in the rest of the world for that matter. I glanced sideways. Next to Lola was Clare, Jasper's daughter. She was dark-haired, small-featured, with narrow shoulders and long pale hands. She looked straight ahead of her, her lips closed but not compressed.

'And I told him I wasn't so sure that there are laws out there any more, not after a summer like this one.' The long hot weeks did have an unreal quality now, like scenes in a film. 'But Mel's her own law, as we all know, and she came back to us. Most of all, she came back for Jasper.'

Mel lifted her head and laughed out loud, momentarily her old brash self again. 'Was I ever going to let him go, once I'd found him? Not for any old knife wound, believe me.'

Everyone else laughed too. 'I'm not surprised you didn't want to let him go,' Caz called. Clare turned towards her father, her pale cheeks colouring, proud of him and wary and possessive all at the same time.

'Let's drink a toast to them,' I said. 'To Jasper and Mel. May you always be as happy together as you look tonight.'

Everyone stood up, pushing back their chairs and lifting their glasses. *Jasper and Mel.* Clare smiled gamely too as she called their names.

Mel picked up the knife I had laid beside her plate and sliced deep into the heart of the Chocolate Nemesis.

Amid the cheering and clapping I was thinking that evenings like this were the best reward. Evenings like this, when everything shimmered with happiness and a sense of rightness, made sense of all the work that had to be done in an ordinary day and of life's routine that occasionally seemed too tedious to endure.

The faces went all blurred and I blinked.

Ted was here again, standing close beside me. He would have loved this party. 'Well, Princess.' He chuckled. 'Not so bad, is it?'

An arm slid round me. The touch made me jump and then I saw that in the noisy aftermath of the toast Paul had left his seat. His breath warmed my neck.

Jasper was standing up now. He looked solemn, and then couldn't maintain the solemnity. He was too happy to be serious.

'Get on with it,' Graham called. 'I want my cake.'

Jasper thanked Caz and me for the dinner. Then he turned to Mel. A glance passed between them and at the same time a little arrowhead of anxiety pressed in my throat. 'I want to propose another toast. To the woman I am more proud of than anything else in my life.'

Oh, be careful, I thought. The dart's pressure was actually painful now. The room seemed to have stopped its collective breathing.

'To my daughter, Clare.'

Relief made me almost gasp. We clapped again and echoed her name, and Clare's flush darkened. She scrambled out of her chair, hesitated, then crossed to Mel and briefly laid her cheek against Mel's hair. She was doing the right thing because this was what was expected of her and she expected it of herself too, but there was reluctance as well as compliance showing in the stiff angles of her head and limbs. Mel tried to draw her closer, but Clare evaded her and circled round to her father and nestled triumphantly up against him.

It wasn't all a fairy tale. Even for Jasper and Mel there was some rough water ahead.

Mel banged on the table. 'Now it's my turn,' she called out. She looked tired, and she didn't try to stand up. The evening was beginning to tell on her. 'I have another toast. To family and friends.'

'To family. And friends.' We drank to that.

The talk broke up while we ate our chocolate pudding. Lola poked her head round Sam's shoulder and called to me, 'How amazing is this, Mum? Clare knows Chloe and Seb.'

'That is amazing,' I agreed. In fact, it wasn't surprising at all. Lola moved blithely and unquestioningly through a huge, loose web of friends and friends of friends, who intersected one another's social groups in an endlessly complicated Venn diagram.

Sam and Lola and Caz's Dan took Clare off upstairs to Lola's room, while Jack left the table and drifted over to switch on the television. He yawned and stretched out in an armchair as Caz and I handed out cups of coffee.

Soon the evening started winding down. Mel's face was waxy with exhaustion and Jasper nodded when I raised my eyebrows at him.

'Have we got to go? Just let me finish my coffee,' Mel insisted. In the old days she was always among the last to leave the party: she would feel the need to stay at this one that was being given in her honour.

'Mel,' Jasper warned her and she blinked at him.

'So is this how it's going to be? For ever?'

'Yeah. Home by ten thirty, or else.'

'Maybe I'm making a terrible mistake.'

'Don't say that, darling.' Lois looked shocked. Mel always did say that her mother had trouble with irony.

'Where's Clare gone?' Jasper was asking, as he helped Lois with her cashmere wrap. More or less on cue, Lola and the others reappeared.

'Mum, we thought we'd go on to a club, OK?' Lola murmured.

Sam was welded to her side, as usual, and the other two were hovering just behind them. Clare was all slender tapered ovals—face and long feet and fingernails, and big blond Dan looked huge and square-cut next to her. They were very obviously not looking at each other and every movement they made betrayed their interest.

'How'll you get home from this place? Where is it?' Jasper asked.

'I'll see her home,' Dan offered, to no one's surprise.

Then, with amazing rapidity, the four of them were gone.

Mel and I laughed together on the doorstep. 'Doesn't that make you feel *old*? It does me.'

I wasn't drunk enough to consider the question seriously. 'Hey. Maybe we *are* old and haven't noticed.' I kissed her on both cheeks. 'Good night, Mel. I love you.'

'And me. Thanks, Sade, and for this evening. Tell Penny I said hello.'

Penny and Evelyn weren't going out much at the moment, and they seemed happy just looking after Cassie and each other.

'I will,' I promised.

I stood in the doorway until Mel and Lois and Jasper were safely in Jasper's car, then I stayed watching until the red taillights disappeared.

Downstairs again Paul was making tea, with small tidy movements. Jack was staring sightlessly at the television, his knees drawn up defensively against his chest. Silence was silted up in the corners of the room and I could tell that Paul had tried to talk and Jack had rebuffed him.

'It's very late,' I said. 'Jack?'

He ignored me and went on gazing at the screen. In a minute Paul would leave and Jack and I would retreat to our bedrooms. Paul and I hadn't spent the night together since Jack came home from Turnmill Street. I wished he would stay tonight, so that we could drink our tea and do a post-mortem on the evening before going to bed.

Paul tilted his head, semaphoring a question.

Lately his face had become blurred with familiarity but the sudden awkwardness of the moment made me look at him afresh. Neat but unremarkable features, it was true, with kind eyes. A good, mobile mouth; I remembered how it felt against my skin.

My own mouth was stiff.

He watched and waited as my eyes turned to Jack. I didn't know what to say. So I said nothing at all.

I disappointed Paul. I knew it, because he put his mug down very carefully and turned away. The television babbled on between us.

'Jack, could you turn that off, please?' His voice was crisp. Startled, Jack pointed the remote and we descended into silence. Paul went and sat down on the chair nearest to him. He said, 'I'd like to stay here tonight with Sadie. How would you feel about that?'

Jack's back went rigid. But he managed a shrug of indifference.

'You don't mind?'

Jack said coldly, 'You're not my dad, are you?'

'No, I'm not. Only your dad can be your dad. But do you think that no one except him should ever be able to stay here with your mum?'

'Yes.'

'What about in six years, say, when you've gone to college like Lola?'

The shrug. 'Dunno. Well, I'll be gone then, won't I?'

Out of sight, out of mind.

'Hm. It's just that it's quite a long time for her to wait until then.'

'*Is* she waiting?'

I broke in. 'Just a minute. I'm not some . . . some cow in a pen, you know, to be discussed between the two of you.'

Paul's mouth twitched.

Jack glared at him and then at me. 'What do you want?'

'I would like him to stay, Jack,' I said. 'I'm sort of realising that I've been a bit lonely, sometimes, even though I've got you and Lo.'

Jack said tragically, 'Mum, *everyone's* lonely. Not just you.'

I would willingly be crippled with loneliness every hour of my life in order for Jack never to feel such a thing.

Paul was less stricken. 'Everyone feels lonely some of the time, yes. But nearly all of us feel the opposite as well, quite often. I've seen you at school, lately. You like Max McLaren, don't you?'

'He's OK.'

'And what about tonight? It wasn't lonely for any of us, was it?'

Paul waited teacher-like for a reply.

'No,' Jack admitted. And then, logically enough, 'So therefore my mum's all right as well, isn't she? She doesn't need you.'

'She doesn't *need* me, no. That's one of the things I value in her. But there's a difference between needing and enjoying. There are times when it might be nice for her to have a partner, wouldn't you agree?'

Grudgingly he said, 'I suppose.'

'I like your mother very much. I wouldn't do anything to hurt her, you know. If that's what you are worrying about.'

'You mean, if you were her boyfriend?'

'If I were or not. Either way, I wouldn't hurt her. Or you.'

Jack considered this. 'Do you think she'd be less sad?'

I was surprised to learn that my son thought I was sad.

'I hope so. Yes, I think so,' Paul said.

Jack suddenly tired of this. He launched himself out of the armchair. 'Whatever,' he pronounced, that most infuriating of adolescent non-acquiescences that still put an effective stop to all further discussion.

I loved him so much, in his slovenly T-shirt and untied trainers, and the jeans that were growing noticeably too short in the leg.

'Night, then,' he muttered and drifted up the stairs.

Paul and I were left alone in the kitchen.

'I'm sorry,' I said. I was disappointed in myself. I wanted to avoid hurting anyone and all I had managed was a failure to show loyalty in either direction.

'He's more resilient than you think and you should take credit for that.'

'Maybe.' I didn't want to talk about Jack any more. 'I'm glad you're here, anyway.'

Paul Rainbird's face split into a smile. He came to me and put his hands on either side of my face, smoothing my cheeks with his thumbs.

'I'm glad I'm here, too, and Jack will get used to it.'

The next day was a Saturday. Jack came down to breakfast and was no more or less uncommunicative with Paul eating toast at the kitchen table than he would have been if he and I were alone. He was still a regular visitor to Turnmill Street and when I asked him if he was going to Audrey's later he surprised me by saying, 'Isn't it time *you* went to see her? She doesn't have many visitors, you know.'

'I know. You're right. I'll go and see her soon.'

'Good,' he said. 'She's got something to tell you.'

Before I could ask what that was, Paul gathered up his jacket and his bag. 'I've got to go. I've got some marking to do. See you, Jack. Sadie, I'll call you later. It was a great evening, by the way. I'll let myself out.'

We were left on our own. I could see that Jack was looking hard at me now, as if he expected or feared that I might be somehow different and I waited through his scrutiny.

'Did you mind about Paul being here last night?' I asked at length.

'Well. It does feel kind of odd.'

'I know. It must do.'

'You won't, you know . . .?' His voice trailed away.

He hoped that I wouldn't withdraw from him or favour Paul Rainbird over him, and that I wouldn't allow myself to be hurt. In other words, that life would go on as usual. Or maybe even improve.

'I won't,' I promised.

'Good,' Jack said in a tone that indicated that was more than enough discussion of the subject.

'And I'll go and see Audrey this afternoon,' I added.

I knocked at the familiar door and waited.

'You again,' Audrey said when it eventually opened.

'May I come in?'

She stalked back down the hallway, indicating that I could follow her if I chose. 'What are you here for anyway?' she said as I edged round the furniture in the back room and glanced into the garden.

She was as combative as ever. I felt the same antipathy to her as I had done from the beginning, long before our tussle over Jack.

'Jack asked me to call in. He said you had something to tell me.'

'Did he?'

I removed most of the stuff from the nearest chair and sat down. While I waited, a cat unfurled itself on the rug. Its claws emerged, sharp hooks the colour of brittle old celluloid, and were sheathed again.

Audrey seemed to come to a decision. She went over to the drawer in the gate-leg table and took out a sheaf of documents. She leafed through them and slipped one out of the pile, which she handed to me.

'What is it?' I asked.

A pucker of anxiety inside my chest made me lean forward. I studied the document for a long moment. Faded buff-pink squares, names handwritten in ink in an even, official hand: Edwin Lawrence Thompson, Bachelor. Audrey Ann Nesbit, Spinster.

It was a marriage certificate, dated 1956.

'No,' I said, out loud. But it was a vain contradiction.

My parents married in late 1949 and I was born in 1950. My mother died suddenly ten years later. And in the middle of that time, according to this paper, Ted married Audrey Nesbit. As well as a perfumer and con artist, my father was a bigamist. I felt a dull reverberation of shock, and let the certificate drop. 'Did you know?'

'When I married him? No, of course not.'

I had read about men who maintained whole families, living duplicitous lives shared between two wives, two sets of children . . .

My head jerked up. 'Did you have children with him?' I asked.

'No. I had an abortion. He made me do it.'

The words fell out of her mouth like stones. There was such desolation in them that my suspicions melted, and I felt nothing but sympathy for her. 'Audrey. Please tell me about it. It's not too late.'

'Isn't it?' Her eyes were dry but they looked sore, as if it were painful to move them in their sockets. At last, she tipped the cats off one of the chairs and sat down. 'Well, then. I fell in love with a man. This man told me he could create a perfume for me.'

'My father.'

'I worked for a company called Phebus Fragrances. Just a couple of weeks of temporary secretarial work. I was eighteen years old.'

'I remember Phebus.'

'Ted was important there. Very good at what he did, but he was irreverent too. He laughed at everything and he made me laugh with him.

'He never suggested anything while I was working there, but when I moved on to the next job he got in touch. Took me for a drink at a pub by the river. He told me he was lodging with a family in Hendon because he'd had some money problems. He was paying off his debts and he'd soon have a place of his own. I had a room in my cousin's house. I grew up near Macclesfield and I couldn't wait to go to London.'

The picture she painted was clear enough. Audrey, buxom and fresh-faced, Ted cupping her cheeks between his hands and murmuring, *I could create such a perfume for you.*

'It's not what you imagine,' Audrey snapped. 'We made plans. Business plans, for a shop, a perfumery and cosmetics line. We were going places, Ted and me. I loved him. And he was in love with me.'

Audrey lifted her chin and I saw beneath her skin into the face of the young woman she had been. 'I was a decent girl, I'll have you know.'

The kind of girl who insisted on a ring on her finger. Ted loved her, and seeing no other way to get Audrey for himself, he married her and overlooked the detail of an already existing wife.

For the first time in my life I properly understood my mother's pallor, her not-quite-there quality. She must have known. Poor Faye.

'Why didn't you become his proper wife, after my mum died?' I tried, but I couldn't quite keep the harshness out of my voice.

Audrey looked away. She would tell her story at her own pace.

'We rented a little flat. Not so very far from here. I went on working as a shorthand typist, kept house for him, sat and waited for him to come back when he was away.' Audrey gave a little cough of laughter. 'I was a proper fool, wasn't I? But you can make yourself believe what you want to believe. Then my grandma died and left me a legacy. He wanted to start up on his own. It was going to be our big chance, so I made the money straight over to him. Then I got pregnant. I thought he'd be pleased, but he was angry. He told me he didn't want children, and never would. He gave me the money to get myself sorted out. Some of my own money back, it must have been. Really, I paid for my own abortion that I didn't want to have anyway.' She was talking now as if she had forgotten I was listening, talking to herself. 'Afterwards, he was good to me. Flowers, presents, promises. But it didn't work. It was as if my silly innocence had been skewered out of me along with the baby. I started putting two and two together. Anyway, I ended up going through his things one night while he was asleep. Found an address in Hendon and when I went up there, what did I see?'

I said nothing, but I could guess.

'I saw Faye coming home with her shopping bags, and you in hair-slides and white socks skipping along beside her.'

She laughed again, a sound that made the nearest cat stir and turn its yellow eyes to her. 'Ha. Do you remember the perfume? *Innominata*. Nameless, faceless. A wife all right, but one to keep hidden.'

At least there had been a perfume, which there hadn't been for Faye or for me. I left my chair and stooped down in front of Audrey so that our eyes were level. I took her hands in mine. 'What did you do?'

'I told him I'd found him out. He begged me to forgive him, told me he couldn't bear to be without me, but I didn't feel the same about him after that. I shut him out. Changed the locks, all of that. What else could I do? I wasn't going to go to the police, was I?'

'You might have done.'

Audrey glared at me. A lesser woman might have done, I understood her to mean.

'Then, about ten months after, your mother died.'

The wording on her death certificate might read brain haemorrhage, but I was sure that Faye had simply given up.

I looked into Audrey's eyes.

'Then, if my father loved you . . .?'

'Oh, he came back to get me. We went away together, down to Devon. But it was no good for me and we both knew it. I loved him but I couldn't have lived as his wife if he was the last man in the universe.'

That was the worst time for me, too. When Ted came back home at last he had been dejected for reasons that were way beyond my childish understanding. He relit the pilot light and we ate fish and chips.

'There was a problem we couldn't get round. You.'

'But—'

Audrey interrupted. 'You were always there, getting between us. He had you and I didn't have the baby we should have had together. I used to think you were like a splinter under his skin. He couldn't charm you, could he? You were the only one it didn't work on. But he loved you all right because you held out on him.'

I tried the words out. *If my father loved me.* They didn't seem to make much difference now. And I could work out the rest of the story for myself. Audrey was the wife he wanted, but the contract had turned itself inside out. Faye died, Audrey rejected him, and he was left with a beady-eyed and unpliant child. There had been the serial aunties as compensation, and Scentsation followed by a spell in prison, and the uneasiness that lay heavy between the two of us for the rest of his life.

'I think I understand,' I said, meaning the effects of history that had marked us all.

'Maybe. Or maybe not.'

I stood up because my thighs and back were aching. 'Shall I make us a cup of tea?' I asked.

'That would be nice,' Audrey said.

I washed the teapot thoroughly, found tea bags that were still in their hygienic sachets, located two cups. 'What about the money?' I ventured, as I poured the tea and gave a cup to Audrey.

'I never saw it again. I never asked him to pay it back.' That was a matter of pride, I could tell.

'Did you see each other?'

Audrey smiled, for the first time a genuine smile that made her look much younger. 'Once in a while.'

I said, 'I'd like to pay you back. Out of the house sale. We will make it up to you, with the proper interest.'

She looked up to where the laths showed in one corner of the ceiling behind a broken lip of plaster. 'Better late than never, I suppose.'

Optimistic plans were tumbling in my head. 'You and Jack get on well . . .' I began, and in my fired-up imagination I saw snapshots of Sunday lunches, birthday celebrations, Christmases.

'That's between Jack and me,' she snapped.

The pictures dimmed, but I knew she was right. If there was going to be a connection between Audrey and me, it would have to grow of its own accord. 'You're right. I'm sorry,' I said humbly.

Audrey seemed mollified. 'You mean well, Sadie,' she conceded.

And that was our first, teetering step towards friendship.

My cup was empty and so was hers. 'Shall I pour you another?'

'No, thank you. I was having a sort-out when you came. I've got to get on with it.'

That was my cue and I took it. I put my arm, very briefly, round Audrey's shoulders and withdrew before she could nudge me away. 'I'll be getting back home, then. Thank you for telling me the truth,' I said, but she didn't reply.

She walked down the hallway behind me and let me out of the front door. It closed firmly.

'Did you talk to her?' Jack was waiting for me in the kitchen, trying to gauge whether I was upset by what I must have discovered.

'Yes, I did. Jack, what was it like, when you were staying with her?'

He chewed the corner of his mouth but he didn't give even the ghost of a shrug. 'We talked quite a lot. She told me things.'

I imagined Jack sitting in the back room at Turnmill Street with the debris and the peeling wallpaper, listening to Audrey while she told her husband's grandchild all the truths that she kept to herself for so long.

'They weren't always things I wanted to hear, as a matter of fact. Like about Granddad and her, and the way they got married when he was already married and had you.' He glanced at me, checking my reaction.

'I know.'

'But some of it was really interesting. About what it was like in the war and stuff. Children got sent away from London, with labels on their coats, to live with people in the country to be safe from the bombs. Did you know that?'

I nodded. 'Evacuees, they were called.'

'Did she tell you about how she gave Granddad money?'

'Yes, that too.'

'I want to give her my share from selling his house. She hasn't got very much to buy food or anything, you know.'

'That's a good and very generous thought, Jack. But it might be better to keep your money for when you want to go travelling, or to help you through college. I'm going to pay Audrey back out of my share.'

'That's not fair, though.'

I smiled at him. 'Yes, it is, actually.' His face remained clouded for a second, but then an answering smile broke through. It was the same smile that had been his from babyhood, but now the changing planes showed me a brief glimpse of the grown man too: Jack fully formed.

'By the way,' he said. 'The postman came. There's a package for you.'

A brown padded envelope lay on the counter. I picked it up and saw French stamps, half-familiar handwriting, crossed sevens.

As I had already guessed, the letter was from Philippe. 'Your visit', he wrote, 'prompted me to look through some old boxes of my mother's things. And I found this.'

Carefully, I unfolded the second sheet. I recognised a complex perfume formula in Ted's handwriting. I stared at the heading, and my heart thumped in my chest. Then my eyes were drawn to the foot of the page where my father had added a note: *My dear friend Marie-Ange. I think this is a fine fragrance, maybe even one of my best. If you can use it, please take it as part payment of my debt to you.* The date was October 1965, just after the end of my Grasse summer. I looked back at the page heading again. It read, 'Orphan. For Sadie.' Well, I thought, with a lump in my throat. The name isn't going to do much for it.

I took the liberty, Philippe continued, *of making the fragrance up for you.* Very carefully, I unscrewed the gilt stopper and lowered my nose to the neck of the tiny bottle. The scent flowed into the chambers of my head. It was fresh and flowery, innocent with a marked sweetness, like an afternoon's sunshine in a bright garden. A young girl's scent.

'It is a pretty fragrance, I think, but not a record breaker. I think my mother must have shared my opinion, because she put it to one side. But I am sure that you will like to have it, just the same.' He signed himself, 'Your friend PL.' Philippe was quite right. I did like to have it.

My fingers closed round the smooth contours of the scent bottle. 'Thank you for this,' I said aloud to Ted. I couldn't hear his voice or smell his cheating citrus cologne. It was so like him to use my perfume to try to settle a debt. It was so like him that I found myself laughing as if I had just heard the best joke in the world.

'Mum?' Jack said enquiringly.

'I was just thinking about Granddad.'

'Oh. Right.'

Bravo, I was saying in my mind to Ted. You did what you wanted, just as far as you could. Bravo for that.

EIGHTEEN

A WHOLE YEAR HAS GONE by and it's October again.

Mel chose autumn colours and they work well. There are big urns all round the room, filled with thick-petalled bronze chrysanthemums, coppery leaves and sprays of golden ivy. The effect is gorgeously theatrical rather than bridal. Mel herself is wearing a plain pale-gold sheath dress that fits tightly round her curves, but the red lipstick is triumphantly back. Altogether she looks as beautiful as any woman could look on her wedding day.

As her (very) senior bridesmaid, I am sitting at the top table. My partner is one of the Archer brothers who is currently between wives, but he is busy talking to Clare who is seated on his other side. Paul is at another table and I can't even see him from here. There are well over a hundred of us and the circular tables stretch right down the room.

The ceremony made me cry. In front of their families and friends Jasper lifted Mel's hand and kissed the wedding ring before he kissed her on the lips. My tears washed pale runnels in the unaccustomed layers of foundation, even though they failed to dissolve the sob-proof mascara that even now makes my eyelashes feel as if I am peering at the world through spiders' legs.

Jasper and Mel linked hands. The two tiny bridesmaids, nieces from a brother's second marriage, fell in behind them, and Clare and I paired up in their wake. Lois, Jasper's best man, and a couple of brothers made up the procession. The organ music swelled and broke like waves around us as we made our way back down the avenue of beaming faces.

On the broad steps of the church the photographer's assistant lined us up for the lens and posterity. It was a perfect autumn day, with the blue sky softened by a thin veil of mist.

Paul slipped out from the crowds of guests. It was the first time we had seen each other today because I had stayed the night at Mel's. 'I hardly recognised you,' he murmured.

'Good or bad?'

As well as the make-up I am fastened into an unfamiliarly tight arrangment of tiny metallic bronze pleats. The skirt fans out behind in broader pleats like a mermaid's tail and the assistant was busily arrang- ing these on the stone step behind me.

'Good. But I certainly wouldn't dare to touch you.'

'I do dare you.'

'Well. I like a challenge.'

'Could the senior bridesmaid come in closer behind the little ones, please?' the photographer ordered.

'See you later, then.' I smiled at Paul.

It's time for the speeches. Jasper's best man does a good funny one, not too long or too rude, and proposes a toast to the bride and groom. I love this about weddings, the rhythm of them and the way that however dif- ferent and original they try to be they are always the same, with the principals happily reduced from themselves to Bride and Groom fig- urines from the top of the cake. As we stand to drink to their long life and happiness I see Mel smiling at me across the table, as if she can read my thoughts. She wanted a proper big wedding and this is it.

Jasper's is the last speech. His is the easiest job and he does it well. He proposes the toast to Mel's beautiful bridesmaids. I keep my head ducked for this one and so my eyes rest on the single-fold menu, thick cream paper with a thin thread of gold ribbon. As I idly admire my own handiwork, I notice something, and gulp.

The pudding we have just eaten was iced berries, red and black currants, with white chocolate sauce. Very well chosen and very good.

Except I now see that I have spelt it *currents*.

After all the years that Mel and I have joked about and collected menu misspellings, I have made a classic error on her wedding one.

I look up in horror, but Jasper has already taken her hand. According to plan, and exactly on time, they will sail down a grand sweeping staircase to the colonnaded ballroom and lead off the dancing.

Then a hand touches my shoulder.

I look up into Paul's eyes.

'AC or DC?' he murmurs and now I am laughing, full-throated head-back laughter that makes Mel's brothers turn to stare. Mel will laugh too, when the photographs and the menu and the guests' signatures are all pasted into the albums, and we sit and share the memories.

Among the dancers I can see Lola. She has recently split up with Sam and tonight she is thinner in the face, winged with melancholy, and attracting a good deal of attention.

I can see Jack, too. He is occupying a table next to the wall with his inseparable friend Max, and something in their louche postures tells me that they have had a lot of champagne. There will probably be a few problems later on, but whenever were there not, after a wedding?

It's half past ten. Mel and Jasper are due to leave, and suddenly we are all surging out and crowding at the foot of the sweep of stairs.

Mel has changed into a red dress and her leather jacket. She has let her hair loose and her eyes are brilliant. I see that Penny and Evelyn are right next to me. Penny is holding tight to Cassie's hand and Evelyn is cradling the baby, the five-week-old product of Jerry's grudging communion with a jam jar. Mel and Jasper have been laughing and calling out from their vantage point on the stairs but now Mel holds her bouquet up like Liberty's torch. Jasper gently turns her so that her back is to the room.

Evelyn nudges me and I circle the baby's minute rib cage with my hands and his frowning, crunched-up tiny dark features twitch slightly.

Mel's bouquet makes a full loop as it sails upwards and falls. A forest of arms stretches but Evelyn leaps like a basketball player. She catches it securely and then jumps up and down. 'I got it, I got it,' she cries.

Penny grins, not knowing what it means; no one does, with Evelyn.

The crowd separates just enough to let Mel and Jasper pass through. Outside, at the foot of some more steps, a car is waiting. There are ribbons and lipstick scrawls all over it and tin cans tied to the back.

'Oh, no.' Mel laughs. Her wide red mouth blows a kiss and they run down the steps together. The weather has changed and a thin drizzle sets halos round the streetlights. We close round the car, thumping on the roof and shouting good wishes. Slowly it moves forward and we fall back, watching it go, then we turn away with the rain in our faces.

Inside again, we are all blinking in the lights. The band is still playing—there will be some slow numbers now, Mel promised.

I can see Paul standing in the doorway. I thread my way towards him and reach out my hand. He takes it in his familiar grasp.

'Hello, Mr Rainbird.'

'Hello, Mrs Rainbird. Shall we dance?'

I *am* Mrs Rainbird.

Paul and I were married in the summer. Neither of us wanted a big set-piece wedding like this one. Paul's father was his witness and Audrey was mine, with Mel's blessing. Jack and Lola were there too, and no one else at all.

But I was happy then as I am now and I long for everyone around me to feel the same joy. I recognised this yearning months ago in Mel and now I know the force of it. Today comes close to satisfying the wish.

We start dancing together, turning in circles to the slow number.

ROSIE THOMAS

Rosie Thomas knows that life does not always turn out the way that you plan it. When her marriage ended after twenty-five years, she was faced with the choice of either coping alone or going under. 'I knew that I had to take stock, look at myself as a different person and move in a new direction.' She had always loved mountains and diving, and now found that she had the time to fully indulge her passions. 'I've got this little window of opportunity before I'm too old!' the fifty-five-year-old author told me. 'So this year I've spent a month down in Antarctica, on one of the research stations, where I have also been researching my next novel. And I'm just off to ski the Haute Route and then I'm going out to Everest for the fiftieth anniversary celebrations, hoping to reach the North Col.'

Rosie Thomas enjoys researching her novels and takes this aspect very seriously. 'I like to feel that my backgrounds are correct,' she told me. 'For this novel I went out to Grasse and stayed there for a week, visiting perfume factories and museums and what's left of the flower fields. I even made up a fragrance of my own and called it 'If My Father Loved Me'. It smells like a cheap imitation of Madame Rochas!' The author also spent a week working at The Wyvern Bindery in Clerkenwell, stitching, binding and finishing books. 'It was great. Much more fun than being a novelist.

They offered me a job, in fact. So I've always got that to fall back on.'

Like Sadie in *If My Father Loved Me*, Rosie lost her own mother when she was ten and I asked the author how close Sadie's feelings about her father and her childhood are to her own? 'Pretty close, actually,' she replied. 'The loss of a parent in early life creates all kinds of uncertainties in a child and leaves unanswerable questions about what might have been. In adult life it affect your relationships with your own children, and with your partner. My awareness of all this strengthens as I get older, and the recent loss of my father triggered all kinds of other memories. So it was almost inevitable that it would emerge in my fiction. However, Ted isn't anything like my own father any more than Sadie is like me, so it's not remotely autobiographical in that way.'

Rosie Thomas lives and works in north London. 'Before my divorce, we lived in a big Victorian house full of books, picture frames, curtains, mouldings and, like Cass in my novel, milk jugs! Now I live in a bare white loft space. To effect the transition I got rid of just about everything. I gave away the books, sold the pictures and china, weeded out the clothes to three pairs of black trousers and some white T-shirts, almost literally, and put the important memorabilia, mostly photos, in store. It was very liberating. I'm travelling light these days and I love it.'

Jane Eastgate

Blessed are the Cheesemakers

Sarah-Kate Lynch

Hidden away in a peaceful corner of Ireland
lies Coolarney House where, for over fifty years,
Corrie and Fee have been making mouth-watering
Coolarney cheese. The special magic that
they put into their processing is legendary—if
rather unorthodox.
But when the Coolarney cheese turns sour, Corrie
and Fee know they're missing that all-important
ingredient—the one that's almost impossible
to find to order . . .

Chapter One

'You can't hurry cheese. It happens in its own time . . .'
Joseph Feehan, from *The Cheese Diaries*

THE PRINCESS GRACE MEMORIAL BLUE sat on the table in front of Abbey, screaming to be eaten.

Abbey, as always, was smiling her dreamy smile, her eyes half closed and her head slightly thrown back, as though she were preparing to blow out a candle and make a wish. Well, it was her twenty-ninth birthday, after all, and there would have been candles, too, had not the Princess Grace been a particularly fussy cheese, inclined to expel a pungent foul-smelling aroma if fiddled with, in any fashion. Actually, this pernicketyness was what made this cheese so special. She was made with fresh Coolarney milk hand-expressed at daybreak every April 19 and she was treated like royalty from the first tweak of the first teat to the last crumb on the last tongue. At six weeks of age, she was perfect.

Her creators, Joseph Corrigan and Joseph Feehan, better known as Corrie and Fee, could not take their eyes off her. They'd been making the Memorial Blues just one day a year ever since Grace Kelly (with whom they were both in love at the time) broke their hearts by marrying Prince Rainier of Monaco on April 19 in 1956. The resulting cheeses were wildly sought after and cherished throughout the world.

'She's a fine thing,' Fee said, licking his lips in a lascivious manner, his cheeks rosy with anticipation as his fat bottom bounced in its seat.

'She's all right,' agreed Corrie, raising his eyebrows in a show of appreciation. Abbey looked on, smiling.

Princess Grace stood taller than the average Coolarney Blue. Her flesh was palest blonde, the exact shade of her namesake's hair in her heyday, and her veins were a perfect mixture of sky blue and sea green, silvery in some lights, black in others, depending on her mood.

Corrie and Fee had been sitting in the smoking room for nearly two hours, just watching and waiting for the cheese to reach the perfect temperature. The room was their favourite and, unlike almost every other in the rambling country home, was out of bounds to the many Coolarney House comers and goers. Two whole walls were devoted to shelves overflowing with magazines and books, some of them more than 100 years old. The other walls were painted a rich dark green, giving a sombre, hunting lodge sort of appeal.

Corrie was in his brown leather La-Z-Boy rocker recliner, Fee in his overstuffed patched brocade armchair. Between them, on a little round table with unmistakable altar overtones, as befitted this and every cheese-eating occasion, sat the glorious Grace and, of course, Abbey.

At seventy-three Corrie bore the same uncanny resemblance to Jimmy Stewart that he had as a younger man (although the girls commented on this less now that Jimmy was mostly a memory, long since replaced by Mels and Harrisons and Brads). His eyes were sparkling blue, his grey hair thick and slicked back. Always impeccably dressed, he was wearing a pale blue woollen sweater over a crisp white cotton shirt and a dark brown pair of fifties-style high-waisted trousers.

Fee, on the other hand, was wearing a desperate pair of pond-scum green corduroy trousers that were belted round his not insubstantial middle with an old piece of twine. His checked brown shirt and grey cardigan—matched only in the number of holes that happened in the same spot—gave the impression that at some stage, many years earlier, he had perhaps been poked all over with a giant sharpened pencil.

Fee was as short and stout as Corrie was tall and lean, and should they be standing close together, as they often were, from a distance they looked for all the world like the letters 'd' or 'b'—depending on which side Fee was standing.

'Twenty-nine,' Fee said, shaking his head in Abbey's direction, his voice tinged with a peculiar sort of amazement. 'You wouldn't credit it.'

Corrie nodded in agreement, and looked from Abbey to the Princess and back again. God knew he loved his cheeses, but what he felt for Abbey no dairy product of any kind, even an impeccably flawless gem like Princess Grace, could ever hope to match. Yet still he felt sad. He poked at the fire and concentrated on the loud ticktocking of his grandfather's clock as they waited in companionable silence.

'It's time, Joseph,' Fee said finally, when he knew that it was, and he sat forward in his chair and reached for his cheese knife.

'For Grace?' Corrie asked, surprised. He'd have thought it another while away yet, but Fee was the expert, there'd be no argument there.

'For a lot of things,' Fee said cryptically, sucking a wedge of the Princess off the blade of his bone-handled knife and forcing it up against the roof of his mouth. He pushed his tongue against it, soaking up its perfect texture and exquisite flavour.

'Right so,' said Corrie, gently moving in to slice a chunk out of Grace with his own stainless-steel knife. He'd known Joseph Feehan for seventy-three years and for most of them had tried hard to make sense of what he said. In recent years, though, he had given up, realising that it made no difference to the outcome and, anyway, being mystifying was part of Fee's charm, if you could call it that.

Corrie raised his knife, sporting its perfectly balanced creamy-blue wedge, in the direction of Abbey and toasted her.

'Happy birthday, Abbey,' he said. 'I hope you're enjoying it and please God you'll be with us for the next one.'

Abbey kept smiling her dreamy smile, eyes half closed, head slightly thrown back.

Corrie tucked his melancholy away and surrendered his senses to the touch and taste of Princess Grace. How she lingered on his lips! How she sang to his saliva! How she tap-danced on his taste buds! When the last tingle of the first taste had melted away to nothing, Corrie turned to his granddaughter, reached across the table and picked her up, planting a kiss on her smile. He looked at the photo a while, then he sighed and put Abbey back on the table.

It's time all right, Fee thought quietly to himself as he reached for another wedge.

Chapter Two

'Once upon a time, before the world was run by men in fancy suits, "grass roots" meant just that. Grass roots. With cheese, that's where it all begins. You can't make good cheese with bad grass.'

Joseph Feehan, from *The Cheese Diaries*

SOME TIME LATER, across the Atlantic in New York City, another Princess Grace was living a far less fêted existence. Sure, she was sitting in a state-of-the-art refrigerator in a $7,000-a-month loft apartment in fashionable SoHo, but her only companions were two bottles of Budweiser and half a pizza that had gnarled and twisted almost beyond recognition.

This Princess had passed her use-by date and when a good Princess turned bad, it was an eye-watering experience. She'd been sitting there in her waxed wrapper inside a brown-paper bag from Murray's Cheese for nearly three months now, and it had taken this long to permeate all the layers. The time for being tasty was over.

In the bedroom down the hallway Kit Stephens, oblivious to this, opened his eyes and felt the bashing of a thousand tiny hammers against his skull. 'Go away,' he growled to himself. 'Leave me alone.'

The banging continued. Kit moved his head ever so slightly and looked at the other side of the bed. Someone was in it. And it wasn't Jacey. Jacey had long blonde hair, a model's body and the face of an angel. Whoever this was had short black hair, a model's body and a face he couldn't see because she was turned away from him. Actually, thought Kit, almost raising his head off the pillow despite its condition, her shoulder blades were exquisite and the back of her neck . . .

A lump rose in his throat as he thought about the back of Jacey's neck. Would he ever get used to waking up without her? Or worse, waking up with a stranger and wondering how the hell she had got into his bed? It hadn't happened often, but it had happened. He looked over at the beautiful back of whoever she was and felt nothing but an overwhelming sadness tinged with shame. He was feeling a lot of that lately.

Kit took a deep breath, rolled onto his side and swung his legs out of the bed, his head spinning with the movement. Carefully he stood up, waiting to see how the contents of his stomach would cope. Almost immediately he felt rebellion from below and, staggering to the bathroom, he fell to his knees on the tiled floor, clutched the toilet bowl like an old friend and threw up into it.

With a groan he flushed away the contents of his tortured stomach and let himself slide down to the floor until his face hit the tiles and, comforted by their coldness and hardness, he passed out.

'Hey, buddy. You. Buddy. Wake up!'

Coming to some time later was hardly a more enjoyable experience. The girl who had been in his bed was now standing over him, nudging his shoulder with her foot.

'Jesus, I thought you were dead,' she said.

Kit slowly pulled himself up to a sitting position and leaned back against the wall, irrationally embarrassed by being naked in front of this strange woman.

'Yeah, right,' the strange woman snorted derisively at his modesty. 'Don't worry,' she said in a bored tone. 'We didn't do it or anything. Just talked about your dead wife for two hours. I'll see you around.'

She turned and walked away as what she said sunk into Kit's addled brain.

Jacey was dead? The little hammers had stopped banging but Kit was suddenly being deafened by another sound: his heart beating louder and louder inside his chest. Jacey was dead. Jacey was dead. If he said it enough times, maybe . . . He threw on the brakes. The little men with hammers were easier to bear than memories of Jacey. He hugged his knees even closer to his body and started to cry.

What's happening to me? Kit bawled, but he couldn't bear to answer himself. Instead he thought about his breathing, then, when he had controlled the sobbing, he crawled into the shower where he let the hot water deal with his hangover and his tears.

Half an hour later he was dressed and shaved. It was past eight o'clock and he had already missed the seven o'clock trading meeting, not for the first time in recent weeks. He would have hundreds of messages waiting from clients and emails mounting by the moment. George would be fuming.

Kit looked at himself in the hall mirror. Apart from the dark circles under his eyes, he thought he looked OK. The square handsome face looking back at him showed little sign of a late-night binge or, worse, he cringed, a crying jag. But as he stared at the green-eyed image of himself, Kit was sure he saw his face grow pale in the mirror and, unless his imagination was playing tricks on him, each breath was more shallow and coming quicker than the last. Panicked, he tried to get his breathing under control but still it raced away from him. If he was going to be able to cope with the next few moments, let alone the rest of the day, he needed to calm down. He needed peace and tranquillity.

Kit stumbled into the kitchen and looked at the refrigerator for less than a heartbeat before opening the door. The smell hit him like a tsunami but, blind to the Princess and her fury, he had eyes only for the Grey Goose in the icebox.

He poured the contents of the bottle down his throat, his chaotic innards falling into line as they were massaged by the smooth satiny vodka. Relieved and much calmer, he easily took a deep, long breath and headed for the door, looking again in the mirror as he walked by with a confident smile. Now he could face the day.

For once, Kit didn't stop to take in the breathtaking view from the twenty-seventh floor of the glass and stainless-steel building they called the Toast Rack when he arrived at work.

His assistant Niamh stood up from behind her desk when she saw him and intercepted him at the door to his office. 'George wants to see you,' she said, looking at him closely. 'And I don't think he wants to swap recipes.'

Kit closed his eyes and tried to straighten his head. Niamh strode back to her desk and opened her top drawer, returning with some breath-freshening mints.

'Don't blow it now, Kit,' she said, staring at him with her earnest green eyes. 'You've come too far.'

For a moment Kit thought about asking her to let him cry for a while on her shoulder. But even through the jelly in his head he realised now was probably not the time. Now was the time to get yelled at by George, his friend and boss, a guy famous for having very little patience and a lot of sarcasm. He turned and walked past the rows of trading desks where eighty of his colleagues were shouting into headsets and bashing at their telephones and keyboards. Nobody was looking at him but he couldn't remember if that was normal or not.

George's assistant, Pearl, a gorgeous Asian woman with legs that raised the temperature of water coolers the whole floor over, indicated that he should go straight in.

George was behind his desk, on the phone. 'I'll call you right back,' he said into the receiver and placed it carefully in its cradle.

'Kit,' he said, motioning for him to sit down. 'Nice of you to join us.'

George's eyes were as cold as Christmas yet his lips were smiling and the sunlight glinting off his shiny bald head cast a certain jauntiness on the scene. Kit suddenly wondered if he was dreaming and started to smile as well. Maybe the not-really-happening-to-him feeling that had been plaguing him these past few weeks was justified. Maybe it wasn't really happening to him.

'I'm glad to see you have retained your sense of humour, Christopher,' George said, the smile slipping off his face like mud in a landslide. 'That the seriousness of the situation is not dampening your spirits in any way.'

Kit cleared his throat. The chances of it all being a dream, he supposed, were really quite slim but that was OK. He wasn't naturally a dreamer, he had his feet on the ground, everyone said so.

'God, George,' he said. I'm real sorry about this morning. It's just that—'

George suddenly thumped his fist on his desk. 'I've had enough,' he said in a voice that was cold and hard. 'You are messing up big time, buddy, and you are not going to do it on my shift any longer.'

'Your shift?' laughed Kit, albeit nervously. 'Come on, George, what is this, *Hill Street Blues*?'

George took a deep breath. 'What I am saying, Christopher, is that you are no longer an indispensable part of the broking team here at Fitch, Wright and Ray. As of eight thirty this morning your clients were transferred to Ed Lipman, and your office is to be occupied by Tom Foster. We will pay you a month's notice and your stock options can be cashed up with no penalty for choosing not to remain employed here for the required ten years. I believe that will be, luckily for you, in just a couple of weeks' time. In the meantime, goodbye.'

'Jesus, George,' Kit said, trying to laugh and failing. 'You're firing me?'

'No, Kit, you are resigning.'

George paused, then looked at his friend and shook his head, thawing slightly now that the worst part was over. 'Kit, look at yourself,' he said more softly. 'You've been a mess since Jacey and the baby—'

'This is *not* about Jacey,' Kit broke in, his voice shaky but determined nonetheless. 'Do *not* talk about Jacey.'

Kit shut his eyes. Flashes of Jacey lying on the floor invaded his thoughts. Jacey, her face pale and blank, their unborn baby already dead inside her. His heart started beating its terrified tattoo. Jacey was gone. Jacey was gone. Jacey was gone.

'I just need more time, George,' he beseeched. 'More time. That's all.'

'Kit,' said George. 'It has been almost three months. You've had all the time we can afford to give you. Anybody else would've been out weeks ago. You can't do a decent day's work any more, Kit. You don't sleep. You can't concentrate. Your drinking is way out of control. I can't trust you any more. Your clients can't trust you any more. You're a mess, my friend. You are an embarrassment.'

'But, George,' Kit said, feeling the words starting in his throat strong and sure before stumbling over his tongue, tripping on his lips to end up weak and pathetic, 'we're buddies. We built this firm up together, you and me, from almost nothing. Doesn't that count for something?'

George looked at him sadly. 'Kit, the day you met Jacey Grey was the day you stopped being my top guy. It was bad enough when she was here, but since she's been gone you have turned into someone I don't even know any more. Look at you! I can smell the booze from here, Kit.'

Smell the booze? What was he talking about? Kit started to feel the panic rising in his stomach again. A drink would be great, he thought.

'You're not the smart, great-looking guy from Burlington, Vermont, who'll do anything to prove himself to the world any more, Kit,' continued George, sadly. 'You're just another Wall Street burn-out with a drinking problem, and I don't know you any more. Now, I'm calling Niamh to take you home.'

George picked up the phone and as he punched in the numbers, a dangerous crack formed in Kit's wall of resolve. As he sat in his best friend's office, the bricks came down, slowly at first, then in a great gushing, thunderous heap, and for the second time that day, he wept.

Chapter Three

'Of course the grass is only part of it. Without the sun, the rain, a slightly salty sea breeze and whatever you're having yourself, your milk will taste like shite and so will your cheese.'
Joseph Feehan, from *The Cheese Diaries*

ANOTHER PRINCESS GRACE was alive and well, as it happened, and living on the other side of the world in the remote Sulivan Islands. This Princess was occupying the imagination of Abbey Corrigan, who was mud-bathing on the squishy banks of the Ate'ate Stream.

Actually, Abbey thought she was imagining Gorgonzola, as creamy wedges latticed with bluey-green stripes floated in the air around her, but the Princess didn't mind. She was more miffed at having to share Abbey's daydream with an automatic washing machine.

The mud always reminded Abbey of cheese, it was just one of those things. It didn't make sense but then neither did anything else so she didn't worry about it. As for washing machines, she thought about those because she spent hour after infernal hour on the banks of the Ate'ate Stream, soaping and dipping and rubbing and rinsing and wringing out Martin's and her own laundry by hand. That didn't make much sense either as they had an adequate supply of running water in their hut. But Martin wouldn't hear of using this water for washing their clothes—it was a precious resource not to be wasted, he was always telling her, and while this was not, in fact, the case, she knew he didn't like to be reminded of that. All in all it seemed easier to do the laundry the hard way.

Abbey flattened her palms against the soft ground and squelched the silky mud between her fingers, imagining it was the innards of a thousand overripened Camemberts and wondering if the push-up bra really pushed up. She thought about bras a lot these days too—underwear generally but bras in particular. They were the only thing that really made her wish she could jump in a cab and whip up to Harvey Nichols with her mother; in fact, apart from that, she didn't miss Harvey Nicks or her mother at all.

She'd arrived in the Sulivan Islands eleven years ago with two pristine white B-cup bras; perfect for the rosebud breasts she had at the time. Within a year, however, she'd been bursting out all over. Typical that just when she had least access to department stores, her boobs decided to show up. She didn't think she'd grown any taller than the five foot five inches she had been when she arrived. Her hair was still reddy brown, her eyes dark hazel, her waist small, and her thighs firm. OK, so she probably had a few more freckles (after all, she was an Irishwoman in the sun), but otherwise the package was pretty similar—apart from her bosoms.

'Abbey!' Martin's voice at such close quarters jerked her out of her daydream with a gasp. 'What on earth do you think you're doing?'

She sat bolt upright, her body making a large *ploop* as it rose out of the mud, and turned round, into the sun, to see the dark form of Martin surrounded by golden rays, wearing his uniform of Akubra hat, open-neck shirt, bandanna, khaki shorts and sandals.

'You're covered in mud,' Martin said, his posh English accent surprising her as it often did. 'What happened? Did you fall over? Are you all right?' He picked his way down the bank, frowning and staring pointedly at the basket of laundry, and stopped at Abbey's feet, taking off his hat and wiping the sweat on his forehead with his arm.

Abbey rubbed the back of her head, gooey with riverbank, and tried not to act as stupid as she felt. 'I had a bit of a headache,' she lied, fairly feebly, 'so I just lay down for a bit. I'm fine, really.'

She looked up at her husband and smiled, thinking for the millionth time how handsome he was. His hair got blonder with every year, and she loved it long and roughly cut. Eleven years in the sun had weathered his skin but that just made his eyes look bluer, his teeth whiter, his smile all the more radiant when he chose to shine it on her. Is it any wonder, she thought, that she had followed this gorgeous man to the ends of the earth as a dreamy teenager?

'You look completely mad,' said Martin. 'What on earth is the matter with you? Get up.' He held out his hand and pulled her abruptly to her feet. They stood there, achingly close to each other for just a heartbeat, and Abbey felt, in that moment, a glimmer of hope. Dashed almost immediately.

'You haven't forgotten that the Fullers are flying in today, have you?' Martin's voice reminded her. Abbey opened her mouth in silent horror and rolled her eyes heavenwards. How could she have forgotten? Jim Fuller, who flew his Hercules in once a month with provisions from Queensland in Australia, had told them last month that he would bring

Shirley, his wife, with him next visit and they would spend the night. Abbey had stayed with Jim and Shirl six years before on an emergency trip to Brisbane and counted Shirl as just about her closest friend on the planet. How could it have slipped her mind?

'Abbey, are you all right?' Martin said, looking at her, his grumpiness replaced by something else. 'I am really worried about you,' he said, leaning towards her and looking into her face. 'You're not yourself.'

Abbey had to agree. She wasn't herself. She was someone quite like herself, but a bit madder. She couldn't explain it really. Well, not to Martin anyway, but she gave it a try.

'Do you ever feel like you're not attached to your life?' she asked her husband. 'Like you're floating along beside it or on top of it and it's just getting on with things without ever really involving you?'

Martin stared at her, thin lines of impatience quivering on his brow.

'Goddamn it, Abigail,' he said, trying to contain his annoyance. 'Why do you always have to make such a fuss about everything? Women all over the world, wives all over the world, would kill to have your life. Lying in the sun all day on a desert island with nothing more than cooking a simple meal to worry about. What is the matter with you?'

Abbey was right, she hadn't been able to explain it. She gave up. 'I'm just nervous, I think,' she said brightly instead, making it up as she went along. 'It's so long since we had anyone here, Mart, and you know that I can't cook to save myself. I don't suppose there's any chance you told Jim it was pot luck?'

Martin ignored her attempt at humour, sighed and rubbed the bridge of his nose, a sure sign he was irritated. 'How hard can it be to cook a chicken and make a salad?' he said, his exasperation giving the question its own little sea of peaks and troughs.

'Not that hard at all. I don't know what's got into me,' she answered in a conciliatory tone, watching Martin put his hat back on and turn away from her, making his way along the bank towards Irrigation Central, the 'project' with which he had become more and more obsessed over the past decade.

Did women all over the world, wives all over the world, feel lonely and empty and unloved? she wondered. Or was it just her? Abbey checked herself. Of course she was not unloved. Martin loved her. They were meant to be together. They had known that from the moment they first clapped eyes on each other at an introductory meeting of Voluntary Aid Workers Abroad. Just when Abbey had needed rescuing from heartache and betrayal, Martin had ridden in, her knight in shining armour, full of courage and strength and certainty.

A week before that miracle of timing, Abbey had been chugging along in her final year at St Ignatius Catholic boarding school in Knightsbridge, without so much as a clue as to what she was going to do with her life. She'd been a good student, mainly because she loved reading, but her grades were average and she hadn't really fancied college anyway (but nor did she fancy being a hairdresser, which was where her mother felt her skills lay). That her mother had low expectations of her came as no surprise, because they were still higher than Abbey's expectations of herself.

She had nothing against hair, she liked it, felt it was necessary on a head, in fact, but she had no desire to make it her life's work. She wanted her life's work to be something special, something that would make her heart beat quickly. The trouble was, she couldn't quite put her finger on what it was. She thought for a while it might have been writing. Poetry even.

'You must be joking,' her mother had said to her, 'or at least more of an eejit than you look.'

When she was about fourteen she'd dreamed once—literally dreamed, asleep in her bed at night—of going back to her grandfather's farm. But when she woke up she realised she didn't even know where it was, as she hadn't been there since she was five. It was somewhere in Ireland. Somewhere green, but near the sea. She knew better than to discuss this prospect with her mother, though, who was long estranged from her father and hated to be reminded of anything to do with him. So she binned that idea along with the poetry.

So it was that at seventeen, without benefit of a clear plan for the future and in possession of a dreamy, sweet, old-fashioned sort of a disposition, she became an obvious target for recruitment into the convent.

'You're special, Abbey, you know you are,' Sister Clematis had whispered to her during an early career counselling session. 'If Our Lord comes knocking at your door, make sure not to turn him away, Abbey.'

One month into her final year, however, it was Jasper Miles from the neighbouring St Patrick's First Fifteen who came knocking at her door and Abbey let him in, all right—he was gorgeous. Tall, blond, handsome, rich. But Abbey had never considered herself his type. She was small and quiet, bookish, not unpopular but not popular either. Abbey felt like background, and Jasper was pure limelight. So no one was more surprised than she when, at an after-match function, she had found herself kissing Jasper Miles passionately in the hallway after fewer than a dozen words had passed between them.

For the first time in her life, Abbey had felt special. For the first time, real life was better than fantasy and it was a sensation like no other. She felt blessed. Yes, Jasper Miles had unlocked something in Abbey Corrigan: pure unadulterated lust and lashings of it.

For the next few months they'd been at it like mad things: at her mother's place; his parents'; the bike sheds at his school; the science lab at hers. Anywhere, any time, Jasper was up for it and Abbey with him.

To this day, she couldn't remember a single conversation with him, until she told him that her period had failed to show up (for the second time in a row), and that she thought she might be pregnant. That had been the last of Jasper Miles. She never saw him again.

The same night, her mother, ice clinking angrily in her glass, had had a heated exchange over the phone with Mrs Miles. It became clear that Jasper's mother didn't want Abbey's little problem and neither did Jasper, who had been dispatched to his aunt and uncle in America.

Rose had railed and cursed after slamming the phone down in Mrs Miles's ear. 'The way she spoke to me! Nobody speaks to me like that, like I was some bog-Irish little floozy. And if you think I am letting her son's bastard into my house you can think again, Abigail Corrigan, because I'm not.'

Instead, she insisted, she would be accompanying her daughter to an abortion clinic in Richmond, after which the name Jasper Miles would never be mentioned again.

Stunned, Abbey agreed reluctantly to go along with her mother's plan. Rose made it clear that she would not allow her daughter to repeat her own mistake: bringing an unwanted baby into the world when her own life was just beginning. This depressed Abbey on so many levels she felt she had no choice but to climb into a cab with her pinched-faced parent and count telegraph poles all the way to Richmond.

Rose, incensed and inconvenienced by her daughter's stupidity, took out her rage on a bar tab at Quaglino's and, after being waylaid in the back of a family sedan by an insurance salesman called Warren, was nearly three hours late to pick up her daughter.

It was sitting, post-termination, in the waiting room during those three hours, sniffling quietly in the corner, that Abbey had picked up a local newspaper and seen the advertisements for VAWA, Voluntary Aid Workers Abroad. Three days later, sad and lonely and overwhelmed with what she eventually realised must be anger, she found herself walking into a church hall in Wimbledon and there found Martin Kenderdine, a strong, handsome, earnest twenty-six-year-old looking for an adventure and someone to take on it, and her fate had been sealed.

When Martin saw Abbey he knew that she was the perfect mate. He saw in her a lack of armour, never mind chinks, that he knew would allow him to guide her into the sort of life he wanted to live. Plus, Abbey was beautiful. Small and soft and sad and needy in a way that made him want to take care of her. The timing had been perfect. They fell in love and within a month they were married; within two they were in the Sulivan Islands, right plonk in the middle of the Pacific close by the Solomon Islands, with nothing but a headful of dreams about doing something good, something great, something special for the planet.

The Sulivans had a population of about 3,000 people, mostly Melanesians, with the majority living on the three main islands of Ika, Oma and Afo, Ate'ate's closest neighbour. Ate'ate was about two miles long and one mile across, with a tropical sandy beach running the length of the northern side and a village nestling on the southern side. In the sixties, the island had been used by the Americans as a refuelling base, which explained why it had a runway that could land, at a pinch, a Boeing 737. Not that that was ever likely to happen. Despite the idyllic beauty of the island it was largely bypassed by tourists.

In a 1980s United Nations study, the Sulivans had been classified as one of the world's least developed countries. This, of course, was what had attracted Martin, the UN report forming the basis of his case to VAWA to send him and Abbey there for aid and development purposes. Unluckily for them, at exactly the same time, a tiny atoll at the far east of the island group was discovered to be so rich in mineral deposits that the Sulivanese were told they could name their price for international mining rights.

No slouches in the fiscal department, the elders had nutted out a fool-proof trust and benefit deal that would see no man, woman or child want for anything until the year 2090, after which interest on their investments would continue to feed, clothe and educate islanders in perpetuity.

Monthly supply drops from Brisbane in Australia were introduced, courtesy of Jim Fuller's Hercules, providing the villagers with everything from Heinz baked beans to hair gel. Generators were shipped to give the islands electricity and the appliances to go with it. Over the years the islanders had even given up drinking the fresh water on their doorstep in favour of Evian water imported directly from France. They wore clothes from Gap and Country Road, often ordered over the Internet, and at least one hut on each island possessed a cappuccino machine.

Naturally, this was not quite what Martin had had in mind when he brought Abbey to the isolated island group. He had wanted to build bridges, clear jungles and get his hands dirty—and that was precisely what he had proceeded to do, despite there being absolutely no need for it. VAWA had subsequently withdrawn its sponsorship when it became apparent that the country could get along just fine without it.

He and Abbey lived on the meagre interest from Martin's savings, topped up once a year by his parents. Martin filled his days by working on a fantastically complicated irrigation scheme he had devised, which he said could one day grow all the produce the villagers needed to be self-sufficient. That all the evidence pointed to them never needing to was a matter he chose to ignore. His arrogance in this and his other opinions won him few friends on the island although the Sulivanese were a tolerant race, and they liked Abbey.

Her original plan to teach the island children to read and write had been somewhat overshadowed by the Sulivanese government's insistence on providing compulsory schooling for all children aged between six and fifteen without her. Still, she taught an English class every afternoon, baby-sat at any opportunity, tried to keep house like a good wife, read whatever she could get her hands on, and daydreamed way more than was good for her.

It wasn't a bad life, but she wasn't entirely sure it was her life. She clung to her love of Martin like a drowning man to an inflatable life raft. But that afternoon she felt truly troubled. She wasn't herself, Martin was right about that. But then who the hell was she? She didn't belong in this paradise, but she didn't belong anywhere else, either. She was nobody. Nowhere. That was what kept her daydreaming her life away.

That was what drowned out the steady *ppppfffff-sssshhhh* of the air escaping the life raft.

Chapter Four

'*Every good cheesemaker needs a secret ingredient. That's what makes your cheese better than the next man's.*'
Joseph Feehan, from *The Cheese Diaries*

'HOW ARE YOU GETTING on with "The Lonely Goatherd" then?' Fee asked, looking at the girl's fingernails.

She snapped the Discman headphones off her ears and flicked them lower round her neck, where they all but disappeared into her dirty blonde dreadlocks. 'Do me a favour,' she said, in a sweet little voice that belied her tough-girl grubby-ferret look, as she pulled her hands away, 'I'm still puking my way through "My Favourite Things".'

'Will you look at that!' Fee said delightedly, ignoring her rudeness, his short fat cheesemaker's fingers now holding her by the jaw. 'Here's another one of those tongue studs. Jesus, Mary and All The Saints, will you look at it!'

The three fat ginger cats sleeping in front of the fire raised their heads simultaneously and stared at him.

'Your cats are called Jesus, Mary and All The Saints?' said Lucy, a look of disbelief and disdain distorting her small pretty face.

Corrie looked at Fee and smiled. 'We didn't do it on purpose, God bless us,' he explained.

'Didn't they take such a long time to get housetrained they were answering to Jesus, Mary and All The Saints before we'd thought of any names,' added Fee. 'And it could have been a lot worse!'

The two old men laughed.

Lucy looked from one to the other. It was possible they weren't quite right in the head. However, it was the only job advertisement she had ever seen for which she perfectly fitted all the criteria. 'Must have short nails,' the ad pinned to the shop notice board, had read, 'a good singing voice and enjoy a strict vegetarian diet.'

'Right so,' Corrie said, pulling the lever on his recliner and stretching his legs out as the footrest appeared in front of him. 'When did you last eat meat, Lucy?'

'A lamb chop when I was five. And I remember because I stuck the bone in my brother's eye,' Lucy said, defiantly. 'Oh, and some bastard poured meat juice on my vegetarian patties at a barbecue once, but I didn't know until afterwards.'

'What did they taste like?' asked Fee with interest.

'I dunno,' answered Lucy. 'I was bulimic at the time.'

'You could be as mad as a hatter and half the size and we wouldn't give a hoot,' Fee said cheerfully. 'We just want someone to milk our cows.'

Lucy's heart sank down to the tips of her Doc Martens boots, via her torn kilt and holey fishnets. She should have known it was too good to be true. For nearly three hours she had sat here in this overheated, old man's library listening to *The Sound of Music* CD and drinking peppermint tea, and of all the possibilities she had considered none included the job she was applying for being that of a dairymaid. She knew that Corrie and Fee made cheese. In fact, her mother used to buy Coolarney cheese to give to the snooty cows at her endless bloody bridge parties in Dublin.

'I thought cheese was made with machines. In big vats. With milk from a factory,' she said. 'What would you want with cows?'

'She's got that many holes in her head,' sighed Fee, 'the brains have fair seeped out of her.'

'Our cheese, Lucy,' said Corrie patiently, ignoring Fee, 'is the finest in all of Ireland, possibly the world. It's made from our own cows' milk. Do you know, they've been grazing on these fields for hundreds of years?'

'So everything around here's ancient then,' Lucy said rudely, but Corrie continued.

'What we want, Lucy, is for the cows to produce the best milk so that we can make the best cheese.' For generations, he explained, the Feehans and Corrigans had been in the business of making cheese together. The traditional deal had always been that the Corrigans provided the cows, the cows provided the milk, and the Feehans provided the skills to make cheese.

'Fascinating,' Lucy drawled sarcastically. 'What do you need me for then?'

'We need you,' Corrie said, 'because you're the special ingredient.'

'Are you messing?' Lucy asked suspiciously.

'Not at all,' answered Corrie. 'We need girls who can hold a tune and who don't eat meat to hand-milk the cows.'

The milk, Corrie said, was sweeter that way. It was as simple as that. The cheese in turn aged more peacefully, which gave it the almost honey-flavoured, lingering aftertaste that had those who sought it still drooling long after it had been smeared on the last cracker, served with the last grape, sampled with the last drop of red wine.

Corrie and Fee ran a split herd of 100 cows and milked 50 at a time. Each cow produced forty-three pints of milk in a day, in twice-daily milkings, morning and afternoon. They needed five singing vegetarians to deal with this schedule but were currently down to four, Mary-Anne's craving for sausage rolls having resulted in her return to her family in Donegal. It sometimes happened.

'You *are* messing,' said Lucy, twisting a rancid-looking dreadlock in her hand, and scowling. 'You lure me in here, make me listen to Julie bloody Andrews for hours on end, spin me some bullshit story about making stinking bloody cheese and expect me to accept a job "milking"? I've never even seen a cow up close, let alone pulled its tits or whatever the hell you call them. I'm from the city.'

She jumped off the chair and started to extricate herself from the headphones, now tangled in her dreads. The truth was, of course, that she no longer wanted to be from the city. She wanted to be as far away from the city and her parents, her college tutors and that cheating bloody Eamon as she could, which was why she had sold her violin and bought a bus ticket to West Cork in the first place.

'And anyway, it's dangerous, isn't it? Don't cows, like, kick or bite or something?' She had both her hands behind her head now, marching their way from separate sides to find the source of the entanglement.

'We'll pay you a hundred and fifty pounds a week, board and feed you,' said Corrie. 'Meat-free, of course.'

'You'll work a split shift, starting at five in the morning and finishing two to three hours later,' Fee chipped in, 'then the same hours in the evening. In between you can do what you like. Avis has the cottage set up so you can watch videos or paint or play board games with the other girls or you can earn a bit extra working in the curing room. And the pub's only five minutes down the road. The girls—the cows I mean—don't mind the smell of booze, in fact they seem to like it. Anyway, we've told Avis to get your room ready.'

Lucy's fingers slowed and met at the errant dreadlock. Carefully, she untwisted the cable until the headphones came away in her hand.

'And what makes you perverts think I'm staying?' she asked.

There was a moment's silence. 'Nobody listens to three hours of *The Sound of Music* unless they're desperate for a place to be,' answered Fee, not unkindly, but nevertheless Lucy's face burned as she picked up her rucksack, getting ready to leave.

'Did you offer her the job yet?' Corrie asked Fee. 'I don't think you should push her into it, Joseph. Why don't you just give her a place to stay while she thinks about it?'

Lucy stood still, hoping something would happen. Quickly. The fact of the matter was that she did find herself ever so slightly desperate for a place to be, plus she was tired and hungry. A hundred and fifty pounds a week and all the food she could eat sounded like a pretty good deal.

Fee chuckled for no particular reason—other than he'd been there a hundred times before—and eased himself out of his chair. Slowly, he stood up and rubbed his back, his mouth squeezed into a silent 'ow' of pain. 'What's the bet Avis is here already?' he said, shuffling to the door and opening it.

'Talk about timing!' marvelled a middle-aged matronly figure, with ski slopes for breasts and a sparkle behind her spectacles, as she bustled in the door. Her grey hair was twisted up on top of her head in a complicated arrangement that looked like something you'd buy in a French bakery, and she had crab-apple cheeks and an impossibly smiley countenance. She kissed Fee on the cheek.

'The state of you! Have you not had that back seen to yet, Joseph? I tell you, one of those osteopracters will sort it out in no time at all.' As she spoke she grasped Fee by the shoulder and leaned round him to run her fingers up his spine like a piano player. The old man straightened to his full height, about level with her chin.

'And Joseph,' she said, turning to Corrie. 'How are you today?' She leaned down and gave him a quick peck and then turned to Lucy, who was still standing, stunned, next to her chair. 'And this must be our new recruit. How are you there, girl? I'm Avis O'Regan. Did the old so-and-sos give you the full treatment? Take no notice, just come with me and I'll get you settled in. Now, is there anyone I should ring to let them know you're in safe hands? You're not the first to arrive here in a state of confusion and still be in the exact same state four hours later, let me tell you . . .'

Without seeming to notice what was happening, Lucy was steered out of the door by Avis, who paused, only momentarily, to tut-tut at the old men over her head.

Fee settled back in his chair and stared into the fire as Corrie leaned in to poke at the coals.

'Will she stay?' Corrie asked, when the fire was crackling again.

'She will,' said Fee, smiling to himself, 'and be all the better for it. She and the little one.'

Corrie raised his eyebrows. How Fee knew these things, no one could figure, but know them he did. 'I'm thinking of the very last of the Princess with a glass of something sweet and sticky,' he finally said, after pondering the predicament Lucy possibly didn't yet know she was in.

'Is that right?' said Fee, closing his eyes and leaning back in his chair, a happy smile tripping across his face. 'Are you thinking Australian Botrytis Semillon?' he asked.

'I could be.'

'But are you?'

There was a silence while Corrie marvelled at his old friend's gift. 'I don't know how you do it,' he said, standing up to go and get the bottle.

Outside the smoking room, Avis had hold of Lucy's rucksack and was marching through the house. With Lucy almost running to keep up, she strode down the hallway and through a huge cluttered kitchen, then into an anteroom choked with Wellingtons and raincoats and out into a concrete courtyard. Wine-barrel halves singing with red geraniums flanked the back door; their other halves, exploding with giant purple poppies, rimmed a stone building opposite.

'The cheese factory,' Avis said almost reverentially, stopping momentarily and nodding in its direction. To the left of the stone building was the top of the sycamore-lined driveway up which Lucy had walked some hours earlier; to the right was a tall, thick hedge with an archway in the middle, over which was threaded a thick covering of sweet-scented, tiny pink roses.

Avis turned through the archway. Following her, Lucy breathed in the cool country air and almost forgot how unhappy she was. The after-noon's summer light cast a kaleidoscope of green and gold on the ground in front of her tatty boots as she followed Avis up the narrow pathway.

As soon as she realised she felt happy she wondered what she was doing there, following Mrs Doubtfire or whoever the hell she was through the undergrowth to God knew where. Her footsteps slowed and she felt an imaginary cloud block out the sun and leave her feeling chilled and shivery. Suddenly she felt so incredibly tired. And angry. But mostly tired. And alone.

Lucy stopped on the pathway. She couldn't seem to help the single tear that made its way uninvited down her cheek. Shaking, her head bowed in shame, she sniffed and wiped the tear with the too-long sleeve of her scuffed leather jacket. But another followed, and another, and then her nose started to stream, and before she knew it, weeks, or maybe months, years, of tears were making a boisterous bid for free-dom. Unable to control her distress, she seemed equally incapable of avoiding the enormous bosom of Avis O'Regan as it came bearing down upon her, sweeping her up in its ample embrace.

'Your heart might be full of anger or emptiness, Lucy, but the thing is that you're among friends here,' Avis almost whispered in a soothing, singsong voice. 'There's not one of us who hasn't come here looking for something; love usually, my darling, and I'm not talking about the sort of love that can be found inside a farm lad's trousers either. I'm talking about the sort of love that makes you feel warm all over when you're just about to drop off to sleep at night or when you've just opened your eyes in the morning and have worked out it's not a dream you're having, it's real life. I'm talking about the feeling that if you hadn't woken up, you know, ever, that there would be people who would notice. People whose lives would be worse because you're not there any more. You've already got more of those people than you know. And now you've got people like Corrie and Fee. Yes, already! And me. And you're about to get Jack and Wilhimina and Tessie and May. What do you say to that?'

Lucy had calmed down enough to pull herself out of Avis's cleavage. She looked up into the friendly bespectacled eyes and sniffed.

'I thought you were going to suffocate me!' she said, her voice shaky with an emotion that couldn't altogether be described as her usual anger. She wiped her nose on her sleeve again, then looked beyond Avis at the cottage behind her. 'What is this?'

She was looking at a small, two-storey, grey stone cottage, not unlike the cheese factory but with a red corrugated-iron roof and red window boxes brimming with a mixture of the poppies and geraniums she had seen back at the main house.

'This is your new home,' Avis said, opening the wrought-iron gate that enclosed a messy cottage garden and motioning Lucy to walk up the path through the wild lavender to the front door. 'This is the dairy-maids' cottage.'

Avis gave a polite knock before opening the door and showing Lucy in. The ground floor seemed to be an all-in-one kitchen, dining and sitting room. It was small but beautifully sunny and at the rear, straight ahead of them, French doors opened out to a garden patio. On the right were two doors, and the wall that housed the kitchen appliances hid a staircase that led to the next floor.

'There are four bedrooms for the five of you girls, with the twins quite happy to share,' Avis was explaining. 'You can always call on me in the main house, but out here you have your own space.' She then opened the first door on the right and led Lucy in.

'This is your room,' she said, putting the rucksack on the dressing table. 'Wardrobe over there, dressing table here, obviously, writing desk, nice view of the woods and garden, radiator, extra linen in the chest at the end of the bed. Bathroom's through here—you share that with Jack. What do you think of it, then?'

The same dappled light Lucy had walked through earlier shimmied on the pink-and-white-striped bedspread.

'It's a bit Laura Ashley but it will do,' she said, sitting on the edge of the bed and testing its bounce.

'I'll leave you to take a rest then,' said Avis, ignoring the jibe. 'The girls are milking so I'll be over in the dairy if you need me. It's out of the kitchen door and round the side of the hill, about a five-minute walk. We'll be back after seven and the girls usually have something to eat then. Can you cook?'

'Toast,' said Lucy, taking her boots off. A rest was indeed required.

Back at the main house, glowing from the benefit of said sticky Semillon on a summer afternoon, Corrie and Fee were heading for the cheese factory. They crossed the courtyard and stopped in the lobby just inside the factory door. On their left was the door into the shop, and, on their right, the little office where they tried not to spend any time at all but kept their cheesemaking clothes. Corrie pulled on his white overalls and Fee slipped into a white coat. They stepped into white Wellingtons, dipped their feet in the in-tray and pushed open the door into the factory proper.

As always, they took a moment to soak up the smells of the big room where they worked their magic. To the left of them was Old Fart Arse, the pasteuriser; to the right, a vat, teak on the outside like a wine barrel, stainless-steel and gleaming on the inside. It stood chest high, to Fee anyway, and was where their precious milk began its journey to cheese.

Beyond the cheese vat were two long stainless-steel benches, another big half-pipe-shaped vat filled with cleaning solution and equipment, and a stainless-steel salting bin packed with yesterday's cheeses. The concrete floor was painted yellow, with drainage at regular intervals, and, stacked above the benches, in slatted steel racks hanging from the ceiling, were row upon row of gleaming moulds glittering in the late sun, which filtered through the long, shallow windows at the top of the factory walls.

At the back of the room were two staircases heading down in opposite directions to the curing rooms, or 'caves' as they were known. At the top of the stairs, mirroring each other on the side walls, were twin dumbwaiter arrangements, which took racks of cheeses down to the caves below.

If Coolarney was a religion, the factory was the chapel in which Corrie and Fee worshipped.

'She's probably right about that back of yours,' Corrie said, as he watched Fee move stiffly down the factory.

'When did I fall off the ladder turning the top shelf, Corrie? After the Alsace Riesling. Was it 1971?'

'No,' said Corrie. 'It was the year Abbey was born. Remember, she was teething and the two of you were making a racket fit to bring the house down.' He sighed a sad little sigh. 'Twenty-nine years ago.'

'Well,' said Fee, ignoring the melancholy, 'I'll tell you what. If it's still giving me pain in another twenty-nine years' time, I'll go to the osteopath. Now get over here and down these stairs. There's work to be done.'

'What do you think she's doing now, Fee?' Corrie asked as he moved in front of his friend to descend the Blue stairs. It was nearly twenty-four years since he had seen his only grandchild and he felt her absence like a one-armed man feels a tickle in the hand he no longer has. He stalled for a moment and felt the warmth of his old friend's hand on his back.

'It's not too late,' said Fee in his characteristically cryptic fashion. 'It's never too late. Don't worry. How many times do I have to tell you not to worry? Now get your old bones down the stairs before I give you a push.'

Corrie opened the Blue room door, soaking up the smell of a thousand cheeses and relishing the darkness that spared him the shame of letting Fee see his eyes, crinkled with tears. He turned on the dim lighting, his heart giving a little jump at the sight of rack after rack of salty blue cheese. Listening to the sound of 90 per cent humidity, he pushed his sadness aside and surrendered to his Blues, the mindless chore of turning them soothing his broken heart.

Not far away in the dairymaids' cottage, Lucy had been asleep for some time. When she woke up, Jesus, Mary and All The Saints had made themselves at home, one of them on her pillow, nestled in her dreadlocks. Lucy wrenched her head away, dislodging the ginger cat who merely stretched her paws, opened one eye, and went back to sleep where she fell. As Lucy sat up, there was a knock on the door.

'Can I come in?' asked a loud voice in a strange accent.

'Um, 'spose,' Lucy answered, sitting up. The door opened and a large, pale-faced freckly girl with ginger hair plaited and beaded in dozens of unlikely braids stumbled into the room. 'Hiya. Lucy, isn't it? I'm Jack. How're ya?'

She pulled a stool out from Lucy's dressing table and sat on it, facing the bed. ''Spose you're a bit freaked out, eh? Don't worry, we all are when we first arrive. Hey, you guys!' she yelled in the direction of the door in a voice that made Lucy's toes scrunch up. 'She's awake!'

Another braided head peeked round the corner. Its face was black and unspeakably beautiful.

'All right?' she asked Lucy coolly as she brought the rest of her body into the room. 'Cat got 'er tongue?' she asked Jack.

'Oh, bugger off, Wilhie, she's only been here five minutes. Don't worry about her,' Jack said to Lucy. 'Doesn't take much to get her tits in a tangle. She's a hairdresser after all. And this is Tessie and May.'

The last two girls to come into Lucy's room were identical twins. They wore their hair in the same style, in little coiled bunches that seemed at odds with their far less funky thick spectacles and protruding front teeth. They looked at Lucy, then at each other, and giggled.

'You'd better get used to that,' advised Jack. 'They're at it all the time, aren't you, girls?' The twins, on cue, looked at each other and giggled again. Jack rolled her eyes.

Lucy sat stock-still on her bed, unable to speak as her eyes flicked from one girl to the other and back again. She clutched a pillow and pulled it over her midriff. Something was wrong. Horribly wrong. Their bellies!

Each of the four girls crowded in here staring at her was undeniably, completely and utterly, without a shadow of a doubt, 100 per cent pregnant.

'Jesus H. Chrrrist,' Wilhie said, rolling her eyes as she took in Lucy's expression. 'She doesn't know!'

The twins looked at each other and bit their lips.

'Know what?' said Lucy, frowning and doing her best to look tough, even though her insides were heaving with terror.

'Know that you don't end up here unless you've got a bun in the oven and no bastard to help you cook it,' said Jack.

Chapter Five

'Your raw material needs to be pure and good. It doesn't need to be perfect. Between the jigs and the reels you can always sort it out, as long as it's pure and good in the first place.'
Joseph Feehan, from *The Cheese Diaries*

BY THE TIME Kit and Niamh finally hailed the most broken-down taxi on the island, New York was in the throes of its lunchtime bustle. The driver pulled out, oblivious to all other traffic, and Kit felt an ache as they pulled away from the building he had called home for nearly ten years. As angry horns tooted and blared around them, he looked over at Niamh just in time to catch a tear falling from her cheek onto her lap. At that point it occurred to him that she must have been fired, too. He and Niamh had been a team for eight years and her devotion had been beyond extraordinary. Niamh was the daughter of Irish immigrants and she had wriggled her way into Wall Street with two well-made suits, great legs and a determination to be better at what she was doing than anyone else who had ever done it. Kit didn't deserve her. And she certainly didn't deserve him.

The need for a drink washed over him. God, when had he turned into this guy? This guy who woke up with strange women he couldn't remember anything about? This guy who craved a drink from the moment his eyes opened? This guy was not the Kit Stephens he thought he knew.

'I need help,' he murmured, more to himself than anyone else, as he stared out of the window at the Manhattanites dodging the rain.

'I know,' he heard Niamh say and, for a moment, he felt safe. He felt maybe everything would be OK after all. But his happiness was short-lived. It was that kind of a day.

Benny the doorman looked at him sadly when he walked through the lobby of his apartment building. 'You'd better check your mailbox, Mr Stephens,' he said balefully, cheering up only on catching sight of Niamh's legs.

Kit did as he was told. The box held one envelope. It was from the building co-op and it had a Day-Glo orange sticker on it that read URGENT. He stuck it in his pocket and headed for the elevator, Niamh at his side.

'Don't tell me you haven't been paying the rent, either,' she said. 'What kind of eejit are you?'

'The kind of eejit who would get fired and evicted in the same day, I guess,' he answered, unlocking the door to his apartment, dumping his cardboard box of pathetic personal effects on the hall stand and heading straight for the kitchen.

'Can I get you a drink?' he asked Niamh over his shoulder.

'You can certainly show me what you've got,' Niamh answered, look-ing around the kitchen's latest Gaggenau appliances, the jars of Balducci's preserves lining the glistening white shelves, the near-empty bottle of Grey Goose on the spotless bench.

'Well, I've got vodka,' said Kit opening the refrigerator. 'Jesus!'

He might have forgotten Princess Grace but she had certainly not for-gotten him, and showed her contempt by directing a wave of nauseating stench directly at his nostrils.

'What is that?' Niamh moaned, her face contorted in horror as she fanned her hand in front of her nose. 'Something has crawled in there and died. Kit, what is it? You haven't got a cat, have you?'

Kit slammed the refrigerator door closed and leaned against it. The smell really was vile. Jacey had not eaten dairy, but she'd been a regular at Murray's in Bleeker Street because she'd read somewhere that it was THE place to go. It was not the first time a cheese of the week had been left to abduct the atmosphere. This one, though, must have been there for three months.

Thinking of Jacey, he girded his loins as he dived again into the refrig-erator for an unopened bottle of Grey Goose. 'Never mind the cat, there's vodka,' he said, his eyes watering as he spied another two bottles, 'and vodka.'

'And in here?' Niamh had retreated to the open-plan living space, where Grace's toxic fumes couldn't reach her. She bent down to inspect the innards of a wall unit she assumed contained a cocktail cabinet.

'Vodka,' said Kit, watching her as she ferreted around in the cabinet and returned to the kitchen, vodka bottle in hand.

'I guess it'll be vodka, then,' said Niamh, putting her bottle on the bench, then grabbing the two Kit had retrieved from the fridge and the one he was still holding from the icebox. He stood by, helpless and humiliated, as she unscrewed the tops off all four bottles and started to pour the contents down the sink.

'Come on, Niamh,' he said, cringing at the pathetic catch to his voice. 'Do you really have to go that far?'

'You're the one that's gone too far, buster,' she said, viciously sloshing the liquor into the sink. 'You know, I have got better things to be doing than cleaning up after you and your wreck of a life, Kit, but luckily when it comes to boozers I do have some prior experience, and because of that I will impart some advice for your benefit. Now, sit down.'

Kit pulled out a bar stool and sat at the kitchen counter, resigning himself to a lecture, knowing he deserved it, hoping it would be over soon so he could go out and get a drink.

'I come from a long line of alcoholics,' Niamh said, dumping the empty vodka bottles in the trash then replacing the mouldy coffee in his machine with a fresh supply and turning it on. 'I am not going to bore you with the sordid details but the good news is you are not necessarily one yourself.'

She paused to let this sink in, even though Kit was too busy wondering if she had left any dregs in any of the bottles to really hear what she was saying.

'Your drinking, though, Kit, has got to stop.' She pulled out the other bar stool and sat next to him. 'Did you hear what I said?'

'Yeah, yeah,' said Kit. 'The drinking has got to stop.'

'Right,' agreed Niamh. 'And why is that?'

'God, Niamh, don't make me go through the list,' he answered, aggrieved. 'I've been fired, I'm losing the apartment, my refrigerator smells like one of those dumps kids live on in Brazil. You know, I don't really need reminding that my life has suddenly turned to shit.'

Niamh's eyes narrowed and a flush crept up her neck towards her face. 'Your life hasn't suddenly turned to anything, you complete and utter eejit. You've been on a collision course with disaster ever since—' She stopped and regained control, taking a deep breath and sitting up straight. 'Look, Kit,' she said in a softer voice, 'drinking has messed up your life and in case you haven't noticed, you're kind of short on people who give a damn. Now get a grip and help me out here. Help yourself, for God's sake. Can you do that?'

As her words sunk in, Kit realised how grateful he was that she was his friend, that she did give a damn. He didn't deserve her.

'Have you thought about going back to Burlington?' she asked gently.

He shook his head. 'There's nothing for me in Vermont,' he said, feeling sick that he even had to contemplate the thought.

'Well, there's family,' Niamh said. 'Times like this they can come in dead handy, you know. Can't you at least think about going home?'

It had been five years since Kit had been back to Burlington and, in truth, he hadn't called it home for a long time. His dad, Ben, had been assistant manager at one of Burlington's biggest hardware stores for more than twenty-five years before being laid off in the mid nineties, a blow from which his pride had had trouble recovering. Ben Stephens was a good man and Kit loved him deeply and dearly.

'My dad's kind of retired,' he told Niamh, 'and he doesn't have a lot of money. He thinks I'm great, Niamh. He thinks I have really made it. If I go back like this? I just can't.'

They sat in silence for a moment.

'What about your mother?'

Greta. Greta had been the most wonderful mom a kid could ask for. Gorgeous and glamorous and the kindest woman he knew, she'd made him the man he was—or the man he had been. He was glad she would never know about his downfall.

'My mom's in a home,' Kit said, awkward with the words. 'She has an early onset form of Alzheimer's disease, you know, dementia.'

Kit had always sensed, despite her gregarious nature, a solitary sort of sadness in his mother. There were moments when he caught her in a dream world, a faraway look in her eyes and a secret smile on her lips. 'Away with the fairies,' she would laugh when he was little and interrupted her private dreams. 'Away with the fairies again.'

As she got older, Kit could see that his mother was spending more and more time away with the fairies and less at home with her husband and two sons. Eventually the visits to her faraway world became permanent, and no one ever saw the real Greta again. She lived now in a home with locks on the doors because her wandering made it impossible to guarantee her safety. She didn't know Ben, she didn't know Kit, and she didn't know his brother, Flynn, either.

'I am so sorry,' Niamh said when Kit told her all this. 'I had no idea. Where's Flynn now?'

Kit's ache grew. 'At law school, courtesy of yours truly,' he said, banging his forehead with his closed fist. 'He's a pretty bright kid, you know. He only just missed out on a scholarship but he is going to be a great lawyer one day. He really is. What am I going to do?' He was desperate now. 'Jesus, how could I let this happen? They all rely on me.'

'You pay for your mom's retirement home, too?'

'Yeah, and I kind of supplement my dad, although he doesn't know that. I have a deal worked out with the local tennis club where he does odd jobs. You know he visits her twice a day, even though she doesn't know who he is?'

He was crying again, unstoppable tears of anguish. Niamh, her own eyes shining with compassion, leaned over him and rubbed his back.

'I can't believe you've been doing all this without saying anything,' she said, jumping off her stool and heading for the coffee machine.

'What's to say?' said Kit. 'It's no big deal. It's one of the good things about having money. I'm hardly Mother Teresa, I'm just trying to look after my folks because I always thought they'd done a pretty good job of looking after me.'

'It's not the end of the world losing your job, Kit. You can sort your-self out and start somewhere new. You're basically one of the good guys, you've just come off the rails.'

She plonked a steaming mug of coffee in front of him and he stared at it without much enthusiasm. He didn't feel good. He felt far from it.

'The question is,' said Niamh, taking a sip of her own drink then blowing on it to cool it down, 'how are you going to sort yourself out?'

The possibilities had been swimming around Kit's head along with all his other tortured thoughts but so far nothing had risen to the surface. He pulled the co-op envelope out his pocket and ripped it open. There were no surprises there: unless he paid the last month's outstanding rent within forty-eight hours he would be evicted. He sighed and handed it over to Niamh, who bit her bottom lip as she read it.

'I probably know the answer to this already,' she said, slapping the letter down on the counter, 'but do you have any money at all?'

'I can get my hands on some,' he admitted, 'but enough to pay Flynn's fees, look after my mom and pay the rent on this place?' He looked around at the shrine to style in which he'd lived so happily for the past year and shook his head. 'We're talking seven grand a month here.'

Niamh looked at him, her face impossible to read. 'I might have a solution,' she said slowly, 'but you're not going to like it.'

Kit laughed. How could Niamh possibly help him? Her salary was a tenth of his, a twentieth even, a fact that had long embarrassed him given her devotion.

'Tom Foster could sublet the apartment,' she said, flooring him.

'Tom Foster? What's he got to do with anything?' he spluttered.

'I talked about it with him earlier,' said Niamh, squirming uncomfortably. 'Ah, don't look at me like that, Kit. It's not what you think. It's just that—' she looked around at the kitchen walls as she carefully picked out the right words. 'It's just that, well, Tom and I have been seeing each other for a few months. You know, as in going out together.'

She let that hang in the air for a moment.

'You're dating him?' Kit finally asked, incredulously. 'And he fired you?'

'No, Kit. I'm just dating him. You're the one that got fired.'

The trap door that had been threatening to open under Kit's feet all day was finally swung down and swallowed him up. 'But you were crying in the cab,' he said, trying to figure out what was happening. 'I thought you'd been— What was that all about?'

'Well, sue me, Kit, but I'm allowed to feel sorry for you, you know. You mean a lot to me. You really do.'

Suddenly, it all fell into place. Niamh, far from being the tireless supporter, was in fact here because she wanted to check out the place for her new boyfriend Tom Foster. He cursed his naiveté and the drained vodka and stood up.

'You can go now, Niamh,' he said, trying not to sound as hurt as he felt. 'And you can tell Tom Foster I will torch this place to the ground before I let him set one single, solitary foot in it.'

To his surprise, Niamh got up and rammed the stool he had stepped away from into the back of his legs, forcing him to sit down again.

'Sit there and listen to me for a moment, will you?' she said forcefully, her face flushed with emotion. She sat down again and regained her composure, her face returning to its normal colour. 'Think about it this way: can you really afford to blow Tom off right now? I mean, it's not just about money. You need to get away for a while. Sublet the apartment to Tom, Kit. You know it makes sense.'

'And what about me?' Kit asked, cringing again at how he sounded.

'There must be somewhere you can go,' she said, blowing on her too-hot coffee. 'Or there's rehab.'

She let the suggestion hover for a second and then said, 'I'm going to have to put some milk in this coffee,' getting up off her stool and heading for the Princess's tomb, a sour look of apprehension on her face. 'Is it safe?' She opened the door and gagged at the smell. 'Jesus, Kit. What the hell is that?' She reached gingerly for the bag and picked it up, but as she swung it towards the trash, it split and the Princess plummeted to the floor, landing on the marble tiles with a wet slap.

'Jaysus!' shrieked Niamh. 'It's alive!' She snatched a paper towel and crouched next to the Princess, her eyes watering with the cheese's angry stench. Not enough, though, to keep her from reading the label: *Coolarney Farmhouse Cheese, Schillies, Co. Cork, Ireland.* 'I don't bloody believe it!' Niamh said, as she rose slowly to her feet.

'Believe what?' Kit said, agog at the foul-smelling mess.

'Believe that the horrible smell in your fridge is going to save your life,' answered Niamh, excitedly searching the room for her handbag.

'I hate to break it to you,' said Kit morosely, 'but somebody's already discovered penicillin.'

'If you trust me with this,' said Niamh, thumbing through her address book looking for the right page, 'I will get your life back.' Her manicured finger scrolled down the list of names and addresses until it found the right one. 'You, my friend, are going to go somewhere far out of temptation's way that does not involve locked wards and group therapy.'

Kit looked at her, mystified.

'Here we are. Avis O'Regan. I don't know why I didn't think of her before. She's dried out two uncles and a cousin twice removed—that I know of—and trust me, Kit, you will not be bumping into anyone you know where she is.'

'Oh yeah?' said Kit. 'And where is that?'

'A mile out of Schillies. County Cork,' said Niamh, picking up the kitchen telephone. 'What time of day do you think it is in Ireland?'

'Ireland?' Kit repeated dazedly.

'Ireland,' Niamh confirmed with a thrill of certainty.

The Princess, splattered and reeking on the floor, burped an extra stream of steamy grey ooze. The mess on his kitchen floor looked, Kit thought, like he felt.

Chapter Six

'Without starter, the milk would still turn into cheese, but the wait would kill you. The starter gives it a shove—and we all need a shove now and then, God bless us.'

Joseph Feehan, from *The Cheese Diaries*

ABBEY SAT AT IMI'S kitchen table, scratching her head and trying to work out how many times fifty-seven went into 3,970.62. This quite often happened when she wanted to make a special effort on the food front, although, of course, the numbers differed. She could pretty much guarantee, though, that it would be long division, and she hated it just as much as Imi's nephew Junior did—which was why he was plucking her chicken and she was doing his homework.

'So if seven times fifty-seven is three hundred and ninety-nine, then—' she mumbled. 'Oh, Imi. What is six times fifty-seven?'

Imi was reading *American Vogue* and paying little attention to the mental athletics going on across the table.

'You want chicken, you do hum-work,' she said, turning the magazine round to point out a page to her friend. 'Cindy Crawford gain plenty kilos, hey, Abbey? Check it out!'

Abbey looked up from her maths and stared at the photo of the curvaceous supermodel, squinting to read the caption. 'She's pregnant, Imi,' she said, trying not to let her voice betray even a sliver of emotion.

Imi's face fell, leaving her features draped in a mortified expression. She flipped the magazine over, quickly turning the pages in a bid to escape the model's pregnant form. ''Scuse, please, Abbey,' she said, quietly and politely. ''Scuse, please.'

An embarrassed silence mushroomed between the two women. Abbey couldn't think of anything to say so concentrated on Junior's homework, but Imi, worried that she had upset her friend, was doing some mathematical gymnastics of her own.

'Sixty-nine and something!' she suddenly crowed, a look of triumph lighting up her broad, brown face. 'Abbey, sixty-nine point six six. Check it out!'

Abbey never failed to be amazed by her next-door neighbour. Her calculation was spot on: fifty-seven times sixty-nine point six six was indeed 3,970.62, and no sooner had Abbey written down the wretched answer than Junior bounced in the door, holding up her naked chicken.

'Done my homework?' the eleven-year-old wanted to know, looking over Abbey's shoulder. 'Cool! Did you get it right this time?'

Last time Abbey had required Junior's plucking duties, she had answered all but one of his maths questions incorrectly and he had had to fake an epileptic seizure in the classroom to get out of trouble.

'Imi helped me out this time so you won't need to swallow your tongue on my account,' said Abbey, swapping the homework book and notepad for the plucked chicken.

'How's Bing?' she wanted to know. Bing was Junior's five-year-old brother who had just started school and who Abbey knew was having a hard time because of his pale eyes and fairish hair. This wasn't completely uncommon in the islands. 'Genetic throwback' was the term Martin used to explain it. The traces of dalliances with early settlers and missionaries showing up generations later, he said. There were a few older ones dotted about the island but Bing was probably the fairest of them all and a target for bullying because he was small for his age and something of a whiner.

'He ordered a Malibu Barbie on the Internet,' said Junior. 'He's in the crap.'

'Bing knows how to use the Internet?' Abbey asked, amazed.

'Everybody knows how to use the Internet,' Junior said, rolling his eyes as he headed for the door.

'God, Imi,' Abbey said, collapsing back into her chair with a bewildered look on her face. 'A five-year-old can use the Internet and I can't even work your microwave oven? I swear I will never be able to leave this island. What use would I be in the real world?'

Imi, still trying to make up for any hurt she might have caused over Cindy Crawford's pregnancy, ignored the question and nodded in the direction of the plucked chicken. 'You quick-cook him here, den bone-bone cook him at you-place?'

Abbey sighed. Cooking had never been her strong point. Yes, she told her friend, she would cook the chicken first in Imi's microwave then finish it in the traditional bone-bone way. This involved wrapping the food in freshly cut bamboo and searing it over the fire. Martin thought she cooked all their food that way but it wasn't called bone-bone (burn-burn) for nothing. Getting the charred food off the fire without burning herself was a skill Abbey had yet to master. For their first two years on the island her hands had looked as though she was wearing skin-tight brown and beige camouflage gloves, such was the extent of her burns. Then, as Martin had started to pay less attention to her and more to his redundant waterworks project, she had cottoned on to Imi's modern appliances and now cooked most of their food over there. (In fact, Imi or her sister Geen—who had been sponsored by the village on a six-week cordon bleu cooking course in Paris—often cooked the food for her.) By finishing the chicken off bone-bone Abbey knew that she could get their hut to smell like a meal had been home-cooked there without singeing her eyelashes.

Imi swiped the chicken off the table next to Abbey and proceeded to stuff its skin with herbs. 'My Crikey!' she suddenly exclaimed. 'Geen make yummily salad for you and Lady Missus Hercules Man!' She whirled over to the refrigerator and took out a beautiful-looking salad, expertly presented in a traditional wooden bowl, sealed for freshness with layers of Cling Film, Geen's favourite thing in all the world.

'Check it out, Abbey!' She thrust it under Abbey's nose. The salad was made of beans and peppers with papaw and peanuts, and was no doubt dressed with Geen's special vinaigrette using 120-year-old balsamic vinegar. Abbey felt a lump rise in her throat. What would she do without her dear, sweet, loyal neighbours and friends? Geen must have remembered the Fullers were coming even though Abbey couldn't remember mentioning it, and had herself forgotten it.

As the chicken rotated in the microwave, Imi returned to her magazine to work out her autumn wardrobe. The fact that the Sulivans had only two seasons, wet and dry, and you got a bit of each every single day, did not deter her one bit. Like most Sulivan Islanders she was tall and slim-hipped with big firm breasts, a narrow waist and broad shoulders. Her hair grew in an irrepressible Afro and she spent a small fortune in mail-order straightening products, none of which had the slightest effect. Today she was wearing red faux-snakeskin hipsters and a skintight Britney Spears T-shirt, revealing her taut midriff and diamond-studded bellybutton. Abbey always felt the frumpy white woman in comparison, not helped by the fact that she relied solely on Imi castoffs for her own sartorial elegance. This afternoon was no exception: it was last year's cargo pants and a white cotton shirt, both from Banana Republic. Actually, the hand-me-down system worked quite well for her, apart from the fact that Imi was six inches taller so Abbey's trousers were, as usual, rolled up and the shirt was tied at her waist. She looked like someone who had started the day much bigger. Coincidentally, she often felt that way, too.

The microwave boinged just as the faint sound of the Fullers' Hercules heralded its arrival on the island. Abbey jumped to her feet and grabbed the chicken out of the microwave. She would have just enough time to wrap it and stick it in the flames before the guests arrived.

Imi passed over the salad, shaking her head at her friend's panic. 'Go slow-time, Abbey. They jus' friends.'

Abbey balanced the salad on her hip and headed for the door. There was no such thing as 'just friends' where Martin was concerned. Having people to visit was a big deal for him and Abbey didn't want to let him down. She'd done enough of that already.

'Thank you, Imi,' she called as she made her way next door. 'You're a lifesaver.'

'No worries,' came the reply. It was something of an island motto and Abbey wished with all her heart she could embrace it. She wrapped the chicken and threw it in the fire, then pricked up her ears at the unlikely sound of a car engine and the tooting of a horn, followed by great cheers and laughter. Out on the porch, she was flabbergasted to see Tomi Papara, the island chief, driving haphazardly through the village in a brand-new bright red convertible. The top was down and the little car was crammed with local children, all hooting and shrieking at every kangaroo hop and honk of the horn. Tomi looked as though he had died and gone to heaven.

'Check it out, Abbey, Mazda motor car!' he called as he bounced past her house, waving furiously.

Abbey was aghast. Ate'ate had one road. It went from the airstrip to the village and was about 1,500 yards long. It only needed to be 300 yards long, but the villagers had extended it so that they could have more fun driving an ancient Jeep left behind by the Americans. Having one vehicle on Ate'ate had been ridiculous, but two? Martin would be outraged. Still, Tomi's enthusiasm was infectious and Abbey couldn't help laughing.

'What's next, eh? Bloody traffic lights? And here I was thinking you were stuck in the wop-wops.'

Abbey spun round and into the arms of Shirley Fuller. She'd been so preoccupied with Tomi's wheels she hadn't seen her friend approach.

'It is so good to see you,' she said, squeezing Shirley with surprising ferocity.

'Hey, hey, you'll bring tears to my eyes,' joked her friend, pulling herself away and dabbing frantically at her eyes. 'And I wouldn't want to go wasting any water now, would I? It's a precious resource, after all.'

Abbey laughed, embarrassed. 'So, he's already given you the speech then?'

'Try stopping him,' said Shirl.

Abbey grinned at her, delighted at the sound of her harsh and scratchy Queensland accent.

'Are you OK, darl?' Shirl asked. 'You look kinda,' she scrutinised Abbey's features, 'I don't know. Different, I s'pose. Smaller.'

Abbey managed a laugh. 'Well, it has been six years, Shirl, perhaps I've shrunk. Anyway, I'm happy to report you still don't look a day over twenty-one.'

Shirl laughed her smoky laugh. 'Point taken,' she said good-humouredly. 'Now, are you going to show me around the place or what?'

Shirl was wearing her everyday outfit of sleeveless cotton shirt, below-the-knee moleskin skirt and RM Williams boots. She wore the same clobber whether she was going to church, loading crates into the cargo hold or sipping champagne cocktails at a mayoral reception. She was a true-blue Aussie and Abbey adored her.

'Come in, come in,' she said, leading the way into the hut where the smell of home-cooked chicken was making a very good impression. Shirl stopped inside the door and looked around her, aghast. The hut was one big room with woven matting walls and exposed beams, through which she could see the thatched roof and, in places where it met the walls, the blue late-afternoon sky. There were windows on each side covered with bamboo blinds, and beneath the one on the right, surrounded by a flimsy curtain, stood a rickety wooden double bed with a lumpy-looking mattress and a candlewick bedspread.

At the back of the hut was a battered stainless-steel sink, held up on either side with two beer barrels; to the left, a mesh-covered safe and to the right, a sort of indoor/outdoor open fireplace in which the green-wrapped chicken smouldered happily. Other than a shaky-looking set of shelves and the table with its three non-matching chairs, the only piece of furniture in the room was a steamer trunk in which she assumed Abbey kept her clothes. Shirl tried to rearrange her lined, leathery face into a shock-free expression but it didn't work.

'Bugger me, Abbey,' she finally said, showing her usual diplomacy. 'Where's the rest of it?'

'Well, the loo's outside with the freshwater shower,' Abbey said falteringly. 'Go on with you, Shirl. It's not that bad.'

Shirl walked, slightly stunned, towards the table and threw herself into a chair which threatened to topple sideways on its uneven legs.

'We're OK, Shirl, really,' Abbey insisted. 'It's not about money. We have plenty of that. Well, Martin does. This is the way he wants us to live and it's not that bad. Honestly.'

Shirl looked doubtfully around the room once more. 'Well, no offence, darl,' she said. 'But if you think me and the old cheese are going to bunk down on the floor we might as well crank up Old Herc right now and hit the road.'

Abbey laughed. 'And here I was thinking you were the rugged ocker,' she teased. 'Where's your pioneering spirit?'

'I'm fifty-two years old and I live in a sixteen-room house with four bathrooms and climate-controlled air conditioning,' said Shirl. 'If I want to rough it I turn the heating down in the swimming pool. Now tell me I'm not sleeping here, Ab.'

'You're not sleeping here, Shirl,' Abbey said, amused. 'You're sleeping at my friend Pepa's house, three huts away. She's going to stay at her sister's place and she's leaving you and Jim her heart-shaped bed and her Jacuzzi.'

'Now we're talking,' said Shirl. 'So where are those blokes? I could murder a beer.'

Later, as she gnawed on a chicken bone and sipped at a glass of the wine the Fullers had brought with them, Abbey congratulated herself on the meal, which, by her standards anyway, was a roaring success, despite the draining properties of her husband's apparent black mood.

'A bloody Mazda MX5 convertible?' he had railed. 'On a Pacific island with one dirt track not even a mile long? He must be mad. And what about the emissions, eh? Did he ever stop to think about the damage the carbon monoxide could do to a delicate ecosystem like Ate'ate's?'

Abbey felt obliged to keep chatting with Jim and Shirl in between Martin's outbursts, even though she knew it was better to stay silent when he was in this frame of mind. She expected there would be 'a moment', and was barely surprised when it came as she stood up to clear the plates.

'Abbey,' Martin growled, staring at her thigh and throwing his knife and fork onto his chipped plate. 'What is that?'

He motioned for her to move closer and proceeded to pull from the side pocket in her cargo pants a thick wodge of Cling Film. The same Cling Film Geen had used to preserve her beautiful salad and which Abbey had ripped off as Martin and Jim arrived home for dinner. There was nothing Martin hated more than non-biodegradable materials, especially plastics.

Jim and Shirl Fuller had stopped chewing and were watching the scene unfold with matching horror.

'Do you think we came all this way,' Martin said, his voice low and dangerous, 'and worked this hard for this long, so that you can pollute these islands with your disgusting rubbish?'

Abbey, praying silently for him to shut up and not ruin the evening, said nothing.

'Well? Do you?' roared Martin. 'Are you that stupid?'

'Steady on there, mate,' Jim said, saving the situation by casually standing up next to Abbey and reaching for Martin's plate.

Martin fumed silently as Jim clattered and banged the plates while Abbey stood, rooted to the spot, waiting to see what was going to happen.

'Well, don't just stand there, Abbey. Help the man,' Martin said, which meant he had decided not to take his rage any further. She shook with relief as she started stacking the dishes.

'How about you leave the blokes to tidy up and take Shirl for a walk?' said Jim, his eyes friendly and sad above his bushy grey beard. 'You'd like that, eh, darl?' he said, turning to his wife.

Eyes down so that she couldn't see Martin's face and tell what he was thinking, Abbey whispered her thanks to Jim and headed outside, Shirl following. The full moon was shining its giant flashlight on the Pacific as they walked silently down to the water's edge and sat on the jetty, their legs swung over the edge.

'Why, in God's name,' Shirl finally said, as gently as an outspoken Australian could, 'are you still with that blithering idiot?'

Abbey said nothing. She didn't want to have this conversation. She didn't want to think about it.

'I thought he was going to clout you back there, Abbey,' Shirl continued. 'And over what? A bit of Cling Film?'

Abbey, horrified, stared at Shirl aghast. 'You've got it all wrong, Shirl. It's not that bad. He's not that bad. We're actually very happy here. Look at it, it's paradise!' She threw her arms up to emphasise their surroundings. 'You have to give Martin a break. He's really a lovely, lovely man, he just gets frustrated with the way things work here.' She'd had this conversation with herself many times over and found that out loud it sounded quite convincing. 'But hit me? Oh no. He's never laid a finger on me.' She paused for a fraction too long. 'He won't lay a finger on me actually. That's more of a problem.'

Shirl, not one to bite her tongue, didn't. 'So, you're not getting any then?' she said.

Abbey sighed and leaned against the jetty post, watching the moonbeams flitter and flash across the waves. 'He went off me when I got back from Queensland,' she said eventually, when she was sure she could get the words out without dissolving into the tears she had long since trained herself to keep at bay, 'and I told him what the doctor said.'

Martin had sent her to Brisbane six years earlier, when after five years of marriage and no contraception she had failed to conceive. A laparoscopy had revealed that Abbey had only one Fallopian tube and that the poor lonely thing was even more severely hampered by the existence of a large ovarian cyst. When this was removed, it proved to be the size of an orange. The gynaecologist told Abbey that she had just a one-in-a-million chance of getting pregnant.

She had used that one-in-a-million chance, of course, with Jasper Miles.

Abbey had been devastated, as Shirl had seen while she nursed her through her recuperation. But when Martin found out he had fallen apart completely.

'He just lost it totally,' Abbey told her friend as they sat on the jetty. 'I've never seen a man so sad. He just rolled up into a ball and cried for a week, and nothing I could do would bring him out of it. It was awful. Then he disappeared for two days and when he came back it was like he was a different person. He looked the same and he sounded the same, but it was like he wasn't really there or I wasn't really there or—oh, I don't know.' Her voice petered out.

'He doesn't blame you, though, does he?' Shirl asked. 'For not being able to have babies?'

Hearing it out loud really hurt, Abbey realised. 'Well, it is my fault,' she said. 'He should blame me. I had one chance and I wasted it.' She shuddered. 'I've ruined his life and I'm not going to walk away and leave it in tatters. Besides, I've nowhere else to go.'

Shirl, flabbergasted, sat up and cleared her throat. 'For a start, Abbey, it is not your bloody fault and you're not to bloody blame for bloody anything. Second, Martin's life is not ruined but yours is—and if you want to enjoy the rest of it you need to bloody do something. Third, you have got somewhere to go. You've got our place.'

Abbey smiled at her friend and tried to imagine living the rest of her days by the side of the pool in the palace at Brisbane. It wasn't a bad thought, but no, she had made her bed and would lie in it.

'Thank you, Shirl,' she said, trying not to notice the pity in her friend's eyes. 'It might not be my fault about the babies, but it is my fault that Martin is so unhappy, and I couldn't leave him here, I really couldn't.'

'But you're only twenty-eight, Abbey,' Shirl argued. 'You've got your whole life ahead of you. You shouldn't be wasting it on someone you don't love.'

'I'm twenty-nine,' Abbey whispered. 'I'm twenty-nine now. And I do love him. I really do. I'm all he's got and he's all I've got, and I do love him.'

As the words came out Abbey realised, not for the first time, how hard she had to work to make herself believe them. She couldn't bear to think about it any more so rose to her feet and pulled Shirl to hers.

'Enough of all this,' she said, her voice pleading. 'Let me show madam to her boudoir.'

Grabbing Shirl's hand she led her up the path past the meeting house towards Pepa's place. Shirl, disturbed and saddened but recognising the difficulties her friend was facing, let herself be led.

'Oh, look, it's Geen,' Abbey said, passing Imi's sister's house and catching a glimpse of her dancing around the room inside. 'I should go and thank her for the salad. Come in and meet her. You'll love her. Everybody does. She's the life and soul of the island.'

She dragged Shirl inside, where Geen proved to be dancing not on her own but with her three youngest children. Without stopping her butt from swinging or her head from shaking, Geen waved to her visitors and nodded in the direction of Bing and his two blonde little sisters, who were all standing in a row dancing wildly and vigorously without one of them moving a single foot. Abbey burst out laughing and turned round to Shirl, who was standing behind her, to introduce her. But Shirl was looking as though she had just been socked in the jaw. Her face was completely white and her eyes were huge as she stared disbelievingly at the three jiggling children.

'What's the matter, Shirl?' Abbey said. Shirl doubled over and gasped for air, all the while still looking at the children, who had by now stopped jiggling and were staring back.

'Abbey,' said Shirl, clutching her stomach, her face scrunched up in pain. 'Jesus Christ, Abbey.'

'What is it, Shirl?' Abbey cried, panicked, as Geen started to chatter hysterically at the children.

Shirl grabbed Abbey by her middle and twisted her round to face the little blonde disco babies. 'The kids, Abbey,' said Shirl. 'The kids. You can't be that blind. They're the spitting image of Martin.'

As soon as Shirl pointed it out, Abbey saw it for herself, clear as day. Bing and his little sisters, Georgie and Martha, were dead ringers for Martin. He could almost be their father. She started to smile at this cheeky nudge of coincidence, but before her lips had reached even half-stretch she felt her bone-bone chicken 'thunk' to the pit of her stomach. One little Martin lookalike would be a coincidence, she realised, as the colour in her face drained southwards, but three?

He could *almost* be their father?

Her lips abandoned their smile like a released rubber band and regrouped into a wonky 'O' of disbelief.

He could *actually* be their father.

Nobody moved. Nobody said anything. Abbey shook her head. Martin and Geen? It wasn't possible. Gorgeous Geen with her long brown legs and crazy hair? She looked at Geen and in that single moment knew the truth.

'How could I have been so stupid?' Abbey whispered, as Geen, suddenly panic-stricken, hurriedly rounded up her stupefied children and herded them towards their beds.

Shirl had begun to regain her composure but was still frozen with shock and scrutinising Abbey for signs of hysteria, trying to think what would be the best next move. She'd assumed Martin was a bully, but this? How could he do this to someone as sweet and innocent and idiotically devoted as Abbey?

'Right,' said Abbey, snapping out of her daze and shrugging off the cloak of dread. 'Let's go.' She turned on her heel and walked out, Geen crying now and following her.

'So sorry, Abbey. So sorry. Pleeeeease!' she sobbed, but Abbey, her back straight and her head held high, kept going.

Outside the same night sky and carpet of stars twinkled above Abbey's world, yet she knew that in those few moments inside her friend's house her life down on earth had changed and would never be the same again. She walked calmly down the track, wondering how she should feel, where she should go. She'd always imagined that in situations like this people knew exactly what to do next, but she didn't have a clue.

'How could I have been so stupid?' Abbey repeated, half to herself and half to Shirl. Shirl, still stuck for words, stumbled along beside her friend, wondering when the tears, the anger, the emotion, would come.

'I can't have children,' Abbey said calmly, 'so he stops wanting to sleep with me, then Geen gives birth to three blonde babies one after the other and we all, stupidly, say what a miracle it is. It's all so obvi—'

She ground to a halt mid-sentence, at the side of the meeting house, and began to shake uncontrollably. 'Oh my God, Shirl,' she said, her face crumpling like a screwed-up paper bag, as her hands flew to her mouth in horror.

All this time she had thought that the villagers were her friends and she was protecting Martin from their scorn, when really they were laughing at her. Poor dreamy Abbey with her baggy clothes and burnt hands and irritating irrigating husband. How could she have been so stupid?

She gave in to the hysteria that was clawing at her and howled at the awful truth of such mass betrayal. Her ridiculous life had all been a lie and, what's more, she didn't have any other life to go to. The loneliness that she had kept at bay for years enveloped her.

'Everything will be all right,' Shirl was saying in a voice so soft Abbey wondered what she usually used it for. 'Everything will be all right.'

Abbey turned her tear-stained face to look at her friend. 'How?' she said, her voice hollow and hopeless. 'How can everything be all right?'

Before Shirl could answer, Abbey heard the crunch of an encroaching footstep, then Junior's voice. 'Is everything OK?' he said. 'Is Abbey OK?'

'Do us a favour, would you, love?' Shirl said, suddenly efficient. 'Run over to Abbey's house and grab the old bugger with the beard for me, will you? Tell him Shirl says it's a code red and I'll meet him at Old Herc.'

Junior turned immediately to go but Shirl reached for his hand and pulled him back. 'Hang on a minute, love,' she said. 'What's your name?'

'Junior.'

'How fast can you run, Junior?'

'Faster than a speeding bullet,' Junior answered proudly.

Shirl turned to Abbey. 'Where's your passport, darl?' she asked.

'My passport?' Abbey repeated stupidly.

'Come on, Abbey,' Shirl urged. 'Where is your passport?'

'It's in my old handbag inside my trunk,' Abbey said, 'but why—'

Shirl was leaning towards Junior now, her voice urgent. 'Tell the old bugger about the code red,' she said. 'Then get Abbey's bag from the trunk in their hut and run like a speeding bullet to the plane at the landing strip. Can you do that? Abbey needs you to do that.'

Junior looked at Abbey and, nodding, turned on his heels and ran.

Shirl pulled Abbey to her feet. 'Just do what I say, Ab. We can work it all out later on.'

She put her arm round Abbey's shoulders and shuffled her out to the main track round the village. Through a haze Abbey thought she heard voices growing louder and louder, maybe even Imi, but Shirl clutched her close and hurried her forward.

The noise, however, got louder and closer, until Shirl exclaimed, 'Jesus H. Christ!' Before she knew it, Abbey was being thrust into the passenger seat of Tomi's Mazda and Shirl was flooring it in the direction of the airstrip. It wasn't far to go but the car certainly made it faster than the villagers; word had spread quickly that Martin's little secret was out and the gossips were on the warpath. At the Hercules, Shirl squealed to a halt and abandoned the car, pulling open the crew door at the front of the plane and bundling Abbey inside the aircraft before heading to the cockpit and flicking on some interior lights and a bank of switches on the control panel.

'Come on, Bullet Boy,' Shirl whispered as she pulled down a seat in the cargo hold for Abbey to sit on. She reached through the cargo net beside her to pull out a thick woollen blanket and wrapped it tightly round Abbey, who was rocking backwards and forwards.

'I'm a bit out of my league, love,' she said in her normal gravelly voice, looking nervously out of the door. 'But I think you should come home with me.' She craned her neck towards the darkness, looking for Junior. At that moment the thunder of boots alerted them to Jim's pending arrival.

'Bugger,' said Shirl. 'Where's the kid?'

Looking red-faced and puffed but not particularly surprised or angry, Jim sprinted towards them, a flurry of villagers in his wake, and dived in the door. 'What kid?'

'She's my wife,' Abbey heard Martin roar close by. 'She's my wife. Let her out. Give her back.'

As Shirl pulled Jim across the floor and lurched over to pull the door closed, a red leather missile came flying through the air and landed on the back of Jim's neck.

'You beauty, Speeding Bullet,' Shirl roared out of the door before pulling it closed with an almighty thud and locking it.

'What the bloody hell is going on here?' Jim asked, breathing heavily and rubbing his neck where an angry welt had already formed.

'Your friend out there is starting a new breed of little Martins behind his wife's back is what the bloody hell is going on here,' said Shirl, pushing her husband towards the cockpit. 'Now get this thing in the air.'

'Steady on, darl. How do you know about this? Who told you?'

'I saw them with my own eyes,' said Shirl. 'Now get this thing in the air or I'll thrash you, you great galah. Come on!'

Jim slipped into the pilot's seat and the engines sputtered into life just as Martin appeared in front of the plane on the airstrip, his face bulging with rage and a string of expletives pouring from his angry, spitting lips.

The Hercules shuddered into motion and lurched forward.

Martin, wanting his wife back but not willing to end up splattered on the nose of the Hercules, moved out of the way at the last possible moment, throwing his hat to the ground and kicking the dust in fury. A weeping gaggle of villagers clutched each other behind him but Abbey was oblivious to their cries. As the plane rose higher and higher, she pulled the blanket closer round her shoulders and, despite her emptiness, her loneliness, her despair, felt the smallest weight lift off them.

She never wanted to see Ate'ate nor her cheating husband again.

Chapter Seven

'Remember, despite all the rules, there really are no rules. Some of the best cheeses in the world have only been discovered by the cheesemaker making a ballyhays of something else.'
Joseph Feehan, from *The Cheese Diaries*

IT WAS PITCH-BLACK and freezing cold when Jesus sat on Lucy's face. It was her third night in the big feather bed in the dairymaids' quarters, and so far she had done little since she arrived but lie in her room, sleeping and thinking dark thoughts. Jack had insisted on bringing her food, which she had done her best to eat, but the truth was she felt ill a lot of the time.

Jesus, Mary and All The Saints, the three fat ginger cats she had met during her interview with Corrie and Fee, had seemingly sensed her despair and draped themselves supportively around her, only leaving the room, one at a time, through the window for their ablutions. That it was the sunniest room in the house was probably just a coincidence.

This morning, though, cracks were showing in Jesus's supportiveness.

'Get off me,' Lucy croaked into the cat's fur, giving her a good shove. Jesus stood on all fours by Lucy's neck and yowled meanly back at her, prompting Mary and All The Saints to lift their drowsy heads from either side of the bed. Jesus soon stopped his yowling but the cats' heads stayed up, their ears twitching as they watched the bedroom door. Just as Lucy was pulling herself up to a sitting position to see what the cats were looking at, her door burst open, flooding the room with warm yellow light from the hallway.

'Awake already?' Avis said, smiling delightedly. 'How about that? Talk about meant to be! Ready to start work today then, Lucy? There's breakfast on the table and cocoa in the pot. Pull on your woollies, we'll wait for you. Come on, girls!'

The cats stretched and jumped languidly off the bed, padding lazily in single file towards Avis, who opened the door wider for them to walk out. Only Jesus stopped to look back snootily at Lucy, who was still sitting, speechless, in her bed. Avis shut the door again and Lucy stayed there in the darkness for a minute or two, furious at being bullied into working at such a despicable hour. Although, she supposed, it couldn't strictly be called bullying. Avis had asked her if she was ready to come to work and she could have said no. But for some reason, probably the hour, she had said absolutely nothing.

Angry at herself for being awake to listen to the question in the first place, she threw back the covers and jumped out of bed, gritting her teeth against the shock of the cold floorboards and the wave of nausea that washed over her. At the breakfast table Wilhie, Jack and the twins looked most surprised to see her; she concentrated on her food and ignored their interested stares. Once the plates and cups were stacked in the dishwasher, the girls assembled themselves at the back door.

'Blimey,' said Wilhie, catching Lucy's scowl. 'You don't have to look quite so miserable, you know. It can actually be fun, this job.'

The girls were helping themselves to duffle coats hanging on a rack by the door. Lucy pulled on the last remaining one and stomped out after them. It was still dark outside and there was a chill in the air, but this didn't seem to deter anyone except Lucy as they chattered happily all the way round the hill to the dairy. They were a funny sight from behind, all walking in various stages of what could only be called a waddle.

Lucy wondered for a moment if she had been sucked in by an evil cult. She doubted, though, that Corrie and Fee had brainwashed her, and they hadn't asked her for any money. In fact, they were giving her some. When they rounded the corner to the dairy her suspicious thoughts were interrupted as the smell of a hundred cows' effluent hit her in the face like a game-show cream pie. She gagged and tripped at the same time, falling into Jack, who turned round to steady her.

'Pretty gross, eh?' Jack said cheerfully.

'Does it always stink like this?' Lucy asked, trying to get her dry retching under control and still clutching desperately to Jack as Avis and a tall ginger-haired boy herded the cows towards the milking shed. The cows were diverted at the front into five different walk-through bails, their heads leaning over wooden doors on the other side. Up closer, all Lucy could see was five bony cows' bums, covered in muck and smelling like shit. She was green with revulsion and fear, and Jack looked at her with sympathy.

'You are in a bad way, aren't you, Luce?' she said, pityingly. 'I have to say yes, it does always stink like this. But,' she said quickly as Lucy made to leave, 'you get a hundred and fifty pounds a week and you don't need to spend a single penny while you're here. You get a roof over your head, and you get good food. All you have to do is sing a few harmless songs, lay off the burgers and do a bit of milking. And where else are we going to get that? You know, in our condition.'

Before Lucy could contemplate the matter of her condition any further, Avis arrived at her side with a stool and a pail and directed her to the closest bail, which contained a sad-eyed cow called Maria.

'Actually,' Avis said sheepishly, 'they're all called Maria for the purposes of ease and convenience. Now!' she pulled Lucy round to face her, then sat herself down on the little stool, rested her shoulder on Maria's undercarriage and reached for her udder. 'Oooh, I nearly forgot!' she said, standing up again with surprising haste for someone quite so top-heavy. 'Have you got the remote, Tessie?'

'Yes, Avis,' came the reply from down the shed.

'Then what are you waiting for, girl?' Avis called good-humouredly. 'Hit it, why don't you!' The gentle soundtrack of *The Sound of Music* permeated the fetid area. The cowshed, quiet up until then apart from the sound of scraping stools and shuffling hoofs, suddenly reverberated to the swelling strains of Rodgers and Hammerstein. Lucy stared open-mouthed as the four pregnant milkmaids and Avis O'Regan began milking in time to the title track. Avis was beaming and pulling

Maria's teats in accord with the swell of the music. The milk seemed to emphasise the beat as it hit the bottom of the pail and the whole strange scenario seemed to swim around Lucy like a dream.

'You try, Lucy,' Avis said over the music as she jumped spryly off the stool again.

Lucy, for want of any alternative opportunity presenting itself, sat on the stool. Under Avis's instruction, she leaned her cheek against Maria's warm side and reached for her udder. Her shoulder fitted neatly under the cow's belly, her head into the soft curve of Maria's flank. Reaching the udder was a bit of a stretch but once she curled her violin-player's hands round the teats, Lucy felt as though she was just the right size for the job. Slowly she squeezed with one hand. Nothing happened. She squeezed again. Still nothing. Maria shuffled uncomfortably and stamped a hoof in impatience, startling Lucy who reared back, only just keeping her balance on the stool. She looked at Avis, who was smiling patiently and miming in the air the gentle but firm massage required for milking. Lucy moved in once more, her angry scowl replaced by her concentrating scowl, and within ten minutes she was milking Maria for all she was worth. It was hard work, but quite satisfying once she got the hang of it. She looked up to share her achievement with Avis, but her supervisor had moved on. Only then did Lucy realise she was the only person in the shed who was not singing about the hills and how alive they were. She thanked God she didn't know the words, and poked her tongue out at the ginger-haired boy who was watching her. He blushed and bobbed down behind another Maria.

Across in the factory, Corrie and Fee were cranking up the pasteurising machine. Corrie loved the factory first thing in the morning when it was just he and Fee. The smell of cheese just made and milk about to arrive seeped out of the factory walls and floorboards like a comfortable old blanket. And the quiet! How he loved the quiet. Once, when the demand for their product had been smaller, they had been the only ones who worked in the building, managing the packing and the orders themselves. As their reputation grew, however, they had been forced to bring in outside help. Fee had wanted Carmelite nuns, who he thought would work hard and not say much. They proved to be a bit thin on the ground, however, so instead they ended up with Marie Lonegan from the village and her sister-in-law Ruby O'Toole. The pair arrived on the dot of 8.30 every morning and neither drew breath until they left again.

Still, Ruby and Marie were worth their not insubstantial weight when it came to running the shop and processing the orders. Their mindless blathering never interfered with their weighing, labelling, phoning, faxing and (in recent years) emailing, and this left Corrie and Fee free to weave their magic in the cheese factory. They didn't want to know about orders and invoices and delivery dates and schedules. They cared only for milk and curd and the sorcery of cheesemaking.

Apart from Grace and another private speciality or two, they produced just two types of cheese at Coolarney: Gold and Blue. The Gold was a washed-rind cheese, which meant that once it had been shaped and salted, it was smeared every two to three days with a special Coolarney yeast culture, giving it a sticky, glistening rind. This provided the perfect conditions inside to turn the curd into a strong, meaty, smooth, super-succulent cheese-lovers' cheese, while the rind started out pale yellow and moved on to gold, then orange, then deep tangerine.

On alternate weeks, Corrie and Fee made Coolarney Blue. The secret to this cheese was in Avis's legendary home-baked barmbrack. Once a year, in early September, she made 200 of the fruity loaves, using her ancient family recipe. The loaves were then stored in the Blue curing room, where after three months they were covered in spores of blue mould. This mould was then sieved and added to the young curd to give Coolarney Blue the spicy, sharp taste and blue-green veins for which it was so well known (and which no one anywhere else on the globe could match, despite many attempts).

Princess Grace was a variation on this cheese. Her taste was quite different though, because it was made from the milk produced in April with the new spring grass and because, unlike a regular Blue, she was not pierced to encourage her blue veins, but was made with a looser curd and developed the veins on her own. As a general rule the less the cheesemakers had to do with Grace, the better.

This week was a Gold week. Corrie and Fee stood ready to weave their magic, and watching Old Fart Arse as he huffed and puffed his way up to the heat that was required to kill the allegedly life-threatening bugs in their milk. The sound of his clattering and banging usually riled Fee into a whole new face colour. For generations, Coolarney cheese had been happily unpasteurised, but in recent years it had come to the attention of high-ranking health authorities that cheese contained bacteria and this evil, unnatural substance must be stomped out.

New European Union restrictions required the cheese to be pasteurised and, as a result of this interference, they had been forced to install, at great expense, Old Fart Arse, who was clattering and banging this very morning. Yet, strangely, Corrie thought, he was having little effect on Fee's complexion. If anything, Fee might be considered a little peaky, he thought, but then he was wearing an orange T-shirt and a purple vest and had a green and red scarf wrapped twice round his neck. No one could look a good colour surrounded by quite such a palette, thought Corrie, noticing also that Fee had two different shoes on. Ah well, they matched his socks.

When the two old friends finally heard the rattle of Avis's tractor delivering the mother lode of milk to the vat outside the east door of the factory, they moved towards the noise in unison, the same smile playing across their different lips.

The cheesemaking was about to begin.

Corrie and Fee set about their separate routines: for Corrie it was cleaning and preparing the surfaces and moulds, for Fee it was overseeing the delivery of the milk.

'You were right, Joseph,' Avis said, putting the tractor in neutral and climbing down to ground level. 'Little Lucy's going to work out just fine. I've hardly seen anyone take to it so quick. Mind you, isn't it always the way when Jesus, Mary and All The Saints take such a shiner. Hardly a word at all this morning and the face on her! And Jamie spoke. Can you believe it? He asked what Lucy's name was. What a day!'

Jamie was Avis's cowherd and almost pathologically shy, thanks to a speech impediment. She'd discovered him hiding in the hayshed when he was twelve, shaking like a leaf after a belting in the Schillies school playground, and he'd helped her with the Marias ever since, albeit most days without saying a single word. That he had come up with an entire question thrilled her to bits.

She and Fee each grabbed a side of one full milk churn and heaved its contents into the tank through a handmade copper funnel, continuing until the churns were all emptied and the tank was nearly full. Within an hour the day's milk had been pumped through Old Fart Arse; had reached, according to the gauge, the required 72 degrees Celsius for the required fifteen seconds; and was pouring into the cheese vat, its sweet comforting smell slowly warming the whole factory. The room was coming to life.

Fee and Corrie worked silently and separately, weaving in and around the vat and the surrounding benches like so many threads of wool following an intricate pattern. When the vat was full and the temperature a steady 35 degrees, Fee added his starter, the first part of the secret to ripening the milk and kick-starting the cheese's flavour.

Like most cheesemakers they used a commercial brand of freeze-dried starter, which came in sachet form. They had spent much of the fifties arguing over whether to make the switch to this commercial product, Fee initially being keen to stick with making his own even though it was labour-intensive and slightly unreliable. By the sixties, though, he had come round to the idea. The rennet—the coagulating agent—they similarly bought in, having not enough calves' stomachs on hand for the making of it. Despite the fact that this had weighed on Fee's conscience heavily for decades, he had to admit that the cheese had never suffered. Quite the opposite, in fact. And the cheese was the thing. The cheese was always the thing.

Once the rennet was added, the magic of the cheesemaking began in earnest. Before their very eyes, the milk disappeared and the cheese began to emerge. In more than sixty years on the factory floor, there had not been one single day when this point in the cheesemaking had not given each man a tingle of excitement up his spine. As the minutes ticked by, the thick creamy milk dissipated into a watery whey, leaving a shiny, solid, beautiful mass floating in its wake. This was the curd. And the curd was their gold. Every blade of grass they grew for every Maria to chew for every vegetarian to milk for Avis to unload led to this moment.

The curd. The first taste of what was to come. An inkling of the cheese it would one day be. The promise of perfection.

The secret potential of every cheese was locked up in the warm, soft curd and it smelt glorious. When the time was right, Corrie and Fee picked up their blades and, starting at opposite sides of the vat, began to cut the curd. The blades, like enormous, long-toothed combs, each had an ancient wooden handle shaped like a baseball bat. Each handle was worn away in a different place according to the fit of its own cheese-maker's hands.

Corrie and Fee wove their blades through the soft curd like synchro-nised ice-skaters, cutting patterns that changed the shiny surfaces into melted draughtboards. They stirred and sliced and twisted and turned, until the curd was finally broken into tiny even pieces. At this point they abandoned their blades, and Fee started to drain off some of the whey.

As the grate in the factory floor spat and hissed with the barrage of watery waste, the sweet smell of grass and passion filled the air. Corrie and Fee looked at each other with identical satisfaction. In every batch, this was the moment they waited for, the moment that kept them in love with Coolarney cheese.

It was tasting time.

Breathing in the warm, sweet air, Corrie leaned over the vat and dipped his arm into the curd, savouring its soft silky squelch before bringing a handful to his lips. On the other side of the vat, Fee too was savouring his first mouthful, his head back and his eyes pointed at the factory ceiling in full concentration.

No sooner had the first microbe of the closest curd hit Corrie's lips, though, than he knew something was wrong. His heart beating in his chest, he looked across at Fee, who had turned to stare at him, open-mouthed, his own half-swallowed curd sitting unwanted on his tongue.

Corrie threw the remaining curd in his palm at the drain and dipped his hand again into the vat, his fingers trembling. He brought a fresh handful to his nose, crumbling it softly to release the aroma. To his horror, sure enough, there it was: the faint scent of failure. It wasn't bitter, or sour, or rancid. It wasn't even unpleasant. It just wasn't right. That was all. Just plain not right.

Fee was still staring at Corrie, open-mouthed and stunned.

'Could it be the starter?' Corrie asked, already knowing the answer. 'Did something contaminate the starter? Or the new girl,' he remembered, almost excitedly. 'Could it be the new girl?'

Fee slowly spat the errant curd into his hand and sat down on an upturned bucket. He looked sadly at the curd, then at his old friend. His blue eyes had lost their glimmer, his round face had collapsed into a new, miserable shape. He opened his mouth to speak.

'It's fecked,' he said.

With those words Corrie felt the temperature in the room drop ten degrees. Of course, it shouldn't be coming as such a surprise, they were both seventy-three after all, but in good health, apart from Fee's back.

Corrie staggered backwards and leaned against the draining bench, cheese moulds clattering to the floor as his hands reached behind to steady him. Fee's back! He felt a hole open up in his chest and swallow his hope. Fee. In the many, many years that the Corrigans and Feehans had been making cheese together the curd had soured on just a handful of occasions and not a week following each such incident, they'd been dressed in black and praising the dead.

The souring of Coolarney curd signalled a changing of the cheesemaking guard from one generation to the next, and Corrie knew in his heart that this was no exception. Fee's back. His refusal to seek medical treatment. His peaky condition. God help him. God help them both. Corrie stared at the little round man and wondered how much time he had left.

'Don't give me the eye,' said Fee, surprisingly robustly for someone in such poor health. 'Wasn't it allus going to happen?'

Corrie stayed where he was, stunned at the turn a day could take.

'I wonder would Abbey come home,' Fee said, looking craftily at Corrie. 'And I wonder would Abbey make the cheese?'

Fee never wondered things, thought Corrie. He was too busy already knowing them. 'I could try writing and asking,' he said, the calm tone belying the hammering in his chest. 'But with Rose, you know . . .' he trailed off. 'Are you sure, Fee?'

Fee looked at him with his beady blue eyes and said nothing.

'Well, I don't think we should rely on Abbey,' Corrie said eventually. 'It's been twenty-four years since we even laid eyes on her, and she's a million miles away. We're going to have to go outside.'

They had talked about this before, of course. About the possibility of bringing non-Corrigans and non-Feehans on board for cheesemaking purposes in the event of a disaster such as this. It had never been done before and there was no telling whether it would work or not. But Fee had never married and Corrie's only daughter, Rose, had not spoken to him since she had run away with her daughter all those years ago.

'Outsiders it is then,' said Fee, standing up. 'Feck it.'

Chapter Eight

'There's a bit of thinking time between adding the rennet and cutting the curd. Different cheesemakers use this in different ways. Personally I favour planning elevenses.'

Joseph Feehan, from *The Cheese Diaries*

IN THE PARLOUR of her little pink B & B in the West Cork town of Schillies, Maureen McCarthy was attempting to drive Kit back to drink. He'd arrived in the village after a hellish trip from New York, expecting to be able to fall into bed. This, however, was clearly not on Maureen McCarthy's agenda.

'From New York are you?' Maureen had asked, snatching away his bags and pushing him into an armchair in her stuffy drawing room. 'It looks like a wonderful place sure it does, despite the twin towers—what a tragedy, all those lives, God rest their souls—and didn't Pauline O'Brien just down the lane have an uncle who moved there a few weeks back?' she said, disappearing to make a cup of tea but eerily leaving her voice in the room with Kit. 'Run over by a yellow taxicab and killed stone-dead the poor man was,' the voice said, enthusiastically. 'Do you take milk?'

'Yes, thanks,' Kit answered, although she was already back in the room with a mug full of milky tea.

'In the street with all the theatres. Do you know it?'

'Broadway?' Kit offered.

'The very one. Fancy that,' Maureen beamed.

A small, wiry woman, with curls set in rows of military precision, she perched like a bird on an uncomfortable little stool by the fireplace and took in every detail of her guest with eyes that didn't miss a trick.

'He's not the only one from around here to end his days under the wheels of a fast-moving motor vehicle actually,' she said, as if Kit had just announced he were doing a thesis on the subject and did she have any other data that might be useful?

'There was Patsy Mulligan bowled over by a bus on her way to Mass over in Cork,' Maureen said, shaking her head. 'Of course, she'd been into the sherry and hadn't she got Sunday morning confused with Friday rush hour, but she was bowled over, nonetheless.'

She stopped and looked mournful for a moment before adding rather brightly, 'I ended up with her toilet-seat cover as it happens. It's purple. It looks like carpet.'

Kit had no response to that. He felt sick. The tea had gone cold and there was something oily floating on the top of it. Actually, he didn't really like tea. He liked vodka. And a lot of it, right now, would have made him feel a whole lot better.

'So,' Maureen said brightly. 'What brings you here? Touring? Sailing? The Ikebana Festival in the village hall this weekend?'

'Much as I like raw fish,' Kit joked, 'I'm actually going to stay at a farm. They make cheese there. It's called Coolarney, and it's run by a couple of old guys and this woman, Avis something . . . Avis O'Regan. I don't suppose you would happen to know where that is?'

Maureen's eyes darkened. 'Don't we all know where that is,' she said. 'A fine old time you'll be in for up there, no doubt. A fine old time indeed. Applying for the cheesemaker's job there, are you? I wouldn't have picked it. Not at all. Still, it wouldn't be the strangest thing to happen, a fancy fella like yourself turning up to make cheese at Coolarney House, that's for sure.'

Kit was intrigued by her insinuations about Coolarney House.

'So what goes on up at this cheese farm, then?' he asked. 'You make it sound kind of weird.'

'Well, I really couldn't say,' Maureen said, with pinched lips. 'I'm not one to gossip but let's just say there's more people gone into Coolarney House than have come out again—unless it's babies you're talking about, in which case it is entirely the other way round.'

'Babies?' Kit wanted to know.

'You'll find out soon enough, no doubt,' Maureen snipped. 'Being as you are headed there yourself. Two old men with a houseful of expectant mothers, it's not right. And Mr High-and-Mighty Corrigan's own daughter the first to turn her back on them. If you don't count his wife, that is, God rest her soul, wherever it might be with only those two old devils and your man upstairs a hundred per cent certain.'

Kit was confused. 'So his wife what? Died?' he asked. He'd put money on there being an automobile involved.

'Just try asking him yourself,' Maureen said, surprising him by remaining stingy with details.

'What about Avis O'Regan?' he asked. 'Is she, you know—?'

'What?' Maureen prompted unhelpfully. 'Is she what?'

'Well, is she all right?' Kit continued, wishing he were dead or asleep or just somewhere else.

'As well as any married woman living with two single men and not a husband in sight would be. There's been no sign of Mr O'Regan in more than thirty years.'

Kit couldn't help but laugh. 'Well, you make it sound like a great place,' he said, 'and I can't wait to get there. But I'm telling you now I'm not interested in making babies or whatever else goes on up there.'

Maureen raised her eyebrows. 'So you are going for an interview then, are you?' She answered her own question. 'Typical, just typical they'd draft a blow-in rather than help out a local lad. Cheesemaker, my elbow!'

Kit rubbed his temples and sighed. 'I'm not going there for an interview,' he said, struggling to come up with a plausible reason for why he was going there. 'I don't know anything about any interview. I'm just going to be staying there a while. I'm working on a, ah, on an investment project with—'

He could see Maureen leaning towards him to glean as much as she could.

'Avis has some, er, financial issues that she—'

Maureen was in danger of toppling off her stool.

'You know what,' Kit said suddenly, standing up. 'I lost my wife a few months back. I've been drinking a lot since then and I got fired from my job, so a friend of mine suggested I come and stay with Avis for a while to get myself cleaned up, you know? So if I could just go and lie down for a while and maybe get some sleep, I would really appreciate it, Maureen, I really would.'

Maureen's eyes glistened with this new-found knowledge.

'I'm so sorry for your troubles, Christopher,' she said, trying hard to keep the glee out of her voice. 'Come and I'll show you to your room.'

Kit picked up his luggage in the hallway and followed her up the narrow stairway to a room with a door so low he had to bend down to walk through it. His room consisted of a single bed, a nightstand, a framed picture of the Sacred Heart of Jesus, and an even smaller door that opened into a tiny bathroom, complete with purple, frighteningly carpet-like toilet-seat cover.

'Would you be after me waking you in the morning, Christopher?' she asked, kindly. 'I'll be up anyway making your breakfast.'

'Thank you, Maureen. If I'm not downstairs by eight thirty please rap on my door.'

He guided her out into the hallway and retreated to his tiny room, banging his head in both directions, then stripped off down to his boxers and T-shirt and flopped onto the bed, every fibre of his being crying out for sleep. Unfortunately, the mattress appeared to be stuffed with porcupine quills, every fibre of his being poked by a different one. Sleep, Kit realised, was to elude him for a while longer yet.

He let his mind drift to the events of the past few days. They seemed to have passed in a long, frightening blur and it hurt to think about it. A tear slid down towards his ear as Kit contemplated the possibility that his reason for existing had disappeared down the plughole with his vodka collection. There didn't really seem any point in anything, he thought miserably. He didn't have a home or a wife or a job, and without any of it, his job especially, he didn't know who he was. Hell, even with it he'd got confused. Kit moved his gaze from the ceiling to the Sacred Heart and prayed with all his heart that Avis O'Regan could help him. Then he fell into a deep, deep sleep.

Chapter Nine

*'Some people should never make cheese. Liars make bad cheesemakers:
it looks good but tastes desperate. Cheats make bad cheesemakers too,
and there's never as much of it as they say there's going to be.'*
Joseph Feehan, from *The Cheese Diaries*

'HI, ROSE,' SAID ABBEY. 'I've come home.' She had forgotten just how exquisitely beautiful her mother was. Her dark red hair was shoulder length and set like a movie star's from the 1940s, and her skin was the colour of milk. The delicate bones around her mother's neck and shoulders that she remembered so clearly were still in prime condition, every stitch of clothing worn to show this feature off to its maximum potential. The make-up was perhaps a layer or two thicker, but the eyes were still an incredible shade of spring-forest green. Her mother, Abbey thought with a jolt, didn't look a day older than when she had last seen her eleven years ago.

'Jaysus,' her mother said, holding on to the front door of her Kensington home. She was wearing an off-white floaty negligee arrangement with impossibly wide sheer long sleeves, feathered at the wrists. It was a strange get-up for the late afternoon but just the romantic sort of Zsa Zsa Gabor outfit her mother had always favoured.

'I think I'm in shock,' Rose said.

Abbey moved cautiously half a step closer. 'You do know who I am, don't you?' she said, only half joking. There was a frightening corridor of silence, then the curtain was lifted and Rose the actress emerged.

'Darling,' she said, suddenly dramatic, holding her arms out for Abbey to walk into them, her face rearranging itself into warm maternal repose. 'It's so wonderful to see you, of course it is. Just such a shock, that's all. A terrible shock. Mind the hair.'

She kissed the air on either side of Abbey's face and then pulled back, but Abbey didn't mind. She'd never really been comfortable in her mother's embrace and now was no exception.

'I just can't believe it's you, Abbey,' Rose said in a strange tone, giving her daughter the once-over. 'Just look at you. That's quite a body you have on you now, girl. Give us a spin.'

Abbey dropped her bag and dutifully did as she was told. It came as no shock that her mother would check out her measurements before her mental health, marital status or plans for the future. Some things would never change.

'I've been in the air for twenty-seven hours,' Abbey explained, picking her T-shirt away from her slightly sweating midriff. She doubted that the too-big hand-me-downs that she couldn't afford to ditch despite their awful memories were doing her justice.

'Come in, you must be exhausted,' Rose said, guiding Abbey with the tip of her talon towards the sitting room. 'Have you been working out?'

'I have been in the islands for more than eleven years, Rose,' Abbey pointed out. 'Gyms are kind of in short supply in that part of the world.' Actually, there had been an entire Nautilus weights system, two treadmills and a running machine in Tomi Papara's back room but she'd never felt the urge to use them.

'Of course you were, darling,' Rose said, arranging herself on the sofa and pretending to scoff at her own silliness. 'The shock of it all. Did you get my letter?'

Abbey looked at her mother. 'The letter you wrote me, what, eight years ago?' she said brightly. 'Yes, Rose, I got it. Did you get the letters I wrote you, you know, every Christmas and birthday and most months in between?'

Her mother caught the tenor of her tone and looked momentarily chastised. 'Ah, don't look at me like that, Abbey. You know I was never much good at writing letters.'

Abbey swallowed her response. She felt shaky and emotional and didn't want to be sitting here bickering about letter writing. She wanted to tell her mother what she had been through. She wanted to cry and be showered, if not with sympathy then at least with advice for how to get on with her life. Rose certainly had the experience when it came to men.

'Oh, Rose, you won't believe—' she started.

'You won't believe how much—' her mother said at the same time, ignoring the intrusion and continuing to talk over the top of her daughter, 'has gone on here since you left, Abbey.' She lit a cigarette and kept talking. 'I got a part in an ongoing tea-bag commercial not long after you went. It was huge. I was voted one of the top ten most popular TV stars. Can you believe it? From a tea commercial? Anyway, that led to a tiny role on *EastEnders* as one of Phil Mitchell's girlfriends. Well, I just blew the producers away, Abbey. Totally blew them away. Next thing you know I have a starring role in *What Am I Like?* Did you get that over in Bali Hai? It was a sitcom, Abbey, you'd have loved it. Four seasons it lasted. Four wonderful seasons. And now I'm playing Marilyn Monroe's part in a West End production of *Bus Stop*. Me and Marilyn Monroe, the critics have said we could be sisters. What do you make of that?'

Her mother, Abbey slowly realised, was displaying all the symptoms of extreme nervousness, not a Rose-like condition by any stretch.

'Rose,' Abbey said, 'are you not going to ask me what I'm doing here?' She examined herself for signs of being hurt by her mother's apparent lack of interest and self-obsession, but nothing painful seemed to have penetrated her. She supposed she must be immune to Rose, and this was, after all, vintage Rose.

'What you're doing here?' Rose repeated, stubbing out her cigarette, then plastering on an empty smile. 'Well, I think I know what you are doing here. Let me see,' she said, unconsciously checking her wrist-watch, 'yourself and the lovely Martin are back for reprogramming or whatever it is you people go in for, you've dropped in for a visit to show me that you're still alive and haven't been cooked up in a big stew, and in a few minutes you'll be out the door back to Bula-Bula and then it'll be another ten years before I see you again.' She launched a sad little frown across the wrinkle-free terrain of her brow and let her eyes fall mournfully to her hands, which sat in her lap as she fidgeted with her rings. 'I've learned to live with the pain of your abandonment, Abbey,' she said. 'I've moved on. I've had to. I couldn't just sit here for year after year weeping and wailing and waiting for my only daughter to stop turning her back on me.'

Abbey had actually forgotten what a brilliant actress her mother was. She could have sworn she even saw her bottom lip quivering. She wondered why she didn't find the woman's gall more offensive.

'Actually, Martin and I are not together any more,' she said as calmly and confidently as she could. 'I've left him in the islands. I've come home, Rose.'

Her mother's mournful look was instantly twisted into one of extreme panic. 'You've come home?' she asked, appalled. 'Home where?' She was having trouble lighting another cigarette. 'What about Martin? What about your marriage vows?'

'What do you care about marriage vows?' Abbey asked, suppressing the nugget of anger she felt over her mother's about-face on the subject of Martin, a man she had described on the only occasion she had met him (their wedding) as giving a new definition to the expression 'damp squib'.

Rose opened her mouth as if to say something, then thought better of it. 'I just want what's best for you, Abbey, you know that,' she said in a sugary tone. 'And you were such a delightful couple. What could possibly have gone wrong with such a match made in heaven?'

'Martin was cheating on me, Rose,' Abbey said. 'He was fathering children with another woman. Not me.' Hearing herself say the words out loud, Abbey felt sure, for the first time really, that leaving Martin behind had been absolutely the right thing to do. At the mention of children, however, her mother choked on a lungful of smoke.

'And you?' she said, waving at the cloud in front of her face, her voice unable to hide her horror. 'Are there grandchildren?' She tiptoed over the last word as if it were green slime about to swallow her mules.

Abbey dug her nails into the palms of her hands to help maintain her composure. 'No,' she said, trying to look at Rose but only managing a spot on the floor. 'I can't have children. That was a one-in-a-million chance. You know. Before. With Jasper's baby. You must remember that? Mum? The termination?'

Rose's face drained to match the colour of her spotlessly cream calico couch. 'That was a long time ago, Abbey, and there's no need to be dragging it up now,' she said. 'It's water under the bridge.'

'I'm dragging it up now because it's affecting me now,' Abbey said carefully. 'Jasper's baby was it, Rose, my one chance in a lifetime to be a mother.'

Her mother shook her words away, turning her head to one side and holding up both hands to stop any more reaching her.

'For God's sake, Abbey, stop it,' she said. 'Being a mother isn't all it's cracked up to be, you know. You don't know the half of it.' She stood up and straightened her gown before looking at her watch again, edgy and flustered. 'You really should try to get over it.'

'Get over it?' Abbey said in amazement, watching her mother suck up her panic and metamorphose into a perfect hostess again. She felt like she was riding a roller coaster.

'Would you like something to eat before you go?' Rose said, gesturing for Abbey to stand up and completely ignoring the point the previous exchange had reached. 'You must be starving. Look at you, you're a stick figure, Abbey, apart from that bosom. You need feeding up. How did you get here again?'

Abbey chastised herself for thinking that the subject of her painful past could be talked about with the woman who had designed it. 'I'm not hungry, Rose,' she said. 'I've come from Australia. I was staying with friends for a few days after I left Martin in the islands. I got the Heathrow Express to Paddington and a cab here. But what do you mean, before I go? I haven't got anywhere to go, Rose. I thought I would stay with you. Here in the flat. I've got nowhere else to go.'

Her mother seemed to be battling a complete nervous collapse. Her face hovered on horror then switched on terror, then settled on something between the two and stayed that way.

'Jaysus Christ Almighty A-bloody-men,' her mother cried, wringing her hands in exasperation. 'I can't deal with it, Abbey. I just can't. Oh, what have I done to deserve this?'

With the clink and tinkle of the wringing hands, something clicked in Abbey's brain. The rings. Her mother was wearing rings. On her wedding finger. Quite a collection.

'You're married,' she said stupidly.

'Oh, Abbey,' her mother said, grabbing her cigarettes and lighter from the arm of the sofa. 'It'll be the end of me. You've no idea. The very end of me, Abbey,' and with that she burst into tears that Abbey knew were real because they streamed down her cheeks.

'Rose, Rose, calm down,' she said as soothingly as she could in the circumstances. 'Let's sit down. It's all right, I understand. Don't worry. I understand.' Her mother laughed through her tears and said, 'I don't think you do.'

'He's young, isn't he?' Abbey asked, once she had settled her trembling mother back on the sofa. Rose laughed and nodded, then cried even harder.

'And he doesn't know about me?'

'It's not that,' Rose sobbed. 'It's just that he's due home any minute. You've got to go, Abbey.'

'I've told you, Rose,' Abbey said tightly. 'I haven't got anywhere else to go. In case you've forgotten, you're it. It'll only be for a couple of days. You can tell him I'm the daughter of an old schoolfriend or something, can't you? Lying to him obviously isn't a problem.'

'Abbey,' her mother said, choosing a pitiful look over an angry one, her eyes dramatised and aged now by blackened mascara smudges, 'you have got to go. You can't stay here. You just can't.' She pushed herself off the sofa, suddenly looking every one of her forty-six years, and moved towards Abbey's bag, picking it up off the floor with shaking hands and holding it out towards her daughter.

'You're kicking me out?' Abbey asked aghast. 'But, Rose . . .'

'I'll give you money,' Rose said, shaking the bag at her daughter. 'I'll give you money to go somewhere else, Abbey, please, just—'

The sound of a key rattling on the other side of the flat's front door paralysed Rose mid-sentence.

'Don't come in,' her mother whispered hoarsely, her back to the door as she stared at her daughter, as the fumbling of the key stopped and the latch clicked. 'Go away,' Rose croaked as the door swung open and Abbey reeled at the shock of who it was stumbling through and slamming it behind him.

His hair was longer and slightly thinning, there was the beginnings of a business-lunch paunch lurking under his suit and he wore a chunky gold bracelet on the wrist of the hand that was twisting at his collar to release his tie. He looked so grown-up that Abbey barely recognised him, yet how could she ever forget him? It was Jasper Miles and he was wearing a wedding ring.

'I say,' he said, shocked, as he registered just who it was gawping at him from the sitting room. 'Goodness.' He put his briefcase underneath the telephone table the way, no doubt, he always did.

'This could be embarrassing,' he said awkwardly. 'Rose? Darling?'

For a split second, Abbey felt a thrill at seeing him, this smudged version of her first, perhaps her only true love. She had imagined this moment many times over the years. The moment when the Jasper Miles of her dreams, young and handsome and pulsating with hormones, would see her, smiling and gorgeous and happy, and curse the day he let her slip away.

But here she was, none of those things, and here he was married to her mother. The quiver she felt in her stomach wasn't a thrill of joy, she suddenly realised, as it gathered momentum and started roaring through her body. It was white-hot, pure and overwhelming rage.

'You complete and utter bastard,' Abbey said in a voice she didn't know she had the venom to produce. Rage engulfed her and pushing past her paralysed mother, she found herself springing at Jasper and punching him hard in the throat.

'Jesus,' he gurgled, clawing at his neck. 'Help.'

But Abbey wasn't finished. Bringing her knee up swiftly she planted it smack in the middle of his groin, then as he doubled over in pain, she brought it up again, catching him under the chin with a sickening crunch. Jasper staggered back onto the telephone chair, moaning, as Abbey stood in front of him, shaking like a leaf, and wondering how else she could hurt him. She drew back her arm and whacked him with a right hook to the side of the head that spun him off the chair and onto the floor.

It took a moment to realise that although she had stopped screaming, she was still being engulfed by noise and pain. Her mother was slapping her from behind and shrieking at her to leave Jasper alone.

'Get off him,' Rose was howling. 'Leave him alone. Leave my beautiful baby alone!'

As quickly as the despicable rage had swept Abbey up and claimed her as its own, it deserted her, leaving her huffing and puffing and staring in horror at the spectre of her mother kneeling at Jasper's side, weeping as she kissed his balding head.

'Leave my beautiful baby alone,' she sobbed again. The words clanged around the hallway as Abbey tried to gather herself. They said it all. The father of Abbey's unborn child was now her mother's baby.

The flat was quiet apart from the soft sound of Rose weeping as she soothed Jasper, who was bleeding slightly from the mouth, and Abbey felt a sudden enormous embarrassment at what had just gone on. Yet in the surreal aftermath of such a raw and exhausting scene, she felt compelled to dig deeper.

'How long,' she asked, 'has this been going on?'

'He came to see me not long after you left for the islands,' her mother wept, holding Jasper's head and looking at her daughter. 'We consoled each other, Abbey,' she said defiantly, trying, despite her distress, to regain a dramatic edge. 'Can you blame us for that? Is that such a crime?'

Abbey looked straight at her mother. 'I think you know exactly what it is,' she said, and in her mother's emerald-green irises she saw that she did.

Rose, just like Martin, had chosen betrayal over love without so much as a backward glance.

Jasper was coughing into his hands, Rose was still weeping softly, but Abbey was silent as she reconciled herself with her situation. Really, she realised, she had only one option left.

'Where is my grandfather?' she asked her mother. 'Where is the farm?'

Rose stopped crying.

'I will not let you go to that wicked old man, I will not,' she said. 'We swore we would never go back.'

'No, Rose,' said Abbey, 'you swore we would never go back. I was only five and, from what I can remember, perfectly happy there.'

'How can you say that when I told you what he did to my mother?'

'How can I believe anything you've ever told me? Especially after this? After him?' Abbey looked at the still-cowering Jasper. Rose stayed silent.

'Tell me how to find my grandfather or I will sell my story to *OK!* magazine along with your real age,' Abbey continued. 'I will tell them that you made me get rid of my boyfriend's baby and then you banished me to the other side of the world and ran off with him.'

'I'll never speak to you ever again,' Rose said.

'I never want you to,' answered Abbey. 'Tell me.'

'Coolarney House,' Rose whispered. 'Schillies. County Cork.'

Abbey turned and picked her bag up from the sitting room, then swept past Rose and Jasper and opened the front door of the flat.

'Go to your grandfather and that is it between you and me,' her mother said in a cold, dead voice. 'I mean it.'

Abbey turned to look at her again, feeling a strange empty blackness inside. She felt humiliated and dirty. 'What is there between you and me, anyway, Rose?' she said. 'Apart from our two names on my birth certificate?' She looked at Jasper, still with his head hidden in his hands so he could avoid any involvement. 'Oh, and him.'

Her mother looked suddenly furious and, abandoning all question of glamour, scrambled undaintily to her feet. 'Just ask that old bastard what happened to your grandmother,' she spat from the entrance to her flat as Abbey walked towards the lift. 'Just ask him what's buried in his precious factory,' she wept as the lift arrived and Abbey stepped into it.

'You'll see,' Rose cried out. 'You'll find out. That'll wipe the—' but the lift doors snapped shut and Abbey was left with nothing but the silent, sweeping cloak of her own remorse and shame.

Chapter Ten

'Once you've done your stirring and your waiting and your thinking and the time is right, there is a single moment, and I'm not messing with you here, there is one single moment when it all comes together and you realise that your milk has gone and your cheese is on its way.'
Joseph Feehan, from *The Cheese Diaries*

BY THE TIME KIT had reached the cheese farm after a mile-long walk, he was dreaming of a friendly face, a darkened room, and a cool glass of water. But found himself confronting a small, troll-like creature with a scowl on her face.

'Have you seen Jesus?' the troll asked him.

Kit blinked and stared at the troll.

'Hello-o-o-o,' the troll said again, quite sarcastically for a Christian, Kit thought. 'I asked you had you seen Jesus?'

'I'm a Baptist,' Kit answered. 'Well, my folks are anyway, so I guess that means, yes, I have seen Jesus.'

The troll looked at him confused, and then smiled a smile so radiant Kit wondered if perhaps he was asleep and she was a dream.

'You've got me all wrong. Jesus is a cat. A fat ginger cat. I'm Lucy, by the way,' said the troll, smiling again, and he saw at once that she wasn't a spooky creature at all. In fact, she was pretty cute in a punky, little girl sort of a way, with a pile of dreadlocks scooped up on top of her head, too many layers of black clothes, and feature ladders in her tights.

'I'm Kit,' he said, with a smile which was not lost on Lucy either. He held out his hand and took hers when she finally offered it, enjoying its smallness and warmth as he did.

'I've come to see Avis O'Regan,' he explained.

'Avis?' said Lucy, thinking how handsome Kit was. 'She'll be up at the dairy now but you can wait inside the house. Corrie and Fee won't care. Well, they won't even know. They're interviewing for a new cheese-maker today and a bigger load of peckerheads you've never seen in all your life. Come on, I'll bring you inside.'

Kit followed her round to a glass- and wood-framed conservatory on the opposite side of the house. Inside, a dark passage led to a big cosy kitchen where Lucy indicated Kit should wait at the big wooden table pushed up close to the rear wall.

'I'd better go,' she said, pulling her heavy leather jacket closer around herself. 'I'll tell Avis you're waiting.'

Outside, Lucy headed up the path to the cottage to get her milking gear. Halfway up she was disconcerted to see a blue-denimed rear poking out of the greenery.

'It's all right,' the other end of the rear was saying into the ground. 'It's OK. Sccchhh. Scchh.'

The noise was frightening so before she could think much about it, Lucy gave the rear a boot.

'Owwwww,' Jamie Joyce cried as he extricated himself from the foliage. He turned to see Lucy scowling at him. 'What did you do that for?' he asked in a hurt voice.

Lucy took in his blushing sweet face and thought perhaps the kick in the arse might have been a bit previous.

'It was poking out,' she said, nevertheless keeping her scowl in place. 'And making the place look untidy.'

Jamie decided to get over it. 'There's a cat in here and I think it's having kittens,' he said.

Lucy hardly had time to notice his speech impediment. 'Is it ginger?' she asked, suddenly fearful. 'Is it small and ginger?'

Jamie nodded.

'Jesus! Show me where.'

Jamie moved over to let Lucy into the foliage. 'Right under the lowest branches of this rhododendron,' he guided her. 'There's a sort of a nest.'

'Jesus,' Lucy crooned. 'Jesus!'

'It's OK,' Jamie said, alarmed at Lucy's distress. 'She's managing fine.'

'No,' said Lucy. 'It's Jesus, the cat. Jesus is having kittens. God, I have to go. I have to milk. Could you stay here with Jesus until I get back? It'll only be an hour. Two at the most. Do you know about kittens?'

'They come from cats,' smiled Jamie. 'Yeah, I do.'

Lucy looked at him suspiciously, then jumped up and started to run for the cottage. 'Oh, by the way,' she said, stopping and turning back. 'I thought you didn't speak.'

'I've usually got nothing to say,' answered Jamie.

'Right,' said Lucy, accepting his excuse without doubt. 'See you in an hour. Don't let anything happen to Jesus.' As she skipped up the path, Jamie settled back into the undergrowth.

Corrie supposed he shouldn't be disappointed that they had not found a successful applicant. It was unlikely they would find somebody the first day. The first month. The first year, even. Not just anybody could be a cheesemaker, after all. Hardly anybody in fact. And even Corrie wasn't sure exactly who they were looking for. Just somebody with a certain sort of something. The curd would recognise him. So, probably, would Fee.

He walked into the kitchen and was surprised to see a sad-looking man of about thirty sitting at the table. Behind him, he heard Fee gasp.

'I hope you don't mind,' the man said in an American accent, 'but I made myself a coffee. I think Avis O'Regan may have forgotten me.'

In a moment, Corrie took in the strong, smooth hands holding the coffee mug and noted the square kind face. He turned to Fee, who was beaming so hard his smile seemed to be doing laps of his head.

'I'm Kit Stephens,' Kit said, standing up and holding out his hand.

'Joseph Corrigan,' said Corrie, offering his own, 'and this is Joseph Feehan.'

'You're the cheesemakers,' said Kit.

'Well,' said Fee, 'we'd like to talk to you about that.'

'To me?' said Kit.

'How long have you been waiting?'

Kit looked embarrassed. 'Well, I arrived around four and the girl with the, you know, hair, looking for the cat, told me to come in here. That was about three hours ago—'

Kit's explanation was interrupted by a feeble knock at the kitchen door.

'Thanks all the same,' Fee called out, his eyes still on Kit. 'We've found someone.'

'I know you've been interviewing for cheesemakers,' Kit started, 'and I think there's been some confusion . . .'

The knock on the door was back again, only louder.

'Position filled,' Fee said again. 'Thanks anyway. Maybe next time.'

'I'm here to see Avis O'Regan,' Kit was trying to explain. 'I'm going to stay for a while. It's just that I—'

But the knock was back again, more persistent than ever.

Fee was about to say something when he froze, the only movement that of his eyes widening with the realisation of what was happening. In a split second he slid wordlessly across the floor and opened the door, standing back to let the knocker in.

She was medium height with big brown eyes and spiky rusty-coloured hair and she looked tired and maybe even a little scared, thought Kit. But nice. As she stood in the kitchen, weighed down by her bag and whatever had brought her here, obviously unsure what to do or say, a strange noise like a cross between a gargle and a gasp emerged from Corrie's throat as he realised who it was. A single tear sprang to his eye and worked its way nimbly down the valley of his wrinkled cheek, as the rest of him stood frozen in an icy mixture of fear and hope.

'Abbey,' he said quietly, as though speaking any louder would blow her away. 'Abbey.'

Chapter Eleven

'Of course, you don't want to get too full of yourself after that one single moment because there's still a fair bit to be done.'
Joseph Feehan, from *The Cheese Diaries*

THE KITCHEN SMELT of sunshine and cinnamon, that was the first thing Abbey noticed. An old Aga built into a brick wall at the far end of the room was half covered in dried lemon and orange skins, and she could sense the citrus lingering invisibly in the air. The floor was covered in big, square, black and white tiles and the benches on either side of the sink in front of the kitchen window were groaning with fruit and vegetables, herbs and flowers, bottles of exotic-looking drink, loaves of bread, an obscene amount of cheese, and many different-coloured jars of fruit and pickles. A rack hanging from the ceiling housed an enormous collection of copper pots and pans that caught the last of the evening sunlight shimmering through the window.

At a long table with bench seats on either side sat a clean-cut preppy-looking guy with bags under his eyes. The big tall man saying her name was her grandfather and the little fat one wasn't. That much Abbey knew. About everything else in the world, she remained in a state of total confusion.

'What's a dote?' the little fat man suddenly asked the preppy guy.

'I'm Kit,' said Kit.

'I'm Abbey,' said Abbey.

'What's a dote?' the little fat man asked again. 'Have you any idea?'

'Fee,' said Corrie, shaking himself out of his paralysis. 'It's Abbey.'

Fee looked as though if he smiled any harder, his head would split in two. He put his hand in his pocket and stepped towards Abbey, pulling out of his indescribably awful corduroys a handful of rainbow-coloured boiled sweets. She took one and slowly unwrapped it, then popped it in her mouth. Corrie looked on in awe. Fee had stopped keeping sweets in his pocket more than twenty years ago. How had he known to have them in there today?

Kit watched the scene with growing unease. He didn't know these people but the air seemed thick with their secrets. Something private and painful was about to happen, he felt sure.

'Do you know, then?' Fee asked again, beaming at him. 'About the dote?'

Common sense dictated that in the circumstances the question was an inappropriate one, but in the absence of anyone else saying anything else, Kit thought of the troll-girl in the garden looking for the cat.

'Is it something small and cute?' he suggested. 'You know, like a little mite? A little dote?'

Fee seemed to flutter clear off the ground with delight. 'This calls for a celebration!' he said, delightedly. 'I'm going to cook a roast.'

'I've just seen Rose,' Abbey said, rolling the sweet around in her mouth, 'and it didn't go particularly well.'

'Would I show you to your room, Abbey?' Corrie suggested, unfazed.

'Would you?' she asked, and she followed her grandfather out into the hall. The house was a maze of hallways and doors and landings and stairs. Dusty sunlight seemed to filter its way around the many corners and crannies, giving the whole place a golden dream-like quality. At the end of the passage on the second level, Corrie stopped and opened a door, standing back to let Abbey step into the room.

It was enormous, with two sash windows, overgrown on the outside with ivy, looking out onto the house's riotous gardens. The double bed was high and puffy, with an old-fashioned patchwork quilt and white linen pillowcases and sheets. The yellow walls were splashed with faint red poppies, and an antique dressing table sat against the wall. The curtains were the same shade of faded red as the poppies, hooked back with handmade swags that looked like braided straw. On a chest of drawers against the far wall sat a buttery-yellow washbowl and jug next to a similarly yellow vase of flowers filled with real poppies, purple ones. The recent hand of Joseph Feehan, Corrie realised.

'This was Rose's room,' he said quietly, looking around and adding, 'You were born in here.'

He could remember the day as clearly as yesterday. Rose, scared stiff and lashing out, cursing and railing and blaming them all for her troubles, yet at the same time needing them desperately and hating herself for it. He'd thought his heart would burst that day, with anguish for his beautiful angry daughter and with fear for the life she was about to bring into the world. But from the moment Abbey arrived, everything changed. Even Rose seemed to fall in love with the little dark-haired, dark-eyed beauty who had given her young mother's soft bones barely a nudge as she made an easy entrance into the world.

Corrie had never felt closer to Rose than on that day, holding her as she held Abbey. He'd thought then that perhaps he could heal his daughter. That perhaps he and Fee and Avis could be enough of a family for her. But it hadn't been long before Rose was back to her old tricks, inflicting her own personal brand of pain and torture on those who loved her. And when Abbey was five she had hurt her father the best way she knew how, by taking his granddaughter far, far away and never bringing her back again.

Yet, here she was.

Abbey had moved over to the bed and was testing its springs. 'I don't know what to call you,' she said, looking at her grandfather with eyes so dark he couldn't begin to understand what was going on behind them.

'Sure, everybody else calls me Corrie,' he said, realising that anything more familial might seem strained at this early stage.

'I didn't have anywhere else to go,' Abbey said, almost apologetically. 'I hope you don't mind.'

Mind? Corrie could barely contemplate that this lovely, lonely, lost little girl might not think she was welcome here. He wanted to hold his granddaughter in his arms and soak up all her sadness and fear and never, ever let her go. But how well he knew that healing wounds inflicted by Rose would not be a quick or an easy job.

'Ah, sure, this is your home,' he said as casually as he could. 'You can stay for as long as you like.'

He made to leave the room. 'I know he doesn't look it,' he said, turning at the doorway, 'but Fee is poorly.' Abbey looked at him quizzically.

'The curd has turned,' he continued, 'which probably doesn't mean much to you at this stage, but it's something of a disaster.'

Abbey sat on the bed, unsure what to say.

Corrie forged on. 'We're too old for cheese—making it—anyway. The thing is, Abbey, Fee was only saying yesterday, would Abbey be a cheesemaker? Would Abbey come home and make the cheese? And here you are. After all these years. It seems . . .'

For the first time since leaving Ate'ate Abbey felt a happy little burr in her brain that she realised could be hope. 'It seems . . . ?' she echoed.

'Well,' said Corrie, trying not to overdo it. 'It seems right. Somehow.'

They looked at each other, a sea of unspoken questions and answers between them.

'I'll let you settle in,' he said. Abbey was holding herself back he knew, but if she would just stay here at the farm surely he, and time, and who knew what else, could help put her back together again. 'You'll make a grand cheesemaker, I can tell,' he said as he slipped out of the door.

Abbey lay back on the bed and tried to stop her head from spinning. The escape from Ate'ate seemed like a dream, as did the days spent crying inconsolably into her pillows at Shirl's house and on the long flight from Brisbane. Then there was the shameful scene the previous day at her mother's house. And the ensuing journey to a dingy b. & b. at Heathrow, then the flight this morning to Cork, the bus to Schillies, and the walk to Coolarney House. She'd come a long way in a short time, she thought, tiredly. She supposed she should have asked about her grandmother. What had happened to her? What did Corrie have to do with it? But the effort involved in finding out seemed just beyond her reach. Besides, the idea of being a cheesemaker had created that little nugget of hope that was humming happily in her belly and she didn't want it to evaporate just yet. Wafts of unconsciousness drifted in and around the pockets in her thoughts until, lulled by the mouth-watering smell of roasting meat juices, she slept.

'Did she look like a vegetarian to you?' Fee asked in the emptiness that had stayed behind in the kitchen.

'I'm not sure,' answered Kit. 'What do vegetarians look like?'

'Never mind,' said Fee.

Kit stood up behind the table. 'Look,' he said, 'I really should go find Avis O'Regan.'

'Not at all,' said Fee. 'You've waited hours, you can wait a bit longer. Besides, I need help peeling the potatoes and I want to talk to you about cheese.'

Nothing this guy said ever quite hung together, Kit had noticed. Yet strangely, it didn't seem to matter. Fee handed him some sheets of old newspaper, a bowl filled with dirty potatoes, and a small instrument with a rubber handle and a blade, which Kit presumed was a peeler of some sort. Where he came from, potatoes didn't have skins and were brought to you on a plate by a whippet-thin would-be actress with attitude. Since Jacey, he had not eaten a single meal in his own apartment, and even with her he'd only cooked a handful of times. He sighed at the thought of Jacey and concentrated instead on trying to operate the peeler without removing the top three layers of skin from his thumb.

Fee, watching Kit slyly out of the corner of his eye, was standing at the kitchen bench preparing a joint of beef. He knew he was right to feel the way he did about Kit. He'd arrived in Coolarney on the right day at the right time. And he had great long fingers on him. These were currently having trouble wrangling potatoes, true, but manual dexterity aside he bore all the signs of a natural cheesemaker. And he had the brains to work out what a dote was.

'So you've not done much with your hands, then?' Fee suggested, as another potato rolled away from Kit's grasp and onto the floor.

'Well, that would depend on what you call much, I suppose,' said Kit, looking under the table for the escapee and locating it with his foot. 'I work in finance, as an investment broker, so I'm on the phone and the computer a lot.'

'Oh, like a secretary?' Fee said, without much interest.

'Kinda,' admitted Kit, 'I guess.' Take away the zeroes and he supposed it was a bit like being a secretary. 'So Abbey and Corrie haven't seen each other in a while, huh?' he asked, changing the subject, his face contorting with the concentration required by the recalcitrant potatoes.

'That's right,' said Fee. 'She's been over in some Pacific islands doing good works.'

That figured, thought Kit. She did have that slightly bad haircut Christian look about her. 'And she's what? Like, his granddaughter?'

'That's right,' said Fee again, bashing thyme, garlic and lemon rind together with olive oil, using an ancient mortar and pestle.

'So where are her folks?' Kit asked.

'Well, we're her folks,' Fee said, as a clatter of feet outside the kitchen door heralded the arrival of what sounded like at least a dozen chattering females. 'Although she has a mother in London.'

At that moment, Lucy, hugely overexcited, burst through the door with Jamie and a string of cranky-looking pregnant women in tow.

'Hasn't Jesus only just gone and had six of the most gorgeous kittens,' Lucy chattered, reaching across the sink to fill a glass with tap water. 'You can fit two in your hand at once, although it's hardly advisable,' she said, holding up a scratched wrist.

As her jacket fell open and he caught the curve of her exposed belly, it dawned on Kit that she too was pregnant.

'She looks totally knackered, poor cow. So who do you think the father is? And what will Mary and All The Saints make of it? Oh, hello,' she said, suddenly noticing Kit and looking horrified. 'Jaysus feck! I'm after forgetting to tell Avis you were here!'

'Hi,' said Jack, sitting down next to Kit and taking the potato peeler away from him and pointing it at Lucy. 'Ignore her. She's high on life. Who are you?'

'I'm Kit,' said Kit, feeling awkward again. What was this place?

'I'm Jack, six months,' said Jack, scooting over so the pregnant twins could fit in beside her and peeling potatoes at lightning speed, 'this is Tessie and May, four and a half, and that,' she said, pointing to Wilhie who was pushing her spine into the doorjamb and squealing with relief, 'is Wilhie. Nearly eight. We are the pregnant singing vegetarian milkmaids.'

Kit laughed but he laughed alone.

'It's not a joke,' said Lucy from the sink. 'We're like a new species.'

'Yeah,' said Wilhie, ferreting through the contents of the cupboards in an overcrowded wooden dresser by the side window, 'the Pregnasaurs.'

Again, Kit laughed. He was sure now that he had stepped through some magical looking glass and was in a parallel universe. Wilhie eventually found the large tin of biscuits she was looking for, at which point the commotion in the kitchen grew to a frightening level. Plates and glasses rattled and banged, cupboards opened and closed, the refrigerator door seemed to be permanently swinging.

Into this melee appeared the figure of someone Kit instantly knew to be Avis O'Regan.

'He's here,' he heard Fee say from somewhere across the clatter.

'You're here,' Avis said. She bent down to where Kit was sitting and pressed her warm, smiling face to his cheek. She smelt of roses and dark chocolate, and for a moment Kit felt faint in her presence. He thought she whispered, 'You're safe now,' but before the words had even tripped over his ear, she seemed to be on the other side of the kitchen inspecting Fee's beef.

'Abbey's come home,' Fee said. 'I'm cooking a roast.'

'Abbey's come home?' Avis stared at him in disbelief, a tremor of excitement jiggling her stays. So that's why he'd been so cool and calm all day, the old fox, she thought. Of course, he'd seen it coming. That's why he'd insisted on sprucing up Rose's room. A less lovely thought occurred.

'So she's seen Rose then?'

Fee nodded as he seasoned the meat. 'She has.'

Avis searched his wrinkly round face. 'And is Abbey all right?'

'I'd say not particularly, just at the moment,' said Fee. 'But I'd say she'll be right soon enough. With a little help from her friends. And perhaps one in particular.' He nodded his head in Kit's direction.

'Oh no! Now you're not cooking things up that don't need cooking are you, Joseph?' Avis warned. 'We're not talking about people in tiptop condition after all. Wilhie—you should not be drinking that orange fizz at your stage,' she said in a louder voice. 'Have milk. God knows there's enough of it. Speaking of which,' she turned her attention back to Fee, 'what are we going to do about a cheesemaker?'

Fee nodded again at Kit. 'We're going to be all right for cheesemakers, Avis. We've got yer man and we've got yer woman. Who could believe such luck?'

Avis looked over as Kit tried unsuccessfully to open a jar of pickles that Lucy had handed him.

'Give it here,' said Jack, snatching it and opening it in half a twist.

'Are you sure, Joseph?' Avis said doubtfully. 'He doesn't look like a cheesemaker. He's not here for cheesemaking.'

'You can trust me on this the way you can trust me on everything else, Mrs O'Regan,' Fee said knowingly.

'Do you know about the wife?' Avis asked, worried.

'I know about the wife.'

'And a man in his state is all right for cheesemaking?'

'In my experience there's not a state in the world,' Fee said matter-of-factly, 'that cannot be greatly improved by close proximity to cheese. Especially our cheese,' he added.

Avis was distracted suddenly by an unfamiliar pair of legs. 'And who's that?'

Fee hadn't really noticed Jamie up until that point, but it was hard to ignore him now, being as he was standing on a stool in the middle of the kitchen, fixing the chain that held the pot rack hanging from the ceiling. It had snapped about thirteen years ago and ever since then the pots had been held up by one of Corrie's old ties. Jamie, though, had a pocket full of tools and was fixing the missing link.

'Oh, it's you,' Avis smiled. 'I didn't recognise you from that angle.' She peered up and watched a blush creep along Jamie's neck to his chin, which was all she could see. It was the first time he had ever ventured into the house and she supposed standing on a stool in the middle of the kitchen must have somehow made him feel less conspicuous.

'May!' Avis called. 'Don't feed Kit biscuits if he doesn't want biscuits. You're scaring the poor man!'

'Yer man and Abbey,' Fee said, smiling again, 'I'm telling you.'

Avis thought about this for a moment. It worried her. But there was no point arguing with Fee. Now or ever. It was better just to wait and see. She thought instead about the thrill that had begun in her toenails and ended at the tips of her Danish pastry hairdo at the thought of Abbey once again being under their roof. After all these years. She and Kit arriving at the same time, just when Corrie and Fee needed a new cheesemaker. It did scream of the magic of coincidence, thought Avis.

'Girls, girls, girls!' she called in a bid to quieten the rabble. The noise was high-pitched and quite deafening, and it was hard to tell who was talking to who. 'Girls!' she shrilled again, finally getting everyone's attention. 'A new and very special addition to the family arrived today.'

Jack clapped Kit so hard on the back he nearly coughed up a lung as the girls cheered raucously around him.

'Shh,' said Avis. 'I'm sure Kit is special, too, but I am talking about Abbey Corrigan, Joseph's granddaughter.'

The girls' babbling bubbled to a stop.

'Abbey has come home today after a long time overseas,' continued Avis, 'so we're going to make a bit of a splash on the dinner tonight. Fee is cooking meat for the carnivores,' she ignored the chorus of 'oooohs' and 'yucks', 'and I suggest you get back to the cottage and perhaps Jack could organise a bean casserole?'

She looked at her watch, it was after 7.30 already. The summer light always had her in a fix over the time. 'Back here at nine, then?'

The girls got to their feet with an astonishing array of different groans and whinges, then filed out noisily, leaving Jamie standing sheepishly under the pot rack and Kit sitting, totally shell-shocked, where he had been for the past three and a half hours.

'I thought I could come back after the cows tomorrow,' Jamie said to the room, looking studiously at his feet, 'and help you with the factory roof. The iron's coming away on the dairy side,' he cringed at his own noisy sibilants, 'and you'll lose three or four sheets if not the whole thing in the next big easterly.'

'Perfect,' said Fee. 'Then would you be staying for a bite to eat in the meantime?'

Jamie blushed again and grinned, then pulled a little screwdriver out of his pocket. 'I'll take the squeak out of that cupboard door while I'm here then?' He jumped down and set to work immediately, as Avis gestured for Kit to follow her to Fee's cottage where he would be staying.

'Three years!' Avis said, shaking her head as she marched across the courtyard. 'Three years and barely a peep out of the boy. What a day.'

'He's not usually that chatty, huh?' Kit asked, making conversation.

'He's been working the herd for three years and I've hardly heard a word,' Avis said. 'The poor thing is so shy he can't even look a Maria in the eye. I must have asked him a hundred times to come into the kitchen for a cup of tea and he's never shown the slightest inclination, but today . . . well, between the jigs and the reels it's a strange one, all right.'

'So Mr Feehan lives here too?' Kit asked.

'Ah, you'll hardly notice him,' said Avis opening the door of the cottage. It was tucked behind a stand of sycamores on the opposite side of the drive from the other farm buildings and had the same red roof as the factory and dairymaids' cottage, but was smooth stone painted white, not the exposed grey slate of its neighbours. Kit, who had to bend his head to get through the doorway, found himself in a single room with a fireplace at one end, another room off to the right and a tiny stairway at the back.

'I'll leave you to make yourself at home,' Avis said. 'You're upstairs. Mind your head. You should be all right without a fire, but if you get cold there's wood in the cupboard beside the hearth and there are extra blankets in your wardrobe upstairs. See you at nine over at the house.'

She turned to go, but Kit found himself suddenly desperate to ask her more. 'Avis,' he said. 'Do they all know why I'm here?'

She turned to look at him and he felt swamped again by her presence. 'Why are you here?' she asked him, more directly than he expected.

'To straighten out?' he said, feeling stupid. 'You know, to get back on my feet?'

'I'm sure you'll work it out eventually,' Avis said cheerfully, as though he had answered the question incorrectly. 'And in the meantime, perhaps a spot of cheesemaking could be considered therapeutic?'

'Cheesemaking?' he repeated doubtfully.

'That's settled then,' said Avis. 'And in case you hadn't noticed, it's a bit of a madhouse here. Nobody really knows much about anybody else and it seems to work pretty well that way.'

Kit looked uncertain.

'No one will judge you here, Kit,' she said, her warm eyes soothing his doubts. 'You are here to get away from it all and away from it all is exactly where you are—although away from what and for how long is your business and your business alone. You can do as much as you want here, or as little. We don't really care. We'll look after you, no matter what.'

In the blink of an eye she left the cottage and Kit, exhausted yet at the same time strangely excited, climbed the narrow staircase to his tiny upstairs room.

Corrie and Fee had escaped to the quiet of the smoking room for a pre-dinner snifter.

'Crack open the Coeur de Coolarney, would you, Joseph,' Fee directed casually, as if he ordered such a thing every day of the week.

Corrie looked at him with surprise. 'The Coeur de Coolarney?' he repeated. 'What would we want with the Coeur de Coolarney?'

Fee looked vaguely uncomfortable. 'Stop flootering around and get on with it, would you?' he commanded, rubbing his back for some diversionary sympathy.

'Well, I would if we hadn't given it to your woman from Goleen with the carbuncle on her face,' Corrie said. 'Unless . . .'

'Your woman with the carbuncle decided being single wasn't such a terrible thing after all,' Fee informed him. 'And you can stop looking at me like that and just fetch the blessed thing.'

Corrie, mostly out of curiosity, did as he was told and went to the C section of the bookcase. He hooked his finger into *Cheeses of the World* and opened a fake section of the library to reveal a small refrigerator-sized *fromagerie*. It never failed to enthral visitors who were keen to read *Cheeses of the World* but got to eat them instead. Corrie delved into this cheese supply on a daily basis and knew for a fact that the Coeur de Coolarney was long gone. Yet when he opened the door, there sat the heart-shaped brie, bold as brass and wrapped in cheesecloth, looking for all the world as though your woman with a carbuncle had taken a vow of chastity after all.

He carefully plucked it out and turned to his friend.

'That's for the new arrivals,' Fee said, by way of an explanation. 'You can bring some Gruyère out for us while you're over there.'

Corrie plucked a wedge of the Swiss cheese from the back of the fridge and carried it with the Coeur over to the cheese altar. He was at a loss to understand what was happening. The Coeur de Coolarney was a secret and scarcely used weapon in the battle for love. They made one of the brie-style cheeses every year on the first of June, the day that Corrie's grandfather Joseph Corrigan had decided to propose to Corrie's grandmother Mary Roberts in 1893. As soon as he'd decided to plight his troth, Grandfather Corrigan had walked up the hill behind the house and cut a tender new branch from the magnificent oak that had stood there as long as anybody knew. He bent and shaped the wood into the shape of a heart and with the milk of his favourite cow developed a soft curd, which he scooped into the mould and left in a dry box in the basement with two glasses of Spanish sherry. Every two days he turned it and after a month it had developed into a firm, smooth, heart-shaped custard covered in a white penicillin mould. Two weeks later, he met Mary under the oak tree where they shared the cheese, drank the sherry and began a love affair that spanned another seventy years and was accepted as the happiest marriage in all the country.

Ever since then, the cheese had been sought after by the lovelorn, and while it couldn't keep people together, it could certainly bring them together. Corrie had used it to help lure his wife-to-be Maggie into his arms, and Fee had used it the following year to help persuade Mary-Therese McGrath into his.

Since then, it had been offered sparingly to those who had heard of its powers, and the previous year bidding for a *Coeur* had reached an all-time high of US$2,067 on eBay. That particular cheese had been given by Corrie and Fee to Maureen McCarthy's niece Sheila, who was thirty-nine and unmarried—and, as Fee pointed out when they heard the price the cheese had fetched, obviously not as silly as she looked.

Corrie looked at this year's version. He couldn't really understand how it was going to help them, but then he couldn't really understand much right now. He had always thought that having Abbey back home would fill in all the gaps in his happiness, but it had been hours now and his heart felt more like Emmenthal than ever.

'It's all happening so fast, Joseph,' he said in a shaky and unfamiliar tone. 'Your back, the curd turning, the boy from New York City, and now Abbey.' His voice tripped uncertainly over her name. Fee said nothing and let him continue. 'I've waited so long for this day, for Abbey to come home, but now that she has, I'm at a loss. She seems so far away from the little dote that lived here all those years ago. I don't know her at all, Joseph. And she seems all sort of broken. Who did that to her? Was it Rose? Am I somehow to blame? I just can't make sense of it.'

Fee found it hard to watch his old friend in such distress. Corrie liked to make sense of things, always had, it was one of the big differences between them. Fee, who didn't much care for sense, trusted fate, perhaps because he usually knew where it was taking them. Most of the time, he could twist what he knew with what Corrie wanted to hear into some semblance of rationality and order, but tonight was different. He knew Corrie wanted to hear that time was a great healer and that if he left well alone it would work out all right in the end. That was Fee's stock advice and he was nearly always, in the end, proved right. But in this instance, Fee happened to know that leaving well alone was not the answer. Time was not on their side. Time was of the essence. He thought carefully about how best to broach this.

'I think Abbey had a bad run on the husband front and the sooner she gets back in the saddle, the better for us all,' he said, flooring his friend.

'Why does everything have to be about the one thing?' Corrie spluttered.

'I don't know,' Fee answered agreeably. 'Peculiar, isn't it?'

'No, no, no,' Corrie shook his head, frustrated. 'What I mean is that not everything *is* about the one thing.'

'It is so,' Fee said robustly. 'But it's also about our cheese and her salvation, so would you stop it with your bellyaching and open a bottle of wine. I'm dying of thirst over here. And you can take that face off you, too, Joseph Corrigan, I know what I'm talking about.'

'And what's wrong with your own arms and legs that makes moving about the place such an impossibility?' Corrie wanted to know, moving nevertheless towards the wine rack.

'So you'd mock a man in constant pain,' Fee said to Corrie's back, arching his own in dramatic fashion until he saw his friend's shoulders slump despondently as he stopped in front of their wine collection. 'Not that I am in constant pain,' he added guiltily.

'I've always felt that I could fix things,' Corrie explained to the wine rack. 'And up till now, apart from Rose, of course, and Maggie, I suppose, I think I've done a pretty good job. But I'm not so sure about this, Joseph, and this is probably the most important thing that needs fixing of them all. What if I can't do it?'

'Abbey is going to be all right,' Fee said in a tone that suggested it was ridiculous that anyone would think otherwise. 'Everything is going to be all right. It's business as usual, Joseph. She's like a fresh Coolarney Gold sitting in the cave. She's got to the right place at the right time, and given a good rub and the chance to let whatever's in the air do its bit, we'll get our result and it will be grand. Like it always is.'

Corrie's hand lingered on a Californian red.

'Saintsbury Pinot Noir,' Fee breathed enthusiastically before Corrie had even slid it out of the rack. 'Perfect.'

Corrie shuffled back to his chair with the wine in his hand and a pain in his heart. He envied Fee his certainty at a time when all he felt was doubt. Doubt that he had lived up to the promise he'd always assumed he had. Doubt that it had all been worth while. Doubt that he had done anything special in the world. He'd thought for a long time that the cheese was his major contribution. He knew that the cheese they made was better than anything with which the previous generations had trifled. That was thanks, mainly, to his thirst for ways to modernise and improve production—something his forefathers might have fought—and Fee's certainty about which direction was the right one. There was never any fiddling around with decision-making when Fee was involved. And, to be sure, the cheese was special, but he knew that wasn't it. That there was more.

Then, when he met Maggie, he thought maybe she was the something special, or the woman with whom he could do something special. When it became clear that was probably not the case, he poured his hope into Rose. As she grew up, however, he had cause to doubt his confidence in himself, and when Maggie left he wondered what he had done wrong to invite so much heartache.

'Would you stop fiddling with the wine and open it?' Fee demanded, snapping Corrie out of his reverie. 'I'm dehydrating in front of your very eyes and the cork is still in the bottle.'

Corrie wound in the corkscrew and felt his heart give a little jump at the happy 'kloop' the cork sang as it popped out, letting the pinot vibes escape.

Fee sniffed the air like a dog at the beach and smiled. 'And by the way,' he said, 'if you could stop wallowing in your misery over there for a minute you might like to remember the small matter of Avis O'Regan and the Coolarney milkmaids.'

Could a man never be alone with his thoughts? Corrie wondered silently.

'No, he cannot, now pour the stuff, would you?' Fee answered.

When Kit walked back into the rattle and hum of the country kitchen at nine, the table was heaving with food. The dairymaids were buzzing around like overstuffed honeybees, rearranging huge platters of food around the cheeses, jams, chutneys, mustards, pickles, loaves and dishes already on the table. Two heavy candelabras, one at each end, glowed with a dozen burning candles and, at their base, bunches of fresh trailing rosemary and violets added to the evening's heavy scent. Avis was heaping more vegetables into a dish and Fee was carving the beef.

Lucy, still ecstatic over Jesus's miracle of birth, grabbed Kit's hand and slid onto the bench seat behind the table, dragging him behind her. 'So,' she said, pointing her little pixie chin at him, 'you're from New York.'

Kit flinched. 'Yeah, I'm from New York,' he said, conscious that everyone could hear him now they were settling down round the table. 'Just flew in yesterday.'

He looked up to see Corrie walk in with Abbey, who looked bleary with sleep and in desperate need of a hairbrush. Her russet-coloured spikes were sticking up in all directions except on the left side of her head where they remained stuck down flat, giving her a hopelessly lop-sided look. She slipped in behind the table on the other side of Kit and slumped back against the wall as Avis did a quick round of introductions during which Abbey just blushed and nodded.

She was a strange fish, thought Kit, almost out of place, despite being, as far as he knew, the only one truly entitled to be there. Fee brought the meat over and sat it at the carnivore end of the table, where the smell of rich, juicy beef gravy reminded Kit he hadn't eaten since

Maureen McCarthy's that morning. He licked his lips and salivated; he couldn't remember the last time he had looked forward to food.

'Joseph,' Avis said, looking at Corrie, 'I think it should be you says grace tonight.'

The dairymaids bowed their heads and Abbey and Kit followed suit.

'Bless us, oh Lord,' said Corrie, his voice clear and strong, despite his earlier brush with doubt and desperation, 'bless this food and each and every one of us sitting here tonight. And thank you, Lord, for bringing Abbey back home and thanks, too, for sending us Kit, and also for giving us a closer look at Jamie Joyce, who could you remind me tomorrow, Lord, to ask would he mind giving us a hand with Old Fart Arse.'

The girls tittered.

'Amen,' said Corrie. A staggered collection of Amens spread around the table like a Mexican wave before food started being piled onto plates with alarming haste.

'So how long are you going to be staying with us then?' Lucy asked Kit, as she put Brussels sprouts onto her plate.

'I'm not really sure. As long as you'll have me, I guess,' Kit answered, taking the sprout bowl out of her hands.

'Oh, we'll have you for as long as you like, won't we, girls?' Lucy said saucily, and the Pregnasaurs fell into a group titter.

Kit looked up, embarrassed, and caught Avis's eye, which was rolling in the direction of Lucy. 'I believe I am going to attempt to make some cheese,' Kit said, to get the conversation back on an even keel.

Abbey felt a twinge of something that she thought could have been resentment. She had thought she was going to be making the cheese.

'Well, we'll be thinking of you tomorrow when we milk,' Lucy said to Kit, making a slightly obscene pulling gesture that had Wilhie ramming a table napkin between her legs to keep from peeing herself.

'Ah, now come on,' Avis said disappointedly. 'Is this any way to behave in front of our new guests?'

'Don't worry on my account,' Kit said, smiling at Lucy, 'I've handled worse.'

'I'll bet you bloody have,' chipped in Jack, 'and now's the time to raise your standards.'

'Stop them, will you, Joseph,' Avis said looking at Fee. 'I've seen all the *Carry On* movies I want to see.'

He stopped carving his beef and looked at her. 'You're a dark horse, Avis O'Regan,' he said, then went back to his dinner. 'Who's got the potatoes?'

Abbey picked the heavy bowl of spuds up from in front of her and handed it to Kit, for passing along. His little flirtation scene had permeated her armour of numbness and annoyed her. She supposed all good-looking husbands were the same. Shameless, the lot of them.

'So what do you know about cheese then?' she asked Kit, trying for a casual tone but getting a slightly snarky one by mistake.

'Not a lot, I guess,' Kit said, 'although my mom was always a big cheese fan so we ate a lot of it when I was a kid. And I used to live around the corner from this great cheese shop in New York, called Murray's. You guys know that?'

Corrie and Fee nodded enthusiastically. Coolarney Gold and Blue sold like hot cakes at Murray's and he imported a healthy percentage of their Princess Graces as well.

'Your mother was a cheese fan, did you say?' Avis wanted to know, a sparkle glittering in her eye. 'Where does your mother live, Kit?'

Kit swallowed and tried not to feel sick. 'She's in Vermont,' he said, wanting a drink.

'And your wife?' Abbey asked, again missing casual and getting snarky instead.

'I'm sorry?'

'Your wife,' Abbey said, pointing at the slim gold wedding ring on Kit's finger. 'How does your wife feel about you being over here in Ireland making cheese for as long as you'll be had?'

The table's jovial feel disappeared as the milkmaids fell quiet and the sound of cutlery slowing on crockery scorched the air.

'My wife,' Kit said, his voice suddenly husky. All eyes were on him, his knife and fork frozen and hovering just above his plate. 'My wife,' he started again, conscious of everybody's attention, as his cutlery clattered clumsily to his plate.

'Leave the poor bugger alone,' Jack suddenly said, crossly. 'It's OK, mate. You don't have to explain anything to anybody.' She leaned across Lucy to glower meanly at Abbey.

Kit tried to manage a smile and failed. He slowly pushed his knife and fork neatly together on his plate, intersecting the meal he no longer had the appetite for, then cleared his throat.

'I lost my wife three months ago,' he said, without looking up.

Fee looked over at Avis who was concentrating studiously on the contents of her own fork. Ah well, he thought to himself.

'Oh,' said Abbey, retreating behind her numbness again. 'Sorry.' She sensed the dairymaids looking at her with contempt and didn't blame them, she was a horrible person. Kit seemed like a nice guy, she didn't know what rubbed her up the wrong way about him—apart from the fact that he seemed perfect and everybody liked him.

'I'm married myself, you know,' Abbey said loudly to the table, wishing as she mouthed the words that she wasn't. 'But my husband was sexing my neighbour.'

Nobody spoke. For a start, no one was quite sure what sexing was. Jamie looked as though his eyes were about to pop out; Jack's mouth, full of food, was gormlessly hanging open; Lucy looked thunderous. Abbey herself couldn't believe what she'd just said. She had meant to say screwing or bonking or shagging but sexing had popped out instead. She felt a wave of dangerous emotion sweep over her.

'And she was having his children.' She abandoned her food and sat up, wiping at the tears on her cheeks and fighting to control herself.

Corrie looked at her flushed face and felt tears prick the back of his own eyes. Such misery! What had happened to his beautiful little girl?

Avis looked across the table and did what she had to. 'I had a husband once, too,' she said cheerfully, 'and a more miserable bollocks you never met in your whole entire life. Now, Abbey, will you pass the greens up to Wilhie, please? She's a demon for skipping her spinach and God knows it's the only iron the girl's ever likely to get.'

'Joseph,' Fee called from the other end of the table, 'would you be unwrapping the Coeur de Coolarney instead of sitting there gawping at the potatoes?'

'I thought we were going to have mashed as well,' Corrie said, entering the spirit of changing the subject as knives and forks around the table were picked up again.

'Well, I didn't see your highness volunteering his services in the kitchen,' Fee returned.

The hum of good-natured banter picked up and slowly buzzed once more around the kitchen, so that only Abbey and Kit were left silent and still at the table. Corrie unwrapped the heart-shaped cheese and, after translating a series of frightening facial expressions from his friend at the other end of the table, pushed it as surreptitiously as he could between them, both too steeped in misery to notice. The fumes of the Irish love cheese rose up and whispered invisibly between them.

'I really am sorry,' Abbey finally said, 'about your wife.'

Kit, still unable to speak or look at her, just shook his head. 'I'm sorry about your husband,' he answered, in time.

The tentacles of the crafty Coeur were sensing resistance, but nevertheless wrapped themselves around him. Kit wanted to get up and leave but he couldn't. He felt frozen to the seat. Naked and exposed and more in need of a drink than ever.

Abbey, too, felt as heavy as lead and was suddenly desperate to undo the damage she'd done. She wasn't a mean person, she knew that, and now she wanted everyone else to know that too.

The love cheese tendrils waved and wafted around her.

'Shake?' she finally offered timidly, holding out her hand to Kit, as, unseen, ghostly coils of ardour essence slid over it like a glove.

'Sure,' Kit said, and he took the hand she had offered in his own.

The *fromage d'amour* screamed with triumph and Kit felt a jolt, like an electric current, run up his arm, across his shoulders, and shoot down through his chest, via his groin, to the tips of his toes. He felt shocked, literally. He let go of Abbey's hand with a gasp and dazedly examined his palm, amazed to find there wasn't a raging red burn mark there. He swore he could still feel the tingle of her touch. He turned back to look at her and noticed, with another tremor, that her formerly flattened hair was now sticking out at right angles to her head. She was staring right back at him with a stunned look in her eyes, and he knew in an instant that she'd felt something too.

Corrie leaned forward and snatched the cheese away, snapping Abbey out of her trance. She looked at him questioningly.

'Smells delicious,' he explained. 'But tastes like shite.'

It was true. Those who had actually eaten the love cheese were repelled by its overambitious flavour and its tendency to give lovebirds breath like the water left too long in the bottom of a vase. Once the thing had done its magic, one was better off by far to stick with Coolarney Gold.

Chapter Twelve

'*If you can see the magic in cheese, you can see the magic in everything.*'
Joseph Feehan, from *The Cheese Diaries*

KIT STOOD NEXT TO AVIS, refusing to believe what he saw.

The morning air in the dairy was thick with the smell of effluent and milk and the sound of raindrops on rosebuds and whiskers on kittens. The Pregnasaurs were milking in time to the soundtrack of *The Sound of Music* and for a moment Kit thought the cows were actually dancing. On close inspection, they proved to be merely shuffling, but he couldn't be 100 per cent sure that it wasn't in time to the beat.

On the other side of Avis, Abbey was equally astounded. She'd had a grim night's sleep, feeling ill at ease with all around her. In the middle of the night she had come to the conclusion that she was once again in the wrong place at the wrong time. Here she was, Corrie's own granddaughter—and yet she felt less like part of the family than anybody else there. It didn't bother her that the place was full of unmarried mothers-to-be and other hangers-on. She felt quite comfortable with the aura of unusual. It was something else that irked her. Something she couldn't quite put her finger on. Something tall and handsome, perhaps, and just a tad goose-bumpy.

'What a sweet song,' she smiled up at Avis as the milkmaids harmonised over their favourite things. 'So when the dog bites or the bee stings, you're supposed to think of something happy. Sounds like that film *Pollyanna*.'

Kit peered behind Avis to see if Abbey was kidding.

'It's from *The Sound of Music*,' he said, incredulously. 'You know, the most successful movie musical of all time?'

Avis climbed aboard the tractor and started to drive towards the dairy.

'Oh, I never saw that,' Abbey said.

'You never saw *The Sound of Music*?' Kit couldn't believe it. 'I thought it was like, compulsory, for every kindergarten pupil.'

'Hello,' said Abbey, 'look around you. How many kindergartens do you see? I lived here until I was five and then we moved to London where, excuse me, I never saw *The Sound of Music* but *Les Mis* and *The Rocky Horror Picture Show*? Ask me anything.'

'Oh, I never saw either of those,' Kit said, moving to where Avis had backed the trailer to help load up the milk.

Avis watched them converse uneasily and wondered where this was all going to lead. She knew Fee had high hopes for the two of them but if she had to put money on it, she wouldn't. They were coming from different directions those two, and there'd already been one collision.

Kit and Abbey sat on the back of the trailer, their legs dangling over the edge, as Avis drove the milk to the dairy.

'So you do know about Julia Roberts and Meg Ryan then?' Kit was asking.

'What? Are they together?'

'No,' he said. 'About them being, you know, the world's biggest box-office stars. And you know about email and mobile phones?'

Abbey rolled her eyes. 'I was in the Sulivan Islands, not,' she tried to think of somewhere more remote, coming up, lamely, with, 'Iceland, you know. We had satellite television and DVDs before most of the rest of the world, including the United States of America.' In fact, she wanted to point out, if he looked very closely he would see that she was currently sporting Meg Ryan's haircut, thanks to the latest *In Style* and Imi's DIY hairdressing kit.

God, but she was a hard nut to crack, thought Kit. Anyone would think he had asked about *her* dead wife in front of a room full of people, not the other way round. Dead wife? He rolled the words over in his mind and wondered where on earth he could go to clear his head of Jacey. He was tired of the claim she had on his thoughts. Every time he started to appreciate where he was, she floated into his mind in a flimsy dress and brought him back down to earth with a dull ache in his stomach where he wanted a drink to be.

He squeezed his eyes shut as the trailer rattled and bumped over the crunchy turf. The morning sun was throwing the beginnings of the day's heat on the back of his neck, and it felt calm and soothing. He relaxed his shoulders and welcomed the warmth.

Abbey was watching him out of the corner of her eye. Something about him just made her want to swing out and give him a good slap. Was it because he was good-looking? she wondered. And well-dressed? And nicely spoken? And confident? And charming? And so at bloody ease with everything it made her want to scream? Or was it because of what had happened between them at the dinner table last night. Not the thing about the dead wife. No. He'd given her a shock, she was sure of it. Or she'd given him one. Either way the two of them had been zapped and she didn't know what it meant but she didn't like it. They had sat there after it happened eating cheese and pretty much ignoring each other until her extreme tiredness—jet lag, she supposed—had provided her with the excuse to sneak off to her room, where she had hardly slept a wink.

Fee had informed them the night before that there was no time like the present, and they were both expected to shape up for cheesemaking duties. All the same, Abbey had been surprised to find Corrie gently knocking on her door at six o'clock.

'Have you ever—'

'Is this the first—'

She and Kit simultaneously tried to break the excruciating silence between them.

'Never mind.'

'Doesn't matter.'

They both laughed humourlessly, relieved to be almost at the factory.

'Holy Mary, Mother of God,' Fee prayed, watching the two of them coming towards him as Avis reversed the trailer up towards the east door and the milk tank. This was going to take more than Coeur de Coolarney, that was for sure. Wordlessly, Kit and Abbey helped pour the milk into the tank, then at Fee's behest entered the factory for the low-down on Old Fart Arse. Inside, Corrie hovered in the background, watching his granddaughter like a hawk.

'So the aim of this heap,' Fee said, giving Old Fart Arse a thump, 'is to heat the milk to seventy-two degrees Celsius for fifteen seconds, a process which kills off a lot of the allegedly harmful bacteria and does the same to most of the flavour.'

'You think pasteurising the milk is bad?' Abbey looked confused.

'Well, didn't we all survive perfectly well without it?' Fee glowered.

Kit opened his mouth to argue, but decided against it. Abbey forged blindly ahead.

'Has the cheese not always been pasteurised?'

'Most certainly not!' said Fee, while Corrie murmured, 'Jaysus! Here we go,' from behind him.

'It's a recent requirement of the Irish health authorities,' Fee said with a forced smile, 'in case one in a million people keels over with some-thing that might or might not have come from an edible substance that might or might not have been cheese that might or might not have been made in this country. In France, of course—' he stopped and smiled a calm, smoothing smile to himself.

'Happy thoughts,' Corrie chipped in drily from the background.

Abbey and Kit shared an uneasy glance.

'We can talk more about that later,' Fee said, with forced serenity. 'Now,' he said, pointing to the outlet from the milk tank, 'our lovely shorthorns' elixir comes out of this pipe here and is pumped directly over here.'

They followed his finger to a collection of similar stainless-steel pipes that ran beneath the pasteuriser and turned corner after corner, like a huge French horn, eventually splitting in different directions around Old Fart Arse's barrel.

'Eventually the milk comes from here,' Fee was following a pipe on the other side of the pasteuriser now, 'to the cheese vat. We call her Anneke.'

'Hang on,' said Kit, still looking at Old Fart Arse. 'The milk goes from the tank through the pasteuriser and comes out here?'

'It comes into this vat here,' Fee said again, patting Anneke on the side, 'like I said the first time.'

'But it goes from this pipe here?' Kit insisted. He was back by the tank, pointing to the first pipe.

'If you can't keep up I can go slower,' Fee said nastily, but Corrie was smiling.

'Exactly what are you getting at?' Abbey asked impatiently.

'Oh, nothing really,' Kit said. 'It's just that if the milk comes out of this pipe and stays in this pipe,' he was tracing the pipe with his smooth, long fingers under and around Old Fart Arse, 'ending up in this pipe—it is in fact all the same pipe.'

Fee looked at the ground.

'And?' prompted Abbey.

'And,' said Kit, 'that would not at any stage involve actually going through the, um, pasteurisation process.'

There was a tiny silence.

'Well, if he's going to be picky,' Fee said in a slightly whinging tone to Corrie, 'he can feck right off.'

Kit chose not to take umbrage. His mother, actually, had always sworn by the locally made unpasteurised cheeses that were sold from farms around Vermont. He'd grown up with the strong earthy flavours of raw farmhouse cheese and didn't object in the slightest to Fee protecting Coolarney's original flavour, although he worried about the consequences of being caught.

'So you only pretend to pasteurise the cheese?' Abbey asked, agog.

'We pasteurise it when we have to,' said Corrie. 'Which tends to coincide with a visit from the local inspector.'

'But don't you have to keep records?' asked Kit.

'We certainly do and they're impeccable,' Fee answered. 'Avis does them on a Thursday night and I swear that woman has the neatest handwriting you ever saw. She could have been a nun with that handwriting.'

Kit was not to be distracted. 'But wouldn't you have to keep the records as you went? You know, times and temperatures and all of that?'

'Is he messing with me, Joseph?' Fee asked Corrie.

Corrie shook his head. 'We have stringent hygiene measures, highly safe and sensitised curing procedures, exceptional packaging skills, and Fee, of course, knows when—' He stopped and changed tack. 'Ah sure, I wouldn't dwell on it if I were you.'

'If we can continue,' Fee said pointedly, opening the valve and letting the milk whoosh into the vat.

The smell as the warm milk hit the clean stainless steel was almost overwhelming. It reminded Kit of babies and homes and kitchens: things he pretty much never needed to think of.

Abbey, too, was soaking up the smell. She could remember now being here as a child, when she didn't even reach the top of the vat. The floor seemed familiar, as too did the slurping and gulping noises of so many gallons of milk starting their journey towards something much, much more interesting. The air in the dairy was warm and wet and yet somehow strangely refreshing. It felt like the beginning of something.

'Once the vat is filled we test the milk to see if it has reached thirty-five degrees like so,' Fee said, sticking his elbow in the milk, closing one eye and poking his tongue out, 'and Bob's your rudd!'

'For heaven's sake,' called Avis through the east door. 'Stop messing.'

Fee looked sheepish and held up a thermometer tied with a chain to the side of the vat.

'There's no getting away with the slightest thing with Herself hovering around in the background,' he grumbled. 'OK, like so.' He dipped the thermometer in the milk where its digital reading showed them the temperature was in fact 35°C. 'You're probably better off using the thermometer to begin with,' he said. 'Then, when you know the milk is the right temperature, you add the starter.'

Corrie handed over a plastic cup that contained what looked like tiny rice bubbles. Fee poured it into the milk and gave the mixture a stir with a long stainless-steel pole that had a sort of potato masher on the end of it.

'Now, I don't want to go all technical on you because you're probably not able for it,' Fee said, giving Kit a particular look as he did so, 'but the bought-in stuff is basically a prescribed lactic bacillus. Good old-fashioned bacteria. We know exactly what's in it, where it's come from, everything about it. No surprises there, feck the lot of them. Put this in your milk and you will get cheese.'

Kit looked from Fee to Corrie and back again. 'And that's a problem?' Kit asked.

'Wouldn't no surprises be a good thing?' Abbey wanted to know. 'Wouldn't always getting cheese be a good thing?'

'Are yis undercover agents for the government or wha'?' Fee said grumpily, his ears turning pink as he concentrated on stirring the milk.

'Very occasionally Joseph has trouble embracing change,' Corrie said. 'Just ignore him on that account.'

'But why wouldn't you want the cheese to be the same every time you made it?' Abbey asked her grandfather.

Corrie answered quickly to head off Fee before he burst a gasket. 'Well, the cheese is basically the same,' he said, 'although really it changes from day to day given the girls, the grass, the milk, and whatever you're having yourself. But the differences now are far milder than they once were and the purists,' he looked at Fee, 'would say that a hundred years ago half the pleasure of a decent Coolarney would not be knowing exactly what to expect, just that you could expect it.'

'I guess that doesn't fit into a modern marketing plan, huh?' Kit ventured. 'The surprise factor's a bit harder to sell these days.'

'Listen to him, with all his modern marketing,' Fee mumbled grouchily under his breath, although privately he was begrudgingly pleased that the boy was onto it so quickly. 'Now, if you could stop talking among yourselves for a moment and pay attention,' he said importantly, 'you'd notice I am now adding the rennet, which is what makes the milk coagulate and form the curd.'

'Where does that come from?' Abbey wanted to know.

'Well, it used to come from the stomachs of baby calves,' Fee said, 'but now we buy that in too.'

'It's an enzyme,' Corrie butted in, 'that turns the liquid into solids and—'

Before Corrie could continue, an almighty cacophony erupted from the factory office.

'What the hell is that?' Kit asked, startled.

'That's Ruby and Marie,' Corrie said. 'They take the orders and deal with the office administration and they work very hard and we greatly appreciate them.'

'Not that they'd ever stop their clattering long enough for us to tell them,' Fee said.

An hour later, Kit and Abbey were exhausted from attempting to translate Ruby and Marie's patchwork of instruction. Corrie and Fee had left them in the capable hands of the two workers who had between them demonstrated the computer ordering system, the packing process, how to make four cups of tea with only one tea bag, and how to dance without using their arms—which came as a particular surprise to Abbey who had never heard of *Riverdance*. When they emerged back into the factory, Corrie and Fee were smiling into the vat. By now, the curd had formed and was floating in the watery whey.

'How about that?' Kit said, impressed. He'd never really thought about the process of cheesemaking that much before. That it started out drinkable and something made it edible.

'Now's the fun part,' Fee said, smiling. He handed Abbey a blade paddle and demonstrated with his own one how to weave and cut through the curd.

'You'd think it wouldn't be stiff enough to stay put and be sliced,' marvelled Abbey as she started cutting through the solid curd. 'But look at it!'

Fee handed Corrie's paddle to Kit and watched his strong, young shoulders manoeuvre the blade through the curd. In the morning light of the dairy, he looked, for a moment, just like Corrie had forty years before. Fee saw that Corrie had seen this too, and felt for his old friend. Of course it was grand to be delivered not one but two cheesemakers on a platter like this, but on the other hand . . . Life would never be the same, and they both knew it.

When the curd was broken down to crumb size, Fee pulled at a plug-like opening on Anneke's side and the whey started to course out onto the floor, flowing down a channel to a grill in the ground.

'Where does it go?' Abbey wanted to know.

'Back out to the farm, usually,' Corrie said. 'It's just water and a bit of protein, but it helps maintain our equilibrium.'

When about a third of the whey was drained off, Fee looked at Corrie. This was an important moment for the future of Coolarney cheese and they both knew it. Everything rode on what was about to happen. Demeanour remaining casual while their hearts beat quickly in nervous anticipation as they entreated their apprentices to taste the curd. Kit scooped up a handful and held it to his nose.

'Smell's sweeter than I would have expected,' he said. Fee felt excitement rising in his chest.

'God, it tastes delicious,' Abbey added, curd spilling from her lips onto the floor.

'Incredible,' agreed Kit. 'It's fantastic.'

Trying not to let them see his excitement, Fee dipped his arm into the vat. He lifted his hand slowly to his lips and closed his eyes to inhale its perfection. But before he even got it to his mouth, he knew something was wrong.

It was still there. Unmistakable. The taint of failure.

He shook his head ever so slightly as Corrie's face collapsed with calamity. He dipped his own hand in and swallowed a mouthful of Kit and Abbey's curd, willing it to sing and dance in his mouth, but it didn't. It sat in the audience. Maybe it even clapped politely, but it still sat in the audience. Ignoring his own disappointment, he nodded encouragingly at the apprentices, then left Fee to show them how to heat the curd again then drain it and pack it into moulds until each last crumb was spoken for.

When Fee found him some time later, Corrie was sitting in the garden on the bench, looking old and grey.

'If you really thought they could get it first time round you're more of a simple old bollocks than I thought,' Fee said, sitting down next to him.

Corrie just sighed. 'Is it him, Joseph?' Corrie asked. 'Are you wrong about him?'

'Well, I don't think so, but shall we give it, oh, I don't know, at least another minute before we give up all hope and shoot ourselves?'

Corrie sighed again. 'I suppose you're right,' he said. 'We'll just wait and see. What else is there for it?' They sat there in silence, watching a gentle breeze run like a ripple through the poppies in the garden.

'Actually, I don't think we should wait for too long,' Fee said eventually, sitting ramrod still on the bench. Corrie went to stand up, but Fee pulled him back. 'I don't mean now,' he said, avoiding his friend's eyes.

Corrie sat back down. 'Well, what do you mean?' he asked.

Fee kicked at the pebbles on the garden path with his filthy tennis shoe. 'I mean generally. I mean there might not be a lot of time.'

Corrie felt a pain rip through his chest as he processed what this meant. For the first time in his life, Fee, who believed in nothing much but time, didn't have any. Fee, who knew that it would heal all wounds. Who always waited, never rushed. Separated from time, Fee was not himself, Corrie thought. He was just a short, fat, cranky cheesemaker with bad shoes. It wasn't possible. He felt the pain in his heart spread and push a lump up into his throat and hot tears to the back of his eyes. He took a moment to compose himself.

'Come on, then,' he said, with a shaky smile and a confidence he felt a million miles away from, 'let's show them how it's done.'

'No, no, no,' Kit was saying to Abbey as they leaned against the benches packed with filled cheese moulds, the factory heavy with the smell of settling curd, 'she was training to be a nun but she got sent to teach the von Trapps instead.'

'Well, who sent her?' Abbey asked.

'The mother superior or whatever they're called,' Kit answered. 'I don't know, but Maria wasn't making a very good nun because she kept running up into the Alps with her guitar and singing.'

'You're clearly not up with what makes a good nun.'

'Well, I know that handwriting is important,' Kit said, but Abbey ignored him as Corrie and Fee appeared again. Kit wasn't sure if he imagined it or not, but she seemed to stiffen at the sight of her grandfather. He supposed they hardly knew each other, but still . . .

Fee looked around with pleasure at the sight of all his cheese moulds filled with curd, dripping happily onto the benches and the floor below. 'A fine mess you've made while my back was turned,' he beamed. 'Tomorrow we'll soak these cheeses in that salty solution in the big stainless-steel tub at the back there. In the meantime, we'll need to turn the moulds every hour to make sure the cheeses take on an even shape and also to squeeze out the last bits of whey.'

'The face on you!' Fee said suddenly to Kit. 'What's your problem?'

'Why do you have to salt it?' Kit asked. Years of nutrition advice at the gym he had frequented, before Jacey used up all his time, had steered him away from salt to the point where he no longer had a taste for it.

Fee huffed in an exasperated fashion. 'Saints preserve us,' he said. 'What do you think is going on inside this contraption?' Fee rapped on the nearest mould, sending droplets of whey spinning into the air. 'We've got something wet and warm to which we have added bacteria. It's alive,' he whispered dramatically. 'What we have in here is the result of our own specific equilibrium. Do you know about equilibrium, Kit?'

Kit nodded. He knew about equilibrium all right. Equilibrium, or lack of it, was why he was here.

'You take the amount of acreage out there,' Fee said, nodding in the general direction of the farm, 'the mood of the shorthorns, the nature of the grass, the amount of milk they give us, the time of year, and whatever's in the air, you mix them together and what have you got?'

'Bibbity-bobbity-boo!' cried Abbey. 'I did see that one!'

Corrie laughed, but Fee rapped his knuckles sharply once more against the cheese moulds, sending an angry message rattling down the bench. 'If you're not going to take this seriously . . .' he warned.

'OK, OK,' said Kit. 'I'm listening.'

You great girlie swot, thought Abbey.

'Just feel the heat, the humidity, the smell, the plain Coolarniness of this place,' Fee said, lifting his round red nose up to the air and waggling it. 'The things that are going on in here . . .'

He closed his eyes and sniffed, Kit and Abbey with him.

'What's going on in these cheeses is dynamite,' he said, snapping his head forward and opening his eyes to look at his apprentices. 'If it keeps going on the way it is now we could be blown to kingdom come.'

Kit felt the hair stand up on the back of his neck.

'What we do with the salt is cancel that bacterial life inside the cheese so we can gain control. The salt locks the flavour, freezes the equilibrium,' he said, 'so we can regroup for a moment.'

Frozen equilibrium, Kit thought. Regrouping.

'We're using alchemy: turning liquid to solids courtesy of acidification, with the catalyst of rennet to trap the proteins,' he continued. 'That much is chemistry. Anybody can do that. Monkeys, three-year-olds, investment brokers . . .'

He beckoned for Kit and Abbey to follow him to the back of the factory, where he headed down the stairs to the Gold room. He stopped reverentially and bowed his head (overkill, thought Corrie) at the door then slipped inside, entreating the others to follow. The smell was tantalising. Nutty, sort of, Abbey thought, and grassy, but with a hint of tamarillo, perhaps, or kiwi fruit. And there was a sourness to it, too.

'So, science can get everybody some of the way,' Fee said, 'but the rest is up to us and this is where it happens.' He looked proudly round the room at the neatly packed racks of cheese. 'We bring Coolarney Gold down here and wipe it every two days with a yeasty smear that gives a bit of a turbo charge to the flavour and makes it this pale yellow hue.' He pointed at the racks closest to them. 'It's not for wimps, Coolarney Gold. It's a cheese-lovers' cheese. Anyway, as the cheese develops and we keep washing it, it changes colour, till it's golden or even orange,' he said, pointing at the racks at the back of the room.

'No offence,' said Kit bravely. 'But it smells like old man's socks.'

'None taken,' Fee said delightedly, 'it's supposed to. Those are our older boys at the back there. Nothing like it anywhere else in the world. We've always had something different. Something unique,' he said.

The four of them stood and soaked up the Coolarniness.

'So what we do,' continued Fee, 'is we bring our perfectly calculated cheese made at the right temperature with the right ingredients at the right time—the stuff you made up there today—down into this room and we let something happen. That's always been the way, whether we made our own starter, our own rennet or not.

'We do what we can upstairs according to fairly rigid calculations, then we stand back and let the farm, the air, the rain, the moon, the room we're standing in make its mark and that becomes Coolarney Gold.'

In the dim light of the curing room he smiled on the racks. 'Can you believe it?' he said. 'The magic of cheese.'

Kit felt a shiver run down his spine. He was thirty-two years old and until recently a well-respected New York investment broker. He wore Prada shoes, Calvin Klein boxers and paid $100 every three weeks to get his hair cut. He had Louis Vuitton luggage, for goodness' sake. But he'd screwed up his equilibrium, and as a result here he was standing in a dingy cellar in Ireland regrouping. It's a strange old world, he thought to himself with a shudder.

Abbey, too, felt trembly and scared, but for a different reason. She wasn't sure if it was tiredness or stress or hope or fear, but the intensity of the curing room making her heart beat in time to the words her mother had hurled at her as she left the London flat.

'Just ask that old bastard what happened to your grandmother,' she heard Rose sob. 'Just ask him what's buried in his precious factory.'

Corrie turned to say something to her, but at the sound of his feet moving in the underground room, panic gripped her. With a strangled cry, Abbey dodged the old man, wrenched open the door and stumbled up the stairs and through the factory.

Chapter Thirteen

'If you think cheese is just food, you're an eejit because it is so much more than that. It's poetry. It's passion. It's pathos. It's no coincidence that milk and human blood are almost the same temperature. Had you thought about that, now?'

Joseph Feehan, from *The Cheese Diaries*

JESUS, AS IT TURNED OUT, was a bad mother. When Lucy ran to check up on the kittens, while Abbey and Kit were having their first cheesemaking lesson, it became clear that she had succumbed to the lure of the night and abandoned her newborns. Two little corpses lay under the tree next to the old blanket that Lucy and Jamie had put there the night before, and of the other four there was no sign.

Lucy was inconsolable. Nothing Avis nor the girls said could calm her down, and when Kit retreated to the garden after lunch for a bit of reflective peace and quiet, he found her sitting on the bench, hiccupping and grief-stricken.

After Abbey's abrupt departure from the curing room earlier on, Corrie had gone in search of his granddaughter while Fee and Kit stayed behind to smear the cheeses, an arduous yet comforting task that had worked up quite an appetite for the vegetarian pies Avis had made for lunch. Kit had gorged himself on Coolarney Blue and was feeling the need for a snooze in the sun, but Lucy's need for a shoulder to cry on was obviously greater—so he resigned himself to that duty.

'How could she leave them like that?' she wailed. 'They were only tiny babies.'

Kit was at a loss to explain. 'Perhaps it just wasn't meant to be,' he said. 'Perhaps it just wasn't their time.'

This only made Lucy cry harder. Her bony shoulders shook with grief and when she lifted her little girl's face to Kit, it was blotchy and mottled and streaked with mascara. She looked about five years old, Kit thought, and his heart went out to her. All traces of the flirtatious minx from last night had been replaced by this tearful girl-child; he scooted closer on the bench and put his arm round her, squeezing her tight.

Lucy sobbed into his T-shirt and Kit felt her tears wet and warm on his skin. He thought of Flynn and wondered how his own kid brother was doing. He'd sent him a cheque and a letter explaining that he was going away for a while, but hadn't quite had the balls to tell him why. Flynn knew about Jacey, of course, but not about Kit's problems since then. He sighed and held Lucy a bit tighter. It was hard to admit to himself that his life had spun out of control. How could he admit it to anyone else, especially Flynn, one of the few people left in the world who still thought the sun shone out of his butt?

Lucy's sobbing subsided mildly but she kept her head on Kit's chest. He'd never seen dreadlocks up close, he realised.

'I just don't understand it,' she said wetly. 'Jesus is normally such a sweet little thing. Mary and All The Saints are the mean ones.'

'Perhaps she just wasn't cut out for motherhood,' Kit said.

'That's what I'm afraid of,' Lucy cried, anguished, pushing her face harder into Kit's T-shirt. 'That's what's so scary.' She wailed even louder and the penny, for Kit, finally dropped. It was sad about the kittens, sure, but her tears were out of proportion. The hysterics, when he thought about it, were unlikely to be truly about Jesus's maternal instincts.

'Lucy,' he said, 'is there anything else that's bothering you?'

She blinked away her tears and nodded her head.

'Is it about the baby?'

She sniffed. 'Maybe,' she said quietly.

Kit started to say something. Thought better of it. Then said it anyway. 'Maybe,' he said, 'you're worried that you're not cut out for motherhood.'

Lucy bit her quivering bottom lip.

'Do you want to talk about it?'

She took a deep breath and sat up straight so she could look at him more easily. 'You're the only one who understands me,' she said.

'I hardly know you,' Kit answered with a brotherly smile. 'I'm sure the others would understand you if you let them.'

'I'm nothing like them,' Lucy said. 'I didn't even know I was pregnant until I got here. I could've been one of those girls that ends up on *Ricki Lake* having a baby in the toilets at a nightclub and not telling anyone.'

'That happens?' Kit asked.

'All the time,' Lucy sniffed again, her bravado making a brief return as she danced around the delicate subject of her condition. 'And then their mothers go ballistic and their friends all turn against them and it's a total nightmare.'

There was no correct response to that, Kit decided. 'So how did you end up here, anyway?'

'I just went to the bus station and got a ticket for as far away as I could afford.'

'Why?' asked Kit. 'What were you getting away from?'

'A great stinking bollocks by the name of Eamon Casey is what,' Lucy said with venom. 'My so-called boyfriend back in Dublin, until, you know—' Lucy faltered.

'Until what?'

'Oh God, I can hardly bear to talk about it,' Lucy said, screwing her face up again. They'd been going out for almost a year, she told Kit. Eamon played bass guitar in a Dublin grunge band called Oktober and she was in her first year of a music degree at Trinity College. They'd met at a mutual friend's party in a rambling student house in Dun Laighoaire and had declared themselves 'exclusive' straight away, or so Lucy had thought.

'Then a couple of months ago we were supposed to meet up one night and I got a message on the answering machine at home saying the band was having an extra practice and he wouldn't be able to make it. They had this huge big gig the next night down at Slane Castle, being the support act for The Red Hot Chili Peppers, so it made sense. Except,' her lip trembled, 'except that he was calling me from his mobile phone and he must have hit the wrong button or not switched it off or something because the message on the answering machine didn't finish when he thought it did, when he said goodbye.'

Kit said nothing. This was not going to be a story with a happy ending.

'He was with some girl, and he was telling her about me, calling me a groupie and a cling-on. He said I was a poor little rich girl with nothing better to do than spend my money on buying pints for him and the band.' Her voice got very small. 'They were laughing at me,' she said. 'And I think maybe they were in bed together. You know, bonking.'

Eamon Casey sounded like a class act, thought Kit. 'So what did you do?' he asked.

'I went out that night, drank seven Red Bull and vodkas and then I shagged Gordy Wilde, Oktober's lead singer,' Lucy answered. 'I knew it would drive Eamon mad because he hates Gordy. Gordy's gorgeous-looking but he can't really sing and he doesn't write any of the songs, but the fans go ape-shit over him. Anyway, he dumped me after the Chili Peppers for some seventeen-year-old who said she was a cousin of the Corrs.'

'What happened with Eamon?' Kit asked.

'Gordy told him but he didn't even care,' said Lucy. 'He told Gordy he could have me. Then the band voted that I couldn't hang out with them any more.'

'Do you know whose baby it is?' Kit asked, although he supposed it didn't make much difference.

'I think it's Gordy's. But I don't really know,' she replied, bursting into tears again. 'All I know is that I don't want it but I don't want it to know that I don't want it.'

She fell into Kit's T-shirt again and he let her, thinking of his own lost baby, which would have been due in a couple of months' time had Jacey not . . . Kit wondered what sort of a father he would have made. He'd never really thought about kids until Jacey came along. She was the first woman he had ever wanted to marry, to have a family with, to hold and never let go.

He sighed and felt Lucy nestle closer into his side.

'You're thinking about things a lot of the time, aren't you?' she asked.

'I suppose I am,' answered Kit.

'Are you thinking about your wife?' Lucy asked.

'Mostly, I guess,' he said, uncomfortably.

'What did she look like? Was she pretty?'

Long blonde hair down past her shoulder blades, a smile that could melt butter, legs like a thoroughbred racehorse.

'She was the most beautiful woman I ever saw in my entire life,' he answered, pulling himself away from Lucy and standing up. He didn't want to talk about Jacey. He wanted peace and quiet. 'I'm going to go take a nap now—I feel kind of whacked—but I want you to promise me that you will come and talk to me whenever you want to, Lucy. Whenever you need to. You know where to find me. Will you do that?'

Lucy looked at him with an adoration he failed to notice was far from little-sisterly. 'I will,' she said. 'Definitely.'

Kit trudged up to Fee's cottage and flopped down on his bed, his belly full of cheese and his head spinning with images of Jacey and babies and Lucy. His eyes drifted down towards his cheeks and, mercifully, he slept.

His dreams were not of his wife or the troubled Dublin teenager, though. They were of Abbey. No sooner had he closed his eyes than images of his fellow cheesemaker filled his head. In the dream, Abbey lay on her side in long warm grass, spreading gooey Coolarney Blue on chunks of farmhouse bread and licking her glossy lips with anticipation. Her dress had ridden up to reveal the curve of her hip and she wasn't wearing any underwear.

He walked towards her and all of a sudden she rolled over and was lying on her back on the floor of the New York Stock Exchange. Kit knelt down in front of her, her big dark hazel eyes pleading with him as he leaned towards her and bent his head, undoing the buttons bursting over her breasts with his teeth. She was wearing the sexiest bra he had ever seen in his whole entire life. It was pale green with pink roses embroidered on it and had tiny cups over which her breasts, blue and milky in the half-light of the abandoned Exchange, burst as the buttons popped open.

'Kit,' she said in a voice that seemed to clash with her 'come hither' body language.

'Kit,' she said again, her clipped tone grating on his subconscious.

'Kit!'

His eyes flew open and he realised with alarm that the object of his dream was standing in his doorway calling his name.

'Are you awake?' Abbey asked, stupidly.

'Yes,' he replied equally stupidly, trying to squash the lust that had him in its grip. He was hot and sweating and throbbing in places that he didn't want Abbey to see. He didn't even like her. Not in that way. Not in any way. She was too small and sad and not at all his type. She was the opposite of his type. She had a boy's haircut and women's hips; no straight edges, just soft round curves and a full heavy bosom that seemed out of place on the rest of her.

'Can I help you?' he asked croakily.

'It's just that Fee wants to know,' Abbey was saying, but when Kit looked at her mouth he couldn't hear the words, he could only imagine those lips on his belly, his thigh, his— Suppressing a groan that was equal parts embarrassment and ardour, he sat up straighter in his bed and surreptitiously pulled a pillow onto his lap.

'He thought that maybe if you and I,' Abbey went on, but still Kit wasn't listening. He was transfixed instead by the way her T-shirt had ridden up just a couple of inches and was now exposing a slice of smooth firm stomach as it dipped to and from her bellybutton. He felt spellbound. Bewitched. Dumbfounded. He hadn't felt like this since, well, obviously, Jacey, and even then—he stopped himself going further down that trail and squirmed on the bed.

'Well?' asked Abbey, stepping unsurely into the tiny room so that she was barely more than an arm's length away from him. 'What do you think?'

'Yes, yes,' Kit croaked, trying so hard not to think about his tongue on her skin that his face was contorted in pain. Jesus. He felt like some badly written character in a Harold Robbins novel.

Abbey faltered. 'Are you OK, Kit?' she asked, worried for him. He looked ill.

'Fine,' Kit gasped, pushing the pillow harder into his crotch and praying to God that she would leave. 'I'm fine. Please. If you could just—' He was about to explode, he was sure. He pulled his knees towards his stomach and twisted away from her, to hide the humiliating throb in his chinos.

'Kit?' Abbey said, alarmed now as she moved even closer, so close he could smell her. He closed his eyes and breathed in through his nose. For just a moment he stopped fighting his lust and concentrated on her scent. She smelt of green grass and passion fruit and limes and it was utterly intoxicating. Vodka, thought Kit. Vodka. I need vodka.

'Abbey,' he heard himself whispering, and her sweet citrus smell loomed closer. He felt the weight of her on his bed and the damp warmth of her hand on his forehead. For a heartbeat, he did nothing. Then he turned slowly towards her and opened his eyes. Her lightly freckled nose was just inches away from his, her dark lashes ringing the inky pools of her eyes.

'Abbey,' he whispered again.

She looked at him.

The moment was there.

It hovered, tantalisingly.

It waited.

And then he took it. With his heart hammering in his ears, he strained forward and pressed his desperate mouth to Abbey's, a groan of knowing it wasn't the right thing to do escaping him as he did. His tongue slipped through her lips and sought out the ridges of her teeth as he felt her hand slip from his forehead to cup his cheek as she pushed her mouth hard against his.

She was kissing him back.

In one movement he pulled her towards him and tugged her onto the bed. Wordlessly he watched her eyes grow bigger and her lips wetter as he pushed one hand up under her T-shirt, under her clinging sports bra, so his thumb could toy with the nipple of his dreams. She closed her eyes and parted her lips with a sharp intake of breath that Kit halted with his own mouth as he felt the full beauty of her delicious breast in his hand.

She pushed her pelvis towards him and he ground his own erection into her hip, feeling her buck underneath him. He lifted himself off her and moved his hand down her belly to the fastening of her cargo pants, which he undid with one deft movement, slipping his hand under her knickers and tracing the line of her hip, then her groin, to the warm, wet, juicy part of her abandoned for so long and crying now for attention.

He'd never noticed before but she had a perfect neck and, as his fingers worked their magic below, he dived gently into her nape and licked an outline with his tongue from her shoulder to her ear. Abbey's eyes were open but her look was far away. The feeling of hands on her body, in her body, was indescribable. It had been so long. She couldn't imagine it had ever felt this good before. Her breathing was getting quicker, she was sweating as Kit lifted her T-shirt and kissed his way down her cleavage. She pushed herself into his hand, then felt him lift himself up on one arm and fumble with his zipper.

This is it, she thought. What am I doing? This is it. What am I doing? Oh, my God! This is it!

She felt Kit stiffen and gasp and closed her eyes in anticipation of the climax. But instead of a host of heavenly angels singing a glorious chorus to her nerve endings, fourteen stone of Kit collapsed heavily on top of her.

'Jesus,' he said, looking at the doorway where Lucy was standing with a face like thunder. She spun round, her dreadlocks whipping round her face, and raced down the stairs in a clomp of Doc Martens—but not before Abbey caught sight of her murderous face.

The moment that before had seemed so magical stopped hovering and suddenly packed up and went, taking Kit's erection with it, leaving him lying on top of Abbey wondering how the hell he was going to explain himself.

'Shit,' he finally said, rolling off her and fumbling again with his zipper. 'Shit.' He closed his eyes and cursed himself for his stupidity.

Abbey, suddenly exposed in a trouser-less fashion, felt the sheer lightweight happiness of the past few moments drain away to be replaced by humiliation. As it seeped into every pore, she wondered how the hell she had got from a polite enquiry at the doorway to lying underneath Kit with his hand down her knickers. With shaking hands she fastened her cargo pants and, without looking at Kit, sat up and swung her legs over the side of the bed.

'I'm so sorry,' Kit said, reaching for her arm to slow her down. 'I don't know what got into me. I shouldn't have—'

'Not at all,' Abbey said quickly, with frightening politeness. 'It's my fault. I—'

'No, no, it's not you,' Kit said vehemently. 'It's just—' He wanted to tell her why it was not right. Why it was too soon. Why he should really thank Lucy for stopping it. But he didn't want to hurt her.

'Let's just forget about it, shall we?' Abbey said, as Kit floundered on the bed. 'I didn't realise that you and Lucy were—' She stood up and straightened her T-shirt. 'Whatever.'

'We're not,' insisted Kit, wondering if the situation could be any worse. 'I told her to come talk to me. She thinks she's going to be a bad mother like Jesus. Abbey, can we talk about this?'

Abbey didn't want to talk. She didn't want to think. She wanted to have sex. Not so badly that she would steal Kit Stephens away from the arms of a pregnant nineteen-year-old. But badly enough all the same. So, they really were all bastards. And she'd thought it was just the two she'd met so far. Well, if Kit Stephens thought she was going to be hurt by this rejection he could think again. There was a queue a mile long in front of him.

'I think all it's safe to say,' she said, turning towards him but not meeting his gaze, which was anyway lingering on a spot on the bedspread, 'is that it's too soon for both of us and we're hardly a perfect match, in the circumstances.'

Kit tried not to look at her neck and nodded. He agreed. Completely. Wholeheartedly. Or at least his head did. His nether regions, inspired no doubt by mere thoughts of the neck, were not so easily convinced.

Chapter Fourteen

'Of course, even a Coolarney Gold will taste like shite if you don't give it enough time to mature. Sure, it's only a matter of weeks but why drink vinegar when you can have Merlot?'
Joseph Feehan, from *The Cheese Diaries*

LUCY WAS MILKING as fast as 'So Long, Farewell' would let her.

The Marias were unimpressed by her ill humour and her fellow milkmaids were not far behind in that consensus although less inclined to kick the bucket. She'd been in a filthy mood for three days now, ever since discovering Abbey fornicating with Kit.

'Well, why shouldn't she?' Wilhie had demanded when they had extracted the truth after the first day of her evil gloom.

'You've got the hots for him, haven't you, you silly cow?' Jack had roared. 'He's too old for you, Lucy. And why would he want a pregnant nineteen-year-old when he can have, um, anyone else?'

She hadn't meant her words to be hurtful but they seared Lucy like a red-hot barbecue grill plate. Jack was right. Who would want a pregnant nineteen-year-old? No one she knew, that was for sure, she thought, wrenching on Maria's udder.

'Lucy.' She felt a tap on her shoulder and Avis's face was suddenly in hers. 'How would you like it if someone pulled your teats like that?'

Lucy narrowed her eyes. 'As long as *The Sound of* bleeding *Music* wasn't playing in the background it would be all feckin' right,' she said.

'Well,' said Avis, standing up and pulling her fawn-coloured cardigan over her middle in a gesture of indignation, 'such a rude and unfeeling young woman probably wouldn't want the sort of news I was about to deliver. You know, young lady, it's about time you faced a few facts,' she said, her smile and kindly face belying her crisp tone. 'You might get away with this sort of behaviour at home but in this family it is not tolerated. We will offer you all the help and support you need, but in return we expect at the least a little kindness, at the most a little gratitude, neither of which you have displayed in the past three days to ourselves or the Marias who have done nothing, as far as I know, to deserve the treatment you are meting out to them.'

Lucy, in her embarrassment, took refuge in her nastiness. 'They're only stupid cows,' she said, sulkily.

'Well, around here, Lucy, we treat stupid cows with the same respect with which we treat everybody else,' Avis said, looking at her pointedly.

Lucy blushed at the inference but bit her tongue.

Avis appreciated this small concession and softened slightly. 'Listen, Lucy,' she said, 'I don't know what is going on inside that pretty little head of yours but the truth of the matter is that no one ends up here, as I think Mr Feehan has already told you, unless there's a shortage of other places who will have them. You had better face the fact that you're pregnant, Lucy. You are working as a milkmaid. You are going to have a baby. You are going to be a mother. Whether you stay a mother or not is up to you—that's a big decision and one there's no rush to make. However,' she continued, 'what you decide will affect the rest of your life and the rest of your baby's life so you need to do quite a bit of growing up between now and the day you bring him or her into the world.'

Lucy opened her mouth to protest but instead burst into tears.

'But Kit's in love with Abbey,' she sobbed. 'I saw them doing it and you can just tell by the way they're horrible to each other.'

Avis looked at her in surprise. You just never knew which way the wind blew in these parts, she thought to herself. 'And what's wrong with Kit being in love with Abbey?' she asked, in a kinder tone all the same.

'I want him to be in love with me,' Lucy wept, seeming younger than ever. 'He's gorgeous.' And she launched herself, sobbing, at Avis's bosom. It was quite some time before Avis eventually managed to deliver the good news that one of Jesus's babies had been found alive and well in Ruby O'Toole's knitting bag.

Fee, meanwhile, was sitting at the kitchen table. It was nearly seven, Abbey and Kit were due any moment now at the factory for their fourth attempt at cheesemaking and Corrie had just announced that today, for the first time since the Greek flu of 1972, he wasn't going to work. He was going to stay at home with a John Le Carré novel and a Camembert and wait for elevenses.

'You can't leave me alone over there with those miserable bollockses,' Fee protested. 'I'll freeze to death stuck between the two of them.'

'It serves you right. You keep telling me everything will be all right,' Corrie said, 'but in the absence of any evidence—'

'All right, all right,' Fee interrupted rudely, banging his mug of tea on the table. The truth was that the cheesemaking was not coming together as quickly as he needed it to. He already knew what today's curd would taste like. Like it had his grandmother's toenail clippings in it. He looked across the table at his old friend and noticed his poor colour. The past few days had taken their toll. Fee straightened up and stretched his aching back.

'You've trusted me before, Joseph,' he said, 'and you can trust me now, evidence or no evidence. They've got the chemistry, even you can see that, they just need the time. And in the absence of time, they need a bit of a shove.'

'You talk about them like they're cheeses but they're not,' Corrie said almost gruffly. 'They're people. Chemistry or not, they don't seem to like each other and they're making cheese that tastes like toe jam.'

And I'm the one supposed to know what people are thinking, thought Fee.

'Not to mention,' Corrie was still going, 'you said there was no time to waste and that was three days ago, which means three days have been wasted.'

Fee said nothing. He didn't make the rules, he just knew when they were going to be broken.

'It can't be Abbey,' Corrie was saying. 'She's family. She's one of us. Our flesh and blood. It must be Kit. We've been fools to think a boy from New York City with no ties to Coolarney at all could make cheese just because he turned up at the right time. I know you like him, Joseph, but don't you think his teeth are too straight?'

Fee looked at Corrie as though he were mad and shook his head in disgust. 'Just because he turned up on time?' he repeated. 'There's only one fool here and it's you, Joseph Corrigan, if you're doubting him on those grounds. Turning up on time is all that matters, as if I need to tell you. It's all about timing. Everything is about timing. I've told you this a million times and still you don't believe me. I'm disappointed in you, Joseph, I really am.'

Corrie sighed. 'I still say it's the teeth,' he muttered as Avis appeared from the hallway with a photo album under her arm and a smile a mile wide.

'Oh, it's the teeth, all right,' she agreed, making much of bustling in between them and opening the 1970s album and pointing to a photo in the top right-hand corner of the page. It was of a beautiful dark-haired woman, about six months pregnant, smiling radiantly at the camera with a very tall, solemn-looking man, slightly balding, standing behind her. She was wearing a red and white gingham sleeveless shirt, flared out to accommodate her pregnancy, and red trousers.

'Greta,' said Corrie, recognising her immediately and running a finger over her face, then stopping, his eyes widening, as he realised the significance of her smile.

'It's the teeth!' Fee whistled.

'They're Kit's teeth,' Avis said proudly. 'I thought I'd seen them somewhere before. And then when he mentioned his mother being a cheese fan. Well, things like that don't happen around here without there being a reason.'

'Greta?' Corrie asked her, in amazement.

'Kit's mother was a Coolarney girl,' Fee said delightedly, clapping his chubby little hands with glee. Corrie looked at him for a split second then reached across and slapped him across the back of the head.

'Jaysus!' Fee was stunned. 'What did you do that for?'

'Why didn't you tell me Kit's mammy was a Coolarney girl?' Corrie demanded.

'I just did,' answered Fee indignantly, rubbing his ear.

'But Avis had already told me,' shouted Corrie.

'Well, why do I always have to be first?' Fee retorted.

'Because you are the one who—'

Avis stepped back and reached round the outsides of the two mens' heads, clapping one hand over each of their mouths as she did so.

'Gentlemen,' she said, resting one head against each enormous bosom, 'we have just made a very reassuring discovery that should be cause for celebration, not shouting at each other like common gutter-snipes. I don't know what has got into everyone today. There's trouble in the air. No wonder the cheese tastes like a certain grandmother's toenail clippings. What would be the chance of a Coolarney getting a bit of peace and quiet around here, I don't know.'

She slowly took her hands away and Corrie and Fee remained silent.

'Tea, anyone?' Avis asked, and they both nodded dumbly.

'A Coolarney mum, eh?' Corrie marvelled eventually, the beginnings of a long-lost smile playing on his lips. 'Next best thing to flesh and blood wouldn't it be, Joey?'

'Remind me about Greta, would you?' Fee asked Avis.

Avis sat down at the table, her hands clasping the teapot as a fond, dreamy look wandered over her face. 'Oh, I remember the day she arrived like it was yesterday, don't you, Joseph?'

Corrie smiled and nodded. He did, as a matter of fact. She'd been a favourite, inasmuch as he let himself have favourites.

Greta, Avis reminded Corrie and Fee, had been on vacation in Europe with her brother when she had succumbed to the charms of a lanky French saxophone player after much cheap Chianti and a jam session at the 606 Club in London's Chelsea. She'd settled in beautifully at Coolarney House, but seven months into her pregnancy was visited by an old schoolfriend with whom she'd been corresponding who begged her to marry him and return home his wife.

'Do you remember him?' Avis asked Fee. 'You must. We've not had that many rescued before. He was that nervous, the long streak of misery. Oh, my heart went out to the poor soul, and she was that happy to see him. Look at the smile on her,' Avis turned to the photo again. 'What a beautiful girl.'

Avis wondered how long the smile had stayed on Greta Stephens's face. She knew that the girl had gone home, seven months pregnant, with Ben Stephens's ring on her finger, but that her father would not speak to her. She knew that Greta had given birth to a bouncing baby boy named Christopher but that was all. Greta had stopped writing when the baby was still small, each letter before then slightly sadder and more disappointed than the last one. Avis filled in the gaps in Greta's life, knowing where she was headed as a twenty-year-old, and where she had ended up, sitting now in a retirement home, her head full of the adventures she'd never managed to have.

'She should have stayed here,' she said to the two old men. 'She should have had the baby here and gone on with her life.'

'I'm sure her family would not agree with you there,' Corrie said. 'I'm sure her family think she did go on with her life. And she certainly seems to have done a fine job of bringing up Kit, more or less,' he added, remembering the reason why Kit was here. 'Anyway,' he said to Avis, 'you know as well as we all do that just because you don't end up leading the life you thought you would, it doesn't mean you've wasted your time.' They had had this conversation many times before.

'You've got it all arse about face,' interrupted Fee. 'If she hadn't gone away, how would Kit have come back? We're one cheesemaker up on the whole deal so you can stop your bellyaching, the two of you.'

'Do you think he knows?' Corrie asked suddenly.

'I'd say he definitely doesn't know,' Avis answered vehemently.

'Can we tell him?' Fee asked excitedly. 'It might speed the whole thing up a bit.'

'No!' Avis and Corrie cried in unison. 'You know our policy on that sort of thing,' Avis scolded. 'What happens on the farm stays on the farm and no exceptions.'

'But doesn't he have the right to—'

'No!' Avis and Corrie closed him down again. 'Don't you breathe a word, Joseph Feehan,' Avis warned. 'Not a word.'

Fee lifted and then dropped his round little shoulders in an exaggerated huff. He knew they were right and he would not interfere, but it wasn't going to be easy.

'Still,' he said to himself, shaking his head as he went out of the kitchen door, 'a Coolarney girl all the same. Now, if that doesn't make sense I don't know what does.' Warmed by this latest development, even if he did have to keep it to himself, he hurried over to the factory where it came as a shock to find the temperature as frosty as it had been the day before, and the day before that. Kit and Abbey were silently cutting the curd, doing an excellent job, Fee had to admit, but he could just as easily have cut the air between them. The tension ricocheted around the well-scrubbed floors and benches and pinged off the vats and moulds, rattling the whole room with its horrible silence.

Fee's back was killing him and he knew without even tasting it that the curd was plain, but Ruby and Marie claimed the so-so cheese they had been producing was actually doing them a favour. They had months of back orders for cooking cheese that they had been unable to fill until now, so producing the stuff wasn't a total waste of time. With this in mind, Fee tried to put his bad temper and aching back behind him, and started to help Abbey and Kit pack the moulds. Before long, though, the chilly atmosphere got to him. It was as plain as day that the two of them had what it took, so why they didn't just get on with it he couldn't fathom.

'For feck's sake,' he growled suddenly at the pair of them, as the last mould was packed and dripping its quick-time drip on the floor. 'If the curd wasn't sour already, it would be now. Will the two of yis go downstairs and turn the Blues, I'm sick of the sound of you.'

Like sulky schoolchildren, Abbey and Kit turned and headed for the stairs, entering the Blue room wordlessly. Kit washed his hands in the basin by the door as Abbey stood behind him waiting to do the same. He swore he could feel her breath on his shoulder blade and started to sweat slightly before heading to the opposite end of the room, leaving Abbey to start on the racks nearest the door.

This was the first time they had been alone in a small place since the near-sex episode of three days before, and he felt slightly panicked. His head and his body had totally different opinions about Abbey and it made being close to her physically difficult, to say the least. There was no doubt in his mind that a weird sort of chemistry existed between the two of them, but he hadn't the faintest clue what to do about it.

She didn't like him and he didn't like her, and as soon as his hormones got a grip on that, the better. Crouching to turn the cheeses on the lowest shelf, he glimpsed through the racks and saw Abbey's hands snake deftly round a perfect Coolarney Blue and flip it. She did have very nice hands.

His own hands sought out his next cheese and turned it. The rind felt cool and slightly damp to touch and the sound it made as he dropped it back on the rack was a good sound. It was as though the cheese sighed a happy sigh when it got back on familiar territory. As though just a nanosecond out of its comfort zone was a nanosecond too long. You knew where you were with cheese, Kit thought. You knew what it needed and how to give it that. He supposed that was what Fee had been trying to tell them the first day they gathered down here, when Abbey had freaked out and run away. All you had to do was look after the stuff to a certain point and then you could rely on it finishing the job itself. He realised that he and Abbey were turning the cheeses in perfect time, the muffled *plumpf* of the cheeses' overturned sides hitting the rack simultaneously forming a fractured almost funky beat. He peered through the racks again as Abbey's hands, a rack higher now, worked their magic. He tried not to think about her and began instead to think of state capitals, starting with Alaska.

Abbey, too, could hardly ignore the uninvited tension that appeared between herself and Kit whenever they were in the same room and was also trying to quash it. Kit was a sexual predator hell-bent on deflowering her, Lucy, most likely Jack, Wilhie and even Avis O'Regan, she tried to convince herself as her fingers sought the moist sides of the fresh Coolarneys and flipped them. He was a prick of the highest order and she should have reported him to the, um . . . she wondered who she should have reported him to. Her grandfather? Hmm. His mother? Hmm. And anyway, what would she report? She was the one who had gone to his bed and felt his head. But he had seemed ill, she argued with herself. But you could have established that from the doorway, herself came back. But I tried that and it didn't work, she continued. And kissing him did? herself countered sarcastically.

It was hopeless trying to think of anything else, she realised. They should just turn all the cheeses and get the hell out of there before the whole place went up in smoke or melted or something. She'd spent the three days since the embarrassing close encounter trying to work out what to do with her life and where to do it. On one hand, it seemed pathetic that she was twenty-nine years old and had nowhere else to go apart from her grandfather's farm in the country. But on the other hand, the feeling that she constantly fought about being in the wrong place at the wrong time had diminished over the past few days to the point where she suspected that the funny little buzz she got in her belly when she woke up in the morning meant she was close to being home. Not to mention, she reminded herself as she moved a rack closer to the middle of the room, the way she felt about the cheese.

The swoosh of the milk into the vat first thing in the morning made her bones tingle. She swore the blood pulsed quicker through her veins at the very sight of it. After just four days she could feel muscles in her arms high-fiving each other with every slice of the curd-cutting paddle. And the feel of the sweet, squeaky stuff between her fingers? It made her want to scream, the same way the feel of the fat, soft spongy arm of a happy milk-fed baby made her want to scream. In a good way.

She leaned in towards a cheese hiding at the back of the rack and found herself staring suddenly into Kit's troubled eyes, peering at her from the other side. Abbey sucked in her breath and stood back. They had met in the middle of the room.

'Do you want to talk about this?' Kit said, mooching down slightly to look at her across the top of a tasty two-week-old.

'Talk?' she repeated, flustered, her heart beating a little too quickly for her liking. 'About what?'

'About this whole thing,' Kit said, absently turning another cheese. He hadn't meant to say anything at all, especially anything like that, but it had just popped out. 'I think you know as well as I do that ever since that first night there has been this great big scary sort of hot kind of thing between us, and whether we like it or not it is there and as mature adults we should decide what we want to do about it.'

Abbey was frightened by his honesty. In a thrilled sort of a way.

'Corrie and Fee want us to make cheese together,' she said lamely, her own hands tightly gripping an as-yet-unturned cheese.

'I'm not talking about cheese,' said Kit, squeezing his own so hard in frustration that he rendered it unsaleable. 'I'm talking about you and me and whatever the hell this zing is between us. Jesus, Abbey, I have spent three days trying to fight it but I just can't stop thinking about you. Every moment of the day you're either there right in front of me or inside my head. I can't explain it but it's driving me nuts and I want to talk about it.'

'You Americans just want to talk about everything,' Abbey said attempting a lighter tone, and failing. Kit said nothing and she felt sorry for him. It had been brave to bring the whole humiliating subject up and the least she could do was admit she knew what he was talking about.

'It's the same,' she finally said, digging her thumbnails into the Coolarney she was still gripping. 'It's the same for me. I don't know what to do about it, either. I don't know what to do about anything.'

'You can't stop thinking about me?' Kit asked, looking at her, a bit of colour creeping back into his cheeks, a light in his eye.

'You're not even my type,' insisted Abbey, ignoring the question.

'Oh, that's OK,' Kit added enthusiastically. 'That's fine. That's great, in fact. You're not my type, either.'

There was another silence.

'It's just that I haven't felt like this about anyone for a long, long time and I'm not sure that I want to now,' Abbey said slowly, realising as she spoke that it was true.

'Well, if it's any consolation, I definitely don't want to, but I still do,' Kit said. 'Does that make sense?'

They looked at each other across the cheeses. Kit had never noticed before how quiet the curing room was. Dead quiet. He could swear the Blues were listening.

'So,' Abbey asked, 'how would it work?'

'You mean us?' Kit answered. 'I don't know. I guess we could decide that as long as we are both here making cheese then we should stop fighting whatever it is that's in the air that's making us so crazy for each other.'

'You're crazy for me?' Abbey asked, smiling, releasing her grip, finally, on the poor mashed Coolarney Blue in her hands and starting to move slowly towards the end of the rack.

'Yeah,' smiled Kit, dumping his own strangled cheese and moving in the same direction. 'I am. You know, in a wanting-to-get-naked kind of way.' They met, face to face, at the end of the rack and looked at each other.

'What about—' Abbey started to say but Kit put his finger to her lips. It tasted of honey and sunshine and blue mould and him.

'What about nothing,' he said, and he took her in his arms and kissed her like he'd never kissed anybody before.

'What in the name of Jesus do you two think you are doing?'

Avis's loud hiss gave Corrie and Fee such a fright that they rose from their crouched positions outside the Blue door with great speed, bonking their heads together in the process.

'Jaysus,' cried Fee, holding his temples with both hands. 'You've broken it.'

'What do you keep in there, you eejit, bowling balls?' Corrie moaned, rubbing the front of his own head where a medium-sized egg was already forming.

'You two should be ashamed of yourselves,' Avis said, towering over them, hands on hips. 'Grown men eavesdropping on two troubled young people. It's disgusting.'

'We were not eavesdropping,' said Corrie, wobbling on his feet. 'I dropped something on the floor and Fee was helping me look for it.'

'Oh yes,' said Avis, 'and what would that be?'

'Something very, very small,' said Fee, concentrating on his head still.

'Is that right?' Avis said, not letting up. 'How small?'

The two men looked at each other. 'So small it doesn't even have a name,' Fee said, proudly.

Corrie rolled his eyes, whimpering at the pain this caused in his head. 'Is that the best you can come up with? So small it doesn't even have a name?'

'It's a terrible thing, concussion,' Fee answered cheerfully, earning an extra headshake from Avis.

'Go away and leave them alone,' she said, 'before I take my broom to the pair of you.'

'Go on,' said Fee, a mischievous glint in his eye, 'you want to know just as much as we do.'

'Of course I do,' said Avis, 'but I'm not going to listen into them. You should know better than to show such disrespect for other people's privacy, Joseph. Anyway, I only came to tell you that it's low-blood-sugar time so I've left a freshly baked brack and a pot of tea in the smoking room. If you get over there now it'll still be hot.'

Abbey was so hungry for Kit she couldn't think straight. Their kisses were desperate with unleashed passion and their hands were tracing hurried routes over each other's bodies as though scared they would never find their way to the good bits again. Abbey was pressed against the wall and had one leg wrapped around Kit's thigh, her groin pushed hard against his as his kisses devoured her. Her bottom half had long surrendered to his touch but her mind was still fighting something, not him, but something.

'I'm not sure,' she whispered to the ceiling as his lips burned up her neck. 'Perhaps we could,' she mumbled as his mouth found hers and nibbled at her lips, a helpless groan escaping him. 'Oh,' she tried again, as she smelt the clean freshness of his hair and he fitted his knee up between her thighs, lifting her higher against the wall.

'Kit,' she cried, louder, suddenly sure what was wrong and pulling her head away from him in panic. 'Not here!'

Her fear finally registered with him and he stepped back, panting. She was trembling, and not, he was certain, because of him.

'What is it, Abbey?' he asked as gently as a man knobbled in the throes of wild passion could. 'What's the matter?'

'Not down here, that's all. Just not down here,' she said, not meeting his eyes. Frustration wasn't a big enough word for what Kit was feeling. He knew she wanted him as much as he wanted her and he couldn't for the life of him work out why she was pulling the plug.

'Here, there, anywhere,' he said. 'Does it really matter?'

'It's not you,' Abbey said. 'It's here.'

Kit thought again of her flight from the curing room on their first cheesemaking day. 'Did something happen to you down here?' he asked.

Abbey felt hysteria nipping at her edges. She knew it was stupid, that she was stupid, but she couldn't fight the fear. 'Not me,' she said, as Kit put his hands on her shoulders and leaned down to make sure he was looking in her eyes.

'Then who? What happened? Tell me.'

'My grandmother,' Abbey whispered, tears gathering in pools at the bottom of her big brown eyes. 'My mother told me . . . Oh my God, I can't believe I'm telling you this.' She took a deep breath. 'I think Corrie buried my grandmother down here,' she said.

Kit's eyes widened.

'You think Corrie buried your grandmother down here in the caves?' he asked.

Abbey nodded, an enormous weight lifting off her shoulders at the relief of having shared her terrible doubts about a man they were all convinced was so kind and sweet and helpful and dear.

'Why?' asked Kit. 'What's wrong with the cemetery?'

'Oooh,' Abbey shook her head and banged her clenched fists against the wall behind her in frustration. 'You don't understand. I think he buried her—in secret—after, you know, doing away with her.'

'Doing away with her?' Kit asked incredulously.

She nodded.

'With his own bare hands?'

She nodded again, although she hadn't actually thought about that.

'You think he did away with his wife with his own bare hands and then buried her down here with all this beautiful cheese under this stone floor that we're standing on right now?'

Abbey nodded, her tears spilling over her cheeks.

'This stone floor?' Kit asked again, stamping one of his feet on the ground. 'This smooth, flat, unlined floor with no body-sized holes in it?'

Abbey nodded again. 'I suppose,' she said.

'What are you? Nuts?' Kit said, lifting his hands off her. 'You think your own grandfather would do something like that? Jesus, Abbey, I mean does the guy really strike you as a murderer?'

It took a few moments for Abbey to realise that Kit was not agreeing with her. The weight came back and landed squarely on her shoulders again. Why had she told him?

'Well, what would you know?' she said, angry at having let down her guard. 'You don't know anything about him.'

'Yeah, well, you don't know anything about him either,' Kit said, not unpleasantly exactly but with some frustration. 'You've been gone since you were five and your mom has obviously been filling your head with garbage about the poor guy. But think about it, Abbey. Would your grandfather really want a rotting cadaver stinking up the very air that he relies on for the flavour of his precious cheese?'

'That's my grandmother you're talking about,' Abbey said angrily but Kit just laughed.

'Corrie, a murderer? Jesus, he must have laughed his head off when you put that to him. I mean, what did he say? Did he confess immediately and beg to be brought to justice?'

Abbey looked away and Kit knew then, for sure, that she had not asked her grandfather about his wife. That that was the reason why she stiffened whenever he came into a room and seemed so uneasy in his presence.

'Oh, for Pete's sake, Abbey,' he said. His heart, to his own surprise, suddenly full of sympathy for her. She was so complicated it wasn't funny. It was very unfunny. She hung her head.

'It sounds silly, I know, now that I say it out loud,' she said. 'But why else would she run away and never come back? Why else would she keep me away from him all these years? You don't do that stuff for nothing, you know.' She wiped her nose with the back of her hand and Kit pulled her towards him and took her in his arms.

'I don't know why she did what she did,' he answered truthfully, 'but I do know you need to talk to your grandfather about all this.' He leaned back and pulled Abbey's chin up so he could look her in the eye. 'And I promise that when he calls the Twinkie-mobile to come and drag you to the nearest nut farm, I will fight him with all the strength in my body.'

If I have any left, he thought to himself, after all the effort of not throwing you to the ground and having you right here and now, dead murdered rotting cadaverous grandmother or not.

Chapter Fifteen

'Your troubles are like germs, you can't bring them into the cheese factory. Cheese is sensitive, it can tell if something is weighing heavy on your heart.'

Joseph Feehan, from *The Cheese Diaries*

CORRIE AND FEE were sitting in the smoking room with an aged Cheddar Fee had fossicked out of the *fromagerie*. Avis's tea had gone cold, and anyway they both felt their separate headaches would be improved with a bit of a tipple.

Corrie had something he knew would be perfect for the match and was not even halfway to the wine rack when Fee crowed with delight.

'You're right,' he said. 'A Chilean Merlot. Who would have thought?'

'You won't know this one,' said Corrie. 'I got it sent over from London specially.'

'Casa Lapostolle Clos Apalta, if that's how you say it,' said Fee. 'Well done yourself.'

Corrie was torn between being highly impressed and highly irritated. Was there nothing he could do to surprise the little toad? The little toad looked at him and shook his head, beaming from ear to ear as he watched the wine being opened.

'Do you think you could do us all a favour and cheer up a bit?' Fee asked.

The truth was, Corrie was scared to be happy. They thought they had overheard hopeful sounds coming from the curing room, but what say they were wrong?

'For the love of God!' cried Fee, reading his thoughts. 'Would it kill you to look on the bright side for a bit? Abbey's come home, there's a fellow wants to make cheese and who knows what else with her, the sun is shining, and everything is going to be all right.'

'I'm not sure she likes him,' said Corrie. 'And I'm not sure she's wild about us either.'

'She seems to like me all right,' Fee said. 'So what could she possibly have against you?'

Corrie sliced off a chunk of mature cheese and scooped it into his mouth, its zesty zing giving him a brief respite from his depression. 'Well, I can't be absolutely sure,' he said slowly, 'but she seems to be scared of me, Joseph, and all I can think is that Rose has been telling her things that have frightened her.'

Fee took a sip of wine and savoured it, then swallowed. 'So,' he said eventually, 'she knows they're not your own teeth?'

Corrie ignored the poor attempt at humour and pressed on. 'It'll be to do with Maggie, like it always was. I think Rose might have been up to her old tricks again, Joseph, telling Abbey stories abut Maggie. Her favourite stories.' For the first time in a long time, he felt his age. He felt old and achey and slightly confused and not sure what to do about any of it. He had thought having Abbey back home would be the best thing that could ever happen to him. He had waited for it for so long. Yet, here she was and here he was. The two of them, miserable.

And the cheese, more miserable again. Fine for cooking, no doubt, but where was the magic? And Fee. You wouldn't know to look at him tucking into the crumbly Cheddar that his days were numbered. But the curd was never wrong. And did he seem even slightly bothered by the distressing turn events had taken? He did not, thought Corrie, sinking further into the mire.

Just then, Abbey burst in the door. It was the first Corrie had seen of her all day and she looked flushed and defiant yet anxious at the same time. He'd been right to think she was scared of him and it saddened his old heart more than anything else that had happened.

Fee's fat hand stretched out for another chunk of cheese and it was all he could do to keep a smile off his face. Perhaps, now, they were going to get somewhere.

'What happened to my grandmother?' Abbey demanded breathlessly, standing, legs apart, arms folded, in front of Corrie. 'What did you do to her?'

Corrie put down his wineglass and looked at Fee in an I-told-you-so sort of a way. 'I don't know what your mother has told you,' he started.

'I've asked you a direct question,' Abbey said, hands on her hips now, 'and I want a direct answer. What happened to my grandmother?'

'There's nothing I can tell you about your grandmother that will make anybody feel any better,' Corrie said calmly, but Fee could see his hands were trembling. 'There's no good can come from it.'

'Well, I can't stay here if I don't know,' Abbey said, stamping her foot like a five-year-old. 'I can't and I won't.'

Good girl yourself, Fee thought from the sidelines. Perhaps she had guts after all.

'Well, I can't tell you,' Corrie said sadly. 'But I don't want you to go.'

'Well, I think you should tell her,' Fee piped up.

'And what would you know?' Corrie said crossly.

'More than the two of you put together,' Fee answered.

'Excuse me,' Abbey said, trying to steer the conversation back to her-self. It was now or never, she knew. 'What can't you tell me?'

'There you go,' said Fee. 'If you tell her what it is you can't tell her then officially you haven't really told her.'

'Don't be ridiculous,' Corrie said to his friend. 'You've been watching too much *Father Ted*. I keep telling you that real life's not like that.'

'Don't be such a stick-in-the-mud,' Fee said robustly. 'Real life's what you make of it. Just put the poor girl out of her misery.'

'Ah, Joseph,' Corrie shook his head, 'didn't we always say . . . ?'

'Ah, Joseph, yourself,' Fee scoffed. 'Didn't we always say we didn't want the truth to hurt anybody but it's not knowing the truth that's hurt-ing yer woman. I don't want to put any pressure on you, Joseph, but as she holds the future to the entire Coolarney empire right there in her hot little hands, why don't you just go ahead and tell her?'

'There's nothing to be gained from dredging up the past,' Corrie insisted.

Abbey could not believe his callousness. 'I'm not asking you to exhume her,' she said incredulously. 'I'm asking you to tell me what you did to her.'

Exhume her? Fee mouthed across the room. So Rose had been up to her old tricks.

'Holy Mary, Mother of God,' Corrie said. 'Sit down, Abbey. It's really not what you think.' There really was nothing else for it. He looked at Fee, took a deep breath and faced his granddaughter. 'Your grandmother left me for another woman,' he said.

Abbey was stunned. 'For another woman?' she repeated stupidly. 'Who?'

'Mary-Therese McGrath,' Fee answered. 'The one-time future Mrs Joseph Feehan.'

Corrie and Fee both reached for the cheese.

'My grandmother ran off with your girlfriend?' Abbey looked at Fee.

'Fiancée,' Fee said nonchalantly, licking his lips, 'and that's the truth of the matter.'

Abbey's head was awhirl. Whatever she had expected Corrie to tell her, it wasn't that. Her defiance fizzled out, leaving confusion in its place. 'So she's not dead then?' she checked.

'Not according to the latest postcard,' Corrie answered.

'Postcard?' echoed Abbey.

'Ah, sure we get a postcard once a year from the two of them. Alive and well and living it up in Portugal,' said Corrie uncomfortably.

'Apparently they cook a very nice chicken in Portugal,' Fee added. 'And of course they have their own swimming pool.'

Abbey was totally flummoxed. So her grandmother was living in Portugal with a woman, eating nice chicken and swimming in a pool. She was not underneath the curing-room floor at all. Which left a flurry of questions to be answered.

'Why didn't Rose tell me that?' she asked Corrie. 'Why would she tell me it was you? Why does she hate you so much?'

The question sent a shooting pain through Corrie's heart. He supposed Rose did hate him and for the millionth time in his life he wondered what he had done and to whom to invite such pain.

'Well,' he said, trying not to let Abbey see how shaken he was, 'there are a couple of reasons for that, the first being that no twelve-year-old girl wants to believe that her mother would abandon her. And rightly so. I didn't want to believe it myself.'

'Well, I can understand that,' said Abbey, because she did, 'but why would she come up with such a horrible story? Why would she be so awful?'

'Ah, now,' said Corrie, 'Rose wasn't so awful. Just confused and resentful on top of being a little bit difficult in the first place.' He shifted uncomfortably in his chair. It wasn't territory he enjoyed going over but he realised now that if Abbey was going to move on in her life, in his, she needed to have all the family secrets laid bare in front of her.

'Before we got the postcard we didn't know for a fact that Maggie and Mary-Therese had run away together,' he explained, 'although the fact they both disappeared at the same time sort of pointed in that direction. Anyway, for the first few days I didn't know what to tell Rose so I just said her mother had gone away and I wasn't sure when she would be coming back.'

'And that was the truth,' Fee interjected, his mouth stuffed with the last of the cheese. 'You were telling her the truth.'

'But a couple of nights after your grandmother left me—Rose was very upset, Abbey, she was very angry—she saw something that she shouldn't have and the poor girl was in such a state she sort of put two and two together and came up with, well . . .' He petered out.

'Came up with what?' Abbey demanded.

'Well, it wasn't four,' Fee added, not particularly helpfully.

'What did you do? What did she see?'

'It's hard to explain,' said Corrie. 'There was a bit of an incident here at the house—you wouldn't be helping me out at all would you, Joseph?—after Rose went to bed and we were sort of trying to clear all that up when . . .' He petered out again, much to Abbey's exasperation.

'When what?' she cried. 'What did Rose see that was so terrible?'

'It was Mr O'Regan,' Avis pronounced from the doorway. 'And may God rot his soul.'

The three of them turned round in surprise.

'Colonel Mustard in the ballroom,' Fee, a big-time Cluedo fan, breathed, impressed.

'I couldn't stand back and let you face the music on your own,' Avis said, moving to Fee's grubby armchair and standing behind him, her hand on his shoulder.

'Music?' Corrie said stupidly.

'It was the dead body of Owen O'Regan,' Avis continued, addressing Abbey, 'and your mother saw these two precious gentlemen lumping his useless lifeless corpse across the courtyard and into the factory where they buried him under the curing-room floor.'

Fee choked on his Merlot while Corrie grew as pale as a Camembert.

'Your mother got up in the night,' continued Avis, looking at Abbey, her chin trembling, 'and saw them from the stairway landing and thought that what she had seen was her own poor mother being done away with.'

'But why was Owen O'Regan dead in the first place?' Abbey asked. 'Why was he even here?'

'He was here because he followed me here after giving me the hiding of a lifetime,' Avis said, tears falling on her crab-apple cheeks. 'I was pregnant with his child and I ran here for help from a mile up the road and then I pushed him down the stairs because the drunken oaf had belted me for the very last time.' She was fierce now. 'And I would kill him all over again if I had the chance.'

There was a stunned silence.

'Actually,' Fee said, 'you might well get it.'

'He wasn't dead, Avis,' said Corrie.

It was Avis's turn to change colour.

'We gave him two hundred pounds and put him on the bus to Limerick,' said Fee.

'Limerick?' whispered Avis.

'Sit down, Avis,' said Corrie. Abbey stood up and helped the stunned woman into her chair then perched on the arm of Corrie's recliner, a tiny gesture that warmed the cockles of the old man's heart.

'I think a glass of wine might help sort your head out,' Fee said, his own hand shaking as he poured more wine into his glass and gave it to Avis.

'All these years, you thought you had killed Owen?' Corrie asked her.

Avis nodded. 'It was an accident,' she said. 'And I really didn't mind. In fact I thought the world was an altogether better place without him.'

'And you thought we got rid of his body?' Fee asked.

'I asked you what had happened and you said not to worry,' Avis replied defensively. 'You said he wouldn't be bothering anyone where he was going.'

'Well, I was talking about Limerick not the great hereafter,' said Fee.

There was another bewildered silence as everyone took in what had just happened.

'So no one is dead, then?' Abbey asked, just to make sure.

'That's right,' agreed Corrie. 'No one that we know of, anyway.'

'Did you never get a funny feeling about Avis thinking she was a murderer and we were accessories?' Corrie asked Fee in a slightly accusing fashion.

Fee blushed to the roots of what little hair he had. 'Not about that, no.'

'Avis,' Corrie said. 'You stayed here all these years thinking we had your dead husband's body buried under the cave floor? Whatever must you think of us?'

'I think you are two of the kindest, dearest, sweetest men in all of Ireland,' Avis said, blushing to the roots of her bun-like arrangement. 'I thank God for the day Owen O'Regan clipped me round the ears and brought me to the two of you. I lived because of it and my baby lived because of it and there's not a minute of the day goes by without me being grateful to the two of you. You're the best sort of men and I love you both.' She sipped weepily at her wine.

'There was a baby?' Abbey asked.

'Yes, there was a baby,' Avis answered, smiling at her with tear-filled eyes. 'The first Coolarney baby. We've had dozens more since then but my Josephine was the first.'

'And she was beautiful,' crooned Corrie. 'Wasn't she, Joseph?'

'Beautiful,' the little man replied, misty-eyed himself.

'Where is she now?' Abbey wanted to know.

'She's living up in Galway, a nurse, with two grown-up children of her own. She was adopted by a lovely couple. They were, weren't they, Joseph? A doctor and his wife. She's had a fantastic life, Josephine, she really has. I see her once or twice a year and I write every week.'

'Why didn't you keep her?' Abbey couldn't keep herself from asking.

'Oh, it wasn't done in those days,' Avis answered, slurping at the bottom of her empty glass, her cheeks glowing but her eyes bright and clear. 'There I was, a widow, or so I thought, with nothing to my name but a month of overdue rent and a baby on the way . . .' Her voice frittered away to nothing. 'That's a point,' she said dazedly. 'I thought I was a widow.'

Fee started to squirm uncomfortably in his chair.

'But you knew I was still married.' She pointed one stout-booted toe at Fee. 'So all these years that's why you never . . .'

Fee's eyes were flicking from wall to wall as though searching for an escape.

'Never what?' Corrie and his granddaughter asked in unison.

Avis suddenly snapped out of her daze. 'Never nothing,' she said brightly, sitting up straight. 'Never nothing at all.'

Abbey looked suspiciously from Avis to Fee and back again. If she wasn't mistaken, there was something in the air. 'You two!' she exclaimed.

Fee and Avis swapped looks of fear and delight and guilt and joy and the absolute horror of being discovered. Corrie felt his heart slow down to a languid, loud *ba-boomp* as he sat forward in his chair, his eyes near-popping out of his head.

'You two?' he whispered.

Fee and Avis remained frozen, their eyes locked on each other.

'How long has this been going on for?' Corrie finally asked in a voice that didn't sound like his.

'Only since 1977,' Avis whispered.

'We were going to tell you but then Rose took Abbey and it didn't seem the right time and I thought we were better off waiting,' said Fee.

'You don't mind do you?' Avis asked, worry crinkling her brow.

'Mind?' said Corrie. 'Mind?' His best friend in the world had been snatched out from underneath his very nose by a woman he'd been harbouring all these years. Did he mind? He thought about it, sitting there in his La-Z-Boy rocker recliner. Well, he hadn't even noticed—so what difference did it make?

'Of course I don't mind,' he said, meaning it. 'In fact, I'm delighted for you, Joseph. I couldn't be more delighted. All this time I've worried about you having no family, being lonely, and here you were—'

'There's no need to forget we're in mixed company,' Avis interrupted rather primly.

'I didn't think you'd mind,' Fee said, rather cautiously, 'but I can't always trust my funny feelings where Avis is concerned.' He looked up at her and smiled as she squeezed his shoulder. 'She jammers my radar, you know.'

'Is there any more of that wine?' Abbey asked. It was all a bit much, really.

'And you never talked between you about whether Owen was dead or in Limerick?' Corrie asked. Fee and Avis both shook their heads.

Please God, don't let them say they've got better things to do than talk, Abbey silently pleaded.

'I heard that,' said Fee, and winked at her.

At the end of the second bottle, Abbey joined Corrie for a walk. He liked to go down the lane to look at the sea, he told her, especially after such excitement. It soothed him. To his great joy, Abbey wanted to go too. She was in the mood for a bit of soothing herself, it seemed. Despite the tying of so many loose ends, she had the oddest sensation that an itch she couldn't pinpoint was still in need of scratching.

'Why didn't Rose believe you about her mam going to Portugal with Mary-Therese and the pool and all that?' she asked Corrie as they strolled in the afternoon sun.

Corrie sighed. 'She couldn't contemplate that option, Abbey. It was too hard for her. She didn't want to believe it. She told me she'd seen me with the body and I told her the truth about exactly whose body it was—and a perfectly healthy one at that. But it just didn't suit her to believe me.'

Abbey took his hand and gave it a squeeze. She knew all about Rose twisting the truth to suit herself.

'It was easier for her to turn her heart against me than believe that her mother would leave her for another woman, of all things,' Corrie went on.

'What was she like?' Abbey ventured softly. 'Before me?'

'Your mother?'

There was so much to say but he didn't want to say it. Corrie wanted to tell Abbey that her mother had loved her with all her heart and that she was a good and kind woman but he knew that simply was not true.

'She was a complicated girl who grew into a complicated woman,' Corrie answered his granddaughter. 'And the best thing she ever did was have you.'

It was his turn to squeeze her hand.

'What about—' she faltered. 'I don't suppose you know . . .'

'About your father?' he prompted.

Abbey bit her lip. It was hard to be this near, yet this far from the truth.

'Rose would have had us believe your father was a famous disc jockey from Dublin,' Corrie continued, 'but Fee says he came from a little closer to home. A lot closer, in fact. Schillies to be precise.'

'He's local?'

Corrie shrugged his shoulders. 'Fee says your man cottoned on to the fact that he was the daddy and had a go at Rose who pretty much came home, packed her bags and was on the next boat across the Irish Sea.'

'But why would she leave and never come back? Why would she do that?'

If there was one thing that Rose was never going to be, Corrie thought to himself, it was an ordinary small-town girl bringing up the local barman's bastard. She had dreams far grander than that.

'She got a job,' he said, 'modelling in London. It was what she always wanted. And she never saw a reason to come home again.'

'But what about me?' Abbey asked, trying not to sound wistful. 'Did you never come looking for me?'

'Abbey, she broke my heart taking you away from me. I must have been to London two dozen times and rung a thousand more,' said Corrie, 'but there was a part of Rose that enjoyed keeping you away from me.'

'And that story about the curing-room floor was to make sure I stayed away from you,' said Abbey slowly. 'She's a one, is she not?'

The two of them looked at each other ruefully. Rose had created a world that focused solely on herself and the miracle was that her father and her daughter had discovered each other again, despite her best efforts.

Abbey thought about her own unknown father. There would be time, she realised, and plenty of it, to smooth out the knots and tangles of her past. In the meantime, she was happy just to be who she was, where she was, with this warm, wonderful old man.

'I feel at home here,' Abbey said, looking at Corrie, her face breaking into a smile he could remember from nearly twenty-five years before. They walked home in silence, swinging their arms and savouring the sweet sensation of whatever it was they were sharing.

'I thought I might take Kit for a picnic,' Abbey said shyly as they walked up the driveway. 'Do you think he'd like that?'

'I think he'd be mad not to,' Corrie answered. 'And he doesn't strike me as being mad, compared to most, anyway. We used to go for picnics when you were small, do you remember? In the field up behind the house, behind the dairy, on this side of the hill, under the old oak tree? It'll be beautiful up there now.'

When they reached the courtyard at the top of the drive, they were surprised to see the tractor idling there.

'What are you doing?' Corrie asked as Fee bustled past him with a flask and a biscuit tin and jumped astride the rumbling machine.

'I'll be back later,' Fee said, settling himself onto the tractor saddle and moving slowly forward, then turning down the drive. 'Don't wait up!'

'Where is he going?' Abbey asked. Corrie shrugged his shoulders. Fee had never learned to drive a car and very occasionally took to the road on the tractor but for what, on this occasion, he didn't know.

'Is it just me,' Abbey asked, looking at Fee's fat round bottom jiggle down the driveway on top of the old machine, 'or is he totally barmy?'

'It's not just you,' Corrie said fondly, and went inside to find the picnic hamper.

Abbey and Kit were sitting on a tartan blanket under the oak tree on the hill behind the house. It was late afternoon and they had pretty much picked over the basket Abbey had filled earlier with fruit and sweets and a flask of coffee before hunting down Kit and inviting him up the hill for a late lunch. Feeling a freedom and happiness that she hadn't known for years, Abbey had shared the events of the smoking room with her fellow cheesemaker, who had listened and laughed and listened some more.

'I can't believe I thought that Corrie would murder his own wife,' Abbey said. 'It seems so ridiculous when I think about it now.'

'Yes, but there's something about this place,' Kit said, 'that makes the ridiculous seem ordinary. Have you noticed that?'

Abbey closed her eyes and let the sun and her thoughts wash over her. The usual merged with the unusual a lot more at Coolarney House than anywhere else, she agreed. But she didn't mind that. She understood it. Just like she understood, perhaps always had, that her mother was a difficult woman, at times even dangerous, but she had survived her and she was going to be the woman that Rose never had been. She had goodness in her genes, thanks to Corrie, she knew that now. And she was going to stay here and make cheese because her heart did a little somersault when she thought about it and her nose was twitching now at the ghost of the warm, wet, yeasty factory smell.

Kit watched her face, wrinkling and beaming as she thought her happy thoughts, and felt an ache that he didn't recognise. He wanted to kiss her, and do more, desperately, right now, he knew that much. But there was more to his longing than that. He wanted to be old with her, he realised as the sun shifted and dropped the dappled shade of an oak branch's giant leafy fingertips over her cheek. He wanted to look across the milk vat in forty years' time and see her aged, wrinkled face break into a smile as she sucked the fresh curd from the palm of her crinkled hand. He wanted to slip up behind her as she packed it into a mould and encircle her with his own ancient arms, adding his strength to hers. He wanted their children, lots of them, to drive them crazy with their constant good-natured bickering and high-falutin labour-saving inventions. The more he thought about it, the more he just plain wanted her.

Abbey opened her eyes and turned towards him, the leafy shadow sliding off her ear and onto the grass. 'Can I help you?' she said, a mischievous glint in her eye.

Kit leaned forward and kissed her, long and hard, his soul soaring as he felt her body rise up to meet him. Her back arched and he slipped his hand behind it and hungrily pulled her closer, on top of himself as he lay back on the grass. She tasted like freedom. Freedom from his troubles, his bent and broken life, his inner ache. As he felt her heart beat against his he knew with a sudden monumental clarity that everything was going to be all right. He pulled away from her mouth and her knees slid down either side of his hips as she sat up, straddling him, licking the taste of him off her lips as he slowly began to unbutton her shirt.

She moaned at the touch of his finger brushing her breast and throwing her head back she was distracted momentarily by the sound of a car speeding up the driveway and in that moment, passion subsided and reason took hold.

'Not here,' she said, brushing away Kit's hands. 'Not up here. Let's go back.'

Kit groaned. 'Don't tell me you have a sister you think is buried underneath this tree,' he said. 'I don't think I could stand it.'

Abbey laughed. 'I told you,' she said, buttoning up her blouse, 'no one is dead.'

Kit groaned again but supposed that she did have a point. Their picnic spot was clearly visible from the house and as their coitus had been twice interrupted already, it made sense to ensure they were really in private this time. He put his hands on Abbey's hips and pushed her down onto his thighs so he could sit up. Then he leaned forward to whisper into her perfect neck. 'You're beautiful,' she felt him say into her collarbone and she wanted him so badly, so immediately, she wondered how she was going to make it down the hill without imploding.

She stood up, smiling, and held out her hand to him. Kit took it, then brought it to his lips to kiss it with a tiny salty lick before he grabbed the picnic hamper and the blanket and they both started down the hill.

Abbey felt so happy it was all she could do to keep from skipping and jumping and screaming. Her body was humming with expectation and her heart was singing with joy. Who cared about anything else? The time was right and she could feel it right to the core of her skeleton. She sidled closer to Kit and kissed him on his arm just below his shoulder. He was such a good man, she thought. Such a good, good man.

Halfway down the hill she spotted the car that she'd heard earlier. It was a yellow convertible with its black roof down that had swung into the courtyard between the house and the dairy.

'I wonder who that could be,' she said, pointing at it. 'Pretty fancy set of wheels for around these parts.'

Kit looked at her, smiling a wicked smile, and shrugged his shoulders. 'Who cares?' he said. 'No one's going to stop us this time.'

'It's not a Coolarney thing, you and me, is it?' asked Abbey, suddenly scared it was all too good to be true. 'It's not one of those ridiculous things that seems ordinary just because of the "Coolarniness" of it all, is it?'

Kit laughed again and swung her arm. 'It doesn't feel ridiculous,' he said, 'and I don't know about you, but it doesn't feel ordinary either.'

He was right, thought Abbey. Of course, he was right. It was right. She could be sure of that now.

They were at the bottom of the hill and Kit was helping her over the gate when an evil, dark cloud rolled over the horizon of their happiness. A voice calling to them from the top of the driveway seemed to freeze Kit to the spot. Abbey looked over his shoulder as he held her round the waist, ready to help her to the ground.

A tall, beautiful blonde woman in a tiny flowery sun frock was walking towards them, teetering in a pair of red stiletto heels. She was almost painfully thin but deliberately so, her spaghetti straps showing off the skeletal bones in her neck and shoulders. Her legs were impossibly long—like those of a thoroughbred racehorse—tanned and bare. She minced closer and shaded her eyes with her hands.

'Hello, y'all,' she drawled, and Abbey saw the life drain from Kit's face as his hands dropped from her waist and he turned slowly towards whoever it was that was coming towards them.

'Jesus Christ,' Kit whispered, a loud buzzing like a pneumatic drill muffled with cotton wool vibrating the inside of his head.

'Who is she?' asked Abbey, confused.

'I said, hello, y'all,' the leggy blonde said again to Kit as she reached him. 'What's the matter, honey? Deaf as well as disappeared?'

Close up, Abbey could see the intruder was perfect. Her skin was golden and clear, her eyes brilliant blue and widely spaced, her mouth big and full and stretched into a smile that showed off two rows of impeccable teeth.

'Aren't you going to introduce me to your little friend?' she asked.

'Jesus Christ,' whispered Kit again, still frozen, as the clear, crisp landscape around him melted like a painting left out in the rain.

'You seem confused,' the blonde said, ignoring him and holding out her hand to Abbey. 'Jacey Stephens. Pleased to make your acquaintance, I'm sure.'

Abbey stared at the hand being offered to her and then at Kit. He looked as though he was seeing a ghost.

'Jacey,' he whimpered, his eyes dark and disbelieving in his pale shocked face.

Abbey, feeling sick to her stomach, forced herself out of her frozen state and half jumped, half fell to the ground, steadying herself as she stood up straight with one hand on top of the fence post.

'I thought . . .' she started, then stopped.

'You thought what?' the blonde asked, her cold tone making a liar of her dazzling smile.

'I thought you were dead,' Abbey said.

There was a split second's silence, then Jacey threw back her long blonde hair and laughed a deep sexy laugh. 'Dead?' she repeated. 'Hell, no, honey. I wasn't dead, I was in rehab.' She turned her gaze again to her stunned husband. 'What on earth have you been telling people, darlin'?'

Abbey looked at Kit for signs that this was all part of some sophisticated prank but something in the look on his face told her it wasn't so.

His shoulders were slumped, his eyes had sunk deeper into his head. He bore almost no resemblance to the man she had been desperate to give herself to only moments before. He looked like a total stranger.

'Kit?' she ventured, a quiver in her voice. 'Kit?'

'You're dead,' Kit said hoarsely to Jacey, ignoring Abbey. 'I thought you were dead.'

'Just because you say I'm dead, honey, doesn't mean I am. It might be wishful thinking but it's still just thinking, sugar.'

Kit closed his eyes and started to shake his head from side to side. He could not take it all in.

'You know what, pumpkin?' Jacey said, turning to Abbey. 'My husband and I could really do with some time alone so if you could just scram that would be great.'

Abbey sought out Kit's eyes for confirmation that this wasn't happening, but still they were closed.

'Kit?' she tried again, but he didn't seem to hear her.

'Run along now, honey,' Jacey smiled with the warmth of a frozen margarita, 'I need to get reacquainted with my man.'

'I have to go,' Abbey said, as if she hadn't twice been asked to. She turned and started to walk, then run towards the house.

Kit listened to the sound of her feet taking her away from him yet was powerless to do or say anything to stop her. He'd been having a dream, he supposed, that had turned into a nightmare. He wanted to wake up and find himself walking down the hill again with the woman of his dreams. He opened his eyes. His dead wife was looking at him.

'What are you doing here, Jacey?' Kit croaked, confused but becoming stomach-lurchingly less so. 'I don't understand.'

'Well, let me refresh your memory, honey. I had a little accident at home and wound up in hospital. Then you dumped me, then I was ordered by the court to spend ninety days in rehab. Now the ninety days are up and I've come to get you, so can we please go? All this fresh air and countryside is getting to me.'

Kit felt the panic that had left him alone these past few days start rising again in his chest. Visions of Jacey lying dead on their floor having lost their baby flickered through his head. Her pale face, her hair spread out like peacock feathers on the floorboards, blood. Paramedics bending over her, the hospital bed, the tubes, the oxygen, the doctor, vodka.

'I thought you were dead,' he said through lips that felt numb and wooden. 'I really thought you were dead.'

A real smile crawled across Jacey's beautiful face as she watched her husband's despair as he pieced together the puzzle of his fractured memories. She reached out and took both his hands in hers. 'Don't think about that now, baby,' she said in a soothing voice. 'It's going to be OK. We're going to be OK.'

Jacey was dead. Jacey was dead. Jacey was dead. The mantra bounced back at him from the recent past. Maybe if he said it enough, he remembered thinking in the days after Jacey's accident—when his wounds were open and raw—it would be true.

Standing there in that moment staring at his wife, Kit suddenly knew why he had been filling the hole deep inside himself with vodka. He had killed his wife. In his head, he had killed her. He had wished her dead and then he had wrapped himself in a shroud of alcoholic mist to keep the painful truth of her survival at bay.

'Jesus Christ,' he said, fighting the urge to retch. 'Jacey, what have I done?'

Jacey moved in, snaked her arms round his neck, and reached up to kiss him on his jaw below the ear. 'Let's not think about that now, darlin',' she whispered. 'Let's just go and get your things. I want you to come back to New York with me. I want our life back, honey. You and me, the way it used to be.'

Corrie watched aghast from the upstairs sitting room as the couple walked down to Fee's cottage, then Kit disappeared inside while Jacey waited impatiently at the door. He and Avis had bumped into a distraught Abbey flying through the kitchen minutes earlier on her way upstairs. Corrie had tried to find out what was wrong, but his granddaughter had cried to be left alone and run, sobbing, to her room. Corrie had wanted to go and find Kit but Avis had stopped him.

'What will be, will be, Joseph,' she had said. 'Leave them. He has to make up his own mind.'

'Who is she?' Corrie asked as he watched Jacey scanning the courtyard for signs that anybody was going to halt Kit's escape.

'His wife,' Avis said.

'The dead one?'

'Not so dead, as it turns out,' she said. 'Though she's not the first one we know of in that category, now is she?' They each looked out of the window at her, thinking their private thoughts. 'She's got a hold on him, all right,' said Avis, 'but Abbey's the one, Joseph. You have to trust that.'

'Does Abbey know that?' Corrie asked, worry gnawing at him, making his arms tingle.

'She has to trust it too.'

Corrie couldn't bear the thought of Abbey's heart being broken again. He was sure it would be too much for her, as it would be for him. 'I wish

Joseph would come back,' he said. 'When's Joseph coming back?'

Avis flicked at the curtain. 'He'll be back when the time is right and it's up to us to trust that, too.' She leaned closer to Corrie as Kit emerged from Fee's cottage with his bag and, seemingly in a daze, lowered himself into the passenger side of the topless yellow sports car. In the roar of an engine and a billow of exhaust, he was gone.

As the car turned out of the leafy driveway and into the lane, Kit felt the wind ruffle his hair and blow the tears that were threatening to fall back into his eyes, for which he was grateful. Over the sombre green of the rolling hills he could see the ocean, but even that had lost its sparkle, still now and slightly listless-looking. A filter of gloom seemed to dull everything he looked at and add to his confusion. He didn't know what he was doing, what he had been doing. Not an hour ago it had all seemed so clear and hopeful, and now here he was desperately bewildered again and going home with his wife. His wife. He looked across at Jacey and her beauty took his breath away. A little smile tripped across her glossy lips as she sensed his gaze, then turned to flash the smile even wider.

That smile. The doctor. The memories were trying to flood back.

Suddenly he remembered standing next to Jacey's hospital bed and telling her it was over, she was not the woman he married, she was dead to him, gone, for ever. Then he remembered leaving the hospital and going to the nearest bar where he had got so drunk that when he finally crawled home he didn't know what day it was, he didn't know anything except that he wanted to pretend his wife had never existed.

And in the weeks that followed, that was just what he had done. He had pretended that Jacey never existed, pretended that she had died, until he didn't need to pretend any more because his anaesthetised mind told him that she was gone, that he had lost her, that she was dead. What sort of a monster was he that he could kill off his wife like that and not even know that's what he had done?

In the bowels of Coolarney House, Lucy was discovering the woeful side of motherhood. In the bowels of Baby Jesus, Jesus's offspring, something had gone horribly wrong and was responsible for this discovery. The kitten, who in all other respects seemed to be enjoying perfectly good health, had been running amok for more than an hour, skittering from floor to floor, hallway to hallway, room to room, leaving foul-smelling piles that Lucy was trying to clean up before anybody caught him in the act and banished him.

On the third floor of the house, the kitten came to an exhausted halt and collapsed against a door.

'I should hope so too,' Lucy said, lunging at him before he could escape and do any more damage. As she picked the little creature up, though, she was distracted by a noise coming from the other side of the door. A crying sort of a noise. Without stopping to think, she opened the door and peered in. The room was very yellow and full of the sound of someone having a very miserable time, a sound to which Lucy was no stranger. She guessed that the lump lying with its back to her on the overstuffed bed was Abbey, and as she watched from the doorway she felt puzzled by an overwhelming sensation to make the back stop shuddering. She felt a warmth towards the back with which she was most unfamiliar. She felt sorry for it. She wanted to make it better.

She cleared her throat. 'Baby Jesus has the squitters,' she announced, stepping into the room. 'He's after re-staining the floors, the poor dote.'

The back froze mid-shudder. 'Go away,' Abbey gurgled, her voice glutinous with crying.

'What's the matter?' Lucy asked, taking no notice of the order as she stepped closer towards the bed.

'I said go away,' Abbey repeated thickly. 'Leave me alone.'

Lucy edged forward and after standing uselessly beside the bed for a moment or two, sprang up and perched on the side of it.

'Go away,' Abbey said again.

Lucy took no notice, she was thinking. The unconnected jigsaw of the afternoon was starting to form a picture. She'd seen the yellow sports car arrive earlier but hadn't thought much of it. People came to visit the factory all the time, after all. Then Jamie had told her he'd seen a gorgous supermodel stepping out of the car, but she'd assumed he was just saying that to make her jealous because he was so desperate for her. Now the car with the gorgeous supermodel was gone and Abbey was very, very sad. Her heart gave a jolt. It could mean only one thing. Well, it could mean a few things but she thought she knew which one.

'Where's Kit?' she asked, boldly.

The back gave another big shudder.

'Did Kit leave?'

The back shuddered some more and Lucy let rip a string of expletives so heartfelt and disgusting she had to hiccup to get her breath back at the end of them. Her enthusiasm wrenched Abbey out of her snivel-fest. She cautiously turned over, then leaned up on her elbows. Her eyes were red and raw from crying and her tears had been soaked up by her hair, which was now stuck close to her face, Beatles-wig style.

As Lucy looked at her, the horror she felt at Kit's disappearance was swallowed by the same sensation she'd felt before. She truly, madly, deeply wanted Abbey to stop being sad. She knew exactly how it felt and it was too horrible to wish on anybody else.

'It was his wife,' Abbey offered, fresh tears springing to her eyes and pouring wetly onto her cheeks. 'His wife came and got him.'

Lucy laughed. 'But his wife is dead,' she disputed matter-of-factly.

'Apparently not,' Abbey answered, a catch in her voice. 'At least she looked pretty bloody alive to me.'

'That was her?' Lucy breathed. 'The gorgeous supermodel? Back from the grave?'

'She was never in the grave,' wailed Abbey, 'she was in rehab. And she looked at me as though I were dirt. Kit just stood there, Lucy. He didn't do anything, he just stood there.'

'That bastard,' exhaled Lucy. 'How could he?'

'He just jumped in the car and took off with her,' Abbey said, sitting up more, her forehead crumpled in uncomprehending misery, 'without saying goodbye to anyone. Can you believe it?'

Lucy couldn't. 'But I thought he was in love with you,' she said bluntly.

'You did?' Abbey sniffed, recognising the pathetic tinge to her voice too late to remove it.

'Only me and everyone else,' Lucy said. 'And Avis said it was meant to be. And he could've had me,' she added with the confidence only a pretty nineteen-year-old possesses, 'but he didn't want to.'

Abbey thought about this as she dried her eyes. 'Then why has he gone back to his wife?' she questioned. 'The wife he told us had died?'

Lucy didn't have an answer to that but after thinking on it for a while, her face unexpectedly brightened. 'Well, look at it this way,' she said, 'it would've been rude to have shagged him just after his wife popped her clogs, wouldn't it? At least you didn't do that.' Abbey managed a weak smile. 'Of course,' Lucy added, 'I suppose that means he was cheating on her with you.'

'He never did anything with me,' Abbey said after the smile departed. 'We always seemed to get interrupted.'

'Jaysus,' gulped Lucy. 'Sorry about that.'

'Well, it wasn't so much you as the dead wife that really put a spanner in the works,' reasoned Abbey. There was a momentary silence, and then she and Lucy looked each other in the eye and burst out laughing. It was nervous laughter, the sort that just as easily could have been crying, but it was laughter all the same.

'It's not funny,' insisted Abbey between near-hysterical giggles. 'It's really not funny.'

'I know,' Lucy kept saying. 'I know, I know, I know.'

'The man I'm madly in love with has left me for ever,' Abbey gasped between belly laughs.

'And I'm having a baby I don't want and haven't a clue who's the father,' laughed Lucy, curled up on the bed now and clutching her own stomach.

'What a pair!' Abbey hooted.

'Twins!' roared Lucy.

They clutched each other and rolled around the bed, laughing uncontrollably, knowing that nothing about their separate situations was funny in the slightest.

'He might come back, you know,' Lucy finally offered, wiping her eyes as her laughter subsided.

'I don't think so,' said Abbey. 'But I suppose you never know.' She sighed and looked at Lucy. 'What about you? Do you think you'll change your mind about the baby and keep it?'

'I don't think so,' Lucy answered. 'But I suppose you never know.'

Distracted abruptly by a monumentally foul stench, Abbey lifted her nose up into the air and sniffed at it. 'Phwoar,' she said, grimacing. 'What the hell is that?'

Lucy's blue eyes bulged in horror. 'Baby Jesus!' she cried. 'I forgot!'

Thirty miles away, contemplating the curves of the Irish countryside, Jacey was growing wary of Kit's silence. He'd been in a world of his own since they left the farm.

Jacey leaned across and put her hand on his knee, ignoring his involuntary flinch, and with one eye on the road, she walked her fingers down his leg until she found the strap of her Prada shoulder bag, nestled at his feet. She scrabbled around inside and pulled out a silver flask. Unscrewing it at the steering wheel, she flipped the lid and threw back her head, gulping at the contents before handing the flask to her husband, who looked at it dumbly.

'Go on,' she smiled, urging him to take it. 'Have some. You know you want to. Besides, you could afford to loosen up a little, sugar. We're going to get back on top, Kit. We're going to start having fun again.' She flicked her hair back over her bare shoulders and raised her face to the sun.

Kit took the flask and fingered it, relishing the cool smooth surface. He wanted a drink, of course he did. Now more than ever. Anything to calm the rising panic that was claiming him. Jacey had lost their baby after overdosing on heroin. He remembered every sad, sordid detail now and her betrayal sickened him almost as much as his own weakness. He knew that the contents of the flask, vodka most likely, would help erase the repulsive truth the way vodka had done a thousand times before but everything seemed different now, now he'd had time to think.

He still couldn't quite fit all the pieces together and it was slowly occurring to him that perhaps the truth shouldn't be erased. Perhaps he should be feeling revulsion and shame. Maybe these sensations were trying to tell him something. The further he got from Coolarney House, he realised, the more he liked the way he had felt there: vodka-free, clear-headed and connected to his thoughts. He didn't want to be sucked back down into the murkiness of drinking, despite its allure at this second. He fought his urge and screwed the top back on the flask.

'So, I see the rehab really took, huh, Jacey?' he said sadly, feeling half-disgusted, half jealous of the buzz she was enjoying.

'Oh, come on,' she grinned. 'I only went because of the court order. I'm not the one with a drinking problem, darlin'. Y'all should know that.' She reached for the flask and wrenched it back from him, fumbling with the top and swerving half off the road before correcting the steering with an unconcerned laugh.

'Jacey,' Kit said anxiously, snatching the flask back after she'd swigged from it again. 'You're going to get us killed. Pull yourself together, will you?' Jacey just laughed again, and held out her hand, waggling her fingers by way of requesting the drink.

'You can't say you don't have a problem, Jace,' Kit said, holding the flask away from her grasp, his voice slow and deliberate. 'You overdosed on heroin, for chrissake. You miscarried our baby on the floor of our apartment. You lied to me from the day I met you until the day you went into detox. Jesus Christ, Jacey, you've never even said you were sorry.'

Jacey's smile faded and her face darkened but she fought the temptation to argue. She didn't want to mess things up now. 'All right, sugar, if that's what y'all want to hear, I'm sorry. Is that better? I am real sorry.'

'And you can cut the Southern crap,' Kit said, his voice sounding tired and empty. 'You're from Jersey, remember? Please, you can drop the charade, Jacey. I know where you're from. I know all about you. And there is nothing wrong with any of it.'

Jacey's eyes hardened. She did not appreciate reality coming along and snapping her thong. Not one bit. 'You're not still mad about that, are you?' she purred. 'Jeez, honey, don't you think you could try to get over it?'

'Get over it?' Kit was aghast. 'Get over it? Jacey, every single thing I knew about you, about my wife, every tiny detail, turned out to be a lie. Do you really think I can just get over that?' yelled Kit, remembering with spine-chilling detail the devastation he felt as the truth about Jacey unfolded in the aftermath of her overdose.

Kit's boss, George, and his wife Mary had arrived at the hospital just as the bald, bespectacled doctor had dropped his big bombshell, and George had launched a mortar attack of his own. Concerned at the downward-spiralling direction of his friend's lifestyle under the influence of his gorgeous party-girl wife, George had been prompted to look into Jacey's background and had attempted to locate the Louisiana newspaper baron Jacey claimed was her father, only, he told Kit, to find out no such man existed.

She was estranged from her family, Kit had protested in the sickly green light of the hospital corridor. She had escaped a bad LA show-biz marriage and was hiding her failure from her wealthy, powerful New Orleans family.

Her family lived in New Jersey, George explained gently, and were neither wealthy nor powerful. Jacey's real name, he informed Kit, was Marlene Blundt. She had run away to LA as a teenager and married the owner of a suburban striptease bar who went bust and wound up stealing cars for a living.

Turned out Kit didn't know anything about Jacey at all.

'You could try to get over it, couldn't you, honey?' Jacey was smiling sweetly at him from the driver's seat. 'For me? For us? Y'all know y'all can do it if you try.'

'Please, Jacey, drop it with the Southern stuff. It's not right to go around pretending you're someone that you're not, that's basically the root of all your problems. And you of all people—well, there's nothing wrong with you the way you actually are.'

'Well, honey, you might not like me the way I actually am,' she replied. 'Had you ever thought of that?'

Kit sighed and shook his head. 'Of course not,' he said sadly. 'You don't think I know the real you?'

'Nobody knows the real me, sugar,' retorted Jacey. She seemed almost proud of the fact. 'And that's just the way I like it.'

'But I'm your husband, Jacey, and if I'm going to stay your husband then you have to be just you. Otherwise, what's the point? I don't want to spend the rest of my life with a woman I'll never really know. What are you so afraid of? What's the big deal with being Marlene Blundt from Freehold, New Jersey?'

Jacey, furious at having her past dragged up again, was having trouble containing her irritation. 'Well, I don't think you can rightly tell me who I should or shouldn't be, Mr Burlington, Vermont,' she declared with venomous sweetness. 'You reinvented yourself too, you know. How come it's only a crime when I do it?'

'I never pretended to be anybody other than who I am,' Kit argued. 'I worked hard and it wasn't until you came along that I started getting messed up. All that partying? The drinking? I was never into that before.'

'Oh, so it's my fault you're an alcoholic,' Jacey declared. 'Of course. Heaven forbid you should ever blame yourself for anything.'

'I'm not talking about that and of course I don't blame you,' replied Kit earnestly. 'I don't blame anybody but myself and I blame me for what happened to you as well, because I was obviously so messed up I didn't even notice what state you were in. What kind of a husband does that make me?'

'Oh Chhheeerist,' groaned Jacey. 'Spare me the analysis. It's like being back in therapy. Could you just hand me the vodka instead?'

'What I'm trying to say,' Kit said, ignoring her request, 'is that I actually used to be pretty happy being exactly who I was and I'd like to be that person again. I think maybe I even have been, these past few days.'

Jacey tossed her head and blew through her lips in a gesture of derision. 'That little bumpkin sure turned your head, didn't she?' she marvelled. 'What did she do—bake you an apple pie? Trust me, sweetie, two days back in the Manhattan swing and you will have forgotten her and this whole stupid country thing altogether.'

'When did you get so hard?' Kit wanted to know. 'I don't remember you being like this.'

'Honey, you don't remember a half of it and you don't need to either. Now why don't you just sit back and relax, huh?'

'You know what?' Kit suggested. 'I think I will. And you know what else? I'm going to do it without this,' and with one swift right hook he threw Jacey's hip flask out of the car, up into the air and into the long grass at the side of the road.

Jacey's pretty face screwed up with anger as she slammed on the brakes and slid the car to a halt.

'Have you lost your fucking mind?' she raged, all Jersey now. 'You get out and go back and get that. Go back and get my flask.'

'I won't,' said Kit, looking at her angry empty eyes and realising that the scattered bits of his life were starting to rise up and rearrange themselves again. 'I don't want our old life back, Jacey. We're better off without it.'

'Don't make me laugh,' Jacey bit back. 'You were just a boring know-nothing bank boy before I met you. You never did anything but go to work and sit around watching TV. Nobody even noticed you before you had me on your arm, honey. You were wallpaper. You want to go back to that?' Her eyes sparkled with fury as she watched him, knowing that no matter what his head told him, she still had the power to make him do what she wanted when it counted.

'I don't want to be noticed,' Kit told her, quietly and calmly. 'I want to be normal. I want a family. I want to stay in some nights and sit around in my sweatpants and watch TV. I want to invite friends over to play cards and have dinner.'

Jacey threw back her head and laughed, a hard mean laugh that came from somewhere deep and dark. 'Give me a break,' she said, 'you've just described my idea of hell. You wouldn't last five minutes living like that, Kit, and neither would I. Maybe that's what your little show-pony girl-friend down there on the farm does for fun but ga-holly, cowboy, any-where else? I don't think so. You want more than that, Kit, you know you do. You and I are the same like that, just admit it.'

Kit felt sadness leach out of his heart and into the rest of his body as he realised that for Jacey this was true. But for him, it was not. In that moment, the staggering emotion he had thought he felt for his gor-geous, graceful, flawless wife and from which he had been running ever since her overdose and betrayal evaporated. He looked at her and for the first time didn't see the mesmerising beauty who had kidnapped his soul and broken his heart, but instead a brittle shell containing nothing but a cold-blooded mass of manipulation. He had been wrong to aban-don his wife and wish her dead, he knew that now. That had not been the right, nor the brave thing to do, and it had led him down a path where escaping reality courtesy of Grey Goose was his best option. But in that moment, in that car, sitting there looking at her, Kit knew as clearly as he knew anything, that even if he had stayed and been a brave understanding husband, he would have arrived at the very same con-clusion he was arriving at now.

Jacey, bored with the resistance she was meeting and fearful of what it meant, lurched out of the car and slammed the door behind her, teeter-ing back down the road in search of her flask. She stepped off the side of the road and got down onto her hands and knees to search for the flask. Kit watched her, horror mounting, as she desperately clawed at the long grass and wild flowers.

Kit slowly got out of the car and started to walk towards her as she grovelled around at the side of the road, her hands searching like a blind woman's for the vodka.

'If you think I am going back to New York without you, you can think again, you selfish bastard,' she said, her voice catching, as she continued scratching at the ground. 'I will not go back to sharing one stuffy little room with three other catty bitches and schlepping around the city for pathetic little jobs that pay nothing.' Her voice was stretched with the effort of controlling herself. 'I will not be groped by one more fat ugly married asshole desperate to get into my pants because he thinks that's where buying me one lousy apple martini will get him,' she railed. 'I am Mrs Kit Stephens and as of next Thursday I am worth a lot of money so screw the lot of them.' She dropped her head down onto her arms, her butt in the air, and roared into the grass as she realised the hopelessness of trying to find the flask.

Next Thursday? Kit thought about the date. It would have been, he realised with another jolt, his tenth anniversary at Fitch, Wright and Ray, and the date on which his vested funds would mature. The final scales fell from his eyes just as Jacey, her head at grass-roots level, spied something glinting in the grass close to the fence and threw herself on it. 'I found it,' she cried, laughing as she grappled with the top, then throwing as much of the vodka as she could down her throat.

When she opened her eyes, her husband was gazing at her with a look she had not seen before but which she suspected was far from mesmerised. Her plan, she realised, had gone slightly awry.

'How did you find out where I was?' Kit asked her.

She looked up at him, squinting into the sun and shading her eyes with the flask. 'That little swamp creature from your office knew.'

'She told you? Niamh told you where I was?'

Getting clumsily to her feet, Jacey started to walk towards him, and it was then that Kit realised how drunk, or stoned, or both, she was. She smiled lazily as she walked up to him, then kissed the tip of her index finger, and ran it across his lips as she passed him.

'Of course she didn't tell me,' she said, over her shoulder, 'she hates me. Her new boyfriend told me. I bumped into him at our old apartment.'

Kit turned and looked at her. 'You bumped into him?'

'Well, I still had my keys, honey. I was a little surprised to find him there, I can tell you, but he was very kind and told me just where I could find you and then he gave me access to your personal effects.'

So Tom wanted to sabotage Kit's chances of returning to his career and Jacey just wanted his money. This was what it all boiled down to.

'Come on, darlin',' Jacey drawled. 'There's a big old jet airliner down the road and it's got our names on it. Yours and mine, baby.'

She pushed her hair back from her face, leaving a smudge on her cheek, and smiled at him, before slipping elegantly into her seat and starting the car. Kit walked deliberately towards her, thousands of cogs moving together in his head, finally synchronising the machinery of his life as he knew it. He stopped at the passenger door. He looked at Jacey, taking a last slug from her now-empty flask, and he knew one thing, just then, and one thing only. He did not want to grow ten minutes older with this woman, let alone forty years. He could not imagine her wrinkled face smiling at him, nor see his own ancient arms adding strength to hers. He could not picture their children. He didn't want to.

'Jacey,' he said, feeling safe and strong outside the car away from whatever it was that made his wife so mortally magnetic, 'why didn't you tell me about our baby?'

Jacey looked at him, calculating, wrongly, how to play it. 'Oh, honey,' she said sweetly, 'the truth is I didn't tell you about the baby because I wasn't planning on having the baby. I wasn't ready for babies. I was having too much fun and so were you.' She smiled her sexiest smile, oblivious to her messy face and sticky hair. 'It's only because I forgot about the Valium and the coke and tried that stupid shit of Violet's that you even knew about it. I was going to deal with it the very next day and you would never have had to worry about it.'

She looked at him and assumed she'd hit her mark. 'We can have all the babies you want when we're done with the good life, darlin',' she added. 'There'll be plenty of time for that.' She leaned over and patted the empty passenger seat. 'Come on home, Christopher honey. I want to go home.'

Kit's smile was sad but Jacey couldn't see that. 'Jacey,' he said, as softly as he could, opening the door and kneeling on the seat, then leaning over as if to kiss her. Her face softened with the glory of triumph as she realised she had won and that he was coming with her.

'I knew y'all'd come around eventually,' she breathed, offering up her face.

But Kit, instead of kissing her, moved quickly past her newly resistible lips and pulled the keys out of the ignition, then jumped out of the car and threw them as hard as he could behind the stone wall at the side of the road. She would never find them.

'Our time is up,' he said calmly as he turned, closed the car door and reached into the back, pulling out his bag. 'I'm going to be a cheesemaker.'

Jacey, her face contorted with shock and rage, bashed at the steering wheel with both hands. 'Fuck you to hell!' she screamed, shaking her head in fury.

'You might not be sorry, Jacey,' he said quietly, 'but I am. Really sorry.'

'I'm going for half of everything you have, you bastard, don't think I won't,' Jacey shrieked at him, her features ugly in their bitterness.

'You're welcome to half of everything I have,' Kit said, 'you deserve it,' and he threw his bag over his shoulder and started to walk back down the lane. He didn't care how long it took, he was going back to Coolarney House—if Coolarney House would have him.

'You can't do this to me,' Jacey screamed at his back. 'What am I going to do?'

'Hitch to the airport,' Kit called over his shoulder. 'Go home, Jace. Good luck.'

Her insults became fainter and fainter as he walked away from her and back to the best thing that had happened to him in his whole entire life. As the road rose up to meet him, his shoulders squared and the emptiness that had swallowed him since Jacey came back in his life was replaced by excitement over his future.

He strode to the brow of a hill and again caught a glimpse of the sea that had earlier seemed so listless and dull. Now, although the light was fading and the sun was hanging lower in the sky, the blue water glimmered and twinkled, the green pastures shimmying at its edge. Kit was not a man to kiss away a marriage lightly, to kiss away anything lightly, but as he walked the winding country lanes of West Cork he knew without a shadow of a doubt that he and Jacey were not meant to be. It had been wrong to run away from her, from their marriage, from the truth, but it would be worse to go back—because he didn't love Jacey. He didn't even like her. He'd been bewitched by her and maybe he did like the way people looked at him when she was on his arm, but the man he was when he was with Jacey was not the man he wanted to be.

Jacey would be all right. He knew that. She would find what she needed with someone else. Someone who wanted what she did. Money. And to be noticed. Kit? He cared for neither of those. He wanted love and honesty and for the people he loved to trust him. He wanted Abbey to trust him. He wanted Abbey.

The steady *chug-chug* of a slow approaching motor intruded into his thoughts, getting louder and louder as he approached a slow bend in the road. Not a single car had passed him since he left Jacey at the side of the road and the only sound had been that of his own steady footsteps and, far away, the sea. The *chug-chug* got louder again as he reached the corner. As he rounded it, the road turned into a corridor of trees that met above the lane to form a canopy that cut out the light and made it hard for him to see. He could hear all right, though, and the *chug-chug* sounded an awful lot, he thought now it was closer, like Avis's tractor.

'Jaysus,' a familiar voice called above the clamour of the familiar old engine. 'Don't tell me I'm late.'

Chapter Sixteen

*'In that fantastic explosive moment when you realise just how good it is,
you know it's all been worth it.'*

Joseph Feehan, from *The Cheese Diaries*

OLD FART ARSE was playing the maggot, knowing full well it was Kit and
Abbey's first solo effort in the cheese factory. Baffled, the pair stood side
by side and looked at the pasteuriser. They'd followed exactly the same
procedure as they'd seen Fee do every single morning, yet still the
machine coughed and spluttered but refused to roar into life.

Abbey gawped uselessly at the wretched contraption, but it wasn't
Old Fart Arse she was thinking about. It was the way her heart had
jumped out of her chest and into her mouth when she had seen Kit
lounging at the factory door as she'd arrived, bleary with spent tears and
sleep, ten minutes earlier.

He had looked up when he heard her footsteps. She had caught his
eye and, with the early-morning sun dark and golden, he didn't
look real. As she got closer, however, she realised that she wasn't dreaming, that it was him, that he'd come back, that perhaps all was not lost.

'We were meant for each other, you know,' he said softly as soon as
she was close enough to hear, 'I realise that now.'

Abbey had looked at him uncomprehendingly and walked straight
past, opening the factory door, pulling on her overalls and Wellingtons,
dipping her feet in the bath, and patting Old Fart Arse on the rump like
a faithful horse as she switched him on and checked the temperature
gauge. Suddenly, Fee's irritating cheerfulness at the breakfast table made
sense. Knowing that he knew Kit was back, his offer of cold cucumber
slices to bring down the swelling in her raw red eyes didn't seem quite
so unsympathetic. Her grandfather, too, had been smiling over his mar-
malade toast, but his good humour had not been quite as convincing.
She could tell he was worried for her and she worried back, but had
loved knowing how much he cared for her.

Now, here she was, eyes puffy and puce, and her heart beating so
loud in her chest she was thankful to Old Fart Arse for making such a
commotion—otherwise Kit would have been deafened by her.

'Who is meant for each other?' she asked, turning to look at Kit.

He snapped out of his own reverie, confused. He'd been thinking that perhaps, 'We were meant for each other,' hadn't been the right thing to say. That he should have said, 'Sorry,' or, 'Please forgive me,' or, 'About the whole wife thing . . .'

'We were meant for each other,' he said again, spreading his hands out in a helpless gesture. It was what he meant. He'd never been so sure of the meaning of anything ever before.

Abbey seemed upsettingly unconvinced. 'Do you mean you and your not-quite-as-dead-as-we-thought gorgeous blonde supermodel wife were meant for each other, or do you mean you and . . . you and . . . ?' Her bluster blew. She was so scared of losing him that she had prepared a lot of anger just in case it was needed, and any hope she had been saving was battling inside her for space. 'Because with all the being-quite-alive and the high heels and the going-away-without-even-saying-goodbye and then sneaking back for who knows how long, a person could get quite confused unless it was made perfectly clear to her,' Abbey jabbered, her face blushing to match her eyes, which were now locked on the belching pasteuriser.

Kit nearly collapsed with relief as he reached out and took Abbey's face in both his hands, turning her towards him and stepping as close to her as he could, so he could feel her sweet breath on his neck, and smell her fresh citrusy smell. He tilted her glowing red eyes up to face him.

He'd been trying all night to rationalise what had happened, was happening, how he felt, but somehow words just didn't fit the picture. There were loose ends. There were problems. But at about four o'clock in the morning, when his bones had finally stopped feeling the after-shock of Fee's tractor, he came to the conclusion that it didn't matter. All he knew was that he wanted to be with Abbey and he wanted to be a cheesemaker. Simple as that. No argument.

'I just have this feeling,' he said, 'that if we could let it all go and just find ourselves, I don't know, magically, in just the right place at just the right time, everything would work out. Do you know what I mean?'

'But your wife—' Abbey started to protest.

'If you could let that go,' Kit said, his eyes not leaving hers.

'But a wife, a living wife, is a pretty big thing to let go,' Abbey answered, with feeling. 'You lied about her and then you ran off with her. You just abandoned me the instant she turned up. I felt invisible.'

'I made a mistake with my wife,' Kit said, his gaze so unswervingly sure that Abbey felt jealous, momentarily, of his certainty. 'I made a lot of mistakes with my wife and when we've got time I will tell you everything you want to know, Abbey. But the guy who deluded himself that his wife was dead? The guy who climbed into her car and drove off with her yesterday? That wasn't me, Abbey, you have to believe me. This is me, here with you, and this is where I want to be.'

'How can I be sure?' Abbey whispered.

'Because I am telling you, Abbey, and I promise you, as sure as I am standing here now in front of this clapped-out excuse for a pasteuriser, that we don't even need because we only pretend to use it, that I will never lie to you ever again as long as we both shall live. I will love you. I will look after you. I will help you make the best goddamn cheese in the universe. I will do anything for you if you will just let me.'

'I'm scared,' Abbey said, realising that she was. 'People loving me hasn't worked out the way I'd hoped so far.'

'But you're here, Abbey, in this place, with me. That's the hard part done. All you have to do now is stand back and let the farm, the air, the rain, the moon, the room we're standing in make its mark, and that's the magic of Coolarney.' He smiled as the words of clever old Fee tripped off his tongue like they belonged there.

'Who are you?' Abbey breathed, her body feeling lighter and lighter with each passing moment.

'I'm just an ordinary guy from Burlington, Vermont, who for some reason I'll probably never know or understand ended up in this particular place at this particular moment with you, Abbey, you. You and I were meant for each other,' he said. 'You and I. Is that clear enough?' And he leaned down and kissed her with the long, languid, slow-burning passion of a man who knew he had a lifetime of this woman ahead of him.

Across in the kitchen, Fee was helping himself to another cup of tea and a fourth crumpet. 'At last,' he sighed, raising his eyes to the heavens.

'At last what?' Corrie said, looking up from the *Irish Times*.

'At last that granddaughter of yours and the boy from New York City are getting on with things.'

'What things?' Corrie said suspiciously, putting down the paper and eyeing up his friend.

'All the things,' Fee smiled, tipping his head in the direction of the factory and taking an enthusiastic bite of his crumpet. 'And I mean all.'

Corrie's face creased with worry. 'Are you sure he's the right one?' he asked again. 'Are you a hundred per cent sure?'

'Joseph, I was sure the moment I clapped eyes on him. And after spending three and a half hours on a tractor with him, I'm doubly, triply, quadruply—what comes after quadruply?' he asked, not waiting for an answer. 'I am as sure as I ever have been. He is the one.'

'What happened out there?' Corrie wanted to know.

'His wife has a touch of the Maggie about her, Joseph; the pull, you know, the pull. But it only took him thirty miles to work out she was messing with his head and on the booze as well so he got her to stop the car, threw away the keys and turned back home to Coolarney.'

'What sort of man leaves his wife in the middle of the countryside though?' Corrie worried.

'That's exactly where some wives should be left,' Fee answered, 'and twice as many husbands. It takes more strength to walk away from the wrong person than it does to stay, Joseph, and I'm not talking about you, I am talking about young Kit Stephens. But having said that, there's a lot of you in the boy and for that we can truly be thankful.'

'But what makes you so sure they're right for each other?'

Fee rolled his eyes. 'What am I always telling you?' he demanded.

Corrie flailed about for an answer. Fee was always telling him so many things, after all, and half of them never made a jot of sense.

'I'm always telling you to trust me,' Fee continued. 'I'm always telling you not to worry, that everything will be all right.'

Corrie must have looked doubtful because Fee sighed and put on his serious look, the impact of which was dented considerably by a large blob of honey on his chin. 'You worry too much, Joseph, did you know that?' he said. 'And I wish you would stop it because you've absolutely nothing to worry about. That girl of yours and that boy over there with her are going to make the most beautiful cheese in the world, Joseph, and they are going to make a grand pair, a couple, into the bargain. It's not often two such good and honest souls meet, you know that. The last time was you and me, Joseph. There are not that many of us but as of right now there are two more. This is no ordinary day, my friend, and certainly no day to be sitting there with a face on you like a wet weekend.'

'Is it any wonder I can't remember what you're always telling me when you're always telling me so much?' Corrie grumbled, but Fee's words had soothed his troubled heart. 'You think she'll stay then?'

'For ever and a day,' Fee beamed, leaning across the table. 'Do yourself a favour, Joseph. Trust me.'

Corrie, tired of his doubts and worries, did himself a favour and trusted him. And as he watched his old friend find the blob of honey on his chin and proceed to lick it off, he even allowed himself the luxury of believing that all was right with the world. He felt better than he had all week.

Old Fart Arse lurched into action with such a thundering crack Kit and Abbey sprang away from each other in panic.

'That infernal machine!' Avis laughed as she popped her head round the door. 'You'd swear it has eyes. Milk's in. Abbey, I don't know what you did to Lucy but she's a different girl this morning. She rang her mammy in Dublin last night, can you believe it? And she got up early and made tea and toast for the girls this morning. If it weren't for the dreadlocks and the earring on her tongue, I'd swear it was an impostor.'

Abbey laughed. 'Oh, it was nothing,' she said. 'Just girl talk.'

They worked side by side unloading the milk and then, after Avis had gone, Kit and Abbey beavered inside the factory getting the moulds and benches ready for the curd, while the milk heated to the right temperature. After an hour, Kit flicked open the valve and the milk whooshed up and around Old Fart Arse and into the cheese vat. The noise made Abbey's blood bubble as she looked at Kit across the vat and wondered how it was possible to feel so happy, so at home, so how she had always imagined the lucky people felt. Kit was standing across from her with a huge grin on his face, mesmerised by the force of the milk as it shot into the vat. When the time was right Kit added the starter, a funny secret smile playing across his lips as he did so.

'Did you ever wonder,' he asked some time later as he was stirring the rennet into the vat, 'how Corrie and Fee make their money?'

'From the cheese, you eejit,' Abbey laughed.

'Think about it,' Kit said. 'They make about a hundred and twenty kilos a day, five days a week. If they were selling that at a fiver a kilo, they would be making about three thousand pounds a week, all up, before tax and overheads—probably leaving them about fifteen hundred pounds to play around with. They pay seven hundred and fifty pounds to the Pregnasaurs, which leaves them another seven hundred and fifty pounds to run the farm and the house and pay themselves and Ruby and Marie.'

Abbey thought about it. When he put it like that, it didn't add up. 'Please don't tell me that they're drug runners,' she pleaded, 'I couldn't bear it.'

Kit laughed. 'They're not.'

'Then what are they?'

'Two very canny old men, that's what they are. Lars and Peder Nielsen. The Nielsen brothers.'

Abbey was confused. 'I don't follow,' she said.

Kit held up the rennet packet. *Brødrene Nielsen Mejeri*, it had stamped on the side. *Denmark*.

'Nielsen Brothers Dairy,' Kit translated for her with a smile. 'When Corrie and Fee realised commercial starters and rennets were the way of the future, they invested back in the sixties. Big time. Those guys are

471

sitting on a gold mine over in Denmark. Fee told me they can't even keep track of the money that pours in. It's an international multi-million-dollar business—I remember when they listed it on the New York Stock Exchange. It went ballistic. And they own some Dutch vat-making company too. They don't even need to make cheese, Abbey. How about that? Coolarney Gold is just a labour of love.'

Abbey seemed stunned by the revelation. She stood there, silently, fiddling with the well-worn handle of her paddle, and Kit was suddenly fearful he had exploded some childhood dream or something.

'Hey, I'm sorry,' he said, coming over to give her a hug. 'I didn't mean to—'

Abbey pushed him back so she could look at him. 'No,' she said, her eyes shining. 'I love that. I love that it's a labour of love.' She pulled herself together and held up her paddle, looking at it and tracing the dents her grandfather's fingers, and his grandfather's before that, had made on it over the decades. Somehow, the more ridiculous it got, the more it made sense. Her life, finally, was falling into place. But there would be time for celebration, lots of it, later. Right now, there was cheese to be made.

A tingle of excitement ran up her spine as she peered into the vat, the minutes ticking by without either of them noticing, as the thick creamy milk disappeared before their very eyes, leaving the sweet watery whey and shiny soft curd in its wake. Wordlessly, they picked up their blades and started the synchronised series of sweeping arcs that would bring them closer to their cheese. Almost instantly they fell into a compatible rhythm, each focusing on the different patterns their blades were slicing through the curd. The factory was silent but for the ever-present sound of dripping water, the friendly occasional clink of blade against steel, and the slip-slop of the whey as the paddles sliced through it. When the curd was as small as it could be, Kit and Abbey looked at each other and grinned, both wet with effort and glowing with satisfaction.

'Bombs away?' Abbey queried. 'Bombs away,' answered Kit, and she pulled the plug on the vat, standing back as the whey hissed and spat its way onto the floor, finding the grate and slinking down it like an escaping snake. The factory never smelt better than at this moment, the whey departing, the curd settling and the air thick with promise, and it was at this moment Corrie and Fee, unable to stay away another second, fell in the door, each pushing the other out of the way and the little fat one, for once, winning.

'Gadzooks!' Fee said. 'I think they've done it!'

'Gadzooks?' repeated Corrie. 'When did you start saying gadzooks?'

But he could feel it too. It wasn't the look or the smell or the feel. It was all of those things and something else, something indefinable, something they had only ever been able to put down to Coolarniness. Kit grinned and invited them to taste the curd but at that moment the door flew open again and a wide-eyed and near-hysterical Lucy burst in, completely out of breath.

'Wilhie,' she gasped. 'Wilhie.'

Abbey handed Kit her paddle and went to Lucy's side, urging her to calm down.

'Wilhie's gone into labour,' Lucy panted. 'I can't find Avis and I don't know what to do and it's happening pretty quickly if you ask me.'

'Where is she?' Abbey urged.

'In the big kitchen,' Lucy said. 'I thought with the boiling water and everything . . .'

'Kit,' said Abbey, immediately taking control. 'You go and find Avis. I'll go with Lucy and get Wilhie up to my room. Can you bring Avis up there when you find her? Are you two all right to pack the moulds?' she asked, looking at Corrie and Fee. 'I'm so sorry, I know today was supposed to be—'

'Go,' said her grandfather, his heart nearly bursting with pride at his wise, warm, wonderful granddaughter. 'Go.'

She went, Kit and Lucy with her, and the two old men were alone in the factory.

'What did I do to deserve her?' Corrie asked, in wonder, and his old friend clapped him on the back and said, 'That you even need to ask, Joseph, makes you the man you are.'

He took up his position on the opposite side of the vat. 'Ready?' he asked. Corrie nodded.

Fee lifted a handful of curd tentatively to his nose.

The curd smelt exquisite. Sweet and special. Warm and inviting. Pure and simple. Exquisite. He pulled his hand back just enough to let Corrie see his smile from across the vat and then brought the curd to his lips, sucked it onto his tongue, clapped his mouth shut, closed his eyes, and savoured the sensation.

Bliss.

It was perfect. Flawless. Faultless. But more than that, it was exceptional. Unique. Unsurpassed.

In a word, it was better.

It was the best.

There was absolutely no doubt about it whatsoever. Kit and Abbey's curd was the best Fee had ever tasted and the thought of the cheese their curd would one day become made him shiver.

His eyes flew open. 'Jaysus, Joseph,' he breathed. 'They've only cracked it. They're only the best fecking cheesemakers in the whole of the world. They're cheeniuses! I knew it. I knew it!'

Corrie felt a warmth flood through his tired old bones and settle calmly on his skin as he cherished the look on his old friend's face. Blissfulness was a wonderful state. This was a grand moment to be relished and remembered.

He leaned in against the vat and stooped down, swinging his arm in a gesture so familiar he couldn't even feel he was doing it. He scooped up the curd and his skin tingled. For a moment he felt as though he could feel every molecule, every atom, every element that was being squeezed by his fingers into his palm. It felt like more than curd. It felt like everything. Everything he had ever done. Every place he had ever seen. Everybody he knew.

With a difficulty he didn't understand, he lifted the sweet soft mass to his lips. It exploded in his mouth with a buzz that was so overwhelming his brain could barely process the deep dark thrill as it quickly spread throughout his body, saturating every single cell.

Suddenly everything was happening in slow motion, flickering in front of him like an old home movie. He tasted. He swallowed. He realised that Fee was right. It was better than perfect. It was the best. His hand fell to grab the side of the vat. His other hand clutched at his chest, numb with the tingling that was taking over him. Still everything was happening in slow motion. Everything. Slow. Tasting. Swallowing. Realising. His eyes widened in panic as he comprehended what was happening and with all his strength he lifted his head to look at his friend.

Fee was standing, stricken, on the other side of the vat, his mouth frozen open in a black, gaping 'O' as tears spilled down his cheeks.

The world stopped moving. The sun stopped shining. The cheese didn't matter.

It's me, thought Corrie, his face paralysed in an expression that was half-rapture over the glory of the cheese, half-terror at what was happening to him. 'It's me,' he whispered as his legs gave way beneath him and he collapsed to the floor, his head bouncing off the smooth brown teak as the cold claw of death squeezed again at his heart.

'It's me, not you,' he whispered again as Fee appeared on the floor beside him and pulled the big man onto his lap, so that Fee was sitting against the vat, his faithful old friend lying, shocked and barely breathing in his arms, his head leaning back against Fee's chest.

Fee kissed the top of his old mate's head and let his tears fall wetly on that glorious mop of silvery hair. 'Ah, sure, it was you,' he whispered. 'But what's a fellow to do?' He rocked Corrie, his short stocky arms looped underneath the big man's armpits, gently rubbing the chest beneath which scarcely pumped the heart that was killing him.

'I didn't want to tell you, Joseph,' he confessed. 'I didn't want you to worry. I wanted you to make the most of it.'

'But I haven't . . .' Corrie's head was muddled.

'Ah, Joseph, you did. You just don't know you did,' Fee whispered. He hugged his friend closer to him and was quiet for a moment. He thought of all the things he'd told Corrie that meant nothing and knew these next words would have to be different.

'You always knew you were here to do something special, Joseph,' he whispered into his bewildered friend's ear. 'You always knew that you were different and that there was a reason for it all and you were right, Joseph Corrigan, you were right, just not in the way you expected.' He felt Corrie shudder in his arms and his own heart contracted with anguish.

'It wasn't the cheese,' Fee said, extricating himself momentarily to wipe at his eyes with his grubby sleeve. 'Ah, the cheese was good, the best even, up until now, but that wasn't it, Joseph. And it wasn't Rose, although God knows you deserve a medal for loving the little wagon after everything she put you through.' He pressed his lips to the old man's bushy eyebrow and kissed him again, his eyes closed and burning with grief.

'Abbey,' Corrie said, or thought he said, but couldn't tell.

'It wasn't even her,' Fee whispered, 'although she's a credit to you, Joseph, and your Corrigan genes. She'll do you proud, Joseph, you know that. She got here in time.'

Corrie smiled, or thought he smiled, until the pain in his chest wrenched him away. 'What was I here for then?' he beseeched his friend although he was well beyond speaking. 'What's it all been for?'

'There's one hundred and seventy-four other babies born happy and healthy here because of you,' wept Fee, 'and that's one hundred and sixty-nine girls no one else wanted when they most needed someone to want them. That's what you were here for, Joseph. It was happening right here under your nose all the time.'

'That was nothing,' Corrie imagined telling his dear old friend. 'It was a pleasure. Sure, anybody else would have done the same.'

'That's why you're different,' wept Fee, 'because not everybody else would do the same.'

'You would,' Corrie felt. 'You would do the same.'

'Not without you,' Fee whispered. 'Not on my own.' He felt Corrie stiffen himself against the monumental physical pain he was fighting and then relax as though the pain had gone away, or he had decided he couldn't fight it any more.

In that moment Corrie thought of all the things he hadn't done. He hadn't made peace with his daughter. He hadn't finished this quarter's tax return. He hadn't told the best friend a man could ever hope to have how much he loved him and how he didn't want to leave him alone in the world.

'You don't need to, old friend,' Fee murmured into his ear. 'I know.'

A single huge fat teardrop leaked out of Corrie's left eye and trickled slowly down his cheek.

'Don't be afraid to let go, Joseph,' Fee whispered into his ear, as a tear of his own fell and landed with a tiny splash on top of Corrie's, hurrying it down his face. 'It won't be the same without you, it won't be perfect, but it will be all right. Trust me.'

And Corrie, knowing that's what friends were for, trusted him. And feeling less than perfect but still lucky and loved and certain, for once, that the time was right, he let go.

Epilogue

FEE BOUNCED BABY CORRIE on his knee and studied the German lesbian.

'My girlfriend knows nothing,' she said. 'I am on safari in Africa and drinking with a young man from Australia when all of a sudden . . .' her eyes widened as if even being there hadn't been proof enough that it had happened, '. . . I am in his sleeping-bag.'

Fee kissed Corrie on the head and marvelled over the baby's soft blonde hair at the breadth of the German lesbian's hands. She had big strong knuckles and no jewellery. Ideal.

'How do you feel about Austrian nuns?' he asked.

'It is a long while since I have thought about Austrian nuns,' she answered, registering little surprise. 'Why?'

'Oh, nothing really,' Fee replied. 'I did mention that you will need to sing to the cows, though, didn't I?'

'Yes,' said the German lesbian. 'You did mention that.'

The door opened and Abbey came in, her face lighting up as she saw her baby jiggling on Grandy Fee's ancient purple track-suit bottoms.

'There you are, you gorgeous girl,' she said reaching for Baby Corrie and lifting her into her arms to be smothered in kisses. 'Oh, hello,' she said, turning to the German lesbian. 'I'm Abbey, the cheesemaker.'

'Hello, I am Lili,' said Lili. 'You have a very beautiful baby. She doesn't look like you.'

'No,' laughed Abbey, kissing the little button nose between the bright blue eyes, 'but she smells like me, that must count for something. Oh, that reminds me,' she turned to Fee, 'Lucy just rang, she's coming down this weekend to see Jamie and us, of course. Lucy is a Coolarney mum,' Abbey explained to Lili, 'and this one's birth mother.'

She held Corrigan Lucy Stephens in the air and blew a raspberry into her fat little stomach.

'You keep all the babies?' Lili asked.

'I'd like to,' laughed Abbey, 'but my husband has other thoughts on the matter. No, most of them go home with their mothers, Lili, but don't panic just yet, there's plenty of time for you to decide what you want to do, as Avis will no doubt explain when she arrives. I think she's over in the cottage getting your room ready.'

'But how could she be?' asked Lili. 'She didn't know I was coming.'

'Yes, well, you'll see,' smiled Abbey. 'Anyway, I'll leave you to it, as soon as I choose a cheese for lunch.' She opened the *Cheeses of the World* section in the library and rustled around in the *fromagerie* while Fee explained to the newcomer the history of the Feehans and the Corrigans.

'The deal has always been,' he said, 'that the Corrigans would provide the cows, the cows would provide the milk, and the Feehans would provide the skills to make cheese—and that's the way we've been doing it for a long, long time now and doing very nicely as a result we are too, thank you for asking.'

Abbey stopped what she was doing and turned round, giving Fee a strange look as she adjusted Baby Corrie on her hip. 'The Corrigans would provide the cows?' she asked. 'And the Feehans would provide the skills to make cheese?'

Fee looked at her and nodded.

'The Corrigans weren't cheesemakers?'

'They helped make the cheese,' he answered, 'but they were mainly cow people. Until your grandfather, God rest his soul.'

Abbey looked at him, aghast. 'The Corrigans were cow people?'

'Before your grandfather, mostly, yes they were.'

'So what happened?' she asked as Lili looked on with passive interest.

'So turns out your grandfather didn't care for cows,' Fee said.

'Couldn't stand the creatures. Hated the look of them, the sound of them, the touch of them, the smell of them. They brought him out in boils. I think it was a phobia. He started selling cheese when he was twelve years old so he could afford to pay someone else to deal with the filthy things. That's sort of how we got going.'

'But what about grand old tradition and it being in the blood and all those things you are always talking about?' Abbey asked, hitching Baby Corrie further up on her hip.

'Ah, the secret's not in following tradition, it's in knowing when to change it,' said Fee, making the baby laugh by poking out his tongue.

Abbey plucked out a chunk of Stilton, closed the refrigerator door, and shook her head disbelievingly, a smile on her face all the same.

'You,' she said, bending to kiss Fee's bald spot as she passed him on her way out of the door, 'just make it up as you go along.'

'Did you hear that, Joseph?' Fee said to the clock. 'Is she a chip off the old block or wha'?'

'You sing to the cows, you talk to the walls,' said the German lesbian. 'What kind of a place is this?'

SARAH-KATE LYNCH

'I had been working as a journalist for a long time before it occurred to me that making things up would be much more fun than trying hard not to,' says Sarah-Kate Lynch, whose last 'real job' provided her with the inspiration she needed for her first novel. 'I was working as a food writer and it was during this stint that I was introduced to the principles of cheesemaking. Do you know that before then, while I had spent a life-time gorging on my favourite dairy product, I had never bothered to find out how it was produced? This all changed in just one day when I was asked to be a judge at some cheese awards. Turns out that cheese comes from milk which comes from cows who eat grass and who, there is some suggestion, provide better milk while listening to music. This appealed to me in terms of a story because it had a beginning, a middle and an end and because, as with love, if you have all the ingredients you are halfway there. But the real key is good timing.

'So there I was, a former food writer, with a love of cheese and the urge to write a book, when what should I spy in my video collection but Monty Python's *Life of Brian*, one of my favourite films. Having had the real Beatitudes—Blessed are the Meek, the Peacemakers etc—drilled into me at convent school, I never really got over the hilarity of the Monty

Python version. Blessed are the Cheesemakers? What an excellent name for my book about the very same, I thought.'

Sarah-Kate Lynch is a New Zealander and lives with her husband Mark and Kerry blue terrier, in Queenstown, a lakeside alpine town on South Island. 'Both my parents descend from Irish stock,' she told me, 'and it was while visiting my mother's last living relative near a seaside town called Schull in Ireland that I found out about an artisan cheese-maker making washed rind cheese on the Beara Peninsula near the Kerry border. I spent some time making cheese with her, and then descended on a different farm that made cheese on a more commercial scale but which became the inspiration for Coolarney House in my novel.'

Back in New Zealand, Sarah-Kate trawled a couple more farms, filling in the gaps in her knowledge 'and naturally ate my own bodyweight in cheddars and creamy blues. In fact, I ate so much cheese in the research, writing and aftermath of the book that I have been forced to go on a dairy-free diet for a while, just so I can fit back into my clothes!

'I enjoy writing about love and friendship because to me those two things are really the food of life. And I love the family ties that bind us, too. My grandfathers were both gone by the time I arrived in this life and I have often imagined what they might have been like. In Corrie and Fee, I found them!'

Jane Eastgate

479

601-021-1